Allan Ramsay

A Dictionary of Lowland Scotch

With an Introductory Chapter on the Poetry

Allan Ramsay

A Dictionary of Lowland Scotch
With an Introductory Chapter on the Poetry

ISBN/EAN: 9783337234119

Printed in Europe, USA, Canada, Australia, Japan

Cover: Foto ©Andreas Hilbeck / pixelio.de

More available books at **www.hansebooks.com**

A DICTIONARY

OF

LOWLAND SCOTCH

WITH AN

INTRODUCTORY CHAPTER ON THE POETRY, HUMOUR, AND
LITERARY HISTORY OF THE SCOTTISH LANGUAGE

AND AN

APPENDIX OF SCOTTISH PROVERBS

BY

CHARLES MACKAY, LL.D.

AUTHOR OF "LOST BEAUTIES OF THE ENGLISH LANGUAGE,"
"THE GAELIC ETYMOLOGY OF THE LANGUAGES OF WESTERN EUROPE,"
"A GLOSSARY OF THE OBSCURE WORDS AND PHRASES IN SHAKSPEARE AND
HIS CONTEMPORARIES," ETC. ETC.

LONDON: WHITTAKER AND CO.
PATERNOSTER SQUARE, E.C.
1888

PREFACE.

THE original intention of the Editor of this work was to make it a guide to the better comprehension by English readers of the immortal works of Robert Burns and Walter Scott, and of the beautiful Scottish poetry to be found in the ancient and modern ballads and songs of the "North Countrie,"—and not only to the English but to all other admirers of Scottish literature, where it differs from that of England, and to present to them in accessible and convenient form such words as are more poetical and humorous in the Scottish language than in the English, or are altogether wanting in the latter. The design gradually extended itself as the compiler proceeded with his task, until it came to include large numbers of words derived from the Gaelic or Keltic, with which Dr. Jamieson, the author of the best and most copious Scottish Dictionary hitherto published, was very imperfectly or scarcely at all acquainted.

"Broad Scotch," says Dr. Adolphus Wagner, the erudite and sympathetic editor of the Poems of Robert Burns, published in Leipzig, in 1835, "is literally broadened,—*i.e.*, a language or dialect very worn off, and blotted, whose original stamp often is unknowable, because the idea is not always to be guessed at." This strange mistake is not confined to the Germans, but prevails to a large extent among Englishmen, who are of opinion that Scotch is a provincial dialect of the English,—like that of Lancashire or Yorkshire,—and not entitled to be called a language. The truth is, that English and Lowland Scotch were originally the same, but that the literary and social influences of London as the real metropolis of both countries, especially after the transfer of the royal family of Stuart from Edinburgh to London, at the commencement of the seventeenth century, favoured the infusion of a Latin element into current English, which the Scotch were slow to adopt.

In the year 1870, the author contributed two papers to *Blackwood's Magazine* on "The Poetry and Humour of the Scottish Language." Those papers are here reprinted with such copious additions as have extended the work to more than treble its original dimensions. The whole has undergone careful revision and emendation, and will, it is hoped, be found to contain not only characteristic specimens of the peculiar humour, but of the abounding poetical genius of the ancient and modern authors who have adorned the literature of Scotland from the days of Barbour, Douglas, and Montgomery to those of Allan Ramsay, Robert Burns, and Walter Scott, and down to our own times.

November 1887.

INTRODUCTION.

—◦—

THE SCOTTISH LANGUAGE AND ITS
LITERARY HISTORY.

THE Lowland Scottish *language* is not a mere dialect, as many English people believe; but a true language, differing sometimes from modern English in pronunciation, and more frequently in the possession of many beautiful words, which have ceased to be English, and in the use of inflexions unknown to literary and spoken English since the days of the author of Piers Ploughman and Chaucer. In fact, Scotch is for the most part old English. The English and Scotch languages are both mainly derived from various branches of the Teutonic; and five hundred years ago, may be correctly described as having been Anglo-Teutonic and Scoto-Teutonic. Time has replaced the Anglo-Teutonic by the modern English, but has spared the Scoto-Teutonic, which still remains a living speech. Though the children of one mother, the two have lived apart, received different educations, developed themselves under dissimilar circumstances, and received accretions from independent and unrelated sources. The English, as far as it remains an Anglo-Teutonic tongue, is derived from the Dutch or Flemish, with a large intermixture of Latin and French. The Scotch is indebted more immediately to the Dutch and Flemish spoken in Holland and Belgium, both for its fundamental and most characteristic words, and for its inflexion and grammar.

The English bristles with consonants.   The Scotch is as spangled with vowels as a meadow with daisies in the month of May.   English, though perhaps the most muscular and copious language in the world, is harsh and sibilant; while the Scotch, with its beautiful terminational diminutives, is almost as soft as the Italian.   English songs, like those of Moore and Campbell,[1] however excellent they may be as poetical compositions, are, for these reasons, not so available for musical purposes as the songs of Scotland.   An Englishman, if he sings of a "pretty little girl," uses words deficient in euphony, and suggests comedy rather than sentiment; but when a Scotsman sings of a "bonnie wee lassie," he employs words that are much softer than their English equivalents, express a tenderer and more romantic idea, and are infinitely better adapted to the art of the composer and the larynx of the singer.   And the phrase is but a sample of many thousands of words that make the Scottish language more musical than its English sister.

The word Teutonic is in these pages used advisedly instead of "Saxon" or Anglo-Saxon.   The word "Saxon" is never applied in Germany to the German or High Dutch, or to any of the languages that sprang out of it, known as Low Dutch. Even in the little kingdom of Saxony itself, the language spoken by the people is always called *Deutsch* (or German), and never Saxon.   The compound word Anglo-*Saxon* is purely an invention of English writers at a comparatively late period, and is neither justified by Philology nor History.

---

[1] Neither of these was an Englishman.   And it is curious to note that no Englishman since the time of Charles II. has ever rendered himself very famous as a song-writer, with the sole exceptions of Charles Dibdin and Barry Cornwall, whose songs are by no means of the highest merit ; while Scotsmen and Irishmen who have written excellent songs, both in their own language and in English, are to be counted by the score—or the hundred.

Philology, even in the advanced period in which we now live, is, at the best, but a blind and groping science. It has made but little real progress since the invention of printing, having been anticipated mainly by shallow sciolists, who based etymology upon fanciful guesses and vague resemblances. A by no means unfair specimen of the class accounted for the vulgar word " sparrow-grass," a corruption of asparagus ; by " sparrow " and " grass," on the assumption that the herb was a species of grass to which sparrows were particularly partial.

Many of the etymologies which English literature owes to Dr. Samuel Johnson, his predecessors and successors, in the lexicographic industry, are frequently as ludicrously ill-founded.

The name of the Southern portion of Great Britain has been derived from a supposed German tribe, who with the Jutes and Saxons invaded the island after the departure of the Romans. It happens, however, that there is no real foundation for the confident statement that the name of " Angles " was ever borne by or known to any German tribes. The invaders of the east coast of Britain, both North and South, came from the opposite coast of the continent, principally from Denmark, Holland, and Belgium, and brought their laws and language along with them. The true origin of the word " Angles " is the Keltic or Gaelic *an*, the definite article, and *gaidheil* (in which the *dh* are not pronounced), which signifies the " Gael " or the *Celts ;* whence *An-gael*, and not Angle. The erroneous interpretation, still too firmly fixed in the minds of both the learned and the unlearned to be easily eradicated, was strengthened by a punning compliment paid by Pope Gregory the Great to a party of British youth of both sexes who were carried into slavery in Rome, and which is recorded in Hume's " History of England." " Struck with the beauty of their fair complexion and blooming countenances," says the historian, " Gregory asked to what country they belonged, and being told they were *Angles*, he replied that they ought more properly to be denominated *Angels*, as it would be a pity that the Prince of Darkness should enjoy so fair a prey, and that so beautiful a frontispiece should cover a mind so destitute of internal graces and righteousness."

The epithet "Anglo-Saxon," now so frequently applied to the natives of South Britain, is of recent origin, and was not known in the golden age of English literature, when Shakspeare and Spenser flourished, nor until the second half of the eighteenth century. Great Britain was known to the Romans as Anglia centuries before the Saxons, or that section of them erroneously supposed to have been called Angles, established themselves in any part of the country. It was not until the Hanoverian family of the Georges had given three sovereigns to the country that courtly writers began to talk of the *Anglo-Saxon* origin of the people, and that the epithet finally became synonymous with "English." It is true that in the time of the Romans a small portion of the eastern coast of Anglia, immediately opposite Belgium and Holland, was called "the Saxon shore." The name was given to it from the fact that successive swarms of Flemish, Dutch, and Danish pirates had succeeded in forming settlements on the littoral, though they had never been able to penetrate into the interior of the country. The Gael, or Celts, called these pirates *Sassenach*, as the Southern English are called to this day by the Gaelic and Keltic-speaking people of Wales, Ireland, and Scotland. The word did not originally signify a German or native of Saxony, but a robber.

The Scottish people, though they do not hate the English as too many of the Irish unfortunately do, remark with pride that Scotland is a nation of itself, that it can boast of an antiquity as venerable and of a history as illustrious as that of its larger realm—the throne of which one of its native kings ascended by hereditary right in the seventeenth century, and in succession to Queen Elizabeth—and they object to being called

Englishmen. By the Act of Union between the two nations, the names of England and Scotland were legislatively abolished, Scotland being called North Britain, and England South Britain, while the army, navy, and government were severally denominated those of Great Britain, and not the army, navy, and government of either England or Scotland.

But popular usage in South Britain and at the seat of government has proved itself stronger than the Act of Parliament, and many of the Scotch themselves, yielding to the literary and colloquial fashion set by the South, find themselves speaking, sometimes in praise, sometimes in blame, of the *English* Government. It cannot, however, be affirmed that the objection taken by the northern nation to the southern usurpation of the epithet *English* is in any way unreasonable, founded as it is upon the commonly received if not universal opinion that the English receive their name from the German "Angles." The Southern English believe this fable, and not aware of the fact that they are not half so much German as they think themselves, make light of the Scottish objection, and call it sentimental, and unworthy of practical consideration. But if Angles are in reality "Angael" or *the Gael*, the Scottish and Northern British people are quite as much *Angael* or English as those of the south, and the *English* Government is rightfully the designation of government of the whole kingdom. This fact should remove the natural jealousy of the Scotch, and cut away from the conceit of the South British the very slender and rotten foundation on which it is based. But until the Southern English admit the fact that a colony of Germans did not give name to England, but that the whole country of Britain, otherwise Anglia, as the Romans called it, derives its name from the Keltic *Angael*, the North British are quite right in objecting and in refusing to recognise in their Southern fellow-countrymen the sole and exclusive title to the honourable designation.

The principal components of the Scottish tongue, as distinguished from modern and literary English, are derived not from German or High Dutch, but from the Low Dutch, comprising many words once possessed by the English, but which have become obsolete in the latter; secondly, words and inflexions derived from the Dutch or Flemish, and Danish; thirdly, words derived from the French, or from the Latin through a French medium; and fourthly, words derived from the Gaelic or Keltic language of the Highlands, and of Ireland. As regards the first source, it is interesting to note that in the Glossary appended to Mr. Thomas Wright's edition of those ancient and excellent alliterative poems, the " Vision " and "Creed" of Piers Ploughman, there occur about two thousand obsolete English or Anglo-Teutonic words, many of which are still retained in the Scottish Lowlands; and that in the Glossary to Tyrrwhitt's edition of Chaucer there occur upwards of six thousand words which need explanation to modern English readers, but fully one half of which need no explanation whatever to a Scotsman. Even Shakspeare is becoming obsolete, and uses upwards of two thousand four hundred words which Mr. Howard Staunton, in many respects his most judicious editor, thinks it necessary to collect in a glossary for the better elucidation of the text. Many of these words are perfectly familiar to a Scottish ear, and require no interpreter. It appears from these facts that the Scotch is a far more conservative language than modern English, and that although it does not object to receive new words, it clings reverently and affectionately to the old. The consequence of this mingled tenacity and elasticity is, that it possesses a vocabulary which includes for a Scotsman's use every word of the English language, and several thousand words which the English have suffered to drop into desuetude.

In addition to this conservancy of the very bone and sinew of the language, the Scoto-Teutonic has an advantage over the modern English, in having reserved to itself the power, while retaining all the old words of the language, to eliminate from every word all harsh or unnecessary consonants. Thus it has *loe*, for love ; *fa'*, for fall ; *wa'*, for wall ; *awfu'*, for awful ; *sma'*, for small ; and many hundreds of similar abbreviations which detract nothing from the force of the idea or the clearness of the meaning, while they soften the roughness of the expression. No such power resides in the English or the French, though it once resided in both, and very little of it in the German language, though it remains in all those European tongues which trace their origin to the Low Dutch. The Scottish poet or versifier may write *fa'* or "fall" as it pleases him, but his English compeer must write "fall" without abbreviation. Another source of the superior euphony of the Scoto-Teutonic is the single diminutive in *ie*, and the double diminutive in *kie*, formed from *och* or *ock*, or possibly from the Teutonic *chen*, as in *mädchen*, a little maid, which may be applied to any noun in the language, as *wife, wifie, wifoch, wifikie*, wife, little wife, very little wife ; *bairn, bairnie, bairnikie*, child, little child, very little child ; *bird, birdie, birdikie ;* and *lass, lassie, lassock, lassikie*, &c.[1] A very few English nouns remain susceptible of one of these two diminutives, though in a less musical form, as *lamb, lambkin ; goose, gosling*, &c. The superior beauty of the Scottish forms of the diminutive is obvious. Take the following lines from Hector MacNeil's song, "My Boy Tammie :"—

> " I held her to my beating heart,
> My young, my smiling *lammie*."

---

[1] The following specimen of the similar diminutives common in the Dutch and Flemish language are extracted from the *Grammaire Flamande* of Philippe La Grue, Amsterdam, 1745 :—*Manneken*, little man ; *wyfken*, little wife ; *vrouwtje*, little woman ; *Meysgie*, little girl (Scottice, *Missie*) ; *Mantje*, little man ; *huysje*, little house ; *paerdje*, little horse ; *schcepje*, little boat (Scottice, *boatie*) ; *vogeltje*, little bird, or *birdie*.

Were the English word *lambkin* substituted for *lammie* in this passage the affectionate and tender would be superseded by the prosaic.

While these abbreviations and diminutives increase not only the melody but the *naïveté* and archness of the spoken language, the retention of the old and strong inflexions of verbs, that are wrongfully called irregular, contributes very much to its force and harmony, giving it at the same time a superiority over the modern English, which has consented to allow many useful preterites and past-participles to perish altogether. In literary and conversational English there is no distinctive preterite for the verbs to *beat*, to *bet*, to *bid*, to *forbid*, to *cast*, to *hit*, to *hurt*, to *put*, and to *set ;* while only three of them, to *beat*, to *bid*, and to *forbid*, retain the past-participles *beaten, bidden,* and *forbidden.* The Scottish language, on the contrary, has retained all the ancient forms of these verbs ; and can say, "I *cast,* I *coost,* and I have *casten* a stone," or "I *put,* I *pat,* or I have *putten* on my coat," "I *hurt,* I *hurted,* or I have *hurten* myself," and "I *let,* I *loot,* or I have *letten,* or *looten,* fa' my tears," &c.

Chaucer made an effort to introduce many French words into the courtly and literary English of his time, but with very slight success. No such systematic effort was made by any Scottish writer, yet, nevertheless, in consequence of the friendly intercourse long subsisting between France and Scotland—an intercourse that was alike political, commercial, and social—a considerable number of words of French origin crept into the Scottish vernacular, and there established themselves with a tenacity that is not likely to be relaxed as long as the language continues to be spoken.· Some of these are among the most racy and characteristic of the differences between the English and the Scotch. It will be sufficient if we cite the following :—To *fash* one's self, to be troubled with or about anything—from *se fâcher,* to be angered ; *douce,* gentle, good-tempered, courteous—from *doux,* soft; *dour,* grim, obdurate, slow to forgive or relent—from *dur,* hard; *bien,* comfortable, well to do in worldly affairs—from *bien,* well; *ashet,* a dish— from *assiette,* a plate; a *creel,* a fish-basket—from *creille,* a basket; a *gigot* of mutton—from *gigot,* a leg; *awmrie,* a linen press, or plate-cupboard—from *armoire,* a movable cupboard or press; *bonnie,* beautiful and good—from *bon,* good; *airles* and *airle*-penny, money paid in advance to seal a bargain— from *arrhes,* a deposit on account; *brulzie,* a fight or dispute —from *s'embrouiller,* to quarrel; *callant,* a lad—from *galant,* a lover; *braw,* fine—from *brave,* honest and courageous; *dool,* sorrow—from *deuil; grozet,* a gooseberry (which, be it said in parenthesis, is a popular corruption from *gorse*-berry)—from *groseille; taupie,* a thoughtless, foolish girl, who does not look before her to see what she is doing—from *taupe,* a mole; and *haggis,* the Scottish national dish ("Fair fa' its honest, sonsie face!")—from *hachis,* a hash; *pawn,* peacock—from *paon; caddie,* a young man acting as a porter or messenger—from *cadet,* the younger born, &c.

The Teutonic words derived immediately from the Dutch and Flemish, and following the rules of pronunciation of those languages, are exceedingly numerous. Among these are *wanhope*—from *wanhoop,* despair; *wanchancie, wanlust, wanrestful,* and many others, where the English adopt the German *un* instead of *wan.* *Ben,* the inner, as distinguished from *but,* the outer, room of a cottage, is from *binne,* within, as *but* is from *beuten,* without. *Stane,* a stone, comes from *steen; smack,* to taste—from *smack; goud,* gold—from *goud; loupen,* to leap—from *loopen; fell,* cruel, violent, fierce—from *fel; kist,* a chest—from *kist; mutch,* a woman's cap—from *muts; ghaist,* a ghost—from *geest; kame,* a comb—from *kam; rocklay* (*rocklaigh*), a short coat—from *rok,* a petticoat or jupon; *het,* hot—from *heet; geck,* to mock or make a fool of—from *gek,* a fool; *lear,* knowledge—from *leer,* doctrine or learning;

bane or *bain*, a bone—from *been ; paddock*, a toad—from *pad ;*
caff, chaff—from *kaf*, straw ; *yooky*, itchy—from *yuk*, an itch ;
clyte, to fall heavily or suddenly to the ground—from *kluyt*,
the sward, and *kluyter*, to fall on the sward ; *blythe*, lively,
good-humoured, from *blyde*, contented.

The Scottish words derived from the Gaelic are apparent
in the names of places and in the colloquial phraseology of
everyday life. Among these, *ben, glen, burn, loch, strath, corrie*,
and *cairn* will recur to the memory of any one who has lived
or travelled in Scotland, or is conversant with Scottish literature. *Gillie*, a boy or servant; *grieve*, a land-steward or
agent, are not only ancient Scottish words, but have lately
become English. *Loof*, the open palm, is derived from the
Gaelic *lamh* (pronounced *laff* or *lav*), the hand ; *cuddle*, to
embrace—from *cadail*, sleep ; *whisky*—from *uisge*, water ;
clachan, a village—from *clach*, a stone, and *clachan*, the stones ;
croon, to hum a tune—from *cruin*, to lament or moan ; *bailie*,
a city or borough magistrate—from *baile*, a town ; may serve
as specimens of the many words which, in the natural intercourse between the Highlanders and the Lowlanders, have
been derived from the ancient Gaelic by the more modern
Scoto-Teutonic.

Four centuries ago, the English or Anglo-Teutonic, when
Chaucer, Gower, and Lydgate were still intelligible, had a
much greater resemblance to the Scoto-Teutonic than it has
at the present day. William Dunbar, one of the earliest,
as he was one of the best of the Scottish poets, and supposed
to have been born in 1465, in the reign of James III. in
Scotland, and of Edward IV. in England, wrote, among other
poems, the "Thrissel and the Rose." This composition was
alike good Scotch and good English, and equally intelligible to
the people of both countries. It was designed to commemorate
the marriage of James IV. with Margaret Tudor, daughter
of King Henry VII. of England—that small cause of many

great events, of which the issues have extended to our time, and which gave the Stuarts their title to the British throne. Dunbar wrote in the Scotch of the literati rather than in that of the common people, as did King James I. at an earlier period, when, a captive in Windsor Castle, he indited his beautiful poem, "The King's Quair," to celebrate the grace and loveliness of the Lady Beaufort, whom he afterwards married. The "Thrissel and the Rose" is only archaic in its orthography, and contains no words that a commonly well-educated Scottish ploughman cannot at this day understand, though it might puzzle some of the clever University men who write for the London press to interpret it without the aid of a glossary. Were the spelling of the following passages modernised, it would be found that there is nothing in any subsequent poetry, from Dunbar's day to our own, with which it need fear a comparison :—

> " Quhen Merché wes with variand windis, past,
> And Apryll haddé, with her silver shouris
> Tane leif at nature, with ane orient blast,
> And lusty May, that mudder is of flouris,
> Had maid the birdis to begyn their houris
> Among the tender odouris reid and quhyt,
> Quhois harmony to heir it was delyt.
> In bed at morrowe, sleiping as I lay,
> Methocht Aurora, with her crystal een,
> In at the window lukit by the day,
> And halsit me with visage paile and grene,
> On quhois hand a lark sang fro the splene :
> ' Awauk luvaris ! out of your slummering !
> See how the lusty morrow dois upspring ! ' "

King James V. did not, like Dunbar, confine his poetic efforts to the speech of the learned, but is supposed to have written in the vernacular of the peasantry and townspeople his well-known poem of " Peblis to the Play." This composition scarcely contains a word that Burns, three hundred years

b

later, would have hesitated to employ. In like manner King James V., in his more recent poem of "Christ's Kirk on the Green," written nearly three hundred and twenty years ago,[1] made use of the language of the peasantry to describe the assembly of the lasses and their wooers that came to the "dancing and the deray," with their gloves of the "*raffele* richt" (right doeskin), their "shoon of the *straitis*" (coarse cloth), and their

> "Kirtles of the *lineum* [Lincoln] licht,
> Weel pressed wi' mony plaitis."

His description of "Gillie" is equal to anything in Allan Ramsay or Burns, and quite as intelligible to the Scottish peasantry of the present day :—

> "Of all thir maidens mild as meid
> Was nane say gymp as Gillie;
> As ony rose her rude was reid,
> Hir lire was like the lily.
> Bot zallow, zallow was hir heid,
> And sche of luif sae sillie,
> Though a' hir kin suld hae bein deid,
> Sche wuld hae bot sweit Willie."

Captain Alexander Montgomery, who was attached to the service of the Regent Murray in 1577, and who enjoyed a pension from King James VI., wrote many poems in which the beauty, the strength, and the archness of the Scottish language were very abundantly displayed. "The Cherry and the Slae" is particularly rich in words, that Ramsay, Scott, and Burns have since rendered classical, and is besides a poem as excellent in thought and fancy as it is copious and musical

---

[1] "This is doubtful," says the late Lord Neaves, in a letter to the editor of this volume. "These obscure questions are fully discussed by Dr. Irving in his History of Scottish Poetry. I should say the probability was that 'Peblis to the Play' and 'Christ's Kirk' are by the same authors or of the same age, and neither of them by James V."

in diction.   Take the description of the music of the birds on a May morning as a specimen :—

> " The cushat croods, the corbie cries,
>   The coukoo couks, the prattling pies
>   To keck hir they begin.
>   The jargon o' the jangling jays,
>   The craiking craws and keckling kayes,
>   They deaved me with their din.
>   The painted pawn with Argus e'en
>   Can on his mayock call ;
>   The turtle wails on withered trees,
>   And Echo answers all.
>   Repeting, with greting,
>   How fair Narcissus fell,
>   By lying and spying
>   His schadow in the well."

The contemporaneous, perhaps the more recent, poetry of what may be called the ballad period, when the beautiful legendary and romantic lyrics of Scotland were sung in hall and bower, and spread from mouth to mouth among the peasantry, in the days when printing was rather for the hundred than for the million, as well as the comparatively modern effusions of Ramsay and Burns, and the later productions of the multitudinous poets and prose writers who have adorned the literature of Scotland within the present century, afford very convincing proofs, not only of the poetic riches, but of the abundant wit and humour of the Scottish people, to which the Scottish language lends itself far more effectually than the English.   Long anterior to the age when the noble art of printing was invented for the delight and instruction of mankind, the poetry of the bards of the "North Countrie" was familiar not only to the people of the North Countrie itself, but to those of the Teutonic south—a far less poetic race than their Keltic brethren ; and northern ballads were recited or sung in hall and bower among the upper classes, and in the popular gatherings of the multitude at fairs and festivals. These ballads, which often received an English colouring in travelling southwards, were highly esteemed for at least three centuries before the days of Shakspeare. The great poet was himself familiar with them, as is shown by more than one quotation from them in his immortal works.

Since the time when James VI. attracted so many of his poor countrymen to England, to push their fortunes at the expense of Englishmen, who would have been glad of their places, to the day when Lord Bute's administration under George III. made all Scotsmen unpopular for his sake, and when Dr. Samuel Johnson, who was of Scottish extraction himself [the son of a Scot, established as a bookseller in Leicester], and pretended to dislike Scotsmen—the better perhaps to disguise the fact of his lineage, and turn away suspicion—up to the time of Charles Lamb and the late Rev. Sydney Smith, it has been more or less the fashion in England to indulge in jokes at the expense of the Scottish people, and to portray them not only as overhard, shrewd, and "canny" in money matters, but as utterly insensible to "wit." Sydney Smith, who was a wit himself, and very probably imbibed his jocosity from the conversation of Edinburgh society, in the days when in that city he cultivated literature, as he himself records, upon a little oatmeal, is guilty of the well-known assertion that "it takes a surgical operation to drive a joke into a Scotsman's head." It would be useless to enter into any discussion on the differences between "wit" and "humour," which are many, or even to attempt to define the divergency between "wit" and what the Scotch call "wut;" but, in contradiction to the reverend joker, it is necessary to assert that the "wut" of the Scotch is quite equal to the "wit" of the English, and that Scottish humour is superior to any humour that was ever evolved out of the inner consciousness or intellect of the English peasantry inhabiting the counties south of Yorkshire. There is one

thing, however, which perhaps Sydney Smith intended when
he wrote, without thinking very deeply, if at all, about
what he said; the Scotch as a rule do not like, and do not
understand banter, or what in the current slang of the day
is called "chaff." In "chaff" and "banter" there is but
little wit, and that little is of the poorest, and contains no
humour whatever. "Chaff" is simply vulgar impertinence;
and the Scotch being a plain and serious people, though
poetical, are slow to understand and unable to appreciate it.
But with wit, or "wut," and humour, that are deserving
of the name, they are abundantly familiar; and their very
seriousness enables them to enjoy them the more. The
wittiest of men are often the most serious, if not the saddest
and most melancholy (witness Thomas Hood, Douglas Jerrold,
and Artemus Ward), and if the shortest possible refutation of
Sydney Smith's assertion were required, it might be found
in the works of Burns, Scott, and Christopher North.
Were there no wit and humour to be found in Scotand except in the writings of these three illustrious Scotsmen,
there would be enough and to spare to make an end of this
stale "chaff;" and to show by comparison that, wit and
humorist as Sydney Smith may have been, he was not equal
as a wit to Robert Burns, Sir Walter Scott, or Professor
Wilson. In what English poem of equal length is there to
be found so much genuine wit and humour mingled with
such sublimity and such true pathos and knowledge of life
and character as in "Tam o' Shanter"? What English novel,
by the very best of English writers, exceeds for wit and
humour any one of the great Scottish romances and tales of
Sir Walter Scott, the least of which would be sufficient to
build up and sustain a high literary reputation? And what
collection of English jests is equal to the "Laird of Logan,"
or Dean Ramsay's "Reminiscences of Scottish Life and
Character"? Joe Miller's "Jest Book," and all the countless

stories that have been fathered upon Joe Miller—one of the most melancholy of men—are but dreary reading, depending as they mostly do for their point upon mere puns and plays upon words, and to a great extent being utterly deficient in humour. It seems to require some infusion of Keltic blood in a nation to make the people either witty or appreciative of wit; for the dullest of all European peoples are without exception those in whom the Keltic least prevails. There is little or no wit or sense of wit in the peasantry of the South of England, though there may be some degree of coarse humour. Whereas the Scottish and the Irish peasantry are brimful both of wit and humour. If any one would wish to have a compendium of wisdom, wit, humour, and abundant knowledge, kindly as well as unkindly, of human nature, let him look to Allan Ramsay's "Collection of Scots Proverbs," where he will find a more perfect treasury of "pawkie," "cannie," "cantie," shrewd, homely, and familiar philosophy than English literature affords. And the humour and wit are not only in the ideas, but in the phraseology, which is untranslateable. Scottish poetry and pathos find their equivalents in English and Teutonic, but the quaint Scottish words refuse to go into any other idiom. "A man's a man for a' that"—strong, characteristic, and nervous in the Scottish Doric, fades away into attenuation and *banalité* when the attempt is made to render the noble phrase into French or German, Italian or Spanish. Even in English the words lose their flavour, and become weak by the substitution of "all that," for the more emphatic "a' that." Translate into literary English the couplet in "Duncan Gray," in which the rejected lover of Maggie

> Grat his e'en baith bleer't and blin—
> Spak o' lowpin ower a lin—

and the superior power of expressing the humorous which belongs to the Scottish language will at once become apparent. In the same way, when Luath, the poor man's dog, explains to his aristocratic friend what a hard time the poor have of it, a literal translation of the passage into colloquial English would utterly deprive it of its tenderness and humour :—

A cotter *howkin* in a *sheugh*,
Wi' dirty stanes *biggin* a *dyke*,
Baring a quarry and sic like ;
Himsel' an' wife he thus sustains
A smytrie o' wee duddie weans,
And nocht but his hand *darg* to keep
Them right and tight in *thack* and *rape*.

The "smytrie o' wee duddie weans" is simply inimitable, and sets a fair English translation and even a paraphrase at defiance.

Time was within living memory when the Scotch of the upper classes prided themselves on their native " Doric ; " when judges on the bench delivered their judgments in the broadest Scotch, and would have thought themselves guilty of puerile and unworthy affectation if they had preferred English words or English accents to the language of their boyhood ; when advocates pleaded in the same forcible tongue ; when ministers of religion found their best way to the hearts and to the understanding of their congregations in the use of the language most familiar to themselves, as well as to those whom they addressed ; and when ladies of the highest rank— celebrated alike for their wit and their beauty—sang their tenderest, archest, and most affecting songs, and made their bravest thrusts and parries in the sparkling encounters of conversation, in the familiar speech of their own country. All this, however, is fast disappearing, and not only the wealthy and titled, who live much in London, begin to grow ashamed of speaking the language of their ancestors, though the sound of the well-beloved accents from the mouths of others is not unwelcome or unmusical to their ears, but even the middle-class Scotch are learning to follow their example. The members of the legal and medical profession are afraid of the accusation of vulgarity that might be launched against them if they spoke publicly in the picturesque language of their fathers and grandfathers; and the clergy are unlearning in the pulpit the brave old speech that was good enough for John Knox [who was the greatest Angliciser of his day, and was accused by Winyet of that fault], and many thousands of pious preachers who, since his time, have worthily kept alive the faith of the Scottish people by appeals to their consciences in the language of their hearts. In ceasing to employ the "unadorned eloquence" of the sturdy vernacular, and using instead of it the language of books and of the Southern English, it is to be feared that too many of these literary preachers have lost their former hold upon the mind of the people, and that they have sensibly weakened the powers of persuasion and conviction which they possessed when their words were in sympathetic unison with the current of thought and feeling that flowed through the broad Scottish intellect of the peasantry. And where fashion leads, snobbism will certainly follow, so that it happens even in Scotland that young Scotsmen of the Dundreary class will sometimes boast of their inability to understand the poetry of Burns and the romances of Scott on account of the difficulties presented by the language!—as if their crass ignorance were a thing to be proud of!

But the old language, though of later years it has become unfashionable in its native land, survives not alone on the tongue but in the heart of the "common" people (and where is there such a common [or uncommon] people as the peasantry of Scotland ?), and has established for itself a place in the affections of those ardent Scotsmen who travel to the New World and to the remotest part of the Old, with the *auri sacra fames*, to lead them on to fortune, but who never permit that particular species of hunger—which is by no means peculiar to

Scotsmen—to deaden their hearts to their native land, or to render them indifferent to their native speech, the merest word of which, when uttered unexpectedly under a foreign sky, stirs up all the latent patriotism in their minds, and opens their hearts, and if need be their purses, to the utterer. It has also by a kind of poetical justice established for itself a hold and a footing even in the modern English which affects to ignore it; and, thanks more especially to Burns and Scott, and, in a minor degree, to Professor Wilson, and to the admiration which their genius has excited in England, America, and Australia, has engrafted many of its loveliest shoots upon the modern tree of actually spoken English. Every year the number of words that are taken like seeds or grafts from the Scottish conservatory, and transplanted into the fruitful English garden, is on the increase, as will be seen from the following anthology of specimens, which might have been made ten times as abundant if it had been possible to squeeze into one goblet a whole tun of hippocrene. Many of these words are recognised English, permissible both in literature and conversation ; many others are in progress and process of adoption and assimilation ; and many more that are not English, and may never become so, are fully worthy of a place in the Dictionary of a language that has room for every word, let it come whence it will, that expresses a new meaning or a more delicate shade of an old meaning, than any existing forms of expression admit. *Eerie*, and *gloaming*, and *cannie*, and *cantie*, and *cozie*, and *lift*, and *lilt*, and *caller*, and *gruesome*, and *thud*, and *weird*, are all of an ancient and noble pedigree, and were the most of them as English in the fifteenth century as they are fast becoming in the nineteenth.

If any Scotsman at home or abroad should, in going over the list in this epitome, fail to discover some favourite word that was dear to him in childhood, and that stirs up the recollections of his native land, and of the days when

he "paidled in the burn," or stood by the trysting-tree
"to meet his bonnie lassie when the kye cam' hame,"—
one word that recalls old times, old friends, and bygone
joys and sorrows,—let him reflect that in culling a posie
from the garden, the posie must of necessity be smaller
than the garden itself, and that the most copious of
selectors must omit much that he would have been glad to
add to his garland if the space at his disposal had permitted.
He must also remember that all the growths of the garden
are not rare flowers, but that weeds, though worthy of respect
in their way, are not always of appropriate introduction into
wreaths and garlands; and that the design of this Dictionary
was not to include all Scotticisms, but only those venerable
by their antiquity, quaint in their humour, touching in their
simplicity, or admirable in their poetic meaning.

The principal writers who have adorned the literature of
Scotland during the last three centuries, in addition to the
nameless and unknown minstrels to whom we owe so many of
the rugged but beautiful ballads of the North Countrie, may
be fairly said to have commenced with Dunbar, Barbour,
Henryson, and Montgomery, and to have ended with Professor
John Wilson, author of the inimitable "Noctes Ambrosianæ"
in *Blackwood's Magazine.* The list is long, and includes in
the seventeenth and early years of the eighteenth centuries
the names of William Crawford, author of many songs in
the purest vernacular of the peasantry; of Hector MacNeil,
whose exquisite ballad of the "Braes of Yarrow" would
be alone sufficient to place him high in the muster roll
of Scottish poets; and of Allan Ramsay, author of the
"Gentle Shepherd," a pastoral poem of which the simple
beauty was universally acknowledged at a time when pastoral
poems were more to the taste of the age than they have been
for the last century, and who collected into four volumes, under
the title of the "Tea-Table Miscellany," all the favourite songs

of the artificial period in which he flourished. Robert Burns had the highest reverence for the songs of Allan Ramsay, and considered it almost as bad as sacrilege to lay a reforming hand upon the compositions of his venerated predecessor, though Ramsay the wig-maker and barber was a star of very inferior magnitude and brilliancy compared with the solar effulgence that radiated from the genius of Burns the ploughman.

Between the period of Ramsay and that of Burns, which included about sixty years of very indifferent poetical manifestations, at least in Scotland, the lyric genius of the country continued as irrepressible, and songs of secondary merit flowed from the lips or pens of literate and illiterate people in a profuse stream. Even the unhappy events of 1715 and 1745, when the adherents of the dethroned and exiled Stuarts made their gallant and heroic attempts to re-establish themselves in the land of their birth and of their love—the land which they believed the Stuarts had a divine right to govern—the voice of song continued to be heard. True and tender-hearted people make love even in times of national peril and calamity, and the Scottish people sang or made love songs as usual in the homely and earnest dialect of the nation; while more earnest spirits gave vent to their political animosities and aspirations in the satirical rhymes and trenchant ballads that are still, under the name of "The Jacobite Minstrelsy of Scotland," known to all the literary students of history, as affording a greater insight into the social spirit of the people than the more staid and solid records of the mere annalist or philosophical historiographer are able to convey. Of the popular Scottish songs of the still more prolific age that commenced with the publication of the poems of Robert Burns, I have spoken in "The Book of Scottish Song," in words that I cannot do better than repeat in this place.

"Scotland is rich in the literature of song. The genius of the people is eminently lyrical. Although rigid in religion, and often gloomy in fanaticism, they have a finer and more copious music, are fonder of old romance and tradition, dance and song, and have altogether a more poetical aptitude and appreciation than their English brethren. For one poet sprung from the ranks of the English peasantry, Scotland can boast of ten, if not of a hundred. Ploughmen, shepherds, gardeners, weavers, tinklers, tailors, and even strolling beggars, have enriched the anthology of Scotland with thousands of songs and ballads of no mean merit. The whole land is as musical with the voice of song as it is with torrents and waterfalls. Every mountain glen, every strath and loch, every river and stream, every grove and grassy knowe, every castle, and almost every cottage, has its own particular song, ballad, or legend; for which the country is not so much indebted to scholars and men of learned leisure and intellectual refinement, as to the shrewd but hearty and passionate common people."

Of the Jacobite ballads, from which many quotations appear in the following pages, I said at the same time :—

"In the Jacobite songs more especially, the humour was far more conspicuous than the pathos. In the heat of the conflict, and when the struggle was as yet unended, and its results uncertain, ridicule and depreciation of the enemy were weapons more effective to stir the passions of the combatants than appeals to mere sentiment, even if the sentiment were as elevated as patriotism, or as tender as love and friendship. It was only when the Jacobite cause had become utterly hopeless, and when its illustrious adherents had laid down their lives for it on the bloody moor of Culloden, or on the cruel block of Tower Hill, or were pining in foreign lands in penury and exile, that the popular bards were so far inspired as to be able to strike the keynote of true poetry.

"As the age was, so were they. In their verse, as in a mirror, were reflected the events and feelings of the time. When the time was hopeful, they were hopeful. When the

time was ribald, insolent, jaunty, and reckless, they responded
to its touch like the harp-string to the harper. From 1688
to 1746 was the day of the common rhymers of the street or
the ale-house, or the lone farmhouse among the hills—the
day when the men of strong feelings, rude humour, and coarse
wit could "say their say" in language intelligible alike to
the clansman and the chief, the ploughman and the gentleman. And they were disputants who could hit as hard in the
battles of the tongue as they could, if need were, in the battle
of swords; and who could wield the musket and claymore in
physical as effectually as the sledge-hammer of invective in
moral warfare. Satire with them was not "a polished razor
keen," but a cudgel or a battering-ram; not a thing that
merely drew blood, but that broke the skull and smashed the
bones. But after the fatal fight of Culloden the voice of the
coarse humorist, if not altogether silenced, was softened or
subdued. There had been a time to sing and to dance, but it
had passed, and the day of lamentation had succeeded it. The
rhymers had flourished in the one epoch,—it was now the turn
of the poets.

"Sorrow for the vanquished and indignation against the
victors superseded all the lighter emotions which had hitherto
found their expression in songs, ballads, and epigrams; and
the echoes of national music that came from Scotland came
from saddened hearts, and from desolate and all but depopu-
lated glens. The voice of the mourner of these days was as
pathetic and often as vehement as the inspired strains of
Isaiah and Jeremiah, and partook of the phraseology as well
as sentiment of the sacred writings. In the hour of their
prosperity the Stewarts had been but common men; but
when adversity befell them, they were elevated to the rank
of heroes and demi-gods. Popular sympathy crowned them
with graces and virtues which, as throned kings, they had
never known; and loyalty, wavering in the sunshine of

fortune, became firm as the rocks in the tempests of calamity."

Among the accomplished ladies who between the '45 and the advent of Burns adorned the poetical literature, the names of Lady Anne Lindsay, Mrs. Grant of Carron, Lady Grizzel Baillie, Mrs. Cockburn, Mrs. Crawford, and Miss Blamire stand conspicuous for the tender, joyous, arch, and melancholy ballads which they wrote to the beautiful old melodies of their country, and which still retain their place amid all the changes of the musical taste and fashion in our time.

Of the contemporaries of Robert Burns, whose reputations seem pale in the light of his genius, but who are still worthy of honourable mention for their contributions to the literature of their country, may be cited the names of the Rev. John Skinner, author of the renowned ballad of "Tullochgorum," "The Ewie wi' the Crooked Horn," and other songs still popular; William Julius Mickle, the author of "There's nae Luck aboot the Hoose," one of the most simply beautiful songs that were ever inspired by the domestic affections; Robert Ferguson, to whom Burns in a burst of poetic enthusiasm generously erected a mortuary memorial in a graveyard at Edinburgh; Lapraik, Semple, and Logan, and in a succeeding generation Dr. John Leyden; James Hogg, better known as the Ettrick Shepherd; the Baroness Nairn, authoress of "The Land o' the Leal" and "Caller Herrin';" and Robert Tannahill, the luckless Paisley weaver, who wrote "Jessie the Flower o' Dunblane;" William Ross, the author of "Eleonore;" and John Beattie, the luckless author of the admirable poem of "John o' Arnha'," that contains passages of wit, humour, and descriptive power only exceeded by the inimitable "Tam o' Shanter" of Burns; William Motherwell, Donald Carrick, Alexander Rogers, James Ballantine, and a very numerous multitude of bards—all more or less esteemed in Scotland—of which it would serve no good purpose to recapitulate the names, even if it were possible to do so. Favourable specimens of their writings may be seen by all who care to look for them in such collections as " Whistle-Binkie," " Scottish Minstrelsy " (six volumes), and the very numerous collections issued from the Edinburgh press from the beginning till the middle of the present century.

But the greatest of all literary preservers of the Scottish language was undoubtedly the illustrious author of the " Waverley Novels." He was aided in the congenial task of perpetuating that language by such lesser lights of literature as Allan Cunningham, John Galt, and Christopher North ; but Sir Walter Scott towered far above them all, and carried the name and fame of Scotland, as well as the quaint graces and tender archaisms of the language, to the remotest parts of the civilised world.

The generations that have arisen since the old Abbey of Dryburgh received the mortal remains of that greatest of the Scottish writers, second to none of British birth, except Shakspeare, have lost sight in some degree of the works of the great Sir Walter. But though partially eclipsed in popularity, they are firmly established among the classics of the nineteenth century, not only in his own country, but in France and Germany. In their original garb—untranslateable to foreign nations in all their native vigour and delicate shades of meaning—they will consecrate to many a future generation that shall have ceased to speak Scottish, the remembrance of a noble old language. Yet it may be said with truth " that even in its ashes will live the wonted fires ; " for modern English in the latter half of the nineteenth century has not disdained to borrow from the ancient Scotch many of the strong simple words that the fashionable English writers of the eighteenth century suffered to fall into desuetude. As there has been pre-Raphaelitism in painting, there have been and will continue to be pre-Addisonianism and even pre-Shakspearianism in

the richly composite language spoken and written in these
islands, and in the vast American and Australian continents
that are rapidly producing a literature of their own. The
English language of the future will in all probability comprise
many words not now used or understood on the south of the
Tweed, but that are quite familiar to the north of it, as
well as in the United States and Australia. Such useful and
poetical words as *thud, gloamin', eerie, dree, weird,* and the others
already cited, and which have been adopted from the ancient
Scotch by the best English writers, are a clear gain to the
language, and are not likely to be abandoned.

Whatever oblivion may attend the works of the great bulk
of Scottish writers, Robert Burns and Walter Scott will certainly live in the affection of posterity; and if some of their
words have already become obsolete, their wit and humour,
their earnestness and their eloquence, and the whole spirit of
their teachings, will survive. To aid English readers in the
comprehension of these immortal books, and to remind Scottish
readers of what they owe to the literary lights of their country,
is one of the main objects of the present compilation. The
author, if he can be called the author, or merely the artificer of
this book, hopes that it will not only answer this particular purpose, but serve more generally to impress upon the minds of the
people of this age how rich is the language of their ancestors,
and what stores of literary wealth lie comparatively unknown
and unregarded in the vernacular of what are irreverently
called the "common people." It is the "common people" who
create and shape the language, and the "uncommon people,"
known as authors, whose duty it is to help to perpetuate it in
books for the pleasure and instruction of posterity.

November 1887.

DICTIONARY OF LOWLAND SCOTCH.

A

Ae, the indéfinite article *a*, or one, and far more emphatic in poetical composition than *ane* or *one*, as in Burns's beautiful song "*Ae* fond kiss and then we sever." Some of the many half - English editors of the Scottish poet have altered *ae* into "one," which to a Scottish ear is the reverse of an improvement. *Ae* does not merely signify ʾone, but *only one*, and is definite and particular, not indefinite and general, in its meaning.

Aboon, above.

Aiblins, perhaps, possibly; from *able*, conjoined with *lin* or *lins*, inclining to, as in the "westlin wind"—wind inclining to the west; hence *aiblins* means inclining to be possible.

> There's mony waur been o' the race,
> And *aiblins* ane been better.
> —BURNS : *The Dream.*
> *To George III.*

Aidle, ditchwater; derivation unknown, but possibly from the Gaelic *adhall*, dull, heavy, stagnant.

> Then lug out your ladle,
> Deal brimstone like *aidle*,
> And roar every note of the damned.
> —BURNS : *Orthodox, Orthodox.*

Ail at. *What ails ye at?* is a peculiarly Scottish synonym for What is your objection to her, him, or it?

An old servant who took a charge of everything that went on in the family, having observed that his master had taken wine with every lady at the table except one who wore a green dress, jogged his memory with the question, "*What ails ye at her in the green gown!*"—DEAN RAMSAY.

Air, early, from the Gaelic *ear*, the east, where the sun rises. "An air winter makes a sair winter;" which may be Englished, "An early winter makes a surly winter."

Airt, a point of the compass; also to direct or show the way. This excellent word ought to be adopted into English. It comes from the Gaelic *ard*, *aird*, a height. "Of a' the *airts* from which the wind can blaw," is better than "of all the *quar-*

A

ters from which the wind can blow."

> O' a' the *airts* the wind can blaw,
> I dearly lo'e the west,
> For there the bonnie lassie lives,
> The lassie I lo'e best.—BURNS.

> But yon green graff (grave), now huskie green,
> Wad *airt* me to my treasure.—BURNS.

Aizle, a live coal that flies out of the fire. It is a superstition in England to call the live coals violently ejected from the fire by the gas generated in them by the names of "purses" or "coffins," according to the fanciful resemblance which they bear to these articles, and which are supposed to be prophetic of money, or of a death in the family. Some such superstition seems to lie at the root of the Scottish word *aizle.*

> She noticed that an *aizle* brunt
> Her braw new worset apron.
>   —BURNS : *Hallowe'en.*

Jamieson says the word was used metaphorically by the poet Douglas to describe the appearance of a country that has been desolated by fire and sword. In the Gaelic, *aisleine* signifies a death-shroud. The derivation, which has been suggested from hazel or hazel-nut, from the shape of the coal when ejected, seems untenable. The Gaelic *aiscal,* meaning joy, merriment, has also been suggested, as having been given by children to the flying embers shot out from the fire ; but the derivation from *aisleine* seems preferable.

Anent, concerning, relating to. This word has only recently been admitted into the English dictionaries published in England. In Worcester's and Webster's Dictionaries, published in the United States, it is inserted as a Scotticism. Mr. Stormonth, in his Etymological Dictionary (1871), derives it from the Anglo-Saxon *ongean* and the Swedish *on gent,* opposite ; but the etymology seems doubtful.

> The anxiety *anent* them was too intense to admit of the poor people remaining quietly at home.—*The Dream Numbers, by* T. A. TROLLOPE.

Arl-penny, a deposit paid to seal a bargain ; earnest-money ; French *arrhes.* From the Gaelic *earlas* or *iarlas,* earnest-money, a pledge to complete a bargain.

> Here, tak' this gowd, and never want
> Enough to gar ye drink and rant,
> And this is but an *arl-penny*
> To what I afterwards design ye.
>   —ALLAN RAMSAY.

Asse, the fireplace; the hearth ; the place where the ashes or cinders fall. Asse-hole or ash-pit is supposed by some philologists to be derivable from the Gaelic *aisir,* a receptacle ; *ais,* the back part of anything, or backwards.

> Do ye no see Rob, Jock, and Hab,
> As they are girded gallantlie,
> While I am hurklin i' the *asse ?*
> I'll hae a new cloak about me.
>   —*Ancient Ballad : Tak' your Auld Cloak about ye.*

Athol brose, whisky with honey, taken as a morning drop; a powerful and indigestive mixture, that no one but a Highlander out in the open air and in active exercise during the whole day can safely indulge in. Why it is named from the district of Athol in preference to any other part of the Highlands is neither known nor perhaps discoverable.

An' aye since he wore tartan trews
He dearly lo'ed the *Athole brose*,
And wae was he, you may suppose,
To play farewell to whisky.
—NEIL GOW.

Auld lang syne. This phrase, so peculiarly tender and beautiful, and so wholly Scotch, has no exact synonym in any language, and is untranslatable except by a weak periphrasis. The most recent English dictionaries have adopted it, and the expression is now almost as common in England as in Scotland. Allan Ramsay included in "The Tea-Table Miscellany" a song entitled "Old Long Syne," a very poor production. It remained for Robert Burns to make "Auld lang syne" immortal, and fix it for ever in the language of Great Britain, America, and the Antipodes. *Lang sin syne* is a kindred, and almost as beautiful a phrase, which has not yet been adopted into English.

A wee, a short time ; contraction of a "*wee* while," or a little while. *Bide-a-wee*, wait a little.

Upon a summer afternoon,
A *wee* before the sun gaed doun.
—*The Lass o' Gowrie.*

Awmrie, a chest, a cabinet, a secretaire ; from the French *armoire.*

Close the *awmrie*, steek the kist,
Or else some gear will soon be missed.
—SIR WALTER SCOTT : *Donald Caird.*

Ayont, beyond or on the other side. A Northumbrian as well as a Scottish word. In the English Border " *ayont* the Tweed " is Scotland, and on the Scottish side of the Border it is England.

B

Bab. Any personal adornment worn by young lovers, either a bunch of flowers on the bosom, or a tassel or bow of ribbons. *Lug-bab*, an ear-ring ; *wooer-babs*, a knot of ribbons tied at the knee by the young peasant lads when they went courting. The word also signifies a cockade or other badge in the hat or bonnet.

Bauble is possibly of similar or the same origin. The word is derived from the Gaelic *babag* or *baban*, a tassel, a fringe, a knot, a cluster ; and *babach*, innocent pleasure, applied to the *bab* as a symbol.

A cockit hat with a *bab* o' blue ribbons at it.
—SIR WALTER SCOTT : *Old Mortality.*

Bairn-time, a whole family of children, or all the children that a woman bears. This peculiarly Scottish word is a corruption of a *bairn-teem ;* from the Gaelic *taom*, the English *teem*, to bear, to produce, to pour out.

> Your Majesty, most excellent !
>   While nobles strive to please ye,
> Will ye accept a compliment
>   A simple Bardie gi'es ye?
> Thae bonny *bairn-time* Heaven has lent,
>   Still higher may they heeze ye !
>   —Burns : *A Dream, Addressed to*
>   *George III.*

The following lines, from "The Auld Farmer's New Year's Salutation to his Auld Mare, Maggie," show that Burns understood the word in its correct sense, though he adopted the erroneous spelling of *time* instead of *teem :*—

> My pleugh is now thy *bairn-time* a',
> Four gallant brutes as e'er did draw,
> Forbye sax mae I sellt awa',
>   That thou has nurst ;
> They drew me thretteen pounds an' twa,
>   The very warst.

Balow ! An old lullaby in the Highlands, sung by nurses to young children, as in the pathetic ballad entitled " Lady Anne Bothwell's Lament : "—

> *Balow !* my babe, lie still and sleep,
> It grieves me sair to see thee weep !

Burns has " *Hee, baloo !* " to the tune of " The Highland *Balow :* "—

> Hee, *baloo*, my sweet wee Donald,
> Picture of the great Clanronald.

The phrase is derived from the Gaelic *bà*, the equivalent of *bye*

in the common English phrase " Bye ! bye ! " an adjuration to sleep—" Go to bye-bye ; " and *laogh*, darling, whence, by the abbreviation of *laogh* into *lao*, *bà-lao* or *balow*—" Sleep, darling." Jamieson has adopted a ludicrous derivation from the French—" *bas là le loup*," which he mis-translates " Be still ; the wolf is coming."

Bandster, one who makes a band or binds sheaves after the reapers in the harvest-field.

> In hairst at the shearing, nae youths now
>   are jeering,
> The *bandsters* are lyart and wrinkled
>   and grey ;
> At fair or at preaching, nae wooing or
>   fleeching,
> The flowers o' the forest are a' weed
>   away.
>   —Elliot : *The Flowers of the Forest.*

In this pathetic lament for " the flowers " of Ettrick Forest —the young men slain at the doleful battle of Flodden—the maidens mourn in artless language for the loss of their lovers, and grieve, as in this touching stanza, that their fellow-labourers in the harvest-field are old men, wrinkled and grey, with their sparse locks, instead of the lusty youths who have died fighting for their country. The air of this melancholy but very beautiful song is pure Gaelic.

Bane-dry, dry as a bone ; *bane-idle*, thoroughly idle ; not only idle in the flesh, but in the bone and marrow.

Bang, to beat, to subdue; *bangie* or *bangsome*, quarrelsome, irritable, apt to take offence; *bangbeggar*, a constable or a constable's staff, and *bangrec*, a scolding, irritable, and contentious woman. The etymology of these words is uncertain. The last seems to be derivable from the Gaelic *ban*, a woman; *banag*, a busy little woman; *ban cheaird*, a female tramp or gipsy.

Bannock, an oatmeal cake, originally compounded with milk instead of water.

> Hale breeks, saxpence, and a *bannock*.
> —BURNS: *To James Tait, Glenconner.*

> *Bannocks* o' bear-meal, bannocks o' barley.
> —*Jacobite Song.*

From the Gaelic *bainne*, milk.

Bap, a small wheaten cake or roll, sold in Scotland for breakfast when porridge is not used. The grandfather of a late Prime Minister of Great Britain kept a small shop in Leith Walk, Edinburgh, where he sold "baps," flour, oatmeal, peas, &c., and where he was popularly known to the boys of the neighbourhood as "Sma' Baps," because his baps were reputed to be smaller than those of his brother tradesmen.

Barken, to clot, to harden on the surface, as some viscous and semi-liquid mixtures do on exposure to the air. The word is derived from the bark or outward covering of trees.

Barm, yeast; old English; not yet obsolete in the rural districts.

Barmkin, a corruption of *barbican*, a watch-tower on a castle or fortress. The derivation of *barbican* (the name of a street in old London, still retained) is from the Gaelic *bar*, a pinnacle or high place; and *beachan*, a place of watching or observation. From *beachan* is derived *beacon*, a watch-fire, a signal light.

> And broad and bloody rose the sun,
> And on the *barmkin* shone.
> .   .   .   .   .   .
> And he called a page who was witty and sage
> To go to the *barmkin* high.
> —*Border Minstrelsy: Lord Soulis.*

Bauch, insipid, tasteless, without flavour, as in the alliterative proverb:—

> Beauty but bounty's but *bauch*.
> —ALLAN RAMSAY.

(Beauty without goodness is without flavour.)

The etymology of this peculiarly Scottish word is uncertain, unless it be allied to the English *baulk*, to hinder, to impede, to frustrate; or from the Gaelic *bac*, which has the same meaning.

Baudrons, a pet name for a cat, for which no etymology has yet been found. The word remains as unaccountable as "Tybert," used by Shakspeare for the same animal.

> Auld *baudrons* by the ingle sits,
> Wi' her loof her face a washin'.
> —BURNS: *Sic a Wife as Willie had.*

Bauk, the cross-beam in the roof of a cottage ; *baukie-bird*, a name given to the bat, that haunts the roof. *Bauk* is from the English *baulk*, of which the primary meaning was from the Gaelic *bac*, to hinder, to frustrate, and was applied to the cross-beam of the roof because it prevented the roof from giving way, and to other wooden partitions necessary for division. It also came to signify to disappoint, because disappointment was the prevention or *hindering* of the fulfilment and realisation of hope.

> When lyart leaves bestrew the yird,
> Or, waverin' like the *baukie-bird*,
>   Bedim cauld Boreas' blast,
> An' hailstanes drive wi' bitter skyte.
>   —BURNS : *The Jolly Beggars.*

Bawbie, a halfpenny—metaphorically used for a fortune by Sir Alexander Boswell, the son of the more famous James Boswell, the biographer of Dr. Johnson. It occurs in the song of "Jennie's Bawbie:"—

> Quoth he, " My goddess, nymph, and queen,"
> Your beauty dazzles baith my e'en,"
> But deil a beauty had he seen
>   But Jennie's *bawbee.*

Sir Alexander took the hint of his song from a much older one :—

> A' that e'er my Jeanie had,
> My Jeanie had, my Jeanie had,
> A' that e'er my Jeanie had
>   Was ae *bawbie.*
> There's your plack, and my plack,
> And your plack, and my plack,
>   And Jeanie's *bawbie.*

Bawsont or **bawsins**, marked with white on the face, as in cattle ; of uncertain etymology, but possibly connected with *bash*, the forehead.

> The stirk stands i' the tether,
>   And our braw *bawsint* yade
> Will carry ye hame your corn ;
>   What wad ye be at, ye jade?
>   —*Woo'd and Married and a'.*

Bawtie, a watch-dog ; apparently from the Gaelic *beachd*, watch, observe, and *tigh* (pronounced *tee*), a house. A favourite name in Scotland for a faithful dog. The English word *Towser*, which is equally common, is also from the Celtic *tuisle*, to struggle or contend with.

Bourd na' in *Bawtie*, lest he bite (*i.e.*, do not play tricks or jest with the watch-dog, lest he bite you).

Bazil, a sot, a fool ; of unknown etymology, but possibly connected with the Gaelic *peasanach*, an impertinent person.

> He scorned to sock mang weirdless fellows,
>   Wi' menseless *bazils* in an alehouse.
>   —GEORGE BEATTIE : *John o' Arnha'.*

Beak or **beek**—common in Ayrshire and Mearns—to sit by a fire and exposed to the full heat of it.

>   A lion,
> To recreate his limbs and take his rest,
> *Beak* and his breast and bellie at the sun,
> Under a tree lay in the fair forest.
> —ROBERT HENRYSON *in The Evergreen:
>   The Lion and the Mouse.*

Beastie, an affectionate diminutive of *beast*, applied to any small and favourite animal.

Wee, sleekit, cowerin', timorous *beastie*,
Oh, what a panic's in thy breastie !
Thou needna start awa sae hastie,
    Wi' bickerin' brattle.
            —BURNS : *To a Mouse.*

Beck, to curtsey.

" It's aye gude to be ceevil," as the auld
wife said when she *beckit* to the deevil.—
ALLAN RAMSAY'S *Scots Proverbs.*

Bed-fast, confined to bed or bed-
ridden. In English, *fast* as a
suffix is scarcely used except in
steadfast, i.e., fast fixed to the
stead place or purpose.

For these eight or ten months I have
been ailing, sometimes *bed-fast* and sometimes not.—BURNS : *Letter to Cunningham.*

An earth - fast or *yird - fast*
stane is a large stone firmly
fixed in the earth. *Faith-fast,
truth-fast,* and *hope-fast* are beautiful phrases, unused by English
writers. If *faithful* and *truth-
ful, faithless* and *truthless,* are
permissible, why not *faith-fast,
truth-fast,* and *hope-fast ?*

Beet, to feed or add fuel to a
fire or flame ; from the Gaelic
beatha, life, food, and *beathaich,*
to feed, to nourish.

May Kennedy's far-honoured name
Lang *beet* his hymeneal flame.
            —BURNS : *To Gavin Hamilton.*

It warms me, it charms me,
    To mention but her name ;
It heats me, it *beets* me,
    And sets me a' aflame.
            —BURNS : *Epistle to Davie.*

I wonderin' gaze on her stately steps,
    And *beet* my hopeless flame.
            —ALLAN CUNNINGHAM : *Bonny
                Lady Ann.*

Beltain, the fire of Bel or Baal,
kindled by the Druids annually
on the first morning of May
direct from the rays of the sun.
Ben Ledi, in Perthshire—the
hill of God, as the name signifies in Gaelic—was the most
sacred of all the hills, on the
summit of which this imposing
ceremony was performed. The
name of Bel or Baal is derived
from the Gaelic *beatha* or *bea*
(*th* silent), life, and *uile,* all ;
whence Bel, Beul, or Baal, the
life of all, and *tain,* a corruption of *teine,* the fire. The ceremony was also performed in Ireland in pre-Christian times on
the 21st of June. The word
" Beltane " is of frequent occurrence in the ballad poetry of
Scotland, and in conjunction
with " Yule " or Christmas is by
no means obsolete ; as in the
phrase, " The love that is hot at
Beltane may grow cauld ere
Yule."

Belyve, by-and-bye, immediately.
This word occurs in Chaucer
and in many old English romances.
            Hie we *belyve*
And look whether Ogie be alive.
            —*Romance of Sir Otuel.*

Belyve the elder bairns come droppin' in.
    —BURNS : *Cotter's Saturday Night.*

Bicker, a drinking-cup, a beaker,
a turn ; also a quarrel.

Fill high the foaming *bicker !*
Body and soul are mine, quoth he,
I'll have them both for liquor.
            —*The Gin Fiend and his Three
                Houses.*

Setting my staff wi' a' my skill
  To keep me sicker;
Though leeward whiles, against my will,
  I took a *bicker.*
—BURNS: *Death and Doctor Hornbook.*

Bicker means rapid motion, and, in a secondary and very common sense, quarrelling, fighting, a battle. Sir Walter Scott refers to the *bickers* or battles between the boys of Edinburgh High School and the Gutterbluids of the streets. In "Hallowe'en" Burns applies *bickering* to the motion of running water :—

Whiles glistened to the nightly rays,
Wi' *bickerin'*, dancin' dazzle.
—R. DRENNAN.

Bide, to stop, to delay, to wait, to dwell or abide.

Bield, a shelter. Of uncertain etymology, perhaps from *build.*

Better a wee bush than nae *bield.*
Every man bends to the bush he gets *bield* frae.
    —ALLAN RAMSAY'S *Scots Proverbs.*

Beneath the random *bield* of clod or stane.
    —BURNS: *To a Mountain Daisy.*

Bien, comfortable, agreeable, snug, pleasant; from the French *bien,* well. Lord Neaves was of opinion that this derivation was doubtful, but suggested no other. If the French etymology be inadmissible, the Gaelic can supply *binn,* which means harmonious, pleasant, in good order; which is perhaps the true root of the word.

While frosty winds blaw in the drift
  Ben to the chimla lug,
I grudge a wee the great folk's gift
  That live sae *bien* and snug.
      —BURNS: *Epistle to Davie.*

Bien's the but and ben.
—JAMES BALLANTINE; *The Father's Knee.*

Bier or beir, a lament, a moan.

As I went forth to take the air
  Intil an evening clear,
I spied a lady in a wood
  Making a heavy *bier*;
Making a heavy *bier*, I wot,
  While the tears dropped frae her e'en,
And aye she sighed and said Alas!
  For Jock o' Hazelgreen.
    —*Old Ballad, on which* SIR WALTER SCOTT *modelled his "Jock o' Hazeldean."*

Jamieson says that *beir* (not *bier*) is allied to the Icelandic *byre,* a tempest, and to old English *bri, byre, bine,* force; but it is of more probable origin in the Gaelic *buir,* to lament, to whine; whence probably the prevalence of the custom among the Celtic nations of moaning over the dead body, and chanting the doleful coronach or death-wail, came afterwards to be applied to the *bier,* or table, board, or plank, on which the corpse was extended, or the coffin in which it was placed.

Bigly, beautiful; origin unknown.

Will ye come to my *bigly* bower,
  An' drink the wine wi' me?
—BUCHAN'S *Ancient Scottish Ballads.*

Billies, fellows, comrades, young men; a term of familiarity and affection.

When chapman *billies* leave the street,
And drouthy neebors neebors meet.
      —BURNS: *Tam o' Shanter.*

Rise up! rise up now, *billie* dear,
  Rise up! I speak these words to see
Whether thou'st gotten thy deadly
    wound,
  Or if God and good leaching may succour thee.—*Border Minstrelsy.*

"This word," says Jamieson,

"is probably allied to German *billig*, the Belgian *billiks*, equals, as denoting those that are on a footing as to age, rank, relation, affection, or employment."

This is an error. In German, *billig* means moderate in price, fair, just, equitable, reasonable. The Lowland Scotch *billie* is the same as the English *fellow ;* and both are derived from the Gaelic *ba-laoch*, a shepherd, a cowherd, a husbandman ; from *ba*, cows, plural of *bo*, a cow, and *laoch*, a lad, a young man.

Bink or **bunker**, a bench ; called in America a *bunk*.

I set him in beside the *bink*,
And gied him bread and ale to drink.
—HERD's *Collection : The Brisk Young Lad.*
A winnock (window) *bunker* in the east,
Where sat Auld Nick in shape o' beast.
—BURNS : *Tam o' Shanter.*

Bird or **burd**, a term of endearment, applied to a young woman or child.

And by my word, the bonnie *bird*
In danger shall not tarry,
And though the storm is raging wild,
I'll row ye o'er the ferry.
—THOMAS CAMPBELL.

Birdalane or **burdalane**. A term of sorrowful endearment, applied to an only child, especially to a girl, to signify that she is without household comrades or companions.

And Newton Gordon, *birdalane*,
And Dalgetie both stout and keen.
—SCOTT's *Minstrelsy.*

Birkie, a young and conceited person ; from the Gaelic *biorach*,

a two-year-old heifer ; *bioraiche*, a colt ; applied in derision to a very young man who is lively but not over-wise.

Ye see yon *birkie* ca'd a lord,
Wha struts and stares and a' that.
—BURNS : *A Man's a Man.*

" And besides, ye donnard carle ! " continued Sharpitlaw, " the minister did say that he thought he knew something of the features of the *birkie* that spoke to him in the Park."—SCOTT : *Heart of Midlothian.*

" Weel, Janet, ye ken when I preach you're almost always fast asleep before I've well given out my text ; but when any of these young men from St. Andrews preach for me, I see you never sleep a wink. Now that's what I call no using me as you should do." " Hoot, sir," was the reply, " is that a' ? I'll soon tell you the reason o' that. When you preach, we a' ken the Word o' God is safe in your hands ; but when thae young *birkies* tak it in hand, ma certie ! but it tak's us a' to look after them."—DEAN RAMSAY.

Birl, to pour out liquor ; probably from the same root as the English *purl*, as in the phrase " a purling stream," probably derived from the ancient but now obsolete Gaelic *bior*, a well ; *bioral*, pertaining to a well or like a well.

There were three lords *birling* at the wine
On the dowie dens o' Yarrow.
—MOTHERWELL's *Ancient Minstrelsy.*
Oh, she has *birled* these merry young men
With the ale, but and the wine.
—*Border Minstrelsy : Fause Foodrage.*

Birs, the thick hair or *bristles* on the back of swine.

The souter gave the sow a kiss.
Humph ! quo' she, it's a' for my *birs* !
—ALLAN RAMSAY's *Scots Proverbs.*

Bismeres or **bismar**, the keeper of a brothel, a bawd ; from the

Gaelic *baois*, lust, lewdness, and *mathair* (pronounced *ma-air*), mother; also a prostitute. Jamieson derives the word from the Anglo-Saxon, and quotes Rudd —"*Bismer*, contumelia, aut *bismerian*, illudere, dehonnorare polluere." The Gaelic derivation is more satisfactory than that from the hybrid language called Anglo-Saxon, which is but inchoate and primitive old English based upon corrupted Celtic, with superadded Dutch and Flemish.

Bit and brat. To earn "bit and brat" is to earn food and raiment; from the Gaelic *biadh*, food, and *brat*, a rag, a garment, or clothing.   .

Bittock, a small bit or piece. When a wayfarer on the road asks of a chance passer-by at what distance is the place to which he is bound, the probable reply is, that it is two, three, or any other number of miles "and a *bittock*," signifying that the respondent will not pledge himself to the exactitude of his reply, adding, with the proverbial cautiousness popularly ascribed in England to his countrymen, that there may be a *bittock* added to his computation; though the qualifying *bittock* has often been found to exceed the primary estimate.

Black-mail. The word *mail* is derived from the Gaelic *màl*, rent, tax, or tribute; and *màla*, a bag, a sack, a purse, a budget to contain the tribute. Why the particular exaction called *black-mail*, levied by many Highland chieftains in former times to ensure the protection of the herds of cattle passing through their territories to southern markets, received the epithet of *black* has never been clearly explained. The word has been supposed by some to designate the moral turpitude and blackness of character of those who exacted such a tax, and by others it has been conjectured that *black*-mail derived its name from the *black* cattle of the Highlands, for whose protection against thieves and caterans the tribute was levied; while yet another set of etymologists have set forth the opinion that *plack*-mail, not *black*-mail, was the proper word, derived from the small Scottish coin— the *plaque* or *plack*—in which the tribute was supposed to be collected. But as *mail* is undoubtedly from the Gaelic, and as *black-mail* was a purely Highland extortion, and so called at a time when few resident Highland chiefs and none of their people spoke English, it is possible that *black* is not to be taken in the English sense, but that it had, like its associated word, *mail*, a Gaelic origin. In that language, *blathaich*—pronounced (the *th* silent) *blá-aich*— signifies to protect, to cherish. Thus *black-mail* meant the tribute or tax of protection. If *black*, the colour, were really intended, the Highlanders would have used their own word and called the tribute *màl-dubh*. The Gaelic *blathaich* has the secondary meaning of to heat. In the same sense, the Flemish has *blakcn*, to warm, to animate, to burn. In connection with the idea of warming, the Scottish language has several words which can scarcely be explained by *black* in the English sense. The first is *black-burning*, which Jamieson says is "used in reference to shame when it is so great as to produce deep blushing, or to *crimson* the countenance." This phrase is equivalent to the English, *a burning shame*, when the cheeks burn or glow, not with black, but with red. The second is *black-fishing*, which Jamieson defines as fishing for salmon by night by means of *torches*. He explains the epithet *black* in this instance by suggesting that "the fish" are *black* or foul when they come up the streams to deposit their spawn, an explanation which is wholly inadmissible. The third and fourth phrases are *black-foot* and *black-sole*, which both mean "a confidant in love affairs, or one who goes between a lover and his mistress endeavouring to bring the cold or coy fair one to compliance." In these instances, *black* is certainly more related to the idea of warming, inciting, animating, than to that

of blackness. *Black-foot* and *black-sole* in reality mean *hot*-foot and *hot*-sole, as in the corresponding phrase, *hot-haste*, applied to the constant running to-and-fro of the go-between. *Black-winter*, which signifies, according to Jamieson, "the last cart-load of grain brought home from the harvest-field," is as difficult as either of the phrases previously-cited to associate with the idea of *blackness*, either moral or physical; but rather with that of comfort, warmth—or provision for the winter months. The winter itself may be metaphorically black, but not by any extension of meaning or of fancy can the epithet *black*, in colour, be associated with a *cart-load of grain*. There are two other equivalent phrases in Scottish use in which *black* is an epithet, namely, *black victual*, meaning pulse, beans and peas, and *black crop*, which has the same signification. Jamieson says these crops are so called because they are always *green*, and extends the meaning to turnips, ¦potatoes, &c., for the same reason! But *black* cannot be accepted as equivalent to *green*.

Of all the derivations ever suggested for *black - mail*, the word on which this disquisition concerning *black* started, the most unfortunate is that of Jamieson, who traces it to "the German *blakmal*, and to the Flemish *blaken*, to rob." It is sufficient for the refutation of

Jamieson to state that there is no such word as *blakmal* in the German language, and that *blaken*, as already observed, does not signify to rob, but to burn. In conclusion, it may be stated that the English *black* has long been a puzzle to the compilers of dictionaries. There is no trace of it to be found in the sense of colour in any of the Teutonic languages. *Black* in German is *schwarz;* in Dutch, Flemish, and Swedish, *swart;* in Danish, *svaerte;* and in old English, *swarth* and *swarthy.*

Worcester's Dictionary derives *black* from *bleak.* Mr. Wedgwood, who is one of the latest authorities, says "the original meaning of *black* seems to have been exactly the reverse of the present sense, viz., shining white. It is, in fact," he adds, "radically identical with the French *blanc*, from which it differs only in the absence of the nasal."

Perhaps it may be possible, *ex fumo dare lucem*, to kindle a light out of all this smoke. May not the real root of the English *black* (as a colour) be the Gaelic *blàaich*, or the Flemish *blaken*, to burn? That which is *burned* is *blackened.* A *black* man, or negro, is one whose skin has been tanned or burned by the sun; and *sun-burnt* in this case means *blackened.* It may be said of this explanation, whether correct or not, that it is at all events entitled to as much consideration as those from *bleak*

and *blanc*, and that it is] far more probable than either.

Black saxpence, supposed in Scottish superstition to be a magical sixpence given by the Devil in payment for the soul of the person who accepted it. The virtue of this "black" sixpence consisted in its having always a bright sixpence alongside of it; that as soon as it was taken away and spent, it was replaced by another, and so on to the "crack of doom." Jamieson supposed that the infernal sixpence was so named from its colour; but possibly, and more probably, it was thus designated from the Gaelic *blathaich*, protection, as being a protection against absolute poverty as long as the unholy compact existed. See *Black-mail* and *Black-Watch* for this sense of the word *black.*

Black-Watch, a name given to the Highland regiment, the brave and very distinguished Forty-Second, which has fought, bled, and conquered in many a hard-won field in every part of the world, where its services were required to vindicate the right and uphold the honour of Great Britain. It is generally supposed that the name was given to them on account of the dark colour of the tartan which they wear; but the tartan is not black, but very dark green, like the tartans of many Highland clans, in which green is the predominant hue, varied by black, blue, red, or yellow stripes in some of them. It is possible, however, that *black* in this instance, as in *blackmail*, &c. (which see), signifies protection, and that the popular name of the illustrious regiment in question signifies the "*protecting* watch."

Blae, of a livid blue colour, sickly blue.

Blaeberries, bilberries.

> The morning *blae* and wan.
> —DOUGLAS: *Translation of the Æneid.*

> How dow you this *blae* eastlin' wind,
> That's like to blaw a body blind?
> —BURNS.

> Be in dread, O sirs! Some of you will stand with *blae* countenances before the tribunal of God.
> —BRUCE: *The Soul's Confirmation.*

Blash, a gust of wind.

> Amidst a glint o' sunshine comes a *blash* o' cauld sleet.—*Noctes Ambrosianæ.*

Blate, shy, modest, bashful; of unknown derivation. *Bleid* in Gaelic is the reverse of *blate* in Lowland Scotch, and means impertinent, troublesome, forward, presuming.

> Says Lord Frank Ker, Ye are na' *blate* To bring us the news o' yer ain defeat.
> —*Jacobite Ballad: Johnnie Cope.*

> A *blate* cat makes a proud mouse.
> —ALLAN RAMSAY.

Blaud, to lay anything flat with violence, as the wind or a storm of rain does the corn.

> Curst common sense, that imp o' hell,
>
> . . . . . .
>
> This day M'Kinlay takes the flail,
> And he's the boy will *blaud* her.
> —BURNS: *The Ordination.*

> Ochon! ochon! cries Haughton,
> That ever I was born
> To see the Buckie burn rin bluid,
> And *blauding* a' the corn.
> —*Aberdeenshire Ballad.*

Blavers. The blue cornflower.

> Blavers that grow amid white land.
> —BUCHAN's *Ancient Ballads: The Gardener Lad.*

Blaw-i'-my-lug, a flatterer, a cajoler, a wheedler; one who *blows* fair words into the ear of a ready listener for a selfish or sinister purpose.

Bledoch, skim-milk; from the Gaelic *bleodhach* or *bleoghann*, to milk.

> She kirned the kirn and scummed it clean,
> Left the gudeman but *bledoch* bare.
> —ALLAN RAMSAY's *Evergreen: The Wife of Auchtermuchty.*

Blether, to talk nonsense, to be full of wind like a bladder, *Bletherskite*, nonsense.

Blethers, nonsense, impertinence. *Blaidry*, foolish talk, from the Gaelic *blaidaireachd*, and *bleidir*, impertinence. *Bletherum-skate* or *bletherum-skite*, sometimes corrupted into *bladderskate*, are derivatives of this word, "'Ye *blethrin loon*' and 'ye *skyte*,'" says Cromek, the editor of the "Remains of Nithsdale and Galloway Song, "are terms of familiar reproach still in use, and are applied to those satiric rogues who have the art of mingling falsehood with truth with admirable art."

Stringing *blethers* up in rhyme
For fools to sing.
—BURNS: *The Vision.*

Fame
Gathers but wind to *blether* up a name.
—BEAUMONT AND FLETCHER.

Some are busy *bletherin*
Right loud that day.
—BURNS: *The Holy Fair.*

Right scornfully she answered him,
Jog on your gate, you *bladderskate*—
My name is Maggie Lauder.
—SEMPLE: *Maggie Lauder.*

"She's better to-night," said one nurse to another. "Night's come, but it's not gone," replied her helpmate, in the full hearing of the patient, "and it's the small hours'll try her." "The small hours'll not try me as much as you do with your *blethering* tongues," remarked the patient with perfect *sang-froid.*—*A Visit to the London Hospitals,* March 23, 1870.

I knew Burns's "Blethering Bitch," who in his later years lived in Tarbolton, and earned a scanty living by breaking stones on the road. In taking a walk round the hill mentioned in "Death and Dr. Hornbook," I came upon Jamie Humphrey (such was his name) busy at work, and after talking with him a short time, I ventured to ask him, "Is it true, Jamie, that you are Burns's *blethering bitch?*" "Aye, deed am I, and mony a guid gill I hae gotten by it!" This was a broad hint; but I did not take it.—R. DRENNAN.

Blinter, to flicker like a flame about to expire for want of nourishment.

Blirt, a sudden burst of grief or anger, also to weep, sob, and lament simultaneously. A "blirt of greeting" signifies an outburst of tears. The English

blurt is akin to the Scottish *blirt,* though not exactly synonymous, and is principally used to signify a sudden and unpremeditated disclosure of what ought to have been kept secret, as in the phrase "He blurted out the truth," or "He blurted out an oath." The root both of *blirt* and *blurt* is the Gaelic *blaor,* to cry out or roar, and *blaorte,* cried out or roared.

Blob, a large round drop of water or other liquid. A similar word, *bleb,* now obsolete, was once used in England to signify an air-bubble, and, in its form of *blebster,* is the root of *blister.*

We look on this troubled stream of the generations of men to as little purpose almost as idle boys do on dancing *blebs* or bubbles on the water. — SIR THOMAS MORE: *Consolations of the Soul.*

Her e'en the clearest *blob* o' dew outshining.—ALLAN RAMSAY.

The bonnie red rose,
Wet wi' the *blobs* o' dew.
—ALLAN CUNNINGHAM.

Blouter, to bluster or talk idly; Gaelic *bladair,* to talk idly.

Cacklin' about] Coleridge or *blouterin'* about Byron.—*Noctes Ambrosianæ.*

Blunk, to mismanage or spoil anything by clumsy, inexpert, or stupid handling; also a dull, stolid, and foolishly inert person. Jamieson thinks it is derived from the Icelandic *blunda,* sleepy-headed. It is more probably from the Gaelic *blonach* or *blonag,* fat, greasy; whence fat-headed and stupid.

Bluntie. In the Dictionary of the Scottish Language by an anonymous author (Edinburgh, 1818), *bluntie* is described as a stupid fellow. Jamieson has "*blunt,* stupid, bare, naked," and "*bluntie,* a sniveller," which he derives from the Teutonic *blutten,* homo stolidus.

They mool me sair, and haud me doun,
And gar me look like *bluntie,* Tam ;
But three short years will soon wheel roun',
And then comes ane-and-twenty, Tam.
— BURNS.

The etymology of the English word *blunt* is uncertain, but as it signifies the opposite of sharp, the Scottish *bluntie* may be accepted as a designation of one who is not sharp or clever. No English dictionary suggests any etymology that can reasonably be accepted, the nearest being *plump,* round, or rounded without a point. "*Blunt,*" the slang word for money, is supposed by some to be derived from the name of Sir John *Blunt,* a rich director of the South Sea Company in the year 1720.

Bob, to make a curtsey, to bend, to bow down.

Sweet was the smell of flowers, blue, white, and red,
The noise of birds was maist melodious,
The *bobbing* boughs bloom'd broad abune my head.
— R. HENRYSON : *The Lion and the Mouse.*

When she cam' ben she *bobbit.*
— CHAMBERS'S *Scottish Songs.*

Weel done, quo' he ; play up, quo' she ;
Weel *bobb'd,* quo' Rob the Ranter.
It's worth my while to play indeed
When I hae sic a dancer.
— *Maggie Lauder.*

When she came ben she *bobbit.*—BURNS.

Out came the auld maidens a' *bobbin'* discreetly.
—JAMES BALLANTINE : *The Auld Beggar Man.*

When she came ben she *bobbit* fu' low,
And what was his errand he soon let her know.
Surprised was the laird when the lady said Na !
As wi' a laigh curtsie she turned her aw a.
—*The Laird o' Cockpen.*

Bodle, a small Scottish coin, of less value than a *bawbee,* the sixth part of an English penny.

Black Madge, she is prudent, has sense in her noddle,
Is douce and respectit ; I care na' a *bodle.*
—JOANNA BAILLIE.

Bonailie, a parting drink, a stirrup-cup ; a *deoch an dorus,* offered to and partaken with a departing guest, with wishes for a good and pleasant journey ; a *bon voyage.* The word, sometimes written *bonalais* or *bonally,* is a corrupt spelling of the French *bonne allée,* or *bon aller.*

Bonnie, beautiful, good-natured, and cheerful—the three qualities in combination—as applied to a woman ; applied to natural objects, it simply signifies beautiful, as in "Ye banks and braes o' *bonnie* Doon." This is an old English word, used by Shakespeare and Ben Jonson, and still current in the Northern English counties, as well as in Scotland.

Bonnieness, a word that conveys the sense of both prettiness and goodness, that are sometimes, but ought never, to dwell apart.

Bonnieness gaed to the water to wash,
And prettiness gaed to the barn to thrash ;
Gae tell my maister to pay me my fee,
For *bonnieness* winna let prettiness be.
—CHAMBERS'S *Scottish Songs.*

Bonspiel, sport or play.

I hae been at mony a bonspiel, but I ne'er saw such a congregation on the ice before.—*Noctes Ambrosianæ.*

Boodie, a ghost, a sprite, a hobgoblin ; by some derived from *bode*, a message, the German *bote*, a messenger, and by others, with more probability, from the Gaelic *bodach*, a spectre—a word which is also applied irreverently to an ill-favoured and churlish old man.

Borrow, to ransom, and not, as in English, to effect a loan.

And in cam' her brother dear,
   A waeful man was he.
I'd gie a' the lands I hae,
   Bonnie Jean, to *borrow* thee.
Oh, *borrow* me, brother, *borrow* me,
   Or *borrowed* I'll never be,
For I gar'd kill my ain dear lord,
   An' life's nae pleasure to me.
   —*The Laird o' Warristoun.*

Bourack or **bourock**, a name given by children to the little mounds of sand or earth that they raise on the sea-shore or in their playgrounds in imitation of castles or houses ;—a diminutive, apparently, of the word *bower*, a lady's chamber. The word is sometimes used for a shepherd's hut or shieling. In

some parts of Scotland it signifies a heap or mound of any kind, and also metaphorically a heap or crowd of people.

We'll ne'er big *bourocks* i' the sand together (*Old Proverb*), *i.e.*, we'll never be familiar or closely allied in sentiment or purpose.

Bourd, a jest, a joke ; also to jest, to play tricks with. In old English, *bord*. From the Gaelic *burt*, mockery.

The wizard could no longer bear her *bord*,
But, bursting forth in laughter, to her said.
   —SPENSER : *Faerie Queene.*

I'll tell the *bourd*, but nae the body.
A sooth *bourd* is nae *bourd.*
They that *bourd* wi' cats may count upon scarts.
   —ALLAN RAMSAY'S *Scots Proverbs.*

Bouse, to drink deeply, to revel ; whence the colloquial English word "boozy."

Then let him *bouse* and deep carouse
Wi' bumpers flowing o'er,
Till he forgets his loves and debts,
And minds his griefs no more.—BURNS.

And though bold Robin Hood
Would with his Maid Marian
Sup and *bouse* from horn and can.
   —KEATS.

Brae, the brow or side of a hill ; from the Gaelic *bruaich*, a hill side, a steep.

We twa hae run about the *braes*,
And pu'd the gowans fine,
But mony a weary foot we've trod
Sin auld lang syne.—BURNS.

Brander, a gridiron, also a toasting-fork ; from the Teutonic *brennen*, to burn ; *gebrannt*, burned.

Brander, a gridiron, *i.e.*, a burner, on which to submit food to the direct action of the fire without the intervention of water; from the Teutonic *brennen*, to burn, and *gelvannt*, burnt.

Brander-bannock, a cake heated on a gridiron; a common mode of preparing oaten cakes in Scotland.

Brankie, gaudy, showy. *Brankit*, vain, conceited, proud of one's fine clothes. *Brankin'* a great show of finery.

Where hae ye been sae braw, lad?
 Where hae ye been sae *brankie*, O?
Where hae ye been sae braw, lad?
 Cam' ye by Killicrankie, O?
 —JOHNSON's *Musical Museum.*

Branne, the calf of the leg; whence the English *brawny*, muscular.

Your stocking shall be like the cabbage leaf,
 That is baith braid and lang,
Narrow, narrow at the cute (the instep or ankle),
 And braid, braid at the *branne*.
 —*Ballad of the Gardener, from Kinloch's Collection.*

Brash, a sickness, a rash, an eruption.

The lady's gane to her chamber,
 A moanful woman was she,
As gin she had taken a sudden *brash*,
 An' were about to dee.
 —*The Gay Gosshawk.*

Brash, a sudden gust of wind, also a tuzzle or fight; *brashy* or *braushie*, stormy.

Brat, a rag or clothes; from the Gaelic *brat*, a covering, a mantle,

a rag; also *bratach*, a flag, a banner; whence perhaps the contemptuous English term of *brat*, for a beggar's child, in allusion to the rags in which it is clad.

We've aye had *bit* and *brat*, John,
 Great blessings here below;
And that helped to keep peace at home,
 John Anderson my jo.
 —*From the old version of "John Anderson my Jo," abridged, amended, and purified by* ROBERT BURNS.

Bratchet, a contemptuous or angry term for a troublesome or mischievous child; a diminutive of *brat*, a child, so called from the Gaelic *brat*, a rag; synonymous with another Scottish phrase for a poor man's child, as used by Burns, "a smytrie o' wee *duddie* (ragged) weans."

Brattle, clatter, or any noise made by the rapid collision of hard substances; possibly from *be-rattle*, the augmentative of the English word *rattle*.

List'ning the doors an' windows rattle,
I thought me on the ourie cattle,
Or silly sheep, that tide the *brattle*
 O' winter war.
 —BURNS: *A Winter Night.*

Breathin'. "I'll do't in a *breathin'*," instanter, in the time which it would take to draw a breath. This phrase is far superior to the vulgar English "in a jiffy," or to the still more intolerable slang "the twinkling of a bedpost."

Bree, the juice, the essence, the spirit. Barley-*bree*, the juice of the barley, *i.e.*, whisky or ale.

B

Brew is to extract the spirit or essence of barley, malt, hops, &c. Both *bree* and *brew* are directly derived from the Gaelic *brigh*, spirit, juice, &c. The Italians have *brio*, spirit, energy, life, animation. From this source is derived the English slang word a "*brick*," applied to a fine, high-spirited, good fellow. Various absurd attempts have been made to trace the expression to a Greek source in a spurious anecdote borrowed from Aristotle, who speaks of a *tetragonos aner* or "four-cornered man," supposed in the slang of the Universities to signify a *brick*.

Breeks, the nether garments of a man, trousers, trews, breeches. The vulgar English word *breeches* is derived from the *breech*, the part of the body which they cover. The Scottish word has a more dignified origin in the Gaelic *breaghad*, attire, dress, ornament, and *breaghaid*, adorn, embellish, "from which Celtic word," says Ainsworth in his Latin Dictionary, "the Romans derived *bracca* and *braccatus*, wearing trews, like the Gauls."

> Thir *breeks* o' mine, my only pair,
> I wad hae gien them aff my hurdies
> For ae blink o' the bonnie burdies.
> —Burns: *Tam o' Shanter.*

Brent or **brant,** high, steep; also smooth.

> Her fair *brent* brow,
> Smooth as the unwrinkled deep.
> —Allan Ramsay.

> John Anderson my jo, John,
>   When we were first acquaint,
> Your locks were like the raven,
>   Your bonnie brow was *brent*.
> —Burns: *John Anderson my Jo.*

In "John Anderson my Jo," the auld wife means that her husband's brow was smooth. I believe that *brent* in this passage is the past-participle of *burn*. Shining is one of the effects of burning. I think the word is always used to mean smooth, unwrinkled—as in the Scottish phrase *brent* new, the English! *bran* new, shining with all the gloss of newness.—R. Drennan.

Brim, fierce, disastrous, fatal, furious; from the Gaelic *breamas*, mischief, mischance.

> The *brim* battle of the Harlaw.
> —Allan Ramsay: *The Evergreen.*

Bring home, to be delivered of a child.

> Now when nine months were past and gone,
> The lady she *brought home* a son.
> —Buchan's *Ballads : Lord Dingwall.*

Brook, to spot, or soil, or blacken with soot; *brookit*, having a dirty face; and *brookie*, a nickname either for a sweep or a blacksmith. *Bruckit* is tanned by the sun or freckled. The root is the Gaelic *brucach*, spotted, freckled, speckled, particularly in the face.

Broostle, to perspire profusely; also to be in a great hurry, bustle, or confusion. From the Teutonic *braus*, bustle, noise, or tumult; *brausen*, to ferment, to rush, to roar, to snort with anger or impatience.

Brownie, a household sprite in the ancient and not yet extinct superstition of Scotland, who, if conciliated, performed domestic duties, and made himself useful and agreeable, similar in his character to Puck or Robin Good-fellow in England. From the Gaelic *bronn*, a gift, a favour.

Brown study. This phrase, to signify deep, sad, or melancholy meditation, was originally Scotch, but has long become familiar in English. It has puzzled all the philologists, who persist in deriving almost every English word and phrase from the Teutonic, the Greek, or the Latin, to the exclusion of the Celtic, from which even these three languages are largely derived. But they have made no guesses superior to that which would trace it to a *brow* study, because those who fall into brown studies often knit their brows in deep thought! The real source of the word is the Gaelic *bron*, sorrow, grief, sadness, melancholy, mourning; *bronag*, a sorrowful woman; *bron bhrat*, a mourning cloth, a cerement or mortcloth; *bronach*, sorrowful, and *bronadh*, lamentation. This explanation ought to satisfy even the Keltophobists, and teach them to "rest and be thankful" in their study of this particular colloquialism.

Bruik, to enjoy, to possess; from the Teutonic *brauchen*, to make use of. *Was braucht es?* What is the use of it?

Weel *bruik* ye o' yon broun, broun bride,
Between ye and the wa',
And sae will I o' my winding-sheet,
That suits me best of a'.
—JAMIESON's *Collection: Ballad of Lammikin.*

Brulzie or **brulyie**, a disturbance, a commotion, a quarrel. This word seems to be the root of the English *brawl*, *broil*, *embroil*, and *embroilment*, and the French *embrouiller;* all derivable from the Gaelic *bruill*, to crush, to beat, to fight, to thrash.

Bannocks o' bear-meal, bannocks o' barley!
Wha' in a *brulzie* will first cry a parley?
Never the lads wi' the bannocks o' barley;
Here's to the Highlandman's bannocks o' barley!
—JOHNSON's *Musical Museum.*

Brumble, to make a rumbling noise. The English *rumble* and the Lowland Scotch *brumble* are synonymous, and both appear to be derived from the Teutonic *brummen*, to rush audibly like a rapid stream ; to gurgle, to growl.

Bryttle, to cut up venison.

And Johnnie has *bryttled* the deer sae weel,
And has feasted his gude blude-hounds.
—*Border Minstrelsy: Johnnie of Braidislie.*

Bubbly-jock, a turkey-cock.

Some of the idiot's friends coming to visit him at a farmhouse where he resided, reminded him how comfortable he was, and how grateful he ought to be for the care taken of him. He admitted the fact, but he had his sorrows and troubles like wiser men. He stood in awe of the great turkey-cock of the farm, which used to run and gobble at him. "Aye! aye!" he

said, unburthening his heart, " I'm very
weel aff, nae doubt; but eh! man, I'm
sair hadden doun by the *Bubbly-jock!*"
DEAN RAMSAY.

Buckie, a whelk or periwinkle.

An' there'll be partans [crabs] an' *buckies.*
    —*The Blithesome Bridal.*

Buckle-to, to marry; derived from
the idea of fastening or joining
together. The word occurs in
a vulgar English song to a very
beautiful Scottish air, which
was written in imitation of
the Scottish manner by Tom
D'Urfey in the reign of Charles
II. It has been long popular
under the title of "Within a
Mile of Edinburgh Town."

Buckle-beggar signified what was
once called a *hedge-priest,* who
pretended to perform the ceremony of marriage. To "*buckle*
with a person" was to be engaged in argument with another.

" **Buff nor stye,**" a common colloquialism. To say of any one that
"he would neither buff nor stye,"
means that he would neither do
one thing or another, that he
did not know his own mind,
or that he was so obstinately
wedded to his own purpose that
nothing could make him deviate
from it. It is probably a corruption of "he would neither
be off nor *stay.*" Jamieson,
however, derives *buff* from the
Teutonic *bof,* a cheer made by
mariners; and thinks that *stye*
may refer to the act of mounting
the shrouds, from the Swedish

stiga, to ascend! He has thus
had recourse to two languages to
help him out of a difficulty, when
one, and that his own, would
have been sufficient.

He would neither *buff nor stye* for father
or mother, friend or foe.—GALT: |*The
Entail.*

Buirdly, strong and stalwart,
hearty, well-built.

Buirdly chiels [fellows]
Are bred in sic a way as this is.
    —BURNS: *The Twa Dogs.*

Burnewin, a contraction of
"Burn-the wind," the popular
and familiar name for a blacksmith.

Busk, to adorn, to dress; from
the Gaelic *busgadh,* a head-dress,
an adornment for the person;
busgainnich, to dress, to adorn,
to prepare.

A bonnie bride is soon *buskit.*
    —ALLAN RAMSAY'S *Scots
        Proverbs.*
Busk ye, busk ye, my bonnie bride,
Busk ye, busk ye, my winsome marrow.
    —HAMILTON *of Bangor.*

But. This word in Scotland long
preserved the meaning it once
had in England of "without,"
and was derived etymologically
from "be out," of which it is
an abbreviation. It remains in
the heraldic motto of the Clan
Chattan, "Touch not the cat
but the glove!" It does duty in
the humorous Jacobite song, in
ridicule of George I., the Elector
of Hanover :—

Wha the deil hae we gotten for a king,
  But a wee, wee German lairdie ;
And when we gaed to bring him hame,
  He was delvin' in his yairdie,
Sheughin kail and layin' leeks,
But the hose, and *but* the breeks,
And up his beggar duds he cleeks,
  The wee, wee German lairdie.

But and ben, the out and in, the front and back rooms of a cotter's hut.

Toddlin *but* and toddlin *ben,*
I'm nae sooner slockened, than drouthy again.
        —SIR ALEXANDER BOSWELL : *A Matrimonial Duet.*

Had siller been made in the kist to lock by,
It wadna been round, but square as a dye,
Whereas by its shape ilka body may see
It aye was designed it should circulate free.
Then we'll toddle *but,* and we'll toddle *ben,*
An' aye when we get it, we'll part wi't
again.—*Ibid.*

Byspel, an accidental piece of good fortune ; a wonderful stroke of luck or dexterity. An epithet applied, generally in a half-hearted spirit of laudation, to any person of rare good qualities or successful rise in the world ; as in the phrase " He's just a *byspel.*" The word is from the Teutonic *beispiel,* an example ; literally a *by-play.* In this sense it is sometimes held to signify an illegitimate or a love-child, a " by-blow," a bastard.

Byssim, a monster, also a worthless and shameless woman. Supposed to be from the Icelandic *byan,* a monster, a prodigy. The German *böse,* wicked, and the Gaelic *baois,* lust, libidinousness, and also madness, have been suggested as the root of this word. A third derivation is worthy of study, that from *baoth* (*bao*), wicked, and *smuain,* thoughts, whence *bao - smuain,* quasi bissim or byssom, a wicked thought, or a person with wicked thoughts. The word *Bezonian,* which has puzzled Shakespearian commentators to explain, may be allied.

C

Ca', to drive, or drive in, to smite ; also to contend or fight ; from the Gaelic *cath,* pronounced *ca',* to smite, to fight.

I'll cause a man put up the fire,
  Anither *ca'* in the stake,
And on the head o' yon high hill
  I'll burn you for his sake.
BUCHAN'S *Ballads : Young Prince James.*

Every naig was *ca'd* a shoe on,
The smith and thee got roaring fu' on.
        —BURNS : *Tam o' Shanter.*

Ca' cannie ! an exhortation to beware, to take heed or care as to what you are doing or saying ; *ca',* to drive, and *cannie,* cautious or cautiously.

Cadgie—sometimes written *caigie* —cheerful, sportive, wanton, friendly ; possibly from the old Gaelic *cad,* a friend, whence, according to some philologists, *cadie*, a lad (used in the sense of kindness and familiarity); but, according to others, from the French *cadet*, a younger born.

> A cock-laird fu' *cadgie*
> Wi' Jeanie did meet ;
> He haused her, he kissed her,
> And ca'd her his sweet.
> —CHAMBERS's *Scottish Songs.*

> Yon ill-tongued tinkler, Charlie Fox,
> May taunt you wi' his jeers and shocks ;
> But gie't him het, my hearty cocks,
>   E'en cowe the *cadie !*
> And send him to his dicing-box
>   And sportin' lady.
> —BURNS : *Author's Earnest Cry and Prayer.*

Cair, to strain through. "This word," says Jamieson, "is used in Clydesdale, and signifies to extract the thickest part of broth or hotch-potch while dining or supping." It is probably from the Gaelic *cir*, a comb ; whence also the English word to *curry* a horse, and *curry*-comb, the comb used for the purpose.

Caird, a tinker.

> Close the awmrie, steek the kist,
> Or else some gear will soon be miss'd ;
> Tell the news in brugh and glen,
> Donald *Caird's* come again.
> —SIR WALTER SCOTT.

From the Gaelic *ceard*, a smith, a wright, a workman ; with the prefix *teine*, fire, is derived the English *tin-caird* or *tinker*, a fire-smith. Johnson, ignorant of Celtic, traced *tinker* from *tink*, because tinkers struck a kettle and produced a tinkling noise to announce their arrival.

Caller, fresh, cool. There is no exact English synonym for this word. "*Caller* herrin," "*Caller* haddie," and "*Caller* ow" are familiar cries to Edinburgh people, and to all strangers who visit that beautiful city.

> Sae sweet his voice, sae smooth his tongue,
> His breath's like *caller* air ;
> His very foot has music in't
> When he comes up the stair.
> —MICKLE : *There's nae Luck about the House.*

> Upon a simmer Sunday morn,
>   When Nature's face is fair,
> I walked forth to view the corn
>   And snuff the *caller* air.
> —BURNS : *The Holy Fair.*

Camsteerie, crooked, confused, unmanageable ; from the Gaelic *cam*, crooked, and *stiuir*, to steer or lead.

> . The phalanx broken into pieces like *camsteerie* clouds.—*Noctes Ambrosianæ.*

Cannie, knowing, but gentle ; not to be easily deceived, yet not sly or cunning. A very expressive word, often used by Englishmen to describe the Scotch, as in the phrase, "a canny Scotsman," one who knows what he is about. The word also means dexterous, clever at a bargain, and also fortunate. It is possibly derived from the Gaelic *ceannaich*, to buy ; and is common in the North of England as well as in Scotland.

> Bonny lass, *canny* lass, wilt thou be mine ?
> —*The Cumberland Courtship.*

> He mounted his mare and he rode *cannilie*.
> —*The Laird o' Cockpen.*

Hae naething to do wi' him; he's no *canny.*

They have need of a *canny* cook who have but one egg for dinner.
—ALLAN RAMSAY's *Scots Proverbs.*

Cantie, joyous, merry, talkative from excess of good spirits; from the Gaelic *cainnt,* speech, or *can,* to sing.

Contented wi' little and *cantie* wi' mair.
—BURNS.

Some cannie wee bodie may be my lot,
An' I'll be *cantie* in thinking o't.
—BROCKETT's *North Country Glossary:
Newcastle Song.*

The *cantie* auld folks.
—BURNS: *The Twa Dogs.*

The clachan yill had made me *cantie.*
—BURNS: *Death and Dr. Hornbook.*

Cantrip, a charm, a spell, a trick, a mischievous trick. The word is a corruption of the Gaelic word *ceann,* head, chief, principal, and *drip,* a trick.

Coffins stood roun' like open presses,
That showed the dead in their last dresses;
And by some devilish *cantrip* slight,
Each in its cauld hand held a light.
—BURNS: *Tam o' Shanter.*

Burns, in the "Address to the Deil," has another example of this word, in which the humour is great and the indecency greater.
—LORD NEAVES.

Capernoity, peevish, crabbed, apt to take offence, of singular and uncertain humour.

"Me forward!" answered Mrs. Patt; "the *capernoity,* old, girning ale-wife may wait long enough ere I forward it!"—
SCOTT: *St. Ronan's Well.*

Gaelic, *cabair,* a gabbler, a tattler; *naitheas,* mischief.

Cappernoytit, slightly deranged.

D'ye hear what auld Dominie Napier says about the mirk Monday? He says it's an eclipse—the sun and the moon fechting for the upper hand! But, Lord! he's a poor *capernoytit* creature.—*Laird of Logan.*

Carfuffle, agitation of mind, perplexity; from the Gaelic *ccarn,* a twist or wrong turn, and *baob, baobach,* and *baobhail,* an alarm, a fright, a perplexity; and with the aspirate, the *b* pronounced as *f, bhaobail,* fuffle.

Troth, my lord may be turned fule outright an' he puts himsell into a *carfuffle* for ony thing ye could bring him, Edie.—SCOTT: *The Antiquary.*

Carkin', grinding, oppressively wearying, vexatious. The root of this word is the Gaelic *garg,* rough, from whence also *gargle,* the rough noise produced by a liquor to foment the throat, but not to be swallowed.

The lisping infant prattlin' on his knee
Does a' his weary *carkin'* cares beguile,
An' makes him quite forget his labour and his toil.
—BURNS: *Cotter's Saturday Night.*

Carle, a man, a fellow; from the Teutonic *kerl.* This word, which was used by Chaucer, has been corrupted into the English *churl,* which means a rude fellow. In Scotland it still preserves its original and pleasanter signification.

The miller was a stout *carle* for the nones;
Full big he was of braune, and eke of bones.
—CHAUCER.

The pawky auld *carle* cam' ower the lea,
Wi' mony guid e'ens and guid days to me,
Saying, Kind sirs, for your courtesy,
Will you lodge a silly poor man?
—RITSON's *Caledonian Songs.*

Oh ! wha's that at my chamber door ?
 Fair widow, are ye waukin' ?
Auld *carle*, your suit give o'er,
 Your love lies a' in talkin'.
    —ALLAN RAMSAY.

When lairds break, *carles* get land.
 —ALLAN RAMSAY's *Scots Proverbs.*

Up starts a *carle*, and gains good,
And thence comes a' our gentle blood.
      —*Idem.*

My daddie is a cankered *carle*,
 He'll no twine wi' his gear ;
But let them say or let them dae,
 It's a' ane to me ;
For he's low doun, he's in the broom,
 That's waiting for me.
    —JAMES CARNEGIE, 1765.

 Carle, a man, or fellow, is also used adjectively for male, manly, strong, vigorous : as in *carle-hemp*, the largest seed-bearing stalk of hemp ; *carle-dodder*, the largest stalk of dodder-grass ; *carle-heather* or *carlin-heather*, the largest species of heather or *erica ; carle-tangle*, the largest species of tangle or sea-weed ; *carle-wife*, a man who does women's work ; *carle-cat*, a tom-cat, a male cat, &c.

Ye have a stalk o' *carle-hemp* in you.
 —ALLAN RAMSAY's *Scots Proverbs.*

The *carle-stalk* of hemp in man—
Resolve.—BURNS.

Carle-wife, a husband who meddles too much with the household duties and privileges of the wife ; a much better word than its English equivalent—a "molly-coddle."

Carline or **carlin**, an old woman.

Cats and *carlines* love to sleep i' the sun.
 —ALLAN RAMSAY.

That auld capricious *carlin* Nature.
 —BURNS : *To James Smith.*

The Rev. Mr. Monro of Westray, preaching on the flight of Lot from Sodom, said : "The honest man and his family were ordered out of the town, and charged not to look back ; but the auld *carlin*, Lot's wife, looked owre her shouther, for which she was smote into a lump of sawt." And he added, with great unction : "Oh, ye people of Westray, if ye had had her, mony a day since ye wad hae putten her in the parritch-pat !"—DEAN RAMSAY.

Carp, by some commentators considered to signify to sing, by others to rehearse, from the oft-recurring phrase in old ballads recording the performances of bards and minstrels—"he *harpit* and he *carpit*."

And ay he *harpit*, and ay he *carpit*,
 Till a' the nobles ga'ed o'er the floor ;
But and the music was sae sweet,
 The groom forgot the stable door.
  —SCOTT's *Border Minstrelsy: The Lochmaben Harper.*

 To this passage Mr. Robert Chambers, in his "Collection of Scottish Ballads," appended the note :—"In the 'Minstrelsy of the Scottish Border' *carpit* is explained as meaning sung, but I suggest, with great deference, that it appears, from the use made of it in Barbour's 'Bruce,' that it refers to the *narrative* which the ancient minstrels accompanied on their instruments." But Mr. Chambers has left the doubt exactly where he found it, for the old minstrels sometimes sang and sometimes merely recited or declaimed their stories. The etymology and meaning are both as doubtful as ever. The English to *carp*, to cavil or find fault, is probably connected.

Carry, the driving clouds.

> Mirk and rainy is the night,
> No a starn (star) in a' the *carry.*
> —TANNAHILL.

The word is derived from the Gaelic *caraich*, to move, to stir; *caraidh*, movement.

Castock, sometimes written **custock**, a cabbage-stalk.

> There's cauld kail in Aberdeen,
> An' *castocks* in Stra'bogie.
> —DUKE OF GORDON.

Every day's no Yule-day;—cast the cat a *castock.*—ALLAN RAMSAY'S *Scots Proverbs.*

In their hearts they're as callous as *custocks.*—*Noctes Ambrosianæ.*

Cateran. A Highland *cateran* was a term formerly applied in the Lowlands to a Highland marauder or cattle-stealer, and generally to the Highlanders, who were all supposed to be lawless depredators on the wealth of the Lowlands. The word is probably from the Gaelic *cath*, a battle, a fight; *cathach*, a fighter or warrior; and *ran*, to shout, to roar; whence, by emphatic denunciation, a roaring, a violent warrior or depredator.

> My love he was as brave a man
> As ever Scotland bred,
> Descended from a Highland clan,
> A *cateran* to his trade.
> —*Gilderoy.*

Cauld bark. To live in "the cauld bark," is to be dead and buried. *Bark*, in this metaphorical euphemism, is evidently not traceable to *bark*, a boat or ship, or to the *bark* of an animal; but is possibly from *bark*, skin (which see), or from *berg* or *burg* or *burrow*, a hill or hillock, or slight mound raised over a grave.

Cauld coal. "He has a *cauld coal* to blaw," *i.e.*, he is engaged in a hopeless undertaking; there is no spark of fire in it which can be blown into a flame.

Cauldrife, cold-hearted, cool in love or friendship, indifferent-minded.

> Gae, get you gone, you *cauldrife* wooer,
> Ye sour-looking *cauldrife* wooer.
> I straightway showed him to the door,
> Sayin', Come nae mair to me, oh !
> —HERD'S *Collection: The Brisk Young Lad.*

Cavée. According to Jamieson, this is an Aberdeenshire word, signifying a state of commotion or perturbation of mind. He suggests its derivation from the French *cas vif*, a matter that gives or requires activity (of mind). Is it not rather the Gaelic *cabhag* (*ca-vag*), hurry, haste, dispatch, trouble, difficulty? whence *cabhagach*, hasty, impetuous, hurried. *Cave* is used in the "Noctes Ambrosianæ" as synonymous with toss. "Gallopin' on a grey horse that *caves* the foam from its fiery nostrils."

Chandlers, candlesticks; the English chandeliers.

> Hae ye ony pots or pans,
> Or ony broken *chandlers*;
> I am a tinker to my trade,
> An' newly come frae Flanders.

As scant of siller as of grace,
    Disbanded, I'd a bad run ;
Gae tell the lady o' the place
    I've come to clout the cauldron.
    —*The Tinker, or Clout the Cauldron.*

Channer, to contend, to complain, to grumble, to chide, to remonstrate ; from the Gaelic *canran*, a contentious murmuring, chiding ; *canranach*, querulous murmuring, contentions ; and *canranacha*, petulance, illhumour.

The cock doth craw, the day doth daw,
The *channerin'* worm doth chide.
    —*Border Minstrelsy: The Clerk's Twa Sons o' Ouenford.*

How the worm could *channer* or chide in the grave is incomprehensible, unless one of the meanings of the word is to fret or cause to fret with vexation. This interpretation has led to the supposition that "fret," in the sense of its former signification of "gnaw" or "eat," from the German *fressen*, Flemish *freten*, as in the Scripture phrase "The moth *fretteth* the garment," is synonymous with *channer*. This, however, is not the case, as the Gaelic etymology suffices to prove. But neither *channering* nor *fretting* supplies an intelligible or satisfactory explanation of the ballad-writer's meaning.

Chap, to knock ; *chaup*, a blow.

I dreamed I was deed, and carried far,
far, far up, till I came to Heaven's yett—
when I *chappit*, and *chappit*, and *chappit*,
till at last an angel keekit out and said,
" Wha are ye ?"—DEAN RAMSAY.

The chiel was stout, the chiel was stark,
    And wadna bide to *chap* nor ca',
And Girzie, faint wi' holy wark,
    Had na the power to say him *na* !
    —*Holy Girzie.*

The Burnewin comes on like death at every *chaup*.
    —BURNS : *Scotch Drink.*

Chark, to make a grinding or grunting noise, also to complain petulantly and obstinately. A form of *cark*, with the substitution of *ch* for *c* or *k*, as in *church* for *kirk*, &c.

Cheep, to chirp or chirrup like a bird.

Ye're nae chicken for a your *cheepin'*.—*Proverb.*

Chiel, a fellow, a youth ; the same as the ancient English *childe*, as used by Byron in " *Childe Harold.*" From the Gaelic *gille*, a youth.

The brawny, bainie ploughman *chiel*.
    —BURNS : *Scotch Drink.*

A *chiel's* amang ye takin' notes.
    —BURNS.

Clachan, a village ; from the Gaelic *clach*, a stone, and *clachan*, the stones or houses.

The *clachan* yill (ale) had made me cantie.
    —BURNS : *Death and Dr. Hornbook.*
Ye ken Jock Hornbook o' the *clachan*.
    —*Idem.*

The *clachan* of Aberfoyle.
    —SIR WALTER SCOTT : *Rob Roy.*

Many English and American tourists in Scotland, and other readers of the works of Sir Walter Scott, imagine that the " clachan of Aberfoyle " means the *mill* of Aberfoyle.

They derive the word from the English *clack*, the noise of the mill-wheel, and knowing nothing of *clachan*, the village, are disappointed when they find neither windmill nor watermill on the classic spot.

Clart, to defile, to make dirty.

Clarty, dirty; from the Gaelic *clabar* or *clabhar*, filth, mud, mire.

Searching auld wives' barrels;
    Ochon the day!
That *clarty* barm [dirty yeast] should stain
    my laurels!
      But—what'll ye say?
Those movin' things ca'd wives and weans
Wad move the very hearts o' stanes.
      —BURNS: *On being Appointed
        to the Excise.*

Clatch, to daub, to do any kind of work carelessly, awkwardly, recklessly, or ignorantly; *claught*, snatched.

Claur or **glaur**, mud, dirt, mire; "a gowpen o' *glaur*," a handful of mud; "a humplock of *glaur*," a heap of mud.

The wee laddie, greetin', said his brither Jock had coost a gowpen o' *glaur* at him and knockit him on the neb.—JAMES BALLANTINE.

Claut, to snatch, to lay hold of eagerly; something that has been got together by greed; a large heap.

Ken ye what Meg o' the Mill has gotten?
She's gotten a coof wi' a *claut* o' siller,
And broken the heart o' the barley miller.
      —BURNS: *Meg o' the Mill.*

Claut is undoubtedly from the English word *claw*, which had the sense in olden time of to scratch, to gather together, and is in that sense still in use in some parts of England. *Claut*, in Scotch, is most frequently used as a noun, and is the name given to a hoe used to gather mud, &c., together; to *claut* the roads, to gather the mud. I don't think the world itself contains the idea of getting together a large heap by *greed*. I don't recognise the other meanings, "to snatch," "to lay hold of eagerly." I would use a different word to express these meanings,—*to glaum, to play glaum*, would fit them exactly.—R. DRENNAN.

Clavers, idle stories, silly calumnies.

Hail Poesie! thou nymph reserved;
In chase o' thee what crowds hae swerv'd
Frae common sense, or sunk unnerv'd
    'Mong heaps o' *clavers*.
      —BURNS: *On Pastoral Poets.*

Claw, to flatter; from the Gaelic *cliù*, praise, and not, as ignorantly supposed, from the English *claw*, to scratch with the nails, in allusion to the itch.

Claw me and I'll *claw* you.—*Scottish Proverbs.*

I laugh when I am merry, and *claw* no man in his humour.
      —SHAKESPEARE: *Much Ado about
        Nothing.*

Claymore, the Highland broadsword; from the Gaelic *claidheamh*, or *glaive*, a sword, and *mor*, great.

Wha on the moor a gallant clan
    From boastin' foes their banners bore,
Who showed himself a better man
    Or fiercer waved the broad claymore?
      —SIR ALEXANDER BOSWELL.

Clepie, deceitful; from the Gaelic *clibe*, deceit.

Clishmaclaver, idle talk, foolish gossip, incessant gabble.

What further *clish-ma-claver* might been said.—BURNS: *The Brigs o' Ayr.*

From the Gaelic *clis* (*clish*), nimble, rapid, and *clab* (*clabh*), an open mouth; *clabach,* garrulous; *clabairê,* a babbler, a loud disagreeable talker; *clabar,* the clapper of a mill.

Clocking-hen, a hen engaged in the act of incubation; from *clock* or *cluck,* the cry or cackle of the hen when hatching. The word is sometimes used jocularly or contemptuously for an elderly woman or nurse.

Clocksie, lively, sprightly, vivacious, talkative; possibly from *clack,* talk; and that, again, from the Gaelic *clach* or *cloch,* a bell; applied derisively to the tongue of a garrulous person, likened to the clapper of a bell.

The *clocksie* auld laird o' the Warlock Glen,
Wha stood without, half cowed, half cheerie,
Raised up the latch and cam' crousely ben.
　　　　　—JOANNA BAILLIE.

Cloot, a cloven foot; *Clootie,* one who is hoofed or cloven-footed, *i.e.,* the devil.

O thou, whatever title suit thee,
Auld Hornie, Satan, Nick, or *Clootie.*
　　—BURNS: *Address to the Deil.*

Cloot (pronounced *clute,* long French *u*) is not a hoof, but the half of a hoof. We speak of a horse's hoof, and of a cow's cloots, and apply this latter word only to the feet of those animals that divide the hoof.—R. DRENNAN.

Clour, a lump on the flesh caused by a heavy blow.

That cane o' yours would gie a *clour* on a man's head eneuch to produce a phrenological faculty. — PROFESSOR WILSON: *Noctes Ambrosianæ.*

Clour is a heavy blow—the lump is only the *result* of a *clour.*—R. DRENNAN.

Clout, a rag; **cloutie,** a little rag, baby-clouts, baby-clothes. *Clout* also signifies a patch, or to patch, to mend, as in the old song of "Clout the Cauldron" (mend the kettle).

Wha my *baby-clouts* will buy?
　　　　　—*Old Song.*

A countryman in a remote part of Aberdeenshire got a newly coined sovereign in the days when such a thing was seldom seen, and went about showing it to his friends and neighbours for the charge of a penny each sight. Evil days unfortunately overtook him, and he was obliged to part with his beloved coin. A neighbour one day called upon him and asked for a sight of his sovereign. "Ah! man," said he, "it's gane; but I'll let ye see the *cloutie* it was rowed (wrapped) in for a *bawbee!*"— DEAN RAMSAY.

Cluff, to strike with the fist, to slap; "a *cluff* i' the lug," a box on the ear. The word is akin to the English *fisticuff* and to *cuff.*

Clunk, the gurgling, confused sound of liquor in a bottle or cask when it is poured out; equivalent to the English *glug* in the song of "Gluggity Glug." It is derived by Jamieson from the Danish *glunk* and the Swedish *klunka,* which have the same meaning.

Sir Violino, with an air
That showed a man o' spunk,
Wished unison between the pair,
And made the bottle *clunk*.
—BURNS : *The Jolly Beggars.*

An old English song has "and let the cannikin *clink*," which is obviously from the same root, though *clunk* is more expressive of a dull sound than *clink* is.

Clyte, a fall; to stop in the midst of a set speech for want of words or ideas, and sit down suddenly. "I couldna find words to continue my speech," said a Glasgow bailie, " and sae I *clyted.*"

I fairly *clyted*
On the cauld earth.
—ALLAN RAMSAY.

Clyte, a heavy, sudden kind of fall. I have generally heard the word as a verb used in connection with the word *played* —" It played *clyte* at my heels," " He got as far as the road, and then played *clyte.*" —R. DRENNAN.

Clytie-lass, a servant girl whose duty is to carry out of the house all filth or ordure, and to deposit it on the midden or elsewhere. The first word is apparently from the Gaelic *cuil-aite*, the back place or latrine, from *cuil* or *cul*, back, and *aite*, a place, whence by abbreviation *clyte* and *clytie.*

Cock. This syllable, which enters into the composition of many words and phrases both in Lowland Scotch and modern English, has generally been associated with its supposed derivation from *cock*, the name given to the male of birds, and especially to the familiar gallinaceous barn-door fowl that " crows in the morning." Its true derivation, however, is from the Gaelic *coc*, which means to elevate, to erect, to stand up, to throw high, to lift, as in such phrases as a " *cocked-hat*," a " *cockade*," " *cock* up your beaver," " *cocksure*" (manifestly or presumedly sure, or pretending to be so), " *cock-a-hoop*," and many others. It is more common in Lowland Scotch than in English. To *cock*, signifies to mount one boy on the back of another for punishment on the posteriors ; to *cock-shy*, to throw a stone or other missile high in the air; *cock-a-penny* or *cock-a-pentic*, to live beyond one's income for pride or ostentation, or the disinclination to appear as poor as one is in reality by expending more pennies than one has honestly got ; *cockie-vain*, conceited, arrogant, stuck up ; *cockie-ridie*, a game among children, when one rides on the shoulders of another ; a *cock-horse*, a wooden horse, on which children mount for amusement ; *cock-laird*, a small landed proprietor, who affects the dignity and gives himself the airs of a great one ; *cock-headed* or *cockle-headed*, vain, conceited, whimsical, stuck up ; *cockernonie* (which see) ; *cock-raw*, manifestly or plainly raw, underdone ; *cock-up* nose, a turned-up nose, " tip-tilted," as Lord Tennyson more elegantly describes it, and *cock-eye*, a squint-eye, that cocks up or awry when it should look straight.

None of these words have any connection with the male bird of the Gallinaceæ, but all are traceable etymologically to the Gaelic root of *coc*. Philologists, if so disposed, may trace to this same source the vulgar and indecent English and Scottish words which may be found in Juvenal and Horace as *Mentula*.

Cockernonie, a gathering up of the hair of women, after a fashion similar to that of the modern "chignon," and sometimes called a "cock-up." Mr. Kirkton, of Edinburgh, preaching against "cock-ups"—of which chignons were the representatives a quarter of a century ago — said : "I have been all this year preaching against the vanity of women, yet I see my own daughter in the kirk even now with as high a 'cock-up' as any one of you all."

Jamieson was of the opinion, that *cockernonie* signified a snood, or the gathering of the hair in a band or fillet, and derived the word from the Teutonic *koker*, a cape, and *nonne*, a nun, *i.e.*, such a sheath for fixing the hair as nuns were accustomed to use ! The word was a contemptuous one for, false hair—a contrivance to make a little hair

appear to be a good deal—and seems to have been compounded of the Gaelic *coc*, to stand erect, and *neoni*, nothing.

I saw my Meg come linkin' ower the lea,
I saw my Meg, but Meggie saw na me,
Her *cockernonie* snooded up fu' sleek.
　　　　　—ALLAN RAMSAY.

But I doubt the daughter's a silly thing : an unco *cockernony* she had busked on her head at the kirk last Sunday.—SCOTT : *Old Mortality*.

My gude name ! If ony body touched my gude name I wad neither fash council nor commissary. I would be down upon them like a sea-falcon amang a wheen wild geese, and the best o' them that dared to say onything o' Meg Dods but what was honest and civil, I wad soon see if her *cockernonie* was made o' her ain hair or other folks' !—SCOTT : *St. Ronans' Well*.

Cod, from the Gaelic, *cod*, a cushion, a pillow, a bag, a receptacle ; *peas-cod*, the shell in which the peas are formed and retained. The word is retained in English in an indelicate sense for the *scrotum*.

I hae guid fire for winter weather,
　A *cod* o' caff (chaff) wud fill a cradle,
A halter an' a guid hay tether,
　A deuk about the dub to paidle.
　　—*The Wooin' o' Jenny and Jock.*

Cod-crune or cod-crooning, a curtain lecture ; from the Gaelic *cod*, a pillow, and *croon*, to murmur, to lament, to moan. Jamieson derives the word from the Teutonic *kreunen*, and says it is sometimes called a "bowster (bolster) lecture." No such word, however, as *kreunen* or *kruncn* is to be found in the German dictionaries.

Codroch, miserable, ugly, detestable. These are the meanings assigned to the word by Allan Ramsay, though Jamieson, who cites it as used in Fifeshire and the Lothians, explains it as a rustic, or one who is dirty and slovenly.

A *codroch coffe*, he is sure sich,
And lives like ony wareit wretch.
—*Pedder Coffe: The Evergreen.*

The final syllable seems to be the Gaelic *droch*, bad, evil, wicked, mischievous. *Co* is doubtless the Gaelic *comh* (pronounced *co*), a prefix equivalent to the Latin *co* and *con*. Jamieson derives it from the Irish Gaelic *cudar*, the rabble, a word that does not appear in O'Reilly's excellent Irish Dictionary, though *cudarman* and *cudarmanta* appear in it as synonymous with "vulgar and rustic."

Coffe, a fellow; in vulgar English, a *chap*. From the German *kaufen*, to buy; and *kaufmann*, a merchant, a tradesman.

Coft, bought, purchased. *Cooft*, to buy, from *kaufen*, has become obsolete; but *cooper*, a buyer or seller, survives in horse-cooper or horse-dealer.

Then he has *coft* for that ladye
A fine silk riding-gown;
Likewise he *coft* for that ladye
A steed, and set her on.
—BUCHAN'S *Ancient Ballads:
Jock o' Hazelgreen (old version).*

Cog and **cogie,** a bowl or cup, also a basin. From the Gaelic *cuach*, a cup, used either for broth, ale, or stronger drink.

I canna want my *cogie*, sir,
I canna want my *cogie*;
I winna want my three-girred *cog*
For a' the wives in Bogie.
—DUKE OF GORDON.

It's good to have our *cog* out when it rains kail!—ALLAN RAMSAY'S *Scots Proverbs.*

Coggle, to shake, to waggle; from the Gaelic *gog* or *cog*, to shake; *gogail*, wavering, unsteady. Whence probably the French *coquette*, a flirt, or one who wavers or is unsteady in the bestowal of her favours to male admirers.

It *coggled* thrice, but at the last
It rested on his shoulders fast.
—GEORGE BEATTIE: *John o' Arnha'.*

Collie-shangie, a loud dispute, a quarrel, an uproar, a noise of angry tongues.

How the *collie-shangie* works
Betwixt the Russians and the Turks.
—BURNS: *To a Gentleman who Sent him a Newspaper.*

"It has been supposed," says Jamieson, "that from *collie*, a shepherd's dog, and *shangie*, a chain, comes the word *collie-shangie*, a quarrel between two dogs fastened with the same chain." Under the word "collie," he explains it to mean a quarrel, as well as a dog of that species; as if he believed that the gentle and sagacious shepherd's dog was more quarrelsome than the rest of the canine species. In Gaelic, *coileid* means noise, confusion, uproar; and *coileideach*, noisy, confused, angry; which is no doubt the etymology of *collie* in the compound word *collie-shangie*. The meaning of *shangie* is difficult to trace, unless it be from the Gaelic *seang* (pronounced *shang*), slender, lean, hungry.

Conundrum, a kind of riddle suggestive of resemblances where no resemblances exist; a wordy puzzle. The word is of comparatively recent introduction into English, and has been supposed by some etymologists to be derivable from the German *kennen*, to know. Stormonth was content to trace it to the Anglo-Saxon *cunnan;* but on its being pointed out to him by the present writer, in a private note, after the issue of the first edition of his Dictionary, that the derivation was so far unsatisfactory that it did not account for the final syllable, and that it was an ancient Scottish word, of which the components were the Gaelic *conn*, sense or meaning, and *antrom*, heavy or difficult, he abandoned the Anglo-Saxon derivation, and expressed his resolve to adopt the Gaelic etymology if his Dictionary ever reached a second edition. He died, unfortunately, before preparing a second edition for the press.

Coof, cuif, gowk, a fool, a simpleton, a cuckoo.

Ye see yon birkie ca'd a lord,
  Wha struts an' stares an' a' that;
Though hundreds worship at his word,
  He's but a *cuif* for a' that.
    —BURNS : *A Man's a Man.*

Coof and *gowk*, though apparently unlike each other in sound, are probably corruptions of the same Gaelic words, *cuabhag* (*cuafag*) and *cuach*, a cuckoo :—

Ye breed of the *gowk* (cuckoo), ye hae but ae note in your voice, and ye're aye singing it.—ALLAN RAMSAY'S *Scots Proverbs.*

In England, a "fool" and a "goose" are synonymous; but in Scotland the cuckoo is the bird that symbolises stupidity.

Cuif, fool, and blockhead, are not exact synonyms,—rather a useless fellow, a sort of male tawpie. A man may be a *cuif*, and yet the reverse of a fool or blockhead. —R. DRENNAN.

Coo-me-doo, a term of endearment for a turtle-dove, wood pigeon, or cushat.

O *coo-me-doo*, my love sae true,
  If ye'll come doun to me,
Ye'se hae a cage o' guid red gowd
  Instead o' simple tree.
    —BUCHAN'S *Ballads : The Earl o'
      Mar's Daughter.*

Corbie, the hooded-crow; also the raven; from the French *corbeau.*

Corbies will no pick out *corbies'* e'en (*Old Proverb*). [Signifying that two of a trade ought not to divulge the tricks of the trade; also applied among thieves to a confederate who informs against them, or *peaches*.]

The adder lies i' the *corbie's* nest,
  Beneath the *corbie's* wing;
And the blast that rives the *corbie's* nest
  Will soon bring hame the king.
    —*Jacobite Song,* 1745.

Cosh, quiet, snug. (*See* COZIE.)

And sang fu' sweet the notes o' love,
Till a' was *cosh* within.
—*Border Minstrelsy : The Gay
Gosshawk.*

Cosie, cozie, comfortable, snug,
warm.

While some are *cozie* in the neuk,
And forming assignations
To meet some day.
—BURNS : *The Holy Fair.*

Jamieson says that *cosie*, snug,
warm, comfortable, seems to be
of the same derivation as *cosh*, a
comfortable situation, and comfortable as implying a defence
from the cold. It is evidently
from the Gaelic *coiscag*, a little,
snug, or warm corner, a derivation from *cos* and *cois*, a hollow,
a recess, a corner.

Couthie, well - known, familiar,
handsome, and agreeable — in
contradistinction to the English
word *uncouth.*

Some kindle, *couthie*, side by side,
And burn together trimly.
—BURNS : *Hallowe'en.*

My ain *couthie* dame,
O my ain *couthie* dame ;
Wi' my bonny bits o' bairns,
And my ain *couthie* dame.
—*Ingleside Lilts.*

Cowp, to tumble over ; akin to the
French *coup*, a blow ; whence to
suffer a blow in falling.

I drew my scythe in sic a fury,
I near had *cowpit* in my hurry.
—BURNS : *Death and Dr. Hornbook.*

Crabb, to find fault, to be angry,
to complain for slight cause,
or without real necessity. This

word is traceable in the English
crabbed, ill-tempered.

He that *crabbs* without cause should
mease (apologise) without mends (making
amends).—*Scottish Proverb.*

Crack, talk, gossip, conversation,
confidential discourse, a story ;
from the Gaelic *crac*, to talk ;
cracaire, a talker, a gossip, and
cracaireachd, idle talk or chat.
To "*crack* a thing up" in English is to talk it into repute
by praise. A *crack* article is a
thing highly praised. Jamieson
derives the word from the German *kraken*, to make a noise,
though there is no such word in
that language.

But raise your arm, and tell your *crack*
Before them a'.
—BURNS : *Earnest Cry and Prayer.*

They're a' in famous tune
For *cracks* that day.
—BURNS : *The Holy Fair.*

The cantie auld folk *crackin'* crouse,
The young anes rantin' through the house ;
My heart has been sae fain to see them,
That I for joy hae barkit wi' them.
—BURNS : *The Twa Dogs.*

A lady on hiring a servant girl in the
country, told her, as a great indulgence,
that she should have the liberty of attend-
ing the kirk every Sunday, but that she
would be expected to return home immediately after the conclusion of the service. The lady, however, rather unexpectedly found a positive objection raised
against this apparently reasonable arrangement. "Then I canna engage wi' ye,
mem, for indeed I wadna gie the *crack* i'
the kirkyard for a' the sermon."—DEAN
RAMSAY.

Craig, the neck.

Ane got a twist o' the *craig*,
Ane got a punch o' the wame ;

C

Symy Hair got lamed o' a leg,
And syne ran wabblin' hame.
  —*Border Minstrelsy : The Death of
    Featherstonehaugh.*

Crambo-clink or **crambo-jingle**, a contemptuous name for doggerel verse, and bad or mediocre attempts at poetry, which Douglas Jerrold, with wit as well as wisdom—and they are closely allied — described as "verse and *worse.*"

A' ye wha live by *crambo-clink*, .
A' ye wha write and never think,
Come mourn wi' me.
  —BURNS : *On a Scotch Bard.*

Amaist as soon as I could spell,
I to the *crambo-jingle* fell,
Tho' rude and rough ;
But crooning to a body's sel'
Does weel enough.
  —BURNS : *Epistle to Lapraik.*

Crambo seems to be derived from the Gaelic *crom*, crooked, or perhaps from "cramp" or "cramped." "Clink" and "jingle," assonance, consonance, or rhyme, are from the English.

Creel or **creil**, a fish-basket ; from the French *creille*, with the same meaning.

The boatie rows, the boatie rows,
The boatie rows fu' weel,
And muckle luck attend the boat,
The merlin, and the *creel.*—*Old Song.*

Creepie, a low stool ; from the Gaelic *crub*, to bend low.

I sit on my *creepie* and spin at my wheel,
An' think on the laddie that lo'es me sae
weel.—*Logie o' Buchan.* .

Creeshie, greasy.

Kamesters (wool-combers) are aye *creeshie* (*Old Proverb*), *i.e.*, people are ever tainted with their trade, as in the phrase, "Millers are aye mealy."

Crone, an old woman, a witch. Worcester, in his Dictionary, derives this word from the Scottish "croon" "the hollow muttering sound with which old witches uttered their incantations." (*See* CROON.)

Crony, a comrade, a dear friend, a boon companion ; derived in a favourable sense from *crone.* This Scottish word seems to have been introduced to English notice by James I. It was used by Swift and other writers of his period, and was admitted into Johnson's Dictionary, who described it as a "cant word."

To oblige your *crony* Swift,
Bring our dame a New Year's gift.
  —SWIFT.

My name is Fun, your *crony* dear,
The nearest friend ye ha'e.
  —BURNS : *The Holy Fair.*

And at his elbow Souter Johnny,
His ancient, trusty, drouthy *crony.*
  —BURNS : *Tam o' Shanter.*

Croodle, to coo like a dove : "a wee *croodlin'* doo," a term of endearment to an infant.

Far ben thy dark green plantin' shade
The cushat (wood-pigeon) *croodles* amorouslie.—TANNAHILL.

There's ae thing keeps my heart light,
Whate'er the world may do ;
A bonnie, bonnie, bonnie, bonnie,
Wee *croodlin'* doo.—*Old Song.*

Croon, to hum over a tune, to prelude on an instrument. The word seems derivable from the Gaelic *cronan,* a dull, murmuring sound, a mournful and monotonous tune.

The sisters grey before the day
Did *croon* within their cloister.
                    —ALLAN RAMSAY.

Whiles holding fast his guid blue bonnet,
Whiles *croonin* o'er some auld Scots sonnet.
                    —BURNS: *Tam o' Shanter.*

Where auld ruined castles grey
    Nod to the moon,
To fright the nightly wanderer's way
    Wi' eldritch *croon.*
                    —BURNS: *Address to the Deil.*

        Plaintive tunes,
Such as corpse-watching beldam *croons.*
                    —*Studies from the Antique.*

Crouse, merry, lively, brisk, bold, from the Gaelic *craos,* greedy, sensual, gluttonous, eager for any pleasure of the senses.

A cock's aye *crouse* on his ain midden.—ALLAN RAMSAY's *Scots Proverbs.*

The cantie auld folk crackin' *crouse,*
The young anes rantin' through the house.
                    —BURNS: *The Twa Dogs.*

Crowdie, oatmeal boiled to a thick consistency; *crowdie-time,* breakfast-time or meal-time.

Jamieson goes to the Icelandic for the origin of the word *crowdie,* once the favourite and general food of the Scottish people, in the days before the less nutritious potato was introduced into the country. But the name of *crowdie* is not so likely to be derived from the Icelandic *graut-ur,* gruel made of groats, as from the Gaelic *cruaidh,* thick, firm, of hard consistency. Gruel is thin, but porridge or crowdie is thick and firm, and in that quality its great merit consists, as distinguished from its watery competitor, the nourishment of the sick-room, and not to be compared to the strong wholesome "parritch," which Burns designated "the chief of Scotland's food."

Oh, that I had never been married,
    I'd never had nae care ;
Now I've gotten wife and bairns,
    An' they cry *crowdie* evermair !
Once *crowdie,* twice *crowdie,*
    Three times *crowdie* in a day !
                    —BURNS.

Then I gaed hame at *crowdie-time,*
    And soon I made me ready.
                    —BURNS: *The Holy Fair.*

My sister Kate came up the gate
    Wi' *crowdie* unto me, man ;
She swore she saw the rebels run
Frae Perth unto Dundee, man.
                    —*The Battle of Sheriffmuir.*

Crowdie, properly, is oatmeal mixed with cold water ; but it is also used for food in general, as in the expression, "I'll be hame about *crowdie*-time."—R. DRENNAN.

Crummie, a familiar name for a favourite cow ; from the crooked horn. Gaelic *crom,* crooked. In the ancient ballad of "Tak' your auld cloak about ye," quoted by Shakespeare in "Othello," the word appears as *Crumbock.*

Bell, my wife, who loves no strife,
    She said unto me quietlie,
Rise up and save cow *Crumbock's* life,
    And put thine auld cloak about thee.

The word appears as *Crummock* in Burns's "Epistle to Major Logan."

Hale be your heart, hale be your fiddle,
Lang may your elbuck jouk and diddle,
To cheer you through the weary widdle
    O' this wide warl',
Until you on a *crummock* driddle,
    A grey-hair'd carl.

Crunt, a smart blow with a cudgel or fist on the crown of the head.

And mony a fellow got his licks
    Wi' hearty *crunt.*
    —BURNS : *To Willie Simpson.*

This word seems to come either from the English *crown*, the head (hence a blow on the head), or from the Gaelic *crun*, which has the same meaning. The crown of the head, the very top of the head, is a common phrase ; the *croon* of the causeway—the top ridge of the road, or the middle of the road—is a well-known Scotticism. In slang English, a *crunt* is called a *nopper*, or one for his "*nob.*"

Cuddie, a donkey ; supposed by some to be derived from the Gaelic *cutach*, bob-tailed, or from *ceutach*, grace, elegance, beauty, applied to the animal by its owner either in affection or derision.

One day my grandfather saw Andrew Leslie's donkey up to the knees in a field of clover. " Hallo, Andrew ! " said he, " I thought your *cuddie* wad eat nothing but thistles and nettles." " Ay," said he, " but he misbehaved himself, and I put him in there just to punish him."—DEAN RAMSAY.

Cuddle. This word, which in the English vernacular means to embrace, to fondle, to press to the bosom, simply signifies in Scottish parlance to *sleep*, and is derived from the Gaelic *cadail*, sleep.

An auld beddin' o' claes
    Was left me by my mither ;
They're jet black o'er wi' flaes ;
    Ye may *cuddle* in them thegither.
. . . . . .
The bride she gaed to her bed,
    The bridegroom he came till her,
The fiddler crept in at the foot,
    An' they a' *cuddled* together.
    —*Maggie's Tocher: The Tea-Table Miscellany.*

Where shall I *cuddle* the night?
    —GALT : *Mansie Wauch.*

Cuif or **coof**, a fool, a blockhead. (*See* COOF, *ante.*)

Cupar.

He that will to Cupar, maun to Cupar.

This proverb, applied to an obstinate man who will have his own way, has puzzled many commentators. Dean Ramsay asks, " Why Cupar? and whether is it the Cupar of Angus or the Cupar of Fife ? "

It has been suggested that the origin of " Cupar," in the sense employed in the proverb, is the Gaelic *comhar* (*covar*), a mark, a sign, a proof, and that the phrase is equivalent to " he who *will* be a marked man (by his folly or perversity) *must* be a marked man." It has also been suggested that " Cupar " is from *comharra* (*covarra*), shelter or protection of the sanctuary, to which a man resorted when hard pressed by justice for a crime which he had committed.

Curn, a grain of corn; whence *kernel,* the fruit in the nut; curny-gutty.

Mind to splice high with Latin—a *curn* or two of Greek would not be amiss: and if ye can bring in anything about the judgment of Solomon in the original Hebrew, and season with a merry jest or so, the dish will be the more palatable.—SCOTT: *Fortunes of Nigel.*

Allied words to *curn* are "kern" and "churn," a hand-mill for grinding corn, and "churn," a mill for stirring the milk so as to make butter.

Cushat, a turtle-dove, a wood-pigeon.

O'er lofty aiks the *cushats* wail,
And echo coos the dolefu' tale.
　　—BURNS: *Bess and her Spinning Wheel.*

Custock or **castock,** the edible stalk of cabbage; a kail-runt.

There's cauld kail in Aberdeen,
An' *custocks* in Stra'bogie,
An' ilka lad maun hae his lass,
An' I maun hae my cogie.
　　—HERD'S *Collection: The Three-Girred Cog.*

Cutty or **cuttie,** short; from the Gaelic *cutach,* that has been cut, abridged, or shortened; whence *cutty*-pipe, a short pipe.

I'm no sae scant o' clean pipes as to blaw wi' a burnt *cutty.*—ALLAN RAMSAY'S *Scots Proverbs.*

Till first ae caper, then anither,
Tam tint his reason a' thegither,
And roared out "Weel done, *cutty* sark!"
And in an instant a' was dark.
　　—BURNS: *Tam o' Shanter.*

Her *cutty* sark, o' Paisley harn,
That when a lassie she had worn,

In longitude though sorely scanty,
It was her best, and she was vaunty.
　　—*Ibid.*

Cuttie-stool, a three-legged stool; a short stool, such as Jennie Geddes is reported to have thrown from the pulpit stairs at the head of the heretical minister.

A circumstance connected with Scottish church discipline has undergone a great change in my time—I mean the public censure from the pulpit of persons convicted of a breach of the seventh commandment. . . . This was performed by the guilty person standing up before the whole congregation on a raised platform called the *cutty-stool.*—DEAN RAMSAY.

The culprits did not always take the admonition patiently. It is recorded of one of them in Ayrshire, that when accused of adultery by the minister, he interrupted and corrected his reverend monitor by denying the imputation, and calling out, "Na! na! minister; it was simple *fornie* (fornication), and no *adultery* ava."—*Ibid.*

Cutty-mun and tree-ladle. These words, according to Jamieson, were the names of old tunes once popular in Scotland. No trace of them, however, has hitherto been discovered, and the interpretation given to them by Jamieson remains a mere supposition on his part. *Cutty-mun,* he says, means a spoon with a short handle. *Cutty* no doubt signifies short or small, as in *cutty-stool* and in *cutty-pipe;* but Jamieson should have been aware that in no known language does *mun* signify a spoon. Investigation would have shown him that the same language from which *cutty* is derived supplied the true etymology of *mun*, from *mainne*, delay, and that *cutty-mun* signified short delay. In like manner *tree-ladle* has no reference to a wooden spoon or ladle, as he supposed, but is derived from the Gaelic *triall*, departure on a journey, and *luathaich*, speed; *luathailteach*, swift, speedy. Thus the old tune mentioned by Jamieson resolves itself into a Lowland rendering of the Gaelic, and signified "a short shrift and speedy exit." This would be an appropriate phrase applied to the hanging of a Highland criminal by a feudal chief, or to the more formal but equally efficacious justice as administered in the Lowlands, and is, there can be little or no doubt, the real meaning of the name of the old song on which Jamieson relied for his interpretation.

D

Daff, to make merry, to be sportive; **daffin',** merriment.

> Wi' *daffin'* weary grown,
> Upon a knowe they sat them down.
> —BURNS : *The Twa Dogs.*

Dr. Adam, Rector of the High School of Edinburgh, rendered the Horatian expression "desipere in loco" by the Scottish phrase "weel-timed *daffin'*"—a translation which no one but a Scot could properly appreciate.—DEAN RAMSAY.

Daff has long ceased to be current English, though it was used by Shakespeare in the sense of to befool. In the scene between Leonato and Claudio in "Much Ado About Nothing," when Claudio refuses to fight with an old man, Leonato replies:

> Canst thou so *daff* me—thou who killed my child ?

The Shakespearean commentators all agree that this word should be *doff* me, or put me off.

They interpret in the same way the line in King Lear :—

> The madcap Prince of Wales, that
> *daff'd* the world aside !

It would appear, however, that in both instances, *daff* was used in the sense which it retains in Scotch, that of fool or befool.

Daft, crazy, wild, mad.

> Or maybe in a frolic *daft*
> To Hague or Calais take a waft.
> —BURNS : *The Twa Dogs.*

Daidle, to trifle, to dawdle.

> *Daidlin'* in the mock-turtle ! I hate a' things mock.—*Noctes Ambrosianæ.*

Daiker or **daker,** to saunter, to stroll lazily or idly, or without defined purpose or object.

Dambrod, draught - board or chess-board ; from the Flemish *dambord ;* the first syllable from the French *dame*, or *jeu aux dames*, draughts.

Mrs. Chisholm entered the shop of a linen-draper, and asked to be shown some table-cloths of a *dambrod* pattern. The shopman was taken aback at such apparently strong language as "damned broad," used by a respectable lady. The lady, on her part, was surprised at the stupidity of the London shopman, who did not understand so common a phrase.—DEAN RAMSAY.

Dapperpye, brilliant with many colours; from *dapper*, neat and smart, the German *tapfer*, brave, English, *bravery* in attire, and *pied*, variegated.

Oh, he has pu'd off his *dapperpye* coat,
The silver buttons glanced bonny.
—*Border Minstrelsy: Annan Water.*

Darg or **daurk,** a job of work; from the Gaelic *dearg*, a plough.

You will spoil the *darg* if you stop the plough to kill a mouse.—*Northumbrian Proverb.*

He never did a good *darg* that gaed grumbling about it.—ALLAN RAMSAY'S *Scots Proverbs.*

Monie a sair *daurk* we hae wrought.
—BURNS: *To his Auld Mare Maggie.*

Darger, a day-labourer, one who works by the piece or job; also a ploughman.

The croonin kye the byre drew nigh,
The *darger* left his thrift.
—*Border Minstrelsy: The Water Kelpie.*

Daud, to pelt; also a large piece.

I'm busy too, an' skelpin' at it,
But bitter *daudin'* showers ha'e wat it.
—BURNS: *To J. Lapraik.*

He'll clap a shangan on her tail,
An' set the bairns to *daud* her
Wi' dirt this day.
—BURNS: *The Ordination.*

A *daud* o' bannock
Wad mak' him blithe as a body could.
—ALLAN RAMSAY.

Daud and *blaud* or *blad* are synonymous in the sense of a large piece of anything, and also of pelting or driving, as applied to rain or wind.

I got a great *blad* o' Virgil by heart.
—JAMIESON.

Dauner or **daunder,** to saunter, to stroll leisurely, without a purpose.

Some idle and mischievous youths waited for the minister on a dark night, and one of them, dressed as a ghost, came up to him in hopes of putting him in a fright. The minister's cool reply upset the plan. "Weel, Maister Ghaist, is this a general rising, or are ye jist taking a *dauner* frae your grave by yoursel'?"—DEAN RAMSAY'S *Reminiscences.*

Daunton, to subdue, to tame, to daunt, to dominate, to break in (applied to horses); from the Gaelic *dan*, bold, daring, and *danaich*, to exert boldness, to dare, to challenge, to defy.

To *daunton* me, and me sae young,
Wi' his fause heart an' flatterin' tongue,
That is the thing ye ne'er shall see,
For an auld man shall never *daunton* me.
—*Old Song, altered by* BURNS.

Daut, to fondle, to caress.

Dautie, a darling, one who is fondled and affectionately treated; allied to the English *doat, doat upon,* and *dotage.*

Whae'er shall say I wanted Jean,
When I did kiss and *daut* her.
—BURNS : *Had I the wyte.*

My *dautie* and my doo (dove).
—ALLAN RAMSAY.
To some it may appear that *dawtie* may
have had its origin from the Gaelic *dalt*, a
foster-child.—JAMIESON.

Yestreen ye were your daddie's doo,
But an your mither's *dautie.*
—BUCHAN'S *Ancient Ballads: The
Trooper and Fair Maid.*

Daw, a slut, akin to the colloquial
English *dowdy*, an ill-dressed
woman or sloven.

See-saw, Margery *Daw*,
Sold her bed and lay in the straw.
—*Nursery Rhyme.*

Dawds and blawds is a phrase
that denotes the greatest abundance.—JAMIESON.

Dawk, a drizzling rain; *dawky*,
moist, rainy, not exactly a downpour of steady rain, but of inter-
mittent drizzle.

Day-daw, abbreviation of day-
dawn, or dawn of day.

Dead is often used in the sense of
very, extremely, or entirely, as in
the English word *dead-beat.* It
occurs in Scottish parlance as
dead-loun, very calm and still;
dead-cauld, extremely cold; *dead-
ripe*, very ripe, or ripe to rotten-
ness; *dead-sweir*, extremely lazy
or tired out.

**Dear me! Oh dear me! Deary
me!** These colloquial exclamations are peculiar to the English and Scottish languages, and
are indicative either of surprise,
pain, or pity. If the word
"dear" be accepted as correct,
and not a corruption of some
other word with a different
meaning, the explanation, if
literally translated into any
other language, would be non-
sensical ; in French, for instance, it would be *O cher moi !*
and in German, *Ach theuer mich !*
The original word, as used by
our British ancestors, and
misunderstood by the Danes,
Flemings, and Dutch, who succeeded them in part possession of the country, appears to
have been the Gaelic *Dia (dee-a),*
God. *Oh Dia !* or *Oh dear !*
and *Oh dear me !* would signify,
God! Oh God! or Oh my God!
synonymous with the French
Mon Dieu ! or *Oh mon Dieu !* and
the German *Mein Gott !* or *Ach
mein Gott !*

Deas, a stone seat in the porch,
or at the porch of a church,
probably so named from its
usual position at the right hand
side ; from the Gaelic *deas*, the
right side, on the right hand.

An' when she came to Marie's kirk,
An' sat down in the *deas,*
The licht that came frae fair Annie
Enlichten't a' the place.
PERCY'S *Reliques: Sweet William
and Fair Annie.*

The etymology of the Eng-
lish and French word *dais* has
given rise to much diference of
opinion. Stormonth's English
Dictionary defines *dais* as " a
canopy over a throne, afterwards the whole seat," and sug-

gests a derivation from the "old French *dais*, a table, from Latin *discus*, a quoit—the raised floor at the upper end of a dining-room; a raised seat, often canopied." Brachet's Etymological Dictionary, in which the compiler follows Littré, says that "*dais* in old French *always* meant a dinner-table, but especially a state table with a canopy; that gradually the sense of table has been lost, and that of canopy prevails; whereas in England the sense of canopy is lost, while that of the platform on which the table stands has taken its place."

May not all these apparent discrepancies between canopy, platform, table, seat, and disk or discus, be explained by the Gaelic *deas*, as the real origin of dais? The right-hand side of the host was the place of honour, reserved for the most distinguished guest; and the canopy was raised, as a matter of course, at the upper end of the banqueting hall, where kings and great nobles held their festivals. The suggestion will be taken by philologists *quantum valeat*. It is certainly as well deserving of consideration as the derivation from *discus* is, which has hitherto found favour with philologists who are ignorant of the Gaelic.

Deave, to deafen.

Last May a braw wooer came down the lang glen,
An' sair wi' his love he did *deave* me ;

I said there was naethin' I hated like men,
The deil gae wi'm to believe me.
—Burns.

A drunken wife I hae at hame,
Her noisome din aye *deaves* me ;
The ale-wife, the ale-wife,
The ale-wife she grieves me ;
The ale-wife an' her barrelie
They ruin me an' *deave* me.
—Buchan's *Scots Songs and Ballads.*

Deil's-buckie or **Deevil's-buckie**, an angry epithet applied to any mischievous lad or small boy. Jamieson says *buckie* signifies a spiral shell of any kind, and adds that a refractory urchin is not only designated by irate persons as a *deil's buckie*, but as a *thrawn* or twisted *buckie*. It may be questioned, however, whether *buckie* is not derived from the Gaelic *buachaille*, a cowherd, and not from a shell, as far more likely to be in use among a pastoral and agricultural peasantry than a shell, that is not in any way suggestive of either a good boy or a bad one.

Deray, disorder, disarray. The word is also applied to any amusement of a boisterous character.

Sic dancin' and *deray.*
—*Christ's Kirk on the Green.*

The word is used by the old poets Barbour and Douglas, but seldom or never by those of the seventeenth and eighteenth centuries, and is all but obsolete.

Dern, dismal, gloomy.

> Auld Dourie never saw a blink,
> The lodging was so dark and *dern.*
> —*Border Minstrelsy: Chirstie's Will.*

Deuch, a drink, a draught; a corruption of the Gaelic *deoch*, which has the same meaning. Jamieson has *deuch-an-dorach* and *deuch-an-doris*, both corruptions of the Gaelic *deoch-an-dorus*, a drink at the door, the parting cup, the stirrup-cup. The alehouse sign, once common in England as well as in Scotland, "The Dog and Duck," appears to have had no relation to aquatic sports, but to have been a corruption of the Gaelic *deoch an diugh*, a drink to-day. In the same manner, "Mad Dog" —once set up as a sign at a place called Odell, as recorded in Hotten's "History of Signboards"—is merely the Gaelic of *math deoch* or *maith deoch*, good drink. In the London slang of the present day, *duke* is a word used among footmen and grooms for gin.

Deuk. A vulgar old song, which Burns altered and sent to "Johnson's Museum," without much improvement on the coarse original, commences with the lines :—

> The bairns gat out wi' an unco shout,
> The *deuk's* dang o'er my daddie, oh !
> The fient may care, quo' the ferlie auld wife,
> He was but a paidlin' body, oh !

The glossaries that accompany the editions of Burns issued by Allan Cunningham, Alexander Smith, and others, all agree in stating that *deuk* signifies the aquatic fowl the duck. But "the *duck* has come over, or beaten over, or flown over my father," does not make sense of the passage, or convey any meaning whatever. It is probable— though no editor of Burns has hitherto hinted it — that the word *deuk* should be *deuch*, from the Gaelic *deoch*, drink, a deep potation, which appears in Jamieson without other allusion to its Gaelic origin than the well-known phrase the *deoch-an-dorus*, the stirrup-cup or drink at the door. (*See* Deuch, *ante.*) Seen in this light, the line "the *deuch's* dang o'er my daddie " would signify "the *drink* or drunkenness has beaten or come over my daddie," and there can be little doubt that this is the true reading.

Dew-piece, a slight refreshment, a piece of bread, a scone, or oatcake, given out to farm-servants in the early morning before proceeding to out-of-door work.

Dight, to wipe, or wipe off.

> *Dight* your mou' ere I kiss you.
> —*Old Song.*

> Just as I *dight* frae the table the wine drops in ma sleeve.—*Noctes Ambrosianæ.*

Dilly castle. This, according to Jamieson, is a name given by boys to a mound of sand which they erect on the sea shore, and stand upon until the advancing tide surrounds it and washes it away. He thinks the name comes from the Teutonic "*digle* or *digel*, secretus, or from the Swedish *doelja* or *dylga*, occultare suus, a hiding-place." The etymology was not so far to seek or so difficult to find as Dr. Jamieson supposed, but is of purely home origin in the Gaelic *dile* (in two syllables), a flood, an inundation, an overflow of water.

Ding, to beat, or beat out; from the Gaelic *dinn*, to trample, to tread down.

If ye've the deil in ye, *ding* him out wi' his brither. Ae deil *dings* anither.

It's a sair *dung* (beaten) bairn that manna greet.—ALLAN RAMSAY, *Scots Proverbs.*

Ding only survives in English in the phrase *ding*, dong, bell; and is the slang of working people out on the strike for an advance of wages, who call a comrade who has left the confederacy, and yielded to the terms of the employer, a *dung*, i.e., one who is beaten in the conflict.

The following ludicrous example of the use of *dung* as the past tense of *ding*, to beat, is given by Dean Ramsay in an anecdote of two *bethrels* or *beadles*, who were severally boasting of the fervour of their two ministers in preaching :—

"I think," said one, "our minister did weel. Ay! he gart the stour fly out o' the cushion." To which the other replied with a calm feeling of superiority, "Stour out o' the cushion! Hoot! our minister, sin' he cam' till us, has *dung* the guts out o' twa Bibles!"

Dink, from the Gaelic *diong*, worthy, highly esteemed, proud, is suggested by Jamieson to mean neat, prim, saucy. The word occurs in the song, "My lady's gown there's gairs upon't," in which a lover draws a contrast between the great lady of his neighbourhood and the humble lass that he is in love with, to the disadvantage of the former. To "*dink* up" is to dress gorgeously or ostentatiously. *Gair*, in the title of the song, signifies an ornamental fold in the dress.

My lady's *dink*, my lady's dressed,
The flower and fancy o' the West;
But the lassie that a man lo'es best,
That's the lass to make him blest.

Dinsome, noisy, full of din.

Till block an' studdie (stithy or anvil) ring and reel
Wi' *dinsome* clamour. '
　　　—BURNS: *Scotch Drink.*

Dirdum, noise, uproar; supposed to be a corruption of the Gaelic *torman*, noise, uproar, confusion.

Humph! it's juist because—juist that the *dirdum's* a' about yon man's pockmanty.—SCOTT: *Rob Roy.*

Sic a *dirdum* about naething.
　　　—*Laird of Logan.*

What wi' the *dirdum* and confusion, and the lowpin here and there of the skeigh brute of a horse.—SCOTT: *Fortunes of Nigel.*

Dirl, a quivering blow on a hard substance.

> I threw a noble throw at ane,
> . . . . . .
> It jist played *dirl* upon the bane,
> But did nae mair.
> ' —BURNS: *Death and Dr. Hornbook.*

Divot, a piece of turf ready cut and dried for burning.

> The deil sat girnin' in the neuk,
> Rivin' sticks to roast the Duke,
> | And aye they kept it hot below,
> Bonnie laddie ! Highland laddie !
> Wi' peats and *divots* frae Glencoe,
> Bonnie laddie ! Highland laddie !
> —*Jacobite Ballad.*

Doited, confused, bewildered, stupid; hopelessly perplexed; of a darkened or hazy intellect.

> Thou clears the head o' *doited* lear,
> Thou cheers the heart o' droopin' care,
> Thou even brightens dark despair
> Wi' gloomy smile.
> —BURNS: *Scotch Drink.*

> Ye auld, blind, *doited* bodie,
> And blinder may ye be—
> 'Tis but a bonnie milking cow
> My minnie gied to me.
> —*Our Gudeman cam' Hame at E'en.*

This word seems to be derivable from the Gaelic *doite*, dark-coloured, obscure.

Doited evidently has some connection with the modern English word *dotage*, which again comes from *dote*, which anciently had, in addition to its modern meaning, that of to grow dull, senseless, or stupid.—R. DRENNAN.

Do-nae-guid and **Ne'er-do-weel.** These words are synonymous, and signify what the French call a *vaurien*, one who is good for nothing. *Ne'er-do-weel* has lately

become much more common in English than "never-do-well."

Donnart, stupefied.

> "Has he learning?" "Just dung *donnart* wi' learnin'."
> —SCOTT: *St. Ronan's Well.*

Jamieson traces this word to the German *donner*, thunder; but it comes most likely from the Gaelic *donas*, ill-fortune, or *donadh*, mischief, hurt, evil—corrupted by the Lowland Scotch by the insertion of the letter *r*. The English word *dunce* appears to be from the same source, and signifies an unhappy person, who is too stupid to learn.

Donnot or **donot,** a ne'er-do-weel, usually applied to an idle or worthless girl or woman; a corruption of *do-nought*, or do-nothing.

> Janet, thou *donot*,
> I'll lay my best bonnet
> Thou gets a new gudeman afore it be night.
> —*Minstrelsy of the Scottish Border.*

Donsie, unlucky; from the Gaelic *donas*, misfortune; the reverse of *sonas*, sonsie or lucky.

> Their *donsie* tricks, their black mistakes,
> Their failings and mischances.
> —BURNS: *Address to the Unco Guid.*

Jamieson admits that the word may be derived from the Gaelic *donas*, and says that it means not only unlucky, but pettish, peevish, ill-natured, dull, dreary. But all these epithets resolve themselves more or less intimately into the idea of unluckiness.

Doo, a dove, a pigeon; *doo*-tart or tert, a pigeon-pie. "My bonnie *doo*" is a familiar and tender salutation to a lover. *Doo-cot*, a dove-cot.

Oh, lay me doun, my *doo*, my *doo*,
 Oh, lay me doun, my ain kind dearie;
For dinna ye mind upo' the time
 We met in the wood at the well sae
 wearie.
 —BUCHAN'S *Ancient Ballads.*

Dook or **douk**, to dive under water. Colloquial English, to duck or dive.

'Gae *douk*, gae *douk*, the king he cried,
Gae *douk* for gold and fee,
Oh, wha will *douk* for Hunter's sake.
 —HERD'S *Collection; Young Hunter.*

Dool or **dule**, pain, grief, dolefulness; from the Gaelic *dolas*, the French *deuil*, mourning.

Of a' the numerous human *dools*,
 Thou bear'st the gree.
 —BURNS: *Address to the Toothache.*

Though dark and swift the waters pour,
 Yet here I wait in *dool* and sorrow;
For bitter fate must I endure,
 Unless I pass the stream ere morrow.
 —*Legends of the Isles.*

Oh, *dule* on the order
 Sent our lads to the Border—
The English for once by guile won the day.
· —*The Flowers of the Forest.*

Dorty, haughty, stubborn, austere, supercilious; from *dour*, hard (q.v.)

Let *dorty* dames say na!
 As lang as e'er they please,
Seem caulder than the snaw
 While inwardly they bleeze.
 —ALLAN RAMSAY: *Polwarth on the
 Green.*

Then though a minister grow˗*dorty*,
 Ye'll snap your fingers
 Before his face.
 —BURNS: *Earnest Cry and Prayer.*

Douce, of a gentle or courteous disposition; from the French *doux*, sweet.

Ye dainty deacons and ye *douce* conveners.
 —BURNS: *The Brigs of Ayr.*

Ye Irish lords, ye knights and squires,
Who represent our brughs and shires,
An' *doucely* manage our affairs
 In Parliament.
 —BURNS: *The Author's Earnest Cry
 and Prayer.*

Doun - draught. A pull - down, draw-down, or drag-down.

Twa men upon ae dog's a sair *doun-
draught.—Noctes Ambrosianæ.*

Dour, hard, bitter, disagreeable, close-fisted, severe, stern; from the French and Latin, *dur* and *durus.*

When biting Boreas, fell and *dour*,
Sharp shivers through the leafless bower.
 —BURNS: *A Winter Night.*

I've been harsh-tempered and *dour* enough, I know; and it's only fitting as they should be hard and *dour* to me where I'm going.—A. TROLLOPE: *Vicar of Bull-hampton.*

Dous or **Doos**, *i.e.*, doves. To "shoot amang the *dous*" is a metaphorical phrase for making an assertion at random or without knowledge. It is sometimes applied to any wilfully false assertion. The true meaning is merely that of an indiscriminate shot, in the hope of hitting or killing something — as in the barbarous practice, miscalled *sport*, which was the fashion under royal patronage at Hurlingham, of firing into a cloud of pigeons with the chance or the certainty of killing some of them.

Dow, to be able, of which the synonym in the infinitive mood *to can*, from the Teutonic *kannen*, has long been obsolete. The misuse and perversion of this word in English in the customary greeting "How do you do?" is a remarkable instance of the corruption of the popular speech by the illiterate multitude, and its adoption after long currency by the literate, until it acquires an apparent authenticity and a real vitality which no correction however authoritative can rectify. "How do you *do?*" originally meant, and still means, how do you *dow?* *i.e.*, how is your strength or ability? how do you thrive or prosper or get on? as in the German phrase *Wie geht's?* or *Wie befinden sie sieh?* the Italian *Come state?* or *Come sta?* in the French *Comment vous portez vous?* or *Comment vous va-t-il?* or the Gaelic *Cia mar tha sibh an diugh*, pronounced *ca-mar-a shee an dew*, equivalent to the English *How are you?* The ancient word *doughty*, strong, is a derivative of *dow*, able. *Dow* is provincial in England, but common in Lowland Scotch.

Facts are chiels that winna ding,
And *downa* be disputed.—BURNS.

And now he goes daundrin' about the dykes,
An' a' he *dow* do is to hund the tykes.
—LADY GRIZZEL BAILLIE.

Dowd, stale, flat; from the Gaelic *daoidh*, weak, feeble, worthless.

Cast na out the *dowd* water till ye get the fresh.—ALLAN RAMSAY'S *Scots Proverbs*.

Dowf, doof, doofing, doofart. All these words are applied to a stupid, inactive, dull person, and appear to be the originals of the modern English slang a *duffer*, which has a similar meaning.

Her *dowff* excuses pat me mad.
—BURNS: *Epistle to Lapraik.*

They're *dowf* and *dowie* at the best,
Dowf and *dowie*, *dowf* and *dowie*,
    Wi' a' their variorum;
They canna please a Highland taste
    Compared wi' Tullochgorum.
—Rev. JOHN SKINNER.

Dowie, gloomy, melancholy, forlorn, low-spirited; from the Gaelic *duibhe*, blackness.

It's no the loss o' warl's gear
That could sae bitter draw the tear,
Or mak' our bardie, *dowie*, wear
    The mourning weed.
—BURNS: *Poor Mailie's Elegy.*

Come listen, cronies, ane and a',
While on my *dowie* reed I blaw,
And mourn the sad untimely fa'
    O' our auld town.
—JAMES BALLANTINE.

Down. The Scottish language contains many more compounds of *down* than the English, such as *down-drag* and *down-draw*, that which drags or draws a man down in his fortunes, an incumbrance ; *down-throw*, of which the English synonym is *overthrow ; down-way*, a declivity or downward path ; *down-put* or *down-putting*, a rebuff ; *down-coming*, abandonment of the sick-room on convalescence ; *down-look*, a dejected look or expression of countenance; all of which are really English, although not admitted into the dictionaries.

Downa-do, impotency, powerlessness, inability.

I've seen the day ye buttered my brose,
And cuddled me late and early, O !
But *downa-do's* come o'er me now,
And oh I feel it sairly, O !
—BURNS : *The Deuk's Dang o'er my Daddie.*

Dowp, the posterior, sometimes written *dolp*. This word applies not only to the human frame, but to the bottom or end of anything, and is used in such phrases as the "*dowp* of a candle," "the *dowp* of an egg," as well as in the threats of an angry mother to a young child, " I'll skelp your *dowp.*" "Where's your grannie, my wee man ?" was a question asked of a child. The child replied, " Oh, she's ben the house, burning her *dowp*," *i.e.*, her candle-end.

Deil a wig has a provost o' Fairport worn sin auld Provost Jervie's time, and he had a quean o' a servant lass that dressed it hersel' wi' the *dowp o' a candle* and a dredging-box.—SCOTT : *The Antiquary.* .

Dowp-skelper. A humorous word applied to a schoolmaster ; from *skelp*, to smite with the palm of the hand. A similar idea enters into the composition of the English phrase " a bum-brusher," with the difference that *brusher* refers to the rod, and not to the palm of the hand. Burns applies the epithet to the Emperor Joseph of Austria, with what allusion it is now difficult to trace :—

To ken what French mischief was brewin'
Or what the drumlie Dutch were doin'—
That vile *dowp-skelper* Emperor Joseph,
If Venus yet had got his nose off.
—BURNS : *To a Gentleman who had Promised to send him a Newspaper.*

This word is not to be mistaken for *dub*-skelper—from *dub*, a pool, a pond, a puddle—and applied to one who rushes on his way recklessly, through thick and thin, heedless of dirt or obstruction.

Draibles or **drabbles**, drops of liquor or crumbs of food allowed to fall from the hand upon the clothes in the act of drinking or eating ; akin to the English *driblets*, signifying small quantities of anything.

Draidgie. A funeral entertainment ; from the French *dragée*, a comfit, a sweetmeat. This word does not appear in Jamieson, but is to be found in a small and excellent handbook of the Scottish vernacular, published in Edinburgh, 1818.

Dram. This ancient Scottish word for a small glass or "nip" of whisky or any other alcoholic liquor has long been adopted into English, but has no synonym of any allied sound in any other European language. The French call it a "*petit verre*," and the Germans a "*schnapps*," while the Americans have recently taken to calling it a "*smile*," or "*an eye-opener*." Philologists have been contented to derive it from the Greek *drachma*, though, if this be the fact, it is curious that the word has not found its way into the vernacular of any other people than those of the British Isles. But though the classic etymology be too firmly rooted in popular estimation to be readily abandoned, it may be interesting to note that in Lowland Scotch *dram* originally signified melancholy, heaviness of mind, from the Gaelic *truime*, heaviness, and that the *dram* was resorted to in order to raise the spirits and drive out melancholy—an idea which seems to have suggested the current American slang of a "*smile*."

ᶠ A story is told in Scotland of an old farmer too much addicted to his "dram" and his toddy, who was strictly forbidden by his medical attendant to indulge in more than an *ounce* of whisky per *diem*, if he hoped to escape a serious illness. The old man was puzzled at the word "ounce," and asked his son, who had studied at the University of St. Andrews and was qualifying for the Scottish ministry, what the doctor meant by an *ounce*. "An ounce," said his son, "why, every one knows that an ounce is sixteen *drams* (drachms)." "Ah! weel," said his sire, "if I may tak' saxteen drams i' the day, it's a' *richt*, an' I'll dae weel eneuch. The doctor, nae doot, kens his business. I've already had twa the day, and I've still fourteen to the fore!" Tradition does not record the ultimate fate of the old farmer.

Dreder, terror, apprehension, dread of impending evil; sometimes written *dredour.*

What aileth you, my daughter Janet,
    You look so pale and wan?
There is a *dreder* in your heart,
    Or else you love a man.
    —BUCHAN'S *Ancient Ballads : Lord Thomas and the King's Daughter.*

Dree, to endure, to suffer; probably from the Teutonic *trüben*, to trouble, to sadden, and thence to endure trouble or suffering; or from *tragen*, to bear, to carry, to draw.

Sae that no danger do thee deir
    What dule in dern thou *dree*
(What soon thou mayst suffer in secret).
    —*Robyn and Makyn : The Evergreen.*
Oh wae, wae by his wanton sides,
    Sae brawlie he could flatter,
Till for his sake I'm slighted sair,
    And *dree* the kintra clatter.
    —BURNS : *Here's his Health in Water.*

In the dialects of the North of England, to *dree* is used in the sense of to draw or journey towards a place.

In the summer-time, when leaves grow green,
    And birds sing on the tree,
Robin Hood went to Nottingham
    As fast as he could *dree*.
    —*Robin Hood and the Jolly Tinker.*

Dreigh, difficult, hard to travel, tedious, prolix, dry.

Hech, sirs! but the sermon was sair *dreigh!*
    —GALT.
Dreich at the thought and dour at the delivery.—*Noctes Ambrosianæ.*

Driddle. This is a word of several meanings, all more or less significant of anything done by small quantities at a time, such as to urinate often, to move with slow steps, to spill a liquid by unsteady handling of the vessel which contains it. It appears to be traceable to the Gaelic *drudh* or *druidh*, to ooze, to drip, to penetrate, and *drudhag*, a small drop.

Droddum, a jocular name for the breech, the posteriors, but more popularly known as the *hurdies* or *dowp* (which see).

My sooth ! right bauld ye set your nose out,
As plump and grey as ony grozet ;
Oh, for some rank mercurial rozet,
    Or fell red smeddum,
I'd gie ye sic a hearty dose o't,
    Wad dress your *droddum.*
—BURNS : *To a Louse, on seeing one on a Lady's Bonnet at Church.*

The word seems to be of kin to *drod*, thick, squat, fleshy. The derivation is uncertain.

Droich, a dwarf ; from the Gaelic *troid* or *troich*, with the same meaning.

Only look at the pictures (of the aristocracy) in their auld castles. What beautiful and brave faces ! Though now and then, to be sure, a dowdy or a *droich.*—*Noctes Ambrosianæ.*

Drook, to wet ; **drookit,** wet through, thoroughly saturated with moisture ; from the Gaelic *druchd*, dew, moisture, a tear, a drop ; *drudhag (dru-ag)*, a drop of water ; and *drughadh*, penetrating, oozing through. The resemblance to the Greek δακρυ, a tear, is noteworthy.

There were twa doos sat in a dookit,
The rain cam' doun and they were *drookit.*
    —*Nursery Song.*
The last Hallowe'en I was waukin'
My *drookit* sark sleeve, as ye ken,
His likeness cam ben the house stalkin',
And the vera grey breeks o' Tam Glen.
    —BURNS : *Tam Glen.*

My friends, you come to the kirk every Sabbath, and I lave you a' ower wi' the Gospel till ye're fairly *drookit* wi't.—*Extract from a sermon by a minister in Arran :* ROGERS'S *Illustrations of Scottish Life.*

Drouth, thirst ; **drouthie,** thirsty ; from *dry, dryeth.*

Tell him o' mine and Scotland's *drouth.*
    —BURNS : *Cry and Prayer.*
Folks talk o' my drink, but never talk o' my *drouth.*—ALLAN RAMSAY'S *Scots Proverbs.*
When *drouthie* neebors neebors meet.
    —BURNS : *Tam o' Shanter.*

Drumlie, turbid or muddy (applied to water), confused, not clear ; applied metaphorically to thoughts or expression. This word would be a great acquisition to the English language if it could be adopted, and lends a peculiar charm to many choice passages of Scottish poetry. All its English synonyms are greatly inferior to it, both in logical and poetical expression. It is derived from the Gaelic *trom* or *truim*, heavy (and applied to water), turbid. The word appears at one time to have been good English.

Draw me some water out of this spring. Madam, it is all foul, *drumly*, black, muddy !—*French and English Grammar*, 1623.

D

Haste, boatman, haste ! put off your boat,
Put off your boat for golden monie ;
I'll cross the *drumlie* stream to-night,
Or never mair I'll see my Annie.
—*Minstrelsy of the Scottish Border.*

When blue diseases fill the *drumlie* air.
—ALLAN RAMSAY.

Drink *drumly* German water
To make himself look fair and fatter.
—BURNS : *The Twa Dogs.*

They had na sailed a league, a league,
A league but barely three,
When dismal grew his countenance,
And *drumlie* grew his e'e.
—LAIDLAW : *The Demon Lover.*

There's good fishing in *drumlie* waters.
ALLAN RAMSAY'S *Scots Proverbs.*

I heard once a lady in Edinburgh objecting to a preacher that she did not
understand him. Another lady, his great
admirer, insinuated that probably he was
too deep for her to follow. But her ready
answer was, " Na, na !—he's no just deep,
ut he's *drumly.*"—DEAN RAMSAY.

Drummock, cold porridge.—*Noctes Ambrosianæ.*

Drunt, draunt, to drawl, to whine,
to grumble; a fit of ill-humour,
pettishness. Both of these words
are from the Gaelic *dranndan,*
grumbling, growling, mourning,
complaining ; *dranndanach,* peevish, morose, though erron-
ously derived by Jamieson from
the Flemish *drinten,* tumescere.

May nae doot took the *drunt,*
To be compared to Willie.
—BURNS : *Hallowe'en.*

Nae weel-tocher'd aunts to wait on their
drunts,
And wish them in hell for it a', man.
—BURNS : *The Tarbolton Lasses.*

But lest he think I am uncivil,
To plague you with this *draunting* drivel.
—BURNS.

Dub, a small pool of dirty water.
The *Goose-dubs* is the name of a
street in Glasgow. *Deuk-dub,* a
duck-pond.

O'er *dub* and dyke
She'll run the fields all through.
—*Leader Haughs and Yarrow.*

There lay a *deuk-dub* afore the door,
And there fell he, I trow.
—HERD'S *Collection : The Brisk
Young Lad.*

Dud, a rag ; **duddies,** little rags.

Then he took out his little knife,
Let a' his *duddies* fa',
An' he was the brawest gentleman
That stood amang them a'.
—*We'll Gang nae Mair a Rovin'.*

A smytrie o' wee *duddie* weans.
—BURNS.

The *duddie* wee laddie may grow a braw
man.—DAVID HUTCHESON.

Dunnie-wassal, a Highland gentleman.

There are wild *dunnie-wassals* three
thousand times three
Will cry *oich* for the bonnets o' Bonnie
Dundee.—SIR WALTER SCOTT.

This word, generally mis-
printed in the Lowlands, and
by Sir Walter Scott in his excellent ballad of " Bonnie Dundee," is from the Gaelic *duine,* a
man, and *uasal,* gentle, noble, of
good birth.

Dunsh, to sit down hastily and
heavily.

His dowp *dunshin'* down.—*Noctes Ambrosianæ.*

Dunt, a blow, a knock ; from *dint,*
to deal a heavy blow that leaves
a mark on a hard substance.

I am naebody's lord,
I am slave to naebody;
I hae a gude broad sword,
I'll tak' *dunts* frae naebody.
—BURNS: *Naebody.*

Dush or dish, to push with the head or horns like animals, to butt, to ram; also to give a hard blow, to destroy or discomfit.

Ye needna doubt I held my whisht,
The infant aith, half-formed, was crusht;
I glower'd as eerie's I'd been *dusht*
In some wild glen;
Then sweet, like modest worth, she blusht,
And steppit ben.
—BURNS: *The Vision.*

The English slang *dish*, to defeat or conquer, seems to be of similar origin; as when the late Lord Derby made use of the expression "*Dish* the Whigs," he meant to discomfit, circumvent them, or defeat them as a party. The root seems to be the Gaelic *dith* (*di*), to press, to squeeze, and *disne*, a die or press.

Duxy, ugly, mischievous; from the Gaelic *duaich* and *duaich-nidh*, ugly.

You *duxy* lubber, brace your lyre;
Still higher yet! you fiend, play higher.
. . . . . .
Sic themes were never made to suit
Your dozen o' lugs, ye *duxy* brute.
—GEORGE BEATTIE: *John o' Arnha'.*

Dwam, a swoon, a fainting fit.

Fast congealin' into a sort of *dwam* and stupefaction.—*Noctes Ambrosianæ.*

Dyke-louper, an immoral unmarried woman, or mother of an illegitimate child. The *dyke* in this phrase means the marriage tie, obligation, or sacramental wall that prohibits the illicit intercourse of the sexes; and *louper*, one who treats the wall and its impediment as nonexistent, or who despises it by *louping*, jumping, or leaping over it.

Dyvor, a bankrupt; from the Gaelic *dith* (*di*), to destroy, to break; and *fear*, a man—a broken man or bankrupt. Jamieson derives the word from the French *devoir*, duty, or to serve.

Smash them, crash them a' to spails,
And rot the *dyvors* in the jails.
—BURNS: *Address of Beelzebub.*

E

Eastie-wastie, a person who does not know his own mind, who veers round in his purpose from one side to the other, *i.e.*, from *east* to *west*.

Eee-bree, an eyebrow.

There's no a bird in a' this forest
Will do as muckle for me

As dip its wing in the warm water
An' straik it on my *ee-bree*.
—*Johnnie o' Braidislee (when dying alone in the forest).*

Eerie, gloomy, wearisome, full of fear.

In mirkiest glen at midnight hour
I'd rove and ne'er be *eerie*, O!
If thro' that glen I gaed to thee,
My ain kind dearie, O.—BURNS.

It was an *eerie* walk through the still chestnut woods at that still hour of the night.—*The Dream Numbers, by* T. A. TROLLOPE.

Aft yont the dyke she's heard you bummin'
Wi' *eerie* drone.
    —BURNS: *Address to the Deil.*

Eerie is a most difficult word to explain. I don't know any English word that comes near it in meaning. The feeling induced by eerieness is that sort of superstitious fear that creeps over one in darkness,—that sort of awe we feel in the presence of the unseen and unknown. Anything unusual or incongruous might produce the feeling. "The cry of howlets mak's me *eerie*," says Tannahill. The following anecdote illustrates the feeling when a thing unusual or incongruous is presented : —An Ayrshire farmer, who had visited Ireland, among other *uncos* he had seen, related that he went to the Episcopal church there, and this being the first time he had ever heard the English service, he was startled by seeing a falla' come in with a long white sark on, down to his heels. "Lord, sir, the sicht o' him made me feel quite *eerie*."—R. DRENNAN.

Eith, easy; etymology uncertain, but neither Gaelic, Flemish, nor German.

It's *eith* defending a castle that's no besieged.
It's *eith* learning the cat the way to the kirn.
Eith learned, soon forgotten.
It's *eith* working when the will's at hame.
    —ALLAN RAMSAY'S *Scots Proverbs.*

Eke, to add to, an addition; "*eik* to a testament," a codicil to a will. This English word has acquired a convivial meaning in Scotland among toddy-drinkers. When a guest is about to depart, after having had a fair allowance of whisky, the host presses him to "tak an eke"—*i.e.,* another glass, to eke out the quantity. "I hate intemperance," said a northern magistrate, who was reproached by an ultra-temperance advocate for the iniquity of his trade as a distiller, "but I like to see a cannie, respectable, honest man tak' his sax tumblers and an *eke* in the bosom o' his family. But I canna thole intemperance!"

Eldritch, fearful, terrible. Jamieson has this word *elrische,* and thinks it is related to *elves* or evil spirits, and that it is derived from two Anglo-Saxon words signifying *elf* and *rich,* or rich in elves or fairies! The true derivation is from the Gaelic *oillt,* terror, dread, horror, which, combined with *droch,* bad, wicked, formed the word as Burns and other Scottish writers use it.

On the *eldritch* hill there grows a thorn.
    —PERCY'S *Reliques: Sir Carline.*

The witches follow
Wi' mony an *eldritch* screech and hollow.
    —BURNS: *Tam o' Shanter.*

I've heard my reverend grannie say,
In lonely glens ye like to stray,
Or where auld ruined castles gray
    Nod to the moon,
To fright the nightly wanderer's way
    Wi' *eldritch* croon.
    —BURNS: *Address to the Deil.*

Eme, an uncle; from the Teutonic *oheim.*

The pummel o' a guid auld saddle,
And Rob my *eme* bocht me a sack,
Twa lovely lips to lick a ladle,
Gin Jenny and I agree, quo' Jock.
    —*The Wooin' o' Jenny and Jock.*

Ettle, to try, to attempt, to endeavour.

For Nannie, far before the rest,
Hard upon noble Maggie prest,
And flew at Tam wi' furious *ettle*,
But little wist she Maggie's metal.
—BURNS: *Tam o' Shanter.*

I *ettled* wi' kindness to soften her pride.
—JAMES BALLANTINE: *The Way to Woo.*

They that *ettle* to get to the top of the ladder will at least get up some rounds.—They that *mint* at a gown of gold will always get a sleeve of it.—SCOTT: *The Monastery.*

Ettle.—The correct synonyms are to intend, to expect, to aim at. Intention is the essential element in the meaning of this word.—R. DRENNAN.

Everly, continually, always, for ever.

To be set doun to a wheelie (spinning wheel),
An' at it for ever to ca',
An' syne to hae't reel by a chielie (fellow)
That *everly* cryed to draw.
—*Woo'd an' Married an' a.*

Ewe-bucht, a sheepfold; **buchtin'**, or **buchtin'-time**, the evening time or gloaming, when the cattle are driven into the fold.

When o'er the hill the eastern star
Tells *bughtin'-time* is near, my jo,
And owsen frae the furrow'd field,
Return sae dowf and wearie, O.
—BURNS: *My Ain Kind Dearie, O.*

Oh, the broom, the bonnie, bonnie broom,
The broom o' the Cowden knowes!
And aye sae sweet as the lassie sang,
In the *ewe-bucht*, milking her ewes.
—*The Broom o' the Cowden Knowes.*

The word *bught* seems to be an abbreviation of the Gaelic *buaigheal*, a cow-stall, and *buaichaille*, a cowherd, a shepherd; *buaile*, a fold; *buailte*, folded, or driven into the fold. Jamieson goes to Germany for the root of the word and does not find it.

Eydent, diligent, earnest, zealous; from the Gaelic *eud*, zeal.

My fair child,
Persuade the kirkmen *eydently* to pray.
—HENRYSONE: *The Lion and the Mouse: The Evergreen.*

Their master's and their mistress's command
The youngsters a' were warned to obey,
An' mind their labours wi' an *eydent* hand.
—BURNS: *Cotter's Saturday Night.*

Eyrie, an eagle's nest; from the Gaelic *eirich*, to rise, and *eirigh*, a rising.

The eagle and the stork
On cliffs and cedar tops their *eyries* build.
—MILTON.

'Tis the fire shower of ruin all dreadfully driven
From his *eyrie* that beacons the darkness of heaven.
—CAMPBELL: *Lochiel's Warning.*

Eytyn, Etyn, Etaine, Aiten, Red-Aiten. This word, with its different but not unsimilar spellings, appears to be a corruption of the Norse *Jotun*, a giant. It was formerly used in England as well as in Scotland. *Hynde Etyn*, or the gentle giant, is the title of a Scottish ballad in Kinloch's Collection.

They say the King of Portugal cannot sit at his meat, but the giants and *etyns* will come and snatch it from him.—BEAUMONT AND FLETCHER: *Burning Pestle.*

F

Fa', the Scottish abbrevation of *fall*. The word is used by Burns in the immortal song of "A man's a man for a' that," in a sense which has given rise to much doubt as to its meaning :—

> A king can mak' a belted knight,
> A marquis, duke, and a' that ;
> But an honest man's aboon his might,
> Gude faith, he mauna *fa'* that.

The context would seem to imply that *fa'* means to try, to attempt. No author except Burns uses the word in this sense ; and none of the varieties of words in which *fall* or the act of *falling*, either physically or metaphorically, is the primary meaning, meets the necessities of Burns's stanza. Halliwell has *fay* as an archaic English word, with five different meanings, of which the fourth is to succeed, to act, to work. The *fa'* of Burns may possibly be a variety of the English word, current in Ayrshire in his time. It finds no place in Jamieson.

Burns did not originate the idea, so well expressed, and to which he has given such wide currency. It is to be found in an anecdote recorded of King James VI. and his faithful old nurse, who came uninvited from Edinburgh to pay him a visit. It is told that the King was delighted to see her, and asked her kindly what he could do for her. After some hesitation, she replied that she desired nothing for herself, only that she wanted his Majesty to make her son a gentleman. "Ah, Jeanie, Jeanie!" said the King, "I can mak' him a duke, if ye like ; but I canna mak' him a gentleman unless he mak's himsel' ane ! "

Faird, a journey, a course. Jamieson thinks it signifies a hasty and noted effort, and quotes a Mid-Lothian phrase, "Let them alane ; it's but a *faird*, it'll no last lang; they'll no win (arrive) far afore us." The word is evidently from the same source as *fare*, to travel, as in way-*farer ;* the Teutonic *fahren*, to go, to travel ; and *fähre*, a ferry, a passage over the water, and *gefährlich*, dangerous ; as originally applied to travelling in primitive and unsettled times.

Fairdy, clever, tight, handy ; fair to do.

> With ane ev'n keel before the wind,
> She is right *fairdy* with a sail.
> *The Fleming Bark—belonging to Edinburgh.*
> —ALLAN RAMSAY: *The Evergreen.*

Fairin' signifies either reward or punishment; one's deserts. *Fair fa'!* may good or fair things befall you! is equivalent to a benison or benediction.

Jamieson derives the word from *fair* or market, and thinks it means a present bought at a fair. But this is guess-work, and does not meet the sense of the passage in "Tam o' Shanter." Possibly it has some connection with the Teutonic *gefahr*, danger, also a doom or punishment; supposed, in its favourable term, to be derived from a present purchased at a fair to be bestowed as a gift on one who was not at it.

Fair fa' your honest, sonsie face,
Great chieftain o' the puddin' race.

    —BURNS: *To a Haggis.*

Ah, Tam! ah, Tam! thou'lt get thy *fairin'*;
In hell they'll roast thee like a herrin'.

    —BURNS: *Tam o' Shanter.*

Fank, a coil, a tangle, a noose; possibly from *fang*, to take hold of. To *fank* a horse in a field, to catch him with a rope noose or lasso; *fankit*, entangled; *a fank o' tows*, a coil of ropes. It may also be the root of the English *funk*, *i.e.*, to be in a coil of perplexity or dread. The common derivation of *funk*, from the German *funk*, a sparkle of light, is not tenable. The Gaelic *fainnich* signifies to curl, from *fainne*, a ring.

Farle, a small oaten or wheaten cake, the fourth part of a bannock; from *farthel*, or fourth part; the Flemish *viertel* and German *fiertel*.

An' there'll be gude lapper-milk kebbucks,
An' sowens, an' *farles*, an' baps.

    —*The Blithesome Bridal.*

Fash, to bother, to worry, to distress one's self; from the French *se fâcher*, to be angry.

Fashious, troublesome.

Speak out, and never *fash* your thumb. |
    —BURNS: *Earnest Cry and Prayer.*

The Rev. John Brown of Whitburn was riding out one day on an old pony, when he was accosted by a rude youth. "I say, Mr. Brown, what gars your horse's tail wag that way?" "Oh!" replied Brown, "just what gars your tongue wag; it's *fashed* wi' a weakness."—DEAN RAMSAY.

Fazard, dastard, coward.

They are mair fashious nor of feck;
Yon *fasards* durst not, for their neck,
  Climb up the crag with us.
    —MONTGOMERY: *The Cherry and the Slae.*

The root of this word would appear to be the Gaelic *fas*, vacant, hollow, good-for-nothing, with the addition of *ard*, as in dast*ard*, cow*ard*, wiz*ard*, a suffix which signifies eminent, or in a high degree. Thus, *fazard* or *fasard* means worthless in the extreme.

Feck, power, activity, vigour. *Feck* seems to be derivable from the Gaelic *fiach*, worth, value. *Feckful*, full of power. *Feckless*, without power or vigour of body or mind. Worcester, in his dictionary, derives this word from *effectless*.

Many a *feckful* chield this day was slain.
    —BLIND HARRY'S *Wallace.*

The lazy luxury which *feckless* loons indulge in.—SCOTT.

> *Feckless* folk are aye fain o' ane anither.
> —ALLAN RAMSAY's *Scots Proverbs.*

> Poor devil! see him o'er his trash,
> As *feckless* as a withered rash.
> —BURNS: *To a Haggis.*

That *feckless* fouter!—*Noctes Ambrosianæ.*

Fell, to kill.

The sister of a lady, who had died of a surfeit from eating too bountifully of strawberries and cream, was consoled with by a friend, who said to her, "I had hoped your sister would have lived many years." "Leeve!" she replied, "how could she leeve, when she just *felled* hersel' at Craigo wi' strawberries an' cream?"—DEAN RAMSAY.

Fend, to ward off — probably a contraction from defend. Fend also means to prosper or do well, to provide, to live comfortably — possibly from the idea of warding off want or poverty.

Can she mak' nae better *fend* for them than that?—SCOTT: *The Monastery.*

> But gie them guid coo-milk their fill,
> Till they be fit to *fend* themsel'.
> —BURNS: *Dying Words of Poor Mailie.*

> Here stands a shed to *fend* the showers,
> And screen our countra gentry.
> —BURNS: *The Holy Fair.*

How is he *fendin'*, John Tod, John Tod?
He is scouring the land wi' a song in his hand.
—CHAMBERS's *Scots Songs: John Tod.*

Fendy, clever at contrivances in difficulty, good at making a shift.

"Alice," he said, "was both canny and *fendy*."—SCOTT: *Waverley.*

Ferlie, a wonder, to wonder, wonderful.

Who harkened ever slike a *ferlie* thing.
—CHAUCER: *The Reeve's Tale.*

> On Malvern hills
> Me befel a *ferly.*
> —*Piers Ploughman.*

Never breathe out of kin and make your friends *ferly* at you.
The longer we live the more *ferlies* we see.
—ALLAN RAMSAY's *Scots Proverbs.*

> And tell what new taxation's comin',
> And *ferlie* at the folk in Lunnon.
> —BURNS: *The Twa Dogs.*

Ferlie and wonner. In this phrase *wonner* is a corruption of the English *wonder*; a contemptuous and ludicrous term to designate a person or thing that is strangely, wondrously ugly, ill-favoured, or mean; almost synonymous with the modern English slang a *guy* or a *cure*. Burns uses both words in the same poem:—

> Ha! where ye gaun, ye crawlin' *ferlie* !
> . . . .
> Ye ugly, creepin', blastit *wonner*,
> Detested, shunned by saint and sinner?
> —*To a Certain Insect, on seeing one
> on a Lady's Bonnet at Church.*

Ferrikie. Jamieson cites this as an Upper Clydesdale word for "strong, robust." He derives it from the German *ferig*, which he translates *expeditus, alacer*; but there is no such word as *ferig* in the German language. It is more probably from the Gaelic *fear*, a man, *fearachas*, manhood, and *fearail*, manly, virile, strong, lusty. The Welsh has *ffer*, solid, strong.

Feu, to let land for building; a possession held on payment of a certain rent to the feudal proprietor, heritor, or owner of the soil. Where the English

advertise "land to let for building purposes," the Scotch more tersely say "land to *feu.*"

There is, or was lately, a space of unoccupied ground on the "Corran" at Oban, contiguous to Dunolly Castle, in the midst of which on a pole was a board inscribed "This land to *feu.*" An English bishop on his holiday tour having observed the announcement, and wondering what it meant, turned to his wife and asked her if she knew. She did not, and the bishop thereupon hazarded the conjecture that it meant to "fire," from the French *feu.* "Very likely," replied the lady, "to burn the grass." Before the bishop left Oban his ignorance on the subject was dispelled by a guest at the *table-d'hôte* of the hotel to whom he applied for information. "Curious language, the Scotch!" was his lordship's rejoinder.—C. M.

Fey, fated, bewitched, unlucky, doomed ; one whose fate is foreknown or prophesied ; from the Gaelic *faidh,* a prophet, the Latin *vates.*

Let the fate fall upon the *feyest.*
Take care of the man that God has marked, for he's no *fey.*
    —ALLAN RAMSAY'S *Scots Proverbs.*

We'll turn again, said good Lord John,
But no, said Rothiemay,
My steed's trepanned, my bridle's broke,
    I fear this day I'm *fey.*
    —*Minstrelsy of the Scottish Border.*

They hacked and hashed, while broadswords clashed,
And through they dashed, and hewed, and smashed,
Till *fey* men died awa, man.
    —*The Battle of Sheriffmuir.*

Fidgin'-fain, extremely anxious ; from *fidge,* the English *fidget,* to be restless or anxious, and *fain,* willing or desirous.

It pat me *fidgin'-fain* to hear it.
    —BURNS : *Epistle to Lapraik.*

Fiel. The glossaries to Burns explain this word to mean " smooth and comfortable," apparently from the context :—

Oh, leeze me on my spinnin'-wheel,
And leeze me on my rock and reel,
Frae tap to tae that cleeds me bien,
And haps me *fiel* and warm at e'en !
    —*Bess and her Spinning-Wheel.*

Jamieson, who has *feil* and *fiel,* defines the words to mean " soft and smooth like velvet, silky to the touch, and also clean, neat, comfortable." The word must not be confounded with *feil, feill, fele,* which signify much, many, and very, and are clearly derivable from the Teutonic *viel,* which has the same meaning ; as *viel gelt,* much money. Jamieson derives the word used by Burns from the Icelandic *felldr, habitis idorem* ; but this is exceedingly doubtful. The Gaelic has *fial,* generous, liberal, bountiful, good, hospitable ; and possibly it is in this sense that Bess applies the word to the spinnin'-wheel that provides her with raiment.

Fient, none, not a particle of ; equivalent to " the devil a bit," from *fiend,* the devil ; *fient-hait,* not an iota, the devil a bit.

But though he was o' high degree,
The *fient* o' pride—nae pride had he.
    —BURNS : *The Twa Dogs.*

The queerest shape that e'er I saw,
For *fient* a wame it had ava !
    —BURNS : *Death and Dr. Hornbook.*

Fient-haet o't wad hae pierced the heart
O' a kail runt.—BURNS : *Idem.*

Fiere, a friend, a comrade. This word is supposed by some to be a misprint for *frere,* a brother.

> And here's a hand, my trusty *fiere,*
> And gie's a hand o' thine.
> —BURNS : *Auld Langsyne.*

This word may either be a synonym for the Latin *vir* and the Gaelic *fear,* a man, or may be derived from *fior,* true, or a true man. The Scottish poet Douglas has *fior* for sound and healthy. It is sometimes spelt *feer.*

First-foot, the first person who is met by lad or lass in the morning.

> Early morning she drest up
> And all her maides fair,
> The ploughman chiel was her *first-foot*
> As she went to take the air.
> —BUCHAN'S *Ancient Ballads.*

Flaff, a momentary display.

> Ga' I ever for a *flaff* in the Park forget
> my ain cosie bield.—*Noctes Ambrosianœ.*

Flamfoo. According to Jamieson this word signifies a gaudily-dressed woman, or any gaudy ornament of female dress. He derives it from an alleged old English word meaning " moonshine in the water ! " It seems, however, to come from the Gaelic *flann,* corrupted into *flam,* red, the showy colour so much admired by people of uneducated taste ; conjoined with the Scottish *fu'* for full. The English word *flaunting,* and the phrase *flaunts,* fiery red ribbons, are from the same root.

Flannen, the Scottish as well as the English vernacular *flannen* for *flannel,* seems to be preferable to *flannel* as the correct pronunciation of the word. Both are correct if the etymology be correct, which traces the word to the Gaelic *flann,* red, and *olann,* wool. In the early ages of civilisation, when wool was first woven for garments to clothe mankind, the favourite colours were red and yellow. In Hakluyt's Voyages it is said—" By chance they met a canoe of Dominicans, to the people whereof he gave a waistcoat of *yellow* flannel." Probably red was the first dye used, whence *flann-olann,* red wool. At an after time, when gaudy colours were not so much in request, the wool was bleached, whence *blanket* or *blanquette,* whitened.

> I wadna be surprised to spy
> You on an auld wife's *flannen* toy (cap),
> Or aiblins some bit duddie boy,
>   On's wylie-coat ;
> But Miss's fine Lunardi, fy !
>   How daur ye do't ?
> —BURNS : *To a Louse, on seeing one*
>   *on a Lady's Bonnet at Church.*

Flaucht or **flaught,** a flash of lightning, a sudden blaze in the sky ; from the Flemish *flakkeren* and *flikkerin,* to flicker, to shine out quickly or instantaneously.

> The thunder crack'd, and *flauchts* did rift
> Frae the black vizard o' the lift.
> —ALLAN RAMSAY : *The Vision.*
> Fierce as ony *fire-flaught* fell.
> —*Christ's Kirk on the Green.*

Flaw, a burst of bad weather, from the Gaelic *fliuch,* a rainstorm.

> Like an auld scart (cormorant) before a
> *flaw.—The Antiquary.*

Fleech or **fleich**, to pet, to wheedle, to cajole; also, to entreat or supplicate with fair words. *A fleeching day* is a day that promises to be fine, but that possibly may not turn out so. Possibly from the French *flechir*, to give way, to ask humbly, instead of demanding loudly.

Duncan *fleeched* and Duncan prayed—
Ha! ha! the wooin' o't.—BURNS.

Expect na, sir, in this narration,
A *fleechin'*, flatterin' dedication.
—BURNS: *Epistle to Gavin Hamilton.*

Hoot! toot! man—keep a calm sough.
Better to *fleech* a fool than fight wi' him.
—SCOTT: *The Monastery.*

Fleer, a gibe, a taunt—etymology doubtful. The Flemish has *fleers*, a box on the ear.

Oh, dinna ye mind o' this very *fleer*,
When we were a' riggit out to gang to Sherramuir,
Wi' stanes in our aprons?
—CHAMBERS's *Scottish Ballads: The Threatened Invasion.*

Fley, to scare, to frighten. Etymology unknown, but possibly from *flee*, to run away for fear, whence *fley*, to cause to run away for fear, to frighten.

A wee thing *fleys* cowards.—ALLAN RAMSAY's *Scots Proverbs.*

It spak' right howe, My name is Death,
But be na' *fley'd.*
—BURNS: *Death and Dr. Hornbook.*

Flichter, to flutter, to fly feebly; a great number of small objects flying in the air, as "a *flichter* of birds;" a multitude of small objects flying, floating, or fluttering in the air, as a *flichter*

or flight of birds; a *flichter* of motes in the sunbeams; a *flichter* of heavy or large snowflakes. To *flichter* is to flutter, to quiver with joyous excitement, and also to startle or alarm. The word is evidently akin to the English *flight* and the Teutonic *flucht.*

The bird maun *flichter* that has but ae wing.—ALLAN RAMSAY's *Scots Proverbs.*

The expectant wee things, toddlin', sprachle through,
To meet their dad, wi' *flichterin'* noise and glee.
—BURNS: *Cotter's Saturday Night.*

Flinders, fragments, splinters.

He put his fingers to the lock,
I wat he handled them sickerlie;
And doors of deal and bands of steel
He gart them all in *flinders flee.*
—BUCHAN's *Ancient Ballads: The Three Brothers.*

Flinging-tree, a flail, the pole of a carriage, a bar of wood in any agricultural implement.

The thresher's weary *flingin'-tree*
The lee-lang day had tirèd me,
And when the day had closed his e'e
Far i' the west,
Ben i' the spence, right pensivelie,
I gaed to rest.
—BURNS: *The Vision.*

Flit, to remove from one residence to another; a *flittin'*, a removal.

As doun the burnside she gaed slow in the *flittin'*,
Fare ye weel, Lucy, was ilka bird's sang;
She gaed by the stable where Jamie was stannin',
Richt sair was his kind heart the *flittin'* to see.
—*Lucy's Flittin'*, *by* WILLIAM LAIDLAW (*the steward, amanuensis, and trusted friend of Sir Walter Scott*).

Flite or **flyte**, to reproach, to blame, to animadvert, to find fault with.

They *flyte* me wi' Jamie because he is poor ;
But summer is comin', cauld winter's awa,
An' he'll come back an' see me in spite o' them a'
—George Halket : *Logie o' Buchan.*

Hed I gude-wife I ye're a *flytin'* body ;
Ye hae the will, but ye want the wit.
—Sir Alexander Boswell : *A Matrimonial Duel.*

Floan, to flirt. Jamieson says that "*floan* means to show attachment, or court regard in an indiscreet way," and derives the word from the Icelandic *flon*, stolidus. Is it not rather from the old English *flone*, arrows (Halliwell and Wright), whence metaphorically to dart glances from the eye, and consequently to flirt or cast amorous looks ? The Kymric Celtic has *ffloyn*, a splinter, a thin wand, an arrow.

And for yon giglet hussies i' the glen,
That night and day are *floaning* at the men.—Ross's *Helenore.*

Flunkey, a servant in livery ; metaphorically applied to a person who abjectly flatters the great. The word was unknown to literature until the time of Burns. Thackeray and Carlyle in our own day have made it classical English, although the most recent lexicographers have not admitted it or its derivative, *flunkeyism*, to the honours of the dictionary.

Our laird gets in his rackèd rents,
. . . .

He rises when he likes himsel',
His *flunkeys* answer to his bell.
—Burns : *The Twa Dogs.*

The word is supposed to be derived from the Gaelic *flann*, red, and *cas*, a leg or foot—red-legs, applied to the red or crimson plush breeches of footmen. The word red-shanks was applied to the kilted Highlanders by the English, and hence the Highland retort of flunkey to the English.

I think this derivation wrong ; *vlonk* in Danish signifies proud, haughty.—Lord Neaves.

Fodgel, sometimes written and pronounced *fodyell* plump, short, corpulent, and good-tempered. A man in Scottish parlance may be stout and plump without being *fodgel*, as *fodgel* implies good nature, urbanity, and cheerfulness, as well as plumpness.

If in your bounds ye chance to light
Upon a fine, fat *fodgel* wight,
Of stature short, but genius bright,
    That's he, mark weel.
—Burns : *On the Peregrinations of Captain Grose Collecting Antiquities throughout the Kingdom.*

Fog, moss ; from the Gaelic *bog* or *bhog*, moist, soft.

"And so, John," said the minister, " I understand ye have gone over to the Independents?" " Deed, sir," said John, " that's true." " Oh, John," rejoined the minister, " I'm sure ye ken that a rowin' stone gathers nae *fog.*" "Aye," said John, " that's true, too ; but can ye tell me what gude the *fog* does to the stone?"—Dean Ramsay.

Fogie, a dull, slow man, unable or unwilling to reconcile himself to the ideas and manners of the new generation. The derivation of this word, which Thackeray did much to popularise in England, is uncertain, though it seems most probable that it comes from "foggy," for a foggy, misty, hazy intellect, unable to see the things that are obvious to clearer minds; or it may be from the Gaelic *fogaire*, an exile, a banished man. In the United States the word is generally applied to an ultra-Conservative in politics.

> Ay, though we be
> Old *fogies* three,
> We're not so dulled as not to dine ;
> And not,so old
> As to be cold
> To wit, to beauty, and to wine.
> —*All the Year Round.*

Fog-moss, foggage, tall grass used for fodder. The etymology is uncertain. The English *fodder* is from the Gaelic *fodar ;* but this scarcely affords a clue to *fog* or *foggage.* Though possibly *foggage* may be a corruption of the old and not yet obsolete *fodderage.*

> Thy wee bit housie too in ruin !
> Its silly wa's the winds are strewin',
> An' naething left to big a new ane,
> O' *foggage* green,
> An' bleak December's winds ensuin',
> Baith snell and keen.
> —BURNS : *To a Mouse.*

Forbears, ancestors.

Forbye, besides, in addition to, over and above.

> *Forbye* sax mae I sell't awa.
> —BURNS : *Auld Farmer.*

> *Forbye* some new uncommon weapons.
> —BURNS : *Death and Dr. Hornbook.*

Foreanent, directly opposite.

Foremost. In English this word signifies first as regards place. In Scottish parlance it also signifies first as regards time.

> They made a paction 'twixt them twa,
> They made it firm and sure,
> That whoe'er should speak the *foremost* word
> Should get up an' bar the door.
> —*The Barrin'.o' oor Door.*

Forfoughten, sometimes written and pronounced *forfoughen,* worn out with struggling or fatigue.

> And though *forfoughten* sair eneugh,
> Yet unco proud to leave.—BURNS.

> I am but like a *forfoughen* hound,
> Has been fighting in a syke (ditch).
> —*Border Minstrelsy : Hobbie Noble.*

Forgather, to meet.

> Twa dogs
> *Forgathered* ance upon a time.
> —BURNS : *The Twa Dogs.*

Forjeskit, wearied out, jaded, exhausted ; derivation uncertain, but probably from the Flemish or Dutch patois.

> The fiend, *forjeskit,* tried to escape
> Thro' frequent changing o' his shape.
> —BEATTIE : *John o' Arnha'.*

Fou, drunk, is generally supposed to be a corruption of *full* (*i.e.,* of liquor) ; but if such were the fact the word ought to be contracted into *fu'*, as wae*fu'*, sorrow*fu'*, which cannot be written wae*fou* or sorrow*fou.* *Fou,* in French, signifies insane, a word that might be applied to an intoxicated person ; but if the Scottish phrase be not derived from the French, it ought to be written *fu'*, and not *fou*. Possibly the root of the word is the Gaelic *fuath* (pronounced *fuà*), which signifies hatred, abhorrence, aversion, whence it may have been applied to a person in a hateful and abhorrent state of drunkenness. This, however, is a mere suggestion. Jamieson has *fowsom*, filthy, impure, obscene.

We are na' *fou*, we're na' that *fou*,
We've just a wee drap in our e'e.
—BURNS : *Willie Brewed a Peck o' Maut.*

Fouter, an expression of extreme contempt for a hateful person. The French *foutre* has the same, and even a worse meaning. Both the Lowland Scotch and the French are from the Gaelic and Celtic *fuath*, hatred.

Fouth or **rowth**, abundance. *Fouth* is from *full*, on the same principle as the English words *tilth* from *till*, *spilth* from *spill*, *youth* from *youngeth*, *growth* from *grow*, *drouth* from *dryeth*. *Rowth* has the same signification, and is from *row* or *roll*, to flow on like a stream.

He has a *fowth* o' auld knick-nackets,
Rusty airn and jinglin' jackets.
—BURNS : *To Captain Grose.*

They that hae *rowth* o' butter may lay it thick on their scones.—ALLAN RAMSAY'S *Scots Proverbs.*

Fremit, **frammit**, strange, unrelated, unfamiliar ; from the Teutonic *fremd*, foreign.

Ye ha'e lien a' wrang, lassie,
In an unco bed,
Wi' a *fremit* man.—BURNS.

And mony a friend that kissed his caup
Is now a *frammit* wight,
But it's ne'er sae wi' Whisky Jean.
—BURNS : *The Five Carlins.*

Frist, to delay, to give credit ; from the Teutonic *fristen*, to spare, to respite.

The thing that's *fristed* is nae forgi'en.
—ALLAN RAMSAY'S *Scots Proverbs.*

Frush, brittle.

Oh, woe betide the *frush* saugh wand (willow wand),
And woe betide the bush o' briar,
It brak into my true love's hand.
—*Border Minstrelsy : Annan Water.*

Fulzie, surfeited with gluttony and over-eating ; full of meat and food.

Enough to sicken a *fulzie* man.—*Noctes Ambrosiana.*

Furth, out of doors, to go forth, to go out. The *muckle furth*, is the full, free open air. *Furthy*, forward, frank, free, affable, open in behaviour. *Furth-setter*, one who sets forth or puts forth ; a publisher, an author.

Sir Penny is of a noble spreit,
A *furthy* man, and a far seeand ;
There is no matter ends compleit
Till he set to his seil and hand.
—*A Panegyrick on Sir Penny : The Evergreen.*

Fusionless, pithless, silly, sapless, senseless ; corrupted from "foison," the old English word for plenty ; the opposite of "geason," scarce.

For seven lang years I ha'e lain by his side,
And he's but a *fusionless* bodie, O !
　—BURNS : *The Deuks Dang o'er my Daddy.*

The mouths of fasting multitudes are crammed wi' *fizzenless* bran, instead of the sweet word in season.—SCOTT : *Old Mortality.*

Fusionless.—In Bailey's Dictionary the word *foison* means "the natural juice or moisture of the grass or other herbs, the heart and strength of it :" used in Suffolk.—R. DRENNAN.

Fy ! or **fye !** This exclamation is not to be confounded with the English *fye !* or *O fye !* or the Teutonic *pfui !* which are used as mild reproofs of any act of shame or impropriety.

Fy ! let us a' to the bridal,
　For there will be lilting there ;
For Jock's to be married to Jeanie,
　The lass wi' the gowden hair.
　　　—*Old Song.*

In this old song, all the incidents and allusions are expressive of joy and hilarity. Jamieson suggests that *fy* means "make haste !" "*Fye-gae-to,*" he says, "means much ado, a great hurry ; and *fye haste,* a very great bustle, a hurry." He gives no derivation. As the Teutonic cannot supply one, it is possible that the root is the Gaelic *faich,* look ! behold ! lo ! in which sense "*Fye !* let us a' to the bridal," might be translated "Look ye ! let us all go to the bridal."

Fyke, to be ludicrously and fussily busy about trifles, to be restless without adequate reason, akin to *fidget,* which is possibly from the same root. The word is also used as a noun. *Fiddle-fyke* and *fiddle-ma-fike* are intensifications of the meaning, and imply contempt for the petty trifling of the person who *fykes.*

Some drowsy bummle,
Wha can do nought but *fyke* and fumble.
　—BURNS : *On a Scotch Bard.*

Gin he 'bout Norrie lesser *fyke* had made.
　—Ross's *Helenore.*

Weening that ane sae braw and gentle-like
For nae guid ends was makin' sic a *fyke.*
　—Ross's *Helenore.*

Fytte, the subdivision of a long poem, now called a canto. Percy, in a note in his "Ancient Reliques," considers the word to signify no more than a division, a part to "fit" on to another. As the bards of the Druids, who sung in their religious festivals, and who delivered their precepts to the people in short verses of couplets or triads—better for committal to memory than long prose homilies would have been —were called *fiadhs* or prophets, it is possible that that word, and not the English *fit,* as Dr. Percy says, was the origin of *fytte* as applied to the subdivision of a sacred song.

G

Gabbock, a hunk, a large piece or slice.

> And there'll be
> Fouth o' gude *gabbocks* o' skate.
>   —*The Blithesome Bridal.*

Gaberlunzie, a wallet or bag carried by beggars for collecting in kind the gifts of the charitable; whence *gaberlunzie-man,* a beggar.

> Oh, blithe be the auld *gaberlunzie-man,*
> Wi' his wallet o' wit he fills the lan';
> He's a warm Scotch heart an' a braid Scotch tongue,
> An' kens a' the auld sangs that ever were sung!—JAMES BALLANTINE.

> To love her for aye he gied her his aith,
> Quo' she, To leave thee I will be laith,
>   My winsome *gaberlunzie-man.*
>   —*The Gaberlunzie-Man (a ballad attributed to King James V.)*

Much research and ingenuity have been exercised to find the etymological origin of this peculiarly Scottish word. Jamieson says that *gaberlunzie* or *gaberlunyie* means a beggar's bag or wallet, and implies that the word has been transferred from the bag to the bearer of it.

Gae-through-land, a wanderer, a vagrant, a pilgrim, an exile, a gangrel.

> Oh, God forbid, said fair Annie,
>   That e'er the like fa' in my hand;
> Should I forsake my ain gude lord,
>   And follow you, a *gae-through-land.*
>   —BUCHAN'S *Ancient Scottish Ballads,* 1828.

Gair, the English *gore,* an insertion in a skirt, robe, or other article of dress; also a strip of a different colour inserted as a plait or ornament, sometimes signifying a coloured belt from which the sword or other weapon was suspended; *gaired* or *gairy,* streaked with many colours; piebald, as a *gairy* cow or horse.

> Young Johnston had a nut-brown sword
> Hung low down by his *gair,*
> And he ritted it through the young colonel,
> That word he never spak' mair.
>   —HERD'S *Collection: Young Johnston.*

Gale, to sing, whence *nightingale,* the bird that sings by night. The word is usually derived from the Teutonic, in which language, however, it only exists in the single word *nachtigall.* Jamieson refers it to the Swedish *gäll* (gale), a sharp, penetrating, or piercing sound. Probably, however, it is akin to the Gaelic *guil,* to lament, and *guileag,* that which sings or warbles; and a *gale* of wind is referable to the Kymric or Welsh *galar,* mourning, lamentation; *galw,* (galu), to call, to invoke; and *galaries,* mournful, sad, so called because of the whistling, piping sound of a storm.

> In May the gowk (cuckoo) begins to *gale,*
> In May deer draw to down and dale,
>   In May men mell with feminie,
> And ladies meet their lovers leal,
>   When Phebus is in Gemini.
>   —ALLAN RAMSAY: *The Evergreen.*

Gallie - hooin', making a loud noise, blustering, talking violently without sense or reason. *Gullie-hoolie*, a loud, blustering, talkative, and conceited fool. These two words seem to be derivable from the Gaelic *gal* or *guil*, to cry out, and *uille*, all; whence *gal-uille*, all outcry or bluster, or nothing but outcry and noise. *Gilhooly*, a well-known Irish patronymic, is possibly of the same Gaelic origin, applied to a noisy orator.

Gang, gae, gaed, gate. These words, that are scarcely retained even in colloquial English, do constant duty in the Lowland Scotch; they are all derived from the Flemish. *Gang* and *gae* are the English *go;* *gaed* is the English *went*, and *gate* is the road or way by which one goes. " *Gang* your ain *gate*," means go your own road, or have your own way. The English *gate*, signifying a doorway, a barred or defended entrance, is a relic of the older and more extended meaning of the Scotch.

> I gaed a waefu' *gate* yestreen,
> A *gate* I fear I'll dearly rue.
> —BURNS.

Gangrel, vagrant, vagabond wandering ; from *gang*, to go.

> Ae night at e'en, a merry core
> Of randie *gangrel* bodies
> At Posie Nansie's held the splore.
> —BURNS: *The Jolly Beggars.*

This word is sometimes employed to designate a young child who is first beginning to walk.

Gardies, defensive weapons ; from the Gaelic *gairdein*, an arm or armour, and the French *garde;* as in the phrase *prenez-garde*, take care, or defend yourself.

> He wields his *gardies*,
> Or at the worst his *aiken rung* (oaken staff).
> —GEORGE BEATTIE : *John o' Arnha'.*

Garraivery. This curious word signifies, according to Jamieson, " folly and revelling of a frolicsome kind." He thinks it is evidently corrupted from *gilravery* and *gilravage*, which are words of a similar meaning. *Gilravage* he defines as " to hold a merry meeting with noise and riot." He attempts no etymology. It seems, however, that *garraivery* is akin to the French *charivari*, or the loud, discordant uproar of what in England is called " marrow bones and cleavers," when a gang of rough people show their displeasure by serenading an unpopular person—such, for instance, as a very old man who has married a very young wife—by beating bones against butchers' axes and cleavers, or by rattling pokers and shovels against iron pots and pans under his windows, so as to create a painful and discordant noise. The word and the custom are both of Celtic origin, and are derived from the Gaelic *garbh*, rough, and *bairich* or *bhairich*, any obstreperous and disagreeable noise ; also the lowing, roaring, or routing of cattle. The initial *g* or *c* of the Gaelic is usually softened into

E

the English and French *ch*, as the *k* in *k*irk becomes *ch* in the English *ch*ur*ch*, and as the Latin *carus* and the Italian *caro* become *cher* in French.

Gash, sagacious, talkative. Jamieson defines the word, as a verb, "to talk much in a confident way, to talk freely and fluently;" and as an adjective, "shrewd, sagacious." It seems derivable from the Gaelic *gais* (pronounced *gash*), a torrent, an overflow; the English *gush, i.e.,* an overflow or torrent of words, and hence by extension of meaning applied to one who has much to say on every subject; eloquent, or, in an inferior sense, loquacious.

He was a *gash* and faithful tyke.
—BURNS: *The Twa Dogs.*
Here farmers *gash* in ridin' graith.
—BURNS: *The Holy Fair.*
In comes a gaucie *gash* good-wife,
And sits down by the fire.—*Idem.*

Gaucie, jolly, brisk, lively.

His *gaucie* tail in upward curl.
—BURNS: *The Twa Dogs.*
In comes a *gaucie* gash good-wife,
And sits down by the fire.
—BURNS: *The Holy Fair.*

Gaucie, big, of large dimensions; jolly, perhaps. It has almost the same meaning as *gash,* with the additional idea of size; very like the English use of the word "jolly"—a jolly lot—a jolly pudding, &c. The Scotch use *gaucie* in precisely the same way.—R. D.

Gaud, a bar, the shaft of a plough; **gaudsman,** a plough-boy. The English *goad* signifies a bar or rod, and to *goad* is to incite or drive

with a stick or prong. The word is derived from the Gaelic *gat*, a prong, a bar of wood or iron, and *gath*, a sting.

Young Jockie was the blithest lad
In a' our town or here awa';
Fu' blithe he whistled at the *gaud,*
Fu' lightly danced he in the ha'.
—BURNS: *Young Jockie.*

I've three mischievous boys,
Rum deils for rantin' and for noise—
A *gaudsman* ane, a thrasher t'other.
—BURNS: *The Inventory.*

They'll turn me in your arms, Janet,
A red-hot *gaud* o' airn.
—*Ballad of the Young Tamlane.*

Gauf or **gawf,** a loud, discordant laugh; the English slang *guffaw.* According to Jamieson, it was used by John Knox. *Gawp,* a kindred word, signifies a large mouth wide opened; whence, possibly, the origin of the Flemish *gapen,* and the English *gape,* which, according to the late John Kemble, the tragedian, ought to be pronounced with the broad *a*, as in *ah. Gauffin,* a giggling, light-headed person, seems to be a word of the same parentage. *Gawpie* is a silly person who laughs without reason.

Tehee, quo' she, and gied a *gawf.*
—ALLAN RAMSAY: *A Brash of
Wooing: The Evergreen.*

Gauner, to bark, to scold vociferously.

Gaunt, to yawn. *Gaunt-at-the-door,* an indolent, useless person, who sits at the door and yawns; an idler, one without mental resources.

This mony a day I've groaned and *gaunted*
To ken what French mischief was brewing.
—BURNS.

Auld gude-man, ye're a drunken carle,
And a' the day ye *gape* and *gaunt*.
—SIR ALEXANDER BOSWELL.

Gaupie, a silly fellow, from *gaup*, to yawn or gape; one who yawns, from weariness, indifference, or stupidity, when he is expected to pay intelligent attention to what is said of him. A word of similar import, founded upon the same idea of listless and foolish yawning, is found in the English phrase to go *mooning* about, a word that has no reference to the moon, but that is derived from the Gaelic *meunan*, a yawn; *meunanach*, yawning; and *dean-meunan*, to yawn or make a yawn.

Gawk, to romp, applied to girls who are too fond of the society of men, and who either play roughly themselves or suffer men to play roughly in their company. The word is probably a variety of *geck*, to sport or mock (*see* that word).

Gawkie, a clumsy or inexpert person, from the French *gauche*, the left hand, and *gaucherie*, clumsiness. The word is colloquial in England as well as in Scotland.

Gear, money, wealth, property, appurtenance; from the Teutonic *gehörig*, belonging to, appertaining to.

He'll poind (seize) their *gear*.
—BURNS : *The Twa Dogs*.

And gather *gear* by every wile
That's justified by honour.
—BURNS : *Epistle to a Young Friend*.

Geck, to bear one's self haughtily, to toss the head in glee or scorn, to mock; possibly from the Flemish *gek*, a vain fool.

Adieu, my liege ! may freedom *geck*
Beneath your high protection.
—BURNS : *The Dream. To George III.*

Gee. To *take the gee*, is an old colloquialism, signifying to take umbrage or offence, to give way to a sudden start of petulance and ill-humour. Jamieson derives it from the Icelandic *geig*, offence, in default of tracing it to another origin. But the derivation is doubtful.

On Tuesday, to the bridal feast,
Came fiddlers flocking free ;
But hey ! play up the rinaway bride,
For she has ta'en the *gee*.

Woman's love a wilfu' thing,
An' fancy flies fu' free ;
Then hey ! play up the rinaway bride
For she has ta'en the *gee*.
—HERD'S *Collection*.

" My wife has ta'en the *gee*," is the title of an old and once extremely popular song.

Gell, brisk, keen, sharp, active; from the Gaelic *geall*, ardour, desire, love; *geallmhor*, greatly desirous ; and *geallmhorachd*, high desire and aspiration.

Gell, intense, as applied to the weather ; a *gell* frost is a keen frost. "There's a gey *gell* in the market to-day," *i.e.*, a pretty quick sale; "in great *gell*," in great spirits and activity; "on the *gell*," a phrase applied to one who is bent on making merry.—JAMIESON.

Gerss. "This term," says Jamieson, "is well known in the councils of boroughs. When a member becomes refractory, the ruling party vote him out at the next election. This they call *gerssing* him, or turning him out to *gerss*. The phrase," he adds, "is evidently borrowed from the custom of turning out a horse to *graze* when there is no immediate use for his service." Perhaps, however, the etymology is not quite so evident as Jamieson supposed. The Gaelic *geur* or *gearr* signifies to cut, to cut off, to shear ; *gearraich* or *geurraich*, to shorten, and *geariadh*, a cutting ; *gearran*, a gelding ; *gearrta*, cut. To cut or shorten, rather than to graze or turn out to graze, appears, *pace* Jamieson, to be the real root of the word. Jamieson has the same word differently spelled as *girse*, to turn out of office ; *girse-folk*, cotters at will, liable to be ejected at short notice, to which the Gaelic etymology of *geurr* and its derivatives applies with more force than that which he suggests from *grass*.

Gey, a humorous synonym for *very*. This word in Jamieson's Dictionary is rendered "tolerable, considerable, worthy of notice." "A *gey* wheen," he says, means "a great number." It is doubtful whether the derivation be from the English *gay* or the Gaelic *gu*. In vulgar English, when "jolly" is sometimes used for "gay," "a jolly lot" would be equivalent to the Scottish "a *gey* wheen." In Gaelic *gu* is an adverbial prefix, as in *gu leoir*, plentiful or plentifully, whence the phrase, "whisky *galore*," plenty of whisky ; *gu fior*, with truth or truly.

A miller laughing at him (the fool of the parish) for his witlessness, the fool said, "There are some things I ken and some things I dinna ken." On being asked what he knew, he said, "I ken a miller has aye a *gey* fat sow !" "And what do ye no ken ?" said the miller. "I dinna ken at wha's expense she's fed."—DEAN RAMSAY's *Reminiscences*.

The word is sometimes followed by *an'*, as in the phrase "*gey an* toom," very empty ; "*gey an* fou," very drunk. The word *gaylies*, meaning tolerably well in health, is probably from the same source as *gey*, as in the common salutation in Glasgow and Edinburgh, "How's a' wi' ye the day ?" "Oh, gailies, gailies !" The editor of *Noctes Ambrosianæ*, Edinburgh, 1866, erroneously explains *gey an* to mean *rather*.

Your factors, grieves, trustees, and bailies, I canna say but they do *gailies*.
        —BURNS : *Address of Beelzebub*.

Mr. Clark, of Dalreach, whose head was vastly disproportioned to his body, met Mr. Dunlop one day. "Weel, Mr. Clark, that's a great head of yours." "Indeed, it is, Mr. Dunlop ; it could contain yours inside of it." "Just sae," replied Mr. Dunlop, "I was e'en thinking it was *gey an* toom (very empty)."—DEAN RAMSAY.

Gielanger, one who is slow to pay his debts ; etymology unknown. It has been thought that this word is an abbreviation of the request to *give longer* or *gie langer* time to pay a debt, but this is doubtful. The Flemish and Dutch *gijzelen* signifies to arrest for debt, *gijzeling*, arrest for debt, and *gizzel kammer*, a debtor's prison; and this is most probably the origin of *gielanger*.

The greedy man and the *gielanger* are well met.—ALLAN RAMSAY's *Scots Proverbs.*

Gillravage, to plunder, also to live riotously, uproariously, and violently; from the Gaelic *gille*, a young man, and *rabair*, litigious, troublesome; *rabach*, quarrelsome.

Ye had better stick to your auld trade o' blackmail and *gillravaging*. Better steal nowte than nations.—SCOTT: *Rob Roy.*

Gilpie or **gilpey,** a saucy young girl.

I was a *gilpey* then, I'm sure
I wasna past fifteen.
    —BURNS: *Hallowe'en.*

I mind when I was a *gilpie* o' a lassock, seeing the Duke—him that lost his head in London.—SCOTT: *Old Mortality.*

Gin (*g* hard, as in *give*) signifies *if*.

Oh, *gin* my love were yon red rose
That grows upon the castle wa;
And I myself a drap o' dew,
Into her bonnie breast to fa'.
    —HERD's *Collection,* 1776.

Gin a body meet a body
Comin' through the rye.
—*Old Song (rearranged by* BURNS).

Horne Tooke, in his letter to Dunning, Lord Ashburton, on the English particles, conjunctions, and prepositions, derives

if from *given;* "*if* you are there," *i.e., given* the fact that you are there. The more poetical Scottish word *gin* is strongly corroborative of Horne Tooke's inference.

Girdle, a gridiron or brander, a circular iron plate used for roasting oat-cakes over the fire.

Wi' quaffing and daffing,
    They ranted and they sang,
Wi' jumping and thumping
    The very *girdle* rang.
    —BURNS: *The Jolly Beggars.*

The carline brocht her kebbuck ben,
Wi' *girdle-cakes* weel toasted broon.
    —*Tea-Table Miscellany: Andro and his Cutty Gun.*

On reading the passage in the Bible to a child where the words occur, " He took Paul's *girdle*," the child said with much confidence, "I ken what he took that for." On being asked to explain, she replied at once, "To bake his bannocks on!"—DEAN RAMSAY.

Girnagain, from *girn* or *grin;* a derisive epithet applied to a person who was always on the *grin,* with or without reason.

An' there'll be *girnagain* Gibbie
An' his *glaikit* wife, Jeannie Bell.
    —*The Blithesome Bridal.*

Girnel, a meal-chest; from *corn, kern,* and *kernel.*

Amaist as roomy as a minister's *girnel.*
—*Noctes Ambrosianæ.*

Glack, a ravine, a cleft in the ground.

Deep i' the *glack* and round the well,
Their mystic rites I canna tell.
    —*John o' Arnha'.*

Glaik, glaikit, giddy-headed, thoughtless, dazed, silly, foolish, giddy, volatile. From the Gaelic *gleog*, a silly look ; *gleogach*, silly, stupid ; *gleogair*, a stupid fellow ; *gleosgach*, a vain, silly woman.

That frequent pass douce Wisdom's door
For *glaikit* Folly's portals.
—BURNS : *Address to the Unco Guid.*
Wi' his *glaikit* wife, Jeannie Bell.
—*The Blithesome Bridal.*

Glamour, enchantment, witchcraft, fascination ; once supposed to be from the Gaelic *glac*, to seize, to lay hold of, to fascinate ; and *mor*, great ; whence great fascination, or magic not to be resisted. Lord Neaves thought the word was a corruption of *grammar*, in which magic was once supposed to reside. This word, once peculiar to the Scotch, has within the present century been adopted by English writers both of prose and verse, and has become familiar in the conversation of educated people. It signifies the kind of halo, fascination, and magical charm that a person or thing receives from the imagination ; the high and fanciful reputation which the French language expresses by *prestige*, a word which has also striven to naturalise itself in English. Its etymology has scarcely·been attempted by English philologists, some few of whom, however, have discovered, as they think, a kindred origin for it in *clamor*, from the Latin *clamare*, to cry out, or make a great noise. It is possible that this idea lies in reality at the root of the poetical word

glamour, in its signification of a glorified repute ; repute itself being the outward manifestation of the popular belief in the excellence of the person or thing spoken of, and which would not be known unless for the spoken opinion or voice of the multitude, which gives and extends fame and glory. In the Gaelic and British languages, *fuaim* signifies noise, sound, recalling the classical embodying of Fame as an angel blowing a trumpet, making a loud sound ; and *gloir* signifies praise loudly expressed, and therefore *glory*. In like manner, *glamour* may resolve itself into the two Gaelic words, *glaodh*, pronounced *ylao*, a shout, and *mor*, great, whence *glao-mor* or *glamour*, a great or loud cry or shout, attesting the applause and approbation of those who raise it. Stormonth, the latest etymologist who has attempted to explain the word, adopts the etymology that found favour with Jamieson, and derives it from *glimmer* or *glitter*, " a false lustre, a charm on the eyes, making them see things different from what they are." This etymology is plausible, and will possibly be accepted by all to whom the Gaelic derivation has not been offered for consideration ; but the Gaelic, supported as it is by the primitive but highly philosophic ideas that gave rise to the simple but now grandiose words of " fame " and " glory," merits

the attention and study of all
students who love to trace
words to their origin, and endeavour by their means to sound
the depths of human intelli-
gence in the infancy of society
and of language.

And one short spell therein he read,
It had much of *glamour* might,
Could make a lady seem a knight,
The cobweb on a dungeon wall
Seem tapestry in a lordly hall.
—SCOTT: *The Lay of the Last
Minstrel.*

As soon as they saw her weel-faur'd face,
They cast their *glamour* o'er her.
—*Johnnie Faa, the Gipsie Laddie.*

Ye gipsy gang that deal in *glamour*,
And you, deep read in Hell's black gram-
mar,
Warlocks and witches.
—BURNS: *On Captain Grose.*

This Scottish word has been
admitted into some recent English dictionaries. Mr. Wedgwood seems to think it is akin
to *glimmer.* The fascination of
the eye is exemplified in Coleridge's *Ancient Mariner :—*

He holds him with his glittering eye,
The wedding-guest stood still,
And listens like a three-year child—
The mariner hath his will.

Glamp, to clutch at, to seize
greedily or violently; from the
Gaelic *glaim,* to seize voraciously.

Some glower'd wi' open jaws,
Syne *glampit* on the vacant air.
GEORGE BEATTIE: *John o' Arnha'.*

Glampin round, he kent nae whither.
—*Ibid.*

Glaum, to grasp at, to clutch, to
endeavour to seize, without
strength to hold; from the

Gaelic *glam,* to devour greedily;
glamair, a glutton.

Clans frae wuds in tartan duds,
Wha *glaumed* at kingdoms three, man.
—BURNS: *The Battle of Sheriffmuir.*

Gled or glaid, a kite, a hawk, a
vulture; etymology uncertain.

And aye as ye gang furth and in,
Keep well the gaislings frae the *gled.*

He ca'd the gaislings forth to feed,
There was but sevensone o' them a',
And by them cam' the greedy *gled,*
And lickit up five—left him but twa.
—*The Wife of Auchtermuchty.*

The name of Gladstone is
derived from *gled-stane,* the
hawk or vulture stone, and
synonymous with the German
Geir-stein, the title of one of
the novels of Sir Walter Scott.

Gleed or gleid, a burning coal,
a temporary blaze, a sparkle, a
splinter that starts from the fire.

And cheerily blinks the ingle *gleed*
Of honest Lucky.—BURNS.

Mend up the fire to me, brother,
Mend up the *gleed* to me ;
For I see him coming hard and fast
Will mend it up for thee.
—*Ballad of Lady Maisry.*

Gleg, sharp, acute, quick-witted;
gleg-tongued, voluble ; *gleg-
lugg'd,* sharp of hearing; *gleg-
ee'd,* sharp-sighted.

Sae for my part I'm willing to submit
To what your *glegger* wisdom shall think
fit.—Ross's *Helenore.*

Unskaithed by Death's *gleg* gullie.
—BURNS: *Tam Samson's Livin'.*

He'll shape you aff fu' *gleg*
The cut of Adam's philibeg.
—BURNS: *Captain Grose.*

Jamieson derives *gleg* from the Icelandic and Swedish, unaware of the Gaelic etymology from *glac*, to seize, to snatch, to lay hold of quickly.

Glent, glint, a moment, a glance, a twinkling; also to glance, to shine forth, to peep out. From the same root as the English *glance*, the Teutonic *glänzen*, and Flemish *glinster*.

And in a *glent*, my child, ye'll find it sae.
   —Ross's *Helenore*.
Yet cheerfully thou *glinted* forth
Amid the storm.
   —Burns: *To a Mountain Daisy.*
The risin' sun owre Galston muir
Wi' glowing light was *glintin'*.
   —Burns: *Hallowe'en.*

Gley, to squint; *aglee* or *agley*, crooked, aslant, in the wrong direction; probably from the Gaelic *gli*, the left hand, awkward.

There's a time to *gley* and a time to look even.—Allan Ramsay's *Scots Proverbs.*
Gleyed Sandy he came here yestreen,
And speired when I saw Pate.
   —James Carnegie, 1765.
The best-laid schemes of mice and men
Gang aft *aglee.*
   —Burns: *To a Mouse.*

Glib-gabbet, having "the gift of the gab," speaking glibly with voluble ease; apparently derived from the Gaelic *glib* or *gliob*, slippery, and *gab*, a mouth.

And that *glib-gabbet* Highland baron,
The Laird o' Graham.
   —Burns: *Cry and Prayer.*

Gliff, a moment, a short slumber, a nap.

I'll win out a *gliff* the night for a' that,
to dance in the moonlight.—Scott: *The Heart of Midlothian.*
" Laid down on her bed for a *gliff*,"
said her grandmother.—Scott: *The Antiquary.*

Gloaming, the twilight; from the English *gloom* or darkness. This word has been adopted by the best English writers.

When ance life's day draws near its
gloaming.
   —Burns: *To James Smith.*
'Twixt the *gloaming* and the mirk,
When the kye come hame.
   —Hogg, *the Ettrick Shepherd.*

Glower, to look stupidly or intently, to glare, to stare.

Ye *glowered* at the moon and fell in the midden.—Allan Ramsay's *Scots Proverbs.*
I am a bard of no regard,
Wi' gentle folks and a' that;
But Homer-like, the *glowrin'* byke (swarm)
Frae town to town I draw that.
   —Burns: *The Jolly Beggars.*
He only *glowered* at her, taking no notice whatever of her hints.—A. Trollope: *Vicar of Bullhampton.*

Glunch, an angry frown, a sulky or forbidding expression of countenance. "To glunch and gloom," to look angry, discontented, sulky, and gloomy. *Glunschoch*, one who has a frowning or morose countenance; from the Gaelic *glonn*, a qualm, a feeling of nausea; *glonnach*, one who has a disagreeable or stupid expression on his face:—

A *glunch*
O' sour disdain.
   —Burns: *Scotch Drink.*
Does ony great man *glunch* and gloom?
   —Burns: *Cry and Prayer.*

Glunch and gloom.—*Glunch*, giving audible expression to discontent in a series of interjectional *humphs*; *gloom*, a frowning, silent expression of displeasure.— R. DRENNAN.

Gomeril, a fool, a loud-talking fool; from the Gaelic *geum*, to bellow. The English and Cockney slang " Give us none of your *gum*," *i.e.*, of your impudence or loud bellowing, is from the root of *geum*.

He's naught but a *gomeril*, never tired of talking.—*Noctes Ambrosianæ.*

Gowan, a daisy; *gowany*, sprinkled with gowans or daisies. Chaucer was partial to the word daisy, which he derived from " day's eye ; " though it is more probably to be traced to the Gaelic *deise*, pretty, a pretty flower. The word *gowan*, to a Scottish ear, is far more beautiful.

Where the blue-bell and *gowan* lurk lowly unseen.—BURNS.

The night was fair, the moon was up, The wind blew low among the *gowans*. —*Legends of the Isles.*

Her eyes shown bright amid her tears, Her lips were fresh as *gowans* growing. —*Idem.*

In *gowany* glens the burnie strays. —BURNS.

I'd not be buried in the Atlantic wave, But in brown earth with *gowans* on my grave, Fresh *gowans* gathered on Lochaber's braes.—*All the Year Round.*

Gowdspink, the goldfinch.

Nancy's to the greenwood gane, To hear the *gowdspink* chattering ; And Willie he has followed her, To win her love by flattering. —*Scornful Nancy.*

Gowff or **gouff**, to pull violently.

She broke the bicker, spilt the drink, And tightly *gouff'd* his haffets (long hair). —HERD'S *Collection: The Three-Girred Cog.*

Gowk, the cuckoo ; also a fool, or a person who has but one idea and is always repeating it ; from the Gaelic *cuach*, with the same meaning.

Ye breed o' the *gowk*, ye hae never a song but ane.—ALLAN RAMSAY'S *Scots Proverbs.*

Conceited *gowk*, puffed up wi' windy pride. —BURNS : *The Brigs of Ayr.*

Gowl, to weep loudly, to whine and blubber ; from the Gaelic *gul*, with the same meaning. The French has *gueule*, a mouth that is very wide open. *Gowl* also signifies large and empty, as " a *gowl* or *gowlsome* house," and " a *gowl* (a hollow) between the hills ; " possibly allied in idea to the French *gueule*.

Ne'er may Misfortune's *gowling* bark Howl through the dwelling o' the clerk. —BURNS : *To Gavin Hamilton.*

Gowl means to bawl, to howl, but has the additional idea of threatening or terrifying. To *gowl* at a person is to speak in a loud threatening tone—" He gied me a *gowl*," " What mak's ye *gowl* that way at the weans?" I have an idea that this is one of the words that have crept into the Scotch through the French.—R. DRENNAN.

Gowpen, two handfuls ; from the Flemish *gaps*, which has the same meaning.

Those who carried meal seldom failed to add a *gowpen* to the alms-bag of the deformed cripple.—SCOTT : *The Black Dwarf.*

Gowpen means placing the two palms together, and the hollow formed thereby is a *gowpen*. The miller would have had but a scanty "mouter" if his *gowpen* had been only a handful. An ordinary beggar would get a nievefu' o' meal, but a weel kent ane and a favourite would get a *gowpen*. Hence, you never heard the crucial test of an Englishman's knowledge of Scotch when he was asked "What's a *gowpen* o' glaur?" and his acquaintance with the tongue failing him, he was enlightened by the explanation that it was "twa neivefu' o' clairts."—R. DRENNAN.

Gracie, well-behaved, graceful, of pleasant manners and behaviour.

"A wife's ae dochter is never *gracie*."
—*Proverb.*

Signifying that an only daughter is likely to be spoiled by over-indulgence, and therefore not likely to be as agreeable in manners as if she had sisters to compete with her for favour.

Gradden, the coarse meal that is ground in the quern by hand.

Grind the *gradden*, grind it;
We'll a' get crowdie when it's done,
An' bannocks steeve to bind it.

Whisky gars the bark of life
Drive merrily and rarely,
But *gradden* is the ballast gars
It steady gang and fairly.
—R. JAMIESON : *The Queen Lily.*

Graith, tools, requisites, implements, appurtenances of a business or work, harness ; *graithing-clothes*, accoutrements.

Then he in wrath put up his *graith*—
" The deevil's in the hizzie."
—*Jacob and Rachel: attributed
to* BURNS, 1825.

And ploughmen gather wi' their *graith*.
—BURNS: *Scotch Drink.*

Ye'll bid her shoe her steed before
An' a gowd *graithing* was behind.
—BUCHAN'S *Ancient Ballads.*

Gramarye, magic ; French *gri-moire*, a magic-book. Attempts have been made to derive this word from *grammar*. It is more likely, considering the gloomy ideas attached to the French *grimoire* (the immediate root of the word), that it comes originally from the Gaelic *gruaim*, gloom, melancholy, wrath, intense sadness or indignation ; and *gruamach*, sullen, surly, morose, gloomy, grim, frowning.

Whate'er he did of *gramarye*,
Was always done maliciously.
—SCOTT : *Lay of the Last Minstrel.*
The wild yell and visage strange,
And the dark woods of *gramarye*,
—*Idem.*

Grandgore, sometimes written **glengore** and **glandgore**, the venereal disease. Jamieson suggests its origin from the French *grand*, great, and *gorre;* but does not explain the meaning of *gorre*, which does not appear in French dictionaries.

The word appears to be rightly *grandgore*, and not *glen* or *gland gore*, and to be derived from the Gaelic *grain*, horrid, disgusting, and *gaorr*, filth.

Gree, to bear the *gree*, to excel, to be acknowledged to excel. The origin of this phrase is uncertain, though supposed to be connected with *degree*, *i.e.*, a degree of excellence and superiority.

Then let us pray that come it may,
As come it will for a' that,
That sense and worth, o'er a' the earth,
Shall bear the *gree* and a' that.
        —BURNS.

I wad hae nane o' them, though they wad
    fancy me,
For my bonnie mason laddie he bears
    awa' the *gree*.
    —CHAMBERS'S *Scottish Songs : The
        Mason Laddie.*

Greetie, the affectionate diminutive of *greet*, to weep or cry ; not to be rendered into English except by a weak paraphrase and dilution of the touching Scottish phrase, such as a small, faint, or little cry or lament, The same remark applies to the diminutive of *feet* in the subjoined verse.

We'll hap an' row, we'll hap an' row,
  We'll hap an' row the *feetie* o't ;
It is a wee bit wearie thing,
  I downa bide the *greetie* o't.
    —WILLIAM CREECH, *Lord Provost of
        Edinburgh, and publisher of the
        Poems of Robert Burns.*

Gregorian, a popular name for a wig in the seventeenth century, introduced into England by the Scottish followers of James VI. when he succeeded to the English throne. Blount, in his "Glossographia," says : " Wigs were so called from one Gregorie, a barber in the Strand, who was a famous perruquemaker."

He cannot be a cuckold that wears a *gregorian*, for a periwig will never fit such a head.—NARES.

Yet, though one Gregorie, a wig-maker, may have lived and flourished in London in the early part of the seventeenth century, it does not follow that the word *gregorian* was derived from his name, any more than that of the designation of a tailor by trade had its origin in the patronymic of *taylor.* At all events, it is worthy of note that in Gaelic *gruaig* signifies a wig ; *gruagach,* hairy ; *gruagag,* a little wig, or a bunch of hair ; and *gruagair,* a wig-maker and hairdresser.

Grien or **grene,** to covet, to long for, to desire ardently and unreasonably ; *grening,* longing, akin to the English *yearn,* "a *yearning* desire," German *gern,* Flemish *gearne,* willingly, desirous of. From this comes probably "*green* sickness," a malady that afflicts growing girls when they long for unwholesome and unnatural food, and would eat chalk, charcoal, unripe fruit, and any kind of trash. The medical name of this malady is *chlorosis,* a Greek translation of "*green* sickness," arising from the fact that English physicians understood the popular word *green,* the colour, but not *grien* or *grene,* to covet, which is the main symptom of the disease.

Teuch Johnnie, staunch Geordie an' Walie,
That *griens* for the fishes an' loaves.
    —BURNS : *The Election.*

They came there justice for to gett,
  They'll never *grene* to come again.
    —*Border Minstrelsy : The Raid of the
        Redswire.*

Grip, tenacity, moral or physical;
  to hold fast.

Will Shore couldna conceive how it was
that when he was drunk his feet wadna
haud the *grip.—Laird of Logan.*

But where you feel your honour *grip*,
Let that be aye your border.
—BURNS: *Epistle to a Young Friend.*

I like the Scotch; they have more *grip*
than any people I know.—SAM SLICK.

Grog, a mixture of spirits and
  water; usually applied to hot
  gin and water, as distinguished
  from rum-punch and whisky-
  toddy. The word is now common in England, and is supposed by careless philologists,
  who follow blindly where their
  predecessors lead them, to have
  been first used by the sailors in
  a ship of war commanded by
  Captain, afterwards Admiral
  Vernon, commonly called "Old
  Grog," from the grogram jacket
  or coat which he usually wore.
  But *grog* was known and named
  long before the days of Admiral
  Vernon, and was in common
  use in Scotland, as well as in
  England, as *croc*, afterwards
  corrupted into *grog*. The word
  croc in Gaelic signifies a horn,
  used in districts and in houses
  where glass was too expensive
  for purchase. A horn or *croc* of
  liquor was synonymous with a
  glass of liquor, and to offer a
  guest a *croc* or *grog* of spirit
  of any kind was the same as
  to invite him to take a social
  glass; and in time *croc* came to
  signify the liquor in the horn,
  as well as the horn itself. To

invite a man to take a friendly
glass is not to invite him to
take the glass itself, but the
drink that is in it. Hence the
word *grog*, which has no more
connection with the grogram
suit of Admiral Vernon than it
has with "the man in the
moon." The French have the
phrase "cric et *croc*" in the
slang vernacular.

Groof, the belly, so called from its
  rumbling when deprived of food;
  from the Gaelic *gromhan (grovan)*,
  to growl.

Rowin' yoursel' on the floor on your
groof, wi' your hair on end and your e'en
on fire.—*Noctes Ambrosianæ.*

Grue or **grew**, a greyhound.

I dreamed a weary dream yestre'en,
  I wish it may come to gude;
I dreamed that ye slew my best *grew-*
  hound,
And gied me his lapper'd blude.
            —*Ballad of Sir Roland.*

What has come ower ye, Muirland Tam?
Your leg's now grown like a wheelbarrow
  tram;
Ye'd the strength o' a stot, the weight o' a
  cow,
Now, Tammy, my man, ye have grown
  like a *grew.*
  —HEW AINSLIE: *Tam o' the Balloch.*

A *grew* is a female *greyhound* in
the South of England, according
to Mr. Halliwell Phillips, while
in the eastern counties the word
is a *grewin*, and in Shropshire
groun. In old French *grous*
signifies any kind of hunting-
dog—a greyhound among the
rest.

  The modern French do not

call the animal a "chien *gris*," but a *limier*, which means a dog which leaps or springs, from the Celtic *leum*, to leap, or a *levrier*, because it courses the *lièvre* or hare. In "Anglo-Saxon," which is merely Teutonic with a large substratum of Gaelic, it appears that this word is *grig-hound*. The pure Teutonic calls it a *windel spiel*, a grotesque term, for which it is difficult to account. The Dutch and Flemish call it a *speurhond*, or tracking-hound. The Italians call the animal a *véltro*. It is evident from all these examples that the dog was not named from *grey*, which is not its invariable colour. *Grey* is not adopted as its designation by any other nation than the English. Philology is thus justified in seeking elsewhere for the root of *grue*, which the Teutonic nations do not afford. The old grammarian Minshew thought he had found it in *grœcus*, and that the hound was so called because the Greeks hunted with it; but this derivation is manifestly inadmissible, as is that from *grip*, the hound which grips or snatches. Possibly the Scottish hound came from the Highlands and not from the Lowlands, or may be derived from *gaoth*, wind or breath, and *gaothar* (pronounced *gao-ar*), long-winded, strong-winded, provided with wind for rapid motion. *Gaothar* is rendered in the Gaelic dictionaries as a *lurcher*, half foxhound and half greyhound, and anciently

as greyhound only. As *gaor* is easy of corruption, first into *grao*, and afterwards into *grew* or *grue*, it is extremely probable that this is the true derivation of a word that has long been the despair of all lexicographers who were not so confident as Minshew and Dr. Johnson.

Gruesome, highly ill-favoured, disagreeable, horrible, cruel. *Grue*, to shudder, to be horrified. From the Teutonic *grau*, horror ; *grausam*, horrible, cruel ; and *grausamkeit*, cruelty. This word has been recently used by some of the best English writers, though not yet admitted to the honours of the dictionaries.

Ae day as Death, that *gruesome* carle,
Was driving to the ither warl (world).
—BURNS : *Verses to J. Rankine.*

And now, let us change the discourse. These stories make one's very blood *grew*.
—SCOTT : *Fortunes of Nigel.*

"They're the Hieland hills," said the Bailie ; "ye'll see and hear eneuch about them before ye see Glasgow Green again. I downa look at them, I never see them, but they gar me *grew*."—SCOTT : *Rob Roy.*

Grugous or **allagrugous,** grim, ghastly, disagreeable, morose, ill-natured ; from the Gaelic *grug*, morose, ill-conditioned and surly, and *uille*, all.

Whilk added horror to his mien,
A *grugous* sight he was, I ween.
—GEORGE BEATTIE : *John o' Arnha'.*

An *allagrugous*, gruesome spectre,
A' gored and bored like Trojan Hector.
—*Ibid.*

Gruntle, a word of contempt for a snub nose or snout ; erroneously rendered by "countenance" in some of the glossaries to Burns; *gruntle-thrawn*, crooked in the nose.

May gouts torment him, inch by inch,
Wha twists his *gruntle* wi' a glunch
    O' sour disdain,
Out owre a glass o' whisky-punch
    Wi' honest men.
      —BURNS : *Scotch Drink.*

Akin to the Gaelic *graineil*, ugly, loathsome ; *graineilachd*, ugliness.

Grunzie, a ludicrous name for the nose or mouth ; possibly applied originally to the snout of a hog, in reference to the grunting of the animal. (*See* GRUNTLE.)

But Willie's wife is nae sae trig,
    She dights her *grunzie* wi' a hushon
(*i.e.*, she wipes her nose with a cushion).
    —BURNS : *Sic a Wife as Willie had.*

Grushie, of rapid growth, thickly sown.

The dearest comfort o' their lives,
Their *grushie* weans and faithful wives.
    —BURNS : *The Twa Dogs.*

Gryce, a young pig.

A yeld (barren) sow was ne'er good to *gryces.* — ALLAN RAMSAY'S *Scots Proverbs.*

My bairn has tocher o' her ain,
    Although her friends do nane her len',
A stirk, a staig, an acre sawn,
    A goose, a *gryce*, a clocking-hen.
    —*The Wooing o' Jenny and Jock.*

Gryme, to sprinkle ; **gryming,** a sprinkling. The English word *grimy* signifies foul with dirt. The Scottish *gryme* has a wider meaning, and is applied both to pure and impure substances when out of place.

The sun wasna up, but the moon was down,
It was the *griming* of new fa'n snaw.
    —*Border Minstrelsy: Jamie Telfer.*

Guller, an indistinct noise in the throat. (*See* GOWL.)

Between a grunt, a groan, and a *guller*
—*Noctes Ambrosianæ.*

Gullie or **gully** (sometimes written *goolie*), a large pocket-knife ; *gullie-gaw*, a broil in which knives are likely to be drawn and used. *Gullie-willie*, according to Jamieson, is a noisy, blustering fool—possibly from his threatening the knife, but not using it.

I rede ye weel, tak' care o' skaith—
    See, there's a *gullie.*—BURNS.

The carles of Kilmarnock had spits and had spears,
And lang-hafted *gullies* to kill Cavaliers.
    —SIR WALTER SCOTT : *Bonnie Dundee.*

Stickin' gangs nae by strength, but by right guidin' o' the *gully.*—ALLAN RAMSAY'S *Scots Proverbs.*

"To guide the *gullie*," is a proverbial phrase, signifying to have the management of an affair. The derivation is uncertain, but is perhaps from the Gaelic *guaillich*, to go hand in hand, to accompany ; applied to the weapon from its ready conveniency to the hand in case of need.

Gumlie, muddy, turbid, synonymous with *drumlie* (*q.v.*). Etymology obscure.

O ye wha leave the springs o' Calvin,
For *gumlie* dubs [pools] o' your ain delvin'.
    —BURNS : *To Gavin Hamilton.*

Gump, a stupid old woman, of the kind so well portrayed in the Mrs. Gamp of Dickens, and which possibly may have suggested the name to the brilliant novelist, who married a Scotswoman, the grand-daughter of George Thompson, the celebrated correspondent of Robert Burns. **Gumphie**, a fool; **gommeril**, a foolish or stupid person; **gomf** or **gomph**, an idiot. The root is possibly the Gaelic *geum*, to low or bellow like a cow or a bull, and which finds its equivalent in the English slang, " Give us none of your *gum*."

Gump not only signifies an old woman not over-wise, but a fat and chubby infant, so that the Gaelic etymology for *geum*, if correct, can only be accepted in the case of the child, on the supposition that the child is a noisy one, and bellows or lows in expression of its wants or its ill-temper. To take the *gumps* is to indulge in a fit of ill-temper. Jamieson defines *gomeril* or *gomrell* as a stupid fellow, so called, he intimates, from the French *goimpre*, " one who minds nothing but his belly." The word, however, is not to be found in the " Dictionnaire Etymologique" of Noel and Carpentier (1857), nor in the comprehensive dictionary of " argot," or French slang, by the erudite and industrious Professor Barrère, published in 1887, nor in that of M. Brachet, published by the Clarendon Press in 1882, or in the voluminous work of M. Littré, the last recognised exponent of the French language. Professor Barrère, however, has *goinfre*—slang of thieves—from a pie-eater, " an allusion to his opening his mouth like a glutton," which may possibly be the word which Jamieson adopts as *goimfre*. But neither *goinfre* nor *goimfre* throws any light upon *gump* or the closely-related words that spring out of it, unless it be in support of the Gaelic derivation from *geum*, to low or bellow, and consequently to open the mouth widely.

Gumption, wit, sense, knowledge. This word is akin to the Gaelic *cuimse* (*cumshe*), moderation, adaptation, and *cuimsichte*, well-aimed, that hits the mark.

Nor a' the quacks with all their *gumption*
Will ever mend her.
—Burns: *Letter to John Goudie.*

Gurl, to growl; **gurly**, boisterous, stormy, savage, growly; from the German and Flemish *grollen*, the English *growl*, to express displeasure or anger by murmurs, and low, inarticulate sounds.

The lift grew dark and the wind blew sair,
And *gurly* grew the sea.
—*Sir Patrick Spens.*

Waesome wailed the snow-white sprites,
Upon the *gurly* sea.
—Laidlaw: *The Demon Lover.*

There's a strong *gurly* blast blawing snell frae the south.—James Ballantine: *The Spunk Splitters.*

Gurr, to snarl, to growl like an angry dog; **gurrie**, a loud and angry disputation, and also the growling, yelping, and barking of dogs in a fight. Allied in meaning and derivation, though spelled with *i* instead of *u*, are *girnie*, peevish; *girnigoe* and *girnigoe-gibbie*, a snarling and ill-natured person; and *girnin' gyte*, a fractious child.

Gurthie, corpulent, obese, large round the waist or *girth*.

Applied especially to what burdens the stomach. Roquefort renders it *pesant*, ponderous, burdensome.—JAMIESON.

Gutcher, a grandfather. This ungainly word seems to be a corruption of *gude-sire*, *gude-sir*, *gudsir*, or *good sir*, a title of reverence for a grandfather.

God bless auld lang syne, when our *gutchers* ate their trenchers. — ALLAN RAMSAY'S *Scots Proverbs*.

This was a reproach directed against over-dainty people who objected to their food.

Gae 'wa wi' your plaidie, auld Donald,
   gae 'wa;
I fear na the cauld blast, the drift, nor the sna',
Gae 'wa wi' your plaidie—I'll no sit beside ye;
Ye might be my *gutcher!* auld Donald, gae 'wa!
   —HECTOR MACNEIL: *Come under my Plaidie.*

The derivation from *good-sire* is rendered the more probable by the common use of the word *good* in Scotland to express degrees of relationship, as *good*-mother, a mother-in-law; *good*-brother, a brother-in-law; *good*-sister, a sister-in-law; *good*-son, a son-in-law, &c., as also in the familiarly affectionate phrases of *good*-wife for wife, and *good*-man for husband. The French use *beau* or *belle* in a similar sense, as *beau*-père, a father-in-law; *belle*-fille, a daughter-in-law; *belle*-mère, a mother-in-law. Possibly the English words *god*-father and *god*-mother, applied to the sponsors at the baptism of a child, were originally *good*, and not *god*.

Gyre - carline. This is in some parts of Scotland the name given to a woman suspected of witchcraft, and is from *gyre*, the Teutonic *geier*, a vulture, and *carline*, an old woman. The harpies in Grecian mythology are represented as having the beaks and claws of vultures, and are fabled to devour the bodies of warriors left unburied on the battle-field. The name of "Harpy," given in the ancient mythology to these supposed malevolent creatures, has been conclusively shown to be derived from the Gaelic, and to be traceable to *ar*, a battle-field, and *pighe* (pronounced *pee*), a bird, whence *ar pighe*, a harpy, the bird of the battlefield, the great carrion hawk or vulture.

I wad like ill to see a secret house haunted wi' ghaists and *gyre-carlines*.— SCOTT: *The Monastery.*

Gyte, deranged, mad; from the Flemish *guit*, mischievous, roguish; *guitenstuk*, a piece of mischief.

Surprised at once out of decorum, philosophy, and phlegm, he skimmed his cocked-hat in the air. "Lord sake," said Edie, "he's gaun *gyte*."—SCOTT: *The Antiquary.*

H

Hadden and dung, a phrase that signifies "held down and beaten," *i.e.*, held in bondage and ill-used; from *hadden*, preterite of *hold*, and *dung*, the preterite of *ding*, to beat or strike. (*See* DING.)

Haddin, furniture, plenishment, household stuff.

Oh, Sandie has owsen an' siller an' kye,
A house an' a *haddin*, an' a' things forbye;
But I'd rather ha'e Jamie wi 's bonnet in hand,
Than I wad ha'e Sandie wi' houses an' land.
  —*Logie o' Buchan.*

Haet, a whit, an iota; *deil a haet*, the devil a bit.

But gentlemen, an' ladies warst,
Wi' evendoun want o' wark are curst;
They loiter, lounging, lank and lazy,
Though *de'il haet* ails them, yet uneasy.
  —BURNS: *The Twa Dogs.*

In Bartlett's "Dictionary of Americanisms" the word occurs as *hate*.

I don't care a *hate*—I didn't eat a *hate*.

Haffets or **haffits**, the long hair of men, also applied to the long hair of women when old, but never when they are young. Jamieson says that *haffits* means the cheeks, but as used by Burns in "The Cotter's Saturday Night" it clearly signifies the front hair on the venerable cotter—"His lyart *haffits* wearin' thin an' bare." His lyart (grey) *haffits* are evidently not meant for grey cheeks, and cheeks, though they may grow thin, do not necessarily grow bare. The etymology of *haffits* as long hair is unknown; but supposing it to be cheeks, Jamieson derives it from the Anglo-Saxon *healf heafod*, half head, a semi-cranium.

His lyart *haffits* wearin' thin an' bare.
  —BURNS: *Cotter's Saturday Night.*

Lyart signifies *grey*, from the Gaelic *liath*, grey, and *liathach*, grey-headed.

Hafflins, almost or nearly one-half, formed from *half* and *lins*, pertaining to or approaching towards half, as in *aiblins* (which see).

While Jeanie *hafflins* is afraid to speak,
Weel pleased the mother hears he's nae wild worthless rake.
  —BURNS: *Cotter's Saturday Night.*

When it's cardit, row'd and spun,
Then the work is *hafflins* done.
  —*Tea-Table Miscellany: Tarry Woo.*

Haggis, the national dish *par excellence* of Scotland, which shares with cock-a-leekie and hotch-potch the particular favour of Scotsmen all over the world. Sir Walter Scott describes it in the introduction to "Johnnie Armstrong," in the "Minstrelsy of the Scottish Border," as "an olio composed of the liver, head, &c., of a sheep, minced down with oat-

F

meal, onions, and spices, and boiled in the *stomach* of the animal by way of bag." In Tim Bobbin's Glossary *hag* and *haggus* are defined as meaning the *belly*.

> Fair fa' your honest, sonsie face,
> Great chieftain o' the puddin' race ;
> Aboon them a' you tak' your place,
> Painch, tripe, or thairm ;
> Weel are ye worthy o' a grace
> As lang's my arm.
> —BURNS : *To a Haggis.*

Even a *haggis*, God bless her! could charge down the hill.—SCOTT : *Rob Roy.*

An illustrious American, travelling in Scotland, was entertained at a public dinner, when towards the end of the repast a very large haggis was brought in on a gigantic dish, carried by four waiters, to the tune of "See the Conquering Hero Comes," played by the band. He was very much amused at the incident, and having heard much of the national dish, but never having tasted it, was easily induced to partake of it. He did not appear to ike its flavour very much, and being asked his opinion of it, replied that "the *haggis* must have been invented to give Scotsmen an excuse for a dram of whisky after it, to take the taste out of the mouth," adding, "But if I were a Scotsman, I should make it a patriotic duty to love it, with or without the dram—but especially with it!" —C. M.

The word, formerly spelled *haggass*, is usually derived from the French *hachis*, a hash of viands cut into small pieces, from *hacher*, to mince, the English *hack*, to cut. The dish is quite unknown to the French, though the etymology is possibly correct. The allusion of Burns to the "sonsie face" of the pudding which he praised so highly, renders it possible

that he knew the Gaelic words *aogas*, a face, and *aogasach*, seemly, comely, sonsie. Anyhow, the coincidence is curious.

Haimert, homely, home-like, or tending *homewards*, of which latter word it is a variety or corruption.

> Quoth John, They're late ; but, by jingo,
> Ye'se get the rest in *haimert* lingo.
> —GEORGE BEATTIE : *John o' Arnha'.*

Hain, to preserve, to economise, so as to prevent waste and extravagance ; to protect with a hedge or fence ; to spare for future use. *Hain* seems to be derived from the German *hagen*, to enclose with a hedge or fence; the Danish *hegne*, with the same meaning ; and the Dutch and Flemish *heenen; omheenen*, to fence around, and *onheining*, an enclosure. From the practical idea of enclosing anything to protect it came the metaphorical use of this word in Scotland, in the sense of preservation of a thing by means of care, economy, and frugality.

> The weel-*hained* kebbock (cheese).
> —BURNS : *Cotter's Saturday Night.*

> Wha waste your weel-*hained* gear on
> damned new brigs and harbours.
> —BURNS : *The Brigs of Ayr.*

> Kail *hains* bread.—ALLAN RAMSAY'S
> *Scots Proverbs.*

> We've won to crazy years thegither,
> We'll toyte about wi' ane anither ;
> Wi' tentie care I'll flit thy tether
> To some *hain'd* rig.
> —BURNS : *The Auld Farmer.*

Hain, to preserve, does not seem to me

to be a correct synonym; the word rather means to use economically. " Her weel-hain'd kebbuck" does not mean that the cheese had been preserved from danger, from mites, or the cheese-fly and maggots, but that it had not been used wastefully; *haining clothes*, means a second goodish suit to save your best one. The English expression "eke it out" comes very near the meaning of *hain*. In Fifeshire the word used instead of *hain* is *tape—tape* it, make it last a good while, don't gobble up a nice thing all at once; in fact, *hain* it.— R. DRENNAN.

Haiver, to talk in a desultory manner, foolishly, or idly, to drivel.

> Wi' clavers and *haivers*
> Wearin' the day awa'.
> —BURNS.

Haiver or *haver* seems to be a corruption of the Gaelic *abair*, to talk, to say.

Hale - scart, without *scratch* or damage; from *scart*, to scratch, and *hale*, well or intact.

Hale-scart frae the wars without skaithing,
Gaed bannin' the French awa' hame.
—ANDREW SCOTT : *Symon and Janet*.

Hallan-shaker, a sturdy, importunate beggar. Jamieson derives the word from *hallan*, a partition in a cottage between the "but" and the "ben;" and *shaker*, one who shakes the *hallan* by the noise he makes. If he had sought in the Gaelic, he might have found a better derivation in *alla, allan, allanta*, wild, ferocious, savage ; and *seachran* (the Irish *shaughraun*), a vagrant, a wanderer, a beggar.

Right scornfully she answered him,
Begone, you *hallan-shaker!*
Jog on your gate, you *bladderskate*,
My name is Maggie Lauder.
—FRANCIS SEMPLE.

Hantle, a good deal, a quantity; from the Flemish *hand*, a hand, and *tel*, to count or number; a quantity that may be reckoned by the handful.

A Scottish clergyman related as his experience after killing his first pig, that " nae doot there was a *hantle* o' miscellaneous eating about a swine."—DEAN RAMSAY.

Some hae a *hantle* o' fauts; ye are only a ne'er-do-weel.—ALLAN RAMSAY's *Scots Proverbs*.

Are we better now than before? In a few things better; in a *hantle* waur.— *Noctes Ambrosianæ*.

Hap, to cover, to wrap up.

I digged a grave and laid him in,
And *happ'd* him wi' the sod sae green.
—*Lament of the Border Widow*.

Hap and rowe, *hap* and rowe the feetie o't,
It is a wee bit ourie thing,
I downa bide the greetie o't.
—CHAMBERS's *Scottish Songs*.

Happer, thin, lank, shrunken; *happer*-lipped, having thin lips; *happer*-hipped, having small or shrunken hips.

An' there'll be *happer*-hipped Nannie,
An' fairy-faced Flora by name ;
Muck Maudie, and fat-luggit Girzie,
The lass wi' the gowden wame.
—*The Blithesome Bridal*.

Harns, brains; from the German *hirn* or *gehirn*, the brain; *hirn-schale*, the brain-pan; Dutch and Flemish, *hersens*.

A wheen midden-cocks pike ilk others' *harns* out (a lot of dunghill cocks pick each others' brains out).—SCOTT : *Rob Roy*.

Lastly, Bailie, because if I saw a sign o'
your betraying me, I would plaster that
wa' wi' your *harns*, ere the hand o' man
could rescue ye.—SCOTT : *Rob Roy.*

Hatter (sometimes written **hotter**)
signifies, according to Jamieson,
to bubble, to boil up and also a
crowd in motion or in confusion.
The English slang expression
" Mad as a hatter " does not
apply—though commonly supposed to do so—to a hat-maker,
any more than it does to a tailor
or a shoemaker. It seems to
have been borrowed by the Lowland Scotch from the Gaelic
at, to swell like boiling water,
and *ataircachd,* the swelling
and foaming of waters as in
a cataract, and, by extension
of the image, to the tumultuous action of a noisy crowd.
In Tim Bobbin's Lancashire
Glossary *hotter* signifies to vex,
and *hottering,* mad, very mad,
very vexed.

Haugh, low ground or meadows
by the river-side ; from the
Gaelic *ac, ach,* and *auch ;* the
Teutonic *aue,* a meadow. *Holm*
and *hagg* have the same meaning. The word *acre* is from the
same etymological root.

> By Leader *haughs* and Yarrow.
>
> Let husky wheat the *haughs* adorn,
> And aits set up their awnie horn.
> —BURNS : *Scotch Drink.*

Haur, an easterly wind; and **hoar,**
frost produced by an easterly
wind.

> The sleet and the *haur*—misty, easterly
> *kaur.*—*Noctes Ambrosianæ.*

Hause-bane, the neck-bone; from
the Flemish and German *hals,*
the neck.

> Ye shall sit on his white *hause-bane,*
> And I'll pike out his bonny blue een ;
> Wi' ae lock o' his yellow hair
> We'll theek our nest when it grows bare.
> —*The Twa Corbies.*

To *hause* or *hals* signifies to
embrace, *i.e.,* to put the arms
round the neck.

Haveril, a half-witted person, a
silly talker ; from *haiver,* to talk
nonsense ; the Gaelic *abair,* to
talk.

> Poor *haveril* Will fell aff the drift,
> And wandered through the bow-kail,
> And pu'd, for want o' better shift,
> A runt was like a sow-tail.
> —BURNS : *Hallowe'en.*

Havers, oats; **haver-meal,** oatmeal; from the French *avoine.*

> Oh, where did ye get that *haver-meal*
> bannock ?
> Oh, silly auld body, dinna ye see ?
> I got it frae a sodger laddie
> Betwixt St. Johnstoun and Bonnie
> Dundee.
> —HERD'S *Collection: altered and
> amended by* BURNS.

Havins, good manners and behaviour, courteous and kindly de-
meanour, personal accomplishments which one *has* ; thence
havings or acquirements.

> Awa, ye selfish warldly race,
> Wha think that *havins,* sense, and grace,
> E'en love and friendship, should give place
> To catch-the-plack (the money) ;
> I dinna like to see your face
> Or hear you crack (talk).
> —BURNS : *Epistle to Lapraik.*

Hawkie, a pet name for a favourite cow or one who is a good milker.

> Dawtit twal-pint *Hawkie's* gaen
> As yell's the bull.
> —BURNS : *Address to the De'il.*

> I'd rather sell my petticoat,
> Though it were made o' silk,
> Than sell my bonnie broun *Hawkie*,
> That gies the sup o' milk.
> —CHAMBERS'S *Scottish Songs.*

"Brown hawkie," says Jamieson, "is a cant name for a barrel of ale"—*i.e.*, the milk of drunkards and topers. The word is traceable to the Gaelic *adhach* (pronounced *awk* or *hawk*), lucky, fortunate.

Heartsome, cordial, hearty; full of heartiness.

> Farewell to Lochaber, fareweel to my Jean,
> Where *heartsome* wi' her I ha'e mony a
> day been.—*Lochaber no More.*

Hech, an exclamation of surprise, of joy, or of pain; softened from the Gaelic *oich*. On the shore of Loch Ness, near the waterfall of *Abriachan*, where the road is steep and difficult, the rock near the summit of the ascent has received from the shepherds and drovers the name of "Craig Oich," from their stopping to draw breath and exclaiming, "*Oich! oich!*" (in the Lowland Scottish, *hech*). The English *heigho* is a kindred exclamation, and is possibly of the same etymology. *Hech-howe* signifies *heigh-ho!* "In the *auld hech-howe*," *i.e.*, as in the old *heigho* condition, a mode of complaining that one is in the customary state of ill-health.

Hecht, to offer, to promise. This verb seems to have no present tense, no future, and no declensions or inflexions, and to be only used in the past, as :—

> Willie's rare, Willie's fair,
> And Willie's wondrous bonny,]
> And Willie *hecht* to marry me,
> Gin e'er he married ony.
> —*Tea-Table Miscellany.*

> The miller he *hecht* her a heart leal and
> loving,
> The laird did address her wi' matter mair
> moving.—BURNS : *Meg o' the Mill.*

> He *hecht* me baith rings and mony braw
> things,
> And were na my heart light I wad die.
> —LADY GRIZZEL BAILLIE. †

The word is of doubtful etymology : perhaps from the Teutonic *echt*, sincere, true, genuine —which a promise ought to be.

Heckle, a sort of rough comb used by hemp and flax dressers. Metaphorically the word signifies to worry a person by cross-questioning or impertinence. To *heckle* a parliamentary candidate at election time is a favourite amusement of voters, who think themselves much wiser than any candidate can possibly be ; and of insolent barristers in a court of law, who cross-examine a hostile witness with undue severity—an operation which is sometimes called "badgering." There was a well-known butcher in Tiverton who always made it a point to *heckle* the late Lord

Palmerston when he stood as candidate for that borough. Lord Palmerston bore the infliction with great good-humour, and always vanquished the impudent butcher in the wordy warfare.

Adown my beard the slavers trickle,
I throw the wee stools o'er the mickle,
As round the fire the giglets keckle
        To see me loup ;
While raving mad I wish a *heckle*
        Were in their doup !
—BURNS : *Address to the Toothache.*

He was a hedge unto his friends,
A *heckle* to his foes, lads,
And every one that did him wrang,
He took him by the nose, lads.
        —CHAMBERS's *Scottish Ballads :
        Rob Roy.*

This was the son of the famous Rob Roy, and was called Robin *Og*. Chambers translates Robin *Og*, "Robin the *Little*." *Og*, in Gaelic, signifies not *little*, but *young*.

Heership, plunder ; from *herry* or *harry*, to rob, to pillage.

But wi' some hope he travels on while he
The way the *heership* had been driven
could see.—Ross's *Helenore.*

Heft, the haft or handle of a knife. The *heft* of a sword is called the hilt. To give a thing "heft and blade," is to give it wholly and without restriction, "stock, lock, and barrel."

A knife, a father's throat had mangled,
Whom his ain son o' life bereft—
The grey hairs yet stuck to the *heft ;*
Wi' mair o' horrible and awfu',
Which e'en to name would be unlawfu'.
        —BURNS : *Tam o' Shanter.*

Hein-shinn'd, having large ankles. *Ain* or *an*, the augmentative prefix in Gaelic to nouns and adjectives, signifying size, or excess, is probably the root of *hein* in this word.

She's bough-houghed and *hein-shinn'd.*
        —BURNS.

Her nain sel', "his own self," and "my own self." This phrase is supposed by the Lowland Scotch to be the usual mode of expression employed by the Highlanders, on account of the paucity of pronouns in the Gaelic language.

Oh, fie for shame, ye're three for ane,
Her nain sel's won the day, man.
        —*Battle of Killiecrankie.*

Mr. Robert Chambers, in a note on this passage, says : "*The Highlanders have only one pronoun,* and as it happens to resemble the English word *her*, it has caused the Lowlanders to have a general impression that they mistake the masculine for the feminine gender." Mr. Chambers, knowing nothing of Gaelic, was utterly wrong in this matter of the pronouns. The Gaelic has the same number of personal pronouns as the English, namely — *mi*, I ; *do*, thou ; *e*, he ; *i*, she ; *sinn*, we ; *sibh*, you or yours ; *iad*, they or theirs. They have also the possessive pronouns—*mo*, mine ; *ar*, ours ; *bhur* and *ur*, yours ; and all the rest of the series. It was doubtless the *ur* or the *ar* of the Gaelic which, by its resemblance to *her*, suggested to Mr. Chambers the error into which he fell.

Herryment, plague, devastation, ruin ; from *herry* or *harry*, to plunder and lay waste.

> The *herryment* and ruin of the country.
> —BURNS : *The Brigs of Ayr.*

Heuchs and haughs, hands, legs, or thigh. *Heuchs* is probably a corruption of *hooks*, as applied to the hands, or, as Shakespeare calls them, "pickers and stealers." *Haughs* is the Scottish form of the English *hocks*, the hind part of the knee.

> The kelpie grinned an eldrich laugh,
> And rubbed his *heuchs* upon his *haughs*.
> —GEORGE BEATTIE : *John o' Arnha'.*

Hiddil, a hiding-place, the hole or refuge of a shy or wild animal.

> The otter yap his prey let drap,
> And to his *hiddil* flew.
> —*Water Kelpie : Border Minstrelsy.*

Hinnie or **honey**, a term of endearment among the Scottish Highlanders, and more particularly among the Irish.

> Oh, open the door, my *hinnie*, my heart,
> Oh, open the door, my ain true love.
> —CHAMBERS'S *Scottish Songs : Legend of the Padda.*

Honey, in the sense of *hinnie*, occurs in the nursery-rhymes of England :—

> There was a lady loved a swine ;
> "*Honey!* my dear," quoth she,
> "My darling pig, wilt thou be mine?"
> "Hoogh, hoogh!" grunted he.

The word *hinnie* is supposed to be a corruption of *honey*, though *honey* in the English may be a corruption of *hinnie*. They both express the idea of fondness ; and those who believe honey to be the correct term explain it by assuming that the beloved object is as "sweet as *honey*." But if this be really the fundamental idea, the Gaelic-speaking population of Ireland and the Highlands might be supposed to have used the native word *mil*, rather than the Teutonic *honey* or *honig*, which does not exist in their language. However this may be, it is at all events suggestive that the Gaelic *ion* signifies fitting ; and the compound *ion-amhuil* means like, equal, well-matched ; and *ion-mhuin*, dear, beloved, kind, loving. The Irish Gaelic has *ionadh* (pronounced *hinna*), admiration, or an object of admiration ; whence *ionadh-rhuigte*, adorable. The Scotch and old English *marrow* is a term of endearment to a lover, and signifies mate, one of a pair, as in the ballad :—

> Busk ye, busk ye ! my bonnie bride,
> Busk ye, busk ye ! my winsome *marrow*.
> —HAMILTON *of Bangour.*

In Scotland *hinnie* and *joe* (Jamieson) signify a lass and her lover who are very fond of each other. This phrase is equivalent to the English "Darby and Joan," and describes a greatly-attached wedded pair. The opinions of philologists will doubtless differ between the Teutonic and the possible Gaelic derivation of *honey* or *hinnie;* but the fact that the Teutonic nations do not draw the similar expression of fondness, as applied to a woman, from *honey,* is worthy of consideration in attempting to decide the doubtful point.

Hirple, to limp, to run with a limping motion.

'The hares were *hirplin'* doun the furs.
            —BURNS: *The Holy Fair.*

And when wi' age we're worn doun,
An' *hirplin'* at the door.
                —*The Boatie Rows.*

I'm a pair silly auld man,
An' *hirplin'* at the door.
        —*Gin Kirk wad Let me be.*

Hirsel, a flock, a multitude; derived by Jamieson from the Teutonic *heer,* an army; but more probably from the Gaelic *earras,* wealth (in flocks and herds), and *earrasail,* wealthy. *Hirsel,* among shepherds, means to arrange or dispose the sheep in separate flocks, and *hirseling,* the separating into flocks or herds; sometimes written and pronounced *hissel.*

Ae scabbed sheep will smit the hale *hirsel.* — ALLAN RAMSAY'S *Scots Proverbs.*

"Jock, man," said he, "ye're just telling a *hirsel* o' e'endown [downright] lies."
—HOGG: *Brownie of Bodsbeck.*

The herds and *hissels* were alarmed.
        —BURNS: *Epistle to W. Simpson.*

Hirsel or hersel. The primary idea of this word is to remove the body, when in a sitting position, to another or contiguous seat without absolutely rising. Jamieson suggests the derivation from the coarse word applied to the posteriors in all the Teutonic languages, including English. He is probably correct; though, as a verb, *aerselen,* which he cites, is not to be found in the Swedish, Danish, Dutch, Flemish, or German dictionaries.

An English gentleman once boasted to the Duchess of Gordon of his familiarity with the Scottish language. "*Hirsel* yont, my braw birkie," said she. To her great amusement, as well as triumph, he could not understand one word except "my."—DEAN RAMSAY.

Hizzie, a lass, a huzzy; a term of jocular endearment. Supposed to be a corruption of *housewife.*

Buirdly chiels and clever *hizzies*
Are bred in sic a way as this is.
        —BURNS: *The Twa Dogs.*

Hoast, a cough, or to cough.

Jamie Fraser, a poor half-witted person, who was accustomed to make inconvenient or unseemly noises in the kirk, was one day cautioned not to make fidgety movements during divine service, under the penalty of being turned out. The poor creature sat quite still and silent, till in a very important part of the sermon he felt an irresistible inclination to cough. Unable to restrain himself, he rose in his seat, and shouted out, "Minister, may not a pair body like me gie a *hoast!*"—DEAN RAMSAY.

Hodden-grey. In the glossary to the first edition of Allan Ramsay's "Tea-Table Miscellany," 1724, "*hodden*" is described as a coarse cloth. *Hodden* appears to be a corruption of the Gaelic *adhan,* warm; so that *hodden*-grey would signify warm grey. It was usually home - made by the Scottish peasantry of the Lowlands, and formed the material of their working-day clothes.

What though on homely fare we dine,
  Wear *hodden-grey*, and a' that ;
Gi'e fools their silks an' knaves their wine,
  A man's a man for a' that.—BURNS.

If a man did his best to murder me, I should not rest comfortably until I knew that he was safe in a well-ventilated cell, with the *hodden-grey* garment of the gaol upon him.—*Trial of Prince Pierre Bonaparte, Daily Telegraph*, March 26, 1870.

Hogmanay or Hogmenay. This is a peculiarly Scottish name for a festival by no means peculiar to Scotland—that of New Year's Day, or the last hours of the old year and the first of the new. On these occasions, before the world grew as prosaic as it is with regard to old customs and observances, the young men, and sometimes the old, paid visits of congratulation to the girls and women of their acquaintance, with words of goodwill or affection, and very commonly bore with them gifts of more or less value according to their means. It was a time of good-fellowship, conviviality, and kindly offices. Many attempts have been made to trace the word. Some have held it to be from the Greek *hagia* (αγια), holy, and *μηνε*, a month. But as the festival lasted for a few hours only, the etymology is unsatisfactory. Others have thought to find its source in

the French *gui*, the mistletoe, and *mener*, to lead—*au gui mener*, to lead to the mistletoe ; and others, again, to the Gaelic *oige*, youth ; and *madhuin*, the morning, because the celebration took place in the earliest hours of the daylight. It cannot be admitted that any one of these derivations is wholly satisfactory. Nobody has ever thought of looking to the Flemish— which has supplied so many words to the vocabulary of the Lowland Scotch—for a solution of the difficulty. In that language we find *hoog*, high or great ; *min*, love, affection, and *dag*, a day—*hoog-min-dag*, the high or great day of affection. The transition from *hoog-min-dag* to *hog-man-ay*, with the corruption of *dag* into *ay*, is easily accomplished. This etymology is offered with diffidence, not with dogmatic assertion, and solely with this plea on its behalf—that it meets the meaning better perhaps than any other, or, if not better, at least as well as the Greek, French, or Gaelic.

Holme, holm, sometimes written *houm*, a meadow.

Doun in a glen he spied nine armed men,
  On the dowie *holms* o' Yarrow.
  —*Border Minstrelsy: The Dowie Dens
    o' Yarrow.*

Hoodock, the hooded owl.

The harpy, *hoodock*, purse-proud race
Wha count a' poortith as disgrace,
  They've tuneless hearts.
  —BURNS : *Epistle to Major Logan.*

The glossaries to Burns explain this word as meaning "miserly," which is a mere conjecture from the context, to fit it into "purse-proud;" whereas it is but a continuation of the ornithological idea of harpy, a vulture. The origin is the French *duc*, an owl, of which in that language there are three varieties—*grand duc*, or great owl; *petit duc*, or little owl; and *haut duc*, large, great owl. Possibly, however, the first syllable in *hood*ock is the English *hood*. The idea in Burns is that of a greedy bird or harpy. Jamieson has "*hoodit craw*" for carrion crow; and *hoody*, the hooded crow.

Hool, the husk of grain, the integument, the case or covering.

> Ilk kind o' corn has its ain *hool;*
> I think the world is a' gane wrang
> When ilka wife her man wad rule.
> —*Tak' your Auld Cloak about ye.*

> Poor Leezie's heart maist lap the *hool,*
> Near laverock height she loupit.
> —BURNS: *Hallowe'en.*

In Dutch, *hülle*, cover, integument, veil; Swedish, *holja*, cover, envelope, case, or hull; whence also the English *holster*, the case of a pistol; and *upholster*, to make cases or coverings for furniture, and *upholsterer*, one who *upholsters*. The unnecessary and corrupt prefix of *up* to this word has led philologists to derive it erroneously from *uphold*.

The English *hoils*, applied to the beard and husks of barley, and *hull*, a husk or shell of peas and beans, seems to be from the same source as the Scottish *hool*, and in like manner the *hull* or outer case of a ship.

> Sad was the chase that they ha'e gi'en to me,
> My heart's near out o' *hool* by getting free.
> —Ross's *Helenore.*

Hoolie or **hooly**. This word is commonly used in conjunction with "fairly," as in the phrase "*hooly* and fairly." Jamieson renders it "slowly and cautiously." It is derived from the Gaelic *tigheil, ui-eil*, heedful, cautious. The glossaries to Burns render it "stop!" There is an old Scottish song—"Oh, that my wife would drink *hooly* and fairly." In the glossary to Mr. Alexander Smith's edition of Burns, where "stop" would not convey the meaning, the explanation that the word means "stop" is a mere guess from the context, which proves that the editor did not really understand the word.

> Still the mair I'm that way bent,
>   Something cries "*Hoolie!*"
> I rede you, honest man, tak' tent,
>   You'll show your folly.
>   —BURNS: *Epistle to James Smith.*

> Sin' every pastime is a pleasure,
> I counsel you to sport with measure;
> And, namely now, May, June, and July,
> Delight not long in Lorea's leisure,
> But weit your lipps and labour *hooly.*
>   —*On May:* ALEX. SCOTT *in the Evergreen.*

> Oh, *hooly, hooly*, rose she up
>   To the place where he was lyin',

And when she drew the curtain bye—
"Young man, I think ye're dyin'."
—*Ballad of Barbara Allan.*

Hooly and fair gangs far in a day.—
ALLAN RAMSAY'S *Scots Proverbs.*

In the North of England *hooly* means
tenderly, gently.—HALLIWELL.

Hootie, a ludicrous but expressive word, applied to a man like Pococurante in Voltaire's romance, who impresses the ingenuous Candide with an idea of the immensity of his wisdom, because nothing could please him. The word is derivable from *hoot !* or *hoots !* an interjection expressive of contempt, or of more or less angry dissent. *Hoot ! toot !* is an intensification of the same idea. The English have *pshaw ! pish !* and *tut !* The word in the form of *ut ! ut !* is very common among Highlanders.

Horn. Drinking vessels, before glass was much used for the purpose, were made of horn, and are still to be found both among the poor and the rich. "To take a *horn*" ultimately came to signify to take a drink —just as the modern phrase, "Take a glass," does not mean to take the glass itself, but the liquor contained in it. (*See* GROG, *ante.*)

By the gods of the ancients ! Glenriddel
replies,
Before I surrender so glorious a prize,
I'll conjure the ghost of the great Rorie
More,
And *bumper his horn* with him twenty
times o'er.—BURNS: *The Whistle.*

Horn-dry, according to Jamieson, means "dry as a horn ; eager for drink ; an expression frequently used by reapers when exhausted by the labours of the harvest." But the obvious etymology—viewed in the light of the other words that have been cited—is not *dry* as a horn, but dry for want of a *horn* of liquor. (For further reference to horn as signifying a drink, see GROG, *ante.*) To take a *croc*, or *grog* (the same as to take a *horn* or a *glass*), meant simply to take a drink. The French have *cric* and *croc* for a glass of spirits, as in the chorus of the old song :—

Cric, croc ! à ta santé !

Horn-mad is defined in the Dictionary of Lowland Scotch (1818) as signifying quite mad; though the compiler did not seem to be aware that the madness was that which came from intoxication or the too frequent emptying of the horn. *Horn-daft* is of similar meaning and origin, though expressive of a minor degree of intoxication. Jamieson renders it "outrageous," and imagines it may be an allusion to an animal that pushes with its horns. *Horn-idle* is defined by Jamieson to mean "having nothing to do, completely unemployed." He derives the first syllable from the Saxon, and the second from the Gaelic. *Horn* is certainly Teutonic or Flemish, but *idle* is as certainly not Gaelic. The allusion in this case is obviously to the sloth or drowsiness that in lethargic persons often results from intoxication.

Hornie is a word used in Ayrshire, according to Jamieson, to signify amorous, lecherous, libidinous. Still, with the notion in his head that *horn* is to be taken literally, and not metaphorically, he suggests that a *hornie* person is one who is apt to reduce another to the state of cuckoldom, or a *cornutus;* and to confer upon him the imaginary horns that are supposed to grace the forehead of those ill-used and unfortunate persons. It is evident, however, that *hornie* meant nothing more than intoxicated to such an extent as to excite the intoxicated person to take improper liberties with women. Burns employs the word as one of the names popularly and jocularly bestowed upon the devil.

Host, to cough with effort or difficulty. The colloquial phrase, "It didna cost him a *hoast* to do it," signifies that the thing was done easily and without effort. From the German *husten,* the Flemish *hosten,* to cough. (*See* HOAST, *ante.*)

——— Joyless Eild (old age),
   Wi' wrinkled face,
Comes *hostin'*, hirplin' ow'r the field
   Wi' creepin' pace.
   —BURNS: *Epistle to James Smith.*

Houghmagandie, child-bearing; wrongly supposed to mean the illicit intercourse of the sexes. This word has not been found in any author before Burns, and is considered by some to have been coined by that poet. But this is not likely. It is usually translated by "fornication." No etymology of the word has hitherto been suggested. Nevertheless, its component parts seem to exist in the Flemish. In that language *hoog* signifies high or great, and *maag,* the stomach or belly; *maagen,* bellies; and *je,* a diminutive particle commonly added to Flemish and Dutch words, and equivalent to the Scottish *ie* in *bairnie, wifie, laddie, lassie,* &c. These words would form *hoog-maagan-je*—a very near approach to the *houghmagandie* of Burns. If this be the derivation, it would make better sense of the passage in which it occurs than that usually attributed to it. The context shows that it is not fornication which is meant—for that has already been committed—but the possible result of the sin which may appear "some other day," in the enlarged circumference of the female sinner.

There's some are fu' o' love divine,
   And some are fu' o' brandy;
And mony a job that day begun
   May end in *houghmagandie*
   Some other day.
   —BURNS: *The Holy Fair.*

Ayrshire and Dumfriesshire retained for a longer time than the eastern counties of Scotland the words and phrases of the Gaelic language, though often greatly corrupted; and in the poems and songs of Burns words from the Gaelic are of frequent occurrence. It is not likely that Burns ever took it upon himself to invent a word; and if he did, it is even more than unlikely that it should find acceptance. Whatever it may mean, *houghmagandie* does not mean fornication, for the whole spirit and contents of the "Holy Fair" show that fornication is what he stigmatises as the practice of the gatherings which he satirises; and that which he calls *houghmagandie* is, or is likely to be, the future result of the too promiscuous intercourse of the sexes, against which he jocosely declaims. The Gaelic *og* and *macan*, a little son, may possibly afford a clue to the word; but this is a suggestion merely.

I don't remember to have met with this word anywhere except in the "Holy Fair." It may have been a word in use in Burns's day, or it may have been a coinage of Burns, that would readily convey to the minds of his readers what he meant. It may have conveyed the idea of a "dyke-louper" appearing before the Session, the "snoovin' awa afore the Session" for a fault, the doing penance for "jobbing." *Gangdays* were the three days in Rogation week, on which priest and parishioners were accustomed to walk in procession about the parish; a remnant of the custom is still to be seen in London in the perambulations of boys about the bounds of the parish. *Gandie* would not be a very violent alteration of *gandeye*, the more especially that the spelling of Scotch words partook a good deal of the phonetic, and *gangday* was very probably pronounced *gandie*. Now, we know as a fact that, in the lapse of time, many of the ceremonies of the Church became corrupted from their origi-

nal intention, and processions became in time a sort of penance for faults, and in this way it is just possible that *gandie* came itself to mean a penance, and *houghmagandie* conveyed the idea of doing penance for some wrong action that the *hough* or leg had something to do with.— R. DRENNAN.

Howdie or **howdie-wife**, a midwife, an accoucheuse. This word is preferable to the English and the foreign term borrowed from the French. *Howdie-fee*, the payment given to a midwife.

When skirlin' weanies see the light,
Thou makes the gossips clatter bright,
How funkin' cuifs their dearies slight—
    Wae worth the name!
Nae *howdie* gets a social night
    Or plack frae them.
    —BURNS: *Scotch Drink.*

No satisfactory clue to the etymology of this word has been made known. In Gaelic the midwife is called the "knee-woman," *beangloinne;* in French, the *sage femme*, or wise woman; in Teutonic, the *weh mutter;* in Spanish, *partera*, and in Italian, *comare*, the latter word signifying the French *commère*—the old English and Scotch *cummer* —or gossip. Possibly the true origin of the Scottish word is to be found in *houd* or *haud*, to hold, to sustain; and the midwife was the *holder*, helper, sustainer, and comforter of the woman who suffered the pains of labour; the *sage femme* of the French, who was wise and skilful enough to perform her delicate function.

Howff, a favourite public-house, where friends and acquaint-ances were accustomed to re-sort; from the Gaelic *uamh* (*uaf*), a cave. " Caves of harmony," as they were called, were formerly known in Paris, and one long existed in London under the name of the *Coalhole*. They were small places of convivial resort, which, in London, have grown into music-halls. Jamie-son traces *howff* to the Teutonic *hof*, a court-yard, and *gast-hof*, an inn or yard. It is possible that he is right, though it is equally possible that the German *hof* is but a form of the Gaelic *uamh*.

This will be delivered to you by a Mrs. Hyslop, landlady of the Globe Tavern here, which for many years has been my *howff*, and where our friend Clarke and I have had many a merry squeeze.—BURNS : *Letter to George Thompson.*

Burns's *howff* at Dumfries.—CHAMBERS.

Where was't that Robertson and you were used to *howff* thegither?—SCOTT : *Heart of Midlothian.*

Howk, formerly spelled **holk**, to dig, to grub up, to root up, to form a hole in the ground.

Whiles mice and moudieworts (moles)
they *howkit*.
—BURNS : *The Twa Dogs.*

And in kirkyards renew their leagues
Owre *howkit* dead.
—BURNS : *Address to the De'il.*

He has *howkit* a grave that was lang and
was deep,
And he has buried his sister wi' her baby
at her feet.
—MOTHERWELL : *The Broom
Blooms Bonnie.*

Howk the tow out o' your lug an' hear
till a sang.—*Noctes Ambrosianæ.*

How-towdies, barndoor fowls ; origin of the word unknown, though it has been suggested that it may be a corruption of the Gaelic *eun-doide*, a fowl to the hand, or a fowl ready to the hand if wanted.

Hunting the fox prevents him from growing ower fat on *how-towdies.*—*Noctes Ambrosianæ.*

Huggers, stockings or hose with-out feet.

But a' her skill lies in her buskin,
And oh, if her braws were awa,
She soon would wear out o' the fashion,
And knit up her *huggers* wi' straw.
—*Woo'd and Married and a'.*

Hummel-corn, mean, shabby, of small account ; a term applied to the lighter grain which falls from the rest when it is win-nowed.

A lady returning from church ex-pressed her low opinion of the sermon she had heard by calling it a *hummel-corn* discourse.—DEAN RAMSAY.

The derivation is unknown, though *humble-corn* has been suggested.

Hummel-doddie, dowdy, ill-fit-ting, in bad taste.

Whatna *hummel - doddie* o' a mutch
[cap] hae ye gotten?—DEAN RAMSAY'S
Reminiscences.

Humple, to walk lamely and painfully, to hobble.

Then *humpled* he out in a hurry,
While Janet his courage bewails.
—CHAMBERS'S *Scottish Songs.*

Hunkers, the loins ; to *hunker down*, to squat on the ground.

The word seems to be allied to the English *hunk*, a lump; whence to squat down on the earth in a lumpish fashion.

> Wi' ghastly ee, poor Tweedle Dee
> Upon his *hunkers* bended,
> And prayed for grace wi' cuthless face
> To see the quarrel ended.
> —BURNS: *The Jolly Beggars.*

Hurdies, the hips, the *podex* of the Romans, the *pyge* of the Greeks. From the Gaelic *aird*, a rounded muscle or swelling; plural *airde*, also *airdhe*, a wave, or of a wavy form.

> His tail
> Hung o'er his *hurdies* wi' a swirl.
> —BURNS: *The Twa Dogs.*

Ye godly brethren o' the sacred gown,
Wha meekly gie your *hurdies* to the smiters.—BURNS: *The Brigs of Ayr.*

Thir breeks o' mine, my only pair,
That ance were plush, o' guid blue hair,
I wad ha'e gi'en them aff my *hurdies*,
For ae blink o' the bonnie burdies!
—BURNS: *Tam O'Shanter.*

Pendable? ye may say that; his craig wad ken the weight of his *hurdies* if they could get haud o' Rob.—SCOTT: *Rob Roy.*

The old French poet, François Villon, when condemned to be hung, wrote a stanza in which the above idea of Sir Walter Scott occurs in language about as forcible and not a whit more elegant:—

> Je suis Français (dont ce me poise),
> Né de Paris, emprês Ponthoise,
> Or d'une corde d'une toise
> Sçaura mon col que mon cul poise.

Burns also uses the word in the sense of "rounded or swelling," without reference to any portion of the human frame, as in the following:—

> The groaning trencher there ye fill;
> Your *hurdies* like a distant hill.
> —*To a Haggis.*

Hurkle, to yield obedience or deference.

> Grant, an' Mackenzie, an' Murray,
> An' Cameron will *hurkle* to nane.
> HOGG, *the Ettrick Shepherd.*

Hurl, to wheel; *hurl-barrow*, wheel-barrow; a corruption of *whirl*, to turn round; *hurlcyhacket*, a contemptuous name for an ill-hung carriage or other vehicle.

> It's *kittle* for the cheeks when the *hurlbarrow* gangs o'er the brig o' the nose.
> —ALLAN RAMSAY'S *Scots Proverbs.*

"I never thought to have entered ane o' these *hurley-hackets*," she said, as she seated herself, "and sic a thing as it is—scarce room for twa folk."—SCOTT: *St. Ronan's Well.*

Hynde, gentle, courteous. An illiterate member of Parliament in the unruly session of 1887 objected to the use of this word as applied to an agricultural labourer, believing that it signified a deer or other quadruped, and never having suspected that it was a term of courtesy. The member himself, called honourable by the courtesy of Parliament, was ignorant of the fact that courtesy was extended even to farm-labourers by all gentlemen and men of good heart and good manners.

Then she is to yon *hynde* squire's yetts,
And tirled at the pin,
And wha sae busy as the *hynde* squire
To let the lady in.
—BUCHAN's *Ancient Ballads : Hynd*
Horn.

Hyte, joyous; excited unduly or overmuch.

Ochone for poor Castalian drinkers !
: The witchin', cursed, delicious blinkers
Ha'e put me *hyte.*
—BURNS : *Epistle to Major Logan.*

This word is derived from the Gaelic *aite,* joy, gladness, fun, and appears to be related to the English *hoity-toity.*

I

Ier-oe, a great grandchild; erroneously spelled *jeroy* in the new editions of Jamieson, and cited as a " Shetland word."

May health and peace with mutual rays
! Shine on the evening o' his days,
Till his wee curlie John's *ier oe,*
When ebbing life nae mair shall flow,
The last sad mournful rites bestow.
—BURNS : *A Dedication to Gavin*
Hamilton.

The word is from the Gaelic *oghe,* a grandchild, and *iar,* after; whence an after grandchild, or great grandchild.

Igo and ago, iram, coram, dago.
The chorus of ancient Gaelic boat-songs, or *Ramh-rans,* introduced by Burns in his song, " Ken ye aught o' Captain Grose ?" The words resolve themselves into the Gaelic *aighe, aghach, iorram, corruig-heamh dachaidh,* which signify " Joyous and brave is the song of the boat that is rowing homewards."

Ilka, each, as " ilka ane," each one; *ilk,* that same. *Ilk* is used

for the designation of a person whose patronymic is the same as the name of his estate—such as Mackintosh of Mackintosh—*i.e.,* Mackintosh of that *Ilk.* This Scottish word has crept into English, though with a strange perversion of its meaning, as in the following :—

We know, however, that many barbarians of their *ilk,* and even of later times, knowingly destroyed many a gold and silver vessel that fell into their hands.—*St. James's Gazette.*

Matilda lived in St. John's Villas, Twickenham ; Mr. Passmore in King Street of the same *ilk.—Daily Telegraph.*

Ingine, genius, " the fire of genius" or "poetic fire," are common expressions. Burns, in an " Epistle to John Lapraik," whose poetry he greatly admired, and thought equal to that of Alexander Pope or James Beattie, made inquiries concerning him, and was told that he was " an odd kind o' chiel about Muirkirk."

An' sae about him there I spier't,
Then a' that ken'd him round declar't
    He had *ingine*,
That nane excelled it—few cam near't,
    It was sae fine.

It would seem on first consideration that this peculiarly Scottish word was of the same Latin derivation as genius, ingenious, ingenuity, and the archaic English word cited in Halliwell, "ingene," which is translated "genius or wit." It is open to inquiry, however, whether the idea of *fire* does not underlie the word, and whether it is not in the form in which Burns employs it, traceable to the Gaelic *ain*, an intransitive prefix or particle signifying great, very, or intense; and *teine*, fire.

The late Samuel Rogers, author of the "Pleasures of Memory," in a controversy with me on the character of Lord Byron, spoke very unfavourably of his poetical genius, which I praised and defended to the best of my ability. Mr. Rogers, however, always returned to the attack with renewed vigour. Driven at last to extremity, I thought to clench all argument by saying —"At least you will admit, Mr. Rogers, that there was *fire* in Byron's poetry?" "Yes," he answered, "*hell-fire !*"—C. M.

I n g l e, the fire; *ingle-side*, the fireside, the hearth; *ingle-neuk*, the chimney corner; *ingle-bred*, home-bred, or bred at the domestic hearth; *inglin*, fuel.

Better a wee *ingle* to warm you, than a muckle fire to burn you.—ALLAN RAMSAY'S *Scots Proverbs*.

His wee bit *ingle* blinkin' bonnilie.
                        —BURNS.

It's an auld story now, and everybody tells it, as we were doing, in their ain way by the *ingle-side*.—SCOTT : *Guy Mannering*.

The derivation of *ingle*, in the Scottish sense of the word, is either from the Gaelic *aingeal*, the Kymric *engyl*, heat, fire, or from *ion*, fit, becoming, comfortable; and *cuil*, a corner. That of the English *ingle*, meaning a favourite, a friend, or lover, is not easy to discover. The word occurs in a passage from an Elizabethan play, with a detestable title, quoted by Nares :—

Call me your love, your *ingle*, your cousin, or so ; but *sister* at no hand.

Also in Massinger's "City Madam" :—

His quondam patrons, his dear *ingils* now.

Ingle, from one signifying a lover in the legitimate use of that word, was corrupted into an epithet for the male lover of a male, in the most odious sense. In "Donne's Elegies," it is used as signifying amorous endearment of a child to its father :—

Thy little brother, which like fairy spirits,
Oft skipped into our chamber those sweet nights
And kissed and *ingled* on thy father's knee.

No satisfactory etymology for the English word has ever been suggested, and that from the Spanish *yngle*, the groin, which finds favour with Nares and other philologists, is manifestly inadmissible. It is possible, however, that the English *ingle* was originally the same as the Scottish, and that its first

G

meaning as " love " was derived from the idea still current, that calls a beloved object a *flame.* Hotten's Slang Dictionary has "*flame*, a sweetheart." *Ingle* was sometimes written *enghle*, which latter word, according to Mr. Halliwell, signifies, as used by Ben Jonson, a gull—also, to coax or to wheedle.

Intill, into ; *till*, to. What's *in-till't?* What's in it ?

An English traveller, staying at a great hotel in Edinburgh, was much pleased with the excellence of the hotch-potch at dinner, and asked the head-waiter how it was made, and of what it was made? The waiter replied that there were peas *intill't*, and beans *intill't*, and onions *intill't.* " But what's *intill't?* " asked the Englishman. " I'm just tellin' you that there's beans *intill't*, and peas *intill't*, and neeps *intill't*, and carrots *intill't* "——
"Yes! yes! I know—beans, peas, onions, turnips, and carrots," said the Englishman ; " but what's *intill't?* Is it salt, pepper, or what? Please tell me what's *intill't?* "
" Eh, man ! " replied the impatient waiter, " ye maun be unco' slow o' comprehension. I was tellin' ye owre and owre again that there are beans *intill't*, and peas *intill't* "——
" And *tult!* What the devil is *tult*, or *intill't*, or whatever the name is? Can you not give a plain answer to a plain question? Does *tult* mean barley, or mutton, or mustard, or some nameless ingredient that is a trade secret, or that you are afraid to mention? "

" Oh, man ! " said the waiter, with a groan, " if I had your head in my keeping, I'd gie it sic a thumpin' as wad put some smeddum *intill't.* "
Tradition records that the Englishman has never yet ascertained what *intill't* means, but wanders through Scotland vainly seeking enlightenment.—*Knife and Fork*, edited by BLANCHARD JERROLD.

I wish ye were in Heckie-burnie.
"This," says Jamieson, "is a strange form of imprecation. The only account given of this place is that it is three miles beyond *hell.* In Aberdeen, if one says, 'go to the devil!' the other often replies, 'go you to *Heckie-burnie!*" No etymology is given. Possibly it originated in the pulpit, when some Gaelic preacher had taken the story of Dives and Lazarus for his text ; and the rich Dives, amid his torments in hell, asked in vain for a drop of water to cool his parched tongue. The intolerable thirst was his greatest punishment ; and in Gaelic *Aicheadh* is refusal, and *buirne*, water from the burn or stream, whence the phrase would signify the refusal or denial of water. This is offered as a suggestion only, to account for an expression that has been hitherto given up as inexplicable.

J

Jamph, to trudge, to plod, to make way laboriously, to grow weary with toil; also, to endeavour to take liberties with an unwilling or angry woman; to pursue her under difficulty and obstruction.

"Oh bonnie lass!" says he, "ye'll gie's a kiss,
And I shall set you right on, hit or miss."
"A hit or miss, I want na help of you,—
Kiss ye sklate stanes, they winna wat your mou."
And off she goes;—the fellow loot a rin,
As gin he ween'd with speed to tak her in;
But as luck was, a knibbloch took his tae,
And o'er fa's he, and tumbles down the brae;
His neebor leugh, and said it was well wair'd—
"Let never *jamphers* yet be better sair'd."
—Ross's *Helenore.*

The etymology of *jamph*—whether it means to plod or flirt, or both—is obscure. It is possibly, but not certainly, from the Gaelic *deanamh* (*de* pronounced as *je*), doing, acting, performing. Jamieson thinks that, in the sense of flirting, it may come from the Teutonic *schimpfen*, to mock; and in the sense of plod or trudge, from *schampfen*, to slip aside.

Jauner, idle talk; to wander listlessly about without any particular object.

Oh, haud your tongue now, Luckie Laing,
Oh, haud your tongue and *jauner.*
—Burns: *The Lass of Ecclefechan.*
We'se had a good *jauner* this forenoon.
—Jamieson.

In the sense of wandering idly, this word seems to be but a variety or corruption of *dauner.*

Jawp, to bespatter with mud or water. To "*jawp* the water" is a metaphor for spending time in any negotiation or transaction without coming to a definite conclusion, "I'll no *jawp* water wi' ye"—"I'll not enter into further discussions or wrangles with you." "To *jawp* waters with one," to play fast and loose, to strive to be off a bargain once made.

Then down ye'll hurl, deil nor ye never rise,
And dash the gumly *jawps* up to the skies.
—Burns: *The Brigs of Ayr.*

Jawthers, quasi synonymous with the English slang "to *jaw*," to dispute or argue abusively, as in the phrase "let me have none of your *jaw.*" *Jawthers*, idle wranglings, and also any frivolous discourse.

Jee, to move. This word survives in English as a command to a horse, in the phrase *jee-up* and *jee-wo.*

I am sick an' very love sick,
Ae foot I canna *jee.*
—Buchan's *Ancient Ballads.*

Jimp, slender in the waist.

She is as *jimp* i' the middle sae fou'
As is a willow wand.
—*The Laird o' Warriston.*

Jink, to play, to sport, to dodge in and out, from whence the phrase "high-jinks," sometimes used in England to describe the merriment and sport of servants in the kitchen when their masters and mistresses are out; a quick or sudden movement; also to escape, to trick, "to gie the *jink*," to give the slip, to elude.

And now, auld Cloots, I ken ye're thinkin'
A certain bardie, rantin', drinkin',
Some luckless hour will send him linkin'
  To your black pit;
But faith he'll turn a corner *jinkin*',
  And cheat ye yet!
    —BURNS: *Address to the Deil.*

¦ Lang may your elbuck *jink* and diddle.
    —BURNS: *Second Epistle to Davie.*

Oh, thou, my muse! guid auld Scotch drink,
Whether through wimplin' worms thou *jink*,
Or, richly brown, ream o'er the brink
In glorious faem.
    —BURNS: *Scotch Drink.*

Jamieson derives the word from the Swedish *dwink-a*, and the German *schwinken*, to move quickly, but no such word appears in the German dictionaries, and the etymology is otherwise unsatisfactory. The Gaelic *dian* (pronounced *jian*) and *dianach* signifies brisk, nimble, which is probably the root of *jink* as used by Burns.

Jirble, jirgle. Both of these words signify to spill any liquid by making it move from side to side in the vessel that contains it; to empty any liquid from one vessel to another; also, the small quantity left in a glass or tea-cup.

The waur for themselves and for the country baith, St. Ronan's; it's the junketing and the *jirbling* in tea and sic trumpery that brings our nobles to ninepence, and mony a het ha' house to a hired lodging in the Abbey.—SCOTT: *St. Ronan's Well.*

Jock in Scottish, and in English *Jack*, are used as familiar substitutes for the Christian name John, and are supposed to be derived from the French *Jacques.* This word, however, means James, and not John. The use of the prefixes *Jack* and *Jock* in many English and Scottish compounds that have no obvious reference to the Christian names either of James or John, suggests that there may possibly be a different origin for the word. Among others that may be cited, are *Jack*-tar, *Jack*-priest, *Jack*-of-all-trades, and such implements in common use as boot-*jack*, roasting-*jack*, *jack*-knife, the *jacks* or hammers of a pianoforte, the *jack* or clapper of a bell, *jack*-boots, *jack*-chain, the Union-*jack* or flag, *jack*-staff, *jack*-towel, *jack*-block, and many others which are duly set forth in the dictionaries, without suggestion of any other etymology than that from John. Shakspeare in his sonnets uses the word *jack* for the hammers of the virginal, and in *Richard II.* employs it to signify a working-man:—

Since every *jack* became a gentleman,
There's many a gentle person made a *jack.*

Besides the Scottish term of familiarity or affection for a man, the word *Jock* occurs in two singular words cited by Jamieson—*Jock-te-leer*, which he says is a cant term for a pocket almanack, "derived from *Jock* the liar," from the loose or false predictions with regard to the weather which are contained in such publications; and *Jock-te-leg*, a folding or clasp-knife.

It is difficult to connect either the Scottish *Jock* or the English *Jack* in these words with the name of John, unless upon the supposition that John and Jack are synonymous with *man*, and that the terms are transferable to any and every implement that aids or serves the purpose of a man's work. Is it not possible that *Jock* and *Jack* are mere varieties of the Gaelic *deagh* (the *de* pronounced as *j*), which signifies good, excellent, useful, befitting? or the Kymric *iach*, whole, useful? and *deach*, a movement for a purpose? This derivation would meet the sense of all the compound words and phrases in which *jock* and *jack* enter, other than those in which it indubitably signifies a Christian name.

The word *jocteleer*—an almanack, in Jamieson—tried by this test, would signify, good to examine, to learn; from *deagh*, good, and *leir*, perception.

In like manner, the English words and phrases, *Jack*-tar, *Jack*-priest, *Jack*-of-all-trades, might signify good, able-bodied sailor, good priest, and good at all trades. Even jockey, a good rider, may be derivable from the same source. Thus, too, in Shakspeare's phrase, *Jack* may signify, not a John, as a generic name, but *deagh* (*jeack*), as applied in the common phrase "my good man," and in French *bon homme*— epithets which, although in one sense respectful, are only employed by superiors to inferiors, and infer somewhat of social depreciation.

In reference to *Jocteleg* or *Jocktelag*, it should be mentioned that Burns spells the word in the first manner, and Allan Ramsay in the second. Jamieson says that there was once a famous cutler of Liege, in Belgium, named Jacques, and that his cutlery being in repute, any article of his make was called a *Jacques de Liege*. As no mention of this man or his business has been found anywhere except in the pages of Jamieson, it has been suspected that the name was evolved from the imagination of that philologist. Whether that be so or not, it is curious that the Gaelic *dioghail* signifies to avenge, and *dioghail taiche* (pronounced *joy-al taiche*), an avenger. In early times it was customary to bestow names of affection upon swords, such as *Excalibur*, the sword of King Arthur, *Durandarte*, and many others, the swords of renowned knights of romance and chivalry; and if upon swords, probably upon daggers and knives; and no epithet in a barbarous age—when every man had to depend upon his own prowess for self-defence or revenge for injuries—could be more appropriate for a strong knife than the "avenger."

Joe or Jo, a lover, a friend, a dear companion; derived not from Joseph, as has been asserted, nor from the French *joie* or English *joy*, as Jamieson supposes, but more probably from the Gaelic *deo* (the *d* pronounced as *j*), the soul, the vital spark, the life; Greek ζῶη.

> John Anderson my *jo*, John.
> —BURNS.

> Kind sir, for your courtesy,
>   As ye gae by the Bass, then,
> For the love ye bear to me,
>   Buy me a keeking-glass, then.
> Keek into the clear draw-well,
>   Janet, Janet,
> There ye'll see your bonnie sel',
>   My *jo*, Janet.
> —*Old Song: remodelled by* BURNS.

Joram, a boat song; a rowing song, in which the singers keep time with their voices to the motion of the oars; from the modern Gaelic *iorram.* This word is often erroneously used in the phrase "push about the *jorum*," as if *jorum* signified a bowl of liquor which had to be passed round the table. An instance of this mistake occurs in Burns:—

> And here's to them that, like oursel',
>   Can push about the *jorum*;
> And here's to them that wish us weel—
>   May a' that's guid watch o'er 'em.
> —*Oh May, thy Morn.*

The ancient and correct Gaelic for a boat song is *oran iomraidh* or *iomramh;* from *oran,* a song; *iom,* many, and *ramh,* an oar, of which *iorram,* or the song of many oars, is a corruption. The connection between *iorram,* a boat song, and *jorum,* a drinking vessel, is probably due to the circumstance that the chorus of the boat song was often sung by the guests at a convivial party, when the bottle or bowl was put in circulation.

Jouk, to stoop down; in the English vernacular to duck the head, or duck down; also to evade a question. *Jouker,* a dissembler, a deceiver.

> Neath the brae the burnie *jouks.*
> —TANNAHILL: *Gloomy Winter.*

> *Jouk* and let the jaw go by (*Proverb*)— *i.e.,* evade replying to intemperate or abusive language.

Jow, the swing or boom of a large bell.

> Now Clinkumbell
> Began to *jow.*
> —BURNS: *The Holy Fair.*

> And every *jow* the kirk bell gied.
> BUCHAN's *Ancient Ballads.*

> *Jow* means to swing, and not the "clang or boom of a large bell."

> Now Clinkumbell, wi' rattling tone
> Began to *jow* and croon.

> The bell-rope began to shake,—the bell began to swing (*jow*) and (croon) ring out.
> —R. DRENNAN.

Jowler. This word is used by Burns in the "Address of Beelzebub to the President of the Highland Society," in which, speaking of gipsies, he says:—

An' if the wives an' dirty brats
E'en thigger at your doors an' yetts,
Get out a horsewhip or a *jowler*,
.   .   .   .   .   .
An' gar the tattered gipsies pack
Wi' a' their bastards on their back.

Jamieson does not include the word in his Dictionary, nor do the glossaries to Allan Ramsay or Burns contain it. By the context, it would seem to mean a cudgel. In this sense the word has support in the northern counties of England. *Jolle,* according to Mr. Halliwell Phillips, signifies to beat ; and *jowler* means thick and clumsy—epithets which describe a bludgeon and a cudgel.

"Did you give him a good drubbing?"
"I gave him a good tidy *jowling.*"—
WRIGHT'S *Archaic Dictionary.*

In the sense of thick and clumsy, *jolle* and *jowl* are apparently the roots of English *jolter-head,* a thick-headed fellow. *Jowler,* as the name of an instrument of punishment, whether a cudgel or not, is probably from the Gaelic *diol* (*jole, d* pronounced as *j*), to punish, to avenge, to requite, to pay ; *diolair,* an avenger. In colloquial English the threat, "I'll pay you out," has a similar meaning.

Jundie, to jostle, to struggle, to contend and push in a crowd ; to *hoy-shouther,* or push with the shoulders in order to force a way.

If a man's gaun down the brae, ilk ane gi'es him a *jundie.*—ALLAN RAMSAY'S *Scots Proverbs.*

The warldly race may drudge and drive,
Hog-shouther, *jundie,* stretch, and strive.
—BURNS : *To William Simpson.*

Jute, a term of reproach applied to a weak, worthless, spiritless person, especially to a woman. It is also used in reference to sour or stale liquor, and to weak broth or tea. It seems to be derived from the Gaelic *diùid* (*diù* pronounced as *ju*), sneaking, mean-spirited, silly, weak ; and *diu,* the worst, the refuse of things.

K

Kail, cabbage, the German *kohl ;* a word that survives in English in the first syllable of *cauliflower.* By an extension of meaning *kail* sometimes signifies dinner, as in the familiar invitation once common, "Come an' tak' your *kail* wi' me," *i.e.,* come and dine with me.

Kail-runt, a cabbage stalk ; *kail-blade,* a cabbage leaf.

When I lookit to my dart,
It was sae blunt,
Fient haet it wad hae pierced the heart
O' a *kail-runt.*
—BURNS : *Death and Dr. Hornbook.*

Just —— in a *kail-blade* and send it,—
Baith the disease and what'll mend it,
At ance he'll tell't.—*Idem.*

Kain, tribute, tax, tithe; from the Gaelic *cain*, tribute; *cain-cach*, tributary.

> Our laird gets in his racked rents,
> His coal, his *kain*.
> —BURNS: *The Twa Dogs.*
> *Kain* to the King.
> —*Jacobite Song* (1715).

Kain-bairns, says a note in Sir Walter Scott's "Minstrelsy of the Scottish Border," were infants, according to Scottish superstition, that were seized in their cradles by warlocks and witches, and paid as a *kain*, or tax, to their master the devil. Jamieson is in error in deriving *kain* from the Gaelic *cean*, the head.

Kaur-handit, left-handed. In this combination, *kaur* does not signify the left as distinguished from the right, but is from the Gaelic *car*, signifying a twist or turn. The hand so designated implies that it is twisted or turned into a function that ought to be performed by the other.

Kaury-maury is used in the "Vision of Piers Ploughman."

> Clothed in a *kaury-maury*
> I couthe it nought descryve.

In the glossary to Mr. Thomas Wright's edition of this ancient poem, he suggests that *kaury-maury* only means care and trouble; a conjecture that is supported by the Gaelic *car*, and *mearachd*, an error, a mistake, a wrong, an injustice.

Kebar, a rafter, a beam in the roof of a house; from the Gaelic *.cabar*, a pole, the trunk of a tree. "Putting" or throwing the *cabar* is a gymnastic feat still popular at Highland games in Scotland.

> He ended, and the *kebars* shook
> Above the chorus roar.
> —BURNS: *The Jolly Beggars.*

Kebbuck, a cheese; *kebbuck heel,* a remnant or hunk of cheese. From the Gaelic *cabag*, a cheese.

> The weel-hained *kebbuck*.
> —BURNS: *Cotter's Saturday Night.*
> In comes a gaucie, gash, gude wife,
> An' sits down by the fire;
> Syne draws her *kebbuck* and her knife—
> The lasses they are shyer.
> —BURNS: *The Holy Fair.*

Keck or **keckle,** to draw back from a bargain, to change one's mind, to flinch; from the Gaelic *caochail*, to change.

> "I have *keck'd*"—I decline adhering to the offer.—JAMIESON.

Keckle is also a form of the English *cackle*, and has no affinity or synonymity with *keck*.

Keek, to peep, to pry, to look cautiously about; possibly from the Gaelic *cidh*, pronounced *kidh* or *kee*, to see; a *cidhis*, a mask to cover the face all but the eyes, a vizor.

> The robin came to the wren's nest
> And *keekit* in.—*Nursery Rhyme.*
> Stars dinna *keek* in,
> And see me wi' Mary.—BURNS.
> When the tod [fox] is in the wood, he
> cares na how many folk *keek* at his tail.—
> ALLAN RAMSAY'S *Scots Proverbs.*

A clergyman in the West of Scotland once concluded a prayer as follows :—" O Lord ! Thou art like a mouse in a drystane dyke, aye *keekin'* out at us frae holes and crannies, but we canna see Thee."— ROGERS' *Illustrations of Scottish Life.*

Keeking-glass, a looking-glass, a mirror.

She. Kind sir, for your courtesy,
    As ye gang by the Bass, then,
For the love ye bear to me,
    Buy me a *keeking-glass,* then.

He. *Keek* into the draw-well,
    Janet, Janet !
There ye'll see your bonnie sel',
    My jo, Janet.—BURNS.

Keel or keill, a small vessel or skiff, a lighter, and not merely the *keel* of any ship or boat as in English. It is synonymous with *coracle*, or the Gaelic *curach,* and is probably derived from the Gaelic *caol,* narrow, from its length as distinguished from its breadth.

Oh, merry may the *keel* row,
The *keel* row, the *keel* row ;
Oh, merry may the *keel* row,
The ship that my love's in.
    —*Northern Ballad.*

Keelivine, a crayon pencil. Origin unknown.

Kell, a woman's cap; from the Gaelic *ceil,* a covering.

Then up and gat her seven sisters,
    And served to her a *kell,*
And every steek that they put in
    Sewed to a silver bell.
    —*Border Minstrelsy : The Gay Goss-hawk.*

Kelpie, a water-sprite. Etymology unknown ; that suggested by Jamieson from *calf* is not probable.

What is it ails my good bay mare ?
    What is it makes her start and shiver ?
She sees a *kelpie* in the stream,
    Or fears the rushing of the river.
    —*Legends of the Isles.*

The *kelpie* gallop'd o'er the green,
    He seemed a knight of noble mien ;
And old and young stood up to see,
    And wondered who this knight could be.
    —*Idem.*

The side was steep, the bottom deep,
    Frae bank to bank the water pouring ;
And the bonnie lass did quake for fear,
    She heard the water-*kelpie* roaring.
    —*Ballad of Annan Water.*

Keltie, a large glass or bumper, to drain which was imposed as a punishment upon those who were suspected of not drinking fairly. "Cleared *keltie* aff," according to Jamieson, was a phrase that signified that the glass was quite empty. The word seems to be derived from *kelter,* to tilt up, to tip up, to turn upside down, and to have been applied to the glasses used in the hard-drinking days of our great-grandfathers, that were made without stems, and rounded at the bottom like the Dutch dolls that roll from side to side, from inability to stand upright. With a glass of this kind in his hand, the toper had to empty it before he could replace it on the table. Jamieson was probably ignorant of this etymology, though he refers to the German *kelter,* which signifies a wine-press. *Keltern,* in the same language, is to tread the grapes. But these words do not apply to either the Scottish *keltie* or *kelter.*

Kemmin, a champion, a corruption of *kemp (q.v.)*.

> He works like a *kemmin*.
> He fechts like a *kemmin*.
> —JAMIESON.

The Kymric has *ceimmyn*, a striver in games; the Flemish *kampen;* and German *kämpfen*, to fight, to struggle, to contend.

Kemp, a warrior, a hero, a champion; also to fight, to strive, to contend for the superiority or the mastery. *Kemper* is one who *kemps* or contends; used in the harvest field to signify a reaper who excels his comrades in the quantity and quality of his work. *Kempion*, or *Kemp Owain*, is the name of the champion in two old Scottish ballads who "borrows," or ransoms, a fair lady from the spells cast upon her by demoniacal agency, by which she was turned into the shape of a wild beast. *Kempion*, or *Kemp Owain*, kisses her thrice, notwithstanding her hideousness and loathsomeness, and so restores her to her original beauty. *Kempion* is printed in Scott's "Border Minstrelsy," and *Kemp Owain* in Motherwell's "Minstrelsy, Ancient and Modern."

Kennawhat, a nondescript, a "je ne sais quoi," or know-not-what.

Kenspeckle, noticeable, conspicuous, noteworthy.

Kep, to catch, to receive; from the Gaelic *ceap*, to intercept, to stop, to receive.

> Ilka blade o' grass *keps* its ain drap o' dew.
> —JAMES BALLANTINE.

> Ilk cowslip cup shall *kep* a tear.
> —BURNS.

Ker haund or **ker-handed**, left-handed, awkward; from the Gaelic, *cer*, a twist; and *cearr*, wrong, awkward. See KAUR-HANDIT, *ante*.

> It maun be his left foot foremost, unless he was *ker-haund.—Noctes Ambrosianæ*.

Ket, a fleece; *tawted ket*, a matted or ropy fleece. From the Gaelic *ceath*, a sheep or sheep-skin.

> She was nae get o' moorland tips,
> Wi' *tawted ket* an' hairy hips.
> —BURNS.

Kevil, a lot; to cast *kevils*, to draw lots.

> Let every man be content with his ain *kevil.*—ALLAN RAMSAY'S *Scots Proverbs*.

> And they coost *kevils* them amang
> Wha should to the greenwood gang.
> —COSPATRICK : *Border Minstrelsy*.

Kidney. "Of the same *kidney*," of a like sort. The Slang Dictionary has, "Two of a *kidney*, or two of a sort—as like as two pears, or two *kidneys* in a bunch." Sir Richard Ayscough says that Shakspeare's phrase, which he put into the mouth of Falstaff, means "a man whose *kidneys* are as fat as mine—*i.e.*, a man as fat as I am." A little knowledge of the original language of the British people would show the true root of the word to be the Gaelic *ceudna*—pronounced *keudna*, sort, or of the same sort ; *ceudnachd*, identity, similarity.

> Think of that ! a man of my *kidney*, that am as subject to heat as butter.—*Merry Wives of Windsor*.

Your poets, spendthrifts, and other fools of that *kidney.*—BURNS: *Letter to Mr. Robert Ainslie.*

Kill-cow, an expressive colloquialism which signifies a difficulty that may be surmounted by resolution and energy. Jamieson translates it "a matter of consequence, a serious affair; as in the phrase, 'Ye needna mind; I'm sure it's nae sic great *kill-cow;*'" and adds, "in reference, most probably, to a blow that is sufficient to knock down or *kill a cow!*" Jamieson forgot the reference in his own Dictionary to *cow,* in which the word signifies a ghost, spectre, or goblin. The phrase might be rendered, "a ghost that might be laid without much difficulty."

Killicoup, a somersault, head-over-heels.

That gang tried to keep violent leasehold o' your ain fields, an' your ain ha', till ye gied them a *killicoup.*—HOGG's *Brownie of Bodsbeck.*

Kilt, a garment worn by Highlanders, descending from the waist to the middle of the knee; to lift the petticoats up to the knee, or wear them no lower than the knee; to raise the clothes in fording a stream. "High kilted" is a metaphor applied to conversation or writing that savours of immodesty. From the Gaelic *ceil,* to cover; *ceilte,* covered.

Her tartan petticoat she'll *kilt.*
—BURNS: *Cry and Prayer.*

She's *kilted* her coats o' green satin,
She's *kilted* them up to the knee,
And she's off wi' Lord Ronald M'Donald,
His bride and his darling to be.
—*Old Song: Lizzie Lindsay.*

Kimmer, a female friend, gossip, or companion; from the French *commère;* synonymous with the English *gammer.*

My *kimmer* and I gaed to the fair
Wi' twal punds Scots on sarkin' to wear;
But we drank the gude braw hawkie dry,
And sarkless cam hame, my *kimmer* and I.
—CROMEK's *Remains.*

Kink, a knot, an entanglement, an involution; the same in Flemish; whence *kink-host,* or *kink-cough,* the hooping-cough, or generally a violent fit of coughing, in which the paroxysm seems to twist knots into each other. The word *kink* is sometimes applied to a fit of irrepressible laughter. *Kink-cough* has been corrupted in English into *king*-cough. Mr. Robert Chambers, on a note on *kink,* which occurs in the "Ballad of the Laird o' Logie," explains it as meaning to wring the fingers till the joints crack, which he says is a very striking though a simple delineation of grief.

And sae she tore her yellow hair,
Kinking her fingers ane by ane,
And cursed the day that she was born.

Kinnen, rabbits; corruption of the English *coney.*

Make *kinnen* and caper ready, then,
And venison in greit plentie,
We'll welcome here our royal King.
—*Ballad of Johnnie Armstrong.*

Kinsh. According to Jamieson, this word signifies kindred.

The man may *eithly* tine a *stot* that canna count his *kinsh.*—ALLAN RAMSAY'S *Scots Proverbs.*

"The man may easily lose a young ox that cannot count his *kinsh.*" The meaning of *kinsh* in this passage is not clear. It has been suggested that it is a misprint for either *kine* or *kindred.* Perhaps, however, the true meaning is to be sought in the Gaelic *cinneas* (*kinneash*), which means growth or natural increase. This interpretation renders the proverb intelligible—a man may afford to lose one stot who cannot count the increase of his flocks and herds.

Kintra cooser, one who runs about the country; a term sometimes applied to an entire horse, which is taken from place to place for the service of mares.

If that daft buckie, Geordie Wales,
Was threshin' still at hizzie's tails,
Or if he was grown oughtlins douser,
And no a perfect *kintra cooser.*
    —BURNS : *To one who had sent him a newspaper.*

The word *cooser* appears in Shakspeare as *cosier* or *cozier*, and has puzzled all the commentators to explain it. *Cosier's catches* were songs sung by working men over their libations in roadside ale-houses. Johnson thought that *cosier* must mean a *tailor*, from *coudre*, to sew; and *cousue*, that which is sewed ;

while others equally erudite were of opinion that *cosiers* were *cobblers* or *tinkers.* The *cosiers* who sang *catches* might have belonged to all or any of these trades ; but the word, now obsolete in English, and almost obsolete in Scotch, is the Gaelic *cosaire*, a pedestrian, a wayfarer, a tramp. Up to the time of Dr. Johnson's visit to the Hebrides, Highland gentlemen of wealth or importance used to keep servants or gillies to run before them, who were known as *cosiers*—misprinted by Boswell as *coshirs.* Jamieson, unaware of the simple origin of the word, as applied to a horse made to perambulate the country, states that *cooser* is a stallion, and derives it from the French *coursier*, a courser. But courser itself is from the same root, from *course*, a journey. The coarse allusion of Burns to the Prince of Wales expressed a hope that he had ceased to run about the country after women.

Kipper, to split, dry, and cure fish by salting them. Kippered herrings, haddocks, and salmon are largely prepared and consumed in Scotland, and to a much smaller extent in the large cities of England. The mode of *kippering* is scarcely known to the south of the Tweed, and where known, is not so successfully practised, or with such delicate and satisfactory results, as in Scotland. The derivation of the word is uncertain.

Kirk, is the original form of the word, which has been Anglicised into *church*. It is derived from the idea of, and is identical with, circle or *kirkle*, the form in which, in the primitive ages of the world, and still later, in the Druidical era, all places of worship — whether of the supreme God or of the Sun, supposed to be His visible representative—were always constructed. The great stone circle, or *kirkle*, of Stonehenge was one of the earliest kirks, or churches, erected in these islands. The traces of many smaller stone circles are still to be found in Scotland. The word is derived feom the Gaelic *coir*, a circle; whence also *court*, and the French *cour*.

Kirnie, a forward boy who gives himself prematurely and offensively the airs and habits of a man. Shakspeare speaks of "kerns and gallowglasses," *kern* being a contraction of the Gaelice *eathairneach* [*kearneach*], an armed peasant serving in the army, also a boor or sturdy fellow. Jamieson derives *kirnie* from the Kymric *coryn* or *cor*, a dwarf or pigmy; but as the Lowland Scottish people were more conversant with their neighbours of the Highlands than with the distant Welsh, it is probable that the Gaelic and not the Kymric derivation of the word is the correct one.

Kist, a chest, a trunk, a box; from the French *caisse*.

Steek the awmrie, shut the *kist*,
Or else some gear will soon be mist.
—SIR WALTER SCOTT: *Donald Caird.*

A man who had had four wives, and who meditated a fifth time entering the marriage state, was conversing with a friend on the subject, who was rather disposed to barter upon his past matrimonial experience, as having made a good deal of money by his wives. " Na! na!" said he, "they came to me wi' auld *kists*, an' I sent them hame (to the grave) wi' new anes."—DEAN RAMSAY.

Kith, known to or acquainted with; from *kythe*, to show, and the old English *couth*, to know or see; a word that survives in *concouth*, with a somewhat different meaning, as strange, odd, or unfamiliar. *Kith* is generally in modern English used in combination with *kin*, as *kith* and *kin*, whence the word is erroneously supposed to mean relationship in blood and ancestry, and to be synonymous with *kin* and *kinship*.

Whether thousands of our own *kith* shall be sacrificed to an obsolete shibboleth and the bloodthirsty operations of an artificial competition.—*Letter on Large Weights,* by ARNOLD WHITE—*Times, November 30,* 1887.

Kittle, difficult, ticklish, dangerous. From the Dutch and Flemish *kittelen*, to tickle.

It's *kittle* shooting at corbies and clergy.
It's *kittle* for the cheeks when the hurlbarrow gangs o'er the brig o' the nose.
Cats and maidens are *kittle* ware.
It's *kittle* to waken sleeping dogs.
—ALLAN RAMSAY's *Scots Proverbs.*

As for your priesthood I shall say but little,
Corbies and clergy are a shot right *kittle*.
—BURNS: *The Brigs of Ayr.*

Kivan, kivin. These words signify a covey, a bevy, a troop, a company, a flock, a crowd, or an assemblage. They are evidently from the Gaelic *coimh* (*coiv*), equivalent to the prefix *co* or *con*, and *feadhain* (*d* silent), a troop or band of people, or of living animals of any description.

Klem or clem. In Lancashire and other parts of England, *clem* signifies to become stupefied or worn out with hunger, to starve. In Scotland, *klem* sometimes means perverse, obstinate, insensible to reason and to argument; and, according to Jamieson, "means low, paltry, untrustworthy, unprincipled; and, as used by the boys of the High School of Edinburgh, curious, singular, odd, queer." He derives it from the Icelandic *kleima*, macula, a blot or stain—*i.e.*, having a character that lies under a stain. But the Icelandic does not convey either the Scottish or the English meaning of the word, which is in reality the Flemish *kleum*, lethargic, stupefied either from cold, hunger, or by defect of original vitality and force of mind or body. The Flemish *verkleumte* is translated in the French dictionaries as *engourdi*, benumbed, stupefied, stiffened. By a metaphorical extension of meaning, all these physical senses of the word apply to mental conditions, and thus account for all the varieties of the Scottish meaning.

The English *clem* may be possibly traced to the German *klemmen*, to pinch, to squeeze; from *klemme*, a narrow place, a strait, a difficulty, whence *clemmed*, pinched with hunger.

Knack, to taunt, to make a sharp answer; the same apparently as the English "nag," as applied to the *nagging* of a disagreeable woman. *Knacky*, or *knacksy*, quick at repartee.

Knappin-hammer. A hammer with a long handle used for breaking stones on the road, or in houses of detention for vagrants or criminals. From the English *knap* or *nap*, a smart blow on the head, as in the colloquial threat to an unruly boy, "you'll *nap* it."

What's a' your jargon o' the schools—
Your Latin names for books or stools;
If honest Nature made you fools,
    What sairs your grammars?
Ye'd better ta'en up spades or shools
    Or *knappin hammers*.
        —Burns: *Epistle to Lapraik.*

Kneef, active, alert; "ower *kneef*" or over active suggests, according to Jamieson, the charge of illicit intercourse. The derivation is probably from the Gaelic *gniomh* (gniof), a doer, to do, or a *deed*. The word is sometimes pronounced *griomh*, whence *grieve*, a factor, bailiff, or agent.

Jenny sat jouking like a mouse,
    But Jock was *kneef* as ony cock,
Says he to her, Haud up your brows,
    And fa' to your meet.
        —*The Wooing o' Jenny and Jock.*

Knowe, a hillock, a knoll.

Ca' the yowes [ewes] to the *knowes*.
—ALLAN RAMSAY.

Upon a *knowe* they sat them down,
And there began a long digression, ·
About the lords of the creation.
—BURNS: *The Twa Dogs.*

Knowe-head, the hill top.

Yon sunny *knowe-head* clad wi' bonnie
wild flowers.—JAMES BALLANTINE.

Knurl, a dwarf; *knurlin*, a dwarfling, or very little dwarf.

The miller was 'strappin', the miller was
ruddy—
A heart like a lord, and a hue like a lady,
The laird was a widdiefu' fleerit *knurl*—
She's left the good fellow, and taken the
churl.—BURNS: *Meg o' the Mill.*

Wee Pope, the *knurlin*, rives Horatian
fame.—BURNS: *On Pastoral Poetry.*

These words are apparently derived from the English *gnarl*, twisted, knotted, as in the phrase, "the *gnarled* oak," and the Teutonic *knorren*, a knot, a wart, a protuberance. They were probably first applied in derision to hunch-backed people, not so much for their littleness as for their deformity. Burns, when speaking of Pope as a *knurlin*, seems to have had in memory the ill-natured comparison of that poet to a note of interrogation, because "he was a *little crooked thing* that asked questions."
Through an English misconception of the meaning of "*a knurl*" (pronounced exactly like "*an earl*"), arose the vulgar slang of the London streets used to insult a hunchback.

· "My Lord" is a nickname given with mock humility to a hunchback.—HOTTEN's *Slang Dictionary.*

Koff or **coff**, to buy; from the Teutonic *kaufen*, Flemish *koopen*, to buy; whence by corruption *horse-kooper*, a dealer in horses.

Kindness comes wi' will; it canna be
kofft.—ALLAN RAMSAY's *Scots Proverbs.*

Kute, coot, or **queete**, the ankle. *Cutes* or *kutes*, according to Wright and Halliwell, is a Northern word for the feet. "To let one cool his *cutes* at the door (or in the lobby)," is a proverbial expression for letting a man wait unduly long in expectation of an interview. *Cootie* or *kutie* is a fowl whose legs are feathered. *Cootikins*, spatter-dashes or gaiters that go over the shoe and cover the ankle.

Your stockings shall be
Narrow, narrow at the *kutes*,
And braid, braid at the braune
[the brawn or calf].
—CHAMBERS' *Scottish Ballads.*

The firsten step that she steppit in [the
water],
She steppit to the *kute.*

· · · · · · ·
The neisten step that she wade in,
She waded to the knee;
Said she, "I wad wade further in,
Gin my true love I could see."
—*Willie and May Margaret.*

It is difficult to trace the origin of this peculiarly Scottish word. The French call the ankle the "*cheville* du pied." Bescherelle defines *cheville* as "part of the two bones of the leg which rise in a *boss* or *hump* on each side of the foot." The

Germans call the ankle the "knuckle of the foot." Jamieson derives *cute* from the Teutonic *kyte*, "*sura;*" but the Latin *sura* means the calf of the leg and not the ankle; and *kyte* is not to be found in any German or Teutonic dictionary. *Kyte*, in the Scottish vernacular, has nothing to do with *kute*, and signifies a part of the body far removed from the ankle, viz., the belly. Possibly the Swedish *kut*, a round boss or rising, as suggested in the extract from Bescherelle, may be the root of *cute*. The Gaelic affords no assistance to the discovery of the etymology. The word does not appear in the glossaries to Ramsay or Burns.

Kyle, a narrow strait of water between islands, or between an island and the mainland, as the *Kyles* of Bute, and *Kyle* Akin, between Skye and the continent of Scotland. The word is derived from the Gaelic *caol*, a narrow passage, a strait, whence *Calais*, the French town on the *straits* of Dover.

Kyte, the belly. *Kytie*, corpulent, big-bellied. The Gaelic *cuid*, victuals, food, has been suggested as the origin of the word, on the principle that to "have

a long *purse*," signifies to have money, or much money, so that to have a *kyte* is to have food to put into it. But this etymology is not satisfactory, nor is that given by Jamieson from the Icelandic.

Then horn for horn, they stretch and strive—
Deil tak' the hindmost—on they drive,
Till a' their well-filled *kytes* belyve
    Are stretched like drums.
        —BURNS: *To a Haggis.*

But while the wifie flate and gloom'd,
The tither cake wi' butter thoomb'd,
    She forced us still to eat,
Till our wee *kites* were straughtit fou,
When wi' our hearties at our mou',
    We felt maist like to greet.
—JAMES BALLANTINE: *The Pentland Hills.*

Kythe, to show or appear; and *kythesome*, of pleasant and prepossessing appearance. Jamieson has the phrase "*blythsome* and *kythsome*," used in Perthshire, and signifying, as he thinks, "happy in consequence of having abundance of property in *cows*." If he had remembered his own correct definition of *kythe*, "show, to be manifest," he would not in this instance have connected it with cows or *kye*, but would have translated the phrase, "blythe and pleasant of appearance."

Kythe is your ain colours, that folk may ken ye.—ALLAN RAMSAY.

L

Laigh, low, or low-down, short.

The higher the hill, the *laigher* the grass.
—ALLAN RAMSAY's *Scots Proverbs.*

Dance aye *laigh* and late at e'en.
—BURNS : *My Jo, Janet.*

Laired, overthrown, cast to the ground. From the Gaelic *lar*, the ground; the English *lair*, as applied to the retreat of a wild animal; or possibly from *lure*, to entice or inveigle.

Laired by *spunkies* i' the mire.
—GEORGE BEATTIE : *John o' Arnha'.*

Lammas, the first day of August; supposed to be derived from the Anglo-Saxon *hlaf*, a loaf, but more probably from *lamb*, the Lamb of God. All the ancient festivals appropriated to particular days had an ecclesiastical origin—such as Mary-mass (now called Lady Day), from the Virgin Mary ; Michaelmas, Hallowmas, Candlemas, Christmas, &c.

Landart, rural, in the country ; from landward.

There was a jolly beggar,
  And a begging he was boun',
And he took up his quarters
  Into a *landart* town.
—Song : *We'll Gang nae mair a Roving.*

Then come away, and dinna stay,
  What gars ye look sae *landart ?*
I'd have ye run, and not delay,
  To join my father's standard.
—COCKBURN : CHAMBERS's *Scottish Songs.*

Landlash, a great fall of rain, accompanied by a high wind. Jamieson is of opinion that this word is suggested by the idea that such a storm *lashes* the land. It is more probably from the Gaelic *lan*, full ; and *laiste*, fury ; whence *lanlaiste* (pronounced *lanlashte*, and abbreviated into *lanlash*), the storm in full fury. A *lash* of water signifies a great, heavy, or furious fall of rain.

Landlord and **landlady**. These words, commonly pronounced *lanlord* and *lanlady*, do not solely imply the proprietorship of land, as their constant application to the owners of public-houses, and to house-owners generally, as well as to women who merely let lodgings, are sufficient to show. The Scottish *laird*, without the prefix *land*, conveys the idea of proprietorship. *Landlord* and *landlady*, in one of the senses in which the words are continually used, both in English and Scottish parlance, are traceable not to *land* in the Teutonic sense of the word, but to *lan*, the Gaelic for full, or an enclosure, and all that it contains or is full of. Thus the keeper of a public, or the owner of a private house, is lord or master of the *lan* or enclosure which he occupies or possesses.

H

Land-louper, a vagabond, a wanderer from place to place without settled habitation; sometimes called a *forloupin* or *forlopin*, as in Allan Ramsay's "Evergreen."

Lane, alone, lone, or lonely; this word, which in the English lone or lonely is an adjective, is a noun in the Scottish *lane*. "I was all alone," or "we were all alone," are in Scottish, "I was a' my lane," and "we were a' our lane." "I canna lie my lane," is, "I cannot sleep alone."

> I waited lang beside the wood,
>   Sae wae and weary *a' my lane*,
> Och hey! Johnnie lad,
> Ye're no so kind's ye should hae been.
>   —TANNAHILL.

> "But oh, my master dear," he cried,
> "In a green wood, ye're gude *your lane*."
>   —*Ballad of Gil Morrice.*

> I wander my *lane* like a night-troubled ghaist.—BURNS.

Lanrien (sometimes written **landrien**). Jamieson defines this word as meaning "in a straight course; a direct, as opposed to a circuitous course," and quotes a phrase used in Selkirkshire— "He cam rinnin' *landrien*," or straight forward. It seems to be a corruption of the Gaelic *lan*, full, complete; and *rian*, order, method, arrangement, regularity.

Laroch or **lerroch**, the site of a building which has been demolished, but of which there are remains to prove what it once was. From the Gaelic *lar*, the ground or earth; and *larach*, the ground on which an edifice once stood.

Lave, the residue, the remainder, that which is left, or, as the Americans say in commercial fashion, the "balance."

> We'll get a blessing wi' the *lave*,
>   And never miss't.
>   —BURNS: *To a Mouse.*

> First when Maggie was my care,
>   Whistle o'er the *lave* o't.—BURNS.

Laverock, the lark. This word, so pleasant to the Scottish ear, and so entirely obsolete in English speech and literature, was used by Gower and Chaucer:—

> She made many a wondrous soun',
> Sometimes like unto the cock,
> Sometimes like the *laverock*.
>   —GOWER: *Quoted in* HALLIWELL'S
>   *Archaic Dictionary.*

> Why should I sit and sigh,
>   When the wild woods bloom sae briery,
> The *laverocks* sing, the flowerets spring,
>   And a' but me are cheery.
>   —BUCHAN'S *Songs of the North of
>   Scotland.*

> Thou *laverock* that springs frae the dews
>   o' the lawn.—BURNS.

Lark and the Teutonic *lerche* are doubtless abbreviations of the primitive word *laverock*, but whence *laverock?* Possibly from the ancient Gaelic *labhra* (*lavra*), and *labhraich*, eloquent, loud— two epithets that are highly appropriate to the skylark.

Law. This word is often used in Scotland to signify a hill or rock, especially to one standing alone, as Berwick *Law*, so familiar by sight to the Mid-Lothian people. It is derived from the Gaelic *leach*, a stone; and *leachach*, the bare summit of a hill. It sometimes signifies the stony or shingly ground by the side of a river, as in the Broomie-*law* in Glasgow. Possibly in this case also the word is of the same derivation as *leach*, and means not only a high stone, but a flat stone, a flag stone, whence *leachaig*, to pave or lay with flat stones.

Lawin. This eminently Scottish word is from the Gaelic *lachan*, the expense of an entertainment; the price of the drink consumed at a tavern; *lachag*, a very small reckoning. "Ye're *lawin-free*," *i.e.*, you are not to pay your share of the bill. The root of the word seems to be *lagh*, law, order, method—the law of the tavern, that the guests should pay before they go. It was formerly written *lauch*.

Aye as the gudewife brought in,
  Ane scorit upon the *wauch* [wall],
Ane bade pay, anither said " Nay,
  Bide while we reckon our *lauch*."
    —*Peblis to the Play.*

Then, gudewife, count the *lawin*,
  The *lawin!* the *lawin!*
Then, gudewife, count the *lawin*,
  And bring a cogie mair.
    —BURNS : *Old Chorus.*

Lawin, the *reckoning* at an inn. Isn't reckoning a Scotticism? I doubt very much if you would be understood if you asked an English landlord for the reckoning, meaning an account of what you have had at his inn. I don't think reckoning is specially associated with an inn bill in this country. In Scotland reckoning has almost entirely superseded the word *lawin*. In Sweden the regular word for a hotel bill is the "reckoning."—R. DRENNAN.

Leal, loyal, true, true-hearted. "The land o' the *leal*," *i.e.*, Heaven.

A *leal* heart never lied.—*Scots Proverbs.*

I'm wearin' awa', Jean,
Like snaw when it's thaw, Jean,
I'm wearin' awa'
To the Land o' the *Leal.*
    —LADY NAIRNE.

Robin of Rothesay, bend thy bow,
Thy arrows shoot so *leal.*
    —*Hardyknute.*

Lear or leer, learning; from the German *lehren*.

When Sandie, Jock, and Jeanitie,
  Are up and gotten *lear*,
They'll help to gar the boatie row
  An' lighten a' our care.
    —*The Boatie Rows.*

Lea-rig, a ridge in a corn or other field, left fallow between two ridges that are bearing grain.

Will ye gang o'er the *lea-rig*,
  My ain kind dearie O.
    —FERGUSSON.

Corn *rigs* and barley *rigs*,
  And corn *rigs* are bonnie ;
I'll ne'er forget that happy night,
  Among the *rigs* wi' Annie.—BURNS.

Leed, a song or incantation, from the German *lied*, a lay or song.

Thrice backward round about she tottered,
While to hersel the *leed* she muttered.
  —GEORGE BEATTIE : *John o' Arnha'.*

Lee-lang, as long as it is light, as in the phrase "the *lee-lang* day," which has hitherto been supposed to mean the "lifelong day." It is more probably from the Gaelic *li*, a colour, and especially a bright colour, the colour of daylight, and from the allied word *liath* (*lia*), pale grey, as distinguished from dark or black.

The thresher's weary flingin' tree
The *lee-lang* day had tired me.
BURNS : *The Vision.*

Leeshin, lazily, in a dilatory manner. From the Gaelic *leise*, lazy.

And cam' *leeshin* up behind her.
—GEORGE BEATTIE: *John o' Arnha'.*

Leesome, agreeable, pleasant, like the light. (*See* LEE-LANG.)

Oh, gear will buy me rigs o' land,
And gear will buy me sheep and kye ;
But the tender heart o' *leesome* luve
The gowd and siller canna buy.
—BURNS : *The Countrie Lassie.*

Fair and *leesome* blew the wind,
Ships did sail and boats did row.
—BUCHAN'S *Ancient Ballads.*

A fairy ballad in Buchan's collection is entitled " *Leesome* Brand." Jamieson derives *leesome* from the German *liebe*, love; perhaps, however, the root of the word is the Gaelic *leus*, light; *li*, colour; and *leusach*, bright, shining.

Leeze or **leeze me on** (a reflective verb), to be satisfied with, to be pleased or delighted with. A Gaelic periphrase for " I love." The Highlanders do not say "I love you," but "love is on me for you." Hence the

Scottish phrase—"*loes* (or *lees*) me " or "love is on me."

Leeze me on my spinning-wheel.—BURNS.

Leeze me on thee, John Barleycorn,'
Thou king o' grain.
—BURNS : *Scotch Drink.*

Leeze me on drink, it gies us mair,
Than school or college.
—BURNS : *The Holy Fair.*

Leglin or **leglan,** a milking-pail.

At buchts, in the mornin', nae blithe lads are scornin',
The lasses are lanely, and dowie and wae,
Nae daffin', nae gabbin', but sighin' and sabbin',—
Ilk ane lifts her *leglin* and hies her away.
—ELLIOT : *The Flowers of the Forest.*

Donald Caird can lilt and sing,
Blithely dance the Highland fling,
Hoop a *leglan*, clout a pan,
Or crack a pow wi' ony man.
—SIR WALTER SCOTT : *Donald Caird.*

Jamieson traces *leglin* to the Teutonic *leghel*. This word, however, has no place in German, Dutch, or Flemish dictionaries. The Gaelic has *leig*, to milk a cow, which, with *lion*, a receptacle (also a net), or *lion*, to fill, becomes *leglin* in Lowland Scotch.

Leister, a three-pronged instrument, or trident, for killing fish in the water ; commonly applied to illegal salmon fishing in the rivers of Scotland.

I there wi' something did forgather
That pat me in an eerie swither,
An awfu' scythe out owre ae shouther
Clear dangling hang,
A three-taed *leister* on the ither
Lay large and lang.
—BURNS : *Death and Dr. Hornbook.*

Donald Caird can wire a maukin (a hare),
Leisters kipper, makes a shift
To shoot a moor-fowl i' the lift.
Water-bailiffs, rangers, keepers,
He can wake when they're sleepers ;
Not for bountitt or reward,
Dare they mell wi' Donald Caird.
—SIR WALTER SCOTT.

Jamieson traces the word to the Swedish *liustra*, to strike fish with a trident. But the derivation may be doubted. "To *leister*," says the Gaelic Etymology of the Languages of Western Europe, "is a mode of taking salmon at night, by attracting them towards the surface by torches held near the water, and then driving a spear, trident, or large fork into them. The word is derived from the light that is employed to lure the fish, rather than from the spear that impales them, and is traceable to the Gaelic *leasdair*, a light, or a lustre." It seems probable that the word is of home origin, rather than of Swedish. Halliwell and Wright claim it as a common word in the North of England. Burns evidently uses it in the sense of a trident, without any reference to the illegal practice of fishing.

Lemanry ; from *leman*, a concubine ; a poetical word for harlotry.

Oh, wed and marry, the knight did say,
 For your credit and fame,
Lay not your love on *lemanry*,
 Nor bring a good woman to shame.
 —BUCHAN'S *Ancient Ballads: Hynd
  Horn.*

Let on, to let appear ; *loot*, appeared ; *lutten*, the past-participle of *let*.

"Weel, Margaret," said a minister to an auld wife, who expressed her dissatisfaction with him for leaving the parish, "ye ken I'm the Lord's servant. If He have work for me in Stirling, ye'll admit that it's my duty to perform it." "Hech !" replied Margaret, "I've heard that Stirling has a great muckle stipend, and I'm thinking if the Lord had gi'en ye a ca' to Auchtertool [a very poor parish], ye wad ne'er hae *lutten on* that ye heard Him."—ROGERS : *Anecdotes of Scottish Wit and Humour.*

Leure, a ray of light, a gleam ; from the French *lueur*, a shining light ; and the anterior Gaelic root *lur*, brightness, splendour, treasure. The Gipsy slang has *lowre*, money ; and *gammy* [or crooked] *lowre*, bad money. The ideas of brightness and beauty go together in most languages. *Lurach*, in Gaelic, is a term of endearment for a beautiful—that is, a bright—young woman.

Levin, the lightning. This word, that has long been obsolete in English literature, is not yet obsolete in the Scottish vernacular. It was employed with fine effect, centuries ago, by Dunbar, the Scottish, and by Chaucer, the English poet. Attempts have recently been made to revive it, by Sir Walter Scott and others, not altogether ineffectually. Chaucer makes splendid use of it when he denounces one who habitually speaks ill of women :

With wild thunder-bolt and fiery *levin*
May his welked [wicked] neck be broke.
                    —*Wife of Bath's Prologue.*
To him as to the burning *levin*,
Short, resistless course was given.
                    —SCOTT : *Marmion.*
The clouds grew dark and the wind grew
    loud,
And the *levin* filled her e'e,
And waesome wailed the snow-white sprites
Upon the gurly sea.
                    —LAIDLAW : *The Demon Lover.*

The etymology is obscure,
There is no trace of it in the
Teutonic or Latin sources of
the language. Spencer, in the
"Faerie Queene," has—

His burning *levin*-brand in hand he took.

The etymology is probably to
be found in the Gaelic *liath*
(pronounced *lia*, *lee-a*) meaning
white or grey, and sometimes
vivid white, which may perhaps
account for the first syllable.
Buin, to shoot, to dart ; *buinne*,
or *bhuinne* (*vuin*), signifies a
rapid motion, which may account for the second—a derivation which is not insisted upon,
but which may lead philologists
to inquire further.

Lewder, lewdering, to flounder
through bog and mire, to plod
wearily and *heavily* on.

Thus *lewdering* on
Through scrubs and crags wi' mony a
    heavy groan.
                    —Ross's *Helenore.*

Jamieson derives the word
from the Teutonic *leuteren*,
morari, a word which is not to
be found in the Teutonic Dic-

tionaries. It is probable that
the root is the Gaelic *laidir*,
strong, heavy. The English
slang, "To give one a good
leathering," is to give him a
strong or heavy beating.

Lib, to castrate, geld, *Libbet*, an
animal on which that operation
has been performed ; a eunuch.
This word still remains current
in the Northern Counties. In
Flemish *lubbing* signifies cas-
tration ; and *lubber*, he who
performs the operation. Burns
speaks contemptuously of Italian
singers as *libbet :*—

How cut-throat Prussian blades. were
    hinging,
How *libbet* Italy was singing.

Lichtly or **lightly**, to treat with
neglect or scorn, or speak lightly
of anybody.

I leaned my back unto an aik,
    And thought it was a trusty tree,
But first it bowed, and syne it brak,
    Sae my true love did *lichtly* me.
—*Ballad of the Marchioness of Douglas.*
Oh is my helmet a widow's cuid [cap],
Or my lance a wand of the willow tree,
Or my arm a lady's lily hand
    That an English Lord should *lichtly* me.
                    —*Kinmont Willie.*
Aye vow and protest that ye care na for me,
And whiles ye may *lichtly* my beauty a
    wee ;
But court na anither tho' daffin' ye be,
For fear that she wyle your fancy frae me.
    —BURNS : *Whistle and I'll come to
            you, my Lad.*

Liddisdale drow, Liddisdale dew ;
the fine rain that is said not
to wet a Scotsman, but that
drenches an Englishman to the
skin. Jamieson defines *drow* to

mean a cold mist heavy with rain, also a squall or severe gust ; and derives the word from the Gaelic *drog*, the motion of the sea, which, however, is not to be found in Gaelic dictionaries. *Drow* is from the Gaelic *druchd*, with the elision of the guttural, signifying *dew*, hence the Liddisdale joke.

Lift, the sky ; from the Teutonic *luft*.

When lightnings fire the stormy *lift*.
—Burns : *Epistle to Robert Graham.*

Is yon the moon, I ken her horn,
  She's glintin' i' the *lift* sae heigh,
She smiles sae sweet to wile us hame,
  But by my troth she'll bide a wee.
          —Burns.

Lil for lal, an ancient Scottish synonym for the English *tit for tat*, that appears in Wynton, who wrote in the sixteenth century. It is supposed by Jamieson to be from the Anglo-Saxon " *lael with laele*," or *stripe for stripe*, though it may be of Gaelic origin ; from *li*, light or colour ; and *là*, day, and *lathail (la-ail)* daily ; or *li-la*, for day, or one light for another.

Lilt, to sing cheerfully, or in a lively manner. Also, according to Jamieson, a large pull in drinking frequently repeated.

Nae mair *liltin'* at the ewe-milkin',
The flowers of the forest are a' wede awa'.
      —*Lament for the Battle of Flodden.*

Mak' haste an' turn King David owre,
An' *lilt* wi' holy clangour.
        —Burns : *The Ordination.*

The origin of this word seems to be the Gaelic *luailte*, speed, haste, rapid motion, and *luailtich*, to accelerate, to move merrily and rapidly forward. This derivation would explain the most common acceptation of the word, as applied to singing, as well as the secondary meaning attributed to it by Jamieson.

Limmer, a depreciatory epithet for a woman ; from the Gaelic *leum*, to leap—one who leaps over the bounds of propriety or moderation, or breaks through the bounds of the seventh commandment.

Linder, a short linen jacket or vest worn next to the skin by both sexes, though Jamieson says only by old women and children.

He'll sell his jerkin for a groat,
  His *linder* for another o't,
And ere he want to pay his shot
  His *sark* will pay the t'other o't.
—Alexander Ross : *The Bridal o't.*

Link, to trip, to leap, to skip, to jump ; **linkin'**, tripping ; from the Gaelic *leum*, to leap, *leumnach*, skipping, jumping, whence *leumanach*, a frog, a creature that jumps. The glossaries to Burns render this word by " trip." Jamieson says it means to walk smartly, or to do anything with cleverness and expedition.

And coost her duddies to the wark,
And *linkit* at it in her sark.
—Burns : *Tam O'Shanter.*

And now, auld Cloots, I ken ye're thinkin'
A certain Bardie's rantin', drinkin',
Some luckless hour will send him *linkin'*
    To your black pit,
But faith ! he'll turn a corner jinkin'
    [dodging],
And cheat you yet.
    —BURNS : *Address to the Deil.*

Lin or lins. This termination to many Scottish words supplies a shade of meaning not to be expressed in English but by a periphrasis, as *westlins,* inclining towards the west. *Aiblins—* perhaps, for able-lins—inclining towards being able, or about to become possible (see AIBLINS, *ante*). *Backlins,* inclining towards a retrograde movement.

The *westlin* winds blaw loud and shrill.
    —BURNS : *My Nannie, O.*

Now frae the east neuk o' Fife the dawn
Speel'd *westlins* up the lift.
    —ALLAN RAMSAY : *Christ's Kirk on*
       the Green.

And if awakened fierce*lins,* aff night flee.
    —Ross's *Helenore.*

This termination properly is *lings,* and is a very common termination in several Teutonic dialects, such as the Dutch, and still more, the German, though not common in English. See Grimm's Grammar. —LORD NEAVES.

Lins corresponds nearly to the English affix *ly,* though not exactly. In Pitscottie's account of the apparition that appeared to James IV. in St. Catherine's Aisle of the Church at Linlithgow, the word *Grofflins* occurs. This has been interpreted to mean gruffly. " He leaned down *grofflins* on the desk before him (the king) and said," &c. *Grufe* or *groff* is a common Scotch word, meaning the belly, or rather the *front* of the body, as distinguished from the back ; and Pitscottie's expression means nothing more than that the apparition leaned the fore part of his body, say his breast, upon the back of the desk at which the king was kneeling.—R. DRENNAN.

Linn, a waterfall ; **Cora Linn,** the falls of the Clyde ; properly, the pool at the bottom of a cataract, worn deep by the falling water ; from the Gaelic *linne,* a pool.

Grat his e'en baith bleer't and blin',
Spak o' lowpin' o'er a *linn.*
    —BURNS : *Duncan Gray.*

Ye burnies, wimplin' down your glens,
Or foaming strang frae *linn* to *linn.*
    —BURNS : *Elegy on Captain Matthew*
       Henderson.

Whiles owre a *linn* the burnie plays.
    —BURNS : *Hallowe'en.*

Lintie, a linnet.

Nae *linties* lilt on hedge or bush,
Poor things, they suffer sairly.
Up in the mornin's no for me,
Up in the mornin' early ;
When a' the hills are covered wi' snaw,
I'm sure it's winter fairly.
    —*Old Song, modernised by* JOHN
       HAMILTON.

Dr. Norman Macleod mentioned a conversation he had with a Scottish emigrant in Canada, who in general terms spoke favourably of his position in his adopted country. " But oh ! sir," he said, "there are no *linties* in the woods, and no braes like Yarrow." The word *lintie* conveys to my mind more of tenderness and endearment towards the little bird than linnet.— DEAN RAMSAY.

Lippen, to incline towards, to be favourable to any one, to rely upon, to trust. Apparently from the Flemish *liefde,* and the German *lieben,* love.

Lippen to me, but look to yoursell.
    —ALLAN RAMSAY'S *Scots Proverbs.*

An ancient lady, when told by the minister that he had a call from his Lord and Master to go to another parish, replied, " Deed, sir, the Lord might ha' ca'd and ca'd to you lang eneuch, and ye'd ne'er hae *lippened* till Him if the steepen [stipend] had na been better."—DEAN RAMSAY.

Lippin' fu', full up to the lip or brim of a glass or goblet, brimful; *owre-lippin'*, full to overflow.

> A' the laughin' valleys round
> Are nursed and fed by me,
> And I'm aye *lippin' fu'*.
> —JAMES BALLANTINE : *Song of the Four Elements—the Water.*

> See ye, wha hae aught in your bicker to spare,
> And gie your poor neighbours your *owre-lippin'* share.
> —JAMES BALLANTINE : *Winter Promptings.*

Lire, sometimes written *lyre*, the complexion. Jamieson defines *lire* as "the part of the skin which is colourless," and "as the flesh or muscles as distinguished from the bones"—"the lean part of butchers' meat." He derives the word from the Anglo-Saxon *lire*, the fleshy part of the body. The word is traceable to the Gaelic *liath* (pronounced *lia*), pale grey, and *liathaich* (*lia-aich*), to become grey.

> As ony rose her *rude* was red,
> Her *lyre* was like the lilies.
> —*Christ's Kirk on the Green.*

Lirk, a crease, a plait, a fold, a hollow in a hill; from the Gaelic *luraich* (see *lar*, ante, p. 114).

> The hills were high on ilka side,
> An' the bricht i' the *lirk*.
> —*Border Minstrelsy—The Broom o' the Cowdenknowes.*

Lith, a joint, a hinge; and metaphorically, the point of an argument on which the whole question turns. To *lith*, to separate the joints; from the Gaelic *luth*, a joint; *luthach*, well-jointed, or having large joints.

> "Fye, thief, for shame !" cries little Sym,
> "Wilt thou not fecht wi' me;
> Thou art mair large of *lith* and limb
> Nor I am "—
> —ALLAN RAMSAY'S *Evergreen : Questioning and Debate betwixt Adamson and Sym.*

> And to the road again wi' a' her pith,
> And souple was she ilka limb and *lith*.
> —Ross's *Helenore.*

Dr. Johnson and Lord Auchinleck were quarrelling over the character of the great Protector, and the sturdy old English Tory pressed the no less sturdy old Scottish Whig to say what good Cromwell had ever done to his country. His lordship replied, "He gart kings ken that they had a *lith* in their necks."—BOSWELL.

> Ye'll tak a *lith* o' my little fingerbane.
> —BUCHAN'S *Ancient Ballads—The Bonnie Bows o' London.*

Littit, coloured; from the Gaelic *liath*, grey.

> Weel dyed and *littit* through and through.
> —GEORGE BEATTIE : *John o' Arnha'.*

Loaning, a meadow, a pasture; a green lane.

> I've heard them lilting at the ewe-milking—
> Lasses a' lilting before dawn of day ;
> But now they are moaning in ilka green *loaning*,
> The flowers o' the forest are a' wede away.
> —*The Flowers o' the Forest.*

> Joy gaed down the *loaning* wi' her,
> Joy gaed down the *loaning* wi' her,
> She wadna hae me—but has ta'en another—
> And a' men's joy but mine ga'ed wi' her !
> —CHAMBERS'S *Scottish Songs.*

Loe-some, or **love-some**, pleasant and amiable, is sometimes wrongly written *leesome*, as in Burns's song of "The Countrie Lassie":—

The tender heart o' *leesome* luve
Gowd and siller canna buy.

Loof, the palm of the hand; from the Gaelic *lamh* (*lav*), the hand.

Gie's yer *loof*, I'll ne'er beguile you.
—*Scots Proverbs.*

Wi' arm reposed on her chair back,
He sweetly does compose him,
Which by degrees slips round her neck,
An's *loof* upon her bosom,
Unkenned that day.
—BURNS: *The Holy Fair.*

Lofa is used by Ulphilas for the open hand; *slaps lofa*, a slap of the hand. The Gaelic *lam*, when the *m* gets aspirate, becomes *lamh—lav* or *laf.*—LORD NEAVES.

Losh, a ludicrous objurgation that does duty as a paltry oath; generally supposed to be a corruption of "Lord!"

Losh me! hae mercy wi' your natch,
Your bodkin's bauld.
—BURNS: *Epistle to a Tailor.*

Losh me! that's beautiful.—*Noctes Ambrosianæ.*

The English corruptions of "Lord!" becomes O Lor'! Lawks! and O La'! The name of the Supreme Being, in like manner, is vulgarised into *Gosh*, as "By *Gosh!*" "*Gosh* guide us!" is a common expression in Scotland, with the object apparently of avoiding the breach of the Third Commandment in the letter, though not in the spirit.

Loup, to leap; to "*loup* the dyke," a proverbial expression, to leap over the dyke (of restraint), applied to unchaste unmarried women; *land-louper*, a vagrant.

Spak o' *loupin'* o'er a linn.
—BURNS: *Duncan Gray.*

He's *loupen* on the bonnie black,
He steer'd him wi' the spur right sairly;
But ere he won to Gatehope slack
I think the steed was wae and weary.
—*Minstrelsy of the Scottish Border—Annan Water.*

I bade him *loup*, I bade him come,
I bade him *loup* to me,
An' I'd catch him in my armis twa.
—*The Fire o' Frendraught.*

Loup-hunting. "The odd phrase, 'Hae ye been a *loup-hunting?*' is a query," says Jamieson, "addressed to one who has been very early abroad, and is an *evident* allusion to the hunting of the wolf (the French *loup* in former days)." The allusion is not so evident as Jamieson imagined. A wolf was not called *loup* either in the Highlands or in the Lowlands. In the Highlands the animal was either called *faol*, or (*madadh alluidh*), a wild dog; and in the Lowlands by its English, Flemish, and German name, "wolf." It is far more likely that "loup" in the phrase is derived from the Gaelic *lobhar*, the Irish Gaelic *lubhar*, a day's work; a hunt more imperative than that after an animal which has not been known in Scotland since 1680, when the last of the race, according to tradition, was killed by Sir Ewen Cameron of Lochiel. Another tradition, recorded in the third volume of Chambers's "Annals of Scotland," fixes in 1743 the date of the last wolf slain, and records the name of the slayer as Macqueen, a noted deer-stalker in the forest of Moray. *Lub* is an obsolete Gaelic word for a youth of either sex. It is therefore possible that *loup-hunting* may have had a still more familiar meaning.

Lout or **loute,** to jump, or leap.

He has *louted* him o'er the dizzy crag
And gien the monster kisses ane.
—*Border Minstrelsy.*

Low, to stand still, to stop, to rest ; *lowden,* to calm ; applied to the cessation of a stormy wind ; also, to silence, or cause to be silent.

Lowan drouth, burning thirst.

With the cauld stream she quench'd her *lowan drouth.*—*Ross's Helenore.*

Lowe, a flame ; *lowin',* burning, to burn, to blaze. *Lò* is the ancient Gaelic word for day, or daylight ; superseded partially by the modern *là,* or *làtha,* with the same meaning. The syllable *lò* appears in the compound word *lo-inn,* joy, gladness, beauty—derived from the idea of light—that which shines, as in the Teutonic *schön* or *schoen,* the old English *sheen,* beautiful.

A vast unbottomed boundless pit,
Filled fou o' *lowin'* brunstane.
—BURNS : *The Holy Fair.*

The sacred *lowe* o' weel-placed love
Luxuriantly indulge it.
—BURNS : *Epistle to a Young Friend.*

The bonnie, bonnie bairn sits poking in the ase,
Glowerin' in the fire wi' his wee round face,
Laughin' at the fuffin' *lowe*—what sees he there ?
Ha ! the young dreamer's biggin' castles in the air.
—JAMES BALLANTINE.

Lown, quiet, calm, sheltered from the wind. The *lown* o' the dyke, the sheltered side of the wall.

"Unbuckle your belt, Sir Roland," she said,
" And sit you safely down."
" Oh, your bower is very dark, fair maid,
An' the nicht is wondrous *lown.*"
—*Ballad of Sir Roland.*

Lown is used in relation to concealment, as when any ill report is to be hushed up. "Keep it *lown,*" *i.e.,* say nothing about it.
—JAMIESON.

Blaw the wind ne'er sae fast,
It will *lown* at the last.
—ALLAN RAMSAY'S *Scots Proverbs.*

Come wi' the young bloom o' morn on thy brow,
Come wi' the *lown* star o' love in thine e'e.
—JAMES BALLANTINE : *Wifie, Come Hame.*

Lounder, to strike heavily right and left.

I brak a branch off an ash, and ran in among them *lounderin'* awa' right and left.
—*Noctes Ambrosianæ.*

Luckie, a term of familiarity applied to elderly women in the lower and middle ranks of society :—

Oh, haud your tongue, now, *Luckie* Laing,
Oh, haud your tongue and jaumer ;

I held the gate till you I met,
   Syne I began to wander.
      —BURNS: *The Lass of Ecclefechan.*

Hear me, ye hills, and every glen,
And echo shrill, that a' may ken
      The waefu' thud
O' reckless death wha came unseen
      To *Luckie* Wood.
            —BURNS.

Mrs. Helen Carnegie of Montrose died in 1818, at the advanced age of ninety-one. She was a Jacobite, and very aristocratic, but on social terms with many of the burghers of the city. She preserved a very nice distinction in her mode of addressing people according to their rank and station. She was fond of a game of quadrille (whist), and sent out her servant every morning to invite the ladies required to make up the game. " Nelly, ye'll gang to Lady Carnegie's, and mak' my compliments, and *ask the honour* of her ladyship's company, and that of the Miss Carnegies, to tea this evening. If they canna come, ye'll gang to the Miss Mudies, and ask the *pleasure* of their company. If they canna come, ye maun gang to Miss Hunter, and ask the *favour* of her company. If she canna come, ye maun gang to *Luckie* Spark, and *bid her come!*"—DEAN RAMSAY'S *Reminiscences.*

It is probable that this word, as a term of respect as well as of familiarity, to a middle-aged or elderly matron, is a corruption of the Gaelic *laoch*, brave. The French say, " une *brave femme*," meaning a good woman; and the Lowland Scotch use the adjective *honest* in the same sense, as in the anecdote recorded in Dean Ramsay's " Reminiscences " of Lord Hermand, who, about to pass sentence on a woman, began remonstratively, " *Honest woman,* what garred ye steal your neighbour's tub ? "

Lug, the ear, a handle; also to pull, to drag or haul. *Luggie,* a small wooden dish with handles. *Luggie,* the horned owl, so called from the length of its ears.

His hair, his size, his mouth, his *lugs,*
Showed he was nane o' Scotland's dogs.
      —BURNS: *The Twa Dogs.*

Up they got and shook their *lugs,*
Rejoiced they were na men but dogs.
            —*Idem.*

How would his Highland *lug* been nobler
   fired,
—His matchless hand with finer touch
   inspired.
      —BURNS: *The Brigs of Ayr.*

Lug, to pull by the ear, or otherwise to haul a load, is still current in English; but *lug*, the ear, is obsolete, except in the Northern Counties, though common in English literature in the Elizabethan era. Two derivations have been suggested for the word in its two divergences. The Gaelic *lag*, genitive *luig*, signifies a cavity, whence it is supposed that *lug* signifies the cavity of the ear. Coles, however, renders *lug* by the Latin, " auris lobus, auricula infinia," not the interior cavity, but the exterior substance of the ear. The derivation of *lug*, to pull, to drag a load, seems to be from another source altogether; from the Gaelic *luchd*—the English for a load, a burden, or a ship's cargo, and for *lugger*, a kind of barge used for the transference of the cargo from the hold of a larger vessel. In this case the meaning is transferred from the load itself to the action of moving it.

Lum, the chimney, the vent by which the smoke escapes from the fireplace. The word is used in the north of England as well as in Scotland. The etymology is uncertain. The Kymric has *llumon*, a beacon, a chimney; the Irish Gaelic has *luaimh*, swift; and the Scottish Gaelic *luath* (*lua*), swift; and *ceum*, aspirated into *cheum* or *heum*, a way, a passage, whence *lua-heum*, the swift passage by which the smoke is carried off.

The most probable derivation is from the Gaelic *laom*, a blaze; whence, by extension of meaning, the place of the blaze or fire.

Lume, a tool, a spinning-machine, a loom.

Lunch, a piece, a slice, whence the modern English *lunch*, a slight meal in the middle of the day.

Cheese and bread frae women's laps
Was dealt about in *lunches*
And dawds that day.
—Burns: *The Holy Fair.*

Lunt, the smoke of tobacco, to emit smoke; from the Flemish *lont*, a lighted wick.

The *luntin'* pipe.
—Burns: *The Twa Dogs.*

Lurder, an awkward, lazy, or worthless person; from the French *lourd*, heavy; *lourdaud*, a heavy and stupid man.

Let alane maks many a *lurder* (neglect makes many a one worthless).—Dean Ramsay.

Lyart, grey; from the Gaelic *liath* (*lia*), which has the same meaning.

His *lyart* haffets [locks of thin grey hair].
—Burns: *Cotter's Saturday Night.*

Twa had manteels o' doleful black,
But ane in *lyart* hung.
—Burns: *The Holy Fair.*

Lyke-wake, the ceremonial of the watching over a dead body. *Lyke* is from the German *leiche*, the Dutch and Flemish *lijk*, a corpse.

She has cut off her yellow locks
A little aboon her e'e,
And she's awa' to Willie's *lyke*,
As fast as gang could she.
—Buchan's *Ballads: Willie's Lyke-Wake.*

M

Machless, lazy, sluggish, indolent. Jamieson derives this word from the Teutonic *macht*, power, strength, might; whence *machtlos*, without might or strength; but the Scottish word is without the *t*, which somewhat detracts from the probability of the etymology. The Gaelic has *macleisg*, a lazy, indolent person, literally a "son of laziness," which is a nearer approach to *machless* than *machtlos*. *Machle* is defined by Jamieson as signifying to busy one's self about nothing, which would seem to be an abbreviation of *macleisg*. He says that *machless* is generally used in an unfavourable sense, as in the phrase, "get up, ye *machless* brute." This supports the Gaelic etymology.

Mad as a hatter. This is English as well as Scottish slang, to signify that a person is more or less deranged in his intellect. Why a hatter should be madder than a shoemaker, a tailor, or any other handicraftsman, has never been explained. The phrase most probably arises from a corruption and misconception of the Gaelic word *atadh*, a swelling, *aitearachd*, swelling, blustering, foaming like a cataract in motion, or the assembling of a noisy crowd. Jamieson, unaware of the Gaelic origin, defined the Scottish *hatter* as a numerous and irregular assemblage of any kind, a *hatter* of stanes, or a confused heap of stones; and *hattering*, as collecting in crowds. So that *mad as a hatter* merely signifies mad as a cataract or a crowd. In the old Langue Romane—the precursor of modern French— *hativeau* meant *un fou, un etourdi*, a madman.

Maggie-rab or **Maggie-rob**, an ancient popular term for a violent, quarrelsome, and disagreeable woman.

He's a very guid man, but I trow he's gotten a *Maggie-rob* o' a wife.—JAMIESON.

This strange phrase, though now so apparently inexplicable, must originally have had a meaning, or it would never have acquired the currency of a proverb. If the word *Maggie* for Margaret be accepted as the generic name for a woman, like Jill in the nursery rhyme of "Jack and Jill went up the hill;" or like Jenny in the old song of "Jock and Jenny;" and *Rob* or *Rab* be held to signify a man, the phrase may mean a virago, a woman with the behaviour and masculine manners of the other sex.

The *rab* or *rob* in the phrase is susceptible of another interpretation. The Gaelic *rab*, or *rabach*, means quarrelsome, litigious, violent, exasperating— while in the same language *rob* means dirty and slovenly. Either of these epithets would very aptly describe the kind of woman referred to in the extract from Jamieson.

But these are suggestions only for students of language, and are not offered as true derivations for the guidance of the unlearned. *Rabagas* was the name recently given by a popular French playwright to a very quarrelsome and litigious character.

Maigs or **mags**, a ludicrous term for the hands, from the Gaelic *mag* or *mog*, a paw.

Haud aff yer *maigs*, man !—JAMIESON.

Mailin', a farm-yard and farm-buildings; a farm for which rent is paid—from *mail*, a tax. Gaelic *mal*, tax, tribute.

A weel-stockit *mailin'*, himself o't the laird,
And marriage off-hand, were his proffers.
—BURNS : *Last May a Braw Wooer.*

Quoth she, my grandsire left me gowd,
A *mailin'* plenished fairly.
—BURNS : *The Soldier's Return.*

Mairly, rather more.

Argyle has raised a hundred men,
A hundred men and *mairly*,
And he's awa by the back o' Dunkeld,
To plunder the house o' Airly.

The lady look't o'er her window sae hie,
She lookit lang and sairly,
Till she espied the great Argyle
Cam' to plunder the house o' Airly.
—*The House of Airly.*

Maks na, or it **maks na**, it does not signify, it does not matter.

Away his wretched spirit flew,
It *maks na* where.
—ALLAN RAMSAY : *The Last Speech of a Wretched Miser.*

Tho' daft or wise, I'll ne'er demand,
Or black or fair, it *maks na* whether.
—ALLAN RAMSAY : *Gie me a Lass wi' a Lump o' Land.*

Malison, a curse. The twin word, *benison*, a blessing, has been admitted into English dictionaries, but *malison* is still excluded; although it was a correct and recognised English word in the time of Langland, the author of Piers Ploughman, and Chaucer.

Thus they serve Sathanas,
Marchands of *malisons*.
—LANGLAND : *Piers Ploughman.*

And all-Hallowes, have ye, Sir Chanone,
Said this priest, and I her *malison*.
—CHAUCER : *The Chanones Yemanne's Tale.*

I've won my mother's *malison*,
Coming this night to thee.
—*Border Minstrelsy.*

That is a cuckold's *malison*,
John Anderson, my joe.
—*John Anderson*, old version.

Mansweir, to commit perjury. This word is almost peculiar to Scotland, though Halliwell has *mansworn*, perjured, long obsolete, but once used in England. The first syllable can have no relation to *man*, homo. The Flemish *meineed*, and the German *meineid*, signify perjury, and one who perjures himself is a *meineidiger*. The Scottish word seems to be derived from the Gaelic *mionn*, an oath, and *suarach*, worthless, valueless, mean, of no account—whence *mionn suarach*, corrupted into *man sweir*, signifying a valueless or false oath. Jamieson thinks it comes from the Anglo-Saxon *man*, perverse, mischievous, and *swerian*, to swear; a derivation which, as regards the syllable *man*, he would have scarcely hazarded if he had been aware of the Gaelic *mionn*, or of the German *meineid*.

Mare's Nest. This originally Scottish phrase is no longer peculiar to Scotland, but has become part of the copious vocabulary of English slang. Hotten's Slang Dictionary defines it to mean "a supposed discovery of marvels, which turn out to be no marvels at all." The compiler accounts for the expression by an anecdote of "three cockneys, who, out ruralising, determined to find out something about *nests.* Ultimately, when they came upon a dung-heap, they judged by the signs that it must be a *mare's nest,* especially as they could see the mare close by." This ridiculous story has hitherto passed muster. The words are a corruption of the Gaelic *mearachd,* an error, and *nathaist* (*th* silent), a fool, whence a fool's error, *i.e.*, mare's nest. Some Gaelic scholars are of opinion that the word is compounded of *mearachd,* an error, and *masaichte,* or *snasta,* reduced into order or system, *i.e.*, systematic error.

Mark and burn. To say of a thing that it is lost, *mark and burn* signifies that it is totally lost, beyond trace and recognition; not that it is marked or burned in the sense of the English words, but in the sense of the Gaelic *marc,* a horse—from whence *march,* a boundary traced by the perambulations at stated periods of men on horseback—and *burn,* a stream of running water, the natural, and often the common boundary, between contiguous estates and territories. *March balk* signifies the narrow ridge which sometimes serves as the boundary between lands of different pro-

prietors. *Marche dyke,* a wall separating one farm or estate from another.

When one loses anything and finds it not again, he is said never to see *mark nor burn* of it.—JAMIESON.

Marmor, an ancient title of nobility equivalent to an earl; from the Gaelic *maor,* an officer, chieftain, and *mor,* great.

Lords of the Isles, and Thanes, and Jarls,
Barons and *Marmors* grim,
With helm on head and glaive in hand,
In rusty armour dim,
Responsive to some powerful call,
Gathered obedient one and all.
—*Legends of the Isles.*

Marrow, one of a pair, a mate, a companion, an equal, a sweetheart — from the Gaelic *mar,* like, similar. This word is beautifully applied to a lover or wedded partner, as one whose mind is the exact counterpart of that of the object of his affection. It appears in early English literature, but now survives only in the poetry and daily speech of the Scottish and northern English people.

One glove or shoe is *marrow* to another.—*Lansdowne MS., quoted in* HALLIWELL's *Archaic Dictionary.*

And when we came to Clovenford,
　Then said my winsome *marrow,*
Whate'er betide, we'll turn aside,
　And see the braes o' Yarrow.
—WORDSWORTH : *Yarrow Unvisited.*

Thou took our sister to be thy wife,
　But ne'er thought her thy *marrow.*
　—*The Dowie Dens o' Yarrow.*

Mons Meg and her *marrow* three volleys let flee,
For love of the bonnets of bonnie Dundee.—SIR WALTER SCOTT.

Meddle with your *marrow* (*i.e.*, with your equal).—*Scottish Proverb.*

Your e'en are no *marrows* (*i.e.*, you squint).—ALLAN RAMSAY.

Marschal, a steward, an upper servant ; from the Gaelic *maor*, an officer, a superintendent, and *sgalag*, a farm-servant, a serf, a hired labourer.

Mart or **mairt**, cow-beef salted for winter provision. So called, says Jamieson, "from *Martinmas*, the term at which beeves are usually killed for winter store." Perhaps the future editors of Jamieson will take note that *mart* in Gaelic signifies a cow ; *mart bainne*, a milch cow ; and *mart fheoil*, beef ; and that consequently the word has no relation to the Martinmas festival. In a note to "Noctes Ambrosianæ," Professor Ferrier says *mart* is an ox killed at Martinmas. *Mart* originally signified a market, where kine and horned cattle were sold, as distinguished from *market*, a horse fair ; from *mare*, a horse.

Mashlum, mixed corn, or rye and oats with the bran.

Twa *mashlum* bannocks (cakes).
—BURNS : *Cry and Prayer.*

Mask, to infuse ; usually employed in connection with the tea-table. To *mask* the tea is, in Scottish phrase, to make the tea, by pouring the boiling water upon it. The word is from the Gaelic *masg*, to mix, to infuse. Jamie-son erroneously derives it from the Swedish *mask*, a mash.

Maughts, power.

They had nae *maughts* for sic a toilsome task,
The barefaced robbers had put off the mask—
Among the herds that played a *maughty* part.
—Ross's *Helenore.*

She starts to foot, but has nae *maughts* to stand.—*Idem.*

The word is from the Teutonic *macht*,' power, might, ability. The root seems to be the Gaelic *maith*, powerful, able, strong, and *maithich* or *maithaich*, to make strong.

Maukin, a hare ; from the Gaelic *maigheach*, and *maoidheach*, with the same meaning.

God help the day when royal heads
Are hunted like a *maukin*.
—BURNS : *Our Thistles flourished Fresh and Fair.*

Mauks, maggots.

I saw the cook carefully wi' the knife scrapin' out the *mauks*.—*Noctes Ambrosianæ.*

Maun, must. This Scottish verb, like its English synonym, has no inflections, no past or future tense, and no infinitive. The peculiarity of the Scottish word is that it sometimes signifies *may*, and sometimes *must*, as in the line of D'Urfey's clumsy imitation of a Scottish song, "Within a Mile of Edinburgh Town "—

I canna, *maunna*, winna buckle to (I cannot, *may* not [or *must* not], will not, be married).

I

Perhaps the use of *may* as *must*, and *vice versa*, was introduced into the Lowland Scotch by the Gaelic-speaking Highlanders. *Feud* in Gaelic signifies *may* or *can*, and *fheudar domh*, " obligation or necessity is to me, or upon me," *i.e.*, I must.

Mavis, the singing thrush. This word, once common in English poetry, is now seldom employed. Spenser, in the following passage from his " Epithalamium," seems to have considered the *mavis* and the thrush to be different birds :—

The thrush replies ; the *mavis* descant plays.

In Scottish poetry the word is of constant occurrence.

In vain to me in glen or shaw
The *mavis* and the lintwhite sing.
—BURNS.

Oh, tell sweet Willie to come doun,
And hear the *mavis* singing ;
And see the birds on ilka bush,
And green leaves round them hinging.
—BUCHAN'S *Ancient Ballads.*

An eccentric divine discoursing on a class of persons who were obnoxious to him, concluded with this singular peroration, " Ma freens, it is as impossible for a *moderate* to enter into the kingdom of heaven as for a soo (sow) to sit on the tap o' a thistle, and sing like a *mavis*."—ROGERS'S *Illustrations of Scottish Life.*

Mawmet, an idol. This word is usually derived from Mahomet,

but as Mahomet was not an idol, but asserted himself to be the prophet of the true God, it is possible that the philologists of an earlier day accepted the plausible etymology, without caring to inquire further. It is, nevertheless, worthy of consideration whether the word does not come from the Gaelic *maoim*, horror, terror, fright ; and *maoimeadh*, a state of terror or awe, such as devotees feel before an idol.

Mawsie, a large, dirty, slovenly, unshapely woman ; a corruption and abbreviation of the Gaelic *maosganach*, a lump, a lumpish person.

May, a lass, a maid, a young girl.

There was a May an' a weel-farèd May
Lived high up in yon glen.
—*Border Minstrelsy : Katharine Ganfarie.*

Meggy Monyfeet, the popular name for the centipede.

Mell, to be intimate with, to mingle or associate ; from the French *meler*, to mix. *Mell* also signifies a company, and *melling* an intermeddling.

Mellder, the quantity of grain sent at one time to the miller to be ground.

Ae market-day thou wast na sober ;
That ilka *mellder*, wi' the miller,
Thou sat as lang as thou hadst siller ;
That every naig was ca'd a shoe on
The smith and thee gat roarin' fou' on.
—BURNS : *Tam o' Shanter.*

Melvie, to soil with meal, as the miller's clothes and hair are soiled from the flying dust of the mill. Erroneously explained in the glossaries to Burns as " to soil with *mud*." It is probably a corruption of *mealy*.

> *Mealie* was his sark,
> *Mealie* was his siller,
> *Mealie* was the kiss
> That I gat frae the miller.
> —*Old Song.*

> To *melvie* his braw claithing.
> —BURNS : *The Holy Fair.*

Mense, mind, good manners, dignity, decorum ; *menseful*, dignified ; *mensefully*, in a proper and respectable manner. From the Latin *mens*, whence mental.

> Auld Vandal, ye but show your little
> *mense*,
> Just much about it wi' your scanty sense.
> —BURNS : *The Brigs of Ayr.*

> I wat she was a sheep of sense,
> And could behave herself wi' *mense ;*
> I'll say't, she never brak a fence
> Thro' thievish greed.
> Our Bardie lanely keeps the spence
> Since Mailie's dead.
> —BURNS : *Poor Mailie's Elegy.*

To *mense* a board, is to do the honours of the table.

> She has a' the *mense* o' the family.—
> JAMIESON.

Mensk, manly dignity ; *menskful*, manly, becoming, dignified ; *menskly*, worthily. Jamieson traces the word to the Icelandic *menska*, humanitas.

Merg or **mergh**, marrow pith ; from the Flemish.

> There was *merg* in his fingers and fire in
> his eye.—*Jock o' Arnha'.*

> And the *mergh* o' his shin-bane,
> Has run down on his spur leather whang.
> —*Border Minstrelsy : Fray*
> *of Suport.*

Merle, the blackbird. The Scottish, which is also the French, name for this delightful songster is far more poetical and distinctive than the prosaic " blackbird" of modern English—a name which might with as much propriety be applied to the rook, the crow, the raven, and the jackdaw. The *merle* is as much noted for his clear, beautiful notes, as for the tribute he levies upon the fruits of the summer and autumn—a tribute which he well deserves to obtain, and amply pays for by his music. The name of *merle*, in Gaelic *meirle*, signifies theft ; and *meirleach*, a thief. In the same language *meirneil*, the English *merlin*, signifies a hawk or other predatory bird. As regards the *merle*, it must be confessed that he is, in the matter of currants and strawberries, deserving of his name. The depredations of the *merle* have created several proverbial phrases in the French language, such as—*C'est un fin merle*, applied to a clever and unscrupulous man ; *un beau merle*, a specious false pretender. The French call the hen-blackbird a *merlette*. The word *merle* was good English in the days of Chaucer, and considerably later.

> Where the sweet *merle* and warbling mavis
> be.—DRAYTON.

Merry Scotland. The epithet "merry" was applied to England as well as to Scotland, and was a common mode of address to a company or multitude of soldiers, hunters, or boon companions.

Old King Cole was a *merry* old soul,
And a *merry* old soul was he,
And he called for his pipe, and he called
   for his bowl,
And he called for his fiddlers three.

. . . .

Of all the girls in *merry Scotland*,
  There's none to compare to Marjorie.
       —Old King Cole.

Few words have puzzled philologists more completely than *mirth* and *merry*. Johnson suggested no etymology; Skinner derived *merry* from the German *mehren*, to magnify; and Junius from the Greek μυριζην, to anoint, because the Greeks anointed themselves with oil when they made *merry* in their public games! The word has no root in any of the Teutonic languages, German, Dutch, Flemish, Danish, or Swedish; and cannot be traced to either French, Latin, Italian, or Spanish. The Gaelic yields *mir*, sport; *mireach*, festive, sportive; *mear*, cheerful, joyous. It thus appears on the evidence of etymology that the pleasant epithet for these islands was given by the Celtic inhabitants, and not by the Saxon and other Teutonic invaders, though it was afterwards adopted by them.

Messan, or **messin,** a cur, a lapdog, a pet dog.

But tho' he was o' high degree,
The fient o' pride, nae pride had he,
But wad hae spent an hour caressin'
E'en wi' a tinker gipsy's *messan*.
       —BURNS: *The Twa Dogs.*

The glossaries to Burns, judging from the context, and the gipsy, imagine *messin* to mean a mongrel, a dog of mixed breeds. Jamieson says it is a small dog, a country cur, so called from *Messina*, in Sicily, whence this species was brought; or from the French *maison*, a house, because such dogs were kept in the house! The word, however, is the Gaelic *measan*, a pet dog, a lap-dog; from *meas*, fancy, kindness, regard.

We hounds slew the hare, quoth the
  blind *messan*.
    —ALLAN RAMSAY's *Scots Proverbs.*

Mess John, the old epithet in Scottish ballad poetry for a priest, derived from the celebration of the mass, so that *Mess John* signified in irreverent phrase, John, who celebrated the mass. The English has the kindred phrase, *Jack Priest.*

The auld folk soon gied their consent,
  Syne for *Mess John* they quickly sent,
Wha ty'd them to their heart's content,
  And now she's Lady Gowrie.
       —The Lass o' Gowrie.

Midden or **midden hole,** the dunghill or dungpit, a receptacle for the refuse, filth, and manure of a farm, situated in the centre of the farmyard, an arrangement not yet wholly superseded :—

Ye glowered at the moon, and fell in the
midden.
—ALLAN RAMSAY's *Scots Proverbs.*

The tither's something dour o' treadin',
But better stuff ne'er claw'd a *midden.*
—BURNS : *Elegy on the Year* 1788.

The word is still used in the
Northern counties of England,
and was derived by Ray from
mud. The true derivation is
from the Gaelic *meadhon,* the
centre, the middle, or midst.

Therein lay three and thirty sows,
Trundlin' in a *midden*
Of draff.
—*Peblis to the Play.*

Mim, meek, modest, prudish,
prim, reticent, affected and
shy of speech; applied only to
young women, or contemptuously to effeminate young men.
This word is usually derived
from the English *mum,* which
means silent or speechless. The
Scottish *mim* means mealy
mouthed, only speaking when
spoken to, over-discreet in conversation, assertion, or reply :—

See l up he's got the Word o' God,
And meek and *mim* he's view'd it.
—BURNS : *The Holy Fair.*

Maidens should be *mim* till they're
married.—ALLAN RAMSAY.

Some *mim*-mou'd pouther'd priestie,
Fu' lifted up wi' Hebrew lore,
And hands upon his breastie.
—BURNS : *To Willie Chalmers.*

Mim, as distinguished from
mum, is an evident rendering of
the Gaelic *min,* soft, delicate,
smooth, mild, meek; *min bheül-
ach* is from *min* and *beul,* a
mouth, the same as the Scottish

mim-mouthed, used by Burns ;
min-bhriathar, a soft word or
expression, from *min* and *bria-
thar,* a word. *Mim* is provincial
and colloquial in England.

First go the ladies, *mim, mim, mim,*
Next come the gentlemen, prim, prim,
prim ;
Then comes the country clown,
Gallop a-trot, trot, trot.
—*Nursery Rhymes of England.*

Minikin, very small, applied in
derision to a little affected person of either sex ; derived possibly from the Gaelic *min,* small;
or from the Flemish *mannikin,* a
little man.

Minnie, a term of endearment for
a mother.

My daddie looks glum, and my *minnie*
looks sour,
They flyte me wi' Jamie because he is
poor.—*Logie o' Buchan.*

From the Flemish *min,* love,
and the Gaelic *min,* sweet, soft,
pleasant, kind, musical ; also
little, used as a term of endearment.

Mint, to attempt, to try, to essay,
to aim at. The resemblance in
the idea of the Scottish *mint,*
to attest, to try, to essay, and
the *Mint,* where the precious
metals are essayed, or tried as
to their purity before they are
coined into money, is curious,
especially when it is remembered
that the Mint was formerly and
is still sometimes called the
Assay Office. The English word
Mint, for the Assay Office, is

usually traced to the German *münze*, the Dutch *munte*, the Latin *moneta*, money. The etymology of the Scottish *mint*, to essay, or try, is unknown; though it is possibly to be found in the Allemanische or German patois *meinta*, to intend, to mean to do a thing.

Mintin's nae makin'.—ALLAN RAMSAY'S *Scots Proverbs.*

A man may *mint* and no' hit the mark. —ALLAN RAMSAY.

Mird, to ogle, to leer, to make amorous signs and advances to a woman.

Donald was smerkit wi' *mirds* and mockery.—JAMES HOGG : *Donald Mac-Gillvray.*

Mird wi' your makes (equals).—JAMIE-SON.

Mirk, dark. Of uncertain etymology, but probably derivable from the Gaelic *murcach*, sad, sorrowful, gloomy.

A man's mind is a'*mirk* mirror.—ALLAN RAMSAY'S *Scots Proverbs.*

Oh *mirk ! mirk !* is the midnight hour, And loud the tempest's roar.
          —BURNS : *Lord Gregory.*

'Twixt the gloaming and the *mirk*, When the kye come hame.
          —JAMES HOGG.

Mirklins, the gloaming, inclining to be mirk or dark.

Mischant, a worthless person; from the French *mechant*, wicked.

Mischanter, a euphonistic name for the devil, synonymous with the English "old mischief,"

sometimes applied to the same personage. It is probable that *mischanter*, as applied to the devil, means the *mischief-maker*, or doer of mischief or wickedness.

Mishanter, misfortune, which is not of the same etymology as *mischanter*, is probably a corrupt abbreviation of misadventure.

Gin Rab Roy hae heard o' this lady's *mishanter*, he wadna be lang o' clearin' the house—Lord Lovat an' a', and letting her gang hame.—MACLEAY'S *Memoirs of the Clan MacGregor.*

Misleard, unmannerly, rude, mischievous, ill-conditioned.

Lord Lovat's sae *misleard* a chap that gin he ken't we were kind to her, he wad mak' whangs o' our hides to mend his Highland brogues wi'.—MACLEAY'S *Memoirs of the Clan MacGregor.*

Missie, a fondling term for a very young girl. The English word *miss*, of which, at first sight, *missie* would seem to be an affectionate diminutive, is of very uncertain derivation. It is commonly supposed to be the first syllable of *mistress*, the French *maitresse* (the feminine of *maitre*). *Miss* and *Missie* are peculiar to Scotch and English, and are unknown in any of the Teutonic and Romance languages. The Teutonic languages use the word *jungfrau*, and *fraülein ;* the French use *demoiselle*, or *mademoiselle ;* the Italians *signorina ;* and the Spanish *senorita.* Perhaps the graceful *miss* and *missie* in Scotch and English are from the Gaelic *maise*, beauty, grace, comeliness, or *maiseach*, pretty, beautiful, elegant. These are more appropriate as the designation of a young unmarried lady than *mistress* would be, implying, as that word does, a sense of command and mastery.

Mister, want, need, great poverty ; *misterful*, necessitous.

> Unken'd and *misterful* in the deserts of Libye.
>> —Gawin Douglas : *Translation of the Æneid.*

> *Misterfu'* folk should nae be mensfu'.
> (Needy people should not be too particular).—Allan Ramsay's *Scots Proverbs.*

The original phrase of *misterfu'* beggars, or needy beggars, was afterwards corrupted into *masterful* beggars, *i.e.*, arrogant or sturdy beggars, as they are called in an edict of James VI., " the whole class of *maisterfull* and ydill beggaris, sornaris (sorners), fulis (fools), and bardis (wandering minstrels or balladsingers)." It is difficult to account for *mister* and *misterful*, unless they be derived from the Scottish Gaelic *misde*, the Irish Gaelic *miste*, the comparative of *olc*, bad or evil. *Mistear* and *mistire* signify a sly, cunning, and mean person, as well as a needy beggar. The corruption to *masterful* in the sense of arrogant is easily accounted for.

Mool, to have carnal intercourse ; sometimes corrupted into *mow* or *mowe*.

> An' there'll be Alaster Sibbie
> That in wi' black Bessie did *mool*,
> Wi' snivellin' Lillie an' Tibbie
> The lass that sits aft on the stool.
>> (the cutty stool, q. v.)
>> —*The Blythesome Bridal.*

Jamieson's Dictionary contains neither *mool* nor *mowe*, in the sense in which they are used in the too libidinous vernacular ; but has *mool*, to crumble, and *mowe* or *mow*, dust or mould.

Moolins, refuse, grains of corn, husks, or chaff ; sometimes crumbs of bread ; from the Gaelic *muillean*, a husk or particle of chaff or grain ; the waste of the meal at the miller's.

> The pawky wee sparrow will peck aff your floor,
> The bauld little Robin hops in at your door ;
> But the heaven-soaring lark 'mang the cauld drift will dee,
> Afore he'll come cowerin' your *moolins* to pree.
>> —James Ballantine : *Winter Promptings.*

Mools, from mould—earth, the grave.

> And Jeanie died. She had not lain i' the *mools*
> Three days ere Donald laid aside his tools,
> And closed his forge, and took his passage home.
>
> . . . .
>
> But long ere forty days had run their round,
> Donald was back upon Canadian ground—
> Donald the tender heart, the rough, the brave,
> With earth and gowans for his true love's grave.—*All the Year Round.*

Moop and mell, to feed together ; *mell*, to associate with ; from the French *meler*, to mingle. Halliwell's Archaic Dictionary contains *mouch* — said to be a Lincolnshire word, signifying to eat greedily.

> The auld West Bow sae steep and crookit,
> Where bawbee pies wee callants *moopit*.
> —JAMES BALLANTINE.

> But aye keep mind to *moop and mell*
> Wi' sheep o' credit like thysel.
> —BURNS : *Poor Mailie.*

> Guid ale hauds me bare and busy,
> Gars me *moop* wi' the servant hizzie ;
> Stand i' the stool when I hae done ;
> Guid ale keeps my heart abune.
> —BURNS : *Good Ale Comes.*

Moop does not mean to keep company with (mell does, meddle with, have to do with), *moop* really means to eat, or rather to nibble, and, if I mistake not, is an old English word,—the present form of the word is *mump*.—R. DRENNAN.

Morn. The Scotch make a distinction between *the morn*, which means to-morrow, and *morn* (without the article), which means morning—thus, "the morn's morn" is to-morrow morning.

Mother-naked, stark-naked, utterly naked ; as naked as the new-born babe at the moment of birth. This word, though a compound of two English ones, has never been admitted into modern English dictionaries, and does not even appear in Nares, Halliwell, or Wright. If it were ever English, there remain no traces of it either in literature or in the common speech of the people. It is still current in the Scottish vernacular, and in poetical composition.

> They'll shape me in your arms, Janet,
> A dove, but and a swan,
> At last they'll shape me in your arms
> A *mother-naked* man.
> Cast your green mantle over me,
> I'll be myself again.
> —*Ballad of the Young Tamlane.*

Readers of the "Arabian Nights' Entertainments" will remember the counterpart of the story of Young Tamlane, in that marvellous compilation of Eastern romance.

Mouter, fee paid to the miller for grinding corn ; old English, *multure ;* French, *moudre*, to grind.

> It's good to be merry and wise,
> Said the miller when he *moutered* twice.
> —ALLAN RAMSAY's *Scots Proverbs.*

> The quaker's wife sat down to bake
> Wi' a' her bairns about her,
> Ilk ane gat a quarter cake
> And the miller gat his *mouter*.
> —CHAMBERS's *Old Song.*

Mowes, jesting, mockery, grimaces ; to make *mowes*, to make faces.

> Affront your friend in *mowes* and tine him in earnest.
> —ALLAN RAMSAY's *Scots Proverbs.*

It has been supposed that *mowes*, which in this sense is only used in the plural, is derived from *mou'*, a Scottish abbreviation of mouth. It would seem so at first blush ; but as the French have "faire la *moue*," "grimace faite par mecontentement, en allongeant les levres," and as *moue* in that language does *not* signify a mouth, it is probable that the source of *mowes* is to be sought in the French and not in the Teutonic. Possibly both the Scottish *mowe* and the French *moue* have a common origin in the Celtic and Gaelic *muig*, a discontented look, an ill-natured frown. In English slang, *mug* signifies the face ; and " ugly *mug* " is a common expression for an ugly face.

Muckle, mickle, meikle, great, large, big ; *muckle-mou'd*, big-mouthed, wide-mouthed, clamorous, vociferous ; *Muckle-mou'd Meg*, a name given to a cannon of large calibre. This word is akin to the English *much*, the Spanish *mucho*, the Greek *mega* and *megala*, and the Latin *magnus*—all implying the sense of greatness. The Gaelic has *meud*, [in which the final *d* is often pronounced *ch*], bulk, great size ; and *meudaich*, to magnify.

> Every little helps to mak a *muckle*.
> —*Scots Proverb.*

> Far hae I travelled,
> And *muckle* hae I seen,
> But buttons upon blankets
> Saw I never nane.
> —*Our Gudeman cam' Hame at E'en.*

Mull, a snuff or tobacco-box, as used in the Highlands. The Lowland Scotch sometimes call a snuff-box " a sneeshin *mill*," mill being a corruption of mull ; from the Gaelic *mala*, a bag, the French *malle*, a trunk or box.

> The luntin' pipe and *sneeshin mill*
> Are handed round wi' right guidwill.
> —BURNS : *The Twa Dogs.*

Jamieson says, with a non-comprehension of the origin of the word *mill* and its connection with *mull*, that the snuff-box was formerly used in the country as a *mill* for grinding the dried tobacco leaves ! If so, the box must have contained some machinery for the purpose. But neither Jamieson, nor anybody else, ever saw a contrivance of that kind in a snuff-box.

Murgullie, to spoil, to mangle, to lacerate, to deform. Sometimes written *margulye.*

> He wadna *murgullie* the howlet on the moudiewort either.—MACLEAY'S *Memoirs of the Clan MacGregor.*

Muslin-kail, an epithet applied by Burns to a purely vegetable soup, without animal ingredients of any kind, and compounded of barley, greens, onions, &c.

> I'll sit down o'er my scanty meal,
> Be 't water-brose or *muslin-kail*,
> Wi' cheerfu' face,
> As lang's the Muses dinna fail
> To say the grace.
> —*Epistle to James Smith.*

It has been supposed that the word *muslin* was applied to it on account of its thinness. The French call it *soupe maigre ;* but as muslin was only introduced to Europe from Mosul in India in 1670, and vegetable broth was known for countless ages before that time in every part of the world, it is possible that *muslin* is an erroneous phonetic rendering of *meslin*, or *mashlum*. Both *meslin* and *mashlum* appear in Jamieson, who translates the former as "mixed corn," and the latter as "a mixture of edibles," but gives no etymology for either. *Mess* is a word that, with slight variations, appears in almost every language of Europe, and which, in its English form, is derived by nearly all philologists from *mensa*, a table. But that this is an error will appear on a little examination, for *mess* originally signified, in nearly every instance in which it was used, a dish of vegetables. The old translation of the Bible speaks of a *mess* of pottage, a purely vegetable compound. Milton speaks of

Herbs and other country *messes*,
Which the neat-handed Phillis dresses.

The Dutch and Flemish *moes* signifies a dish of herbs, or herbs reduced to what the French call a *purée;* the Americans call oatmeal porridge, or any compound of mashed grain, a *mush*. The Gaelic *meas* signifies fruit or vegetables, and this, combined with the word *lan*, full, is doubtless the true root of *meslin* or *mashlum*, rendered *muslin* by Burns's printers. It may be observed that *mash*, to render into a pulp or *purée*, is exclusively used for vegetables, as *mashed* potatoes, *mashed* turnips, &c., and that *hash* or *mince* is the word employed by cooks for the reduction of beef, mutton, and other flesh of animals into smaller portions or particles. *Muslin-kail* seems to be peculiar to Burns.

Mutch, a woman's cap or bonnet; from the Flemish *muts*, the German *mützen*, which have the same meaning.

Their toys and *mutches* were sae clean,
They glancit in our ladies' e'en.
—Allan Ramsay.

A' dressed out in aprons clean,
And braw white Sunday *mutches*.
—Sir Alexander Boswell : *Jenny Dang the Weaver.*

Mutchkin, a pint ; from the Flemish *mudde*, a *hectolitre*, a large quart ; or *muid*, a quart. An English traveller, who prided himself on his knowledge of the Scotch language, called at an inn in Glasgow for a *mutchkin* of whisky, under the idea that *mutchkin* signified a *gill*, or a small glass. "*Mutchkin?*" inquired the waiter, "and a' to yoursel'?" "Yes, a *mutchkin!*" said the Englishman. "I trow ye'll be gey an' fou," said the waiter, "an'yedrinkit." "Never you mind," said the Englishman, "bring it." And it was brought. Great thereanent was the Englishman's surprise. He drank no more than a gill of it ; but he added meanwhile a new Scottish word to his vocabulary.

N

Nae-thing. The English language, or at least the rhymers who write English, have lost many rhymes by not being able to make *nothing* do duty for *nothing;* whence they might have claimed it as a rhyme for *slowthing, low-thing,* and many others too obvious to be specified. The Scottish language, in preserving *nae-thing,* has emphasised the etymology of the word. It is impossible to find a rhyme for the English *nothing,* but for the Scottish *nae-thing* Burns has found that there are many; among others, *ae-thing, claithing, graithing, gaything, plaything,* &c.

Napery, table-linen; from the French *nappe,* a tablecloth, or the English *napkin,* a little cloth.

I thought a beetle or bittle had been the thing that the women have when they are washing towels and *napery*—things for dadding them with.—DEAN RAMSAY: *The Diamond Beetle Case.*

Nappy. This word was used by a few English writers in the eighteenth century, but was never so common in England as it was in Scotland. It always signified strong drink, particularly ale or beer, and not wine or spirits.

Two bottles of as *nappy* liquor
As ever reamed in horn or bicker.
—ALLAN RAMSAY.

Care, mad to see a man sae happy,
E'en drowned himsel' among the *nappy.*
BURNS: *Tam o' Shanter.*

With *nappy* beer, I to the barn repaired.
—GAY's *Fables.*

The word is rendered in French by " capiteux, qui monte à la tete "—that is to say, heady. It seems derivable from the English slang *nob,* the head, as in the pugilistic phrase, "One for his *nob,*" "One (blow) for his head;" whence also the familiar *nopper,* the head. The original word was the German *knob,* a round lump, or ball, in allusion to the shape; whence *knobby,* rounded or lumpy. *Nappie,* in the sense of strong drink that mounts to the head, becomes, by extension of meaning, strong and vigorous; "a *nappie* callant" is a strong, vigorous youth, with a good head on his shoulders.

Nappy.—Bailey's definition of this word in his English Dictionary is " Nappy-ale, such as will cause persons to take or knap pleasant and strong ale."—R. DRENNAN.

N e b, the nose. Flemish *sneb* (with the elision of the *s*), the nose, the beak; a point, as the *neb* or *nib* of a pen.

She holds up the *neb* to him,
And arms her with the boldness of a wife.
—SHAKSPEARE: *Winter's Tale.*

Turn your *neb* northwards, and settle for awhile at St. Andrews.
—SCOTT: *Fortunes of Nigel.*

Neep, a turnip; from the French *navet.*

A late Lord Justice-Clerk of the Court of Session, who was fond of sport, was shooting pheasants in a field of turnips, when the farmer, whose consent had not been asked, and who looked upon the sportsman as an illegal trespasser, rushed out of his house in a towering passion, and called out in a loud voice, " Come oot o' that you, sir! come oot o' that immediately." The Lord Justice-Clerk, unaccustomed to this style of address, confronted the angry man, and asked him if he knew to whom he was speaking? " I dinna ken, and I dinna care; ye'se come oot o' that, or I'll mak it the waur for ye." " I'm the Lord Justice-Clerk," said the legal dignitary, thinking to overawe the irate agriculturist. " I dinna care whose clerk ye are, but ye'se come oot o' my *neeps.*" How the altercation ended is not on record, though it is believed that his lordship left the field quietly, after enlightening the farmer as to his high status and position, and cooling his wrath by submission to an authority not to be successfully contested, without greater trouble than the contest was worth.—*Scottish Wit and Humour.*

Neuk, a corner; English a nook, a small corner. Both words are derived from the Gaelic *uig,* a corner, which, with the indefinite article *an* before it, was corrupted from an *ook,* or an *uig,* into a *neuk,* or a *nook.* The Flemish *uig* and *hoek,* and the German *eck,* a corner, are traceable to the same Celtic root.

The deil sits girnin' in the *neuk,*
Rivin' sticks to roast the Deuk.
—*Jacobite Ballad on the Victory of the Duke of Cumberland at Culloden.*

Nevermas, the time that never comes. This word, equivalent to the "Greek kalends," is formed after the model of Martinmas, Michaelmas, and Christmas. It does not occur in Jamieson. It is found in Armstrong's Gaelic Dictionary as the translation of *Là buain na lin,* the "day of the cutting of the flax," which has in the Highlands the meaning of "never," or "at no time," or "at a very uncertain time."

Nicher, to neigh, to snort; French, *nennir,* sometimes written *hennir;* Flemish, *nenniker,* or *ninniker.*

Little may an auld nag do that maunna *nicher.*
—ALLAN RAMSAY'S *Scots Proverbs.*

Nick, Auld Nick, Nickie-Ben. All these names are used in Scotland to signify the devil; the third is peculiar to Scotland, and finds no place in English parlance.

But fare-you-weel, auld *Nickie-Ben!*
Oh, wad ye tak a thought an' men',
Ye aiblins might, I dinna ken,
  Still hae a stake!
I'm wae to think upon yon den,
  Even for your sake!
—BURNS : *Address to the Deil.*

Why *Nick* came to signify Satan in the British Isles has never been satisfactorily explained. Butler in *Hudibras* supposes that he was so called after Nicholas Macchiavelli.

Nick Macchiavel had no such trick,
Though he gave name to our *Old Nick.*

But the name was in use many ages before Macchiavelli was born; and the passage must, therefore, be considered as a joke, rather than as a philological assertion. It is remarkable, too, that *Nick* and *Old Nick*, whatever be the derivation, is a phrase unknown to any nation of Europe except our own. The derivation from Nicholas is clearly untenable; that from *Nikkr*, a water-sprite or goblin, in the Scandinavian mythology, is equally so; for the *Old Nick* of British superstition is reputed to have more to do with fire than water, and has no attributes in common with Satan, the prince of the powers of evil. To derive the word from *niger*, or *nigger*, black, because the devil is reputed to be black, is but perverted ingenuity. All the epithets showered upon the devil by Burns,

Oh thou, whatever title suit thee,
Auld Satan, Hornie, Nick, or Clootie,

are, with the exception of Satan, titles of irreverence, familiarity, and jocosity; *Hornie*, from the horns he is supposed to wear on his forehead, and *Clootie*, from his cloven hoofs, like those of a goat. It is probable that *Nick* and *Old Nick* are words of a similarly derisive character, and that *nick*, which appears in the glossaries to Allan Ramsay and to Burns, as *cheat* or *to cheat*, is the true origin, and that *Old Nick* simply signifies the *Old Cheat*. It may be mentioned, in connection with the idea of *cheat* or *nick*, that *old gentleman* is a name often given to Satan by people who object to the word *devil*, and that the same name is descriptive, according to the Slang Dictionary, of a card almost imperceptibly longer than the other cards of the pack, used by card-sharpers for the purpose of cheating. To be out on the *nick* is, on the same authority, to be out thieving. The etymology of *nick* in this sense is doubtful. Dr. Adolphus Wagner, the learned editor of the German edition of Burns, derives it from the Greek Νεκω, and translates it "to bite or to cheat." In Wright's Dictionary of Obsolete and Provincial English, *nick* is "to deceive, to cheat, to deny"; also, to win at dice unfairly."

Nidder, Nither, to lower, to depress; *niddered*, pinched with cold or hunger, with the vital energies depressed; also, stunted or lowered in growth. From the German *nieder*, low, or down; the Flemish *neder*, English *nether*, as in the Biblical phrase, "the upper and the *nether* millstone." *Netherlands*, the low countries; the French *Pays Bas*.

Nithered by the norlan' breeze,
The sweet wee flower aft dwines and dees.
—JAMES BALLANTINE.

Nieve, the fist, the closed hand; *nevel*, to strike with the fist, a blow with the fist. From the Teutonic *knuffen*, to beat with the fist, to cuff, to fisticuff.

Though here they scrape, and squeeze,
and growl,
Their worthless *nieve-fu'* o' a soul
May in some future carcass howl
The forest's fright.
—BURNS : *Epistle to John Lapraik.*

Sir Alexander Ramsay of Fasque, showing a fine stot to a butcher, said, " I was
offered twenty guineas for that beast."
"Indeed, Fasque!" said the butcher, "ye
should hae steekit your *nieve* upon that."
—DEAN RAMSAY.

They partit manly with a *nevel;*
God wat gif hair was ruggit
Betwixt thame.
—*Christ's Kirk on the Green.*

He hasna as muckle sense as a cow could
had in her *nieve.*—ALLAN RAMSAY'S *Scots
Proverbs.*

Mark the rustic, haggis-fed,
The trembling earth resounds his tread,
Clap in his walie *nieve* a blade,
He'll mak' it whissle ;
And legs and arms and heads will sned
Like taps o' thrissle.
—BURNS : *To a Haggis.*

Niffer, to barter, to exchange.
Probably, according to Jamieson, from *nieve,* the fist or closed
hand—to exchange an article
that is in one hand for that
which is in the other. This etymology is doubtful, although no
better one has been suggested.

Ye'll no be *niffered* but for a waur, and
that's no possible.—ALLAN RAMSAY'S *Scots
Proverbs.*

Ye see your state wi' theirs compared,
And shudder at the *niffer;*
But, cast a moment's fair regard,
What maks the mighty differ?
—BURNS : *To the Unco Guid.*

Nippit, miserly, mean, parsimonious, near ; from *nip,* to pinch.
The English *pinch* is often applied in the same sense.

Noo or **the noo,** at the present
time, now.

On one occasion a neighbour waited on
a small laird in Lanarkshire, named Hamilton, and requested his signature to an
accommodation bill for twenty pounds at
three months' date, which led to the following characteristic colloquy :—
"Na! na!" said the laird, "I canna
do that."
"What for no, laird? Ye hae done the
same thing for others."
"Aye, aye, Tammas! but there's wheels
within wheels that ye ken naething about.
I canna do't."
"It's a sma' thing to refuse me, laird."
"Weel, ye see, Tammas, if I was to pit
my name till't, ye wad get the siller frae
the bank, and when the time cam round,
ye wadna be ready, an' I wad hae to pay't.
An' then me an' you wad quarrel. So we
may just as weel quarrel *the noo,* an' I' ll
keep the siller in my pouch."—DEAN
RAMSAY.

Nowte, horned cattle ; corrupted
in English into *neat.*

Mischief begins wi' needles and prins,
And ends wi' horned *nowte.*
—ALLAN RAMSAY.

Or by Madrid he takes the route,
To thrum guitars and fecht wi' *nowte.*
—BURNS : *The Twa Dogs.*

Lord Seafield, who was accused by his brother of accepting a bribe to vote for the union
betwixt England and Scotland,
endeavoured to retort upon him
by calling him a cattle-dealer.
" Ay, weel," replied his brother,
" better sell *nowte* than nations."

Noyt, noit, or **nowt,** to injure, to
hurt, to beat, to strike ; from
the French *nuire,* to injure.

The miller was of manly mak,
To meet him was na mowis,

> They durst not come him to tak,
> Sae *noytit* he their powis.
> —*Christ's Kirk on the Green.*

Nugget, a word scarcely known to the English until the discovery of gold in California and Australia, when it was introduced by the miners to signify a large piece of the metal as distinguished from grains of gold dust. Many attempts have been made to trace its etymology, only one of which has found a qualified acceptance— that which affirms it to be a corruption of *ingot.* This is plausible, but not entirely satisfactory. In some parts of Scotland, the word for a *luncheon*, or a hasty repast taken at noon, is *noggit*—sometimes written *knockit*—which means a piece. In other parts of Scotland the word used is *piece*, as, " Gie the bairn its *piece*," and the word *lunch* itself, from the Gaelic *lonach*, hungry, signifies the *piece* which is cut off a loaf or a cheese to satisfy the appetite during the interval that elapses before the regular meal.

> When hungry thou stoodest, staring like
> an oaf,
> I sliced the *luncheon* from the barley loaf.
> —GAY.

All these examples tend to show that *nugget* simply means a lump or piece. In Kent, according to Wright's Archaic Dictionary, a lump of food is called a *nuncheon.*

Nyse, to beat, to pommel, a word in use among the boys of the High School of Edinburgh ; from the Gaelic *naitheas* (*t* silent), a mischief. " I'll *nyse* you," " I'll do you a mischief."

O

Ock, a diminutive particle appended to Scottish words, and implying littleness combined with the idea of tenderness and affection, as in lass, *lassock*, wife, *wifock*. This termination is sometimes combined with *ie*, thus making a double diminutive, as *lassockie*, often spelled *lassickie*, and *wifockie, wifiekie.* *Ock* is probably derived from the Gaelic *og*, young.

Olyte, diligent, industrious, active. According to Mr. Halliwell, this word appears in the Harleian MS., and is still used in some parts of England. Jamieson spells it *olight* and *olite*, and derives it from the Swedish *oflaet*, " too light, fleet," but no such word is to be found in the Swedish dictionaries, nor in those of the other Teutonic languages. Possibly the true origin of the word is the Gaelic *oil*, to rear, educate, instruct, and *oilte*, instructed, *oilean*, instruction, good-breeding ; whence an *olyte* mother, in the proverb quoted below, may signify a woman instructed in the due performance of all her household duties, and performing them so zealously as to leave nothing for her daughter to do. *Oileanta,* more commonly written *ealanta,* signifies quick, nimble, active.

An *olyte* mother makes a sweer daughter.
—ALLAN RAMSAY'S *Scots Proverbs.*

Oo aye ! An emphatic assertion of assent. The French *oui.*

Orra, all sorts of odds and ends, occasional.

Where Donald Caird fand *orra* things.
—SCOTT.

She's a weel-educate woman, and if she win to her English as I hae heard her do at *orra* times, she may come to fickle us a'.
—SCOTT : *The Antiquary.*

Orra,—now and then, unusual, not frequently met with, almost always associated with time.—R. DRENNAN.

Orra man. A man employed to do odd jobs on a farm, that are not in the regular routine of the work of the other farm servants.

Oughtlins, pertaining to duty, or to that which *ought* to be done ; a word composed of *ought,* a *debt* owing to duty, honour and propriety, and *lins* (see AIBLINS, WESTLINS, &c.), inclining towards.

If that daft buckie, Geordie Wales,
Was grown *oughtlins* douser.
—BURNS : *On Receiving a Newspaper.*

Ourie or oorie, cold, shivering. This word, peculiar to Scotland,

is derived from the Gaelic *fuar,* cold, which, with the aspirate, becomes *fhuar,* and is pronounced *uar.*

I thought me on the *ourie* cattle.
—BURNS : *A Winter Night.*

The English *hoar-frost,* and the *hoary* (white, snowy) hair of old age, are traceable to the same etymological root. Jamieson, however, derives *oorie* from the Icelandic *ur,* rain, and the Swedish *ur,* stormy weather, though the origin of both is to be found in the Gaelic *uaire,* bad weather or storm.

Outthrough, entirely or completely through.

They dived in through the one burn bank,
Sae did they *outthrough* the other.
—BUCHAN'S *Ancient Ballads.*

Out-cast, a quarrel, to "cast-out," to quarrel.

O dool to tell,
They've had a bitter black *cast-out*
Atween themsel.
—BURNS : *The Twa Herds.*

I didna ken they had *casten-out.*
—DEAN RAMSAY.

Outlers, cattle left out at night in the fields, ·for want of byres or folds to shelter them.

Amang the brackens on the brae,
  Between her an' the moon,
The Deil or else an *outler quey*
  Gat up and gae a croon.
Poor Lizzie's heart maist lap the hool—
  Near lav'rock height she jumpit,
But miss'd a foot, and in the pool
  Out owre the lugs she plumpit.
—BURNS : *Hallowe'en.*

Outside of the Loof, the back of the hand. "The outside of my loof to ye," is a phrase that signifies a wish on the part of the person who uses it to reject the friendship or drop the acquaintance of the person to whom it is addressed.

"If ye'll no join the Free Kirk," said a wealthy widow to her cousin, to whom she had often conveyed the hint that he might expect a handsome legacy at her death (a hint that never ripened into a fact), "ye'll hae the *outside* o' my loof, and never see the inside o't again."—C. M.

Outspeckle, a laughing - stock ; and *kenspeckle,* to be easily recognised by some outer mark of singularity. These words have a common origin, and are derived either from *speck,* or *speckle,* a small mark or spot; or from *spectacle,* corrupted into *speckle ;* but most probably from the former.

"Wha drives thir kye," gan Willie to say,
"To mak' an *outspeckle* o' me !"
—*Border Ballads : Jamie Telfer.*

Outwittens, unknowingly, without the knowledge of.

Outwittens of my daddie [*i.e.,* my father not knowing it].—JAMIESON.

Overlay or **owerlay,** the burden or chorus of a song ; the *refrain.*

And aye the *owerlay* o' his sang
Was, wae's me for Prince Charlie.
—*Jacobite Ballad.*

The French *refrain,* recently adopted into English, is of Gaelic origin, from *ramh* or *raf,* an oar, and *rann,* a song ; a sea song or boat-song, formerly chanted to the motion of the oars by Celtic boatmen in Brittany and the Scottish Highlands.

Ower Bogie, a proverbial phrase used in regard to a marriage which has been celebrated by a magistrate, and not by a clergyman. Synonymous in Aberdeenshire with the English Gretna Green marriages, performed under similar conditions. The origin is unknown, though it is supposed that some accommodating magistrate, at some time or other, resided on the opposite side of the river Bogie from that of the town or village inhabited by the lovers who desired to be joined in the bonds of matrimony without subjecting themselves to the sometimes inconvenient interrogations of the kirk. Jamieson erroneously quotes the phrase as *owre boggie.*

I will awa wi' my love,
I will awa' wi' her,
Though a' my kin' had sorrow and said,
I'll *ower Bogie* wi' her.
—ALLAN RAMSAY : *Tea Table Miscellany.*

Owergang, to surpass, to exceed.

You're straight and tall and handsome withal,
But your pride *owergangs* your wit.
—*Ballad of Proud Lady Margaret.*

Ower-word, a chorus or burden. A phrase often repeated in a song, the French *bourdon,* the English *burthen* of a song.

K

And aye the *ower-word* of his song
Was, wae's me for Prince Charlie.
　　—GLEN : *A Jacobite Song.*

The starling flew to the window stane,
　It whistled and it sang,
And aye the *ower-word* o' the tune
Was " Johnnie tarries lang."
　　　—*Johnnie of Breadislee.*

Oxter, the armpit and the space
between the shoulder and the
bosom ; sometimes it is used incorrectly for the lap ; and to embrace, to encircle with the arms
in fondness. From the Gaelic
uchd, the breast or bosom ;
whence also the Latin *uxor*, a
wife, *i.e.*, the wife of one's
bosom ; and *uxorious*, fondly attached to a wife·; *uchd mhac*, an
adopted son, the son of one's
bosom. Jamieson derives *oxter*
from the Teutonic *oxtel*, but no
such word is to be found in the
German language. The Flemish
and Dutch have *oksel*, a gusset,
which Johnson defines as "an
angular piece of cloth, inserted
in a garment, particularly at
the upper end of the sleeve of
a shirt, or as a part of the neck."
This word has a clear but remote connection with the Gaelic
uchd.

He did like ony mavis sing,
　And as I in his *oxter* sat
He ca'd me aye his *bosome* thing.
　　—ALLAN RAMSAY : *Tea Table
　　　　Miscellany.*

Here the phrase "sitting in
his *oxter*" is equivalent to sitting
folded in his arms, or clasped
to his bosom.

P

Pack, familiar, intimate, closely
allied.

Nae doubt but they were fain o' ither,
And unco *pack* and thick thegither,
Wi' social nose whiles snuff'd and howkit.
　　—BURNS : *The Twa Dogs.*

Pack is not only used as an
adjective, but is common as a
noun in colloquial English, as
in the phrase, a *pack* of rascals,
and a *pack* of thieves. In this
sense it is derivable from the
Gaelic *pac* or *pacca*, a troop, a mob.

Pad, to travel, to ride. Often in
Scotland when a lady is seen on
horseback in the rural districts,
the children of the villages follow her, crying out, " Lady *pad !*
lady *pad !*" Jamieson says that
on *pad* is to travel on foot, that
pad, the hoof, is a cant phrase,
signifying to walk, and that the
ground is *paddit* when it has
been hardened by frequent passing and repassing. He derives
the word from the Latin *pes*,
pedis, the foot. It seems, however, to be more immediately
derived from *path ; pad*, to go
on the *path*, whether on foot
or on horseback ; from the
German *pfad*, the Flemish *pad*,
and *voet - pad*, the foot - path.
The English dictionaries erroneously explain *pad* in the word

foot-pad, a highway thief. But *pad* by itself is never used in the sense of steal. Grose's Classical Dictionary of the Vulgar Tongue has *pad-borrowers*, horse-stealers, as if *pad* signified a horse. The phrase really means *path-borrowers*, *i.e.*, borrowers on the path or journey.

Padda, Paddock, a frog or toad ; *paddock stool*, a toad-stool, a wild fungus or mushroom. Flemish *pad* and *padde*, a frog.

Says the mother, "What noise is that at the door, daughter?" "Hoot," says the lassie, "it's naething but a filthy *padda.*" "Open the door," says the mother, "to the puir *padda.*" Sae the lassie opened the door, and the *padda* cam loup, loup, loupin' in, and sat doun by the ingle side. —*Scottish Songs collected by* ROBERT CHAMBERS, 1829.

Gowks and fools,
Frae colleges and boarding schools,
May sprout like summer *paddock-stools*,
In glen or shaw.
—BURNS : *Verses written at Selkirk.*

Old Lady Perth, offended with a French gentleman for some disparaging remark which he had made on Scottish cookery, answered him curtly, "Weel I weel ! some folk like parritch, and some like *paddocks.*" —DEAN RAMSAY.

Paidle. This eminently Scottish word has no synonym in the English language, nor in any country where everybody, even the poorest, wears shoes or boots, and where, to go bare-footed, would imply the lowest social degradation. But in Scotland, a land of streams, rivulets, and burns, that wimple down the hills and cross the paths and roads, to go barefooted is a pleasure and luxury, and a convenience, especially to the children of both sexes, and even to young men and women verging upon manhood and womanhood. An Englishman may *paddle* his boat and his canoe, but a Scotsman *paidles* in the mountain stream. How the young children of England love to *paidle*, may occasionally be seen at the sea-side resorts of the southern counties in the summer season, but the Scottish child in the rural districts *paidles* all the year, and needs no holiday for the purpose.

We twa hae *paidled* in the burn,
Frae morning sun till dine,
But seas between us braid hae roared,
Sin' the days of auld lang syne.
—BURNS.

The remembrance of *paidlin'* when stirred by the singing of this immortal song by Scotsmen in America, in India, in Africa, or at the Antipodes, melts every Scottish heart to tenderness, or inspires it to patriotism, as every Scotsman, who has travelled much, very surely knows.

Paik, a beating, to beat, to thrash, to fight, to drub, to strike. Jamieson derives this word from the German *pauken*, to beat ; but there is no such word in that language. *Pauke* in German, *pauk* in Flemish, signifies a kettle-drum ; and *pauken*, to beat the kettle-drum, but not to beat in any other sense. The word is probably from the Gaelic *paigh*, to pay ; and also, by an extension of meaning, to pay one's deserts by a beating, as in the proverb in Allan Ramsay—"He's sairest dung that is *paid* with his own wand," *i.e.*, he is sorest hit who is beaten with his own cudgel.

Paikie, a trull, a prostitute, a *fille de joie,* a euphemism from the Gaelic *peacadh (peaca),* a sinner. *Paik,* a sin ; the French *pecher;* and the Italian *peccare.*

> In adulterie he was ta'en—
> Made to be punisht for his *paik.*
> —Jamieson.

Pang, to fill full, to cram ; *pang-fu',* as full as one can hold. Etymology unknown ; but possibly related to the French *panse,* belly ; *pansu,* large-bellied ; English *paunchy.*

> Leeze me on drink ; it gies us mair
> Than either school or college,
> It kindles wit, it waukens lair,
> It *pangs* us fu' o' knowledge.
> —Burns : *The Holy Fair.*

Parle, a discourse ; from the French *parler,* to speak ; the Italian *parlare.* The Gaelic *beurla* signifies language, and more particularly the English language.

> A tocher's nae word in a true lover's *parle,*
> But gie me my love, and a fig for the warl.—Burns : *Meg o' the Mill.*

Parritch or **porridge.** A formerly favourite, if not essential, food of the Scottish people of all classes, composed of oatmeal boiled in water to a thick consistency, and seasoned with salt. This healthful food is generally taken with milk, but is equally palatable with butter, sugar, beer, or wine. It is sometimes retained in middle and upper class families ; but among the very poor has unfortunately been displaced by the cheaper and less nutritious potato.

> The hailsome *parritch,* chief o' Scotia's food.
> —Burns : *Cotter's Saturday Night.*

Partan, a crab, from the Gaelic ; *partanach,* abounding in crabs ; *partan-handit,* epithet applied to one who is hard-fisted and penurious, who grips his money like a crab grips with its claw.

> An' there'll be *partans* and *buckies,*
> An' singit sheeps' heads and a haggis.
> —*The Blithesome Bridal.*

Pash, the head, the brow, the forehead. Allan Ramsay, barber and wig-maker, sang of his trade :—

> I theek [thatch] the out, and line the inside,
> Of mony a douce and witty *pash,*
> And baithways gather in the cash.

A bare *pash* signifies a bald head, and mad-*pash* is equivalent to the English madcap. Latham's Todd's Johnson has *pash,* to push or butt like a ram or bull, with the head. *Pash* was current English in the time of Shakspeare, who uses it in the "Winter's Tale," in a passage which no commentator has been able to explain. Leontes, suspicious of the fidelity of his wife Hermione, asks his child Mamilius—

Art thou my calf?

To which Mamilius replies—

Yes! if you will, my Lord.

Leontes, still brooding on his imaginary wrong, rejoins moodily—

Thou wants a rough *pash* and the shoots that I have to be full like me.

It is amusing to note into what errors the English editors of Shakspeare have fallen, in their ignorance of this word. Nares thought that *pash* was something belonging to a bull —he did not know what—or a calf, and Steevens thought that it was the Spanish *paz*, a kiss. Mr. Howard Staunton, the editor of Shakspeare, had a glimpse of the meaning, and thought that *pash* meant a "*tufted* head." Jamieson acknowledged the word, but attempted no etymology. *Pash* is clearly derivable from the Gaelic *bathais* (pronounced *bash* or *pash*), and signifies the forehead. The allusion of the unhappy Leontes to the *shoots* on his rough *pash* (wrinkled brow) is to the horns that vulgar phraseology places on the foreheads of deceived and betrayed husbands. Read by this gloss, the much-misunderstood passage in the "Winter's Tale" becomes clear.

Paughty, proud, haughty, repulsive, but without having the qualities of mind or person to justify the assumption of superiority over others. Probably derived from the Flemish *pochen*, to vaunt, to brag, and *pocher*, a braggadocio, a *fanfaron*.

An askin', an askin', my father dear,
An askin' I beg of thee;
Ask not that *paughty* Scottish lord,
For him ye ne'er shall see.
—*Ballad of the Gay Goss-Hawk.*

Yon *paughty* dog
That bears the keys of Peter.
—BURNS: *A Dream.*

Paumie and taws. All Scottish school-boys, past and present, have painful knowledge of the meaning of these two words. *Paumie* is a stroke over the open hand, with a cane or the *taws*. The *taws* is a thong of leather cut into a fringe at the end, and hardened in the fire. It is, and was, the recognised mode of punishment for slight offences or breaches of discipline at school, when the master was unwilling to resort to the severer and more degrading punishment, inflicted *a posteriori*, after the fashion of Dr. Busby. *Paumie* is derived from the *palm* of the hand, the French *peaume*, and *taws* is the plural form of the Gaelic *taod*, a rope, a scourge.

Pawky, of a sly humour, wise, witty, cautious, discreet, and insinuating,—all in one. There is no synonym for this word in English. The etymology is unknown.

The *pawky* auld carle cam owre the lea,
Wi' mony good e'ens and good days to me.

Dear Smith, the slee'est, *pawkie* thief.
—BURNS: *To James Smith.*

Peat-Reek and Mountain Dew.

Peat-Reck is the smoke of peat when dried and burned for fuel, the flavour of which used to be highly appreciated in Scottish whiskey, when made by illicit distillers in lonely glens among the mountains, out of the usual reach of the exciseman. From the solitary places of its manufacture, whiskey received the poetic name of *Mountain Dew*, or the "Dew off Ben Nevis," which it still retains.

Mountain Dew, *clear* as a Scot's understanding,
Pure as his conscience wherever he goes,
Warm as his heart to the friends he has chosen,
Strong as his arm when he fights with his foes !
In liquor like this should old Scotland be toasted,
So fill up again, and the pledge we'll renew ;
Unsullied in honour, our blessings upon her—
Scotland for ever ! and old *Mountain Dew !*—MACKAY.

Pech,

to pant, to blow, for want of breath. Derived by Jamieson from the Danish *pikken*, to palpitate.

My Pegasus I gat astride,
And up Parnassus *pechin'*.
—BURNS : *To Willie Chalmers.*

There comes young Monks of high complexion,
Of mind devout, love and affection ;
And in his court their hot flesh dart (tame),
Fule father-like with *pech* and pant,
They are sa humble of intercession,
Their errand all kind women grant,
Sic tidings heard I at the session.
—ALLAN RAMSAY : *The Evergreen— Frae the Session.*

Pechan,

the stomach.

Ev'n the ha' folk fill their *pechan*
Wi' sauce, ragouts, and such like trashtrie,
That's little short o' downright wastrie.
—BURNS : *The Twa Dogs.*

This word seems to be a corruption of the Gaelic *poc*, a bag, a poke ; and *pocan*, a little bag ; and to be ludicrously applied to the belly or stomach. The English slang *peckish*, hungry, is probably derived from the same root, and not from the beak, or peck of a bird.

Pedder-coffe,

a pedlar. In Allan Ramsay's "Evergreen," a poem ascribed to Sir David Lyndsay is entitled a "Description of *Pedder-coffs*, their having no regard to honesty in their vocation." Both *pedder* and *coffe* are of Teutonic derivation ; *ped*, sometimes written *pad*, from the German *pfad ;* Flemish *pad*, a path ; and *coffe* or *koffe*, from *kaufen*, to buy ; whence a pedlar signified a walking merchant who carried his wares along with him. But it should be observed with regard to the Teutonic derivation, that in the Kymric, or ancient language of Wales, more ancient than the German, *padd* signifies one that keeps a course. Attempts have been made to trace *pedlar* to *ped*, a local word in some parts of England for a basket : but this derivation would not account for *pedder*, a mounted highwayman ; for foot-*pad*, a highway robber on foot, from the slang expression among thieves and beggars to go on the *pad*, *i.e.*, on the tramp.

Jamieson derives the Scottish *pedder* from the barbarous low Latin *pedarius*, i.e., *nudis ambulans pedibus*. Sir David Lyndsay in his poem was exceedingly indignant, both with the *Pedders* and the *Coffes*, who seem to have been in their mode of transacting business with the country people, whom they favoured with their visits on their peregrinations through districts afar from towns, the exact counterparts of the tallymen at the present day. He recommends, in the interest of the people, that wherever the "pedder knaves appear in a burgh or town where there is a magistrate, that their lugs should be cuttit off," as a warning to all cheats and regrators. A similar outcry is sometimes raised against the "tallymen," or travelling linen-drapers and haberdashers, who tempt the wives of working men, and poor people generally, to buy their goods at high prices, and accept small weekly payments on account, until their extortionate bills are liquidated.

Peel, a border tower, a small fortress, of which few specimens are now left standing. A very interesting one, however, still remains in the town of Melrose. Possibly a corruption of *bield*, a shelter.

And black Joan, frae Creighton-*peel*,
O' gipsy kith an' kin'.
—BURNS : *The Five Carlins.*

An' when they came to the fair Dodhead
Right hastily they clam (climbed) the *peel*,
They loosened the kye out, ane and a',
An' ranshackled the house right weel.
—*Border Minstrelsy : Jamie Telfer.*

Peep, to utter a faint cry or sound, like an infant or a young bird. *Peepie-weepie*, a querulous and tearful child ; *peep-sma'*, a feeble voice, a weak person who has to submit to the domination of one stronger ; synonymous with the English "sing small." "He daurna play *peep*," he must not utter a word in defence of himself. In Dutch and Flemish, *pirpen* signifies to cry like an infant ; and *piep-yong* is a word for a very young or new-born child. The etymology is that of *pipe*, or the sound emitted by a flute or pipe, when gently blown upon.

Peesweep, a lapwing, or plover ; *peesweep-like*, a contemptible epithet applied to a feeble, sharp-featured man or woman, with a shrill but not loud voice, like the cry of a plover.

Peerie, **pearie** or **perie**, a humming top ; sometimes a peg-top ; from the Gaelic *beur* (*b* pronounced as *p*), to hum, to buzz. Brand, in his well-known work on Popular Antiquities, quotes Jamieson as his authority. He defines it to mean a peg-top, and adds that the name was apparently derived from its close similarity to a pear, and that the Scotch originally called it a French pear or *pearie*, because it was first imported from France.

Peik-thank, is, according to Jamieson, an ungrateful person, one who returns little or no thanks for benefits conferred. *Peik* in this phrase seems to be a corruption and misspelling of the Gaelic *beag* (*b* pronounced as *p*), little. Jamieson derives it from the Italian *poco*.

The English *pick-thank* appears to have had a different origin and meaning, and signifies, according to the examples of its use in Nares, a sycophant, a favourite, a flatterer, who strove to pick up, acquire, or gather thanks from the great and powerful. Shakspeare has " smiling *pick-thanks*, and base newsmongers;" Fairfax, "a flatterer, a *pick-thank*, and a liar."

Possibly, however, the Scottish and English interpretations of the word may be more akin than might appear at first glance. Sycophants, flatterers, and parasites are proverbially ungrateful, unless it be, as La Rochefoucauld so wittily asserts, " for favours to come."

Pendles, ear-rings ; from pendants.

She's got *pendles* in her lugs,
  Cockle-shells wad set her better ;
High-heel'd shoon and siller tags,
  And a' the lads are wooin' at her.

Be a lassie e'er sae black,
  Gin she ware the penny-siller,
Set her up on Tintock tap,
  The wind will blaw a man till her !
  —HERD'S *Collection : Tibbie Fowler.*

Pennarts. Jamieson says this word means "revenge," and quotes the proverbial saying, " I'se hae *pennarts* o' him yet ; " suggesting that the derivation may be from *pennyworths*. It is more likely to be from the Gaelic *pein*, punishment ; *peanas*, revenge ; and *pein-ard*, high or great revenge.

Penny-fee, wages. *Penny* is commonly used in Scottish parlance for money generally, as in *penny-siller*, a great quantity of money ; *penny-maister*, the town-treasurer ; *penny-wedding*, a wedding at which every guest contributed towards the expense of the marriage festival ; *penny-friend*, a friend whose only friendship is for his friend's money. The French use *denier*, and the Italians *danari*, in the same sense.

Peny is ane hardy knyght,
Peny is mekyl of myght,
Peny of wrong he maketh ryght
  In every country where he go.
  —RITSON'S *Ancient Songs and
    Ballads : A Song in Praise
    of Sir Peny.*

My riches a's my *penny-fee*,
And I maun guide it canny, O.
  —BURNS : *My Nannie, O.*

Pensy, proud, conceited ; above one's station. Probably a corruption of pensive or thoughtful.

Helen Walker was held among her equals to be *pensy*, but the facts brought to prove this accusation seem only to evince a strength of character superior to those around her.—SCOTT : *Heart of Midlothian.*

Perlins or **pearlins**, fine linen ornamented with lace work or knitted work.

Oh where, oh where, is her auld son,
Spak out the Lammikin ;
He's gane to buy *pearlins*
Gin our lady lye in.
These *pearlins* she shall never wear,
Spak out the Lammikin.
—HERD's *Collection: Lammikin.*

Pernickitie (sometimes written *prig-nickitie*), precise about trifles ; finicking, over - dainty, trim, neat, nicely dressed, adorned with trifling articles of finery, or knick - knackets. Etymology doubtful.

The English are sae *pernickity* about what they eat, but no sae *pernickity* about what they drink.—*Noctes Ambrosianæ.*

Peuter or **peuther**, to canvass, to solicit votes, to thrust one's self forward in election times to ask for support ; from the Gaelic *put*, to thrust, and *putair*, one who thrusts ; and the Flemish *peuteren*, to poke one's fingers into other people's business,— rendered in the French and Flemish Dictionary (1868), " pousser les doigts, dans quelque chose."

He has *peuthered* Queensferry and Inverkeithing, and they say he will begin to *peuther* Stirling next week.—JAMIESON.

Philabeg or **fillabeg**, the kilt as worn by the Highlanders ; lite- rally a little cloth ; from the Gaelic *fileadh*, a cloth, a woven garment, and *beag*, little.

Oh to see his tartan trews,
Bonnet blue, and laigh-heeled shoes,
Philabeg aboon his knee—
That's the laddie I'll gang wi'.
—GEDDES : *Lewie Gordon.*

I' faith, quo' John, I got sic flegs (frights)
Wi' their claymore and *philabegs*,
If I face them again, deil break my legs,
So I wish you a good mornin'.
—*Jacobite Ballad : Hey Johnnie Cope.*

They put on him a *philabeg*,
An' up his dowp they rammed a peg,
How he did skip, and he did roar,
The deils ne'er saw sic fun before.

They took him niest to Satan's ha',
There to lilt wi' his grandpapa ;
Says Cumberland, I'll no gang ben
For fear I meet wi' Charlie's men.
—*Jacobite Ballad : Bonnie Laddie Highland Laddie.*

Pickle, a small quantity ; from the Italian *piccolo*, small, akin to the Gaelic *beag* (or *peag*), little. *Pickle* in familiar English, as applied to a small, unruly, and troublesome boy, is of the same origin ; " a wee *pickle* saut," a very small quantity of salt ; " a *pickle* o' tow," a small quantity of flax or hemp for spinning into yarn. *Pickle* is sometimes used for *pilfer*, to steal small things. " To *pickle* in one's ain pock, or peuk," *i.e.*, to take grain out of one's own bag, is a proverbial expression signifying to depend on one's own resources or exertions. A hen is said to "*pickle* up" when she searches for and feeds on grain. The word, in these senses, is not from the same source as *pickle*, to preserve in salt or vinegar.

> She gies the herd a *pickle* nits
> And twa red-cheekit apples.
> —BURNS : *Hallowe'en.*

Pig, an earthen pitcher or other vessel, a flower-pot. *Piggerie,* a place for the manufacture of crockery and earthenware. *Pig-man* and *pigwife,* hawkers of crockery, or keepers of shops where earthenware is sold ; from the Gaelic *pigeadh,* an earthen pot or jar ; *pigean,* a little pot ; *pigeadair,* a potter or manufacturer of crockery. The English *pig iron,* iron in a lump, before its final manufacturing by fire into a superior quality, seems to be derived from its coarse nature, as resembling the masses of clay from which crockery and earthenware are formed by the similar agency of fire.

> My Paisley *piggy*
> Contains my drink, but then, oh,
> No wines did e'er my brains engage
> To tempt my mind to sin, oh.
> —CHAMBERS's *Scots Songs : The Country Lass.*

> She that gangs to the well wi' ill-will
> Either the *pig* breaks or the water will spill.
> —ALLAN RAMSAY's *Scots Proverbs.*

> Where the *pig's* broken, let the shards lie.
> —*Idem.*

An English lady, who had never before been in Scotland, arranged to spend the night at a respectable inn, in a small provincial town in the south. Desiring to make her as comfortable as possible, Grizzy, the chambermaid, on showing her to the bedroom, said—

"Would you like to hae a *pig* in your bed this cauld nicht, mem ?"

"A what ?" said the lady.

"A *pig,* mem ; I will put a *pig* in your bed to keep you warm ! "

"Leave the room, young woman ; your mistress shall hear of your insolence."

"Nae offence, I hope, mem. It was my mistress bade me ask it, an' I'm sure she meant it oot o' kindness."

The lady was puzzled, but feeling satisfied that no insult was intended, she looked at the girl and then said pleasantly—

"Is it common in this country for ladies to have *pigs* in their beds ?"

"Gentlemen hae them tae, mem, when the weather's cauld. I'll steek the mouth o't an' tie it up in a clout."

A right understanding was come to at last, and the lady found the *pig* with hot water in her bed not so disagreeable as she imagined.—DOUGLAS's *Scottish Wit and Humour.*

A rich Glasgow manufacturer, an illiterate man who had risen from the ranks, having ordered a steam yacht, sent for a London artist to decorate the panels in the principal cabin. The artist asked what kind of decoration he required ? The reply was, *Ony thing simple, just a pig wi' a flower.* Great was the surprise of the Glasgow body when the work was completed, to see that the decoration consisted of swine, each with a flower in its jaws, which had been painted on every panel. He made no complaint—paid the bill, and declared the effect to be satisfactory, though "it was no exactly what he had meant in ordering it."—*Traits of Scottish Life.*

Pike, to pick and steal ; *pikie,* one addicted to pilfering and petty thefts.

> By these *pickers* and stealers.
> —SHAKSPEARE : *Hamlet.*

Pinch and drouth, hunger and thirst.

> Nae mair wi' *pinch and drouth* we'll pine
> As we hae done—a dog's propine—
> But quaff our draughts o' rosy wine,
> Carle ! an' the king come.
> —*Jacobite Song.*

Pinkie-small, the smallest candle that is made, the weakest kind of table beer, anything small. The word is also applied to the eye when contracted.

There's a wee *pinkie* hole in the stocking.—JAMIESON.

Possibly this word is from the Latin *punctus*, a point, or from the Dutch and Flemish *pink*, the little finger, and *pink-oogen*, to look with half-closed eyes. The Kymric *pinc* signifies a small branch or twig.

Pirrie-dog, a dog that follows at his master's heels; *pirrie*, to follow and fawn upon one, like a dependant, for what can be gained from or wheedled out of him. Jamieson derives this word from the Teutonic *paeren*, or *paaren*, to pair or couple; and refers to *parry*, an Aberdeenshire word, with a quotation, "When ane says *parry*, a' say *parry*," signifying that when anything is said by a person of consequence, it is echoed by every one else. The true origin both of *pirrie* and the Aberdonian *parry* seems to be the Gaelic *peire*, a polite word for the breech. A dog that follows at the *heels* is a euphemism for a less mentionable part of the person. Jamieson suggests that the Aberdeenshire *parry* is derived from the French *il parait*; but the Gaelic *peire* better suits the humour of the aphorism.

Piss-a-bed, a vulgar name for the dandelion or taraxacum—a beautiful, though despised, wild flower of the fields. The word appears to have originated in Scotland, and thence to have extended to England. It is a corruption of the Gaelic *pios*, a cup, and *buidhe*, yellow—a yellow cup, not, however, to be confounded with buttercup, another wild flower—the companion in popular affection of the daisy.

The daisy has its poets,—all have striven
Its world-wide reputation to prolong ;
But here's its yellow neighbour !—who has given
The dandelion a song?

Come, little sunflower, patient in neglect,
Will ne'er a one of them assert thy claim,
But, passing by, contemptuously connect
Thee and thy Scottish name?
—ROBERT LEIGHTON : *To a Dandelion.*

Several years before Robert Leighton strove to vindicate the fair fame of the dandelion, a couplet in its praise appeared in the *Illustrated London News*, in a poem entitled "Under the Hedge":—

Dandelions with milky ring,
Coins of the mintage of the spring.

Pit-dark, dark as in the bottom of a pit.

'Tis yet *pit-dark*, the yard a' black about,
And the night fowl begin again to shout.
—Ross's *Helenore.*

It is very probable that *pit-dark* was the original form of the English *pitch-dark*, as dark as *pitch*, *i.e.*, as dark as *tar*, or coal tar. The etymology from pit, a hole, is preferable.

Pixie, a fairy. This Scottish word is used in some parts of England, particularly in the south and west. It has been supposed to be a corruption of *puck*, or *puckie*, little *puck*, sometimes called Robin Goodfellow. It is more probably from the Gaelic *beag* (peg), little, *sith* (shee), a fairy, anglicised into *pixie*, a little fairy, a fairy sprite. *Puck* is the name of one particular goblin and sprite in Shakspeare, and in popular tradition; but the *pixies* are multitudinous, and the words *puck* and *pixie* are from different sources. The English *puck* is the word that, in one variety or another, runs through many European languages. The Welsh or Kymric has *pwca* (pooca), a goblin, a sprite, the Gaelic *bocan*, and Lowland Scottish *bogie*, the Russian *bug*, the Dutch and Flemish *spook*, the German *spuk*, &c.

Pixie-rings are fairy-rings, supposed to be made in the grass by the footsteps, not of one *puck*, but of many little sprites that gamble by moonlight on the green *pixie-stool*, a popular name for the fungus, sometimes called toad-stool; *pixie-led*, bewildered and led astray by the *ignis fatuus*, Jack o' Lantern, or Will o' the Wisp.

Plack, an ancient Scottish coin of the value of one-twelfth of an English penny.

> There's your *plack* an' my *plack*,
> Au' Jenny's bawbee.
> —*Old Song.*

> Nae howdie gets a social night,
> Or *plack* frae them.
> —Burns: *Scotch Drink.*

> Stretch a joint to catch a *plack*,
> Abuse a brother to his back.
> —Burns: *To Gavin Hamilton.*

The word is probably derived from the ancient Flemish coin, a *plaquette*, current before the introduction into the Netherlands of the French money, reckoned by francs and centimes.

Plea, a lawsuit; the substitution of the aggregate of law for the segregate. The English verb, *to plead*, has received in Scottish parlance a past tense which does not correctly belong to it, in the phrase, " he *pled* guilty," instead of " he *pleaded* guilty," as if *plead* were a word of Teutonic origin and subject to the Teutonic inflexion which governs most of the ancient English verbs, which are derived from the Dutch, German, or Danish, such as "bleed, bled;" "blow, blew;" "run, ran;" "freeze, froze," &c. &c. Verbs derived from the Latin and French cannot be correctly conjugated in the past tense, except by the addition of *d* or *ed* to the infinitive, as in "coerce, coerced;" "plead, pleaded."

> Nae *plea* is best. (It is best not to go to law at all.)—*Old Proverb.*

> When neighbours anger at a *plea*,
> The barley bree
> Cements the quarrel.—Burns.

Pliskie, a trick, a prank. From the Gaelic *plaosgach,* a sudden noise, a flash, a blaze.

Her lost militia fired her blood,
Deil na they never mae do guid,
Played her that *pliskie.*
—BURNS : *Author's Earnest Cry and Prayer.*

Ghaist ! ma certie, I sall ghaist them ! If they had their heads as muckle on their wark as on her daffins, they wadna play sic *pliskies !*—SCOTT : *St. Ronan's Well.*

Plooky, swollen, blotchy, pimpled. From the Gaelic *ploc,* a tumour, a bunch, a knob, a swelling. The English slang *bloke,* a swell, is probably from the same root.

Plooky, plooky are your cheeks,
And *plooky* is your chin,
And *plooky* are your armis twa
My bonnie queen's layne in.
—SCOTT's *Minstrels of the Scottish Border : Sir Hugh Le Blonde.*

Plotcock, the devil ; the dweller in the pit of hell, the fiend, the arch enemy. This singular word, or combination of words, appears in Jamieson as "from the Icelandic *Blotgod,* a name of the Scandinavian Pluto ; or *blotkok* —from *blot,* to sacrifice ; and *koka,* to swallow—*i.e.,* the swallower of sacrifices." May not a derivation be found nearer home than in Iceland : in the Gaelic *blot* (pronounced *plot*), a pit, a cavern ; and *cog,* to conspire, to tempt, to cheat ?

Since you can *cog,* I'll play no more with you.
—SHAKSPEARE : *Love's Labour's Lost.*

Lies, *coggeries,* and impostures.
—NARES.

The Kymric has *coegiaw,* or *cogio,* to cheat, to trick. To *cog* dice was to load the dice for the the purpose of cheating ; and *cogger,* in old English, signified a swindler, a cheat. This derivation would signify the cheat, the tempter who dwells in the *cavern* or bottomless pit of hell; and might have been included by Burns in his "Address to the Deil," among the other names which he bestows upon that personage.

Plout, plouter, to wade with difficulty through mire or water ; akin to the English *plod,* as in the line in Gray's Elegy :—

The ploughman homewards *plods* his weary way.

From the Gaelic *plodan,* a clod of mud or mire, a small pool of water ; *plodanachd,* the act of paddling in the water or the mud.

Plouting through thick and thin.
—GROSE.

Many a weary *plouter* she cost him
Through gutters and glaur.
—JAMIESON : *Popular Ballads.*

Had it no been, Mr. North, for your *plowterin'* in a' the rivers and lochs o' Scotland, like a Newfoundland dog.
—*Noctes Ambrosianæ.*

Ploy, a plot, scheme, contrivance.

I wish he mayna hae been at the bottom o' the *ploy* himsel'.—SCOTT : *Rob Roy.*

Pluff, a slight emission or short puff of smoke, either from a tobacco-pipe or of gas from a burning coal ; possibly of the same derivation as the English *puff*, a slight, short or sudden movement of the wind or the breath.

Pockpud, an abbreviation of the contemptuous epithet of *pock-pudding* applied by the Scottish multitude to the English, in the bygone days when the English were as unpopular in Scotland as the Scotch still are among the more ignorant of the lower classes in England.

They gloom, they glower, they look sae big,
At ilka stroke they fell a Whig;
They'll fright the fuds o' the *Pockpuds*,
For mony a buttock 's bare coming.
                    —*Jacobite Song*, 1745.

The English *pockpuddings* ken nae better.—SIR WALTER SCOTT: *Waverley*.

Pock-shakings, a humorous and vulgar term applied to the last born child of a large family, expressive of the belief that no more are to be expected.

Poind, to lay a distraint on a debtor's goods, to make a seizure for non-payment or arrears of rent. The word was once current in English, and survives in a corrupt form, as *impound*, and *pound*, an enclosure for stray cattle. The officer whose duty it was to *impound* was formerly called a *pindar*, a word that survives in tradition or legend in the "*Pindar* of Wakefield," celebrated in connection with the deeds, real or fabulous, of Robin Hood and his merry band of poachers and out-

laws. The etymology is from the French *poigne*, the closed fist, and *empoigner*, to seize. Multiple-*poinding* is a Scottish law-phrase, expressive of a series of *poindings*.

An' was na I a weary wight,
They *poin'd* my gear and slew my knight:
My servants a' for life did flee,
An' left me in extremitie.
                    —*Lament of the Border Widow.*

"A puir *poind*" signifies a weak, silly person, metaphorically applied to one who is not substantial enough to take hold of, intellectually or morally; one of no account or importance.

Point, an old Scottish word for state of body; almost equivalent to the modern "form," which implies good condition generally of body, mind, and manners.

Murray said that he never saw the Queen in better health or in better *point*.—RODERTSON: *History of Mary Queen of Scots.*

This is a French idiom, nearly allied to that which is now familiar to English ears, *en bon point.* "In better *point*" signifies more plump, or in fuller habit of body.—JAMIESON.

The word *point* has so many meanings, all derivable from and traceable to the Latin *punctus*, such as the *point* of a weapon; *puncture*, the pinch of a sharp weapon; *punctual*, true to the *point* of time, or the time appointed, &c., as to suggest that the etymology of *point*, in the sense of the French *en bon point*, and of the old Scotch, as used by Robertson in his reference to

Queen Mary, must be other than *punctus*. *En bon point* is euphemistic for stout, fat, fleshy, inclining to corpulency — all of which words imply the reverse of *pointed*. It is possible that the true root is the Gaelic *bun* (*b* pronounced as *p*), foundation, root ; applied to one who is in solid and substantial health or condition of body ; well formed and established, physically and morally. The word is indicative of stability rather than of sharpness or pointedness. The now current slang of "form," derived from the language of grooms, jockeys, and racing men, springs from the same idea of healthiness and good condition. The Gaelic *bunanta* signifies firm, well-set, and established. The colloquial and vulgar word *bum* is from the same root of *bun*, and produces *fundament ;* the French *fondement*, the bottom, the foundation.

Post, to tramp, to tread. To *post* the linen was to tread upon it with the bare feet in the washing-tub, a common practice among the women of the working-classes in Scotland. Seen for the first time by English travellers in the far North, the fashion excited not only their surprise, but sometimes their admiration, by the display of the shapely limbs of the bonnie Highland and Lowland lassies engaged in the work, with their petticoats kilted up to the knee,

without the faintest suspicion of immodesty. *Post* is derived from the Gaelic, "to tread ;" *postadh*, treading ; *postanach*, a little child that is just beginning to walk or tread. The word is thus of a different origin and meaning from *post*, an office, a station, a place, which is derived from the Latin *positum*. The *post - office* and the postal service, words which are common to nearly all the European languages, are more probably traceable to the Gaelic and Celtic source, in the sense of tread and tramp, than to the Latin *positum*. The postman *treads* his accustomed rounds to the great convenience of the public in all civilised countries.

In scouring woollen clothes or coarse linen when the strength of arm and manual friction are found insufficient, the Highland women put them in a tub with a proper quantity of water, and then with petticoats tucked up commence the operation of *posting*. When three women are engaged, one commonly tramps in the middle, and the others tramp around her. This process is called *postadh.*—ARMSTRONG's *Gaelic Dictionary*, 1820.

Pot, a deep pool, or eddy in a river.

> The neist step that she waded in,
>   She waded to the chin;
> The deepest *pot* in Clyde water
>   They gat sweet Willie in.
> —*Ballad of Willie and May Margaret.*

Pow or **powe**, the head ; from the old English *poll*. The impost called the "Poll-tax," that created such great dissatisfaction in the days of Wat Tyler, was a personal tax on the *head* or *poll.*

There is little wit in his *pow*
That lights the candle at the low [or fire].
—ALLAN RAMSAY'S *Scots Proverbs.*

The miller was of manly make,
To meet him was nae *mows* [joke];
There durst not ten cum him to take,
Sae noytit [thumped] he their *pows.*
—*Christ's Kirk on the Green.*

Fat pouches bode lean *pows.*—ALLAN RAMSAY'S *Scots Proverbs.*

Blessings on your frosty *pow,*
John Anderson, my jo.
—BURNS.

Powsoudie. Sheep's head broth. This word occurs in the humorous ballad by Francis Semple, "Fy let us a' to the bridal," which contains an ample list of all the dainty eatables served up at a marriage-feast among the rural population of Scotland in the seventeenth century.

And there'll be fadges and bracken,
And fouth o' gude gebbocks o' skate,
Powsoudie and drammock and crowdie,
And caller nowte-feet on a plate.
—WATSON'S *Collection,* 1706.

The word is compounded of *pow,* the head, and *soudie,* broth.

Powt, a young fowl or chicken; from the French, *poule* and *poulte;* in English, *poultry* and *poulterer.*

Ye peep (chirp or pipe) like a *powt,*
O Tammy, my man, are ye turned a saunt?
—HEW AINSLEE: *Tam o' the Balloch.*

Pree, to taste, to sip, "to *pree* the mou," to kiss the mouth. A story has long been current that

a young English nobleman, visiting at Gordon Castle, had boasted that during his six weeks' shooting in the north he had acquired so much Scotch that it was impossible to puzzle him. The beautiful and celebrated Duchess of Gordon took up his challenge, and defied him to interpret the sentence, "Come *pree* my bonnie mou, my canty callant." It was with intense disgust that he afterwards learned what a chance he had lost by his ignorance.

Ye tell me that my lips are sweet,
Sic tales I doubt are a' deceit,
At any rate it's hardly meet,
To *pree* their sweets before folk.
—CHAMBERS'S *Scotch Songs: Behave Yoursel before Folk.*

Preen, a pin; from the Gaelic *prine,* a pin; *prineachan,* a little pin; *prinich,* to secure with pins.

Prick-me-dainty, prick-ma-leerie. These two apparently ridiculous phrases have the same meaning, that of a finical, conceited, superfine person, in his manners or dress, one who affects airs of superiority—without the necessary qualifications for the part he assumes. Jamieson suggests that *prick-me-dainty* is from the English *prick-me-daintily!* Of *prick-ma-leerie,* he conjectures nothing. Both phrases seem to be traceable to the Gaelic *breagh,* fine, beautiful, braw; and *deanta,* complete, finished, perfected; and *leor* or *leoir,* enough, sufficient, entirely; so that *prick-me-dainty* resolves itself into a corruption of *breagh-me-deanta*, I am beautifully perfect; and *prick - ma - leerie* into *breagh - ma-leor*, I am beautiful entirely. A comic and scornful depreciation underlies both phrases.

Prig, to cheapen, to beat down the price; whence the English word *prig*, a conceited person, who thinks he knows better than other people. The English, "to *prig*," in the sense of committing a petty theft, appears to have no connection with the Scottish word.

Men who grew wise *priggin'* ower hops and raisins.
—BURNS: *The Brigs of Ayr.*

Ane o' the street-musician crew
Is busy *priggin'* wi' him now ;
An' twa auld sangs he swears are new,
    He pawns on Jock ;
For an auld hod o' coals half fou,
    A weel-matched troke.
—JAMES BALLANTINE : *Coal Jock.*

Jamieson defines to *prig* as to haggle, and derives it from the Flemish *prachgen*, to beg ; French *briguer*, barter, from *brigue*, " rechercher aveo ardeur."

Prig.—I don't know how this word in Scotch means to cheapen, and in English to steal ; perhaps there is some connection which a knowledge of the root from which it comes would help us to understand. *Prig*, as a conceited person, is purely a conventional use of the word. *Prig* in Scotch has also the meaning of earnestly to entreat. " I *prigged* wi' him for mair nor an' hour that he shouldna leave me."
—R. DRENNAN.

Prink and preen. *Prink* signifies to adorn, to dress out in finery ;

preen or *prein*, a pin—or to pin ; and *preen-head*, a pin's head.

She has *prinked* hersell and *preen'd* hersell
By the ae light o' the mune,
And she's awa to Castelhaugh
To speak wi' young Tamlane.
—*Minstrelsy of the Scottish Border :*
    Ballad of the Young Tamlane.

Prinkling, a slight pricking; a tingling sensation, either of pain or pleasure.

Her wily glance I'll ne'er forget,
    The dear, the lovely blinkin' o't,
Has pierced me through and through
    the heart,
And plagues me in the *prinkling* o't.
The parson kissed the tinker's wife,
    An' coudna preach for thinking o't.
—CHAMBERS's *Scottish Songs: Love's
    Like a Dizziness.*

Prog, to goad, to stab, to thrust, to prick, to probe; metaphorically, to taunt, to gibe, to provoke by a sarcastic remark; a sting, a lance, an arrow. From the Kymric *proc*, a thrust; and *prociaw*, to thrust or stab.

Propine, a gift, or the power of giving. Also drink-money — equivalent to the German word *trink-geld*, the French *pour boire*, and the English *tip*. To *propine* also means to pledge another in drinking, or to touch glasses in German fashion.

If I were there and in thy *propine*,
Oh, what wad ye do to me.
—*Border Minstrelsy: Lady Anne.*

Puirtith, poverty.

Oh *puirtith* cauld, and restless love,
    Ye wreck my peace atween ye ;
Yet *puirtith* a' I could forgi'e,
    An' 'twerna for my Jeanie.
—BURNS.

L

Punchy, thick, short, squat, and broad; applied to the human frame. From the Gaelic *bun*, foundation; and *bunaich*, to establish firmly on a broad foundation.

Purlicue, the unnecessary flourish which people sometimes affix at the end of their signatures; also, a whim, a caprice; and, in derision, the summing up of a judgment, and the peroration of a sermon or a speech. The French *par la queue*, by the tail or finish, has been suggested as the derivation.

Puslic (more properly *buslick*), a cow-sherd, gathered in the fields when dried by the weather. and stored for winter fuel by the poor. According to Jamieson, this is a Dumfriesshire and Galloway word, and used in such phrases as "dry as a *puslick*," and "as light as a *puslick*." It is compounded of the two Gaelic words *buac*, cowdung; and *leag*, a dropping, or to drop or let fall: used in a similar sense to the English "horse-droppings," applied to the horse-dung gathered in the roads.

Pyle, a small quantity; small as a hair, or as a grain. From the Latin *pilus*, French *poil*.

The cleanest corn that e'er was dight
   May hae some *pyles* o' caff in.
      —BURNS : *The Unco Guid.*

Pyot, a magpie ; from the Gaelic *pighe*, a bird.

I tent it a *pyot*
Sat chatterin' on the house heid.
   —ANDREW SUTAR : *Symon and Janet.*

Q

Quarters, a place of residence or abode, a domicile, an apartment or lodging.

An' it's oh for siccan *quarters*
As I gat yesternight.
   —*King James V.* : *We'll Gang Nae Mair a-Rovin.*

Quarters, in this sense, is not derived from *quatuor*, or from the fourth part, as is generally asserted in the dictionaries, and exemplified by the common phrase, "From which *quarter* does the wind blow?" *i.e.*, from which of the *four* points of the compass? The true derivation of *quarter*, the French *quartier*, and of the military functionary, the Quarter-master General, is the Gaelic *cuairt*, a circle. "Paris," says Bescherelle in his French Dictionary, "was formerly divided into four quarters; it is now divided into forty-eight, which, if *quarters* were translated into *circle*, would not be an incongruous expression, as it is when *quarter* represents a fourth part only." The French use the word *arrondissement* in the same sense, which supports the Gaelic etymology. The *quarter* or habitation of a bird is its nest, which is a *circle*. "The circle of one's acquaintance," and "the social circle," are common expressions; and the points of the compass are all points in a circle, which, as all navigators know, are considerably more than *four*.

Quean, wench, winklot. These are all familiar or disrespectful terms for a woman.

I wat she was a cantie *quean*,
And weel could dance the Highland walloch.
—*Roy's Wife.*

By that the dancin' was all done,
Their leave took less or mair,
When the *winklots* and the woers turn'd
To see it was heart-sair.
—*Peblis to the Play.*

Quean, like *queen*, seems to orinate in the Greek γυν, a woman; Danish *quinde*, a woman; *quindelig*, feminine; Gaelic *gin*, to beget, to generate; *gineal*, offspring. *Wench*, by the common change of *gu* into *w*, as in *war* for *guerre*, is from the same root. *Wink-lot*, or *wench-let*, as a little *wench* or *quean*, is of the same parentage.

Queer cuffin. English and Scottish gipsy slang—a justice of the peace. This phrase is of venerable antiquity, and is a relic of the Druidical times

when the arch-druid, or chief priest, was called *coibhi (coivi)*, since corrupted into *cuffin*. The arch-druid was the chief administrator of justice, and sat in his *coir*, or court (whence *queer*), accessible to all suppliants; like Joshua, Jephtha, Eli, and Samuel, judges of Israel. A Druidical proverb, referring to this august personage of the olden time, is still current among the Gaelic-speaking population of the Highlands, that "the stone is not nearer to the ground on which it rests, than is the ear of *Coibhi* to those who apply to him for justice."

Queet, an ankle; sometimes written *cute* (which see).

The firstan step that she stept in,
She steppit to the *queet;*
"Ochone! alas!" said that lady,
"The water's wondrous deep."
—BUCHAN's *Ancient Ballads: The Drowned Lovers.*

I let him cool his *cutes* at the door.
—JAMIESON: *Aberdeenshire Proverb.*

Quey, a young cow; from the Danish *quay*, cattle, the German *vieh*, the Dutch and Flemish *vee*.

Amang the brachans on the brae,
Between her and the moon,
The Deil, or else some outler *quey*,
Gat up and gae a croon.
—BURNS: *Hallowe'en.*

The cow was eager to browse the pasturage on which she had been fed when she was a young and happy *quey.*—*Noctes Ambrosianæ.*

R

Rad, to fear, to be afraid, or to guess.

> I am right *rad* of treasonry.
> —*Song of the Outlaw Murray.*

> O ance ye danced upo' the knowes,
> And ance ye lightly sang,
> But in herrying o' a bee byke
> I'm *rad* ye gat a stang.
> —BURNS: *Ye hae been a' wrang, Lassie.*

Jamieson derives *rad* from the Danish *raed*, afraid, which meets the sense of the passage in which it is used by Burns. The sense, however, would be equally well rendered by a derivation from the Danish, Flemish, and Dutch *raad*, German *rathen*, to guess or conjecture.

Ram and **ran.** The Scottish language contains many expressive and humorous words commencing with the syllables *ram* and *ran*, which are synonymous, and imply force, roughness, disorder; and which appear to be primarily derived from the Gaelic *ran*, to roar, to bluster. Among others are—*randy*, violent or quarrelsome; *rampage*, a noisy frolic, or an outburst of ill-humour, a word which Charles Dickens revived and rendered popular in the English vernacular; *ramgunshock*, rough, rugged, coarse; *ramshackle*, old, worn out with rough usage.

> Our *ramgunshock* glum gudeman,
> Is out and owre the water.
> —BURNS: *Had I the Wyte.*

Rangunshock. This seems to be a corruption of the Gaelic *ran*, to roar; *gun*, without; and *seach* (pronounced *shach*), alternation, *i.e.*, to roar incessantly, without alternation of quiet.

Rant, to be noisily joyous; *rants*, merry-makings, riotous but joyous gatherings; *ranter*, a merry-maker. From the Gaelic.

> My name is Rob the *ranter.*
> —*Maggie Lauder.*

> From out the life o' publick haunts,
> But thee, what were our fairs and *rants*,
> Ev'n godly meetings o' the saunts
>   By thee inspired.
> When gapin' they besiege, the tents
>   Are doubly fired.
> —BURNS: *Scotch Drink.*

Rattan, rottan, a rat. In Flemish the word is written *rat* or *rot*. *Baudrons*, in the following quotation, is a familiar name for a cat.

> Then that curst carmagnole, old Satan,
> Watches like *baudrons* by a *rattan*,
> Our sinful souls to get a claut on.
> —BURNS: *Colonel De Peysten.*

"Wonderful man, Dr. Candlish," said one clergyman to another. "What versatility of talent. He's fit for onything!" "Aye, aye! that's true; put him doon a hole, he'd make a capital *rottan*!"—*Anecdotes of Scottish Wit and Humour.*

Rax, to reach; *raught*, reached; a corruption, or perhaps the original of the modern English word.

Never *rax* aboon your reach.

The auld guidman *raught* down the pock.
　　　—BURNS: *Hallowe'en.*

And ye may *rax* Corruption's neck,
And gi'e her for dissection.
　　　—BURNS: *A Dream.*

" *Rax* me a spaul o' that bubbly Jock."
Reach me a wing of that turkey.—DEAN RAMSAY.

Ream, to froth like beer, or sparkle like wine, to effervesce, to cream ; from the German *rahmen*, to froth; *rahm*, yeast; Flemish *room.*

Fast by an ingle, bleezing finely,
Wi' *reaming* swats that drank divinely.
　　.　　　.　　　.　　　.
The swats sae *reamed* in Tammy's noddle,
Fair play ! he cared na deils a boddle.
　　　—BURNS: *Tam o' Shanter.*

The nappy reeks wi' mantling *ream.*
　　　—BURNS: *The Twa Dogs.*

That merry night we got the corn in,
Oh sweetly then thou *reams* the horn in.
　　　—BURNS: *Scotch Drink.*

Reaming dish, a shallow dish for containing the milk until it is ready for being creamed.

Red-wud, stark, raging mad.

And now she's like to run *red-wud*
　　About her whisker.
　　　—BURNS: *Earnest Cry and Prayer.*

Red, used as an intensitive prefix to a word, is not uncommon in English and Scottish literature. *Red* vengeance is a vengeance that demands blood ; and possibly *red-wud* may mean a madness that prompts blood.

In Gaelic the great deluge is called the *Dile Ruadh*, or redflood.

Rede, advice, counsel.

Rede me noght, quod Reason,
No ruth to have
Till lords and ladies
Loves.alle truth
And hates alle harlotrie.
　　　—*Vision of Piers Ploughman.*

Short *rede* is good *rede.*
—ALLAN RAMSAY'S *Scots Proverbs.*

I *rede* ye weel—tak care o' skaith—
　　See there's a gullie !
　　　—BURNS: *Death and Dr. Hornbook.*

Ye gallants wight, I *rede* ye right,
　　Beware o' bonnie Anne.
　　　　　—BURNS.

This word was once good English, as appears from the extract from " Piers Ploughman," and was used by Chaucer, Gower, and Shakspeare. It is either from the Flemish and Dutch *raed*, counsel; the German *reden*, to speak; or the Gaelic *radh*, *raidh*, or *raite*, a saying, an aphorism.

Renchel, a tall, lean, lanky person ; from the Gaelic *reang*, or *reing*, thin, lean; and *gillie*, a youth, a young man, a fellow.

He's naething but a lang *renchel.*
　　　　　—JAMIESON.

Rhaim, Rhame. According to Jamieson, these words signify either a commonplace speech, a rhapsody ; or " to run over anything in a rapid and unmeaning way," " to repeat by rote, to reiterate." He thinks

it a corruption of *rhyme*, "because proverbs were anciently
expressed in a sort of rhyme."

Is not the true derivation of
the word the Teutonic *rahm*,
the Flemish *room*, froth ; to
ream, to cream, to froth, to
effervesce like soda-water or
champagne? "A *frothy* speaker"
is a common expression of dis-
paragement.

Rickle or **ruckle**, a loose heap ;
rickler, a term of contempt applied to a bad architect or
builder.

I'm grown so thin ; I'm naething but a
rickle o' banes.—JAMIESON.

The proud Percy caused hang five of
the Laird's henchmen at Alnwick for burning a *rickle* of houses.
                    SCOTT : *The Monastery.*

A wild goose out o' season is but a *ruckle*
o' banes.—*Noctes Ambrosianæ.*

Rigging. In English this word
is seldom used except in reference to ships, and the arrange-
ments of their masts, spars,
ropes, &c. In the Scottish language it is employed to signify
the roof, cross-beams, &c., of a
house.

This is no my ain house,
  I ken by the *rigging* o't ;
Since with my love I've changed vows,
  I dinna like the bigging [building] o't.
                —ALLAN RAMSAY.

There by the ingle-cheek
  I sat,
And heard the restless rattons squeak
  About the *riggin'*.
                —BURNS : *The Vision.*

The word is derived from the
Teutonic *ruck*, the Flemish *rug*,

a ridge, top, or back ; whence
the *ridge* at the top of the house,
the roof. The *rigging* tree is the
roof tree. The *rigging* of a vessel is in like manner the roof, or
ridge of a ship, as distinguished
from the hull. So the colloquial
expression to "rig out," to dress,
to accoutre, to adorn, to put the
finishing touch to one's attire,
comes from the same idea of
completion, which is involved
in the *rigging* of a ship or of a
house.

Rigwoodie, old, lean, withered.

Withered beldams, auld and droll,
  Rigwoodie hags. .
          —BURNS : *Tam o' Shanter.*

Rigwoodie. — " Old, lean, withered."
Mr. Robert Chambers says it means
" worthy of the gallows." Neither of
these meanings is correct. *Rigwoodie* is
the name of the chain or rope which passes
across the saddle to support the shafts of
a cart or other conveyance—what an Englishman would call the back band. This
very likely was anciently made of twisted
woodies or *saugh* or willow *wands*, now it
is generally made of twisted chain and of
iron. By a very evident metonymy Burns
applied the twisted wrinkled appearance
of a *rigwoodie* to these old wrinkled hags.
—R. DRENNAN.

Rind or rhynd, hoar frost ; a corruption of the English *rime*, or
possibly of the Kymric *rhym*,
great cold ; *rhyme*, to shiver.
Jamieson derives the Scottish
rhynd and the English *rime* from
the Anglo-Saxon *hrim*, and the
Dutch and Flemish *rym;* but
in these languages *rym*—more
correctly *rijm*—signifies rhyme,
in versification, not *rime* or

frost. *Rhind* is all but obsolete in Lowland Scotch, and has been superseded by *cranreuch*, sometimes written *crandruch*, a particularly cold and penetrating mist or fog. The etymology is uncertain, but the word is most probably a corruption and mispronunciation by the Lowland Scotch of the Gaelic *grainn*, horrible ; whence *cranreuch*, from *grainn* and *driugh*, penetrate, ooze, drip ; whence also the word *drook*, to saturate with moisture, and *drookit*, wet through. Jamieson derives *cranreuch* from the Gaelic *cranntarach*, but no such word is to be found in the Gaelic dictionaries of Armstrong, Macleod, and Dewar, MacAlpine, or the Highland Society of Edinburgh.

When hailstones drive wi' bitter skyte,
And infant frosts begin to bite
In hoary *cranreuch* drest.
— BURNS : *The Jolly Beggars.*

The French word for hoar-frost or *cranreuch* is *verglas*, which is also of Gaelic origin, from *fuar*, cold, and *glas*, grey.

Ringled-eyed, squinting.

He's out-shinned, in-kneed, and *ringled-eyed* too,
Auld Rob Morris is the man I'll ne'er lo'e.
— ALLAN RAMSAY : *Auld Rob Morris.*

Rink, a space cleared out and set aside for sport or jousting, and in winter for curling or skating on the ice.

Trumpets and shalms with a shout
Played ere the *rink* began,
And equal judges sat about
To see wha tint or wan
    The field that day.
— ALLAN RAMSAY : *The Evergreen.*

Then Stevan cam steppand in,
Nae *rink* might him arrest.
— *Christ's Kirk on the Green.*

Jamieson derives *rink* from the English *ring*, a circle ; but it is more probably from the Gaelic *rianaich*, to arrange, to set in order, to prepare.

Ripp, a handful of unthrashed ears of corn pulled out of the sheaf or stack to give to an animal ; from the Gaelic *reub*, to rend, to pull out.

A guid New Year I wish thee, Maggie ;
Hae ! there's a *ripp* to thy auld baggie.
— BURNS : *Auld Farmer to his Auld Mare Maggie.*

An' tent their duty, e'en and morn,
Wi' teats o' hay and *ripps* o' corn.
— BURNS : *Mailie, the Author's Pet Yowe.*

Rippet, a slight matrimonial quarrel. The word seems to be derived either from the Gaelic *riapaladh*, mismanagement, bungling, misunderstanding, or from *reubte*, a rent, from *reub*, to tear, to rend, to pull asunder ; the English *rip*, or *rip up*.

Mr. Mair, a Scotch minister, was rather short tempered, and had a wife named Rebecca, whom, for brevity sake, he called Beckie. He kept a diary, and among other entries this one was very frequent. " Beckie and I had a *rippet*, for which I desire to be humble." A gentleman who had been on a visit to the minister went to Edinburgh and told the story to a minister and his wife there, when the lady replied, "Weel, weel! he must have been an excellent man that Mr. Mair. My husband and I sometimes have *rippets*, but deil tak' me if *he's* ever humble."—DEAN RAMSAY'S *Reminiscences.*

Rippet means a noise or disturbance of any kind, not specifically and only a domestic quarrel between husband and wife. I have often been told by my mother, when a boy, to be "quate and no breed sic a *rippet.*"—R. DRENNAN.

Rispie, a bulrush; the badge of the clan Mackay, worn in the bonnet.

Among the greene *rispies* and the reeds.
—ALLAN RAMSAY: *The Evergreen—The Golden Terge.*

Jamieson erroneously defines *rispie* to mean coarse grass, and derives the word from the English *rasp,* to scrape, with which, however, it has not the slightest connection. It seems to be derived from the Gaelic *rias,* or *riasg,* a moor, a fen, a marsh, where bulrushes grow; and thus to signify a marsh flower or bulrush.

Ritt, to thrust with a weapon, to stab. The etymology cannot be traced to the Gaelic, the German, the Flemish, or any other of the known sources of the Scottish language. Jamieson seems to think it signifies to scratch with a sharp instrument. It is possibly a corruption of *right;* "*ritted* it through" may mean, drove it *right* through.

Young Johnston had a rust-brown sword Hung low down by his gair [belt],
And he *ritted* it through the young Colonel,
That word he never spak mair.
—MOTHERWELL'S *Collection: Ballad of Young Johnson.*

Roddins, the red berries of the hawthorn, the wild rose, the sweet briar, and the mountain ash, more commonly called *rowan,* or *rodden,* in Scotland; from the Gaelic *ruadh,* red. Jamieson confines the use of the word to the berries of the mountain ash, but in this he is mistaken, as appears from the following :—

I've mair need o' the *roddins,* Willie,
That grow on yonder *thorn.*
.　.　.　.　.　.　.
He's got a bush o' *roddins* till her
That grew on yonder thorn,
Likewise a drink o' Maywell water
Out o' his grass-green horn.
—BUCHAN'S *Ancient Ballads,* vol. ii. :
The Earl of Douglas and Dame Oliphant.

Roop, roup, to call out, especially if the voice be harsh and rough; *roopet* or *roupit,* rendered hoarse by cold or by violent vociferation. This word seems to be from the Flemish *roop,* to cry out; the German *rufen,* to call.

Alas! my *roupit* Muse is *hearse.*
—BURNS: *Earnest Cry and Prayer.*

Here the poet is guilty of a pleonasm, unusual with one so terse in expression, of using in one line the two synonymous words of *roupit* and *hearse* (hoarse). But he was sorely in need of a rhyme for the coarse but familiar word in the third line of the poem. *Roup* also signifies a sale by auction, from the "crying out" of the person who offers the goods for sale.

Roose, rouse, to praise or extol; and thence, it has been supposed, by extension of meaning, to drink a health to the person praised; also, any drinking-bout or carousal. The etymology of *roose*, in the sense of to praise, as used in Scotland, is unknown. *Rouse*, in the sense of a drinking-bout, has been held by some to be a corruption of *carouse*, and by others, of the German exclamation, *heraus!* signifying " empty the cup or glass," drink it !

Roose the ford as ye find it.
Roose the fair day at e'en.
—ALLAN RAMSAY'S *Scots Proverbs.*

To *roose* ye up and ca' ye guid,
An' sprang o' great an' noble bluid.
—BURNS : *To Gavin Hamilton.*

He *roos'd* my e'en sae bonnie blue,
He *roos'd* my waist sae genty sma'.
—BURNS : *Young Jockey.*

Some o' them hae *roosed* their hawks,
And other some their houndes,
And other some their ladies fair.
—MOTHERWELL'S *Ancient Minstrelsy.*

In all the above quotations the meaning of *roose* is clearly to praise or extol. But the English *rouse* has not that meaning.

No jocund health that Denmark drinks to-day,
But the great cannon to the clouds shall tell,
And the kings *rouse*, the heavens shall·
bruit again,
Bespeaking earthly thunder.
—SHAKSPEARE : *Hamlet.*

I have took since supper a *rouse* or two too much.
—BEAUMONT AND FLETCHER.

It is thus clear that the Scottish *roose* and the English *rouse*

are of different origin. The German *rausch*, and the Dutch and Flemish *roes*, signify semi-intoxication; *roesig*, in these languages, means nearly drunk, or, as the French phrase it, " entre deux vins," or, as the English slang expresses it, "half seas over." In Swedish, *rus* signifies drunkenness; *taga rus*, to get drunk; and *rusig*, inebriated. In Danish, *ruus* signifies drunkenness, and *ruse*, intoxicating liquor. Nares rightly suspected that the English *rouse* was of Danish origin. The passage in *Hamlet*, act i. scene 4—

The king doth wake to-night and takes his *rouse*,

signifies the king takes his *drink*, and all the other instances quoted by Nares are susceptible of the same interpretation. Nares quotes from Harman's " Caveat for Common Cursitors," 1567 :—

I thought it my bounden duty to acquaint your goodness with the abominable, wicked, and detestable behaviour of all these *rowsey*, ragged rabblement of rakehells.

He defines *rowsey* in this passage to mean *dirty*, but, in view of the Danish, Dutch, and Flemish derivations, it ought to be translated *drunken*.

Row, to enwrap, to entwine, to enfold, also to roll or flow onwards like the wavelets on the river; from the Gaelic *ruith* (*rui*), to flow, to ripple.

Hap and *row,* hap and *row,*
Hap and *row* the feetie o't,
It is a wee bit eerie thing,
I downa bide the greetie o't.
—*Creech.*

Then round she *row'd* her silken plaid.
—*Ballad of Fremmet Hall.*

Where Cart runs *rowan'* to the sea.
—BURNS.

Rowan, the mountain ash ; a tree
that grows in great perfection
in the Highlands of Scotland,
and named from its beautiful
red berries, *ruadh,* the Gaelic
for red.   This tree, or a twig of
it, is supposed, in the superstition of Scotland, to be a charm
against witchcraft.   Hence, it
has been supposed, but without sufficient authority, that
the phrase, "Aroint thee, witch,"
in Shakspeare, is a misprint for
"a *rowan-tree,* witch ! "   The
word occurs in no author previous to Shakspeare.

The night was fair, the moon was up,
   The wind blew low among the gowans,
Or fitful rose o'er Athole woods,
   An' shook the berries frae the *rowans.*
      —*The Wraith of Garry Water.*

Rowan tree and red thread
Mak' the witches tyne [lose] their speed.
      —*Old Scottish Proverb.*

Rowt, to bellow or low like cattle ;
from the Gaelic *roiteach,* bellowing.   Nares erroneously renders
it "snore."   "The rabble *rowt,*"
i.e., the roaring rabble, the
clamorous multitude.

The kye stood *routin* in the loan. .
      —BURNS : *The Twa Dogs.*

Nae mair thou'lt *rowte* out o'er the dale,
Because thy pasture's scanty.
      —BURNS : *The Ordination.*

And the king, when he had righted
himself on the saddle, gathered his breath,
and cried to do me nae harm ; "for," said
he, "he is ane o' our Norland stots, I ken
by the *rowte* o' him ; " and they a' laughed
and *rowted* loud eneuch.—SCOTT : *Fortunes of Nigel.*

Rowth, plenty, abundance ; a
word formed from *roll* and *roll-
eth,* Scottish *row.*   It is expressive of the same idea as in the
English phrase, applied to a
rich man, "He *rolls* in wealth."
A peculiarly Scottish word
which never seems to have been
English.   It has been suggested
that it is derived from the Gaelic
ruathar, a sudden rush, onset,
or inpouring ; whence metaphorically, a sudden or violent
influx of wealth or abundance.

A *rowth* o' auld knick-knackets,
Rusty airn caps, and jingling jackets.
      —BURNS : *Captain Grose.*

The ingle-neuk, with *routh* o' bannocks
and bairns !—DEAN RAMSAY : *A Scottish
Toast or Sentiment.*

A *rowth* aumrie and a close nieve.—
JAMIESON.

It's ye have wooers mony a ane,
   An' lassie ye're but young, ye ken,
Then wait a wee, and cannie wale,
   A *routhie* butt, a *routhie* ben.
      —BURNS : *Country Lassie.*

God grant your lordship joy and health,
Long days and *routh* of real wealth.
      —ALLAN RAMSAY : *Epistle to
      Lord Dalhousie.*

A houndless hunter and a gunless
gunner see aye *rowth* o' game.—ALLAN
RAMSAY's *Scots Proverbs.*

Fortune, if thou wilt give me still
Hale breeks, a scon, a whisky gill,
And *rowth* o' rhyme to rave at will,
   Take a' the rest.
      —BURNS : *Scotch Drink.*

Roxle, to grunt, to speak with a hoarse voice; Gaelic *roc*, a hoarse voice; French *rauque*, hoarse; English *rook*, a bird that has a hoarse voice in cawing; Gaelic, *rocair*, a man with a hoarse voice; *rocail*, croaking. Mr. Herbert Coleridge, in his dictionary of "The Oldest Words in the English Language," from the semi-Saxon period of A.D. 1250 to A.D. 1800, derives it from the Dutch *rotelen*, but the word does not appear in any Dutch or Flemish dictionary.

Royet, wild, dissipated, riotous, unruly. *Roit*, according to Jamieson, is a term of contempt for a woman, often conjoined with an adjective, denoting bad temper; as, "an *ill - natured roit.*" The resemblance to the English *riot* suggests its derivation from that word, but both *royet* and *riot* are traceable to the Gaelic *raoit*, noisy, obstreperous, or indecent mirth and revelry; and *ruidhtear*, a loud reveller; *riatach*, indecent, immodest. Jamieson, however, derives it from the French *roide*, stiff, which he wrongly translates fierce, ungovernable.

Royet lads may make sober men.
—ALLAN RAMSAY'S *Scots Proverbs.*

Ruddy, to roar like thunder, or to rumble like wind in the stomach. Derivation uncertain, but possibly akin to *rowte* or *rowtin*, the bellowing of cattle.

I in its wame heard Vulcan *ruddy*.
—BEATTIE: *John o' Arnha'.*

Rude, the complexion; the ruddy face of a healthy person. From the Flemish *rood*, red, which has the same meaning; Gaelic *ruath*, red, corrupted by the Lowland Scotch into *Roy*, as in Rob *Roy*, Gilde*roy*, and applied to the hair as well as to the complexion.

Of all their maidens myld as meid
Was nane sae gymp as Gillie,
As ony rose her *rude* was reid,
Her lyre was like the lillie.
—*Christ's Kirk on the Green.*

She has put it to her *roudes* lip,
And to her *roudes* chin,
She has put it to her fause, fause mouth,
But never a drap gaed in.
—*Border Minstrelsy: Prince Robert.*

Sir Walter Scott, in a note to this ballad, glosses *roudes* by "haggard." Surely this is wrong?

Rug, to pull. Derivation uncertain.

Trying to *rug* them off, tae an' heel.—
Noctes Ambrosianæ.

Rugg, a great bargain, a thing ridiculously cheap; to spoil, to plunder, to seize. From the Gaelic *rug*, the past tense of *beir*, to take hold of.

When borrowers brak, the pawns were *rugg*,
Rings, beads of pearl, or siller jug,
I sold them off—ne'er fashed my lug
Wi' girns or curses;
The mair they whinged, it gart me hug
My swelling purses.
—ALLAN RAMSAY: *Last Speech of a Wretched Miser.*

Rule the roast. This originally Scottish phrase has obtained currency in England, and excited much controversy as to its origin. It has been derived from the function of a chief cook, to be master or mistress in the kitchen, and as such, to "rule the *roasting*." It has also been derived from the mastery of the cock among the hens, as ruling the place where the fowls *roost* or sleep. In the Scottish language *roost* signifies the inner roof of a cottage, composed of spars or beams reaching from one wall to the other; the highest interior part of the building. Hence, to rule the *roast*, or *roost*, or to rule the house, to be the master.

Rummel, to make a confused sound; from *rumble*.

> Your crackjaw words of half an ell,
> That *rummel* like a witch's spell.
> —GEORGE BEATTIE: *John o' Arnha'*.

Rump, to break; *rumpit*, broken; or in English slang "to be cleaned out," or exhausted of money by losses at gambling. "Perhaps," says Jamieson, "in allusion to an animal whose tail has been cut off near the *rump!*" The etymology did not need the "perhaps" of the non-erudite author, and is to be found in the French *rompre*, to break, and *rompu*, broken.

Rumple-bane, the lowest bone of the spine.

> At length he got a carline grey,
>   And she's come hirplin' hame, man,
> And she fell o'er the buffet stool,
>   And brak her *rumple-bane*, man.
> —JOHNSON's *Musical Museum*.

Rung, a cudgel, a staff, a bludgeon, the step of a ladder; any thick strong piece of wood that may be wielded in the hand as a weapon. From the Gaelic *rong*, which has the same meaning. The modern Irish call a bludgeon a *shillelah;* also a Gaelic word for *seileach*, a willow, and *slaith* (*sla*), a wand.

> Auld Scotland has a raucle tongue,
> She's just a deevil wi' a *rung*.
> —BURNS.

Runk, to whisper secret slanders, also a term of opprobrium applied to an old woman, a gossip, or a scandal-monger. From the Gaelic *runach*, dark, mysterious, also a confidant; *run*, a secret, a mystery; and by extension of the original meaning, a scandal repeated under the pretence of a secret and confidential disclosure.

Runt, a deprecatory or contemptuous name for an old woman; from the German *rind*, and the Flemish *rund*, an ox, or a cow that calves no longer; also, the hard stalk of kail or cabbage left in the ground, that has ceased to sprout.

Ruther. This word, according to Jamieson, means to storm, to bluster, to roar, also an uproar or commotion. It is probably from the Gaelic *rutharach*, quarrelsome, contentious, and *rutharachd*, quarrelsomeness.

Ryg-bane, or **rig-bane**, the spine or backbone; from the Flemish *rug,* the German *rucken,* the back, and *bein,* a bone. The original meaning of *rug* and *rucken* is that of extension in length; from the Gaelic *ruig,* to extend, to reach, and *ruigh,* or *righe,* an arm; *ruighe* (the English *ridge*) is the extension of a mountain, or of a series of hills forming, as it were, the spine or backbone of the land.

S

Saikless, innocent, guiltless; from the Teutonic *sach,* the cause; whence *sachless,* or *saikless,* without cause.

. "Oh, is this water deep," he said,
"As it is wondrous dim;
Or is it sic as a *saikless* maid,
And a leal true knicht may swim?"
—*Ballad of Sir Roland.*

Leave off your douking on the day,
And douk upon the night,
And where that *saikless* knight lies slain,
The candles will burn bright.
—*Border Minstrelsy: Earl Richard.*

Sain, to bless, to preserve in happiness; from the German *segnen,* to bless, and *segen,* a benediction; Flemish *zegenen*— all probably from the Latin *sanus.*

Sain yoursel frae the deil and the laird's bairns.
—ALLAN RAMSAY'S *Scots Proverbs.*

Sairing, enough, that which satisfies one; used both in a favourable and unfavourable sense. "He got his *sairin,*" applied to a drubbing or beating; in the ironical sense, he got enough of it, or, as Jamieson phrases it in English, "he got his bellyfull of it." A corruption of *serve,* or serve the purpose—therefore, a sufficiency.

You couldna look your *sairin* at her face,
So meek it was, so sweet, so fu' o' grace.
—Ross's *Helenore.*

Sairy or **sair,** very, or very great; from the German *sehr,* as in *sehr schön, sehr gut,* very fair, very good; sometimes used in English in the form of *sore;* as, "sore distressed," very much distressed.

And when they meet wi' *sair* disasters,
Like loss o' health or want o' masters.
—BURNS: *The Twa Dogs.*

It's a *sair* dung bairn that mauna greet.
—ALLAN RAMSAY'S *Scots Proverbs.*

It's a *sair* field where a' are slain.
—*Idem.*

The state of man does change and vary:
Now sound, now sick, now blythe, now sary,
Now dansand merry, now like to dee.
—ALLAN RAMSAY: *The Evergreen.*

Sak, saik, sake, blame, guilt; whence *sachless, sackless, saikless,* guiltless, innocent; and also, by extension of meaning, foolish, worthless, as in the corresponding English word, "an innocent," to signify an imbecile.

The root of all these words appears to be either the German *jach* (see SAIKLESS, *ante*), or the Gaelic *sag*, weight; whence also *sag*, to weigh or press down, and *sack*, a bag to carry heavy articles. The idea of weight, as applied to guilt and blameworthiness, is obvious, as in the line quoted by Jamieson, "Mary was *sackless* o' breaking her vow," *i.e.*, she was not *burthened* with the guilt of breaking her vow. A *saikless* person, or an imbecile, in like manner, is one who is not weighted with intellect. *Sag*, in English, is said of a rope not drawn tightly enough, and weighed down in the middle. It also signifies to bend or give way under pressure of weight.

The heart I bear
Shall never *sag* with doubt or shake with fear.—SHAKSPEARE.

"It is observable," says Dr. Johnson, "that *sack* (in the sense of a bag for carrying weight) is to be found in all languages, and is therefore conceived to be antediluvian." The phrase "sair *saught*," quoted by Jamieson, and defined as signifying "much exhausted, and especially descriptive of bodily debility," is traceable to the same root, and might be rendered, sorely weighed down by weakness or infirmity. There is, however, in spite of these examples, much to be said in favour of the derivation from the German *sach*.

Sandie, Sanders, Sawney, Sannock, abbreviations of the favourite Scottish Christian name of Alexander; from the last two syllables. The English commonly abbreviate the first two syllables into *Aleck*. In the days immediately after the accession of James VI. to the English throne, under the title of James I., to the time of George III. and the Bute Administration, when Scotsmen were exceedingly unpopular, and when Dr. Samuel Johnson—the great Scoto-phobist, the son of a Scotch bookseller at Lichfield—thought it prudent to disguise his origin, and overdid his prudence by maligning his father's countrymen, it was customary to designate a Scotsman as a *Sawney*. The vulgar epithet, however, is fast dying out, and is nearly obsolete.

An', Lord! remember singing *Sannock*,
Wi' hale breeks, saxpence, and a bannock.
BURNS: *To James Tait.*

Sanshagh or **sanshach**. Jamieson defines this word as meaning wily, crafty, sarcastically clever, saucy, disdainful, and cites—"'He's a *sanshach* callant, or chiel,' is a phrase used in Aberdeenshire and the Mearns." He thinks it is derivable from the Gaelic *saobh-nosach*, angry, peevish, irascible; but it is more probable that it comes from *sean*, old, and *seach* (*shach*), dry or caustic, an old man of a cynical temper.

Sant or **saunter.** Jamieson defines this word as meaning "to disappear, to vanish suddenly out of sight," and quotes it as in use in Ettrick Forest. " It's *santed*, but it will, may be, cast up again." In Wright's " Dictionary of Obsolete and Provincial English," *saunt*, a northern word, is said to signify to vanish; and *saum*, to wander lazily about. The word is nearly, if not quite obsolete, and does not appear either in Burns or Allan Ramsay. *Sant* was formerly current in the same sense as *saunter*, to roam idly or listlessly about ; to *saum*, to disappear from, or neglect one's work or duty. Johnson derived *saunter* from an expression said to have been used in the time of the crusades, in application to the idle vagabonds and impostors who roamed through the country and begged for money to help them on their way to the Holy Land, or *La Sainte Terre. Saunter*, as now used in English, is almost synonymous with the Scottish *dauner*, q.v. But no authoritative derivation has yet been discovered, either for *sant* or *saunter*, unless that given by Mr. Wedgwood, from the German *schlendern*, can be deemed satisfactory. In Sheffield, Duke of Buckingham's Essay on "Satire," *saunter* is used in a curiously unusual sense, an investigation of which may possibly throw light on the original meaning of the word.

While *sauntering* Charles betwixt so mean
a brace [of mistresses],
Meets with dissembling still in either place,
Affected humour or a painted face ;
In loyal libels we have often told him
How one has jilted him, the other sold him.
.   .   .   .   .   .
Was ever Prince by two at once misled,
Foolish and false, ill-natured and ill-bred ?

Sir Walter Scott cites from the same author, in reference to the *sauntering* of Charles II. :—

In his later hours, there was as much laziness as love in all those hours he passed with his mistresses, who, after all, only served to fill up his seraglio, while a bewitching kind of pleasure called *sauntering* and talking without restraint, was the true sultana he delighted in.

In Gaelic *sannt*, and *sanntaich*, signifies to covet, to desire, to lust after; and if this be the true derivation of the word, the passage from the Duke of Buckingham would be exceedingly appropriate. To *saunter* was applied to idle men who followed women about the streets, with libidinous intent of admiration or conversation; *sanntaire*, a lustful man. The French have a little comedy entitled " Un monsieur qui suit les femmes," which expresses the idea of *saunterer*, as applied to Charles II.

Sap, a fool, a simpleton, a ninny. The English has *milk-sop*, an effeminate fool. *Sap* and *sop* are both derived from the Gaelic *saobh*, silly, foolish, as well as the English slang, *soft*, apt to be imposed upon.

Sark, the linen, woollen, silken, or cotton garment worn next to the skin by men and women; a shirt or shift; the French *chemise*, the German *hemde*. Weel-*sarkit*, well provided with shirts.

> The last Hallowe'en I was wauken,
> My droukit *sark*-sleeve as ye ken.
> —BURNS : *Tam Glen.*

> They reel'd, they set, they crossed, they cleekit,
> Till ilka carlin swat and reekit,
> And coost her duddies to the wark,
> And linkit at it in her *sark!*
> . . . . . .
> Tam tint his reason a' thegither,
> And roar'd out, "Weel done! *Cutty sark!*"
> And in an instant a' was dark.
> —BURNS : *Tam o' Shanter.*

Being asked what was the difference between Presbyterian ministers, who wear no surplices, and Episcopalians, who do, an old lady replied, "Well, ye see, the Presbyterian minister wears his *sark* under his coat, the Episcopalian wears *his sark* aboon his coat."—DEAN RAMSAY.

The phrase, "*sark-alane*," is used to signify nude, with the exception of the shirt; and "a *sarkfu'* o' sair banes," to express the condition of a person suffering from great fatigue, or from a sound beating. The etymology of the word, which is peculiar to Scotland and the North of England, is uncertain. Attempts have been made to trace it from the Swedish, the Icelandic, the Anglo-Saxon, and the Greek, but without success. In the "Dictionaire de la Langue Romane, ou du Vieux Langage Française" (Paris, 1768), the Scottish word *sark* is

rendered *screcote*, and *serecot*, "une camisole, une chemisette."

Saugh, a willow; the French *saule*, Gaelic *seileag*.

> The glancin' waves o' Clyde
> Through *saughs* and hanging hazels glide.
> —PINKERTON : *Bothwell Bank.*

Saulie, a hired mourner, a mute, or undertaker's man. The word seems to have been employed to express the mock or feigned sorrow assumed in the lugubrious faces of these men, and to be derived from the Gaelic *sall*, mockery, satire, derision; *samhladh*, an apparition, a ghost, has also been suggested as the origin of the word. The derivation of Jamieson from *salve reginam* is scarcely worthy of consideration.

Saur, to flavour; *saurless*, insipid, tasteless; supposed to be a corruption of savour. The French for a red herring is *saure*; and *saurir*, or *saurer*, is to flavour with salt.

Scaff-raff, rubbish, refuse.

> If you and I were at the Witherspoon's Latch, wi' ilka ane a gude oak hipple in his hand, we wadna turn back—no, not for half-a-dozen o' your *scaff-raff*.—SCOTT : *Guy Mannering.*

Jamieson, unaware of the indigenous roots of these words, derives them from the Swedish *scaef*, a rag, anything shaved off; and *rafa*, to snatch away. The true etymology, however, is from the Gaelic *sgamh* (pronounced *scav*), dross, dirt, rubbish; and *rabh* (*raff*), coarse, idle, useless.

Scag, to shrivel in the heat, or by exposure to the weather, to split, to crack in the heat; a term applied in the fishing villages of Scotland to fish, dried or fresh, that have been kept too long. " A *scaggit* haddie " is a haddock spoiled by long exposure. Jamieson hesitates between the Icelandic *skacka, inquare;* and the Gaelic *sgag,* as the derivation of this word. *Sgag,* in Gaelic, signifies to shrivel up, to crack, to split, or to spoil and become putrid by long keeping; *sgagta,* lean, emaciated.

Scance, skance. To reflect upon a person's character or conduct by charge or insinuation; to censure, to taunt indirectly ; to glance at a subject cursorily in conversation ; also, a transient look at anything. These words are not used in English, though *askance*, a recognised English word, appears to be from the same root. The ordinary derivation of *askance* is either from the Italian *schianco*, athwart, or from the Flemish and Dutch *schuin*, oblique, to squint. The latter etymology, though it meets the English sense of the word, does not correspond with the variety of meanings in which it is employed in Scotland. Neither does it explain the English *scan*, to examine, to scrutinise,—still less the *scan*-

ning, or *scansion* of the syllables or feet in a verse.

Perhaps the Gaelic *sgath,* a shadow, a reflection in the water or in a glass, *sgathan* (*sga-an*), a mirror, and *sgathanaich*, to look in a glass, may supply the root of the Scottish, if not the English words. Tried by these tests, *scance* might signify to cast a shadow or a reflection upon one, to take a rapid glance as of one's self in a glass ; and to *scan*, to examine, to scrutinise, " to hold the mirror up to nature," as Shakspeare has it. In these senses, the word might more easily be derivable from the Gaelic, which does not imply obliquity, than from the Flemish and Dutch, of which obliquity is the leading, if not the sole idea, as in the English *squint.*

Then gently *scan* your brother man,
Still gentler sister woman ;
Though they may gang a kennin' wrang,
To step aside is human.
    —BURNS : *Address to the Unco Guid.*

To *scan* a verse, to examine or scrutinise whether it contains the proper number of feet or syllables, or is otherwise correct, may possibly be an offshoot of the same idea; though all the etymologists insist that it comes from the Italian *scandio*, to climb.

Scarnoch. A *scarnoch o' words* signifies a multitude of words, such as are unnecessarily used by wordy lawyers and by over garrulous Members of Parliament, who use them, as Solomon

M

said in old times, "to darken counsel," and as a wise and cynical man of more modern days—the late Prince Talleyrand —said with equal appropriateness, " pour deguiser la pensée " (to disguise their thoughts). *Scarnoch* also signifies a tumultuous din, the murmur or shouting of a crowd, and *scarochin*, a great noise. Jamieson derives these words from the Swedish *skara*, a crowd, a cohort, but the true root is the Gaelic *sgairn*, to howl as dogs, wolves, or other animals, and *sgarneach*, howling, shrieking, roaring, &c.

Scart, a scratch ; *scart-free*, without a scratch or injury. *Scart* is also a name given, in most parts of Scotland, to the rapacious sea-bird, the cormorant. *Scart*, to scratch, is a softer rendering of the harsher English word ; and *scart*, a cormorant, is a corruption of the Gaelic *sgarbh*, which has the same meaning.

They that bourd wi' cats may count upon *scarts.*—ALLAN RAMSAY.

"To *scart* the buttons," or draw one's hand down the breast of another, so as to touch the buttons with one's nail, is a mode of challenging to battle among Scottish boys.—JAMIESON.

Like *scarts* upon the wing by the hope of plunder led.
—*Legends of the Isles.*

D'ye think ye'll help them wi' skirlin' that gate, like an auld *skart* before a flaw o' weather ?—SCOTT : *The Antiquary.*

Scaur, a steep rock, a cliff on the shore ; *skerrie*, a rock in the sea. Scarborough, a watering-place

in England, signifies the town on the cliff or rock ; *Skerrievore*, or the great rock or *skerrie*, from *sgeir* and *mhor*, is the name of the famous lighthouse on the West Coast of Scotland. The *skerries* are rocks in the sea among the Scilly islands. Both *scaur* and *skerrie* are traceable to the Gaelic *sgeir*, a rock in the sea, and *sgor*, a steep mountain side ; whence also the English *scar* in Scarborough.

Ye that sail the stormy seas
Of the distant Hebrides.
. . . . .
By lordly Mull and Ulva's shore
Beware the witch of *Skerrievore.*
—*Legends of the Isles.*

Where'er ye come by creek or *scaur*,
Ye bring bright beauty.
—JAMES BALLANTINE.

Schacklock. Jamieson imagines this word to mean a pickpocket or burglar, or one who *shakes* or loosens *locks*. It is, however, a term of contempt for a lazy ne'er-do-weel, like the similar English word, *shackaback*, and is derivable from the Gaelic *seac* (*shack*), useless, withered, dried up, and *leug*, dull, sluggish, or incorrigibly lazy.

Schore, a man of high rank ; *schore-chieftain*, a supreme chief. Jamieson derives *schore* from the German *schor* or *schoren*, " altus eminens "—a word which is not to be found in any German dictionary, nor in Dutch or Flemish, or any other Teutonic speech. The etymology is unknown or difficult to discover, unless it be presumed that the word was used metaphorically for *high*, in the sense of an eminence ; from the Gaelic *sgor*, a steep rock, a cliff.

S c h r e w (sometimes written *schrow*), to curse ; allied to the English *shrew*, a scolding and ill-tempered woman, and usually derived from the German *beschreien*, to curse. A *screw*, in English slang, signifies a mean, niggardly person, who, in American parlance, would be called "a mean cuss," or curse. A miserable old horse is called a *screw*, not as the Slang Dictionary says, "from the *screwlike* manner in which his ribs generally show through the skin," but from the original sense of *shrew*, to curse—i.e., a horse only fit to swear at —or possibly from the Gaelic *sgruit*, old, wrinkled, thin, meagre. *Schrewit* signifies accursed, also poisonous, which is doubtless the origin of the slang English *screwed*, intoxicated. The kindred English word *scrub*, a mean person, and *scrubbed*, vile, worthless, shabby, as used by Shakspeare in the phrase, "a little *scrubbed* boy," is evidently derived from the Gaelic *sgrub*, to act in a mean manner, and *sgrubair*, a churl, a niggard, or a despicable person. The true derivation of the Scottish *schrew* remains obscure.

In its form of *shrew* or *schrow* the word was formerly used in reference to the male sex, in the sense of a disagreeable and quarrelsome person ; as in *shrewd*, an epithet applied to a man of penetration and sharp common sense. These words, whether *schrew* or *schrow* be the correct form, have given rise to many discussions among etymologists, which are not yet ended. *Shrew* or *schrow* has been derived not only from the Teutonic *schreien*, to shriek, to call out lustily, but from the little harmless animal called the *shrew* mouse, which was fabled to run over the backs of cattle and do them injury by the supposed venom of its bite. Some of these apparently incongruous or contradictory derivations are resolvable by the Gaelic *sgruth* (*sru*), to run, to flow. A *shrew* is a scold, a woman whose tongue *runs* too rapidly, or a man, if he have the same disagreeable characteristic ; *shrewd* is an epithet applied to one whose ideas *run* clearly and precisely. The *shrew* mouse is the *running* mouse.

Sclaurie, to bespatter with mud ; also metaphorically, to abuse, revile, to asperse, make accusation against, on the principle of the English saying, "Throw mud enough; some of it will stick." The lowland Scotch *claur*, or *glaur*, signifies mud, q.v. This word is derived from the Gaelic *clabar* (aspirated *clabhar* or *claur*), filth, mire, mud ; "A gowpen o' *glaur*," or *claur*, the two hands conjoined, filled with mud. When the initial *s* was either omitted from or joined to the root-word, is not discoverable.

Scogie or **scogie-lass**, a kitchen drudge, a maid-of-all-work, a "slavey;" one unskilled in all but the commonest and coarsest work. From the Gaelic *sgog*, a fool, a dolt, one who knows nothing.

Scoil, shriek; akin to the English *squeel*.

An' smellin' John he gaed a *scoil,*
Then plunged and gart the water boil.
—*John o' Arnha'.*

Till echo for ten miles around
Did to the horrid *scoil* resound.
—*Ibid.*

Scold or **skald.** Fingal and the other warriors whose deeds are commemorated by Ossian, drank out of shells (scallop shells), doubtless the first natural objects that in the earliest ages were employed for the purpose. *Scold* is an obsolete word, signifying to drink a health, evidently derived from *shell,* or scallop; the Teutonic *schale,* a shell or a cup; the Danish *skiall,* the French *escaille* or *ecaille,* the Flemish and Dutch *schelp* and *schaal,* the Norse *skul,* the Greek *chalys,* the Latin *calix,* a shell or cup. Possibly the tradition that the Scandinavian warriors drank their wine or mead out of the *skulls* of their enemies whom they had slain in battle, arose from a modern mis-

conception of the meaning of *skul* — originally synonymous with the skull or cranium, or shell of the brain. *Skul* is used by the old Scottish poet, Douglas, for a goblet or large bowl.

To *scold* or *scoll,* to drink healths, to drink as a toast; *scolder,* a drinker of healths; *skul,* a salutation of one who is present, or of the respect paid to an absent person, by expressing a wish for his health when one is about to drink it.
—JAMIESON.

Skeolach (*sgeolach*), the name of one of Fingal's drinking cups.—MACLEOD AND DEWAR: *Gaelic Dictionary.*

The custom of drinking out of shells of great antiquity, and was very common among the ancient Gael. Hence the expression so often met with in the Fingalian poets, "the hall of *shells,*" "the chief of *shells,*" "the *shell* and the song." The *scallop* shell is still used in drinking strong liquors at the tables of those gentlemen who are desirous to preserve the usages of their ancestors.—ARMSTRONG's *Gaelic Dictionary,* 1828.

Scon or **scone,** a barley cake; from the Gaelic *sgonn,* a lump or mass.

Leeze me on thee, John Barleycorn,
    Thou King o' grain,
On thee auld Scotland chaws her cood,
In souple *scones,* the wale o' food.
—BURNS: *Scotch Drink.*

Sconfice, discomfit, beaten, led astray, subdued; from the Gaelic *sgon,* bad, and *fios,* knowledge.

I'm unco wae for the puir lady; I'm feart she'll grow wud gin she be lang in yon hole, for it would *sconfice* a horse, forbye a body.—MACLEAY's *Memoirs of the Clan MacGregor.*

Scoot, a tramp, a gad-about, a vagrant, a term of opprobrium given to a low woman; from the Gaelic *sguit*, to wander. The English *scout*, a person employed by an army to reconnoitre, by travelling or wandering to and fro, so as to observe the motions of the enemy, is obviously from the same root.

Scottis bed. "This phrase," says Jamieson, "occurs in an' Aberdeen Register, but it is not easy to affix any determinate meaning to it." May it not mean a ship's bed, or a hammock; from *scothach*, a small skiff?

Scouk, to sneak, to loiter idly or furtively ; either a corruption of the English *skulk*, or a derivation with an allied meaning; from the Gaelic *sguga*, a coarse, ill-mannered, ungainly person.

They grin, they glower, they *scouk*,
   they gape.
                  —Jacobite Relics.

Scouth or **skouth**, elbow-room, space, scope, room for the arm in wielding a weapon so as to cut off an enemy or an obstruction at a blow ; from the Gaelic *sgud*, to lop, to cut off; *sgudadh*, act of cutting down by a sudden blow.

An' he get *scouth* to wield his tree,
I fear you'll both be paid.
                  —Ballad of Robin Hood.

By break of day he seeks the dowie glen,
That he may *scouth* to a' his morning len' (lend).
   —Allan Ramsay: Pastoral on the Death of Matthew Prior.

They tak religion in their mouth,
They talk o' mercy, grace, and truth—

For what ? to gie their malice *scouth*
   On some poor wight,
An' hunt him down, o'er right and ruth,
   To ruin straight.
   —Burns : To the Rev. John M'Math.

"*Scouth* and *routh* " is a proverbial phrase for elbow-room and abundance.

That's a good gang for your horse, he'll have *scouth* and *routh.—*Jamieson.

Scowf, a blustering, low scoundrel. Dutch and Flemish *schoft*. Explained in Dutch and French dictionaries as "*maroufle, coquin, maraud*," *i.e.*, a low scoundrel, a rogue, an impudent blackguard.

He's naething but a *scouf;* Danish *scuffer*, to gull, to cheat, to shuffle ; a cheat, a false pretender.—Jamieson.

Scran or **skran**, odds and ends or scraps of eatables, broken victuals ; also applied derisively to food or daily bread.

Scranning is a phrase used by schoolboys when they spend their pocket-money at the pastry-cook's.—Jamieson.

Scran-pock, a beggar's wallet to hold scraps of food. The word *scran* is derived from the Gaelic *sgrath* (pronounced *sgra*), to peel, to pare, to take off the rind or skin, and *sgrathan* (*sgra-an*), a little peeling or paring. In the sense of food, the word occurs in the Irish objurgation, "Bad *scran* to ye ! "

Screed, a lengthy discourse or written article. This word is defined in a note to a passage in the "Noctes Ambrosianæ " as a "liberal allowance of anything."

A man, condemned to death for rape and murder at Inverness, requested that the editor of the *Courier* might be permitted to see him the night before his execution. After some talk, the criminal said, "Oh, Mr. Carruthers, what a *screed* you'll be printin' in your next paper about me !"—M.

Screik (or **scraigh**) o' day, the early dawn, the first flush of the morning light. Jamieson says the radical word is *creek;* from the Teutonic *krieche*, "aurora rutilans." It has been suggested that *screich*, or shriek, of day, means the shrill cry of the cock at early morn, but it is more probable that the phrase is from the Flemish *krieken van den dag*, which the French translate *l'aube du jour, l'aurore*, the dawn of day.

Scrieve, to roll or move or glide easily; from the Gaelic *sgriob*, to scrape, to draw a line or a furrow, to go on an excursion or journey.

The wheels o' life gae down-hill *scrievin'*.
—BURNS : *Scotch Drink.*

Scrimp, bare, scarce ; *scrimply*, barely, scarcely.

Down flowed her robe, a tartan sheen,
Till half a leg was *scrimply* seen.
And such a leg ! my bonnie Jean
  Alone could peer it.
    —BURNS: *The Vision.*

Scrog, a stunted bush, furze ; *scroggy*, abounding in underwood, covered with stunted bushes or furze like the Scottish mountains ; from the Gaelic *sgrogag*, stunted timber or underwood.

The way toward the cite was stony, thorny, and *scroggy.—Gesta Romanorum.*

As I came down by Merriemass,
  And down among the *scroggs*,
The bonniest chield that e'er I saw
  Lay sleeping 'mang his dogs.
    —*Johnnie of Bredislee.*

Sir Walter Scott, when in his last illness in Italy, was taken to a wild scene on the mountains that border the Lago di Garda. He had long been apathetic, and almost insensible, to surrounding objects ; but his fading eyes flashed with unwonted fire at the sight of the furze bushes and scrogs that reminded him of home and Scotland, and he suddenly exclaimed, in the words of the Jacobite ballad—

Up the *scroggy* mountain,
  And down the *scroggy* glen,
We dare na gang a hunting,
  For Charlie and his men.

Scroggam and ruffam. These two words occur as a kind of chorus in a song attributed, but on doubtful authority, to Robert Burns. It is wholly unworthy of his genius, and appears—if he had anything at all to do with it—to have been slightly mended, to make it more presentable in decent company. Burns was almost wholly unacquainted with Gaelic, though he occasionally borrowed a phrase or a word from that language without quite comprehending its meaning.

There was a wife wonn'd in Cockpen,
    Scroggam !
She brewed guid ale for gentlemen,
Sing, Auld Coul lay ye down by me,
  Scroggam, my dearie, *ruffam.*

Scroggam is the Gaelic for *sgroggam*, let me put on my bonnet ; and *ruffam* is *rubham*, or (*ruffam*) let me rub or scratch. An obscene meaning is concealed in the words.

Scrub, a term of contempt for a mean, niggardly person ; a Scottish word that has made good its place in the English vernacular. *Scroppit*, sordid, parsimonious ; from the Gaelic *scrub*, to hesitate, to delay, especially in giving or paying ; *sgrubail*, niggardly ; *scrubair*, a churl, a miser.

Scrunt, a worn-out broom ; *scrunty*, a Northern word, signifying, according to Halliwell, short, stunted. Jamieson gives a second interpretation—" a person of slender make, a walking skeleton." Possibly the word is a corruption of the English *shrink*, *shrank.* There is no trace of it either in the Teutonic or the Gaelic.

Scuddy, stark naked ; from the Gaelic *sguad*, to strip or lay bare.

Strip a country lass o' laigh degree perfectly *scuddy*, and set her beside a town belle o' a noble blood, equally naked, and wha can tell the ewe-milker frae the duchess ?—*Noctes Ambrosianæ.*

Scug or **skug**, to hide, to take shelter, to run to sanctuary, to overshadow.

That's the penance he maun dree
To *scug* his deadly sin.
—*Border Minstrelsy: Young Benjie.*

In this quotation, *skug* seems to mean expiate, rather than hide or take refuge from the consequence of the deadly sin. Jamieson derives this word from the Gothic-Swedish *skugga*, a shade. It does not, however, appear in modern Swedish dictionaries. *Skug* and *scuggery* are noted both by Halliwell and Wright as northern English words for secret, hidden, and secrecy. In a note to the ballad of "Young Benjie," in the "Minstrelsy of the Scottish Border," Sir Walter Scott states that *scug* means to shelter or expiate. Possibly, if the interpretation of "shelter" can be accepted as connected, the etymology of the word is the Gaelic *sgathach*, pronounced *sgach*, or *skug*, a screen.

Scunner or **sconner,** a very expressive word, significant of a loathing or aversion to a thing or person, for which it is sometimes difficult or impossible to account.

And yill and whisky gie to cairds
Until they *scunner.*
—BURNS : *To James Smith.*

From the Gaelic *sgonn*, bad, also rude, boorish, ill-mannered. It enters also into the composite of the English word *scoundrel*, and the Italian *scondruels*, evidently of Celtic and Tuscan origin. Or it may perhaps be derived with equal propriety from *sgeun*, a fright, and *sgeunaich*, to frighten.

Scutch, to bruise or beat, to beat or dress flax. The error of Shakspeare's printers in spelling *scutch* as *scotch*, has led to the all but incorrigible mispronunciation of the word—"We have *scotched* the snake, not killed it"—and to the idea that the word has something to do with Scotland, and with the habits of the Scottish people. *Squids*, pronounced *scuitch* or *scutch*, is the Gaelic for to bruise, to beat ; *sguidscadh*, the act of dressing flax. The word *scutch* is still used in the northern counties of England.

Sea-maw, the sea-gull, or sea-mew ; the beautiful white bird of the ocean.

Keep your ain fish-guts to feed your ain *sea-maws.*—ALLAN RAMSAY's *Scots Proverbs.*

The white sea-mew, and not the white dove, was considered by the Druids the bird that Noah let fly from the ark on the subsiding of the Deluge. The name of *pigeon*, sometimes given to the dove, signifies in Gaelic the bird of security ; from *pighe*, bird, and *dion* (*di* pronounced *ji*), security, protection. The coincidence is curious.

Seile, happiness ; from the German *selig*, happy.

Seile o' your face ! is a phrase in Aberdeenshire, expressive of a blessing on the person to whom it is addressed.—DEAN RAMSAY.

Sokand seil is best—the happiness that is earned is best—*i.e.*, earned by the plough ; from *sock*, the ploughshare, and here used metaphorically for labour of any kind.—FERGUSON's *Scots Proverbs.*

Selkouth or selcouth, seldom seen or known ; rendered "wondrous" by Sir Walter Scott, in the notes to "Thomas the Rhymer." The word is of the same origin as the English uncouth, strange, or unknown ; from *kythe*, to show, or appear.

> By Leader's side
> A *selkouth* sight they see,
> A hart and hind pace side by side
> As white as snow.
>   ʼ—*Thomas the Rhymer.*

Sell or selle, a seat, a chair, a stool. Latin *sedile*, French *selle*, a saddle, the seat of a rider. This was once an English as well as a Scottish word, though obsolescent in the Elizabethan era. Shakspeare uses it in *Macbeth*—

Vaulting ambition that o'erleaps *itself*, And falls on the other—

which, to render the image perfect, as Shakspeare meant—and no doubt wrote—ought to be read—

Vaulting ambition that o'erleaps its *sell*, And falls on the other *side.*

The London compositors of Shakspeare's time, ignorant of the word *sell*, insisted upon making *self* of *it*, and in omitting "side." Ambition, in the guise of a horseman, vaulting to the horse's back, could not fall on the other side of itself ; though it might well fall on the other side of the *sell* or saddle, and light upon the ground, which is the true Shakspearian metaphor.

Shacklebane, the wrist; a word apparently first applied to a prisoner who was handcuffed, or manacled.

Shadow-half, the northern exposure of land. Sir Walter Scott built Abbotsford on the wrong side of the Tweed—in the shadow-half. Land with a southern exposure is called the *sunny-half*, or the *sunnyside*.

Shaghle, sometimes written *shaucle*, to walk clumsily, to shuffle along, to drag or shackle the feet as if they were painfully constrained by the shoes; to distort from the original shape, to wear out.

Had ye sic a shoe on ilka foot, it wad gar ye *shaghle.*
—ALLAN RAMSAY'S *Scots Proverbs.*

And how her new shoon fit her auld *shachl't* feet.
—BURNS : *Last May a Braw Wooer.*

Schachled is metaphorically applied to a young woman who has been deserted by her lover. She is, on this account, compared to a pair of shoes that have been thrown aside, as being so put out of shape as to be unfit to be worn any longer.
—JAMIESON.

Jamieson derives this word from the Icelandic *skaga*, deflectere ; *skaggrer*, obliquus. If he had looked at the Gaelic, he would have found *seac* (*shak*), dried up, worn out, without substance, decayed.

Shairnie-faced, a contemptuous epithet applied to a person with a very dirty face ; from *sharn*, or *shairn*, dung, more especially cow-dung, sometimes called in English cow-*sherd*, a word, in all probability, from the same source.

Flae luggit, *shairnie-faced.*
—*The Blithesome Bridal.*

Shalk, a servant, a workman, a farm-servant ; from the Gaelic *sgalag*, corrupted in America into *scalawag*, and used as a term of opprobrium. The word enters into the components of the French *marechal*, and the English *marshal ;* from the Gaelic *maor*, a bailiff, overseer, steward, or superintendent ; and *syalag*, a servant or workman, whence *marechal*, one in charge of workmen or servants.

Shang, a vulgar term for a hasty luncheon or "snack," and for what Scottish children call a "piece ;" *shangie*, thin, meagre, lean.

A *shang* o' bread and cheese, a bite between meals. In Icelandic *skan*, a crust, a rind.—JAMIESON.

The root is probably the Gaelic *seang* (*sheang*), lean, hungry ; thence, by extension of meaning, a piece taken to satisfy hunger.

Shangie-mou'd, hare-lipped, or with a cleft mouth ; from *shangan*, a cleft stick, or anything cleft or divided.

Shangie-mou'd, haluket Meg.
—*The Blithesome Bridal.*

The word *haluket* in this derisory line appears to be a form of *halse*, a giddy, thoughtless girl.

Shank, the leg. This noun is sometimes used as a verb in Scotland, and signifies to depart, to send away, to dismiss. To *shank* a person is to send him away; equivalent in English, to give him the sack; to *shank* one's self away is to leave without ceremony. The English phrase, to go on *shank's* or *shanks's mare*, *i.e.*, to walk, is rendered in Scottish—to go on *shank's naigie*, or little nag. Jamieson absurdly suggests that the English, to travel by the *marrow-bone* stage, *i.e.*, to walk, or go on *shank's* mare, may be derived from the parish of Marylebone, in London. The etymology of *shank* is the Gaelic *seang* (*shank*), lean, slender, like the tibia, or bone of the leg.

Shannach, or **shannagh**, a word explained by Jamieson in the phrase, "'It's ill *shannagh* in you to do this or that,' *i.e.*, it is ill on your part, or it is ungracious in you to do so." In Gaelic *seanacach* signifies wily, cunning, sagacious, which is clearly the root of *shannagh*, so that the phrase cited by Jamieson signifies it is not wise, or it is ill wisdom on your part to do so.

Shard (more properly *sharg*), a contemptuous epithet applied to a little, weazened, undergrown, and, at the same time, petulant and mischievous child. From the Gaelic *searg* (*s* pronounced as *sh*), a withered, insignificant person or animal, one shrivelled or dried up with age, sickness, or infirmity; *seargta*, withered, dried up, blasted.

Shargar, sharg, a lean, scraggy, cadaverous person. *Shargie*, thin, shrivelled, dried up; from the Gaelic *searg*, a puny man or beast, one shrivelled with sickness or old age; also, to wither, to fade away, to dwindle or dry up, from want of vitality.

Sharrow, sharp, sour or bitter to the taste. Flemish *scherp*, French *acerbe*, Gaelic *searbh*, bitter; *searbhad*, bitterness; *searbhag*, a bitter draught.

Shathmont, a measure, of which the exact length is uncertain, but which is evidently small.

> As I was walking all alane
> Atween the water and the wa',
> There I spied a wee, wee man,
> The wee'est man that e'er I saw,
> His leg was scarce a *shathmont* lang.
>   —*Ballad of the Wee, Wee Man.*

This obsolete English, as well as Scottish word, is sometimes written *shaftmond*, and *shaftman*. It appears in "Morte Arthur," and other early English poems. The etymology has never been satisfactorily traced. *Shacht*, which is also written *schaft*, is Flemish for the handle of a pike, or hilt of a sword; and *mand* is a basket or other piece of wickerwork; whence *schacht-mand*, a basket-hilt, or the length of a basket hilt of a sword, which may possibly be the origin of the word. The length of a *shathmont* is stated to be the distance between the outstretched thumb and little finger — a distance which corresponds with the position of the hand, when grasping the sword-hilt. *Maund*, for basket, is not yet entirely obsolete.

Shaver, a droll fellow, a wag, a funster, or one who indulges in attempts at fun; *shavie*, a trick.

> Than him at Agincourt wha shone,
>   Few better were or braver,
> And yet wi' funny, queer Sir John,
>   He was an unco *shaver*.
>   —BURNS: *A Dream.*

> But Cupid shot a shaft
> That played the dame a *shavie*.
>   —BURNS: *The Jolly Beggars.*

It has been suggested that *shaver*, in the sense of a wag or funster, is derived from Figaro the barber, as the type of a class who were professionally funny in amusing their customers, when under their hands for hair-cutting or hair-dressing. The words are possibly corruptions of the old English *shaver*, described by Nares as a low, cunning fellow, and used by the writers of the early decades of the seventeenth century. *Shaver*, in the United States, signifies a bill discounter who takes exorbitant interest, and a *shave* means a swindle or an imposition. Some have derived the word from *shave*, to cut the beard, itself a word of very uncertain etymology, and not necessarily connected with any idea of dishonesty. The more likely derivation is from the Gaelic *saobh* (or *shaov*), dissemble, prevaricate, take unfair advantage of, also, foolish.

Shaw, a small wood, a thicket, a plantation of trees; from the Teutonic. This word was once common in English literature. It still exists in the patronymics of many families, as *Shawe*, *Aldershaw*, *Hinshaw*, *Hackshaw*, *Hawkshaw* (or *Oakshaw*), and others, and is used by the peasantry in most parts of England and every part of Scotland.

> Whither ridest thou under this green
>   *shawe?*
> Said this yeman.
>   —CHAUCER: *The Frere's Tale.*

> Gaillard he was as goldfinch in the *shaw*,
> Brown as a berry, a proper short fellow.
>   —*Idem.: The Coke's Tale.*

> Close hid beneath the greenwood *shaw*.
>   —FAIRFAX.

> In summer when the *shaws* be shene,
>   And leaves be fair and long, .
> It is full merry in fair forest,
>   To hear the fowles' song.
>   —*Ballad of Robin Hood.*

> To all our haunts I will repair,
>   By greenwood, *shaw*, and fountain.
>   —ALLAN RAMSAY.

> The braes ascend like lofty wa's,
> The foaming stream deep roaring fa's,
> O'erhung wi' fragrant spreading *shaws*,
>   The birks of Aberfeldy.
>   —BURNS.

Gloomy winter's now awa,
Saft the westlin breezes blaw ;
'Mang the birks o' Stanley *shaw*,
The mavis sings fu' cheery, oh.
　　　　　—TANNAHILL.

There's nae a bonnie flower that springs
　By fountain, *shaw*, or green,
There's nae a bonnie bird that sings,
　But minds me o' my Jean.
　　　—BURNS : *Of a' the Airts*.

Shear. The primary meaning of *shear* is to cut or clip. In this sense it is used by English agriculturists, for the operation of cutting or clipping the fleece of sheep. In Scotland it is used in the sense of reaping or cutting the corn in harvest. On the occasion of the first visit of Queen Victoria and the Prince Consort to the Highlands of Scotland, it was duly stated in the *Court Circular* that Her Majesty visited the *shearers*, and took much interest in their labours. In the following week, a newly-started pictorial journal, in opposition to the *Illustrated London News*, published a wood engraving, in which Her Majesty, the Prince, and several members of the Court in attendance, were represented as looking on at the *sheep - shearing*. The Cockney artist, ignorant alike of the seasons of agricultural operations and of the difference between the Scottish and English idioms, and who had no doubt, wished the public to believe that he was present on the occasion on which he employed his pencil, must have been painfully convinced, when his fraud

was discovered, of the truth of the poetic adage, that " a little knowledge is a dangerous thing ; " and that *shearing* and *reaping* had different meanings in England and Scotland.

In hairst, at the *shearing*,
Nae youths now are jeering,
At fairs or at preaching,
Nae wooing and fleeching.
　　—*The Flowers o' the Forest.*

Sheuch, a drain, a furrow or trench.

I saw the battle sair and teuch,
And reekin' red ran mony a *sheuch*.
　　—BURNS : *The Battle of Sheriffmuir.*

Shiel or **shielin,** a hut, a shed, or small cottage on the moor or mountain for the shelter of cattle or sportsmen ; derived by Jamieson from the Icelandic *skala*, a cottage ; probably a corruption of *shield*, or *shielding*, a place where one may be *shielded* or *sheltered* from the weather. *Wintershielins*, winter quarters.

No ; I shall ne'er repent, Duncan,
　And shanna e'er be sorry ;
To be wi' thee in Hieland *shiel*
　Is worth the lands o' Castlecary.
　　　—*Ballad of Lizzie Baillie.*

The craik among the clover hay,
　The paitrick whirrin' o'er the lea,
The swallow jinkin' round my *shiel*,
　Amuse me at my spinnin' wheel.
—BURNS : *Bess and her Spinnin' Wheel.*

Shill. Appears to be a contraction for the sake of euphony of the harsher English word *shrill*. The etymology of *shrill* is doubtful, though some derive it from the

Scottish *skirl*, which they call an *onomatopeia*, or imitation of the sound. This also is doubtful, more especially if the Teutonic *schreien*, and the Dutch and Flemish *schreuwen*, to cry out discordantly, are taken into consideration.

The westlin' wind blaws loud and *shill*,
The night's baith mirk and rainy, O.
    —Burns : *My Nannie, O.*

Shilpit, insipid, tasteless, dull, stale, flat; applied to liquor and sometimes to persons, metaphorically to signify that they are spiritless, timid, cowardly, and of no account.

A *shilpett* (*shilpit*) wretch, a heart stripped of manliness.—Jamieson.

The Laird of Balmawhapple pronounced the claret *shilpit*, and demanded brandy with great vociferation.—Scott : *Waverley.*

According to Jamieson, *shilpit* is used to designate ears of corn that are not well filled. He derives it from the German *schelp*, signifying a reed, a bulrush, which is possibly the word that he referred to. But neither *schelp*, which Jamieson renders by the Latin *putamen*, a paring, a husk, a shell, or *schilp*, a bulrush, can be considered the root of *shilpit*, as applied to the insipidity or flatness of a liquor. The origin of *shilpit* remains unknown, though it may possibly have some remote connection with the Gaelic *sile* (*shile*), saliva, or drivel.

Shool, a shovel.

If honest nature made you fools,
  What sairs your grammars ?
Ye'd better ta'en up spades and *shools*
  An' knappin' hammers.
    —Burns : *To Lapraik.*

Shoon, the old plural of shoe, still used in Scotland, though almost obsolete in England.

If ever thou gave hosen or *shoon*,
  Every night an awle,
Sit thee down and pass them on,
  And Christ receive thy saule.
    —*Funeral Dirge, in use in England
      before the Reformation, quoted
      in* Aubrey's *Miscellanies.*

Short, to divert, to amuse, to shorten the time by agreeable conversation; *shortsome*, diverting, as opposed to *langsome*, or *longsome*, tedious, wearisome. In English, *short* is often applied to a hasty or quick temper. In Scottish parlance, *shortly* or *shortlie*, signifies tartly, peevishly, ill-naturedly.

Shot, shote, a puny or imperfect young animal, especially a pig or lamb. The Americans, who have acquired many words from the Scottish and Irish immigrants, have *shote*, a weakly little pig, and apply the word metaphorically to man or woman as an epithet of contempt or derision. It is derived from the Gaelic *seot* (pronounced *sheot*, or *shote*), a stunted animal, a short tail, a tail that has been docked; and, generally, an incumbrance, impediment, or imperfection; *scotair* signifies an idle, lazy, useless person, a drone; a *vaurien*, a good-for-nothing.

Seth Slope was what we call down East a poor *shote*, his principal business being to pick up chips and feed the pigs.— BARTLETT's *Dictionary of Americanisms*.

Shouther, the shoulder; "High- landers! *shouther* to *shouther!*" the motto of some of the High- land regiments in the British service.

When the cloud lays its cheek to the flood, And the sea lays its *shouther* to the shore.   —CHAMBERS's *Scottish Songs: Hew Ainslie*.

Shue, to play at see-saw; *shuggie- shue*, a swing.

Sib, related, of kin by blood or marriage. Hence the English gossip, from *god-sib*, related by baptismal union. From the German *sippe*, which has the same meaning; and *sippschaft*, relationship.

He was *sibbe* to Arthur of Bretagne.   —CHAUCER.

He was no fairy born or *sib* to elves.   —SPENSER.

A boaster and a liar are right *sib*.

A' Stewarts are no *sib* to the king.

It's good to be *sib* to siller.   —ALLAN RAMSAY's *Scots Proverbs*.

We're no more *sib* than sieve and riddle, Though both grew in the woods together.   —*Cheshire Proverb*.

Siccan, such; *sic like*, such like, or *such a*, as an adjective; *sic like* a time, such a time; *sic like* a fashion, in such a way or fashion; generally used in the sense of inopportune, improper, unseemly.

What the deil brings the laird here At *sic like* a time?   —*The Laird o' Cockpen*.

Wi' *siccan* beauties spread around, We feel we tread on holy ground.   —JAMES BALLANTINE: *Darnick Tower*.

Sicker, siccar, firm, safe, secure; *sickerly*, safely; *sickerness*, safety, security; to *sicker*, to make cer- tain; *lock sickar*, lock securely, or safely—the motto of the ancient Scottish family, the Earls of Morton. *Mak sickar* is another motto of historic origin in Scotland.

Toddlin' down on Willie's mill, Setting my staff wi' a' my skill   To keep me *sicker*.   —BURNS: *Death and Dr. Hornbook*.

Sick-saired, nauseated by reple- tion, served with food to excess, and to consequent sickness and loathing.

Simmer (or summer) couts, the gnats or midges which live for one summer day, born ere noon and dying ere sunset, and which seem to pass their brief life in whirling and dancing in the sun- shine. The word, a *summercout*, is often applied affectionately to a very troublesome and merry young child. Jamieson suggests that *couts* may be a corruption of *colts*, in which supposition he is possibly correct, though the comparison of the tiny midge with so large an animal as a young horse is not easy to ex- plain. According to Wright's Dictionary of Provincial English, *cote* signifies a swarm of bees, which seems to approach nearer to the idea of the midges. In Gaelic, *cutha* signifies frenzy, delirium ; and *cuthaich*, frantic dancing of the midges or other ephemeral flies, allied in idea to the phrase of Shakspeare—"a midsummer madness." This may be the real origin of the phrase.

Sindle, seldom ; from the Teutonic *selten.*

> Kame *sindle*, kame sair.
> —ALLAN RAMSAY'S *Scots Proverbs.*

Skalrag, of a shabby appearance ; from the Gaelic *sgail*, to cover, and *rag*, which is both Gaelic and English. *Skalrag* is synonymous, as Jamieson states, with *tatterdemalion*, one covered with rags, though he is incorrect in the etymology from *skail*, to scatter, and the explanation that it signifies one who "gives his rags to the wind."

Skedaddle, to disperse suddenly. A long obsolete Scottish word, revived unexpectedly in the army of the Potomac during the great American Civil War at the battle of Bull's Run, in 1862, when the Federal troops were seized with unreasonable panic, or alarm, and fled, when there was no pursuit. The word is said to be still occasionally used in Dumfriesshire, and to be applied to the wasteful overflow of the milk in the pails, when the milkmaids do not balance them properly, when carrying them from the byre to the farm. It has been generally considered to be an American coinage, on account of the incident of the retreat at Bull's Run, which brought it into notoriety, but was in reality employed either by the Gaelic-speaking Irish or Scottish soldiers under General MacClellan's command, and derived from the two Gaelic words *sguit*, to wander, to disperse, and *allta*, wild, irregular, ungovernable ; or else from *sgath* (*ska*), to lop or cut off, and *adhl*, a hook ; though some hold that it is derivable from the Greek σκεδαζω, to disperse. It is still doubtful which of these derivations, or either of them, is correct.

Skeigh, proud, scornful, disdainful, mettlesome, insolent in the pride of youth.

> When thou and I were young and *skeigh.*
> —BURNS : *Auld Farmer to his Auld Mare, Maggie.*

> Maggie coost her head fu' heigh,
> Looked asklent and unco *skeigh.*
> —BURNS : *Duncan Gray.*

From the Gaelic *sgeig*, to taunt, deride, scorn ; *sgeigeach*, disdainful. Jamieson has *skeg*, which he says is not clear, though he quotes "a *skeg*, a scorner, and a scolder"—words which might have helped him to the meaning.

Skeely, for skilful, but implying much more than the English word ; sagacious, far-seeing.

Out and spak Lord John's mother,
And a *skeely* woman was she,
" Where met ye, my son, wi' that bonnie
   boy
That looks sae sad on thee ?"
                    —*Ballad of Burd Helen.*

Where will I get a *skeely* skipper
   To sail this ship o' mine ?
   —*Ballad of Sir Patrick Spens.*

Skeerie, easily scared or frightened, timid, shy ; from *scare*.

Skellum and blellum. These words are directed against Tam o' Shanter by his wife, in Burns' immortal poem :

She tauld thee weel thou wast a *skellum*,
A bletherin', blusterin', drunken *blellum*.

They are explained in the glossaries as signifying the first, "a worthless fellow ;" the second, " an idle, talkative fellow." *Skellum* was used by English writers in the seventeenth century, among others by Taylor, the water-poet, and by Pepys in his diary. It is traceable to the German, Dutch, and Flemish *schelm*, a rogue, a rascal, a bad fellow ; and also to the Gaelic *sgiolam*, a coarse blackguard ; and *sgiolomach*, addicted to slander and mischief - making. *Blellum* is also from the Gaelic, in which *blialum* signifies incoherent, confused in speech ; especially applied to the utterances of a drunken man.

Skelp, to smack, to administer a blow with the palm of the hand ; to *skelp* the doup (breech), as used to be the common fashion of Scottish mothers.

I'm sure sma' pleasure it can gie,
   E'en to a deil,
To *skelp* and scaud puir dogs like me,
   And hear us squeal !
   —BURNS : *Address to the Deil.*

This word, of which the English synonym is *spank*, to strike with the palm of the hand in a quick succession of blows, appears to be derived primarily from the Gaelic *sgealbh*, to dash into small pieces, fragments, or splinters ; and to have been applied afterwards, by extension of meaning, to the blows that might be sufficient to break any brittle substance. The English *spank* is to strike with the open hand, and the Scottish *spunk*, a match, signifies a splinter of wood, in which the same extension of meaning, from the blow to the possible results of the blow, is apparent. *Skelp* also means to walk or run at a smart pace, and the slang English phrase, "A pair of *spanking* tits " (a pair of fast-trotting or galloping horses), shows the same connection between the idea of blows and that of rapid motion.

   And, barefit, *skelp*
Awa' wi' Willie Chalmers.
                  —BURNS.

Three hizzies, early at the road,
   Cam *skelpin'* up the way.
         —BURNS : *The Holy Fair.*

Tam *skelpit* on thro' dub and mire,
Despising wind and rain and fire.
      —BURNS : *Tam o' Shanter.*

Skelpie-limmer, a violent woman, ready both with her hands and tongue.

Ye little *skelpie-limmer's* face,
I daur ye try sic sportin'.
—Burns : *Hallowe'en.*

Skene-occle, a dagger, dirk ; from the Gaelic *sgian,* a knife, concealed in the *achlais,* under the arm, or in the sleeve ; *achlasan,* anything carried under the arm ; from whence the verb *achlaisich,* to cherish, to fold to the bosom, or encircle with the arm.

"Her ain sell," said Callum, "could wait for her a wee bit frae the toun, and kittle her quarters wi' his *skene-occle.*"— "*Skene-occle !* what's that?" Callum unbuttoned his coat, raised his left arm, and, with an emphatic nod, pointed to the hilt of a small dirk, snugly deposited under the wing of his jacket.
—Scott : *Waverley.*

Skin, a vituperative term applied to a person whom it is wished to disparage or revile. "Ye're naething but a nasty *skin.*" Jamieson suggests that this word is a figurative use of the English *skin,* as denoting a *husk.* It is more likely to be a corruption of the Gaelic *sgonn,* a blockhead, a dolt, a rude clown, an uncultivated and boorish person, a dunce ; from whence *sgonn bhalaoch,* a stupid fellow ; *sgon* signifies vile, worthless, bad ; whence the English *scoundrel*— from *sgon,* and *droll,* or *droil,* an idle vagabond.

Skincheon o' drink, a drop of drink, a dram ; a pouring out of liquor. *Skincheon* is a misprint for *skinkin'.*

Skink, to pour out ; *skinker,* a waiter at a tavern who pours out the liquor for the guests, a bar tender. From the Flemish and German *schenken,* to pour out. This word is old English as well as Scotch, and was used by Shakspeare, Ben Jonson, and their contemporaries. *Skink* is sometimes contemptuously applied to soup or broth when not of the accustomed flavour or consistency, imparted by vegetable ingredients, such as barley, peas, &c.

Sweet Ned, I give thee this pennyworth of sugar, clapt even now into my hand by an under-*skinker.*
—Shakspeare : *Henry IV.*

Such wine as Gannymede doth *skink* to Jove.—Shirley.

Ye powers wha mak mankind your care,
And dish them out their bill o' fare ;
Auld Scotland wants nae *skinking* ware
  That jaups i' luggies,
But if ye wish her grateful prayer,
  Gie her a haggis.
—Burns : *To a Haggis.*

The wine! there was hardly half a mutchkin,—and poor fushionless *skink* it was.—Sir Walter Scott.

In many of the editions of Burns which have been printed in England, the compositors, or printers' readers, ignorant of the word *skink,* have perverted it in the "Lines to a Haggis," into *stink.*

Auld Scotland wants nae *stinking* wares.
—*Complete Works of* Robert Burns, edited by Alexander Smith. London : *Macmillan & Co.,* 1868.

"These editions," says Mr James M'Kie of Kilmarnock in his Bibliography of Robert Burns, "are known to collectors as the *stinking* editions."

N

Skipper, the captain of a ship, but properly any sailor; *skip*-man, a ship man. This word is fast becoming English, and promises to supersede captain as the designation of officers in the mercantile marine. *Skipper* is from the Danish *skiffer*, the German, Dutch, and Flemish *schiffer*.

> The king sat in Dunfermline tower,
> Drinking the blood-red wine;
> Oh whaur 'll I get a skeely *skipper*,
> To sail this ship o' mine.
> —SIR PATRICK SPENS.

It is related of the late eminent sculptor, Patric Park, that, on an excursion through the beautiful lakes that form the chain of the Caledonian Canal, he was annoyed by the rudeness of the captain of the steamer, and expressed his sense of it in language more forcible than polite. The captain, annoyed in his turn, inquired sharply—"Do you know, sir, that I'm the captain of the boat?" "Captain be hanged!" said the irate man of genius, "you're only the *skipper*, that is to say, you're nothing but the driver of an aquatic omnibus!" The *skipper* retired to hide his wrath, muttering as he went that the sculptor was only a *stone mason!*

Skirl, to shriek, to cry out, or to make a loud noise on a wind instrument.

> Ye have given the sound thump, and he the loud *skirl* (*i.e.*, you have punished the man, and he shows it by his roaring).
> —ALLAN RAMSAY'S *Scots Proverbs.*

> When *skirlin'* weanies see the light,
> Thou mak's the gossips clatter bright.
> —BURNS: *Scotch Drink.*

A family belonging to the Scottish Border, after spending some time at Florence, had returned home, and, proud of the progress they had made in music, the young ladies were anxious to show off their accomplishments before an old confidential servant of the family, and accordingly sang to her some of the finest songs which they had learned abroad. Instead, however, of paying them a compliment on their performance, she showed what she thought of it, by asking with much *naïveté*—"Eh, mem! Do they ca' *skirling* like yon, singing in foreign parts?"—DEAN RAMSAY'S *Reminiscences.*

Skirl-naked, stark naked; naked as a child that *skirls* or squalls at the moment of its birth. *Skirl* is allied to screech, shriek, and shrill, and comes immediately from the Gaelic *sgreuch*, a shrill cry, and *sgreuchail*, shrieking.

Sklent, oblique, slanting; to deviate, to slant off the right line of truth, to cast obliquely; to push away, to look away, to squint.

> Now, if yer ane o' warld's folk,
> Who rate the wearer by the cloak,
> And *sklent* on poverty their joke,
> Wi' bitter sneer.
> —BURNS: *To Mr. John Kennedy.*

> One dreary, windy, winter night,
> The stars shot doun wi' *sklentin'* light.
> —BURNS: *Address to the Deil.*

> The city gent
> Behind a kist to lie and *sklent*,
> Or purse-proud, big with cent. per cent.
> An' muckle wame.
> —BURNS: *Epistle to Lapraik.*

> Ye did present your smootie phiz
> 'Mang better folk,
> And *sklented* on the man of Uz
> Your spiteful joke.
> —BURNS: *Address to the Deil.*

Skrae, or **scrae**, a thin, skinny, meagre person, a skeleton; *skrae-shankit*, having skinny legs; English *scrag*, and *scraggy ;* Gaelic *sgraidh - teach (dh* silent), shrivelled, dried up; *sgraidht*, a lean, shrivelled, ugly old woman.

> But gin she say, lie still ye *skrae*,
>   That's Water Kelpie !
>   —JAMIESON'S *Border Minstrelsy :*
>   *Water Kelpie.*

In the glossary appended by Sir Walter Scott to Jamieson's ballad written in imitation of the antique, *skrae* is glossed as a skeleton.

Skreigh, or **screigh**, a shrill cry, a shriek, a screech.

> The *skreigh* o' duty, which no man should hear and be inobedient.—SCOTT : *Rob Roy.*

> It's time enough to *skreigh* when ye're strucken.—ALLAN RAMSAY'S *Scots Proverbs.*

> When thou and I were young and skeigh,
> An' stable meals at fairs were dreigh,
> How thou would prance and snort, and *skreigh*,
>   An' tak the road.
>   —BURNS : *Auld Farmer to his Auld Mare, Maggie.*

Skulduddery. This grotesque word has been held to signify indulgence in lust, or illicit passion ; but it also signifies obscene language or conversation, or, as it is sometimes called in English, *smut.* Jamieson suggests the Teutonic *shuld*, fault or crime, as the origin of the first syllable, and the Gaelic *sgaldruth,* a fornicator, as the origin of the whole word. *Scaldruth,* however, has long been obsolete, and seems to have been a compound of *sgald,* to burn or scald ; and *druis,* lust ; whence the modern Gaelic *druisear,* a fornicator. If the Gaelic etymology be accepted, the word would resolve itself into a corruption of *sgald-druis,* burning lust, or burned by lust. From the Gaelic *druis* came the old English *druery,* for courtship, intercourse of the sexes, gallantry ; and *drossel,* an unchaste woman. The French, who have inherited many Celtic words from their ancestors, the Gauls, formerly used the word *dru* for a lover (*un ami*), and *drue* for a sweetheart (*une amie*). *Drú,* as an adjective, signified, according to the "Dictionaire de la Langue Romane" (Paris 1768), "un amant vigoureux et propre au plaisir." *Druerie,* in the sense of courtship and gallantry, occurs in the "Roman de la Rose." Another French word, *sgaldrine,* still more akin to the Scottish *skulduddery,* is cited in the "Dictionaire Comique de Le-Roux," as a "terme d'injure pour une femme de mauvaise vie ; femme publique affligée d'une maladie brulante."

> And there will be Logan Macdonald—
>   *Skulduddery* and he will be there !
>   —BURNS : *The Election.*

> That can find out naething but a wee bit *skulduddery* for the benefit of the Kirk Treasury.—SCOTT : *Rob Roy.*

Skybald, apparently the same as the English *skewbald* and *piebald,* terms to designate a horse of two colours, marked as cows and oxen more usually are. Both *skybald* and *piebald,* as well as the English *skewbald,* have their origin in the Gaelic. *Sky* and *skew* are corruptions of *sgiath,* a shade, a dark shade; *pie* comes from *pighe,* a pie, or mag*pie,* a bird whose black plumage is marked with a white streak; *bald* is derived from the Gaelic *ball,* a mark or spot; whence *skybald* is shade-marked, and *piebald* is marked like a bird. Jamieson says that, in Scotland, *skybald* signifies a base, mean fellow, a worthless person, and that it is also applied to a man in rags and tatters. Possibly this metaphorical use of the word arises from the fact that the rags of such a person 'are often of various colours. Locke, the celebrated English metaphysician, uses *piebald* in a similar sense, "a piebald livery of coarse patches." In Yorkshire, according to Wright's Provincial Dictionary, *skeyl'd* signifies parti-coloured, which is apparently from the same Gaelic root as *sky* and *skew.*

Skyre. Jamieson renders this word, pure, mere, utter. The Flemish and German *schier* signifies nearly, almost; while the Danish *skier* means clear, pure, limpid. Thus the Danish, and not the German or Flemish, seems to be the root of this Scottish word.

Skyte or **skite,** to eject liquid forcibly, a flux, or diarrhœa. This vulgar word is often, both in a physical and moral sense, applied in contempt to any mean person. A *skyte* of rain is a sudden and violent shower; *skyter* is a squirt, a syringe; so called from the violent ejection of the liquid. *Bletherum skyte*—more properly, *blether and skyte* (see BLETHER, *ante*)—is a colloquial phrase very often employed by people who are unaware of the grossness of its original meaning, and who are impressed by its aptness as descriptive of the windy trash of conversation and assertion which it but too powerfully designates. The word is derivable either from the English *scud,* fast motion, or the Gaelic *sgud,* to cut, a cutting wind.

When hailstanes drive wi' bitter *skyte.*
　—BURNS : *The Jolly Beggars.*

Slack, slug, a pass, opening, or gap between two hills; from the Gaelic *sloc,* and *slochd,* a hollow, a cavity, a ravine. *Slochd muigh,* or the gap of the wild swine, is a wild pass in the Grampians between Perth and Inverness.

But ere he won the Gate-hope *slack,*
I think the steed was wae and weary.
　—*Minstrelsy of the Border:*
　　Annan Water.

Slanky, slimy.

Twa *slanky* stanes seemed his spule banes.
　—*Border Minstrelsy: The Water*
　　Kelpie.

Slap, a breach, or casual opening in a hedge or fence.

> At *slaps* the billies [fellows] halt a blink [a little while],
> Till lassies strip their shoon.
> —BURNS: *The Holy Fair.*

Slawpie, slaipie, indolent, slovenly; derived by Jamieson from the Icelandic *slapr,* homuncio sordidus. It is rather from the Gaelic *slapach,* slovenly, *slapair* and *slaopair,* a slovenly man, a drawler, an idler; and *slapag,* a slut, a lazy, dirty, slovenly woman or girl; and *slapaireachd,* slovenliness.

Sleuth-hound, a blood-hound, a hound trained to follow by the scent the track of man or beast. From the Gaelic *slaod,* a trace, a trail; and *slot, sliogach,* subtle, keen scented.

> Wi' his *sleuth*-dog in his watch right sure;
> Should his dog gie a bark,
> He'll be out in his sark,
> And die or win.
> —*Ballad of The Fray of Suport.*

Slid, smooth; *sliddery,* slippery.

> Ye had sae saft a voice, and a *slid* tongue.
> —ALLAN RAMSAY: *The Gentle Shepherd.*

Sliddery, slippery; from *slide.* **Slidder,** unstable, changeable in thought or purpose, not to be depended upon.

> There's a *sliddery* stane afore the ha' door.
> [It is sometimes dangerous to visit great houses.]
> —ALLAN RAMSAY'S *Scots Proverbs.*

> Though I to foreign lands must hie,
> Pursuin' fortune's *sliddery* ba'.
> —BURNS: *Farewell to his Native Country.*

Slink, a tall, idle person; a term of depreciation. The word is usually associated with *lang,* as, a *lang slink.* It is sometimes written and pronounced *slunk.* It is derived apparently from the Teutonic *schlang,* the Dutch and Flemish *slang,* a snake. *Slinken* means to grow long, thin, and attenuated; and Jamieson has the adjective *slunk,* lank and slender; and the substantive *slink,* a starveling.

Slint or **slinter,** a slovenly, untidy, awkward man, corresponding with the English *slut* as applied to a woman; from the Gaelic *slaod,* to draggle or trail lazily along the ground; *slaodag,* a slut; *slaodair,* a sluggard. Jamieson derives it from the Teutonic *slodde,* a dirty female; but the word is not to be found in German dictionaries, though it possibly exists in the vulgar patois.

Sliver, a slice, a small piece. The word was employed in this sense by Chaucer, and is akin to the English *slice,* and to the Gaelic *slios,* a side. Stormonth derives it from the Anglo-Saxon *slifan,* to cleave or split. Shakspeare uses the word three times.

> *Slivered* in the moon's eclipse.
> —*Macbeth,* act iv. scene 1.

> An envious *sliver* broke.
> —*Hamlet,* act iv. scene 7.

> *Sliver* and disbranch.
> —*Lear,* act iv. scene 2.

Slocken, to slake, to allay thirst, to extinguish.

Foul water may *slocken* fire.
—ALLAN RAMSAY's *Scots Proverbs.*

It *slockened* not my drouth, but aggravated a thousandfold the torrent o' my greed.—*Noctes Ambrosianæ.*

The Rev. John Heugh of Stirling was one day admonishing one of his people on the sin of intemperance : " Man ! John ! you should never drink except when you're dry." " Weel, sir," said John, " that's what I'm aye doin', but I'm never *slocken'd.*"—DEAN RAMSAY.

Slogan, the war-cry of a Highland clan.

Our *slogan* is their lyke-wake dirge.
—SIR WALTER SCOTT.

When the streets of high Dunedin,
Saw lances gleam and falchions redden,
And heard the *slogan's* deadly yell.
SCOTT : *Lay of the Last Minstrel.*

Jamieson has this word as *slughorn,* and derives it from the Irish Gaelic *sluagh,* an army, and *arm,* a horn. Jamieson might have found the true etymology in the Scottish Gaelic *sluagh,* the people, the multitude, the clan ; and *gairm,* a cry, a shout, a loud call. The *slogan* was not made on a horn ; and *arm* does not signify a horn in Gaelic. *Slogan,* the war-cry, has been used by English writers as synonymous with *pibroch,* especially in a play that enjoyed considerable popularity a quarter of a century ago, on the siege and relief of Lucknow during the Indian Mutiny. When General Havelock approaches with his gallant Highlanders,

Jeanie, the heroine of the piece, who hears the music of the pibroch from afar, exclaims, " Oh ! hear ye not the *slogan ?* " But the " pock puddings," as one of Sir Walter Scott's characters called the English, knew no better, and always applauded the *slogan.*

Slogger, to swallow broth, porridge, or spoon meat awkwardly and voraciously; from the Gaelic *sluig,* to swallow ; *slugair,* or *slogair,* a glutton. Synonymous with the local English *slorp.*

Sloom, a deep sleep, whence the English word *slumber,* a light sleep ; from the Flemish *sluimeren,* to sleep; *sluimerig,* sleepy.

Sloomy, lethargic.

Slorp, slotter, to eat or drink greedily, and with a guttural and vulgar noise ; from the Flemish and Dutch *slorpen,* which has the same meaning.

There's gentle John, and Jock the *slorp,*
And curly Jock, and burly Jock,
And lying Jock himsel'.
—HOGG's *Jacobite Relics.*

Slort, a sloven ; *sloeter,* to work in an idle, slovenly, and bungling manner ; akin to the English *slut,* applied in the same manner to a woman. From the Gaelic *sluodair,* a sluggard ; a lazy, careless person.

Slounge, to go idling about, to go sorning (q.v.), or seeking for a dinner, lounging about and coming into the house of a friend or acquaintance at or near dinner time, as if accidentally. Apparently a corruption of the Gaelic *slugair*, a glutton ; *sluganach*, a voracious person, and *slugan*, the gullet.

Slunk, sometimes written **slung**, an Aberdonian word, which according to Jamieson signifies a tall, cadaverous-looking person of inferior intellect, " a lang, toom, haiverilly kind o' chiel." He derives it from the Icelandic *slani*, an imbecile. The word, however, seems akin to the English *slink*, as its past participle *slunk*, and to be derivable from the German *schlang*, a snake that *slinks* away, and is hence, by association of ideas, applied metaphorically, in the same way as the English *sneak*, which has a similar origin.

Sma' drink, a weak liquor ; the English say *small beer*, for weak beer or ale, and the French *petit vin*, for inferior wine. To " think nae sma' drink o' him-sel'," is a phrase applied to any one who thinks too much of his own dignity or importance.

Smaik, a mean, low fellow, a poltroon, a puny fellow, a person of small moral or physical account.

" Oh, I have heard of that *smaik*," said the Scotch merchant ; "it's he whom your principal, like an obstinate auld fule, wad mak a merchant o'—wad he, or wad he no !"—SCOTT : *Rob Roy*.

This false, traitorous *smaik*. I doubt he is a hawk of the same nest.—SCOTT : *Fortunes of Nigel*.

From the Teutonic *schmach*, insult, ignominy ; *schmächtig*, slender, lank.

Smeddum, spirit, pith, energy. Also dust, powder ; from the Gaelic *smodan*, small dust.

Now and then ye may overhaul an article that's ower lang and ower stupid, and put some *smeddum* into it.—*Noctes Ambrosianæ*.

Oh, for some rank mercurial rozet,
    Or pale red *smeddum*,
I'd gie ye sic a hearty dose o't
Wad dress your droddum.*
            —BURNS : *To a Louse*.

Smeerless, pithless, marrowless ; from the Gaelic *smior*, marrow.

I mark him for a *smeerless* dolt,
Who'd jink to eschew a thunderbolt.
—GEORGE BEATTIE : *John o' Arnha'*.

Smergh, marrow, vigour, pith ; strength either of body or of mind ; *smerghlers*, weak, marrowless, pithless, vapid, insipid ; from the Gaelic *smior*, marrow, and *smiorach*, marrowy, or full of marrow and pith. The Teutonic *mark*, marrow, seems to be of this origin, with the omission of the initial *s*, though Jamieson traces it to the Teutonic *mergh*, which does not mean marrow, but marl.

Smervy, fat and marrowy.

They scum'd the cauldron, fed the fuel, They steer'd and preed, the *smervy* gruel. —GEORGE BEATTIE : *John o' Arnha'*.

---

* *Droddum*, a ludicrous word for the posterior of a child.

Smiddle, to work by stealth; derivation uncertain, but possibly related to *smith, smithy,* and *smiddy.*

Smird, to gibe, to jeer. Jamieson derives this word from the Icelandic *sma'* (the Scottish *sma'* and the English *small*), and *ord,* a word, and supposes it to mean small and contemptuous language. It is more probably from the Gaelic *smioradh* or *smiuradh,* smearing, or besmearing; used metaphorically for *larding* with abuse or ill-natured jests.

Smirl, a roguish or mischievous trick. Jamieson derives this word from the German *schmieren,* illudere; but in the German dictionaries it is defined as "to smear." It is more probably from the Gaelic *smiorail,* strong, active, lively; and "I'll play him a *smirl* for that yet," as quoted by Jamieson, simply means, "I'll play him a *lively* trick for that yet."

> And in some distant place,
> Plays the same *smirle.*
> —T. Scott.

Smirtle, a slight, or half-suppressed laugh or smile.

> And Norie takes a *glack* of bread and cheese,
> And wi' a *smirtle* unto Lindie goes.
> —Ross's *Helenore.*

This word is akin to the English *smirk,* but without any depreciatory meaning.

Smit, the noise, clash, or clank of smitten metal; from the English *smite.*

> As she was walking maid alane
> Down by yon shady wood,
> She heard a *smit* o' bridle reins
> She wished might be for good.
> —*Border Minstrelsy: Lord William.*

Smitch or **smytch,** a term of contempt or anger applied to an impudent boy; from *smut,* dirt, a stain, an impurity. German *schmützig,* dirty; Flemish and Dutch *smotsen,* to soil, to dirty, to defile; the English *smudge.*

Smolt, an epithet applied to the weather when fair and calm, with a blue sky.

> Merry maidens, think na lang,
> The weather is fair and *smolt.*
> —*Christ's Kirk on the Green.*

This word is used, according to Messrs. Halliwell and Wright, in Sussex and other parts of England. It is probable that the root is the Teutonic *schmaltc,* deep blue, applied to the unclouded sky.

> O'er Branxholme Tower, ere the morning hour,
> Where the lift is like lead so blue,
> The smoke shall roll white on the weary night,
> And the flame shine dimly through.
> —*Border Minstrelsy: Lord Inglis.*

Smook, to prowl stealthily about a place, with a view to pilfer small articles; from the Flemish *smuig,* furtive, secret.

Smookie, addicted to petty larceny.

The *smookie* gipsy i' the loan.
—Ross's *Helenore.*

Smoor, abbreviation and corruption of smother.

What's the matter, quo' Willie,
Though we be scant o' claes,
We'll creep the closer thegither,
An' we'll *smoor* a' the fleas.
—*Woo'd an' Married an' A'.*

Smyte, a small particle; possibly derived from the spark of an anvil when smitten; *smytrie*, a large collection of little things, or little children.

A *smytrie* o' wee duddie weans.
—BURNS.

Snack, a slight repast, a cut from the loaf, refreshment taken hastily between meals; to go *snacks*, to share with another. From the Gaelic *snaigh*, to cut. *Snack*, and to go *snacks*, are still used in colloquial English, and are derived by Worcester and others from *snatch*, *i.e.*, as much of a thing as can be snatched hastily. An etymology which may apply to *snack*, a lunch, but scarcely applies so well as the Gaelic *snaigh*, to the phrase of go *snacks*, or shares in any thing.

Snag, to chide, to taunt, to reprove, to snarl; *snaggy*, sarcastical, apt to take offence. This word, with the elision of the initial *s*, remains in English as *nag*, the form of scolding or grumbling, which is peculiarly attributed to quarrelsome women. It is one of the numerous family of words commencing with *sn*, which, in the Scottish and English languages, generally imply a movement of the lips and nose, expressive of anger, reproof, scorn, and in inferior animals, of an inclination to bite; such as snarl, snub, sneer, snort, snap, snack, or snatch (as an animal with its jaws), and many others, all of which, inclusive of snore, sniff, snuff, sneeze, snigger, snivel, snout, have a reference to the nose. They appear to be derivable primarily from the Gaelic *sron*, pronounced *strone*, the nose. The Teutonic languages have many words commencing with *schn*, which also relate to the action of the nose, and are possibly of the same Celtic origin.

Snaggerel, a contemptuous term for a puny, deformed child; from *snag*, a broken bough.

Snash, impertinence, rebuff, rebuke.

Poor bodies . . .
. . . thole (endure) a factor's *snash.*
—BURNS: *The Twa Dogs.*

Sneck or **snick,** the latch, bolt, or fastening of a door. The etymology is uncertain, and cannot be traced to any branches of the Teutonic, either High Dutch, Low Dutch, or Danish and Swedish. The English has *snacket* and *snecket*, a fastening,

a hasp; as well as *sneck* and
snick, with the same meaning
as the Scotch, but the words
are local, not general.

And you, ye auld *sneck*-drawing dog,
Ye came to Paradise incog.
—BURNS: *Address to the Deil.*

Sneeshin', snuff; from *sneeze;*
sneeshin'-mull, a snuff-box.

Snaped haddocks, wilks, dulse an'
tangles,
An' a mull o' gude *sneeshin'* to prie;
When weary wi' eatin' and drinkin'
We'll up an' we'll dance till we die.
—*The Blithesome Bridal.*

Snell, keen, bitter, sharp, quick;
from the Flemish *snell,* and the
German *schnell,* swift.

And bleak December's winds ensuing
Baith *snell* and keen.
—BURNS: *To a Mouse.*
Sir Madoc was a handy man, and *snell*
In tournament, and eke in fight.
—*Morte Arthur.*
Shivering from cold, the season was so
snell.
—DOUGLAS: *Eneid.*
The winds blew *snell.*
—ALLAN RAMSAY.
Snelly the hail smote the skeleton trees.
—JAMES BALLANTINE.

Snirtle, to laugh slily, or in a half
suppressed manner.

He feigned to *snirtle* in his sleeve,
When thus the laird addressed her.
—BURNS: *The Jolly Beggars.*

Snood or **snude,** a ribbon, a
band worn by young unmarried
women in or around the hair.

To tyne one's *snude* is a phrase applied
in Scotland to a young woman who has
lost her virginity. It is singular that the
ancient Romans had the same figure.—
JAMIESON.

The word and the fashion
appears to be peculiar to the
Celtic nations. In Gaelic, *snuadh*
signifies beauty and adornment,
and thence an ornament, such
as the *snood* of the Scottish
maidens. The word appears in
Snowdon, the ancient name of
Stirling, which signifies the fair
or beautiful hill. The Kymric
and Welsh has *ysnoden,* a fillet, a
lace, a band, evidently from the
same root. The much despised
English patronymic *Snooks,*
sometimes alleged to be a corruption of *sevenoaks,* is probably
of Celtic origin, from *snuadhach*
(*snu-ach*), beautiful.

Snool, to flatter abjectly, to cringe,
to crawl. This word also means
to snub, to chide ill-naturedly
and unduly.

They *snool* me sair and haud me down,
And gar me look like bluntie, Tam;
But three short years will soon wheel roun',
And then comes ane and twenty, Tam.
—BURNS.
Is there a whim-inspired fool,
Ow're blate (shy) to seek, ow're proud to
snool.
—BURNS: *A Bard's Epitaph.*
Your *snools* in love and cowards in war,
Frae maidens' love are banished far.
—*John o' Arnha'.*

The etymology of this word
is uncertain. It seems to have
some relation to the nose and
mouth, and expression of the
features in an unfavourable
sense; like many words in the
English language commencing
with *sn.* (See SNAG, *ante.*) The
most probable derivation is that
given by Jamieson from the

Danish *snøfte*, to reprimand unnecessarily, continually, and unjustly—the French *rabrouer*.

Snoove, to glide away easily, like a worm or snake; to sneak. Probably from the Gaelic *sniomh* (pronounced *sni-ov*), to twist, to twine, to wriggle,

> But just thy step a wee thing hastit,
> Then *snoov't* away.
> —BURNS : *Auld Farmer to his*
> *Auld Mare, Maggie.*

Snowk, to snuff, to smell, to scent.

> Wi' social nose they snuffed and *snowket*.
> —BURNS : *The Twa Dogs.*

Snuit, to go about in a careless, half-stupefied manner; *snuitit*, having the appearance of sleepy inebriety.

> He was gaun *snuitin* down the street ;
> he came *snuitin* in.—JAMIESON.

Jamieson traces the word to the Dutch and Flemish *snuit*, the snout. The Gaelic has *snot*, to smell, to snuff up the wind, to turn up the nose suspiciously; and *snotuch*, suspecting, inclined to suspicion.

Snurl, to ruffle the surface of the waters with a wind; metaphorically applied to the temper of man or woman.

> Northern blasts the ocean *snurl*.
> —ALLAN RAMSAY.

Sockdologer, a heavy, knockdown blow. This word is usually considered to be an Americanism. But it clearly comes from the " old country," from the Gaelic *sogh*, easy ; and *dolach*, destructive ; *dolaidh*, harm, detriment, injury, destruction ; thus a *sockdologer* means a blow that destroys easily.

Sodger or **sojer**, a soldier ; *swaddie* or *swad*, a familiar and vulgar name for a soldier.

> My humble knapsack a' my wealth,
> A poor but honest *sodger*.
> —BURNS.

The Scottish word *sodger* is possibly not a mere corruption or mispronunciation of the English *soldier*, or the French *soldat*, as it is generally considered to be. The old Teutonic for soldier was *kriegsman*, warman, or man of war ; a word which was not adopted by the early English of German, Danish, and Flemish descent. The English soldiers were called bowmen, spearmen, archers, &c. The commonly accepted derivation of soldier is from *solde*, pay,—*i.e.*, one who is paid. But in early times, before the establishment of standing armies, people who took up arms in 'defence of their country were not mercenaries, but patriots and volunteers, or retainers of great territorial chieftains. *Sodger*, as distinguished from *soldier*, dates from a period anterior to the invention of gunpowder and the use of fire-arms, when bows and arrows were the principal weapons of warfare over all Europe ; may be derived from the

Gaelic *saighead*, an arrow; and *saighdear*, an arrower, an archer, a bowman; the same as the Latin *saggitarius*. Thus the Scottish *sodjer* appears to be a word of legitimate origin and of respectable antiquity. Soldier, from the French *soldat*, is comparatively modern, and does not appear in the "Dictionary of the First or Oldest Words in the English Language, from the Semi-Saxon Period from A.D. 1250 to 1300," by Herbert Coleridge, published in 1862. It is worthy of mention that Jamieson's Scottish Dictionary does not contain *sodger* or *sojer*, but has *sodgerize*, to act as a soldier, or go a soldiering; and the strange term *sodgertheed*, which he explains to be a low word meaning one that has little or no money, or having "the *thigh* of a soldier!" Had Jamieson, before hazarding this suggestion, looked to another page of his own dictionary, he would have found the word *thig*, to beg, and might have explained the phrase in the sense of a disbanded soldier, begging from door to door, without any particular reference to his *thigh*.

Sokand seil. An old Scottish proverb says, "*Sokand seil* is best." Dean Ramsay, who quotes it, defines it to mean, "The plough and happiness is the best lot." The translation is too loose to be accepted. *Soc* is, indisputably, a ploughshare, in Gaelic, in French, in Flemish (in Latin *soccus*), and other languages. No trace, however, has hitherto been discovered of its employment as a verb, signifying to plough. It would seem, nevertheless, from the terminal syllable in *sockand*, that it was in old time so used in Scotland. *Seil* is from the Gaelic *sealbh*, signifying good fortune, good luck, happiness, — whence the Teutonic *selig*, happy. Ploughing, in the proverb, may be taken to mean labouring generally; and then the proverb might be rendered, "Labouring happiness, or the happiness that results from labour, is the best."

Sonk, a stuffed seat, or a couch of straw; *sonkie*, a gross, coarse, unwieldy man, of no more shapely appearance than a sack of straw. The root of these two words seems to be the Gaelic *sonnach*, anything thick, bulky, or strong; *sonn* is a stout man, also a hero; and *sonnach*, a fat, ill-shaped person.

> The Earl of Argyle is bound to ride,
> And all his habergeons him beside,
> Each man upon a *sonk* of strae.
> —*Introduction to Border Minstrelsy.*

Sonse, happiness, good luck; *sonsie*, strong, happy, pleasant; from the Gaelic *sona*, happy, and *sonas*, happiness. *Sonas agus donas*, happiness and unhappiness.

> His honest, *sonsie*, baws'nt face
> Aye gat him friends in ilka place.
> —BURNS: *The Twa Dogs.*

Sook, a suck, a drop, a sup or sip, a taste of liquor. *Sooch* or *sook* is defined by Jamieson as "a copious draught."

There sat a bottle in a hole,
Ayont the ingle low;
And aye she took the ither *sook*,
To drook the stoury tow.
—*The Weary Pund o' Tow.*

Sool (sometimes written *soul*), a sufficiency of food, also, a relish taken with insipid food to render it more palatable. " *Sool* to a potatoe," often applied to a finnan haddie, or a red herring; sometimes ludicrously used by the Irish as, "potatoes and point," a potato pointed at a red herring hanging from the roof, to whet the imagination with the unattainable flavour of the *sool*.

I have, sweet wench, a piece of cheese as good as tooth may chaw,
And bread and wildings *souling* well.
—WARNER : *Albion's England.*

Sool, anything eaten with bread, such as butter, cheese, &c.—WRIGHT's *Dictionary of Obsolete English.*

Soul, French *saouler*, to satisfy with food. *Soul*, silver, the wages of a retainer, originally paid in food.—*Idem.*

The French have *soul*, full; and *se souler*, to get drunk, *i.e.*, full either of meat or of liquor. The Gaelic *sult* seems to be of kindred derivation, and signifies fat, full, replenished with good things.

Sooth. Old English for *truth*, still preserved in such phrases as, " in *sooth*," "*for-sooth*," &c. In Scottish, *sooth* is used as an adjective, and signifies " true."

A *sooth* boord is nae boord (*i.e.*, a jest with too much truth in it it may be no jest at all).—ALLAN RAMSAY'S *Scots Proverbs.*

Sorn, to go to a person's house, without invitation, and fasten yourself upon him to feast or lodge. The English synonym is "to sponge upon;" a very inferior form of expression, partaking of the character of slang, and not to be compared for force and compactness to the Scottish word. Mr. John Thompson, private secretary to the Marquis of Hastings in India, in his "Etymons of English Words," defines *sorn* to be a corruption of *sojourn*. The true etymon appears to be the Gaelic *saor*, free, and *saoranach*, one who makes free or establishes himself in free quarters. It is related of a noble Scottish lady of the olden time, who lived in a remote part of the Highlands, and was noted for her profuse and cordial hospitality, that she was sometimes overburdened with habitual *sorners*. When any one of them out-stayed his welcome, she would take occasion to say to him at the morning meal, with an arch look at the rest of the company—" Mak' a guid breakfast, Mr. Blank, while ye're about it; I dinna ken whar' ye'll get your dinner." The hint was usually taken, and the *sorner* departed.

Soss, an incongruous, miscellaneous mixture of eatables.

Soss-poke, a ludicrous term for the stomach; usually derived from *sal* and *salsum,* because the ingredients are salted; but the word is more likely to have originated in *soss,* the old French *sause,* the Flemish *sass,* the modern *sauce,* compounded of several ingredients, all blending to produce a particularly piquant flavour. *Soss* is used in colloquial and vulgar English in the Scottish sense of a mixed mess; and *sorzle,* evidently a corruption of *soss,* is, according to Mr. Wright's Archaic Dictionary, a word used in the East of England to signify " any strange mixture."

S o u d i e, broth; from the old English *seethe,* to boil. (See POWSOUDIE, *ante.*)

Sourocks, wild sorrel; any sour vegetable.

Souter, a shoemaker, a cobbler. This word occurs in early English literature, though it is now obsolete.

> Ploughmen and pastourers,
> And other common labourers,
> *Souters* and shepherds.
> —*Piers Ploughman.*

> The devil maks a reeve to preach,
> Or a *souter,* a shipman, or a bear.
> —CHAUCER: *Canterbury Tales.*

> " Mair whistle than woo,"
> As the *souter* said when he sheared the soo.
> —ALLAN RAMSAY'S *Scots Proverbs.*

> *Souters'* wives are aye ill shod.
> —*Idem.*

Sowens, flummery; a mixture of oatmeal and sour milk.

Sowie, diminutive of *sow.* An implement of war for demolishing walls, which the English call a *ram,* and the French *un belier,* or a *battering ram;* the Scotch call it a *sow,* from its weight and rotundity.

> They laid their *sowies* to the wall
> Wi' mony a heavy peal ;
> But he threw ower to them again
> Baith pitch and tar-barrel.
> —SCOTT's *Border Minstrelsy:*
> *Auld Maitland.*

Sowth, to try over a tune with a low whistle, to hum a tune to one's self involuntarily.

> On braes when we please, then,
> We'll sit and *sowth* a tune,
> Syne rhyme till't ; we'll time till't,
> And sing't when we hae done.
> —BURNS: *To Davie, a Brother Poet.*

Sowther, or **soother,** to solder, to make amends for, to cement, to heal.

> A towmond o' trouble, should that be my fa',
> Ae night o' good fellowship *sowthers* it a'.
> —BURNS: *Contented wi' Little.*

Spae, to tell fortunes, to predict. Etymology uncertain; derived by Jamieson from the Icelandic, but probably connected with *spell,* a magic charm or enchantment, or with *spes,* hope; *spae-wife,* a fortune-teller; *spae-book,* magic book, a fortune-teller's book.

> The black *spae-book* from his breast he took,
> Impressed with mony a warlock spell ;

And the book it was wrote by Michael Scott,
He held in awe the fiends o' hell.
—LORD SOULIS : *Border Minstrelsy.*

Spae, which in Scottish means to prophesy, has no connection with the English *spae,* written by Johnson *spay,* to castrate a female animal for the purpose of producing barrenness.

Be dumb, you beggars of the rhyming trade,
Geld your loose wits, and let the muse be *spay'd.*

A singular misconception of the true meaning of a *spay'd,* or one who is *spay'd,* has led to a current English proverb, that will doubtless drop out of use as soon as its true origin is understood. In Taylor's works (1630), quoted by Halliwell, occurs the couplet :—

I think it good plaine English without fraude
To call a *spade* a *spade,* a bawd a bawd.

The juxtaposition of *bawd* and *spade* in this passage suggests that the true reading should be *spay'd.* In Dr. Donne's satires, anterior to the works of Taylor, there appears the line :—

I call a *bawd* a *bawd,* a *spae'd* a *spae'd.*

Nares in his Glossary asks very naturally, "why the *spade* (rather than the poker, or hoe, or plough, or pitchfork, or any other implement) was especially chosen to enter into this figurative expression is not clear." If he had known the true meaning of the word *spay'd* or *spae'd,* the obscurity would have been cleared up.

Spairge, to sprinkle, to scatter about as liquids. From the French *asperger,* to sprinkle with water.

When in yon cavern grim and sootie,
    Closed under hatches,
Spairges about the brimstane cootie.*
        —BURNS : *Address to the Deil.*

Spank, to move rapidly ; *spanker,* one who walks with a quick and lively step ; *spanky,* frisky, lively, sprightly. The phrase "a *spanking* tit" is still employed by the sporting brotherhood of the lower classes to signify a fast horse. The English *spank,* to beat, to slap, seems to be derivable from the same idea of rapidity of motion which pertains to the Scottish word, and to be suggestive of the quick and oft-repeated motion of the hands in *spanking* or slapping the posterior. *Spankering,* nimble, active, alert. The word is derived by Jamieson from the Teutonic *spannen,* to extend. The German word, however, does not exactly mean *extend,* but to put the horses to a carriage, as the French *atteler.*

Spargeon, plaister ; *spargeoner,* a plaisterer ; from the French *asperger,* to sprinkle.

Spartle, from the Flemish *spartcln,* to move the limbs quickly or

---

* Cootie signifies a large dish, and also the broth or other liquor contained in it.

convulsively, to kick about helplessly or involuntarily. *Sprattle,* to struggle or sprawl.

Listening the doors and windows rattle,
I thought me on the ourie cattle,
Or silly sheep, wha bide this brattle
　　O' winter war,
And through the drift deep-lairing *sprattle,*
　　Beneath a scaur.
　　　　—BURNS : *A Winter Night.*

No more was made for that lady,
　For she was lying dead ;
But a' was for her bonnie bairn,
　Lay *spartling* at her side.
　　.—BUCHAN'S *Ancient Ballads.*

Spatch-cock, a fowl split open, to be broiled in haste, on a sudden demand for dinner from an unexpected guest ; a corruption of *dispatch*-cock, a cock quickly cooked. The word is ⎰ common in the United States.

Spate, a flood or freshet, from the overflow of a river or lake ; also metaphorically an overflow of idle talk.

The water was great and mickle o' *spate.*
　　　　—*Kinmont Willie.*

Even like a mighty river that runs down in
spate to the sea.
—W. E. AYTOUN : *Blackwood's Magazine.*

He trail'd the foul sheets down the gait,
　Thought to have washed them on a
　⎰stane,
The burn was risen out of *spate.*
　　—RITSON'S *Caledonian Muse : The
　　Wife of Auchtermuchty.*

While crashing ice, borne on the roaring
spate,
Sweeps dams an' mills an' brigs a' to the
gate.
　　—BURNS : *The Brigs of Ayr.*

And doun the water wi' speed she ran,
　While tears in *spates* fa' fast frae her e'e.
　—*Border Minstrelsy : Jock o' the Side.*

The Laird of Balnamoon was a truly eccentric character. He joined with his drinking propensities a great zeal for the Episcopal Church. One Sunday, having visitors, he read the services and prayers with great solemnity and earnestness. After dinner, he, with the true Scottish hospitality of the time, set to, to make his guests as drunk as possible. Next day, when they took their departure, one of the visitors asked another what he thought of the laird. "Why, really," he replied, "sic a *spate* o' praying, and sic a *spate* o' drinking, I never knew in all the course of my life."—DEAN RAMSAY'S *Reminiscences.*

Spate, or **spaite,** is from the Gaelic *speid,* a mountain torrent suddenly swollen by rain. In the North of England, according to Messrs. Halliwell and Wright, a *spait* signifies a more than usually heavy downpour of rain ; and in the county of Durham it signifies a pool formed by the rain.

Spaul, sometimes written *spald,* a shoulder ; from the French *espaule,* or *épaule,* often used to signify a leg or limb. "To *spaul,*" according to Jamieson, "is to push out the limbs like a dying animal."

The late Duchess of Gordon sat at dinner next to an Englishman, who was carving, and who made it a boast that he was thoroughly master of the Scottish language. Her Grace turned to him and said, "Rax me a *spaul* o' that bubblyjock !" The unfortunate man was completely nonplussed.—DEAN RAMSAY.

The gander being longer in the *spauld.*
　　—*Noctes Ambrosianæ.*

Wi' spur on heel, or splent (armour) on
spauld.
—*Border Minstrelsy : Kinmont Willie.*

The Scotch employ the French word *gigot* for a leg of mutton; but they do not say a *spaul* of mutton for a shoulder.

Spean (sometimes spelled *spane* or *spayn*), to wean. The English *wean* is derived from the German *wohnen*, or *entwohnen;* and the Scottish *spean* from the Flemish and Low Dutch *speen,* which has the same meaning. *Speaning-brash,* an eruption in children, which often occurs at weaning-time.

Withered beldams auld and dröll,
Rigwoodie hags wad *spean* a foal,
Louping and flinging on a crummock,
I wonder did na turn thy stomach.
—BURNS: *Tam o' Shanter.*

The meaning of *spean,* as used by Burns, implies that the hags were so very hideous, that, had they been brood mares, a foal would in disgust have refused to imbibe nourishment from them.

Speer-windit or **spier-windit**, out of breath or wind from asking too many questions, tired of asking; a word most applicable to impudent barristers cross-examining a witness; from *speer,* or *spier,* to inquire.

Spell, an interval. The Scotch and the Americans say : " a *spell* of work," " a *spell* of idleness," " a *spell* of bad weather," " a *spell* of good weather," " a *spell* of amusement," &c. The derivation of the word is supposed to be from the Dutch and

Flemish *spel,* the German *spiele,* to play. Possibly, though not certainly, the root is the Gaelic *speal,* to mow, cut down; and thence a *stroke, i.e.,* a stroke of good or bad weather, &c. The word has recently become current in English.

Spence, a store-room next to a kitchen, where the provisions are kept; an inner apartment in a small house. The word is supposed to be derived from *dispense,* to distribute; whence *dispensary,* the place where medicines are distributed.

Wi' tottering step he reached the *spence,*
Where soon the ingle blazed fu' hie;
The auld man thought himself at hame,
And the tear stood twinkling in his e'e.
—PICKERING: *Dornocht Sea, or the Auld Minstrel.*

Our Bardie lanely keeps the *spence*
Sin' Mailie's dead.
—BURNS: *Poor Mailie's Elegy.*

" Edward," said the sub-Prior, " you will supply the English knight here, in this *spence,* with suitable food and accommodation for the night."—SCOTT: *The Monastery.*

The word is still used in the north of England for a buttery, also for a cupboard, a pantry, and a private room in a farm house.

Yet I had leven she and I
Were both togydir secretly
In some corner in the *spence.*
—HALLIWELL.

Spier, to inquire, to ask after; of unknown etymology. The derivation from the Gaelic *speur,* clear, whence by extension of

O

meaning, an inquiry, to make clear, is scarcely satisfactory.

Mony a ane *spiers* the gate he knows full well.—ALLAN RAMSAY'S *Scots Proverbs.*

> I am Spes, quoth he,
> And *spier* after a knight,
> That took me a mandement
> Upon the mount of Sinai.
> —*Piers Ploughman.*

I *spiered* for my cousin fu' couthie and sweet.
—BURNS: *Last May a Braw Wooer.*

> When lost, folks never ask the way they want,
> They *spier* the gait.
> —ROBERT LEIGHTON : *Scotch Words.*

A very expressive derivation of *spier* is *back-spier*, meaning to cross-examine.—R. DRENNAN.

Her niece was asking a great many questions, and coming over and over the same ground, demanding an explanation how this and that had happened, till at last the old lady lost patience, and burst forth—"I winna be *back-spiered*, noo, Polly Fullerton."—DEAN RAMSAY.

Sperthe, a spear, a javelin, or, more properly, a battle-axe; a word that might well be rescued from oblivion for the use of rhymers, often hardly pushed for a rhyme to earth, birth, girth, and mirth—all well, or too well worn.

> His helmet was laced,
> At his saddle girth was a good steel *sperthe*,
> Full ten pound weight and more.
> —*Border Minstrelsy: The Eve of St. John.*

Spin-drift, sometimes corruptly written and pronounced *speen-drift* and *spune-drift*, snow driven by the wind in whirls or spinnings in the air, and finally accumulates on the ground when the force of the wind is exhausted.

Spirlie, a person with slender legs; *spindle-shanked,* slim, thin, often combined with *lang;* as, "A lang spirlie," a tall slender person. From the Gaelic *speir,* a shank, a claw; *speireach,* having slender limbs.

Spleuchan, a Highland purse ; from the Gaelic *spliuchan,* an outside pouch or receptacle of small matters, and *spliuch,* anything that hangs down.

> Deil mak' his king's-hood [scrotum] in a *spleuchan.*
> —BURNS: *Death and Dr. Hornbook.*

Splore, a riotously merry meeting; to make a *splore,* to create a sensation. The Americans have *splurge,* a word with the same meaning. The derivation is unknown.

> In Poosie Nancy's held the *splore.*
> Wi' quaffing and laughing,
> They ranted and they sang.
> —BURNS: *The Jolly Beggars.*

> The squads o' chiels that lo'ed a *splore,*
> On winter evenings never ca' ;
> Their blythesome moments now are o'er,
> Since Rabbie gaed an' left them a'.
> —RICHARD GALL : *On the Death of Burns.*

Splute, to exaggerate in narrative, to indulge in fiction. Jamieson derives this word from the French *exploit,* but it is more probably a corruption of the Gaelic *spleadh,* a romance, a boast, a gasconade, a vain-glorious assertion; *spleadhaich*, hyperbolical.

Spoacher, a poacher, one who steals game. The Scottish word seems to have been the origi-nal form, and to have become poacher by the elision of the initial *s*, a not uncommon result in words from the Celtic, as the Welsh *hen*, old, is the same as the Gaelic *sean*; the English *nag* is the same as *snag*, to snarl or say provoking things, as is the custom with spiteful women if they wish to quarrel with their husbands. The English *poacher* is usually derived from *poke*, the French *poche*, a pocket, pouch, or bag, because the poacher, like the sportsman, *bags* his game. But if the Scot-tish *spoacher* be the elder word, it will be necessary to account for the lost *s*. This is supplied in the Gaelic *spog*, to seize vio-lently, as birds of prey do with their claws and talons, and *spogadh*, seizure. Jamieson was of opinion that the *s* was *added* in the Scottish word; but this would be a singular instance, contradicted by all previous ex-perience of similar cases.

Spoutie, a word of contempt for a too fluent orator, or a garru-lous boaster; one who, accord-ing to a wealthy Scottish phil-anthropist, is too plentifully endowed with "the pernicious gift of the gab—the curse of all free countries, especially of

Great Britain and the United States." To *spout* is a common English vulgarism that signifies to talk at an inordinate length to a public meeting. The Amer-icans derisively call it to *orate*.

Sprack, lively, alert, animated; common in Scotland and pro-vinces in the south of England.

Spraikle, sprackle, sprauchle, to clamber up a hill with great exertion and difficulty. From the Gaelic *spracail*, strong, ac-tive. The English words *sprawl* and *sprag* seem to be of the same parentage.

> I, rhymer Robin, *alias* Burns,
> October twenty-third;
> A ne'er-to-be-forgotten day,
> Sae far I *sprachled* up the brae,
> I dinnered wi' a lord.
> —BURNS: *The Dinner with Lord Daer.*

Wad ye hae naebody *spraickle* up the brae but yoursel, Geordie.—SCOTT: *For-tunes of Nigel.*

Spring, a lively tune.

> Sae rantingly, sae wantonly,
> He played of *spring*
> Beneath the gallows tree.
> —*Old Song: Macpherson's Farewell.*

Let him play a *spring* on his ain fiddle (*i.e.*, let him have his own way; let him ride his own hobby.)—DEAN RAMSAY.

Ye are as lang in tuning your pipes as anither man wad be in playing a *spring.*— *Scottish Proverb.*

Sproage. This eccentric-looking word signifies, according to Jamieson, to go out courting at night, to wander by the light of the moon or stars. Alexander Ross, in " Helenore, or the

Fortunate Shepherdess," has the lines :—

> We maun marry now ere lang ;
> Folk will speak o's, and fash us wi' the kirk,
> Gin we be seen thegither in the mirk.

Neither Burns, Allan Ramsay, nor Scott employs this word, and its origin is wholly unknown, unless the Gaelic *sporach*, to incite, excite, or instigate, may supply a clue.

Spulzie, to despoil, to ravage, to devastate, to lay waste ; from *depouiller*, to spoil, or despoil.

> *Spulzie* him, *spulzie* him l said Craigievar,
> *Spulzie* him presentlie,
> For I wad lay my lugs in pawn,
> He'd nae gude will at me.
> —Buchan's *Ancient Ballads.: The Death of John Seton.*

Spune - hale, in such restored health as to be able to take one's ordinary food, one's kail or parritch, with a good appetite. *Parritch-hale* and *meat-hale* are synonymous.

Spung, a purse that fastens with a clasp ; *sporan*, the large purse worn by the Highlanders on full-dress occasions.

> But wastefu' was the want of a',
> Without a yeuk they gar ane claw,
> When wickedly they bid us draw
>   Our siller *spungs*,
> For this and that to mak them braw
>   And lay their tongues.
> —Allan Ramsay : *Last Speech of a Wretched Miser.*

Spunk, a match, a spark ; *spunkie*, fiery, high spirited ; also an ."ignis fatuus" or will o' the wisp. The word is derived by Jamieson from the Gaelic *spong*, rotten wood, or tinder, easily inflammable ; but it is questionable whether the root is not the Teutonic *funk*, a sparkle of light ; *funkeln*, to sparkle ; and *ausfunkeln*, to sparkle out, to shine forth. *Ausfunk* is easily corrupted into *sfunk* and *spunk*.

> Erskine, a *spunkie* Norland billie,
>   And mony ithers ;
> Whom auld Demosthenes and Tully,
>   Might own as brithers.
> —Burns : *Earnest Cry and Prayer.*

> If mair they deave us wi' their din
>   O' patronage intrusion ;
> We'll light a *spunk*, and every skin
>   We'll rin them aff in fusion,
>   Like oil some day.
> —Burns : *The Ordination.*

> And oft from moss-traversing *spunkies*,
> Decoy the wight that late and drunk is.
> —Burns : *Address to the Deil.*

Spurtle or **parritch spurtle,** a rounded stick or bar of hard wood, used in preference to a spoon or ladle for stirring oatmeal porridge in the process of cooking. Jamieson—who seldom dives deeper than the Teutonic—derives the word from *spryten*, the Latin *assula*. The Gaelic has *sparr* or *sparran*, a little wooden bar or bolt ; and the Flemish has *sport*, with the same meaning ; and also that of the rung of a ladder (a bar of wood which a Scottish housewife, in default of any better *spurtle*, might conveniently use for the purpose). Good bairns in the olden times when oatmeal porridge was the customary food

of the peasantry, were often re-
warded by having the *spurtle* to
lick in addition to their share of
the breakfast.

> Our gudeman cam' hame at e'en,
>   And hame cam' he ;
> And there he saw a braw broad sword,
>   Where nae sword should be.
>
> How's this ? gude wife,
>   How's this, quo he,
> How came this sword here
>   Without the leave o' me ?'
>
> A sword ! quo she,
>   Aye, a sword, quo he ;
> Ye auld blind doited bodie,
>   And blinder may ye be,
> 'Tis but a parritch *spurtle*,
>   My minnie gied to me.
>
> Far hae I travelled,
>   And muckle hae I seen,
> But scabbards upon *spurtles*,
>   Saw I never nane !
>   —*Our Gudeman.*

Staffa, the name of the well-
known island of the West that
contains the " cave of Fingal."
Colonel Robertson, in " The
Gaelic Topography of Scotland," has omitted to give the
etymology of the word. Many
people suppose it to be English, and akin to *Stafford.* It
is, however, pure Gaelic, and
accurately descriptive of the
natural formation of the cave,
being compounded of *stuadh* (*dh*
silent), a pillar or pillars, column
or columns; and *uamh* (*uav* or
uaf), a cave, whence *stua-uaf*
or *staffa*, the cave of pillars or
columns.

Staig, a young, unbroken stallion.
In the North of England, this
word *stag*, or *staig*, is applied to
any young male quadruped, and,
in contempt, to a strong, vulgar,
romping girl, whose manners are
masculine. The word is also
applied to the Turkey cock and
the gander. From the German
steigen, to mount, to raise, to
stick up, to stand erect. In the
old Norse, *steggr* signifies male.

> It's neither your *stot* nor your *staig* I
>   shall crave,
> But gie me your wife, man, for her I
>   must have.
>   —BURNS : *The Carle o' Kellyburn
>   Braes.*

Stance, situation, standing-place,
or foundation. This word has
not yet been admitted into the
English dictionaries.

> No ! sooner may the Saxon lance,
> Unfix Benledi from his *stance*.
>   —SCOTT : *Lady of the Lake.*

We would recommend any Yankee be-
liever in England's decay to take his
stance in Fleet Street or any of our great
thoroughfares, and ask himself whether it
would be wise to meddle with any member
of that busy and strenuous crowd.—*Blackwood's Magazine*, June 1869.

Stank, a pool, a ditch, an en-
trenchment filled with water
for the defence of a fortress.
This word, with the elision of
the initial letter, becomes the
English *tank*, a receptacle for
water. *Stankit*, entrenched.
From the French *etaing*, or
estaing; the Gaelic *staing*, a
ditch, a pool ; *staingichte*, entrenched.

> I never drank the Muses *stank*,
>   Castilia's burn and a' that ;
> But there it streams, and richtly reams,
>   My Helicon, I ca' that.
>   —BURNS : *The Jolly Beggars.*

Clavers and his Highland men
  Cam down among the raw, man ;
Ower bush, ower bank, ower ditch, ower
    stank,
  She flang amang them a', man.
      —Battle of Killiecrankie.

Stanners, gravel, small stones on
the banks of a stream, shingle
on the sea shore.

Yestreen the water was in spate,
  The *stanners* a' were curled.
    —Border Minstrelsy : Water Kelpie.

Stark, strong ; from the German.
The word, however, is English,
with a different meaning, as in
the phrase, *stark naked,* utterly
naked.

Fill fu' and hand fu' maks a *stark* man.
—Old Proverb.

S t a u m r e l, a stupid person ;
saumer, to stutter, to be incoherent in speech, to stammer ;
from the German *stumme,* dumb ;
and *stumpf,* stupid, the Flemish
and Dutch *stumper,* a fool, a silly
and idle person.

Nae langer, thrifty citizens, an' douce,
Meet owre a pint or in the council house,
But *staumrel,* corky-headed gentry,
The herriment and ruin of the country.
  *—*Burns: *The Brigs of Ayr.*

The lad was aye a perfect *stump.*
      *—*Jamieson.

Staves. "To go to *staves* " is a
proverbial expression used in
Scotland to signify to go to
ruin, to fall to pieces like a
barrel, when the hoops that
bind the staves together are
removed.

Staw, to surfeit, to disgust. Etymology uncertain ; not Flemish,

as Jamieson supposes, but probably from the Gaelic *stad* or
stadh (pronounced *stà*), to desist,
or cause to desist.

Is there that o'er his French ragout,
Or olio that wad *staw* a sow.
  *—*Burns: *To a Haggis.*

Curryin's a grand thing, when the edge
o' the appetite's a wee turned, and ye're
rather beginnin' to be *stawed.—Noctes
Ambrosianæ.*

Steek, to close, to shut, to fasten
with a pin.

Sages their solemn e'en may *steek.*
  *—*Burns : *Cry and Prayer.*

Steek the awmrie.
  *—*Sir Walter Scott : *Donald Caird.*

Ye're owre bonnie ! ye're owre bonnie !
  Sae *steek* that witchin' e'e,
It's light flees gleamin' through my brain.
      *—*James Ballantine.

Your purse was *steekit* when that was
paid for.

When the steed's stown *steik* the stable-
door.
  *—*Allan Ramsay's *Scots Proverbs.*

Steeks, the interstices of any woven or knitted fabric, stitches ;
steek, probably from *stitch,* as *kirk*
from *church.*

He draws a bonnie silken purse,
As lang's my tail, where, through the *steeks,*
The yellow-lettered Geordie [guinea] keeks.
  *—*Burns : *The Twa Dogs.*

Steenies, guineas, foreign or other
gold coins ; derivation unknown,
unless the term be a mock depreciation of the precious metal,
from *stone,* or *stein,* applied upon
the same principle that money
is called dross or filthy lucre.

What though we canna boast of our
guineas, O,
We've plenty of Jockies and Jeanies, O,
   An' these, I'm certain, are
   More daintier by far
Than a pock full of yellow *steenies*, O.
    —Rev. JOHN SKINNER : *The Old
    Man's Song.*

Steeve, or steive, firm, erect,
stout; from the English *stiff*,
and the Flemish *stijf.*

Sit ye *steeve* in your saddle seat,
For he rides sicker who never fa's.
    —JAMES BALLANTINE.

Sten, to spring to one side, a sudden motion in the wrong direction; to turn away, to twist, to
bend; *stennis*, a sprain. From
the Gaelic *staon*, awry, askew;
and *staonaich*, to bend, to twist,
to turn. Jamieson erroneously
derives *sten* from *extend.*

Yestreen at the valentines' dealing,
My heart to my mou' gied a *sten*,
For thrice I drew ane without failing,
And thrice it was written Tam Glen.
    —BURNS : *Tam Glen.*

Stevin or steven. Before the introduction from the Latin *vox*,
and the French *voix*, of the
word *voice* into the English and
Scottish languages, the word
stevin was employed. It was
used by Chaucer in England,
and by Gawin Douglas in Scotland. From its resemblance
to the Teutonic *stimme*, a voice,
and *stimmen*, voices, the Flemish
stem, it is probable that it was a
corruption or variation of that
word.

With dreary heart and sorrowful *steven*.
    —*Morte Arthur.*

Betwixt the twelfth hour and eleven,
I dreamed an angel cam frae heaven,
With pleasant *stevin* sayand on hie,
Tailyiors and soutars, blest be ye !
    —DUNBAR : ALLAN RAMSAY'S
      Evergreen. ·

Lang may thy *steven* fill with glee
The glens and mountains of Lochlee.
    —BEATTIE : *To Mr. Alexander Ross.*

Quoth Jane, " My *steven*, sir, is blunted
   sair,
And singing frae me frighted off wi' care ;
But gin ye'll tak' it as I now can gie't,
Ye're welcome til't—and my sweet blessing
   wi't."
    —Ross's *Helenore.*

The rhymes to "heaven" in
Scottish and English poetry are
few, and *stevin* would be an
agreeable addition to the number if it were possible to revive it.

Steward, a director, a manager,
an administrator. As a patronymic, the word is sometimes
spelled *stewart* and *stuart*, and
has been derived from the Teutonic *stede-ward*, one who occupies the place delegated to him
by another; or from the Icelandic *stia*, work, and *weard*, a
guard or guardian. It seems,
however, to have an indigenous
origin in the Gaelic *stiuir*, to
lead, direct, guide, steer, super-
intend, manage, &c.; and *ard*,
high or chief. The *"Steward*
of Scotland"* was in early times
the chief officer of the crown,
and next in power and dignity
to the king. There was a similar functionary in England :—

The Duke of Norfolk is the first,
And claims to be high *Steward*.

The attributes of the "*Steward of Scotland*" are set forth by Erskine as quoted in Jamieson ; and the last holder of the office —who became king of Scotland —gave the name of his function to his royal descendants. In its humbler sense, of the *steward* of a great household, or of a ship, the name is still true to its Gaelic derivation, and signifies the chief director of his particular department.

It has been suggested in the "Gaelic Etymology of the Languages of Western Europe," that the true etymon of *stew* or *stu* (the first syllable of *steward* and *stuart*) is the Gaelic *stuth*, pronounced *stu*, which signifies any strong liquor, as well as food, sustenance, or nourishment for the body ; and that consequently *steward* means chief butler, or provider of the royal household. There is much to be said in favour of this hypothesis, but the derivation from *stiur* seems preferable.

The Irish Gaelic spells *steward* in the English sense *stiobhard*. The Scottish Gaelic has it *stiubhard ;* but the words thus written have no native etymology, and are merely phonetic renderings of an obsolete Gaelic term, re-borrowed from the modern English. The suggested Teutonic etymology of *steward* from *stede-ward*, has no foundation in the Teutonic languages. *Steward* in Germany is *Verwalter*, administrator or director ; and *Haushofmeister*, master of the household. In Flemish, *bestieren* signifies to administer, to direct ; and *bestierder*, an administrator, a director, a steward.

Stey, steep, perpendicular. In Cumberland and Westmoreland, a mountain of peculiar steepness is called a *sty ;* and in Berkshire, *sty* signifies a ladder. *Stey* and *sty* are both from the German *stiegen*, and the Flemish *stijgen*, to mount, to climb.

Set a stout heart to a *stey* brae.—ALLAN RAMSAY's *Scots Proverbs.*

The *steyest* brae thou wouldst hae face't at.
  —BURNS: *The Auld Farmer to His Auld Mare, Maggie.*

Stickit minister, a term of obloquy in Scotland for a candidate for holy orders who has failed to pass the necessary examination, or to give satisfaction to the congregation before whom he preached the probationary sermon. The phrase is akin to the vulgar English—"old *stick* in the mud."

Puir lad ! the first time he tried to preach, he *stickit* his sermon.—JAMIESON.

A speech is *stickit* when the speaker hesitates and is unable to proceed.—*Idem.*

Still. This word is sometimes employed in the Scottish vernacular in a sense which it possesses no longer in English, that of taciturn, or reticent of speech. "A *still* dour man," signifies a taciturn, reserved, and hard man.

Stirk, a bullock ; *stirkie*, a bull calf.

There's aye water where the *stirkie* drowns (*i.e.*, there's a reason or cause for everything ; or there's never a smoke without fire).

Stob, to push the foot accidentally against a stone or other impediment in the ground. " I have *stobbed* my toe," said the late President Lincoln, in explanation of his temporary lameness ; from the Gaelic *stob*, a stake, a thrust, or anything thrust in the ground ; a stick, a stump, any stalk broken or cut and still projecting from the ground ; whence the English word *stubble*.

Stoit, to stagger.

> And aye as on the road he *stoitit*,
> His knees on ane anither *knockit*
> [knocked together].
> —GEORGE BEATTIE : *John o' Arnha'*.

Stound, a moment, a very short space of time ; also, a quick sudden momentary pain. From the German *stund*, an hour.

> Gang in and seat you on the sunks a' round,
> And ye'se be sair'd wi' plenty in a *stound*.
> —Ross's *Helenore*.

> And aye the *stound*, the deadly wound,
> Came frae her e'en sae bonnie blue.
> —BURNS : *I Gaed a Waefu Gate*.

Stoup or **stoop**, a flagon, a pitcher, a jug. *Pint-stoup*, a bottle or jug containing a pint. This word was used by Shakspeare, Ben Jonson, and other dramatists of the Elizabethan era ; it has long been obsolete in England, but survives with undiminished vitality in Scotland.

> Come, ;Lieutenant ! I have a *stoop* of wine, and here without are a brace of Cyprian gallants, that would fain have a measure to the health of black Othello.—
> *Othello.*

> Set me the *stoup* of wine upon that table.
> —*Hamlet.*

> And surely ye'll be your *pint-stoup*,
> As sure as I'll be mine.
> —BURNS : *Auld Lang Syne.*

> Water-*stoups ?* quo' he ;
> Aye, water-*stoups*, quo' she—
> Far hae I ridden,
> And muckle I hae seen ;
> But silver spurs on water-*stoups*
> Saw I never nane !
> —HERD's *Collection : Our Guidman.*

The etymology of *stoup* or *stoop* has long been contested. Johnson derives it from the Dutch and Flemish *stop*, a cork or stopper of a bottle ; the German *stöpsel ;* but this can scarcely be the origin of the Scottish word, for a milk-*stoup*, a water-*stoup*, a can, a pitcher, a bucket, a pail, are not corked or stopped. In some Scottish glossaries a *stoup* is said to be a tin pot, and in others it is defined as a jug with a handle ; while in Northumberland, according to Wright's Provincial Dictionary, a *stoop* signifies a barrel. In Gaelic, *stop* means a wooden vessel for carrying water, a measure for liquids, or a flagon ; and *stopan* signifies a small flagon. Between the Flemish and Gaelic derivations it is difficult to decide ; but the Gaelic, which applies the word to wide and open utensils, seems to be preferable, at least in comprehensiveness.

Stour, dust in motion, and metaphorically trouble, vexation, or disturbance; *stourie,* dusty. The word is akin to the English *stir,* and in its metaphorical sense is synonymous with the Scottish *steer,* as in the song " What's a the *steer,* kimmer ? " what's the disturbance, or in the broad vernacular, what's the row ? " To kick up a dust" is a slang expression that has a similar origin.

> Yestreen I met you on the moor,
> Ye spak na, but gaed by like *stour;*
> Ye geck at me because I'm poor.
>   —BURNS : *Tibbie, I hae Seen the Day.*

After service, the betheral of the strange clergyman said to his friend the other betheral, "I think our minister did weel. He aye gars the *stour* flee out o' the cushion." To which the other replied, with a calm feeling of superiority, "*Stour* out o' the cushion ! Hoot ! our minister, sin' he cam' wi' us, has dung [knocked or beaten] the guts out o' twa Bibles."—DEAN RAMSAY.

> How blithely wad I bide the *stoure,*
> A weary slave frae sun to sun,
> Could I the rich reward secure
> Of lovely Mary Morrison.
>   —BURNS.

Burns uses the word in the sense of mould, earth, or soil, as in his "Address to the Daisy : "—

> Wee, modest, crimson-tippet flower,
> Thou'st met me in an evil hour,
> For I man crush amang the *stour,*
> Thy slender stem.

Stour, in the sense of strife, was a common English word in the time of Chaucer and his predecessors.

Stowlins, stownlins, by stealth, stealthily, or stolen moments unobserved, or expecting to be unobserved.

> Rob *stowlins* pried her bonnie mou,
> Fu' cosie in the neuk for't
> Unseen that night.
>   —BURNS : *Hallowe'en.*

Stoyte, stoiter, to stagger, stumble, or walk unsteadily ; from the Flemish *stooten,* to push against, to stumble or cause to stumble.

> When staggirand and swaggirand,
> They *stoyter* hame to sleep.
>   —ALLAN RAMSAY : *The Vision.*

> Blind chance let her snapper and *stoyte* on the way.
>   —BURNS : *Contented wi' Little.*

> At length wi' drink and courtin' dizzy,
> He *stoitered* up and made a face.
>   —BURNS : *The Jolly Beggars.*

To *stoitle* over, in consequence of infirmity, without being much hurt. To tyne or lose the *stoyte,* is a metaphor for being off the proper line of conduct.—JAMIESON.

Strae death, straw death, death in bed, natural death. This strong but appropriate expression comes from the Middle Ages, when lawlessness and violence were chronic.

Strappan or **strappin',** strong, tall, burly, well-grown ; the English *strapping,* a strapping youth.

> The miller was *strappin',* the miller was ruddy.
>   —BURNS : *Meg o' the Mill.*

> Wi' kindly welcome Jenny brings him ben,
> A *strappin'* youth—he taks the mother's eye.
>   —BURNS : *Cotter's Saturday Night.*

This word comes from the Gaelic *streap*, to climb up, *i.e.*, in stature, to grow tall.

Streik, to stretch; from the Dutch and Flemish *strekken*, German *strechen*, to extend. This word is used in a variety of ways, unknown to or unfrequent in English; as, "Tak' your ain *streik*," take your own course; *streikin*, tall and active; *streik*, to go quickly, *i.e.*, to stretch out in walking; tight or tightly drawn, *i.e.*, excessively drawn, stretched out, or extended.

Strone or **stroan**, a ludicrous word for the habitual urination of dogs when out on their rambles. It is introduced by Burns in his description of the rich man's dog, Cæsar, the fine Newfoundland, who was the friend and companion of Luath, the poor man's dog:—

Though he was of high degree,
The fient o' pride, nae pride had he.
. . . . .
Nae tauted tyke, though e'er sae duddie,
But he wad stan't as glad to see him,
And *stroan't* on stanes and hillocks wi' him.

The word seems to have been originally applied to the action of the dog in first smelling the place where another dog has been before for a similar purpose, and to be derived from the Gaelic *srone* (pronounced *strone*), a nose; and *sronagaich*, to trace by the scent as dogs do.

Stroop, a spout. *Stroopie*, the spout of a kettle; also a gutter or watercourse.

Struishle, to struggle pertinaciously, and in vain, against continually recurring difficulties; from the Femish *struikelen*, to stumble, to fall down.

A tradesman employed to execute a very difficult piece of carved work, being asked how he was getting on, answered—"I'm *struishling* awn' like a writer [lawyer] tryin' to be honest!"—*Laird of Logan.*

Strunt, alcoholic liquor of any kind; a fit of ill-humour; also, an affront, or a sturdy, arrogant walk.

Strunt and sturt are birds of ae feather,
And aft are seen on the wing thegither.
—*Scots Proverb.*

Burns makes the disagreeable insect that he saw on a lady's bonnet at church "*strunt* rarely over her gauze and lace." The word, in this sense, seems to be a corruption of the English *strut*. *Stront* is a low Teutonic word for *stercus humanum;* but this can scarcely be the root of *strunt* in any of the senses in which it is used in the Scottish language; though *strunty*, an epithet applied to any one in a fit of such ill-humour as to be excessively disagreeable to all around him, may not be without some remote connection with the Teutonic idea.

Study or **brown study.** This expression seems to have first appeared in literature in the

"Case Altered." of Ben Jonson, who was of Scottish parentage, though born in.London :—

Faiks I this *brown study* suits not with your black ; your habit and your thought are of two colours.

(See BROWN STUDY, *ante*, p. 19.)

Stug. This Scottish word is used in a variety of senses—all allied to the idea of stiffness, erectness, rigidity, hardness, prickliness, &c., as the English *stiff*, *stick*, *stock*, *stuck up*, and the corresponding verb derived from the noun ; as *stug*, to stab or stick with a sharp weapon ; *stug*, the trunk or fragment of a decayed tree projecting above the ground; *stug*, a hard, masculine woman ; *stug*, obstinate ; *stugger*, an obstinate person ; *stug*, a thorn ; *stugs*, stubble. From the Dutch and Flemish *stug*, inflexible, stiff, obstinate ; the German *stich*, to stab, to pierce ; *sticheln*, to prick, to sting.

Sturt, strife, contention, disturbance ; also, to strive, to contend ; a word apparently 'akin to *stour* in its poetical sense of confusion. It is akin to, and possibly derived from, the German *stürzen*, to disturb, to overthrow.

And aye the less they hae to *sturt* them,
In like proportion less will hurt them.
—BURNS : *The Twa Dogs.*

I've lived a life of *sturt* and strife,
I die by treachery.
—*Macpherson's Farewell.*

Styme, a particle, an iota, an atom; the least possible quantity; a blink, a gleam, a glimpse.

He held, she drew, fu' steeve that day,
Might no man see a *styme*.
—*Christ's Kirk on the Green.*

I've seen me daz't upon a time,
I scarce could wink or see a *styme*.
—BURNS : *Naething like Nappy.*

The faintest form of an object ; a glimpse or transitory glance, as, "There's no a *styme* o' licht here."—JAMIESON.

From *styme* is formed *stymie*, one who sees indistinctly ; and *stymel*, which, according to Jamieson, is a name of reproach given to one who does not perceive quickly what another wishes him to see. Jamieson hints, rather than asserts, that *styme* is from the Welsh *ystum*, form, or figure ; but as *styme* is the absence of form and figure, something faint, indistinct, and small, rather than a substantial entity, the etymology is unsatisfactory. The word seems to have some relationship to the Gaelic *stim*, or *stiom*, a slight puff, or wreath of smoke ; and thence to mean anything slight, transitory, and indistinct.

Sugh. or **sough**, a sigh, a breath. Greek *psyche*, the breath of life, the soul. To keep a calm *sugh*, is to be discreetly silent about anything, not to give it breath ; *sugh-siller*, erroneously printed *sow-siller* by Jamieson, means hush-money.

Sunkets, scraps of food, scrans (q. v.).

In Scotland there lived a humble beggar,
  He had neither house nor hauld nor hame,
But he was weel likit by ilka body,
And they gied him *sunkets* to rax his wame ;
A nievefu' o' meal, a handfu' o' groats,
A daud o' a bannock, or pudding bree,
Cauld parritch, or the licking o' plates,
  Wad mak him as blithe as a body could be.
  —*Tea Table Miscellany.*

Sunket-time is meal-time. The etymology of *sunket* is uncertain. Herd derived it from *something.*—JAMIESON.

Whenever an uncertain etymology in English or Lowland Scotch is avowed, it would be well if the dubious philologists would look into the Gaelic, which they seldom do. In the case of *sunket* they would have found something better in that language than the English *something. Sanntach* signifies a dainty, or something that is desired, coveted, or longed after ; and *sanntaichte,* that which is desired. This word would be easily convertible by the Lowland Scotch into *sunket.* Halliwell, in his Archaic Dictionary, has *sun-cote,* a dainty, which he says is a Suffolk word.

Sumph, a stupid or soft-headed person. Jamieson derives the word from the German *sumpf,* and Flemish *somp,* a bog, a marsh, a morass ; a possible but not a convincing etymology. Halliwell has *sump,* a heavy weight,

whence he adds, a heavy stupid fellow is so called.

The soul of life, the heaven below,
  Is rapture-giving woman ;
Ye surly *sumphs* who hate the name,
  Be mindfu' o' your mither.
      —BURNS.

Sumph, an admirable word.—*Noctes Ambrosianæ.*

Swack, to deal a heavy blow ; akin to the vulgar English *whack,* to beat severely ; a swashing blow, a heavy blow ; etymology uncertain. The Teutonic *schwach,* weak, has an opposite meaning, though there may be some connection of idea between a heavy blow and a blow that *weakens* him on whom it falls.

When Percy wi' the Douglas met,
  I wat he was fu' fain,
They *swakkit* their swords till sair they swat,
  And the blood ran doun like rain.
      —*Battle of Otterbourne.*

In another stanza of this vigorous old ballad, occur the lines :—

Then Percy and Montgomery met,
  That either of other were fain ;
They *swappit* swords, and they twa swat,
  And the blood run doun between.

Here *swappit* seems employed in the same sense as *swakkit,* and is possibly a variation of *swoop,* to come down with a heavy blow.

Swacken, to grow weak ; from the German *schwach,* weak.

Wi' that her joints began to *swacken,*
And she scour'd like ony *maukin* (hare).
      —GEORGE BEATTIE: *John o' Arnha'.*

Swagers, men married to sisters. Jamieson goes to the Swedish and Icelandic for the derivation of this word, but it is to be found nearer home in the Flemish *zwager*, and the German *schwager*, a brother-in-law.

Swank, active, agile, supple; *swankie*, an active, clever young fellow, fit for his work, and not above it; from the Flemish and German. Halliwell says that *swanky* is a northern English word for a strong, strapping fellow; and *swanking* for big, large.

Thou ance was in the foremost rank,
A filly, buirdly, steeve, and *swank*.
—BURNS : *The Auld Farmer to his Auld Mare, Maggie.*

At e'en at the gloaming,
Nae *swankies* are roaming,
Bout stackin' the lassies at bogle to play.
—*The Flowers of the Forest.*

The etymological root of *swankie* is apparently the Teutonic *schwank*, droll; used in a sense equivalent to the French *drôle*, which means a funny fellow, a droll fellow, or a fellow in a contemptuous and depreciatory sense. Mr. Thomas Wright, in his Archaic Dictionary of Local and Provincial English, says that *swankie* is a northern word for a strapping fellow; and that *swamp* signifies lean, unthriving, which suggests that possibly *swampie* is a corruption of *swankie*, with a slight shade of difference in the phrase; the meaning for "a strapping fellow," though suggestive of

strength, may be also suggestive of tallness and leanness. The Danish has *svang*, withered, lean; but it also has *svanger*, which means large-bellied, and is applied to a pregnant woman; the Flemish and Dutch have *swanger* with the same meaning.

Swankies young in braw braid claith,
Are springin' owre the gutters.
—BURNS : *The Holy Fair.*

Swarf, to faint, to swoon, to stupefy, or be stupefied; also, a fainting fit, a swoon.

And monie a huntit poor red coat,
For fear amaist did *swarf*, man !
—BURNS : *The Battle of Sherriff-Muir.*

He held up an arrow as he passed me ;
and I *swarf'd* awa wi' fright.—SCOTT : *The Monastery.*

Ye hae gar'd the puir wretch speak till she *swarfs*, and now ye stand as if ye never saw a woman in a *dwam* before.—SCOTT : *St. Ronan's Well.*

The etymology of *swarf* is uncertain ; the author of "Piers Ploughman" has *swowe*, to swoon, akin apparently to the Gaelic *suain*, to fall asleep. By some *swarf* has been derived from the Teutonic *auswerfen*, to throw out, or throw off ; and as to fall in a fainting fit is to throw off temporarily the semblance of life, it is probable that the derivation is correct. *Dwam*, in the same sense as used by Sir Walter Scott, was formerly written *dualm*, and *dwalm*. These latter words are evidently allied to the old English *dwale*, one of the popular names of the plant bella donna, or deadly night-shade; a word employed by the early poets Gower and Chaucer, and still in use in the Lowlands of Scotland, and the Northern counties of England.

Swatch, a specimen, a sample. Etymology uncertain.

> On this side sits a chosen *swatch*,
> Wi' screwed-up, grace-proud faces.
> —BURNS: *The Holy Fair.*

> That's just a *swatch* o' Hornbook's way;
> Thus goes he on from day to day,
> Thus does he poison, kill, and slay,
> An's weel paid for't.
> —BURNS: *Death and Dr. Hornbook.*

Swats, new ale or beer.

> Tam had got planted unco right
> Fast by an ingle bleezing finely,
> Wi' reaming *swats* that drank divinely.
> —BURNS: *Tam o' Shanter.*

> I gie them a skelp as they're creeping alang,
> Wi' a cog o' guid *swats* and an auld Scottish sang.
> —BURNS: *Contented wi' Little.*

This word seems to be a ludicrous derivation from the Gaelic *suath*, to mix liquids, to rub or press barley; and *suathadh*, a mode of threshing barley; and thence, by extension of meaning, the juice of the barley. According to Jamieson, *swats*, or *swaits*, signifies new ale only. He derives it from the Anglo-Saxon *swate*, ale or beer; but the anterior root seems to be the Gaelic *suath*.

Sweer, difficult, heavy, slow, wearied; from the German *schwer*, heavy, hard, difficult.

> *Sweer* to bed, and *sweer* up in the morning.—ALLAN RAMSAY'S *Scots Proverbs.*

Sweere - arse and **sweer - tree** are, according to Jamieson, the names of a sport among Scottish children, in which two of them are seated on the ground, and, holding a stick between them, endeavour each of them to draw the other up from the sitting posture. The heaviest in the posterior wins the game.

Sweine, a swoon, a trance; from the Gaelic *suain*, sleep.

> Sometimes she rade, sometimes she gaed
> As she had done before, O,
> And aye between she fell in a *sweine*
> Lang ere she cam to Yarrow.
> —*The Dowie Dens o' Yarrow.*

Swick or **swyke**, to deceive; also, a trick, a fraud, a deception; *swicky* and *swickful*, deceitful. Apparently from the Danish *svige*, to deceive, to cheat, to defraud; and *svig*, fraud, imposture.

> "He played them a *swick*; I had nae *swick* o't," I had no blameableness in it.—JAMIESON.

Swiff, the English *whiff*, a puff of smoke, a breath, a short interval, as a *swiff* of sleep amid pain, a passing odour; *swiff*, the sound of an object passing rapidly by, as of an arrow or bullet in its flight. Whether the English *whiff*, or the Scottish *swiff*, were the original form, it is hopeless to inquire. The Scottish word seems to be a variety of the old English *swippe*, which Halliwell's Archaic Dictionary defines, to move rapidly; and *swipper*, nimble, quick.

Swine. "The *swine's* gone through it," is a proverbial expression which signifies that a marriage has been postponed or unduly delayed. Why the swine should have anything to do with a marriage is so incomprehensible as to suggest that the word does duty for some other, of which it is a corruption. Such a word exists in the Gaelic *suain*, a sleep, a deep sleep, a lethargy, whence the English *swoon*. *Suain* also signifies to entwine, to wrap round, to envelop, to tie up, to twist a cord or rope round anything; and hence may, in the proverbial saying above cited, signify an impediment. Either of the two meanings of *suain* would meet the sense of the phrase better than *swine*.

Swipes, a contemptuous term for small and weak beer; probably first given to it on account of its thinness, and the difficulty, or impossibility, of getting drunk upon it. From the Flemish *zuipen*, to drink to excess; the German *saufen*, to drink as animals do, who, however, wiser in this respect than men, never drink to excess. *Souf*, to drink, to quaff, and *souffe*, a drunkard, are Scottish words from the same root.

Die Juden sind narren die fressen kein schwein,
Die Turken sind narren die *saufen* kein wein.
[The Jews are fools, they eat no swine;
The Turks are fools, they *swite* no wine.]
—*Old German Song; attributed to*
Martin Luther.

Swirl, to turn rapidly, to eddy, to curl.

His tail
Hung o'er his hurdies wi' a *swirl*.
—Burns: *The Twa Dogs.*

The mill wheel spun and *swirl'd*,
And the mill stream danced in the morning light,
And all its eddies curl'd.
—*The Lump of Gold.*

Swither, fear, doubt, perplexity, hesitation, dread. The etymology is doubtful, but is possibly from the German *zwischen*, between, *i.e.*, between two conflicting opinions.

I there wi' something did foregather,
That put me in an eerie *swither*.
—Burns: *Death and Dr. Hornbook.*

Syde, long or low, largely applied to a gown or dress.

Jeanie she gaed up the gate,
Wi' a green gown as *syde* as her smock,
Now, sirs, Jeanie has gotten her Jock.
—Chambers's *Scottish Songs.*

Syke, a ditch, a northern English word, according to Halliwell, for a gutter; probably a corruption of *soak* or *suck*. A *sike*, according to Jamieson, is a rill, or a marshy bottom with a small stream in it.

Through thick and thin they scoured about,
Plashing through dubs and *sykes*.
—Allan Ramsay: *Continuation of Christ's Kirk on the Green.*

Syne, since, time past, a time ago. (See Auld Lang Syne, p. 3.)

Here's a health to them that were here short *syne*,
And canna be here the day.
Johnson's *Musical Museum.*

T

Tabean birben, a comb; probably a side-comb for the adornment of a woman's hair. It occurs in the ancient version of the song entitled "Lord Gregory." Jamieson is of opinion that the phrase, a "*tabean birben* kame" means a comb made at Tabia, in Italy. "Shall we suppose," he adds, "that *birben* is a corruption of *ivour*, or *ivory-bane* (or bone)?" Shall we not rather suppose, as Tabia was not known as a place of manufacture for combs, that the word is of native Scotch origin, and that, uncouth as it looks, it is resolvable into the Gaelic *taobh*, a side; *taobhan*, sides; *bior*, a pin, a point, a prickle, the tooth of a comb; and *bean*, a woman, whence *taobhan bior bean* (corrupted into *tabean birben*), the side-comb of a woman?

Tack, a lease, a holding; *tacksman*, a leaseholder; from *tack*, to hold, to fasten.

Nae man has a *tack* o' his life.
—ALLAN RAMSAY's *Scots Proverbs*.

Taigle, to tease, to perplex, to banter; from the Gaelic *teagamh*, doubt, perplexity.

Two irreverent young fellows determined to *taigle* the minister. Coming up to him in the High Street of Dumfries, they accosted him with much solemnity, "Maister Dunlop, hae ye heard the news?" "What news?" "Oh, the deil's dead!" "Is he?" replied Mr. Dunlop. "Then I maun pray for twa faitherless bairns."—DEAN RAMSAY's *Reminiscences*.

Taigle, "to tease, perplex, banter." I never heard these meanings;—*teigle* is to delay, to hinder—dinna *taigle* me—I was sair *taigled* the day. In the quotation from Dean Ramsay, I suspect that *taigle* is improperly put for *tackle*, or, as pronounced in Scotland, *tackle*, meaning to seize upon, lay hold on. In a description of a meeting of the U.P. Presbytery of Edinburgh, that had what is called the Dalkeith heresy case before it, it was stated that Dr. Peddie proceeded to *tackle* Mr. Ferguson upon his heretical views.—R. DRENNAN.

Tairge, or **targe**, to cross-question severely and rigidly; of uncertain etymology, though possibly connected with the Gaelic *tagair*, to plead, to argue, to dispute.

And aye on Sundays daily, nightly,
I on the questions *tairge* them tightly;
Till, fack, wee Davock's grown so gleg,
Though scarcely larger than my leg,
He'll screed you aff Effectual Calling
As fast as ony in the dwalling.
—BURNS: *The Inventory*.

I'll gie him a *tairgin'*.—JAMIESON.

Tait, joyous, gay; a word used by the old Scottish poet, Douglas, in his translation of the "Eneid." Jamieson derives it "from the Icelandic *teitr*, hilares, exultans;" but its more obvious source is the Gaelic *taite*, which has the same mean-

P

ing. The English exclamation of *hoity-toity*, or *hoite cum toite*, the name of a favourite dance in the reign of Charles II., is from the same Gaelic root—*aite chum taite*—in which *aite* and *taite* are almost synonymous, and signify joy, merriment, pleasure. *Hoyt*, in the sense of revelry, was used by the Elizabethan writers, Donne, Beaumont and Fletcher, and others.

Hoity-toity, whisking, frisking.
—BICKERSTAFFE: *Love in a Village.*

He sings and *hoyts* and revels among his drunken companions. — BEAUMONT AND FLETCHER.

The modern English slang *tight*, applied to a person who is joyously intoxicated, or semi-intoxicated, seems to be of the same Gaelic derivation.

Taity, taitey, matted like hair, entangled. *Tait* (sometimes written *tate* and *tett*), a lock of matted hair.

At ilka *tait* o' his horse's mane
There hung a siller bell,
The wind was loud, the steed was proud,
And they gied a sindry knell.
—*Ballad of Young Waters.*

Her skirt was o' the grass-green silk,
Her mantle o' the ermine fine,
At ilka *tett* o' the horse's mane
Hung fifty siller bells and nine.
—*Ballad of True Thomas.*

The etymology of this word is uncertain, unless it is to be found in the Gaelic *taod*, a rope, a string ; from the ropy, stringy appearance of hair in this condition. There is an old

Scottish song entitled "Taits o' Woo'."

Tak' tellin', take telling ; a phrase that implies that a person either requires or is amenable to advice or admonition, or the reverse.

He wad na *tak tellin*, he would not be advised. . . . She's a clever servant in a house, but she *taks tellin*, *i.e.*, she needs to be reminded of what ought to be done. —JAMIESON.

Tandle (sometimes written *tawnle*), a bonfire ; from the Gaelic *tein*, fire, and *deal*, friendly. From the root of *teine* comes *teind*, or *tynd*, to kindle ; and *tin-egin* (sometimes rendered by the Teutonic *neid-fire*), a fire of emergency, produced by friction of two pieces of dried wood. *Neid-fire* also means a beacon ; possibly a misprint for "need-fire." Jamieson translates *tin-egin*, a force fire, but gives no etymology. *Egin* is from the Gaelic *eigin* or *eiginn*, force, violence, compulsion. See BELTANE, *ante*.

Tangle, long, tall, and feeble, not well jointed ; from the Gaelic *tean*, long, thin, drawn out, extended; and *gille*, a lad ; also the popular name of the long seaweed, *tangle*, often used in conjunction with dulse, for seaweed generally. Dean Ramsay quotes the saying of an old Scottish lady, who was lifted from the ground after a fall, happily not severe, by a very tall, young lieutenant, who addressed him when she afterwards met him—"Eh, but ye're a *lang lad !*"

The English *tangle* and *entangle* are words of a different meaning, and probably a corruption of the Gaelic *seangal*, to tie up, to fasten, to enchain, to fetter. The American phrase applied to whisky or other spirit, when indulged in too freely, of *tangle-foot* and *tangle-footed*, unable to walk steadily from intoxication, is both humorous and appropriate.

Tangleness, contradiction, confusion, dishonesty, entanglement of truth and falsehood.

Donald's the callant, that brooks nae *tangleness*,
Whiggin' and priggin' and a' new fangleness,
They maun be gane, he winna be baukit, man,
He maun hae justice, or faith he will tak it, man.
—JAMES HOGG, *the Ettrick Shepherd.*

Tanterlick, a severe beating. Probably this word is derivable from the Gaelic *deann* (*teann*, see TANTRUM), or *dian*, fierce, hot. This, combined with *lick*, the English slang to beat (a good *licking*, a good beating), and the Gaelic *leach*, a stone, would signify, in the first instance, a stoning, one of the earliest methods adopted in the quarrels of boys for the conquest or punishment of an opponent.

Tantin', hard pressing, squeezing; *rantin'-tantin'*, ranting and raving; or *ranting* and pressing

hard upon or against, from the Gaelic *teantann*, a pressing, a squeezing. A minister in his Sabbath service, asked by his congregation to pray for fine weather during a long continuance of rain that threatened to be injurious to the harvest, put up the following prayer :—

"O Lord, we pray thee to send us wind, no a *rantin'-tantin'*, tearin' wind, but a soughin' (sighing), winnin' wind." More expressive words than these could not be found in any language.—DEAN RAMSAY.

Tantrum. This word, borrowed by the English from the Scotch, is generally used in the plural; and the phrase, "to be in the *tantrums*," most commonly applied to a woman, signifies that she is in a violent fit of illtemper. Jamieson explains it as "high airs," and derives it from the French *tantrans*, nicknacks. This etymology cannot be accepted — firstly, because there is no such word in the French language ; and secondly, because if there were, the meanings are not in the slightest degree related. The "English Slang Dictionary" derives it from a dance called, in Italy, the *tarantula*, because persons in the *tantrums* dance and caper about ! The word is composed of the Gaelic *deann*, haste, violence, hurry ; and *trom*, heavy, whence violent and heavy, applied to a fit of sudden passion.

Tapetless, heedless, foolish ; probably from the Gaelic *tapadh*, activity, cleverness; and *ta-paidh*, quick, active, manly, bold, with the addition of the English *less*, want of cleverness or activity.

The *tapetless*, ramfeezled hizzie,
She's saft at best, and something lazy.
—BURNS: *To John Lapraik.*

Tap-oure-tail, top-over-tail, or topsy-turvy (erroneously printed in Jamieson tap-*our*-tail), has the same meaning as *tapsalteerie*, and the English *head-over-heels*.

Tappiloorie, top-heavy; or *tappie-tourie*, round at the top. From the Flemish, Dutch, and English *top*; and the Flemish and Dutch *loer*, French *lourd*, heavy; *tourie*, from the Flemish, *toere*, round about; the French *tour* and *autour*.

Tappit-hen, a crested hen, or a hen with a top tuft of feathers; a phrase applied to a large bottle or jar of wine or spirits.

Blythe, blythe, and merry was she,
Blythe was she but and ben,
Weel she loo'ed a Hawick gill,
And leuch to see a *tappit-hen.*
—*Tea Table Miscellany: Andrew and his Cuttie Gun.*

Come, bumpers high, express your joy,
The bowl we maun renew it,
The *tappit-hen* gae bring her ben,
To welcome Willie Stewart.
—BURNS.

Their hostess appeared with a huge pewter measuring pot, containing at least three English quarts, familiarly termed a *tappit-hen.*—SCOTT: *Waverley.*

Blithe, blithe, and merry are we,
Pick and wale o' merry men,
What care we though the cock may crow,
We're masters o' the *tappit hen.*
—CHARLES GRAY: *Whistle Binkie.*

"This term," says Jamieson, "denoted in Aberdeen a large bottle of claret, holding three magnums or Scots pints;" but as regards the quantity opinion differs. All agree, however, that a *tappit-hen* held considerably more than an ordinary bottle.

Tapsalteerie, in confusion, upside down, topsy-turvy. Possibly from the Gaelic *toabh*, the side; and *saltair*, to tread, to trample. *Topsy-turvy* is apparently from the same source, and not from "top-side the t'other way," as some etymologists have suggested.

Gie me a cannie hour at e'en,
My arms about my dearie, O,
And warldly cares and warldly men
May a' gang *tapsalteerie*, O!
—BURNS.

In an excellent translation into German of Burns's "Green grow the rashes, O!" appended as a note in Chambers's "Scottish Songs," the two lines in which *tapsalteerie* occurs are well rendered:—

Mag Erdenvolk and Erdenplag,
Kopfuber dann, *Kopfunter* gehen.

Tapthrawn, perverse, obstinate, unreasonably argumentative; from *tap*, the head or brain, metaphorically the intellect; and *thrawn*, twisted wrongly.

Tartar. To catch a *Tartar*, to be overpowered in argument or in fight, by one whose prowess had been denied or unsuspected; to get the worst of it. *Tartar*, says the Slang Dictionary, is "a savage fellow, an ugly customer." To "catch a *Tartar*," is to discover, somewhat unpleasantly, that a person is by no means so mild or good tempered as was supposed.

This saying originated from the story of an Irish soldier in the imperial service, who, in a battle against the Turks, called out to his comrade that he had caught a *Tartar*. "Bring him along then," said he. "He won't come," said Paddy. "Then come along yourself," replied his comrade. "Bedad!" said he, "but he won't let me!" A *Tartar* is also an adept at any feast or game. "He is quite a *tartar* at cricket or billiards."—GROSE's *Classical Dictionary of the Vulgar Tongue.*

Grose's story was evidently invented. Philology had no need to travel into Tartary to explain the source of a peculiarly British phrase, which has no equivalent in any language but English and Scotch: inasmuch as it is of native origin, from the Gaelic *tartar*, a great noise, clamour, bustle, confusion; *tartarach*, bustling, noisy, uproaring, unmanageable.

Tartarian is a word used by the dramatists of the Elizabethan era to signify a strong thief, or a noisy blustering villain.

Tass, a small heap of earth or cluster of flowers; from the French *tas*, a parcel or pack.

There lived a lass in Inverness,
She was the pride of a' the toun,
Blythe as the lark on gowan *tass*
When frae the nest it's newly flown.
—ALLAN CUNNINGHAM.

Tatshie, according to Jamieson, signifies dressed in a slovenly manner; and *tattrel*, a rag.

Tatterdemalion, a ragged, miserable object. A colloquial word introduced into England by the Scotch; and supposed by English philologists to be from the Icelandic *tetur*, a torn garment. The roots, however, are derivable from the Gaelic; that of tatter is from *dud*, a rag; from whence the provincial English *dud*, meaning a scarecrow. *Malion* comes from *meall* and *meallan*, a lump, a heap of confused objects; from whence the primary meaning of *tatterdemalion* would seem to be a "heap of rags," applied contemptuously to the wearer of them. Mr. James M'Kie, of Kilmarnock, quotes in his Bibliography of Burns, "The Jolly Beggars, or *Tatterdemalions*, a cantata by Robert Burns. Edinburgh, Oliver & Boyd, 1808."

Tavern sign of the Dog and Duck. This is usually explained in the English sense of a "Dog" and a "Duck," with a representation on the signboard of a sportsman shooting wild ducks, followed by a dog ready to spring into the water. It is probable, however, that the sign is of greater antiquity than the conquest of England by the Danes and Saxons; and that it dates from the Celtic period, and was originally *Deoch an Diugh*, or "Drink to-day," an invitation to all travellers and passers by to step in and drink; and that it was not by any means confined to the shooters of ducks, or to the watery districts in which such sports were possible. The perversions of the word *deoch* (drink), by the English and Lowland Scotch, are very numerous. One of them in particular deserves to be cited, *dog's nose*, which is, or used to be, a favourite drink of the populace in London, composed of beer and gin. Charles Dickens, in Pickwick, describes *dog's nose* as a warm drink; but the compiler of Hotten's Slang Dictionary affirms it to be a cold drink—so called, because it was "as cold as a dog's nose." The true derivation is most probably from the Gaelic *deoch* and *nos*, custom; and *nosag*, customary, or usual; and thus signifies the "usual drink." Another common and equally ludicrous perversion of the Gaelic is "Old Tom," which is used by the publicans of London, illustrated by a large tom-cat sitting on a barrel of gin. The origin of the phrase is *ol*, drink, and *taom*, to pour out; whence, to pour out the favourite liquor.

Tavey's locker, Davy's locker, Davy Jones's locker. These singular phrases, used princi-

pally among sailors, all signify death simply, or death by drowning in the sea. Their origin has never been very satisfactorily explained or accounted for; and no one has yet told the world whether *Tavey* or *Davy* was a real or a fabulous person, or who *Jones* was, and what was signified by his *locker*. The Teutonic roots of the English and Scotch languages fail to give the slightest hint or clue to the etymology of the expression, and thus compel inquirers to look to the Celtic for a possible solution of the mystery. In Gaelic is found *taimh* (*taiv* or *taif*), death; and *tamh* (*tav*), the ocean; *ionadh*, a place; and *lochd*, sleep, or a closing of the eyes. *Taimh* or *tamh* may account for the corruption into *Tavey* or *Davy*, *ionadh* for *Jones*, and *lochd* for *locker*. This explanation supplies an intelligible and appropriate meaning to *Davy Jones's locker*, the grotesque combination of words in Scotch and English which has become proverbial among seafaring people.

According to Wright's "Provincial English Dictionary," *David Jones* is a name given by sailors to a "sea-devil." But whether the "sea-devil" had or had not a *locker* we are not informed. Nares, in his Glossary, says that one "Davy" was a proficient in sword and buckler exercise, celebrated at the close of the sixteenth century. It does not appear, however, that any of these allusions can shed any light on the origin of *Davy's locker.*

Tawdy, a term of contempt for a child; *tawdy-fee,* a fine for illegitimacy; also, a depreciatory epithet for the *podex.* The etymology is unknown, but may be connected with the Gaelic *todhar,* excrement, and, by extension of meaning, to the senses in which it is applied to the *podex,* or to a child. *Todhar* also signifies a field manured by folding cattle upon it. *Taudis,* in French, signifies a miserable and dirty hole or hovel. In Irish Gaelic, *tod* or *todan* signifies a lump, a clod, a round mass, which may also have some remote connection with the idea of the *podex.*

Tawie, tame, peaceable, friendly, easily led. Gaelic *taobhach (taovach),* friendly, partial, inclined to kindness; erroneously derived from *tow,* a rope, or to be led by a rope.

> Hamely, *tawie,* quiet, cannie,
> An' unco sonsie.
> —BURNS: *Auld Farmer's Address.*

Tawpie, a foolish person, especially a foolish girl.

> Gawkies, *tawpies,* gowks and fools.
> —BURNS: *Verses Written at Selkirk.*

This word is usually derived from the French *taupe,* a mole —erroneously supposed to be blind; but the Gaelic origin is more probable, from *taip,* a

lump, a lumpish or clumsy person.

> Dans le royaume des *taupes,* les *borgnes* sont rois.—*French Proverb.*

Teen, tene, teyne, provocation, anger, wrath, From the Gaelic *teine,* fire; *teintidh,* fiery, angry.

> Last day I grat wi' spite and *teen,*
> As poet Burns cam' by:
> That to a bard I should be seen,
> Wi' half my channel dry.
> —BURNS: *Humble Petition of Bruar Water.*

Teethie, crabbed, ill-natured, snarling; applied metaphorically from the action of a dog which shows its teeth when threatening to bite. The English word *toothsome,* which has no relation in meaning to *teethie,* is often used instead of *dainty,* from the erroneous idea that *dainty* is derived from *dens,* a tooth. The real derivation of *dainty* is from the Gaelic *deanta,* complete, perfect, well formed, and finished. When Shakspeare speaks of his "*dainty* Ariel," or a man praises the *dainty* hand or lips of his beloved, he does not mean that the teeth should be employed upon them, but that they are well-formed, complete, or beautifully perfect.

Teind, a tax, a tribute, a tithe, a tenth; *teind-free,* exempt from tithes or taxation.

> But we that live in Fairy Land
> No sickness know, nor pain,
> I quit my body when I will,
> And take to it again;
> And I would never tire, Janet,
> In Elfin land to dwell:

But aye at every seven years' end,
Ihey pay the *teind* to hell ;
And I'm sae fat and fair of flesh,
I fear 'twill be mysel.
—*Border Minstrelsy: The Young
Tamlane.*

Tendal knife. Jamieson cites
from an inventory, "two belts,
a *tendal knife*, a horse comb,
and a burning iron ;" and at a
loss to account for the word,
asks : "Shall we suppose that
knives celebrated for their temper had been formerly made
somewhere in the dale, or val-
ley of Tyne, in England ? It
might, however, be the name
of the maker ?" These are, no
doubt, ingenious suppositions,
but both appear to be wrong if
tested by the Gaelic, in which
tean signifies long and thin ; and
tail, or *taile*, strong ; whence
tendal knife, a knife with a long,
thin, strong blade.

Tent, to take heed, to act
cautiously and warily, to be
attentive. From the French
tenter, to try, to attempt. *Tentie*, cautious, wary ; *to tak tent*,
to take care, to beware; *tentless*,
careless.

When the tod preaches tak *tent* o' the
lambs.
—ALLAN RAMSAY : *Scots Proverbs.*

But warily *tent* when ye come to court me,
And come na unless the back yett be ajee.
Syne up the back stair and let naebody see,
And come as ye were na comin' to me.
—BURNS : *Oh Whistle and I'll come to
you, my Lad.*

I rede you, honest man, tak *tent*,
Ye'll show your folly.
—BURNS : *Epistle to James Smith.*

The time flew by wi' *tentless* heed,
Till 'twixt the late and early,
Wi' sma' persuasion she agreed
To see me through the barley.
—BURNS : *Corn Rigs and Barley Rigs.*

See ye take *tent* to this !
—BEN JONSON : *Sad Shepherdess.*

Teribus ye teri odin, the war cry
of the men of Hawick at the
battle of Flodden, and still preserved in the traditions of the
town. The full chorus is often
sung at festive gatherings, not
only in the gallant old border
town itself, but in the remotest
districts of Canada, the United
States, and Australia, wherever
Hawick men and natives of the
Scottish Border congregate to
keep up the remembrance of
their native land, and the haunts
of their boyhood.

Teribus ye teri odin,
Sons of heroes slain at Flodden,
Imitating Border bowmen,
Aye defend your rights and common.

Attempts have been frequently
made to connect this Border
ballad with the names of the
Scandinavian and Norse demi-
gods, Thor and Odin; but these
heroes were wholly unknown to
the original possessors of the
Scottish soil, and but very partially known to the Danish and
Saxon invaders, who came after
them. The ballad, of which these
mysterious words form the burden, is one of patriotic "defence
and defiance" against the invaders of the soil. *Teribus ye
teri odin* is an attempt at a
phonetic rendering of the Gaelic

Tir a buaidh's, tir a dion, which, translated, means " Land of victory, and Land of defence."

Teth, spirit, mettle, humour, temper, disposition; usually employed in the sense of high-spirited. The word was English in the Elizabethan era, and was pronounced and written *tith,* from the Gaelic *teth,* hot.

> She's good mettle, of a good stirring strain, and goes *tith.*—BEAUMONT AND FLETCHER.
>
> Take a widow—a good staunch wench that's *tith.—Idem.*
>
> *Ill-teth'd,* ill-humoured.—JAMIESON.

Teuch, a drink, a draught of liquor. This word has been derived by Jamieson and others from the Teutonic *tog,* and *teughe,* to draw or pull. As no such words are to be found in the Teutonic languages, it is possible that Jamieson meant the German *zug,* the English *tug,* to pull or draw; whence, in vulgar language, a long *pull* at the bottle or tankard, a deep draught. It seems more probable, however, that the Lowland Scotch word is a corruption of the Gaelic *deoch,* a drink, as in the phrase, " *deoch* an' doruis," a drink at the door, a stirrup cup. (See DEUK, *ante,* p. 42.)

Tevoo. This nearly obsolete word was formerly used by women in contemptuous depreciation of a male flirt, fond of their society, but who was never serious in his attentions to them.

It has been supposed to be somehow or other derived from the French, but no word similar to it appears in that language. It is probably from the Gaelic *ti,* a person, a creature; and *fu,* an abbreviation of *fuachaidh,* a flirt, a jilt, a deceiver.

Tew is a word of many meanings in Scotland, but most commonly signifies to work hard. It also signifies to struggle, to strive, to fatigue, to overpower, to make tough. " Sair *tews* " signifies old or sore difficulties or troubles; *tewing on,* toiling on; sair *tewd,* greatly fatigued, are common expressions. Jamieson derives the word from the French *tuer,* to kill; Nares cites instances in which it is used in the sense of *tow,* to pull along by a rope. Possibly, however, it is but a misspelling of the Scottish *teuch* (with the omission of the guttral *j,* the English *tough,* in which the omitted guttral is replaced by the sound of *f,* as *tuff*). The Gaelic *tiugh,* thick, stiff, strong, is doubtless an allied word.

Thack and raip, from the thatch of a house; and *rope,* the binding or fastening which keeps the thatch in its place. Hence, metaphorically, the phrase applied to the conduct of an unreasonable and disorderly person, that he acts "out of a' *thack and raip,*" as if the roof of his house were uncovered, and let in the wind and weather;

or, in vulgar slang, as if he had "a slate or a tile loose."

Thairms, the strings of a violin, harp, or other instrument for which wire is not used, called in England cat-gut. The word is derived from the German, Dutch, and Flemish *darm,* gut, intestines; the German plural *därme.*

Oh, had M'Lachlan, *thairm*-inspiring sage, '
Been there to hear this heavenly band engage.
—BURNS: *The Brigs of Ayr.*
Come, screw the pegs wi' tunefu' cheep,
And ower the *thairms* be trying.
—BURNS: *The Ordination.*

The word, though immediately derived from the Teutonic, may, in the sense of gut or entrails, have some connection with the practice of divination by the ancient Augurs, who studied the intestines of sacrificed birds to foretell future events. But this is a·mere conjecture founded upon the fact, that the Gaelic *tairm,* or *thairm,* signifies divination.

From *thairm,* string made from gut, may probably come the Scottish words *thrum,* to play on a stringed instrument, and, in a contemptuous sense, *thrummer,* an inferior fiddler. Possibly the English *strum* is a corruption and euphemism of *thrum.*

Thane, a very ancient title of nobility in Scotland, equivalent in rank to an English earl. Macbeth, according to Shakspeare, was Thane of Cawdor. Jamieson suggests its derivation from the Anglo-Saxon *thegn,* a servant; but as the title was peculiar to the Gael, wholly unknown to the Saxon, and implied rather mastery and dominion than servitude, a Celtic etymology is most probable; that etymology is found in *tanaistear,* a governor, a lord, a prince; one second in rank to the king or sovereign; and *tanaisteach,* governing, acting as a thane, or master.

The noo, or **the now,** a common Scotticism for just now, immediately, presently, by and by.

Theak, theek, to thatch a house. Greek θηκη (*thēkē*), a small house, a repository; German *dach,* a roof; old English *theccan,* to cover; Gaelic *tigh* and *teach,* a house.

Bessie Bell and Mary Gray,
  They were twa bonnie lasses,
They biggit a bower on yon burn brae,
  And *theekit* it o'er wi' rashes.
—*Ballad: Bessie Bell and Mary Gray.*

Ye'll sit on his white hause bane,
And I'll pike out his bonnie blue een ;
Wi' ae lock o' his gowden hair
We ll *theek* our nest when it grows bare.
—*Minstrelsy of the Scottish Border:
  The Twa Corbies.*

The cozy roof *theekit* wi' moss-covered Strae.
—JAMES BALLANTINE.

Them, they, those. These plural pronouns are often used in Scotland instead of the singular *it,* especially when applied to oatmeal porridge, brose, hotchpotch, and broth, or soup. The idea of plurality seems to be attached to porridge, from the multiplicity of the grains of meal, of which the dish is compounded, and to hotch-potch, barley broth, and other soups, for the same reason of their numerous ingredients.

Why dinna ye sup ye're parritch, Johnnie?
Johnnie—I dinna like *them*.
—GALT.

Once at the annual dinner to his tenants, given by the Duke of Buccleuch, the Duchess pressed a burly old farmer, to whom she wished to show attention, to partake of some pea-soup. "Muckle obleeged to your Grace," said the farmer, "but I downa tak' *them*. They're owre wundy!"—*The Ettrick Shepherd*.

Each true-hearted Scotsman, by nature jocose,
Can cheerfully dine on a dishfu' o' brose,
And the grace be a wish to get plenty of *those*;
And it's O for the kail brose o' Scotland,
And O for the Scottish kail brose.
—ALEXANDER WATSON: *Old Song*.

Then-a-days, in former time, as opposed to the English and Scottish phrase, *now-a-days*, in the present time.

Thepes, gooseberries, or more properly *gorse* or thorn berries; in Dutch and Flemish *doorn*, or thorn-berries. Mr. Halliwell, in his Archaic Dictionary, cites *thepes* as an Eastern Counties word, used in Sir Thomas Brown's works. It is also current in the Lowlands of Scotland. The derivation is unknown.

Thetes, traces or harness of a horse drawing a vehicle. To be "out of the traces," is to be out of rule, governance, or control.

To be quite out of the *thetes*, *i.e.*, to be disorderly in one's conduct. . . . To be out of *thete* is a phrase applied to one who is rusted as to any art or science from want of practice.—JAMIESON.

The word is derived by Jamieson from the Icelandic *thatt'r*, a cord, a small rope; but is more probably from the Gaelic *taod*; aspirated *thoad*, a rope.

Thief - like, ugly, disagreeable. This Scottish phrase does not signify dishonest-looking, but simply repulsive, or disagreeable; possibly because the Lowland Scotch who made use of it suffered but too often from the incursions of the Highland cattle-stealers into the pastures and sheep-folds, associated in their minds with all that was most offensive, morally and physically.

That's a *thief-like* mutch' ye have on, *i.e.*, that's an ugly cap you have on.—JAMIESON.

Thief-like occurs in two common proverbial phrases—the *thiefer-like* the better soldier; the aulder the *thiefer-like*. Ye're like the horse's bains, the aulder ye grow the *thiefer-like*.—JAMIESON.

Thig, to beg or borrow; sometimes written *thigger*.

The father buys, the son biggs (builds),
The oye (grandson) sells, and *his* son *thigs*.
—ALLAN RAMSAY'S *Scots Proverbs*.

And if the wives and dirty brats,
E'en *thigger* at your doors an' yetts.
—BURNS: *Address of Beelzebub*.

Think-lang, to grow weary, to be impatient of another's absence ; to think the time long.

But *think* na' *lang*, lassie, tho' I gang awa',
The summer is comin', cauld winter's awa',
And I'll come back and see thee in spite o' them a'.
—*Song: Logie o' Buchan.*

Thistlecock or **thrustlecock**, the thrush, more poetically called the *mavis*, both in Old English and Scottish poetry.

The primrose is the fairest flower
That springs on muir or dale ;
An' the *thistlecock* is the bonniest bird
That sings on the evening gale.
—*Ballad of Proud Lady Margaret.*

Thivel, a cudgel, a large shillelagh. Etymology unknown.

An' for a *thivel* they did use
A sturdy stump o' knotty spruce.
—*John o' Arnha'.*

Tholeable, tholesome, tolerable, that may be endured ; *tholance*, sufferance, endurance. *Thole* is doubtless from the same root as the Latin *tolerare*, and the Gaelic *dolas*, sufferance, dolour, pain.

Thowless. Perhaps a corruption of *thewless*, weak ; without *thews* and sinews. Gaelic *tiugh*, thick, strong ; whence *thowless*, without strength or thickness.

For fortune aye favours the active and bauld,
But ruins the wooer that's *thowless* and cauld.
—ALLAN RAMSAY.

Her dowff excuses pat me mad,
Conscience—says I, ye *thowless* jad,
I'll write, and that a hearty blaud
This very night.
—BURNS: *Epistle to Lapraik.*

Thraine. According to Jamieson, this word signifies to be constantly harping on one subject, and is derived from the Teutonic or Swedish *traegen*, assiduous. He is of opinion also that *rane*, to cry the same thing over and over again, is synonymous, and of the same origin. But more probably, in the sense of harping continually on one subject, of complaint, *thraine* is from the Greek *threnos*, a lamentation. *Rane* is probably from the Gaelic *ran*, to roar.

Thram, to thrive, to prosper. Etymology uncertain. Jamieson supposes it to be from the Icelandic.

Well wat your honour, *thram* for that, quo' she.
—Ross's *Helenore.*

Can you expect to *thram*,
That hae been guilty o' so great a wrang?
—*Ibid.*

Thrang, busy, crowded with work or occupation ; from the English *throng*, to crowd, and the German *drang*, pressure, *drängen*, to press, and the Flemish *dringen*, to press, to squeeze.

Upon a bonnie day in June,
When wearin' through the afternoon,
Twa dogs that were nae *thrang* at hame,
Foregathered ance upon a time.
—BURNS: *The Twa Dogs.*

The deil sat grim amang the reek,
Thrang bundling brimstone matches !
—*Jacobite Song: Awa', ye Whigs,
Awa'.*

Thrapple, the throat ; akin to the English *throttle.*

As murder at his *thrapple* shored ;
And hell mixed in the brulzie [broil].
—BURNS : *Epistle to Robert Graham.*

When we had a Scots Parliament,—deil rax their *thrapples* that reft us o't.
SCOTT : *Rob Roy.*

Thraw, a twist, a fit of ill-humour ; *thrawn,* twisted, contorted. *Thrawn-gabbit,* with a twisted or contorted *gab,* or mouth ; and, metaphorically, a cantankerous, morose person who is always grumbling. *Gabbit* is from the Gaelic *gab,* a mouth ; whence the English slang, "the gift of the *gab,*" the gift of eloquence, or power of much speaking. *Thrawart,* perverse, obstinate ; *thraw,* to contradict ; *thraws, throes,* twists or contortions of pain ; also, a little while, or a turn of time, a twist.

She turns the key wi' cannie *thraw.*
—BURNS : *Hallowe'en.*

When I a little *thraw* had made my moan,
Bewailing mine misfortune and mischance.
—*The King's Quair.*

There are twa hens into the crib,
Have fed this month and mair ;
Make haste and *thraw* their necks about,
That Colin weel may fare.
—MICKLE : *There's nae Luck About the House.*

He's easy wi' a' body that's easy wi' him ; but if ye *thraw* him, ye had better *thraw* the deevil.—SCOTT : *Rob Roy.*

Thraw seems akin to the English *throe,* a throb, a twist of pain, and is probably from the Teutonic.

Threpe, or **threap,** to argue, to contend pertinaciously in argument, to assert obstinately in spite of reason ; from the Gaelic *drip,* or *trip,* to contend, to fight.

It's not for a man with a woman to *threep,*
Unless he first give owre the plea :
As we began we'll now leave off—
I'll tak my auld cloak about me.
—*Old Ballad, quoted by* SHAKSPEARE.

Some herds, weel learned upon the beuk,
Wad *threap* auld folk the thing mistook.
—BURNS : *Epistle to Simpson.*

Threapin's no' provin'.
—ALLAN RAMSAY.

This is na *threapin'* ware [*i.e.,* this is genuine ware, not to be argued about].—ALLAN RAMSAY.

Thrimle, thrimmel, to press, to squeeze ; *thrimp, thrump,* to press as in a crowd, to push. Etymology uncertain, but possibly from the Flemish *drempel,* an entrance—whence to force an entrance, to press through, to push through.

Through. This word, the Gaelic *troimh,* the Kymric *trw,* and the Teutonic *durch,* enters more largely into its structure of Scottish compound terms and phrases, than was ever the case in England. Thus the Scotch have *through-gang,* perseverance ; *through-gaun,* and *through-gang-ing,* persevering, also wasteful, prodigal, going through

one's means ; *through-pit,* activity, energy, that *puts* a thing
through; through-fare, or *through-
gang,* a thoroughfare; *through-
ither,* confused ; *through-stone,*
a stone as thick as the wall;
through-pittin', or *through-bearin',*
a bare subsistence, enough to
get through the world with ;
and the verb *to through,* or *thruch,*
to penetrate, to go through.
Sir Walter Scott uses *through-
gaun* in Rob Roy, in the sense
of a severe exposure of one's
life and conduct, during a rigid
cross-examination.

Throwther, higgledy - piggledy,
helter - skelter, in confusion ;
possibly a corruption of *through-
ither,* or *through-each-other.*

> Till—skelp—a shot ! they're aff a'
> *throwther,*
>   To save their skin.
> —BURNS : *Earnest Cry and Prayer.*

Thrum, a musical sound, also
a thread. *Gray thrums,* the
popular phrase in Scotland for
the purring of a cat, the sound
of a spinning-wheel, the thread
remaining at the end of a web ;
apparently derived from the
Gaelic *troimh,* through.

> Come out wi' your moolins, come out wi'
>   your crumbs,
> And keep in slee baudrons [the cat] to
>   sing ye *gray thrums.*
> —JAMES BALLANTINE : *A Voice from the
>   Woods.*

Thud, a dull, heavy blow : etymology unknown. Lord Neaves
considered it a *comic* word,
though it is difficult to see

why, especially when such
serious use of it was made
by Gawin Douglas and Allan
Ramsay :—

> The fearful *thuds* of the tempestuous tide.
> —GAWIN DOUGLAS : *Translation of
>   the Enid.*

> The air grew rough with boisterous *thuds.*
>   ALLAN RAMSAY : *The Vision.*

> Swith on a hardened clay he fell,
>   Right far was heard the *thud.*
>   —*Hardyknute.*

Tid, tid - bit, tydy. All these
words, like the English *tide,* are
derivable from the idea of time,
the German *zeit,* the Dutch
and Flemish *tijd. Tid,* in the
Scottish language, signifies season ; the English *tid-bit* is a
seasonable bit. *Bit* is from
the Gaelic *biadh,* food, and not
from the English *bite,* or that
which is bitten. The French
morceau, the English *morsel,* is
unquestionably derived from
mordre, to bite. *Tydy,* seasonable; "a *tydy* bride " is a phrase
applied to an unmarried girl who
is about to become a mother,
and in that state is married and
taken home to her bridegroom's
house, in order that the coming
child may be born after wed-
lock, and thus become legiti-
mised.

Tift, English *tiff,* a slight quarrel, a fit of ill-humour ; *tip,* a
slang word for money given to
a servant as a small gratuity
to procure drink or otherwise ;
called by the French a *pour
boire,* and by the Germans *trink-*

geld. No English or Scottish etymologist has succeeded in tracing these words to their sources. Jamieson derives *tift* from the Icelandic *tyfta,* to chastise; Johnson declares *tiff,* a quarrel, to be "a low word, without etymology;" Richardson has *tiff,* a drink, which he thinks a corruption of *tipple,* an allied word ; Ash defines *tiff* to be a corruption of the Teutonic *tepel,* a dug or teat, while the ancient author of "Gazophylacium Anglicanum " surpasses all his predecessors and successors in ingenuity by deriving *tipsy* and *tipple* from the Latin *tipula,* a water-spider, because that insect is always drinking ! Mr. Halliwell, without entering on the etymological question, says that in English provincial dialects *tiff* has three meanings— small beer, a draught of any liquor, and to fall headlong from the effects of drink.

There are several derivatives in the Scottish language from *tift,* a quarrel, viz., *tifty,* quarrelsome, apt to take offence ; *tifting,* an angry scolding ; and "to be in a *tifter,*" *i.e.,* in a difficult and disagreeable position where one is likely to be severely reprimanded. Possibly the Scottish *tift* (a quarrel), the English *tiff* (a fit of ill-humour), are as closely allied in meaning as they are in sound.

Tig, a twitch, a touch, a sharp stroke ; also a slight fit of ill-temper; possibly, in both senses,

derived from the Gaelic *taoig,* anger, and *taoigeach,* angry, and as such disposed to strike a blow.

A game among children. He who in this game gives the stroke, says to the person to whom he has given it, " Ye bear my *tig.*"—JAMIESON.

Tillie-soul. According to Jamieson, this word signifies " a place to which a gentleman sends the horses and servants of his guests, when he does not choose to entertain them at his own expense." He derives it from the French *tillet,* a ticket ; and *solde,* pay. There is, however, no such word as *tillet,* a ticket, in the French language. There is *tiller,* which means, "detacher avec la main les filaments du chanvre," *i.e.,* to remove with the hand the filaments of hemp. But this operation has certainly nothing to do with the explanation given to *tillie-soul.* The true derivation appears to be from the Gaelic *till,* to turn away ; and *sult,* feeding, fatness, good bodily entertainment; whence *tillie-soul* or *till sult,* to turn away for entertainment elsewhere.

Timmer, timber; from the Flemish *timmer.* This word is used not alone as signifying wood, but in the sense of building or constructing out of wood ; and, by extension of meaning, into constructing or fashioning generally ; and, by still wider extension, into doing or performing. "To give one a *tim-merin'*" signifies to beat one with a stick (or piece of timber). *Timmer*-breeks and *timmer*-sark were ludicrous terms for a coffin. *Timmerman*, in the Flemish, and *zimmerman*, in the German, signified a carpenter, an artificer in wood, and also a woodmonger, or woodman.

Timmer up the flail, *i.e.*, to wield the flail; *timmer* up the floor with a dishclout, *i.e.*, to clean it. . . . To *timmer* up the lesson, *i.e.*, to be busily employed in learn-it. . . . Oh, as he *timmers* up the Latin ! *i.e.*, what a deal of Latin he employs.— JAMIESON.

And who in singing could excel
Famed Douglas, Bishop of Dunkel';
He *timmer'd* up, though it be lang,
In gude braid Scots a Virgil's sang.
—INGRAM'S *Poems.*

Tine, to lose; *tint*, lost. This ancient English word has long been confined to Scottish literature and parlance.

What was *tint* through tree,
Tree shall it win.
—*Piers Ploughman.*

He never *tint* a cow that grat for a needle.

Where there is nothing the king *tines* his right.

All's not *tint* that's in danger.

Better spoil your joke than *tine* your friend.

Tine heart—all's gone.
—ALLAN RAMSAY'S *Scots Proverbs.*

Next my heart I'll wear her,
For fear my jewel *tine.*—BURNS.

Tinkle - sweetie. According to Jamieson, *tinkle-sweetie* was a name formerly given in Edinburgh to a bell that was rung at eight o'clock in the evening. A previous bell, which was rung at two in the afternoon, was called the "kail bell," *i.e.*, the dinner bell. *Tinkle-sweetie,* was superseded as a phrase by the "aucht hour bell." Jamieson, at a loss for the etymology, says "it was thus denominated because the sound of it was *sweet* to the ears of apprentices and shopmen, because they were then at liberty to shut up for the night." The conjecture is no doubt ingenious ; but it may be asked whether the kail or dinner bell might not have been as justly entitled to be called sweet as the bell that announced the cessation of labour ? The word is apparently a relic of the very old time when the kings and nobles of Scotland and the merchants of Edinburgh all spoke or understood Gaelic. In that language *diun* (*d* pronounced as *t*) signified to shut up, to close ; *glaodh* (pronounced *glao*) signified a cry, a call ; and *suaitcachd*, labour, work, toil ; whence *duinglao* (*tuinglao*, quasi *tinkle*) and *suai-teachd* corrupted into *sweetie.* Thus the phrase would mean a call or summons, to cease from labour, or, in modern parlance, "to shut up shop."

Tinsel, loss ; from *tine*, to lose.

My profit is not your *tinsel.*
—ALLAN RAMSAY'S *Scots Proverbs.*

Tippenny, from twopence; whence *tippenny*, at the price of two pence; twopenny ale.

Wt' *tippenny* we'll fear nae evil,
Wi' usquebae we'll face the devil.
—BURNS: *Tam o' Shanter.*

Mr. Loève Weimaurs, a once noted French author, who translated or paraphrased Burns into French, rendered the first of these lines by "Avec deux sous, nous ne craindrons rien," with twopence we'll fear nothing, thus leaving the ale out of the question.

Tirl, to turn the knob, the pin, or other fastening of a door. The word is of constant occurrence in the ballad poetry of Scotland.

Oh he's gone round and round about
And *tirled* at the pin.
—*Willie and May Margaret.*

Tirl, to spin round as in a whirlwind, to unroof with a high wind.

Whyles, on the strong-winged tempest flying,
Tirling the kirks.
—BURNS: *Address to the Deil.*

This word has been supposed to be a corruption of the English *twirl,* to turn round; and, by extension of meaning, "*tirling* the roof of the kirk," *i.e.*, sending the materials whirling or twirling in the storm. To *tirl* the pin or knob of a door, is doubtless from twirl, in the English sense; but to *tirl* the roof of a kirk, as in the line of

Burns, is more probably from the Gaelic *tuirl,* and *tuirlin,* to rush rapidly with a great noise.

Tirlie-wirlie, intricate or trifling ornaments.

Queer, *tirlie-wirlie* holes that gang out to the open air, and keep the air as caller as a kail-blade.—SCOTT: *The Antiquary.*

It was in and through the window broads
And a' the *tirlie-wirlies* o't,
The sweetest kiss that e'er I got
Was frae my Dainty Davie.
—HERD'S *Collection: Dainty Davie.*

From the English *twirl* and *whirl,* though Jamieson goes to the Swedish in search of the etymology.

Tirr, a fractious child; *tirran,* one of a perverse and complaining humour; *tirrie,* querulous, peevish. These words seem all to be derived from the Gaelic *tuir,* to moan, to lament, to weep; and *tuireadh,* moaning, complaining, lamentation. Jamieson, however, derives *tirr* from the Greek *tyrannos,* a tyrant, or the Teutonic *terghen,* to irritate; though the latter word is not to be found in German or in any of its dialects. *Tire lire* is often used in French poetry for the song or lament of the nightingale.

Tittie, a sister.

He had a wee *tittie* that loved na me
Because I was true and trim as she
—LADY GRIZZEL BAILLIE.

Tittie-billie, according to Jamieson, who denounces it as vulgar.

Q

This phrase signifies an equal, a match, as in the proverbial saying which he quotes, "Tam's a great thief, but Willie's *tittie-billie* wi' him;" and derives it from *tittie*, a sister; and *billie*, a brother. The true meaning of *billie* is a fellow; from the Gaelic *balaoch*, a mate, or close companion; and *tittie*, in all probability, is a corruption of *taite*, joyousness, jolliness. *Tittie-billie* would thus be synonymous with the English phrase, "a jolly good fellow." (See BILLIES, *ante*, page 8.)

Tocher, a dowry, but principally used as applicable to the fortunes of persons in the middle and lower ranks of life, who are too poor to give their daughters *dowries*. A *tocher* may be either a large or a small one. There is no other *Scotch* word for a daughter's portion. *Tocherless*, fortuneless.

A cow and a calf,
An ox and a half,
Forty good shillings and three;
Is not that enough *tocher*
For a shoemaker's daughter?
  —J. O. HALLIWELL: *Nursery Rhymes of England.*

The bonnie lass *tocherless* has mair wooers than chances of a husband.

The greatest *tochers* make not ever the greatest testaments.

Marry a beggar and get a louse for your *tocher*.

Maidens' *tochers* and ministers' stipends are aye less than they are ca'd.
  —ALLAN RAMSAY'S *Scots Proverbs.*

Oh meikle thinks my love o' my beauty,
And meikle thinks my love o' my kin,

But little thinks my love I ken brawly,
My *tocher's* the jewel has charms for him.
  —BURNS.

Philologists are at variance as to the origin of *tocher*, which is purely Scottish, and has no relation to any similar word in the Teutonic or in the Romance languages of Europe. The French has *dot*, the German *braut-schätz* (bridal treasure), and the Dutch and Flemish *bruid schat*. Dr. Adolphus Wagner, editor of a German edition of Burns (Leipzig, 1825), suggests "the Icelandic *tochar*," which he thinks is either corrupted from the Latin *douarium*, or from *daughter*, the German *tochter*, or the Greek θυγατηρ. The real root of the word is the Gaelic *tacar* or *tocar*, provision or store, a marriage portion; *tocharachd*, well or plentifully dowered; *toic*, wealth, fortune; *toic ard*, high fortune; and *toic-each*, rich.

Tod, usually considered to signify a bush; *ivy tod*, a bush or bunch of ivy. The derivation seems to be from the Dutch and Flemish *tod*, a rag, a fringe; and the Gaelic *dud*, a rag; or *taod*, a string; from the string-like and ragged appearance of ivy when it has grown as high as possible on the supporting tree or wall, and has then fallen downwards. *Tod* also signifies a fox; *tod-laurie* is a jocose word for the same animal.

Ye're like the *tod*; ye grow grey before you grow guid.

The *tod* ne'er sped better than when he gaed on his ain errand.

—ALLAN RAMSAY's *Scots Proverbs.*

The King rose up, wiped his eyes, and calling, "*Todlaurie,* come out o' your den [Fox, come out of your hole]," he produced from behind the arras the length of Richie Moniplies, still laughing in unrestrained mirth. — SCOTT : *Fortunes of Nigel.*

Toddy, a mixture of whisky with hot water and sugar. It has been generally supposed that the name was introduced into Scotland by some retired East Indian, from *toddy,* a juice extracted from various species of palm trees, especially from the *cocos nocifera,* which, when fermented and distilled, was known as *arrack.* But this is doubtful. In Allan Ramsay's poem of " The Morning Interview," published in 1721, occurs a description of a sumptuous entertainment or tea-party, in which it is said "that all the rich requisites are brought from far ; the table from Japan, the tea from China, the sugar from Amazonia, or the West Indies ; but that

Scotia does no such costly tribute bring,
Only some kettles full of *Todian* spring."

To this passage Allan Ramsay himself appended the note— " The Todian spring, *i.e.,* *Tod's well,* which supplies Edinburgh with water." Tod's well and St. Anthony's well, on the side of Arthur's seat, were two of the wells which very scantily supplied the wants of Edinburgh ;

and when it is borne in mind that whiskey (see that word) derives its name from water, it is highly probable that *Toddy* in like manner was a facetious term for the pure element. The late Robert Chambers, when this etymology was first propounded to him by the present writer, rejected the idea, but afterwards adopted it on the strength of Allan Ramsay's poem.

Tol-lol, a slang expression, common to Scotland and England, as a reply to an inquiry after one's health. " How are you ? " " Oh, *tol-lol !* " *i.e.,* pretty well. The word is usually supposed to be a corruption of *tolerable,* or *tolerably well.* Perhaps it comes more probably from the Gaelic *toileil,* substantial, solid, sound, in good condition.

Toman or **tommack,** a small hill, a hillock, a mound of earth ; from the Gaelic *tom,* a hill. This primitive monosyllable is widely spread over all the languages of Western Europe, and enters into the composition of numberless words that imply the sense of swelling above the surface ; as in the Latin *tumulus,* a mound of earth that marks a grave ; the English *tomb,* the French *tombeau,* the Keltic and Kymric *tom,* a mound, a heap ; the Latin *tumor, tume*faction, a pimple, a swelling of the flesh ; *tumescere,* to swell up ; the English and French *dome,* the Italian *duomo,* the German, Dutch, and Flemish *dom*, the Latin and Greek *doma*, the rounded roof or cupola, swelling over a church or cathedral, and also the cathedral itself; as "il *duomo*" at Milan, and the "*Dom* kirke" at Cologne. *Tom*, in the secondary sense, signifies large, from the primary idea of that which is swollen; a *tom* cat is a large cat; *tom* noddy is a great noddy or simpleton; *tom* fool is a great fool; and *tom*-boy, when applied as a reproach to a romping or noisy girl, signifies that she acts more like a great boy than like a girl.

Singing a song to the Queen o' the Fairies, among the *tomans* o' the ancient woods.—*Noctes Ambrosianæ.*

Tongue-ferdy, glib of tongue, loquacious, over ready of speech. From the German *zung*, Flemish and Dutch *tong*, the tongue; and *fertig*, ready.

Tongue-tackit, tongue-tied, either from natural impediment, or from nervous timidity and inability to speak when there is occasion to declare one's self; also, undue reticence, when there is a necessity for speaking out.

Toom or tume, empty, poured out; from the Gaelic *taom*, to pour out, the English *teem*, to produce, to pour out progeny. *Toom-handit*, empty-handed; *toom*-headit, brainless, empty-headed; a *toom* pock, an empty purse. The word is used in Lancashire, according to Tim Bobbin's Glossary.

Better a *toom* house than an ill tenant.
—*Allan Ramsay's Scots Proverbs.*

Scotland greetin' owre her thrissle,
Her mutchkin stoup as *toom's* a whistle.
—*Burns : Earnest Cry and Prayer.*

Mr. Clark of Dalreoch, whose head was vastly disproportioned to his body, met Mr. Dunlop one day. "Weel, Mr. Clark, that's a great head o' yours." "Indeed, it is, Mr. Dunlop; I could contain yours inside o' my own." "Just so," echoed Mr. Dunlop, "I was e'en thinking it was *gey* an *toom*."—*Dean Ramsay.*

On being called upon to give his vote in the choice of a chaplain to the prison of Dunfermline, David Dewar signified his assent to the election of the candidate recommended by the Board, by saying, "Weel, I've no objection to the man, for I understand that he has preached a kirk *toom* already; and if he be as successful in the jail, he'll maybe preach it vacant as weel."—*Dean Ramsay.*

A *toom* pouch maks a sair heart. But why should it? Surely a heart's worth mair than a pouch, whether it's *toom* or brimming ower?—*Donald Cargill.*

"Set on them, lads!" quo' Willie, then,
"Fie, lads! set on them cruellie,
For ere they win to the Ritterford
Mony a *toom* saddle there sall be."
—*James Telfer : Border Minstrelsy.*

Toot, or **tout,** to noise a thing abroad, to spread a rumour or a scandal; also, to blow a horn.

It was *tootit* through a' the country.
. . . The kintra claiks were *tootit* far and wide.—*Jamieson.*

But now the Lord's ain trumpet *touts*,
'Till a' the hills are rairin'.
—*Burns : The Holy Fair.*

An auld *tout* in a new horn.

Every man can *tout* best on his ain horn.

It's ill making a *touting* horn of a tod's tail.
—*Allan Ramsay's Scots Proverbs.*

In English slang, a *tout* is one stationed outside of a shop or place of amusement, to entice people to enter; metaphorical for blowing the trumpet, *i.e.*, praising the goods, or entertainment, to be had within. From the Gaelic *dud*, a trumpet; *dudair*, a trumpeter. The Germans call the bagpipe a *dudelsack*, *i.e.*, a trumpet sack.

Toothills—or hills where in early times a horn was blown to give warning of danger — are frequently mentioned in old records, and the name still subsists. *Tothill* or *Toothill* Fields in London was so called from an eminence of the kind in the borough of Southwark.

Tory, a word of contemptuous anger for a child, equivalent to *brat*. Jamieson cites it as an Ayrshire expression—" Get out of my sight, ye vile little *tory*." It is obvious that the word has no political origin, and is possibly from the Gaelic *torrach*, pregnant, and *toradh* (*dh* silent), the fruit or produce of pregnancy, *i.e.*, a child.

Tosh, neat, trim, cozy, comfortable; *toshach*, a neat, tidy-looking girl; *tossie*, warm and snug, —almost synonymous with *cozie*. Of uncertain etymology. Jamieson derives it from the Flemish *dossen*, to dress, to adorn; but the Gaelic offers *dos*, a bush, a thicket, a bield, a shelter, which has become slang among Eng-

lish tramps and vagrants, to signify a lodging. It is possible that the idea of comfortable shelter, in the sense of the proverb, " Better a wee bush than nae bield," lies at the root of *tosh* and *tozie*.

> She works her ain stockings, and spins her
>   ain cleedin',
> And keeps herself *tosh* frae the tap to the
>   tae.
> —JAMES BALLANTINE : *Auld Janet.*

Tot, a fondling name for a child that is learning to walk; from whence *tottle*, and *toddle*, to walk with slow, feeble, and uncertain step. From the Gaelic *tuit*, to fall. (See TOTUM.)

Tottie, warm, snug, comfortable. From the Gaelic *teth*, warmth ; *teodh*, to warm ; and *teodhaichte*, warmed ; whence also *tottle*, to boil, or the bubbling noise made by boiling liquids.

Totum, a term of affection for a child just beginning to walk, and sometimes falling in the process; from the Gaelic *tuit*, to fall. From the same root comes the name of the spinning and falling toy, the *teetotum ;* and English *tot*, a child.

> Twa-three toddlin' weans they hae,
>   The pride o' a' Strabogie ;
> Whene'er the *totums* cry for meat,
>   She curses aye his cogie.
> —*Song : There's Cauld Kail in Aberdeen.*

The Scotch have carried the word *totum* with them to the United States. It occurs in a ridiculous rhyme concerning the negroes—

De Lord He lub de nigger well,
He know de nigger by um smell;
And when de nigger *totums* cry,
De Lord He gib 'em possum pie.

The English word *teetotum*, is a child's toy, or kind of top to be twisted round by the fingers and spun on a table. Stormonth's Dictionary defines it, in addition to its ordinary use as a toy, to mean "any small thing in contempt," and suggests that the word is probably imitative of its unsteady movements when nearly spent. *Teetotum* is an amplification of the Gaelic, from its tendency to fall; *tuiteam*, let me fall.

Toun's Bairn, a name affectionately applied to the native of a town or city, after he has risen to distinction and established a claim to the respect of the inhabitants.

Toustie, quarrelsome, irascible, contentious, twisty. From the Gaelic *tuas*, and *tuasaid*, a quarrel; *tuasaideach*, quarrelsome.

Mr. Treddles was a wee *toustie*, when you rubbed him against the hair, but a kind, weel-meaning man.—SCOTT: *Chronicles of the Canongate.*

Touttie, totey, irritable, irascible, of capricious and uncertain temper. Derived by Jamieson from the Flemish *togtig*, windy, a word which is not to be found in the Dutch or Flemish dictionaries.

Tove, to associate kindly as friends or lovers; to "*tove* and crack," to hold amorous or friendly discourse. *Tovie*, comfortable; a *tovie* fire, a snug, cozy, or comfortable fire. From the Gaelic *taobh* (pronounced *taov*), a side, a liking, partiality, friendship; *taobhach*, kindly, friendly. *Tovie* is an epithet sometimes used to signify that a man is garrulously drunk.

Tow, a rope, also the hemp of which ropes are made; to pull by a rope. *Towing-path* by a canal, the path by which men or horses *tow* or pull the vessels through the water. To wallop in a *tow*, to dangle from the gallows.

And ere I wed another jade,
I'll wallop in a *tow*.
—BURNS: *The Weary Pund o' Tow.*

I hae another *tow* on my rock [I have other business to attend to].—*Scots Proverb.*

Jamieson derives *tow* from the Swedish *tog*, the substance of which ropes are made. It is more likely from the Gaelic *taod*, a rope, a string, a halter.

Towdy, a jocular term for the breech, fundament, podex, or doup, especially when abnormally large. From this word comes the English *dowdy*, applied to an ill-dressed and unshapely woman, large in the hips. The derivation is possibly from the Gaelic *doideach*, fleshy, muscular.

Towhead, a head with flaxen or very light-coloured hair. A term used in America, according to Bartlett's Dictionary of Americanisms, for "a flaxen-headed urchin."

Towmond, a twelvemonth.

How 'twas a *towmond* auld, sin' lint was
i' the bell.
—Burns : *Cotter's Saturday
Night.*

Surrounded wi' peat an' wi' heather,
Where muircocks and plovers were rife,
For mony a long *towmond* together
There lived an auld man an' his wife.
—Andrew Scott : *Symon and
Janet.*

Towzie, rough, hairy, shaggy; whence *towzer*, the name sometimes applied in England to a terrier.

His *touzie* back
Weel clad wi' coat o' glossy black.
—Burns : *The Twa Dogs.*

A *touzie* tyke, black, grim, and large,
To gie them music was his charge.
—Burns : *Tam o' Shanter.*

Toy, a woman's cap. This word is probably from the Gaelic *toil*, pleasure, applied to the finery with which it is the *pleasure*, and often the *toil*, of women to adorn or attire themselves, and was originally given to the ordinary *mutch* or indoor head-dress when bedizened with ribbons.

Toyte, to dawdle, to take things easily; from the Gaelic *taite*, ease, pleasure.

We've won to crazy years thegither,
We'll *toyte* about wi' ane anither,
Wi' tentie care I'll flit thy tether

To some hain'd rig,
Where ye may doucely rax your leather
Wi' sma' fatigue.
—Burns : *Auld Farmer to his Auld
Mare, Maggie.*

Traik, to lounge, to gad about, to follow idly after women; from the Flemish *trekken*, to walk, to draw or pull along.

There is not a huzzy on this side of thirty that ye can bring within your doors, but there will be chiels, writer lads, 'prentice lads, and what not, come *traiking* after them for their destruction.—Scott : *Heart of Midlothian.*

Trattle. The resemblance of this word to *prattle*, from *prate*, has led Jamieson and others to suppose that its meaning is identical. But it is by no means clear that the supposition is well founded, or that *trattle*, *prattle*, and *rattle* are related in meaning, notwithstanding the similarity of sound. The word seems to be akin to, or to be derived from, the German *trotzen*, the Flemish *trots*, to dare, to defy, to be arrogant or presumptuous ; *trotzig*, violent.

Oh better I'll keep my green cleiding
Frae gude Earl Richard's bluid,
Than thou canst keep thy clattering tongue
That *trattles* in thy head.
—Earl Richard : *Border
Minstrelsy.*

Against the proud Scots clattering
That never will leave their *trattling*.
—Skelton : *Against the Scottis,
quoted by* Sir Walter Scott
in Border Minstrelsy.

The German and Flemish *trotzen* would more fully meet the meaning and spirit of the epithet than any derivation from *prattle* could pretend to.

Treacherous as Garrick, false as Garrick, deep as Garrick. These phrases are current in England as well as in Scotland, and can have no possible connection with the name of Garrick, or to the renowned actor who bore it in the last century. The true origin is unknown. It is possible, however, that *treacherous as Garrick* may mean treacherous as a *caoireagh* (or *caoircach*), Gaelic for a blazing fire. This suggestion is offered *faute de mieux*. A Highlander, however, is of opinion that *Garrick* is a corruption of *coruisg*, a deep, gloomy, and treacherous loch in the island of Skye. "Who shall decide when doctors disagree?"

Trig, neat, clean, attractive; usually derived from the English *trick* or *tricky*, which has not the same meaning. Also, a fop, or a person giving too much attention to his personal appearance.

It is my humour: you are a pimp and a
trig,
An Amadis de Gaul, or a Don Quixote.
—BEN JONSON : *The Alchemist.*

And you among them a', John,
Sae *trig* from top to toe.
—BURNS : *John Anderson.*

The word seems to be derived from the Dutch and Flemish *trek*, to attract. Though Jamieson derives it from the English *trick*, or *trick* out, to dress

gaudily or finely, it is possibly either from the Welsh or Kymric *trig*, firm-set, or the Gaelic *triathach* (*th* silent, *triac*), splendid.

Trimmer, trimmie, disrespectful terms applied to a scolding or irascible woman. From the Gaelic *dream*, or *tream*, to snarl, to grin angrily; *dreamach*, morose, peevish, ill-natured; *dreamag*, or *dréimeag*, a vixen, a shrew.

Troggin, wares exchanged with servant girls for the odds and ends of a household by travelling pedlars ; *trog*, old clothes ; *trogger*, or *trocker*, a pedlar, one who deals in old clothes. It is doubtful whether these words are from the French *troquer*, to barter, the English *truck*, or from the Dutch and Flemish *troggelen*, to beg under pretence of selling trifles that nobody requires. The word appears as *troke* in Halliwell's Archaic Dictionary.

Buy braw *troggin,*
Frae the banks o' Dee ;
Wha' wants *troggin,*
Let him come to me.
—BURNS : *An Election Song.*

Trolollay, a term which, according to Jamieson, occurs in a rhyme sung by young people in Scotland at Hogmanay, the last day of the old year, and the morning of the new. "It has," he says, "been viewed as a corruption of the French *trois rois* *allais,* three kings are come!" In this sentence the word *allais* is ungrammatical and incorrect, for *trois rois sont venus.* But independently of the bad French, the etymology is entirely wrong. The word, or words, are part of a very ancient Druidical chorus, sung two thousand years ago at the dawning of the day, in honour of the sunrise: *trà là là!* From the Gaelic *tràth (tra),* early; and *là,* day, signifying not "the three kings are come," but "Day! early day!" equivalent to the "Hail, early morn!" of a well-known modern song.

Tron. There is a *Tron* Church in Edinburgh and another in Glasgow ; but the Scottish Glossaries and Jamieson's "Scottish Dictionary" make no mention of the word. It would appear from a passage in Hone's "Every-day Book" that *Tron* signified a public weighing-machine, or scale in a market-place, where purchasers of commodities might, without fee, satisfy themselves that the weight of their purchase was correct. Hence a "*Tron* Church" was a church in the market-place near which the public weighing - machine was established. The word is derived from the Gaelic *trom,* heavy, or a weight.

Tronie, a tedious story that has been often repeated, and that causes a sense of weariness in the person condemned to listen to it. From the Gaelic *trom* or *tron,* heavy, tedious. The same epithet is applied to a boy who is unable to learn his lessons.

Trow or **drow,** the evil one. From the Gaelic *droch,* evil, bad, wicked. *Sea trowes,* evil spirits of the sea ; to *trow,* or *drow,* to wish evil, to imprecate.

Trullion, a low, base, dirty fellow. The English has *trull,* the feminine of this word, applied to an immoral woman of the lowest class. The origin is the Gaelic *truaill,* to pollute, to debase; and *truilleach,* a base, dirty person.

Tryste, an appointed place of meeting, a rendezvous ; of the same origin as *trust,* or confidence, from the idea that he who appoints a *tryste* with another *trusts* that the other will keep or be faithful to it. The word occurs in Chaucer, and in several old English MSS. of his period; but is not used by Spenser, Shakspeare, or later writers. "To bide *tryste,*" to be true to time and place of meeting.

"You walk late, sir," said I. "I bide *tryste,*" was the reply, "and so I think do you, Mr. Osbaldistone?"—SIR WALTER SCOTT: *Rob Roy.*

The tenderest-hearted maid
That ever bided *tryste* at village stile.
—TENNYSON.

By the wine-god he swore it, and named the *trysting*-day.
—LORD MACAULAY.

No maidens with blue eyes
Dream of the *trysting* hour
Or bridal's happier time.
—*Under Green Leaves.*

When I came to Ardgour I wrote to Lochiel to *tryste* me where to meet him.—HOGG'S *Jacobite Relics: Letter from Rob Roy to General Gordon.*

Tuath de Danaan. This name has been given to a colony of northmen who early settled in Ireland, and afterwards passed into Argyllshire. From *tuath,* north ; *tuathach,* northern ; and *dan,* bold, warlike ; and *danfher,* (*dan-er*), a warrior, a bold man ; and also a *Dane. Tuath de Danaan* is a corruption, in which the second word *de* ought to have no place of *tuathaich* and *dan* or *dana.* The Very Rev. Canon Bourke, in his work on the Aryan origin of the Gaelic language, says "The *Tuath de Danaans* were a large, fair-complexioned, and very remarkable race, warlike, energetic, progressive, musical, poetical, skilled in Druidism," &c. Mr. Pym Yeatman, in "The Origin of the Nations of Europe," who quotes these and other passages, is of opinion that the *Tuath de Danaans* were Scandinavians, a supposition which their Gaelic designation fully corroborates. Of course they brought with them their own language, many of the words of which were in course of time incorporated with the speech of the people with whom they amalgamated.

This accounts for the many Danish words both in modern Gaelic and in Lowland Scotch.

Tuilyie or **toolzie,** a broil, a struggle, a quarrel ; *tuiliesome,* quarrelsome ; *tuilzeour,* a quarrelsome person, a wrangler. Though Jamieson derives *tuilzie* from the French *touiller*—a word which is not to be found in the French dictionaries—to stir or agitate water, it is probably derived from the same source as the quasi-synonymous English *tussle,* and akin to the Gaelic *tuisleach,* a tumult, a quarrel among several persons ; and *tuileas,* riot ; whence, also, *towzle,* to pull about roughly, to dishevel or disorder.

A *toolying (toolzieing)* tyke comes limping home.—ALLAN RAMSAY'S *Scots Proverbs.*

The *toolzie's* teugh 'tween Pitt and Fox,
And our gude wife's wee birdie cocks.
BURNS : *Elegy on the Year* 1788.

But though dull prose folk Latin splatter
In logic *tulzie,*
I hope we bardies ken some better
Than mind sic *brulzie.*
—BURNS : *To William Simpson.*

What verse can sing, what prose recite,
The butcher deeds of bloody fate
Amid this mighty *tulzie.*
—BURNS : *Epistle to Robert Graham.*

Tulcan. Mr. Gladstone, during his electioneering raid into Midlothian, in November 1879, explained at Dalkeith the meaning of *tulcan.*

My noble friend, Lord Rosebery, speaking to me of the law of hypothec, said that the bill of Mr. Vans Agnew on hypothec is a *Tulcan Bill.* A *tulcan,* I, believe, is a figure of a calf stuffed with straw, and it is, you know, an old Scottish custom among farmers to place the *tulcan calf* under a cow to induce her to give milk.

Jamieson writes the word *tulchane*, and cites the phrase a *tulchane bishop*, as the designation of one who received the episcopate on condition of assigning the temporalities to a secular person. In some parts of Scotland the people say a *tourkin calf*, instead of a *tulcan calf*, and it is difficult to say which of the two words is the more correct, or in what direction we must look for the etymology. *Tulcan*, in the Gaelic, signifies a hollow or empty head, that of the mocked calf stuffed with straw, from *toll*, hollow, and *cean*, a head; while *tourkin* would seem to be derived from *tur*, to invent, and *cean*, a head; therefore signifying a head invented for the occasion, to deceive the mother.

A *tourkin calf*, or lamb, is one that wears a skin not its own. A *tourkin lamb* is one taken from its dam, and given to another ewe that has lost her own. In this case, the shepherd takes the skin of the dead lamb, and puts it on the back of the living one, and thus so deceives the ewe that she allows the stranger to suck.— JAMIESON.

Tumbler, a drinking-glass of a larger size than is ordinarily used for wine. The derivation may be from *tumble*, to fall over; as in the deep drinking days, happily passed away, glasses were round at the base, without stems, and a drinker who held one full in his hand had to drink off the contents, before he could set it down, without spilling the liquor. "Tak' a *tumbler*," *i.e.*, take a glass of toddy, is a common invitation to convivial intercourse. "Three *tumblers* and an eke" were once considered a fair allowance for a man after dinner, or before retiring to rest. A Highland writer once suggested that the derivation was from *taom*, pour out or empty, and *leor*, enough. This was apt, and may perhaps be the true etymology. Jamieson has *tumbler*, the French *tombril*, a cart; but this can have no relation to the convivial glass.

Tum-deif. Jamieson suggests that perhaps this word means *swooning*, and refers it to the Icelandic *tumba*, the English *tumble*, to fall to the ground. It seems, however, to be no other than a mis-spelling of *dumb-deaf*, or *deaf and dumb*.

Tumph, a blockhead. From the German *dumm*, stupid, the Dutch and Flemish *dom*. *Tumfie*, or *tumphie*, is diminutive of *tumph*.

Lang Jamie was employed in trifling jobs on market days, especially in holding horses for the farmers. He was asked his charge by a stranger to the town. "Hoot! I hae nae charge; sometimes a *tumph* offers me twa bawbees, but a gentleman like you always gies me a saxpence!"— *Laird of Logan.*

Tunag, a kind of jacket worn by women in the Highlands

of Scotland and in Ireland, and covering the shoulders, back, and hips; a *tunic.* "If not derived from the Latin *tunica,*" says Jamieson, "*it may be from the same root.*" It *is* from the same root in a language much older than the Latin —the Celtic and Gaelic *ton,* the posterior, the hips. The Greeks called that part of the body πυγη, whence, in the learned slang of the English universities, the coat-tails were called "pygastoles," and by some irreverent undergraduates, "bum curtains." The word in Scottish Gaelic is *tonag,* and in Irish Gaelic *tonach.*

Turnimspike, a name given by the Highlanders to a high road or turnpike road when first made to the north of Inverness. Great consternation is said to have been excited in Ross-shire when a sheriff's officer and a toll-collector first appeared in Tain. "Lord preserve us !" said one townsman to his neighbour, "what'll come next ? The law has reached Tain ! "

Another law came after this,
   She never saw the like, man,
They mak a lang road on the crund
                       (the ground)
An' ca' him *turnimspike,* man.
But she'll awa to Highland hills
   Where deil a ane can turn her,
And no come near to *turnimspike,*
   Unless it be to burn her.
         —*Jacobite Songs and Ballads.*

Tutti, tatie, according to Jamieson, is an interjection equiva-

lent to the English *pshaw !* But *Hey ! tuttie tatie* is the name of an old Scottish martial air, to which Burns adapted his noble song of "Scots wha hae wi' Wallace bled." To this spirited melody, according to tradition, the troops of King Robert Bruce marched to the great victory of Bannockburn. The words are derived from the Gaelic, familiar to the soldiers of Bruce, *aite dudach taite !* from *dudach,* to sound the trumpet, and *taite,* joy, and may be freely translated, "Let the joyous trumpets sound ! " The battle of Bannockburn was fought in an age when the bagpipe had not become common in Scotland, and when the harp was pre-eminently the national instrument in peace as the trumpet was in war. Jamieson, not quite sure of *Pshaw* as an interpretation, adds that "the words may have been meant as imitative of the sound of the trumpet in giving the charge."

It may be remarked that possibly there may be a remote connection between Jamieson's idea of *Pshaw* and that of the blast of trumpets. *Fanfare* in French signifies a blast on a trumpet, and a *fanfaron* is a braggadocio, a vain boaster, a braggart, or one who blows the trumpet of his own praises. For such a one in the full flow of his self-laudation, the impatient interjection, *Pshaw !* would be equally appropriate and well-merited.

When you hear the trumpet sound
  Tutti tatti to the drum,
Up your sword, and down your gun,
  And to the loons again !
    —*Jacobite Relics :* WHEATLEY'S
      *Reduplicated Words in the
      English Language.*

Tut-mute and tuilzie mulzie, described in Wheatley's Dictionary of Reduplicated Words " as a muttering or grumbling between parties that has not yet assumed the form of a broil." This odd phrase, signifying a fierce quarrel that had but slight beginning, is presented in the proverb—

It began in a laigh *tute-mute*,
An' it rose to a wild *tuilzie mulzie*.
    —JAMIESON.

Tut is the Gaelic *dud*, the sound or *toot* upon a wind instrument, a horn, a flute, a whistle or a trumpet—and *mute* is a corruption of *maoth*, soft, gentle. *Tuilzie* is a brawl, a scuffle, a fight, from the ´Gaelic *tuaileas*, riot, disorder, conflict, tumult ; *tuaileasag*, a quarrelsome, foul-mouthed woman ; a scold, and *mileadh*, battle. The proverb expresses a meaning similar to that in Allan Ramsay—" It began wi' needles and pins, and ended wi' horned nowte."

Twasome, threesome, foursome. The numerals two, three, and four, with the addition of the syllable *some*, are used in a sense of which they are not susceptible in English. A *twasome* walk, or a *twasome* interview, is often rendered in English by the French phrase *tête-à-tête*.

Threesome and *foursome* reels, dances in which three or four persons participate.

There's *threesome* reels and *foursome* reels,
There's hornpipes and strathpeys, man,
But the best dance in a' the toun
. Is the Deil's awa' wi' the Exciseman.
    —BURNS.

Tway, a pair, a couple, the English *twain ;* two, sometimes written *twa*.

Every knight had a lady bright,
  And every squire a May ;
Her own self chose Lord Livingstone—
  They were a lovely *tway*.
    —BUCHAN'S *Ancient Ballads : Lord
      Livingstone.*

Twime and thrime, a couplet and a triplet. These are words that have not yet been admitted into the dictionaries.

Twine, to rob, to deprive ; to part with, to relinquish. Etymology uncertain ; supposed to be from the English *twain*, two, thence to separate into two.

The fish shall swim the flood nae mair,
  Nor the corn grow through the day,
Ere the fiercest fire that ever was kindled
  Twine me and Rothiemay.
    —*Ballad of the Fire of Frendraught.*

My duddie is a cankert carle
  Will no *twine* wi' his gear.
    —JAMES CARNEGIE.

Brandy . . .
Twines many a poor, doylt, drucken hash
  Of half his days.
    —BURNS : *Scotch Drink*.

Tyke, a mongrel, a rough dog ; originally a house dog ; from the Gaelic *tigh*, or *taigh*, a house. The word is common in Yorkshire, and in all the Northern Counties of England.

Tyke-tyrit or **tired.** Tired or wearied, as a dog or *tyke* after a long chase.

> Base *tyke*, call'st thou me host?
> —SHAKSPEARE: *Henry V.*

Nae tawted (uncombed) *tyke*.
—BURNS: *The Twa Dogs.*

He was a gash and faithful *tyke*.
—*Idem.*

I'm as tired of it as a *tyke* of lang kail.

You have lost your own stomach and found a *tyke's*.
—ALLAN RAMSAY'S *Scots Proverbs.*

U

Ug, ugg, to feel extreme loathing or disgust. *Ugsome,* frightful; *ugsomeness,* frightfulness, horror.

> They would *ug* a body at them.
> —JAMIESON.

> *Ugsome* to hear was her wild eldrich shriek.
> .   .   .   .   .   .
> The *ugsomeness* and silence of the night.
> —DOUGLAS: *Translation of the Enid.*

> Who dang us and flang us into this *ugsome* mire.
> —ALLAN RAMSAY: *The Vision.*

This word seems to be akin to the English *ugly,* which all the philologists who ignore the Gaelic as one of the sources of the English language, derive either from the Danish *huggern,* to shiver, or from other equally improbable Teutonic roots. In Gaelic *aog* (quasi *ug*), signifies death, a ghost, a skeleton, and *aogail,* ghastly, deathlike, *ugly.*

Ultimus eekibus, the very last glass of whisky toddy, or *eke,* one drop more at a convivial gathering before parting for the night; the last of the *ekes.*

Umbersorrow, hardy, rough, rude, uncultivated. This corrupt word, of which Jamieson cites a still corrupter, "a *number sorrow*," is clearly derived from the Flemish and Teutonic *unbesorgt,* uncared for, wild, neglected, growing in the strength of nature without human assistance. Jamieson cites its use in the Lothians in the sense of "rugged, of a surly disposition," applied to one whose education has been neglected, and who is without good manners.

Umquhile or **umwhile,** at one time, formerly; used also in the sense of departed or late, in such phrases as, "my late husband," "my departed wife," my *umquhile* husband, my *umquhile* wife; from the Flemish *om,* past, and *wijl,* a short time, the same as the English *while,* a short time past, a short while ago.

Unco, strange, unknown, a wonder, a strange thing; an abbreviation of *uncouth*. *Unco guid*, extremely good, very good.

The *unco* guid, and the rigidly righteous.
—BURNS.

An *unco* cockernony.—GALT.

Nae safe wading in *unco* waters.

Like a cow in an *unco* loan.
—ALLAN RAMSAY'S *Scots Proverbs*.

Each tells the *uncos* that he sees or hears.
—BURNS : *Cotter's Saturday Night*.

Unfurthersome, unpropitious; applied to the weather, if too cold, or too rainy, and preventing the due ripening of the crops.

Ungainly, awkward, uncouth, insufficient, clumsy ; *gainly*, pleasant, fit, proper, pleased ; *gane*, to serve, to suffice, to fit, to be appropriate ; *unganed*, inappropriate. *Gainly* and *ungainly* are not exactly synonymous in Scottish parlance with the English word. *Gainly* is nearly obsolete in England ; and *ungainly* merely signifies awkward, clumsy. The root of the words in the Scottish sense is the Gaelic *gean*, good-humour, fitness, comeliness ; *geanail*, comely, fit, proper, pleasant, serviceable. In the following quotation *gane* means to serve or suffice :—

But there is neither bread nor kale
'To *gane* my men and me.
—*Battle of Otterbourne, Old Version.*

Unkensome, not to be known or recognised, not to be traced.

A smith ! a smith ! Dickie, he cries,
A smith, a smith right speedilie !
To turn back the caukers o' our horses'
shoon
For its *unkensome* we wad be.
—*Border Minstrelsy : Archie o' Ca'field.*

Unmackly, mis-shapen, deformed.

Up then sterts the stranger knight,
Said Ladye be not thou afraid,
I fight for thee with this grim Soldan
Though he's sair *unmackly* made.
—*Ballad of Sir Cauline.*

Untholeable, intolerable, unendurable, insufferable ; from *thole*, to endure.

He got *untholeably* divertin', and folk complained o' pains in their sides wi laughin'.—*Noctes Ambrosianæ.*

Updorrock, worn out, bankrupt. According to Jamieson, a Shetland word, which he derives from " Icelandic *app* and *throka*, also *thruka*, urgere, primere." It seems to be rather from the Flemish *op drogen*, dried up, exhausted.

Uppil, to clear up ; applied to the weather.

When the weather at any time has been wet, and ceases to be so, we say it is *uppled*.
—JAMIESON.

From the Teutonic *aufhellen—auf*, up ; *hellen*, to become clear, to clear up.

Upon luck's head, by chance. " I got it on *luck's head*," I got it by chance.

Urisk, according to Jamieson, was a name given in the Highlands of Scotland to a satyr. It was in reality the name given to a *Brownie* or Puck, the Robin Goodfellow of English fairy mythology ; from the Gaelic *uirisg*, a goblin. (See WIRRY-COW.

V

Vanquish, a disease among sheep and lambs, caused by their eating a certain unwholesome grass. Jamieson says the disease is so called because it *vanquishes* the sheep! He might as well account for the name of Kilmarnock, by stating that one Marnock was killed there. *Vanquish* is a corruption of the Gaelic *uain*, pale green, and *cuiscach* or *cuiscag*, a species of rank grass with a long stalk that grows on wet soil and is deleterious to cattle, and especially to sheep. *Cuiscach* is possibly the same as *couch* grass, described in Halliwell's Archaic and Provincial Dictionary as a kind of coarse grass that grows very quickly, and is sometimes called *twitch* grass.

Vaudy or **vaudie,** gay, showy; a corruption of the English *gaudy*.

Our land shall be glad, but the Whigs shall be sorry
When the King gets his ain, and heaven gets the glory;

The rogues shall be sad, but the honest man
vaudie
When the throne is possessed by our ain bonnie laddie.
—*Jacobite Relics of Scotland.*

Vauntie, proud, vain, also a braggart; from the French *vanter*, to boast.

Her cutty sark
In longitude though sorely scanty,
It was her best, and she was *vauntie.*
—BURNS: *Tam o' Shanter.*

Vir, force, vigour. Sometimes written *bir*, a vein; from the Latin *vis*, *vires*. Possibly the English *burly*, strong, is of kindred origin.

Swith with *vir* he whirled her round.
—GEORGE BEATTIE: *John o' Arnha'.*
Wi' vengeful *vir*, and Norland twang.—*Ibid.*

Vlonk, or **Wlonk,** splendidly dressed, richly attired; from the "Anglo Saxon" or old English *vlonke*, which has the same meaning. Possibly this may be the origin of the modern word *flunkey*, in contemptuous allusion to the grayish colours of the liveries of male servants in great ostentatious families. (See FLUNKEY, *ante*, p. 60).

W

Wa', abbreviation of wall. " His back is at the *wa'*," *i.e.,* he is driven into a corner; his back is at the wall, fighting against opposing enemies or creditors.

Wabster, a weaver; from weave and web.

Willie Wastle dwalt on Tweed,
The spot they ca'd it Linkum-doddie,
Willie was a *wabster* gude.
BURNS.

An honest *wabster* to his trade,
Whose wife's twa nieves were scarce weel bred.
—BURNS: *Death and Dr. Hornbook.*

Wad, to wager, to bet; from the Flemish *wedden*, which has the same meaning. *Wads* also signify forfeits; a game at *wads*, a game at forfeits; *wad-set*, a mortgage; *wad*, a pledge.

The gray was a mare and a right good mare,
But when she saw the Annan water,
She could not hae ridden a furlong mair,
Had a thousand merks been *wadded* at her.
—*Minstrelsy of the Scottish Border:
Annan Water.*

Wads are nae arguments.
—ALLAN RAMSAY'S *Scots Proverbs.*

My Sunday's coat she has laid it in *wad*,
And the best blue bonnet e'er was on my head;
At kirk or at market I'm covered but barely,
Oh that my wife would drink hooly and fairly.
—HERD'S *Collection: The Drucken
Wife o' Galloway.*

Waddie, vigorous, willing, alert, ready to do.

What fee will you give me for now and for aye—
Was e'er a young laddie sae *waddie* as I.
—BUCHAN'S *Ancient Ballads: The
Rigwoodie Carlin'.*

Wae's! woe is; unlucky, unhappy, in ill plight.

Wae's the wife that wants the tongue,
but wee's the man that gets her.
—ALLAN RAMSAY'S *Scots Proverbs.*

And aye the o'erword o' his sang
Was—*wae's* me for Prince Charlie.
—*Jacobite Song.*

Waesuck! wae's-heart! wae's-me! Interjections or expressions of surprise or sorrow, like *alas!*

Waesuck! for him that gets nae lass,
Or lasses that hae naething.
—BURNS: *The Holy Fair.*

The derivation of *wae's-heart* and *wae's-me*, from *wae*, sorrow, is obvious; that of *waesuck* is not so clear. It is probably from the Flemish *wee*, sorrow or love, and *sugt* or *zucht*, a sigh. Jamieson derives it from the Danish *usig*, woe to us; *vae nobis*, woe to us. The word, however, is not to be found in Danish dictionaries.

Waff, wauf, waft. A freak, a whiff, a wave of sound or of wind, a sudden and slight impression upon the senses, a transient glance, a glimpse, a passing odour. "A *waff* o' cauld" is a slight attack of cold. "I had a *waff* o' him i' the street;" I had a glimpse of him. "There was a *waff* o' roses;" there was a sudden odour of roses. The primitive idea at the root of the word is sudden and of short duration, rising and subsiding like a wave.

Waff, worthless, or shabby in appearance and conduct; idle, dissipated; *waffie*, a loafer, an idler, a vagrant, a vagabond; *waff-like*, resembling a vagabond in manners and appearance; *waffinger*, a confirmed vagrant and idler. These words are of uncertain etymology, though it is probable that they are all from the same root as the English *waif*, a stray, a vagrant, one who, like the

R

Italian *traviato* and *traviata*, has gone astray from the right and respectable path, and formed on the same principle from *way off*, or off the way. Another possible root is the Flemish *zwerfen* (with the elision of the initial *z*), to go astray, to vagabondise.

Wa'gang or **awa'-gang**, departure; *ganging awa'*, going away; an escape.

> Winter's *wa'gang*.
> —JAMES BALLANTINE.

A *wa'gang* crop is the last crop gathered before a tenant quits his farm; also the name given to the canal, through which the water escapes from the mill wheel.— JAMIESON.

> Its dowie in the end o' hairst,
> At the *wa'gang* o' the swallow,
> When the wind grows cauld and the burn grows bauld,
> And the weeds are hanging yellow;
> But oh, it's dowier far to see
> The *wa'gang* o' her that the heart gangs wi'.
> —HEW AINSLIE.

Waghorn. In the North of Scotland it is a proverbial phrase to say of a great liar that "he lies like *Waghorn*," or is "waur than *Waghorn*," that "he is as false as *Waghorn*, and *Waghorn* was nineteen times falser than the devil." Jamieson records that "*Waghorn* is a fabulous personage, who being a greater liar than the devil, was crowned King of Liars." Why the name of *Waghorn*, any more than that of *Wagstaffe*, both respectable patronymics, should be selected to adorn or to disfigure the proverb is not easy to explain, except on the supposition that the traditionary "*waghorn*" is a corruption of a word that has a more rational as well as a more definite meaning. And such it is found to be. In Gaelic *uaigh* (quasi *wag*) signifies the grave, the pit, and *iutharn* (*iuarn*, quasi *horn*) signifies hell, whence he lies like *Waghorn*, would signify he "lies like hell" or like the "pit of hell," consequently worse than the devil, who is supposed to be but one, while the other devils in the pit are supposed to be multitudinous.

Waif, a derelict, a wanderling; one found by accident after having been lost or gone astray. The word in this sense has lately been adopted into English literature as a noun; but in Scotland it is employed both as a noun and an adjective.

> Wi' her I will get gowd and gear,
> Wi' thee, I sall get nane;
> Ye cam to me as a *waif* woman,
> I'll leave thee as the same.
> —HERD'S *Collection: Fair Annie.*

This word, sometimes written and pronounced *waff, waffie,* and *waffinger,* signifies a wanderer, a strolling vagabond, lost to civilised life and society; *wafflike,* of vagabond and disreputable appearance.

Waith, to wander, a wandering and straying. The English *waif,* waifs and strays, things or persons that have wandered or gone astray. The etymology is doubtful; perhaps from *waft*, to be blown about by the wind, or carried by the waters.

Wale, to choose, to select, a choice; *waly*, choice. From the German *wahlen*, to choose.

> Scones, the *wale* o' food.
> —BURNS: *Scotch Drink.*

> There's auld Rob Morris that wons in yon glen,
> He's the king o' guid fellows and *wale* o' auld men.
> —BURNS.

The Laird of Balnamon, after dinner at a friend's house, had cherry brandy put before him in mistake for port. He liked the liquor, and drank freely of it. His servant Harry or "Hairy" was to drive him home in a gig. On crossing the moor, whether from greater exposure to the blast, or from the Laird's unsteadiness of head, his hat and wig fell to the ground. Harry got off to pick them up and restore them to his master. The Laird was satisfied with the hat, but demurred to the wig. "It's no my wig, Harry lad; it's no my wig." "Ye'd better tak it, sir," said Harry; "for there's nae *wale* o' wigs on the moor."—DEAN RAMSAY'S *Reminiscences.*

> He *wales* a portion wi' judicious care,
> And let us worship God, he says, wi' solemn air.
> —BURNS: *Cotter's Saturday Night.*

Wallageous. This obsolete word is used by the ancient Scottish poet, Barbour, in the sense of sportive, wanton, lustful. It is evidently a corruption of the Gaelic *uallach*, which has the same meaning; *uallachās*, cheerfulness, gaiety, frolicksomeness, conceitedness, wantonness; *uallachag*, a coquette.

Wallie, a toy; a *bonnie wallie*, a pretty toy; from *wale*, choice; from the Teutonic *wahlen*.

Walloch, a name applied in the Lowlands to the Highland fling, or other dance, and not to the reel, which is less active and boisterous. The word also means a *frisk* or *kick*. The word seems to be derived from the Gaelic *uallach*, joyous, frisky.

> I wat she was a cantie quean,
> And weel could dance the Highland *walloch*.
> —*Roy's Wife of Aldivalloch.*

> Auld Roy look'd as he gaed by,
> And oh! he gaed an unco *walloch;*
> And after them he soon did hie,
> And followed through the braes of Balloch.
> —BUCHAN'S *Collection of Old Scottish Ballads.*

The word is sometimes written *wallop*, as in the favourite song of "Maggie Lauder":—

> Meg up and *wallop'd* o'er the green,
> For brawly she could frisk it.

Walloch-goul, an abusive epithet applied to a wanton or arrogant blusterer; from the Gaelic *uallach*, and *guil*, to cry out. (See YOWL.)

Wallop, to dangle, to hang, to sway about with quick motion, to swing.

> Now let us lay our heads thegither,
> In love fraternal;
> May Envy *wallop* in a tether,
> Black fiend, infernal!
> —BURNS: *To Lapraik.*

Wallow, to fade away ; *wallowed*, faded, withered by cold, blight, or natural decay ; the etymon doubtless of the word *wilt*, in common use in America, and in some parts of England, of which a ludicrous example is given by the humorist, Artemus Ward : "I said to her, *wilt* thou ? and she *wilted.*" The derivation is uncertain, though probably from the Teutonic *welken*.

> The last time that I saw her face
> She ruddy was and red,
> But now, alas ! and woe is me,
> She's *wallowed* like a weed.
> —Scott's *Border Minstrelsy* : *Ballad of the Gay Goss-Hawk.*

Waly ! waly ! an interjection of sorrow ; *alas !* or, *woe is me !* Derived from *wail*, to lament, or *wail* ye ! lament ye ; the Teutonic *weh*, woe, and *wehlich*, woful.

> Oh *waly ! waly !* but love is bonnie,
> A little time while it is new ;
> But when it's auld it waxes cauld,
> And fades 'awa' like morning dew.
> —*Ballad of the Marchioness of Douglas.*

> Oh *waly ! waly !* up the bank,
> And *waly ! waly !* down the brae,
> And *waly ! waly !* yon burn side,
> Where I and my love wont to gae.
> —*Lady Anne Bothwell's Lament.*

Wame, the belly ; also the English word *womb*, which is from the same etymological root. The Scottish derivatives of *wame* are numerous ; among others, *wamie*, having much *wame*, *i.e.*, corpulent ; *wamieness*, corpulency ; *wamyt*, pregnant ; *wame-tow*, a belly-band or girth, from *wame*,

the belly, and *tow* (the Gaelic *taod*), a rope, a band ; *wamefu'*, a bellyfull.

> I never liked water in my shoon ; and my *wame's* made o' better leather.

> Wae to the *wame* that has a wilfu master.
> —Allan Ramsay's *Scots Proverbs.*

> Food fills the *wame*, and keeps us livin',
> Though life's a gift no worth receivin',
> When heavy dragged wi' pine and grievin'.
> —Burns : *Scotch Drink.*

> A *wamefu'* is a *wamefu'*, whether it be of barley-meal or bran.—Scott : *St. Ronan's Well.*

Wame has disappeared from English literature, but still survives in the current speech of the northern counties. *Womb*, in English, was formerly applied to the male sex, in the sense of the Scottish *wame*, or belly, as appears from Piers Ploughman :—

> Paul, after his preaching,
> Paniers he made,
> And wan with his handes
> What his *wombe* needed.

(Gained with his hands what his belly needed.) In recent times the word is restricted in its meaning to the female sex, though used metaphorically and poetically in such phrases as the "*womb* of Time."

> The earth was formed, but in the *womb* as yet
> Of waters, embryon immature.
> —*Paradise Lost.*

> Caves and *womby* vaultages of France
> Shall chide your trespass.
> —Shakspeare : *Henry V.*

Among the three interpretations of the word, as given by

Johnson, the last is "a cavity." The only traces of anything like *wame*, or *womb*, that appears in any of the Teutonic languages, or in high or low Dutch, is the Swedish *wam*, signifying tripe. Though Johnson derives *womb* from the Anglo-Saxon and from Icelandic, it may be suggested that the more ancient Celtic and Gaelic provides the true root of both *wame* and *womb* in *uaimh* and *uamh*, a cavity, a cave, a hollow place. The Shakspearean adjective *womby* finds its synonym in the Gaelic *uamhach*, abounding in cavities or hollows.

Wan, pale green, as applied to the colour of a river in certain states of the water and the atmosphere. Many philologists have been of opinion that *wan*, both in English and Scotch, always signifies pale. Jamieson, however, thought differently, and translated *wan* as "black, gloomy, dark-coloured, or rather filthy," not reflecting, however, that these epithets, especially the last, were hardly consistent with the spirit or dignity of the tender or tragical ballads in which *wan* occurred. The etymology of the English *wan* has been traced to *wane*, to decrease in health and strength, as well as in size, whence *wan*, the pallor of countenance that attends failing health. That of the Scottish *wan*, as applied to the colour of the streams, was for the first time suggested in "The Gaelic Etymology of the Languages of Western Europe." It is from the Gaelic *uaine*, a pale blue, inclining to green. This is the usual colour of the beautiful streams of the Highlands, when not rendered "drumlie" or muddy by the storms that wash down sand and earth from the banks.

On they rade, and on they rade,
  And a' by the light o' the moon,
Until they came to the *wan* water,
  And then they lighted down.
    —*The Douglas Tragedy.*

Deep into the *wan* water
  There stands a muckle stane.
    —*Earl Richard.*

The ane has ta'en him by the head,
  The ither by the feet,
And thrown him in the *wan* water
  That ran baith wide and deep.
    —*Lord William.*

There's no a bird in a' this forest
  Will do as muckle for me
As dip its wing in the *wan* water,
  And straik it ower my e'e bree.
    —*Johnnie o' Bradislee.*

In English, *wan* is never used as an epithet except when applied to the countenance, as in such phrases—"His face was pale and *wan*," and occasionally by poetic license, to the face of the moon, as in the beautiful sonnet of Sir Philip Sidney.

With how sad steps, oh moon! thou
  climb'st the sky,
How silently, and with how *wan* a
  face.

Wanchancie, unlucky, mischanceful.

Wae worth the man wha first did shape
That vile *wanchancie* thing—a rape.
    —BURNS: *Poor Mailie's Elegy.*

Wandought, weak, deficient in power; from *dow*, to be able; *doughty*, brave; and *wan*, or *un*, the privative particle. *Wandocht*, a weak, silly creature.

By this time Lindy is right well shot out
'Twixt nine and ten, I think, or thereabout,
Nae bursen-bailch, nae *wandought* or mis-
    grown,
But plump and swack, and like an apple
    roun'.
    —Ross's *Helenore.*

Wanhope, despair. Jamieson incorrectly renders it "delusive hope." This is an old English word which is nearly obsolete, but still survives in Scotland.

I sterve in *wanhope* and distress,—
Farewell, my life, my lust and my
    gladnesse.
    —CHAUCER: *The Knight's Tale.*

Good Hope that helpe shulde
To *wanhope* turneth.
    —*Piers Ploughman.*

Some philologists, misled by the prefix *wan*, have imagined that the word was synonymous with *wane*, and have interpreted *wanhope* as the "waning of hope." But *wan* is the Dutch and Flemish negative prefix, equivalent to the English and German *un*. Among other beautiful Scottish words which follow the Flemish in the use of the negative prefix, are *wanearthlie*, preternatural or unearthly; *wanfortune*, ill-luck; *wangrace*, wickedness, ungraciousness; *wanrest*, inquietude; *wanworth*, useless, valueless; *wanthrift*, prodigality, extravagance; *wanuse*, abuse; *wanwit* or *wanwith*, ignorance.

An' may they never learn the gaets (ways)
Of ither vile *wanrestful* pets.
    —BURNS: *Poor Mailie.*

Wanwierd, misfortune, ill-luck, calamity.

Nor wit, nor power, put off the hour
For his *wanwierd* decreed.
    —*Border Minstrelsy: The Water
        Kelpie.*

Wap, in England written *wad*, a bundle of straw, a wisp, used in the Scottish sense in the North of England; from the Flemish *hoop*, a bundle, a pile of hay or straw. To be in the *wap* or *wad*, to lie in the straw.

Moll i' the *wap* and I fell out,
I'll tell ye what 'twas a' about,—
She had siller and I had nane,
That was the gait the steer began.
    . —*Gipsy Song.*

The English version among the gipsies is—

Moll i' the *wad* and I fell out,
She had money and I had none,
That was the way the row began.

Ware, to spend, to guide, to control or guide one's expense discreetly.

My heart's blood for her I would freely
    ware,
Sae be I could relieve her of her care.
    —Ross's *Helenore.*

But aiblins, honest Master Heron
Had at the time some dainty fair one,
To *ware* his theologic care on.
    —BURNS: *To Dr. Blacklock.*

This word is most probably a corruption of the Teutonic *führen*, the Flemish *voeren*, to lead or guide.

Ill-won gear is aye ill *wared.*
—ALLAN RAMSAY'S *Scots Proverbs.*

[Ill-acquired money is always ill guided or spent.]

The best o' chiels are whyles in want,
While cuifs on countless thousands rant,
And ken na how to *ware't.*
BURNS : *Epistle to Davie.*

Warklike, Warkrife, industrious, fond of work.

Warklume, a tool, a working tool. The second syllable of this word remains in the English *loom,* part of the working apparatus of the weaver. In Scotland *lume* signifies any kind of tool or implement with which work can be done. Burns uses it in a very ludicrous sense in the "Address to the Deil."

Thence mystic knots mak great abuse
On young gudemen fond, keen, and crouse,
When the best *warklume* i' the house
 By cantrip wit,
Is instant made na worth a louse
 Just at the bit.

This peculiar superstition prevails among all the Celtic peoples of Europe, and is thought to be the favourite and most malignant diversion of the devil and his instruments, the wizards and witches, to prevent the consummation of marriage on the bridal night. A full account of the alleged practices of several sorcerers who were burnt at the stake in France in the Middle Ages, for their supposed complicity in this crime, appears in the "History of Magic in France," by Jules Garinet, Paris,

1818. The name given in France to the "cantrip" mentioned by Burns was *nouer l'aiguillette,* or, tie the little knot. One unhappy Vidal de la Porte, accused of being a *noueur d'aiguillette* by repute and wont, was in the year 1597 sentenced to be hung and burned to ashes for having bewitched in this fashion several young bridegrooms. The sentence was duly executed, amid the applause of the whole community.

Warld's gear, worldly wealth ; a word used for any valuable article of whatever kind, as in the phrases "I have nae *warld's gear,*" I have no property whatever ; "there's nae *warld's gear* in the glass but cauld water," nothing more costly than cold water.

But *warld's gear* ne'er fashes me,—
 My thocht is a' my Nannie, O.
 —BURNS.

Warlock, a wizard. The Scottish word, though admitted into the English dictionaries, is not common either in English conversation or literature.

She prophesied that late or soon
Thou would be found deep drowned in Doon,
Or catch'd by *warlocks* in the mirk,
By Alloway's auld haunted kirk.
 —BURNS : *Tam o' Shanter.*

In the ancient time of Druidism, a wizard, an augur, a prophet, or fortune-teller, was called a Druid, a name that is still retained in modern Gaelic. The Lowland Scotch *warlock* is derived, according to Jamieson, from the Icelandic *vardlokr*, a magic song or incantation for calling up evil spirits. Mr. Stormonth, in his Etymological Dictionary, refers the word to the Anglo-Saxon *waer*, wary, and *loga*, a liar. It is more probable, however, that the word had not this uncomplimentary meaning ; and that as *wizard* is derived from the German *weise* or *wise*, *warlock* has its root in a similar idea, and may come from the Gaelic *geur*, sharp, acute, cunning ; and *luchd*, folk. It was not customary in the days when witches and fairies were commonly believed in, to speak disrespectfully of them. The fairies were "the good folk," the wizard was "the wise man," and the witch, in Irish parlance, was the Banshee (*Bean-sith*), or woman of peace ; and *warlock*, in like manner, was an epithet implying the sagacity rather than the wickedness of the folk so designated. The change of the syllable *geur* into *war* is easily accounted for. The French *guerre* becomes *war* in English by the change—not uncommon —of *g* into *w*, as in *wasp*, from the French *guespe* or *guêpe*. Another possible derivation is suggested in the "Gaelic Etymology of the Languages of Western Europe," from *barr*, head, top, chief; and *loguid*, a rascal ; but the first is preferable.

Warple, to entangle, to intertwine wrongly. From the English

warp, to twist or turn aside, as in the phrase, "His judgment is *warped*." The root of both the Scottish and English is the Flemish *werwele*, to turn, or turn aside.

That yarn's sae *warplit* that I canna get it redd.
—JAMIESON.

Warsle, to wrestle, to contend, also to tumble violently after a struggle to keep the feet.

Upon her cloot (hoof) she coost (cast) a hitch
And ower she *warsled* in the ditch.
—BURNS : *Poor Mailie.*

Wast, west; often used in the north-east of Scotland for beyond, further off.

Sir Robert Liston, British Ambassador at Constantinople, found two of his countrymen who had been especially recommended to him in a barber's shop, waiting to be shaved in turn. One of them came in rather late, and seeing he had scarcely room at the end of the seat, addressed the other—"Neebour, wad ye sit a wee bit *wast ?*" What associations must have been called up in his mind by hearing, in a distant land, such an expression in Scottish tones!"—DEAN RAMSAY.

Wat, to know, to wit. Obsolete English *wot ;* Dutch and Flemish *weten.* *Watna*, wits not, knows not.

Little *wats* the ill-willy wife what a dinner may haud in't.

Dame! deem warily ; ye *watna* wha wytes yoursel.

Mickle water runs by that the miller *wats* na of.
—ALLAN RAMSAY's *Scots Proverbs.*

Wath, a ford ; a shallow part of the river that may be waded across. Either from the Flemish *waad*, or the Gaelic *ath*, a ford. Scotis-*wath* is the name given to the upper part of the Solway Firth, where, in certain states of the tide, people from the English side can wade across to Scotland.

Watter, water. The word is used in Scotland in the sense of a stream, a brook, a river; as in the phrase, "the *water* of Leith," and the Glasgow phrase, "Down the *water*," signifying down the Clyde. It is recorded of the noted Edinburgh advocate, John Clerk, afterwards Lord Eldin, that, in arguing a case of water privilege in Scotland before Lord Chancellor Eldon, he annoyed his lordship by constantly repeating the word *watter* with a strong Scottish accent. "Mr. Clerk," inquired his lordship, "is it the custom in your country to spell water with two *t's*?" "No, my lord," replied Clerk; "but it's the fashion in *my* country to spell *manners* wi' twa *n's*."

Wattie - wagtail. From *Walter Wagtail*, a name given to the beautiful little bird, the *hochequeue* of the French; the *motacilla yarrellie* of the naturalists. The English have corrupted the word, not knowing its Scottish origin, into "*water-wagtail*." *Walter*, or *Wattie*, is a fond alliteration formed on the same principle as that of *Robin Redbreast*. *Water-wagtail* is an appellation

given by the English to the pretty little creature, founded on the erroneous notion that it is an aquatic bird, or that it frequents the water more than it does the land. It comes with the flies and departs with the flies, which are its only food, and, unlike many other attractive birds, does no harm to fruit, blossoms, seeds, or any kind of vegetation. In some parts of Scotland it is called "*Wullie*," or "*Willie-wagtail*."

Wauchle, to weary; also, to puzzle, to sway from side to side ; English, to *waggle;* Flemish *waggelen*, to vacillate, to stagger.

The road *wauchlit* him sair (made him stagger with fatigue).

That question *wauchlit* him (staggered him.

—JAMIESON.

Waught, a large deep draught of liquor. The etymology is uncertain. In most of the glossaries to Burns' Poems the word is erroneously joined with "willy," and converted into "willy-*waught*," and described as meaning "a hearty draught." The line in "Auld Lang Syne," usually printed—

We'll drink a right gude willy-*waught*,

should be

We'll drink a right gude-willie *waught*:

i.e., we'll drink with right good will a deep or hearty *waught* or draught.

Dean Ramsay, whose undoubted knowledge and appreciation of the Scottish language should have taught him better, has fallen into the mistake of quoting *willie - waught* as one word in the following lines :—

Gude e'en to you a', and tak your nappy,
A "*willywaught*," a gude night cappy.

The word is introduced with fine effect in a translation from the Gaelic, by the Ettrick Shepherd, of the Jacobite Ballad, " The Frasers in the Correi : "—

Spier na at me !
Gae spier at the maiden that sits by the sea,
The red coats were here, and it was na for good,
And the ravens are hoarse in " the *waughting*" o' blood.

And meantime gies a *waught* o' caller whey,
The day's been hot, and we are wondrous dry.
—Ross's *Helenore.*

I'm sure 'twill do us meikle guid, a *waucht* o' caller air,
A caller douk, a caller breeze, and caller fish and fare.
—*Whistle Binkie : Doun the Water.*

Wauk, to render the palm of the hand hard, callous, or horny, by severe toil.

I held on high my *waukit* loof,
To swear by a' yon starry roof,
That henceforth I wad be rhyme proof,
Till my last breath.
—BURNS : *The Vision.*

Waukrife, watchful, wakeful, unable to sleep; the suffix *rife*, as in cauld*rife*, very cold, is used as an intensitive, so that *waukrife* signifies not only unable

to sleep, but unable in an intense degree.

What time the moon, wi' silent glower,
Sets up her horn,
Wail through the dreary midnight hour,
Till *waukrife* morn.
—BURNS : *Elegy on Captain Matthew Henderson.*

'Tis hopeless love an' dark despair,
Cast by the glamour o' thine e'e,
That clouds my *waukrife* dreams wi' care,
An' maks the daylight dark to me.
—JAMES BALLANTINE.

Waullies or **waulies.** Jamieson defines *wallies* as meaning the intestines. The word is not to be confounded with *waly* or *walie*, choice, large, ample, as Burns uses it.

But mark the rustic haggis-fed,
The trembling earth resounds his tread ;
Clap in his *walie* nieve a blade,
He'll mak it whistle.
—*To a Haggis.*

In " Jacob and Rachel," a song attributed to Burns, published in an anonymous London edition of his songs, dated 1825, the word occurs in the following stanza :—

Then Rachel, calm as ony lamb,
She claps him on the *waulies*,
Quo' she, " ne'er fash a woman's clash."

In this song, omitted on account of its grossness from nearly all editions of his works, the word is not susceptible of the meaning attributed to it by Jamieson, nor of that in the poem in praise of "The Haggis." Jamieson has the obsolete word . *wally*, a billow, a wave, which affords a clue to its derivation.

The name of *waulie* was given to the hips or posteriors on account of their round and wavy form, as appears from the synonymous words in Gaelic— *tonn*, a wave, and *ton*, the breech. The idea is involved in the words, now seldom used, which are cited by Jamieson, *wallie-drag*, and *wallie-dragglie*, signifying a woman who is corpulent and heavy behind, and makes but slow progress in walking. The connection with *wallies*, intestines, as rendered by Jamieson, is exceedingly doubtful.

Waur, worse. To *waur*, or *warr*, to conquer, to give an enemy the worst of the conflict; from *worst*, to put a person in the wrong, or in a worse position.

> Up and *waur* them a', Willie.
> —*Jacobite Ballad.*

An advocate was complaining to his friend, an eminent legal functionary of the last century, that his claims to a judgeship had been overlooked, adding acrimoniously, "And I can tell you, they might have got a *waur*," to which the only answer was a grave "*whaur?*"—DEAN RAMSAY.

> Sax thousand years are near hand fled,
> Sin I was to the butcherin' bred,
> And mony a scheme in vain's been laid
>   To stop or scaur me,
> Till ane Hornbook's ta'en up the trade,
>   An faith he'll *waur* me.
> —BURNS: *Death and Dr. Hornbook.*

> Want o' wit is *waur* than want o' wealth.

> In his case, the water will never *waur* the widdie.
> —ALLAN RAMSAY's *Scots Proverbs.*

(*i.e.*, in his case the water will never get the better of the gallows; equivalent to the English saying, "He that's born to be hanged will never be drowned").

Wax, to grow, or increase; the reverse of *wane*, to decrease. *Wax* is almost obsolete; but *wane* survives, both in Scotland and England, as in the phrases: "the *waning* moon," "the *waning* year," "his *waning* fortunes." *Wax* remains as a Biblical word, in the noble translations of the Old Testament by Wickliffe and the learned divines of the reign of James I., which has preserved to this age so many emphatic words of ancient English, which might otherwise have perished. It is derived from the German *wachsen*; the Flemish *wassen*, to grow.

> The man *wox* well nigh wud for ire.
> —CHAUCER.

> And changing empires wane and *wax*,
> Are founded, flourish and decay.
> —SIR WALTER SCOTT: *Translation of Dies Irae.*

Wazie, jolly, brisk; probably a variation for *gaucie* (q.v.), with the common change of *g* into *w*, as in *war* for *guerre*, &c.

> Right *wazie* wax'd an' fou' o' fun,
> They whistled down the setting sun.
> —BEATTIE: *John o' Arnha'.*

Wean, a little child; a *weanie*, a very little child—from "wee ane," little one. This word has not yet been admitted to the dictionaries, though becoming common in English parlance.

A smytrie o' wee duddie *weans*
(a lot of little ragged children).
—BURNS : *The Twa Dogs.*

When skirlin' *weanies* see the light.
—BURNS : *Scotch Drink.*

Wearin' awa', decaying gradually.

I'm *wearin' awa'*, Jean,
Like snaw when it's thaw, Jean,
I'm *wearin' awa'*
To the Land o' the Leal.
—LADY NAIRNE.

Hope's star will rise when
Life's welkin grows grey,
We feel that within us which ne'er can
decay,
And Death brings us Life as the
Night brings the Daw' [dawn],
Though we're *wearin' awa'*, an'
we're *wearin' awa'*.
—JAMES BALLANTINE.

Weatherie, stormy or showery
weather; a word formed on the
same principle as the Teutonic
ungewitter, very bad weather.
Weather gleam, a streak of light
on the horizon in cloudy weather.

Wee, little, diminutive, very little ;
generally supposed to be derived
from the first syllable of the
German *wenig*. This word
occurs in Shakspeare, and is
common in colloquial and familiar English, though not in literary composition. It is often
used as an intensification of littleness, as "a little *wee* child,"
" a little *wee* bit."

A *wee* house well filled,
A *wee* farm well tilled,
A *wee* wife well willed,
Mak' a happy man.

A *wee* mouse can creep under a great
haystack.
—ALLAN RAMSAY's *Scots Proverbs.*

Weed or weeds, dress, attire,
clothing. The only remnant of
this word remaining in modern
English is the phrase, a
" widow's *weeds*," the funeral
attire of a recently bereaved
widow.

They saw their bodies bare,
Anon they pass'd with all their speed,
Of beaver to mak themselves a *weed*,
To cleith (clothe) them was their care.
—*On the Creation and Paradyce Lost*,
by SIR RICHARD MAITLAND, *in*
ALLAN RAMSAY's *Evergreen.*

Weed is in many Etymological
Dictionaries said to be derived
from *weave*, the Teutonic *weben.*
Possibly it comes from the
Gaelic or *eudadh*, a dress or
garment, also the armour of a
knight. The author of the
Scottish poem of " Paradyce
Lost," which appears in the
" Evergreen," was born in 1496,
and died in 1586, at the advanced age of 90, and was
consequently long anterior to
Milton, who afterwards adopted
the same title, and rendered it
as enduring as the English language.

Weeder-clips, shears for clipping
weeds.

The rough burr thistle spreading wide
Among the bearded bear,
I turned the *weeder-clips* aside
And spared the symbol dear.
—BURNS.

The patriotic poet turned the
clips aside in order that he might

not cut down a thistle, the floral badge of his country.

Weeks or **weiks** of the eye or mouth signify, according to Jamieson, the corners of the mouth or eyes. To hang by the *weeks* of his mouth, is to keep hold of a thing or purpose to the utmost, to the last gasp; an exaggerated phrase similar to that in Holy Writ to "escape by the skin of the teeth." *Week* or *weik* is a corruption of the Gaelic *uig*, a corner. The word occurs in Tim Bobbin's Yorkshire Glossary.

Weigh-bauk, the cross beam of a balance.

> Come like a *weigh-bauk*, Donald MacGillivray,
> Come like a *weigh-bauk*, Donald MacGillivray,
> Balance them fairly, balance them cleverly,
> Off wi' the counterfeit, Donald MacGillivray.
> —JAMES HOGG, *the Ettrick Shepherd.*

Weil or **wele**, an eddy in the water; a whirlpool.

Weil-head, the centre of an eddy. These words appear to be a corruption of *wheel* or *whirl*, having a circular motion, and to have no connection with *well*, a spring of water.

> They doukit in at a *weil-head.*
> —*Border Minstrelsy: Earl Richard.*

Weill, good fortune, the English *weal*, as in the phrase, "Come weal, come woe."

> He is na worth the *weill* that canna thole the wae.—*Old Proverb.*

Weir, war; *wurman*, a soldier, a man of war, a combatant; *wier-like*, warlike; *weirigills*, quarrels; *wedded weirigills*, disputes between husband and wife; from the French *guerre*, the Italian *guerra*, with the change of the *gu* into *w*. The primary root seems to be the Flemish *weeren*, to defend; the English *be ware!* *i.e.*, be ready to defend yourself;—a noble origin for resistance to oppressive and defensive war, that does not apply to offensive war—the "bella, horrida bella," of the Latin, and the *krieg* of the Teutonic, which signify war generally, whether offensive or defensive;—the first a crime, the second a virtue.

Weir or **wear**, to guard, to watch over, to protect, to gather in with caution, as a shepherd conducts his flock to the fold.

> Erlinton had a fair daughter;
> I wat he *wiered* her in a great sin,
> And he has built a high bower,
> And a' to put that lady in.
> —*Ballad of Erlinton.*

Motherwell translates "*wiered* her in a great sin," placed her in danger of committing a great sin, which is clearly not the meaning. But the whole ballad is hopelessly corrupt in his version.

Weird or **wierd.** Most English dictionaries misdefine this word, which has two different significations: one as a noun, the other as an adjective. In English literature, from Shakspeare's time downwards, it exists as an adjective only, and is held to mean unearthly, ghastly, or witch-like. Before Shakspeare's time, and in Scottish poetry and parlance to the present day, the word is a noun, and signifies "fate" or "destiny"—derived from the Teutonic *werden*, to become, or that which *shall* be. Chaucer, in "Troilus and Cressida," has the line—

O Fortune ! executrice of *wierdes !*

and Gower, in a manuscript in the possession of the Society of Antiquaries, says—

It were a wondrous *wierde*
To see a king become a herde.

In this sense the word continues to be used in Scotland :

A man may woo where he will, but he maun wed where his *wierd* is.

She is a wise wife that kens her ain *wierd.*—ALLAN RAMSAY's *Scots Proverbs.*

Betide me weel, betide me woe,
That *wierd* shall never danton me.
—*Ballad of True Thomas.*

The *wierd* her dearest bairn befel
By the bonnie mill-dams o' Binnorie.
—SCOTT's *Minstrelsy of the Border.*

Shakspeare seems to have been the first to employ the word as an adjective, and to have given it the meaning of unearthly, though pertaining to the idea of the Fates :—

The *wierd* sisters, hand in hand,
Posters of the sea and land.
—*Macbeth.*

Thane of Cawdor ! by which title these *wierd* sisters saluted me.—*Idem.*

When we sat by her flickering fire at night she was most *wierd.*—CHARLES DICKENS : *Great Expectations.*

No spot more fit than *wierd*, lawless Winchelsea, for a plot such as he had conceived.—*All the Year Round*, April 2, 1870.

It opened its great aisles to him, full of whispering stillness, full of *wierd* effects of light.—*Blackwood's Magazine*, April 1870.

Jasper surveyed his companion as though he were getting imbued with a romantic interest in his *wierd* life. — CHARLES DICKENS : *The Mystery of Edwin Drood.*

She turned to make her way from the *wierd* spot as fast as her feeble limbs would let [permit] her.—T. A. TROLLOPE : *The Dream Numbers.*

Wierd is sometimes (but rarely) used as a verb, signifying to doom.

I *wierd* ye to a fiery beast,
And relieved sall ye never be.
Border Minstrelsy : Kempion.

Weise, to direct, to guide, to draw or lead on in the way desired. This word is akin to the English *wise*, a way or manner, as in the phrase, " Do in that *wise*," and in the word *likewise*, in a like manner, and is derived from the French *viser* and the Dutch and Flemish *wijzen* or *wyzen*, to indicate, to show or point the way.

Every miller wad *weise* the water to his ain mill.—ALLAN RAMSAY's *Scots Proverbs.*

Weise also signifies to use policy for attaining any object, to turn to art rather than by strength, to draw or let out anything cautiously so as to prevent it from breaking, as in making a rope of tow or straw one is said to *weise* out the tow or straw.—JAMIESON.

The wean saw something like a white leddy that *weised* by the gate.—SCOTT : *The Monastery.*

Wem, a scar; *wemmit*, scarred, *wemless*, unscarred; and, metaphorically, blameless or immaculate. Probably from the Flemish and English *wen*, a tumour or swelling on the skin.

Wersh, insipid, tasteless; from the Gaelic *uiris*, poor, worthless, trashy.

A kiss and a drink o' water are but a *wersh* disjune.—ALLAN RAMSAY.

Why do ye no sup your parritch? I dinna like them; they're unco *wersh*. Gie me a wee pickle saut!—JAMIESON.

That auld Duke James lost his heart before he lost his head, and the Worcester man was but *wersh* parritch, neither gude to fry, boil, nor keep cauld.—SCOTT: *Old Mortality*.

The word was English in the seventeenth century, but is now obsolete, except in some of the Northern Counties, where it survives, according to Brocket's Glossary, in the corrupted form of *welsh*.

Her pleasures *wersh*, and her amours tasteless. — *Translation of Montaigne*, 1613.

Helicon's *wersh* well.—ALLAN RAMSAY.

Wet one's whistle. *Whistle* is a ludicrous name for the throat, whence to "*wet one's whistle*" signifies to moisten the throat or take a drink.

But till we meet and *weet our whistle*, Tak' this excuse for nae epistle. —BURNS: *To Hugh Parker*.

Whalp, to bring forth young dogs or *whelps*. Burns says of Cæsar, the Newfoundland dog

in his well-known poem of the "Twa Dogs" that he was—

Whalpit some place far abroad, Where sailors gang to fish for cod.

The Jacobite ballad-singers and popular poets of the '45, when Prince Charles Edward made his forlorn but gallant attempt to regain the throne of his ancestors, made frequent derogatory and contemptuous allusions to the family name of the House of Hanover, which they persisted in calling *Whelp* instead of *Guelph*.

Now our good king abroad is gone, A German *whelp* now fills the throne, *Whelps* that are desired by none, They're brutes compared wi' Charlie.

Oh, Charlie, come an' lead the way, No German *whelp* shall bear the sway: Though ilka dog maun hae his day, The right belongs to Charlie. —PETER BUCHAN'S *Prince Charlie and Flora Macdonald*.

Whalpit is the past tense of the verb to *whelp*, or bring forth *whelps* or young dogs. In Dutch and Flemish, *welp* signifies the cub of the lion or the bear, but in Scotch and English the word, though formerly applied to the progeny of the wolf and the fox, is now almost exclusively confined to that of the dog. Dr. Wagner, in his Glossary to the German edition of Burns, conjectures that the word is derivable from the Latin *vulpes*.

Whang, a large slice, also a thong of leather, and by extension of meaning, to beat with

a strap or thong, or to beat generally.

> Wi' sweet-milk cheese i' mony a *whang*,
> And farlies baked wi' butter.
> —BURNS : *Holy Fair.*

> Ye cut large *whangs* out of other folk's leather. — ALLAN RAMSAY'S *Scots Proverbs.*

Whang, in the sense of to beat with a strap, is local in England, but in the sense of a large slice, or anything large, it is peculiar to Scotland ; and in one odd phrase, that of *slang-whanger*, to the United States of America. According to Bartlett's " Dictionary of Americanisms " it signifies political vituperation largely intermingled with *slang* words. It appears, however, in Hood's " Ode to Rae Wilson : "—

> No part I take in party fray
> With tropes from Billingsgate's *slang-whanging* Tartars.

To which Mr. Bartlett appends the note, " If the word, as is supposed, be of American origin, it has been adopted in the mother country."

> This day the Kirk kicks up a stour,
> Nae mair the knaves shall wrang her ;
> For Heresy is in her power,
> And gloriously she'll *whang* her,
> Wi' pith this day.
> —BURNS : *The Ordination.*

The Glossaries translate *whang*, by beat, belabour ; but it is probably derived from the Teutonic *wanke*, the Flemish *wankelen*, to shake, to totter, to stagger, or cause to shake and stagger.

What ails ye at ? This question signifies, what is the matter with a thing named ? What dislike have you to it ? as to a child that does not eat its breakfast, " *What ails ye at your parritch ?* "

Lord Rutherford having, when on a ramble on the Pentlands, complained to a shepherd of the mist, which prevented him from enjoying the scenery, the shepherd, a tall grim figure, turned sharply round upon him. " *What ails ye at* the mist, sir ?* It weets the sod, slockens the yowes, and " —adding with more solemnity—" it is God's wull."—DEAN RAMSAY.

An old servant who took charge of everything in the family, having observed that his master thought that he had drank wine with every lady at the table, but had overlooked one, jogged his memory with the question, " *What ails ye at* her wi' the green gown ?"— DEAN RAMSAY.

Whaup, a curlew.

> The wild land-fowls are plovers, pigeons, curlews, commonly called *whaups.*—*Statistical Account of Scotland,* article ORKNEY.

Whaup-nebbit, having a nose like the neb or bill of a curlew.

Wheen, a lot, a small quantity.

> What better could be expected o' a *wheen* pock-pudding English folk ?— SCOTT : *Rob Roy.*

A young girl (say at St. Andrews) sat upon the cutty stool for breach of the seventh commandment, which applies to adultery as well as to the minor, but still heinous, offence of illicit love, was asked who was the father of her child ? " How can I tell," she replied artlessly, "among a *wheen* o' divinity students ?"—DEAN RAMSAY.

> But in my bower there is a wake,
> And at the wake there is a *wane* ;
> But I'll come to the green wood ere morn.
> —*Border Minstrelsy : Erlinton.*

Wane means a number of people, a *wheen folk.*—SIR WALTER SCOTT.

The derivation, which has been much disputed, seems fairly traceable to the Teutonic *weniy*, little or few.

Wheep, a sharp, shrill cry or whistle. *Penny-wheep,* a contemptuous designation for sour, weak, small beer, sold at a penny per quart or pint, and dear at the money; so called, it is supposed, from its acidity, causing the person who swallows it, thinking it better than it is, to make a kind of whistling sound, expressive of his surprise and disgust. Formed on the same principle as the modern word "penny dreadful," applied to a certain description of cheap and offensive literature. *Wheep* seems to be akin to *whoop*, a shrill cry, and *whaup*, the cry of the curlew or plover.

Be't whisky gill or penny-*wheep*,
  Or ony stronger potion,
It never fails, on drinking deep,
  To kittle up our notion.
    —BURNS: *The Holy Fair.*

Wheeple, the cheep or low cry of a bird; also, metaphorically, the ineffectual attempt of a man to whistle loudly.

A Scottish gentleman, who visited England for the first time, and ardently desired to return home to his native hills and moors, was asked by his English host to come out into the garden at night to hear the song of the nightingale, a bird unknown in Scotland. His mind was full of home, and he exclaimed, "Na, na! I wadna gie the *wheeple* o' a whaup (curlew) for a' the nightingales that ever sang."—*Statistical Account of Scotland.*

Wheericken or **queerikens,** a ludicrous term applied to children who are threatened with punishment, signifying the two sides of the breech or podex, the soft place appropriate for "skelping." Apparently derived from the Gaelic *ciùrr*, to hurt, to cause pain.

Whid or **whud,** an untruth, a falsehood, a lie; usually applied to a departure from veracity which is the result of sudden invention or caprice, rather than of malicious premeditation.

Even ministers they hae been kenn'd,
  In holy rapture,
A rousin' *whid* at times to vend,
  An' nail't wi' Scripture.
    —BURNS: *Death and Dr. Hornbook.*

In the first edition of Burns the word *whid* did not appear, but instead of it—

Even ministers they hae been kenn'd,
  In holy rapture,
Great lies and nonsense baith to vend,
  And nail't wi' Scripture.

This was ungrammatical, as Burns himself recognised it to be, and amended the line by the more emphatic form in which it now appears.

The word *whid* seems, in its primary meaning, to be applied to any sudden and rapid movement, or to a deviation from the straight line. It is akin to the English *scud*. According to Jamieson, to *yed* is to fib, to magnify in narration. This word is probably a variety or hetero-

S

graphy of *whid*, and has the same meaning.

An arrow *whidderan!*
— *The Song of the Outlaw Murray.*

Paitricks scraichin' loud at e'en,
An' mornin' poussie *whiddin* seen.
[Partridges screeching, and the early hare scudding along.]
—BURNS : *To Lapraik.*

Connected with the idea of rapidity of motion are the words *whidder*, a gust of wind ; *whiddie*, a hare ; *whiddy*, unsteady, shifting, unstable ; to *whiddie*, to move rapidly and lightly ; to *twidder* the thumbs, in English twiddle the thumbs. The derivation is uncertain, but is probably from the Teutonic *weit*, the English *wide*, in which sense *whid*, a falsehood, would signify something wide of the truth, and would also apply in the sense of rapid motion through the wideness of space.

Whid, a lie. Bailey has "*whids*, many words "—a cant word, he says. Does not Burns speak of amorous *whids*, meaning, or rather I should say referring to, the quick rapid jumpings about of rabbits ? *Whid* certainly has in Scotch the meaning of frisking about; and applied to statements, it is obvious how *whid* could come to mean a lie.—R. DRENNAN.

Whigmaleeries, whims, caprices, crotchets, idle fancies ; also fanciful articles of jewellery and personal adornment, toys and trifles of any kind.

There'll be, if that day come,
I'll wad a boddle,
Some fewer *whigmaleeries* in your noddle.
—BURNS : *The Brigs of Ayr.*

. I met ane very fain, honest, fair-spoken, weel-put-on gentleman, or rather burgher, as I think, that was in the *whigmaleerie* man's back-shop.—SCOTT : *Fortunes of Nigel.*

The etymology of this word, which is peculiar to Scotland, is not to be found in any of the current languages of Europe. It is probably from the Gaelic *uige*, a jewel, a precious stone ; from whence *uigheam*, adornment, decoration ; *uigheach*, abounding in precious stones ; and *uigheamaich*, to adorn. These words are the roots of the obsolete English word *owche*, a jewel, used by Shakspeare, Beaumont and Fletcher ; and which also occurs in the authorised version of the Bible :—

Your brooches, pearls, and *owches*.
Henry IV., Part II.

Pearls, bracelets, rings, or *owches*,
Or what she can desire.
—BEAUMONT AND FLETCHER.

The last two syllables of *whigmaleerie* are traceable to *leor* or *leoir*, sufficient, plenty. The quotation from the " Fortunes of Nigel " refers to the jewels in George Heriot's shop. The connection of ideas between the fanciful articles in a jeweller's shop and the fancies or conceits of a capricious mind is sufficiently obvious.

Jamieson notices a game called *whigmaleeries*, "formerly played at drinking-clubs in Angus, at which the losing player was obliged to drink off a glass. Perhaps," he adds, " the game was so denominated out of contempt for the severe austerity attributed to the Whigs!"

"This etymology," says Dr. Adolphus Wagner, " is very doubtful and difficult." Confused by the word *Whig*, and unaware of the Gaelic *uige*, and believing in the drinking bouts alluded to by Jamieson, he endeavours to account for the final syllable, *eerie*, by citing from Ben Jonson, " a leer horse," a led horse, as applicable to a drunkard being led in the train of another! The Gaelic derivation makes an end of the absurdities both of Jamieson and the erudite foreign critic.

Whilie, a little while; pronounced *fylie* in Aberdeenshire. A wee *whilie*, a very little while; *whiles*, at times.

On the Bishop (Skinner) making his appearance, the honest man (a crofter) in the gladness of his heart stepped briskly forward to welcome his pastor, but in his haste stepped upon the rim of the iron riddle, which rebounded with great force against one of his shins. The accident made him suddenly pull up, and instead of completing the reception, he stood vigorously rubbing the injured limb, and, not daring in such a venerable presence to give vent to the customary strong ejaculations, kept twisting his face into all sorts of grimaces. As was natural, the Bishop went forward, uttering the usual formulas of condolence and sympathy, the patient meanwhile continuing his rubbings and his silent but expressive contortions. At last his wife, Janet, came to the rescue, and clapping the Bishop coaxingly on the back, said, " Noo, Bishop, just gang ben to the house, and we'll follow when he's had time to curse a *fylie*; and then, I'se warrant, he'll be weel eneuch."—DEAN RAMSAY.

Whyles she sank, and *whyles* she swam,
Binnorie, O Binnorie!
Until she cam to the miller's dam,
By the bonnie mill-dam o' Binnorie.
—Border Minstrelsy: The Cruel Sister.

Whillie-lu, a threnody, a lament, a prolonged strain of melancholy music; but, according to Jamieson, "a dull or flat air." He derives the word from the Icelandic *hvella*, to sound; and *lu*, lassitude. It seems, however, to be a corruption of *waly!* an exclamation of sorrow ; as in the beautiful ballad—

O waly! waly! up the bank,
And waly! waly! down the brae ;

which, conjoined with the Gaelic *luaidh* (*dh* silent), a beloved object, makes *whillie-lu*, or *waly lu*. The final syllable *lu* enters into the composition of the English *lullaby*, a cradle-song, from *lu-lu !* beloved one, and *baigh*, sleep, which thus signifies " Sleep, beloved one!" or " Sleep, darling !"

Whillie - wa', to procrastinate; apparently from *while away* the time.

Whillie-whallie, sometimes abbreviated into *whillie-wha'*. This word in all its variations signifies any thing or person connected with cheaters, cajolers, or false pretenders. Jamieson has *whilly* or *whully*, to cheat, to gull ; *whillie-whallie*, to coax, to wheedle ; *whillie-wha*, one not to be depended upon ; *whillie-*

wa, or *whillie-whal,* one who deals in ambiguous promises. In a South Sea song which appears in Allan Ramsay's "Tea-Table Miscellany" occur the lines—

If ye gang near the South Sea House,
The *whilly-whas* will grip your gear!

The etymology of all these words is uncertain. The English *wheedle* has been suggested, but does not meet the necessities, while *wheedle* itself requires explanation. *Whillie-whallie,* which appears to be the original form of the word, is probably the Gaelic *uilleadh,* oily, and, metaphorically, specious, as in the English phrase, an *oily* hypocrite, applied to a man with a smooth or specious tongue, which he uses to cajole and deceive, and *balaoch,* in the aspirated form, *bhalaoch,* a fellow. From thence *whillie-whallie,* a specious, cajoling, hypocritical person.

Burns, in "The Whistle," speaks of one of the personages of the ballad as—

Craigdarroch began with a tongue
    smooth as oil,
Desiring Glenriddel to yield up the
    spoil.

Whilper or **whulper,** any individual or thing of unusual size; akin to the English *whopper* and *whopping,* of which it may possibly be a corruption.

The late Rev. Rowland Hill, preaching a charity sermon in Wapping, appealed to the congregation to contribute liberally. His text was, "Charity covereth a multitude of sins." "I preach," he said, "to great sinners, to mighty sinners,—ay, and to *whapping* sinners!"—JOE MILLER'S *Jest Book.*

What a *whilper* of a trout I hae gotten!
—JAMIESON.

Whinge, to whine; from the Teutonic *winseln,* to whimper.

If ony Whiggish *whingin'* sot
    To blame poor Matthew dare, man,
May dool and sorrow be his lot,
    For Matthew was a rare man.
—BURNS: *Elegy on Captain Matthew Henderson.*

Whinger, a knife worn on the person, and serviceable as a sword or dagger in a sudden broil or emergency. Jamieson derives it from the Icelandic *hwin,* fununculus, and *gird,* actio; and queries whether it may not mean an escape for secret deeds. The Gaelic *uinich* signifies haste, and *geur,* sharp, whence *uin geur* or *uinich geur,* a sharp weapon for haste. The word is sometimes written *whin-yard,* and is so used in the English poem of "Hudibras," and explained by the commentators as a *hanger* or hanging sword. It is, of course, open to doubt whether *whinger* is not the same as *hanger,* but the Gaelic derivation seems preferable, as expressive of a definite idea, while *hanger* admits of a multiplicity of meanings.

And *whingers* now in friendship bare,
The social meal to part and share,
Had found a bloody sheath.
—SCOTT: *Lay of the Last Minstrel.*
Mony tyne the half-mark *whinger* for the halfpennie *whang.* [Many lose the sixpenny knife for sake of the halfpenny slice.]—FERGUSON's *Scots Proverbs.*

Jocteleg was another name for a *whinger*, which, though susceptible of a Gaelic interpretation (see *ante*), perhaps only signified a hunting-knife or dagger, from the Flemish *jacht*, the chase or hunt, and *dolk*, a dagger, pronounced in two syllables, *dol-ok*, a hunting-knife or dagger, a *jacht-dolok* or *jocteleg*. But whether the Gaelic or the Flemish origin of the word be correct, it is clear that Jamieson's derivation from the imaginary cutler, *Jacques de Liege*, is untenable.

Whinner, to dry up, like vegetation in a long-protracted drought. The derivation is uncertain; probably a corruption of the English *winnow*.

A *whinnerin'* drouth. The word is applied to anything so much dried up, in consequence of extreme drought, as to rustle to the touch. The corn's a *whinnerin'*.—JAMIESON.

Whinner, to snort like a horse, to *whinney;* French *hennir*, to neigh.

An' goblins *whinnered* through the air Wi' *whorled chaps* (distorted faces or jaws).
—GEORGE BEATTIE : *John o' Arnha'*.

Whipper-snapper, a contemptuous term for a little, presumptuous person, who gives himself airs of importance and talks too much. Jamieson says it "might be deduced from the Icelandic *hwipp*, saltus, celer cursus, and *snapa*, captare escam, as originally denoting one who manifested the greatest alacrity in snatching at a morsel!" The true derivation seems to be from the Flemish *wippen*, to move about rapidly and restlessly, and *snapper*, to prate, to gabble, to be unnecessarily loquacious.

Whippert, hasty, irascible, impatient ; *whippert-like*, inclining to be ill-tempered without adequate provocation. Jamieson thinks the root of *whippert* is either the Icelandic *whopa*, lightness, inconstancy, or the English *whip*. He does not cite the Flemish *wip*, to shake in the balance, and *wippen*, to move lightly and rapidly as the scales do on the slightest excess of weight over the even balance. Thus *wippert-like* would signify one easily provoked to lose the balance of his temper.

He also cites *whipper tooties*, as silly scruples about doing anything, and derives it from the French *apres tout*, after all. This derivation is worse than puerile. The first word is evidently from the Flemish root ; the second, *tooties*, is not so easily to be accounted for.

Whish, whist, silence, or to keep silence ; whence the name of the well-known game at cards, formerly called quadrille.

Haud your *whish* (*i.e.*, keep silence, or hold your tongue).—SCOTT : *Rob Roy*.

Whisky, whusky, a well-known alcoholic drink, of which the name is derived from the Gaelic *uisge*, water. The liquor is sometimes called in the Highlands *uisge beatha*, the water of life; in Irish Gaelic written *uisque baugh*. The French pay the same complement to brandy, when they call it *eau de vie*.

Whisky tackets, pimples produced on the face by the excessive use of whisky or other spirituous liquors; from *tacket*, a small nail.

Whistle binkie, a musician, harper, fiddler, or piper who played at penny weddings or other social gatherings, and trusted for his remuneration to the generosity of the company. A *whistle* is a somewhat irrevelant name for a pipe, or for music generally, and *binkie* is a bench, a bunker, or seat. It has been supposed that these two words were the etymological roots of the phrase, but this derivation is open to doubt. *Uasal*, the Gaelic for gentle or noble, and *binkie*, a bunker, a seat, was the seat reserved at the weddings of the peasantry for the chief or landlord, who graced the ceremony by his presence when any of his tenants were married, and the place of honour thus appropriated to him was called the *uasal* (corrupted into *whistle*) *binkie*, and the epithet was thence transferred to the hired musician who stepped into it after the laird's departure. The late David Robertson of Glasgow published, in 1847 and 1853, a collection of Scottish songs by then living Scottish poets under this title, of which the contents proved what was previously known, that the genius of Scotsmen, even among the humblest classes, is pre-eminently lyrical, and produces many effusions of great poetical beauty.

Whistle kirk, a term of contempt applied by bigoted Calvinists and Puritans, who object to all music in churches except the human voice, to Episcopalian and other Protestant churches who make use of organs. That noble instrument is a far greater incentive to devotional feeling than the untrained singing, which is often little better than howling or braying of a miscellaneous congregation of old and young people who know nothing of music and have never been taught to sing in unison. A *whistle - kirk* minister is a contemptuous epithet for an Episcopalian clergyman.

Whitter, to move quickly, to talk quickly, to drink quickly a hearty draught. The etymology is uncertain, but is possibly allied to the English *whet*, the Dutch and Flemish *wetten*, the German *wetzen*, to sharpen.

Whitterin' down the stair.
　　　—JAMIESON.

Syne we'll sit down and tak' our *whitter*
  To cheer our heart,
And faith we'll be acquainted better
  Before we part.
—BURNS: *Epistle to Lapraik.*

Whittle, a clasp-knife ; to *whittle*, to chip or carve a stick.

A Sheffield *thwittle* bare he in his hose.
  —CHAUCER: *The Reeve's Tale.*
Gudeman, quoth he, put up your *whittle*,
I'm no designed to try its mettle.
  —BURNS: *Death and Doctor Hornbook.*

The word is common in the United States, and was scarcely understood in England until its introduction into humorous literature by Judge Haliburton of Nova Scotia, in the inimitable "Sam Slick, the Clockmaker." According to a ballad quoted by Mr. Bartlett, in his Dictionary of Americanisms, the "Yankie or New Englander will *whittle* or cut his way through the world by some 'cute device or other, in spite of difficulties."

Dexterity with the pocket-knife is part of a Nantucket education. I am inclined to think the propensity is national. Americans must and will *whittle*." — N. P. WILLIS.

Whommle, to turn over clumsily and suddenly, and with a loud noise ; transposition of *whelm*.

Coming to the fire with the said pan and water therein, and casting the water therefrom, and *whommeling* the pan upon the fire, with the pronouncing of these fearful words, "Bones to the fire and soul to the devil!" which accomplished the cure.—*Trial of Alison Nisbet for Witchcraft*, 1632.

Whommle means something different from *whelm*. *Whelm* means to cover over, to immerse ; neither does *whommle* mean to turn over clumsily and suddenly with a loud noise. Not one of these ideas is conveyed by the word itself ; it means literally and really nothing more than to turn upside down.—R. DRENNAN.

Whully, to wheedle, to endeavour, to circumvent by fair words and flattery ; in modern English slang to *carny*. *Wully-wha-ing*, insincere flattery.

My life precious ! exclaimed Meg Dods, nane o' your *wully-wha-ing*, Mr. Bindloose. Diel ane wad miss the auld girning ale wife, Mr. Bindloose, unless it were here and there a poor body, and may be the auld house tyke that wadna be sae weel guided, puir fallow.—SCOTT: *St. Ronan's Well.*

Whulte, a blow or hurt from a fall ; Gaelic *buailte* (aspirated *bhuailte* or *vuailte*), preterite of *buail*, to strike a blow.

Whuppie, a term of angry contumely applied to a girl or woman, signifying that she deserves whipping.

Whurlie-burlie. This Scottish word seems to be the original of the English *hurly-burly*, and signifies rapid circular motion ; from *whorl*, a small wheel; *whirl*, to spin round ; *world*, the earth that rotates or whirls in space around the sun.

Whyles, sometimes, occasionally, now and then.

How best o' chiels are *whyles* in want,
While coofs in countless thousands rant.
  —BURNS: *Epistle to Davie, a Brother Poet.*

Whyles crooning o'er some auld Scotch
sonnet.
              —*Tam o' Shanter.*

I took his body on my back,
And *whiles* I gaed, and *whiles* I sat.
         —*Lament of the Border Widow.*

A lady, visiting the poor, in the West
Port, Edinburgh, not far from the church
established by Dr. Chalmers, asked a poor
woman if she ever attended divine service
there. She replied, "Ou ay! there's a
man ca'd Chalmers preaches there, and I
whiles gang in to hear him, just to encour-
age him—puir body!"—DEAN RAMSAY.

Whylock, or a *wee while,* a little
while.

Wi' a blush, as she keepit lookin' roun'
an' roun' for a *whyleock.*—*Noctes Ambrosianæ.*

Widdie, angry contention; *widdiefu',* cross-grained, ill-tempered, half-crazy, cantankerous,
angry without cause.

The miller was strappin', the miller was
    ruddy,
A heart like a lord, and a hue like a lady;
The laird was a *widdiefu',* bleerit knurl,—
She's left the gude fellow and taken the
    churl.
          —BURNS: *Meg o' the Mill.*

Misled by the meaning of *widdie,* the rope, or gallows, Jamieson says that, properly *widdiefu',* or *widdie-fow,* signifies one
who deserves to fill a halter.
But as a man may be peevish,
morose, irascible, contentious,
and unreasonable without deserving the gallows, the etymology is not satisfactory. The
true root seems to be the
Flemish *woede,* the German
wuth, the old English *wode,*
the Scottish *wud*—all signifying
mad, crazy, unreasonable.

Widdle, to turn, to wheel, to
wriggle; and metaphorically, to
struggle; akin to the English
twiddle, to turn the thumbs
round each other in idle movement. *Widdle* is from the Gaelic *cuidhil,* a wheel.

Hale be your heart, hale be your fiddle,
Lang may your elbuck jink and diddle
To cheer you through the weary *widdle*
    O' worldly cares.
         —BURNS: *Epistle to Davie.*

Widdy (sometimes written *woodie*
and *wuddie*), the gallows.

The water will nae wrang the *widdy.*

[The English have another version of this proverb—

He who's born to be hanged will never
be drowned.]

It's nae laughing to girn in a *widdy.*

It's ill speaking o' the *widdy* in the
house o' a man who was hangit.
         —ALLAN RAMSAY'S *Scots Proverbs.*

The French have a similar proverb—"Il ne faut pas parler
de corde dans la maison d'un
pendu."

He'll wintle in a *widdie* yet [he'll wriggle in a rope yet, *i.e.,* he'll be hanged].—
JAMIESON: *Scots Proverb.*

Her Joe had been a Highland laddie,
But weary fa' the waefu' *woodie.*
         —BURNS: *The Jolly Beggars.*

On Donald Caird the doom was stern,
Craig to tether, leg to airn,
But Donald Caird wi' muckle study
Caught the gift to cheat the *wuddie.*
Rings o' airn an' bolts o' steel
Fell like ice frae hand and heel,
Watch the sheep in fauld and glen,
Donald Caird's come again.
         —SIR WALTER SCOTT.

In very primitive times in Scotland the ropes used for hanging those who had offended the chief, or who had rendered themselves amenable to the death penalty, were formed of twisted willow *withes*—whence *withy*, or *widdy*, afterwards came to signify a rope, or, by extension of meaning, the gallows.

Wight, wicht, wichtly, wichty, wichtness. *Wight* remains an English word in mock heroic composition, and means a man, a fellow; originally, a strong or brave man, a sturdy fellow. The Dutch and Flemish *wicht* means a child or a little fellow. *Wight*, in the epithet "Wallace *wight*," given in Scottish poetry and tradition to the great national hero, means "brave Wallace," and was a kind of title of nobility bestowed on him for his prowess, and the patriotic use he made of it.

> A *wight* man never wanted a weapon.
> —ALLAN RAMSAY.

Wilie-wa', to cajole, to flatter, possibly from *wile away;* from *wile*, to trick, to beguile.

Willie. This suffix answers in meaning to the Latin *volens*, or *volent* in the English words benevolent and malevolent. The Scotch renders the former word by *guid - willie*, or *well - willie;* from the Flemish *goed willig;* and the latter by *ill-willie*, in which *ill* is substituted for the Flemish *quad*, or bad. On the same principle of formation, *ill-deedie* signifies nefarious, and *ill-tricky* mischievous, both of which might well become English if they found favour with authors of acknowledged authority.

Willie-winkie, a term of somewhat contemptuous endearment to a diminutive and not over intelligent child. The Jacobites of 1688 to 1715 long applied it to William III., when they did not call him the "Dutchman," "the Hogan Mugan," "Willie the Wag," or "Willie Wanbeard." "The Last Will and Testament of *Willie winkie*," is the title of a once popular Jacobite song.

Wilshoch, wulshoch, changeable of opinion or purpose, a bashful wooer. Jamieson derives the first syllable from the English *will*, and the second from the Anglo - Saxon *seoc aeger*, sick from the indulgence of one's own will. It seems rather to be from the Gaelic *uile*, all, totally; and *seog* (shog), to swing from side to side — whence, metaphorically, one who is continually at variance with his former opinion, and sways from side to side.

Wilt, to shrivel, or begin to decay, as a leaf or flower in the extreme heat or cold—not exactly *withered* in the English sense of the word, inasmuch as a *wilted* leaf may revive, but u withered one cannot. This old Scottish word has been revived in America, where it is in common use. The late Artemus Ward punned upon it, when he said to his lady love, "*Wilt* thou ! and she *wilted.*"

Miss Amy pinned a flower to her breast, and when she died, she held the *wilted* fragments in her hand. —JUDD's *Margaret.*

Wilt, though not admitted into the English dictionaries, is in local use in many northern and eastern counties, and is often pronounced *wilk,* or *wilken,* which seems to have been the original form ; from the German, Dutch, and Flemish *welken,* to decay, to droop. Spenser used *welk,* in speaking of the sunset, to describe the fading light of the day.

When ruddy Phoebus 'gins to *welk* in west.—*Faerie Queene.*

Wimple, to flow gently like a brook, to meander, to purl.

Among the bonnie winding banks, Where Doon rins *wimplin'* clear.
          —BURNS: *Hallowe'en.*

Win, this word in English signifies to gain, to make a profit, to acquire ; but in the Scottish language it has many other and more extended meanings, such as to reach, to attain, to arrive, to get at. It enters into the composition of a great number of compound words and phrases, such as—to *win above,* to surmount ; to *win about,* to circumvent ; to *win awa,* to escape, and,

poetically, to die, or escape from life ; to *win forret,* to advance, to get on ; to *win owre,* to get over, to cajole ; to *win past,* to overtake, or get by ; to *win free,* to get loose ; to *win hame,* to get home ; to *win aff,* to get off, or away, to be acquitted on a trial ; to *win ben,* to be admitted to the house ; to *win up,* to arise, or get up.

Win and tine, a man able to *win and tine,* is a man of substance and energy, able to win and able to lose without hurting himself, and to whom winnings and losings are alike of little consequence.

Winnock, a window corner ; abridged from window-*nook. Winnock-bunker,* a seat, ledge, or bench at the window.

A *winnock-bunker* in the east, Where sat Auld Nick in shape o' beast ; A towsie tyke, black, grim, and large, To gie them music was his charge.
          —BURNS: *Tam o'Shanter.*

Winsome. This pleasant Scottish word is gradually making good its claim to a place in recognised English. The etymology is undecided whether it be from *win,* to gain, or the Teutonic *wonne,* joy, pleasure, or delight.

I gat your letter, *winsome* Willie.
          —BURNS.

She is a *winsome* wee thing, She is a bonnie wee thing, This sweet wee wife o' mine.
          —BURNS.

Wintle, a corruption of *windle*, to gyrate, to turn round in the wind; also, to reel, to stagger, to walk unsteadily; also, to wriggle, to writhe, to struggle.

Thieves of every rank and station,
From him that wears the star and garter,
To him that *wintles* in a halter.
—BURNS : *To J. Rankine.*

He'll *wintle* in a widdie yet.
—JAMIESON.

Winze, an oath, a curse, an imprecation, an evil wish; from the Flemish *wensch*, a wish, which, conjoined with the prefix *ver*, became *verwenschen*, to curse, to wish evil.

He taks a swirlie auld moss-oak
For some black gruesome carline,
And loot a *winze*, and drew a stroke.
—BURNS : *Hallowe'en.*

Wirry-cow, a bugbear, a goblin, or frightful object, a ghost; the devil; also a scarecrow.

Draggled sae 'mang muck and stanes,
They looked like *wirry-cows*.
—ALLAN RAMSAY.

The word was used by Scott, in " Guy Mannering," and is derived by Jamieson from the English " worry," and " to cow." *Wirry*, however, seems to be a corruption of the Gaelic *uruisg*, which, according to Armstrong's Gaelic Dictionary, signified a " brownie," or goblin, who was supposed to haunt lonely dells, lakes, and waterfalls, and who could only be seen by those who had the " second sight." Ruddiman thought that the

uruisg was called a "brownie" in the Lowlands, on account of the brown colour of the long hair which covered his body when he appeared to human eyes; but it is more probable that " brownie" was derived from the Gaelic *bròn*, sorrow or calamity. The attributes ascribed to the *uruisg* are similar to those of the " lubber fiend " of Milton.

The final syllable of wirry-*cow* was sometimes written and pronounced *carl*, a fellow. According to Jamieson, *cow*, or *kow*, signified a hobgoblin, and to " play the *kow*," was to act the part of a goblin, to frighten fools and children.

Wisp, to currycomb a horse, or rub it with a *wisp* of straw.

A short horse is sune *wispit* (*i.e.*, a little job is soon done).—*Old Proverb.*

Wissel, to exchange. *Wissler*, a money-changer; from the Flemish *wissel*, and *geld wisselaar*, a money-changer; the German *wechsel*. To *wissel* words, is to exchange words; usually employed in an angry sense, as in the English phrase, to " bandy words with one," the irritation preceding a quarrel.

Withershins, backwards, against the course of the sun. To pass the bottle *withershins*, or the wrong way, at table, is considered a breach of social etiquette. The word seems to be derived from the Teutonic *wider*, contrary, and *sonne*, the sun;

or perhaps from *wider*, and *sinn*, sense ; whence it would signify, in a "contrary sense." The word *wider*, corrupted in the Scotch into *wither*, enters into the composition of many German words, such as *wider-spruch*, contradiction ; *wider-sinn*, nonsense ; *wider-stand*, resistance. The ancient Druids called a movement contrary to the course of the sun, *car-tual*. On this subject, apropos of the word *withershins*, a curious note appears in Armstrong's Gaelic Dictionary. "The Druids," he says, "on certain occasions moved three times round the stone circles, which formed their temples. In performing this ceremony, *car-deise*, they kept the circle on the right, and consequently moved from east to west. This was called the prosperous course ; but the *car-tual*, or moving with the circle on the left, was deemed fatal or unprosperous, as being "contrary to the course of the sun."

The said Alison past thrice *withershins* about the bed, muttering out certain charms in unknown words. — *Trial of Alison Nisbet for Witchcraft*, 1632.

To be whipped round a'circle *withershins*, or *car-tual*, would thus be considered peculiarly degrading, and probably, as the meaning of Gaelic words was perverted by the Saxon-speaking people, was the origin of the phrase, "to be whipped at the cart's tail."—*Gaelic Etymology of the Languages of Western Europe.*

Witter, to struggle, to fight, to strive in enmity ; from the Teutonic *wider*, against, contrary to ; *wider-sacher*, an antagonist ; *wider-sprechen*, to contradict ; Flemish *weder-partij*, an adversary, an opposing party.

To struggle in whatever way,—often for a subsistence ; as, "I'm *witterin* awa'." A *witterin body* is one who is struggling with poverty or difficulty.—JAMIESON.

Wittering, a proof.

And that was to be a *wittering* true,
That maiden she had gane.
—*Border Minstrelsy: The Broomfield Hill.*

Witterly, knowingly, wittingly ; to do a thing *witterly*, to act on good information, or with full knowledge ; to *witter*, to inform, and also to prognosticate.

Wod or **wud**, stark mad, raging mad ; old English *wode*, *wuth*, and *wouth ;* Dutch and Flemish *woode ;* German *wuth.*

Ye haud a stick in the *wod* man's e'e, *i.e.*, you hold a stick in the mad man's eyes, or you continue to provoke one already enraged.—JAMIESON.

When neebors anger at a plea,
And just as *wud* as *wud* can be,
How easy can the barley bree
Cement the quarrel.
—BURNS : *Scotch Drink.*

The wife was *wud*, and out o' her wit,
She couldna gang, nor could she sit ;
But aye she cursed and banned.
—*The Gaberlunzie Man.*

Won, to dwell, to reside, to inhabit. *Woning*, a dwelling-place. From the German *wohnen*, and *wohnung ;* Dutch and Flemish *wonen*, to dwell ; *wonen-huis*, a dwelling-house, a lodging.

There's auld Rab Morris that *wons* in
  the glen,
The king o' guid fellows, and wale o'
  auld men.
                          —BURNS.

Wonner, wonder; applied in contempt to any odd, decrepit, or despicable creature.

Our whipper-in, wee, blastit *wonner.*
              —BURNS: *The Twa Dogs.*

Wont to be, a phrase applied to any ancient or obsolete custom or observance, a thing that used to be or was *wont to be* in olden time.

Mony *wont to be's*, nae doubt,
An' customs we ken nought about.
  —JAMIESON: *The Piper o' Peebles.*

Wooer-bab. It was formerly the custom among the young men and lads of the rural population in the Highlands and Lowlands of Scotland to wear bows of ribbons of flaunting colours in their garters on high days and holidays, when they expected to meet the lasses, and to dance or flirt with them.

The lasses' feet are cleanly neat,
  Mair braw than when they're fine,
Their faces blythe fu' sweetly kythe,
  Hearts leal an' warm an' kind ;
The lads sae trig wi' *wooer-babs*
  Weel knotted on their garten,
Some unco blate, and some wi' gabs
  Gar lasses' hearts gang startin'.
              —BURNS: *Hallowe'en.*

"*Bab*," says Dr. Adolphus Wagner, the German editor of Burns, " seems akin to the English *bob*, something that hangs so as to play loose, and is a tassel or knot of ribbons, or the loose ends of such a knot." The English word *bob*, in this sense, is a corruption of the Gaelic *bab*, a fringe ; and *babag*, a little fringe. Perhaps the English phrase, "tag, rag, and *bobtail*," is from the same source, and *bobtail* may signify the ragged fringe of a frayed outer garment, *bobbing* or dangling loose in the wind.

Wool or oo'. English ; from the German and Flemish *woll ;* in Scottish parlance, *oo'*. *A' oo'*, all wool ; *a' ae oo'*, all one wool ; *ay, a' ae oo'*, yes, all one wool. There is a popular proverb which formerly ran—

    Much cry and little *oo'*,

to which some humorist added—

As the Deil said when he shear'd the sow.

The addendum was at once adopted by the people, though some strict philologists remain of the opinion that the first line is complete in itself, and that " cry " does not signify the noise or uproar of the animal, but is a corruption either of the Gaelic *graidh*, or *graigh* (*gry*), a flock, a herd, or *cruidh*, which has the same meaning, and signifies a large flock that yields but little wool. However this may be, the idea in the lengthened proverb has a grotesque humour about it, which insures its popularity.

Wooster, a wooer, a lover, a sweetheart.

Wooster-tryste, a lonely meeting.

> At kirk she was the auld folks' love,
> At dance she was the laddies' e'en,
> She was the blythest o' the blythe,
> At *wooster-trystes* on Hallowe'en.
> —ALLAN CUNNINGHAM : CROMEK'S
> *Remains of Nithsdale and Gal-
> loway Song.*

Word. " To get the *word* of,"
i.e., to get the character, or the
repute, of being so and so.
"She gets the *word* o' being a
licht-headed quean," *i.e.,* the
character of being a light-
headed or frivolous woman.

Worl, wurl, wroul, wirr. All
these words of a common origin
express the idea of smallness,
or dwarfishness, combined with
perversity, disagreeableness, and
ill-nature. Jamieson has *wurlie*,
contemptibly small in size; a
wurlie body, an ill-grown person ; *wurlin*, a child or beast
that is unthriven ; *wurr*, to snarl
like a dog ; *wirr*, a peevish and
crabbed dwarf ; *wurr*, to be
habitually complaining or snarling ; and a *wurlie* rung, a knotted stick. He suggests that
wirr and *wurr* are corruptions of
were-wolf, the man-wolf of popular superstition—one afflicted
with the disease called lycan-
thropy, in which the unhappy
victim imagines himself to be a
wolf, and imitates the howlings
of that animal. The true etymology is uncertain. Perhaps
all these words are derivable
from the Teutonic *quer*, oblique,
athwart, perverse—the origin of
the English *queer*, *quirk*, and

quirky. Jamieson has also *wurp*,
a fretful, peevish person ; and
wurpit, afflicted with fretfulness.
These latter seem akin to the
Gaelic *uipear*, a clown, a churl,
a bungler ; and *uipearach*, ill-
tempered, churlish.

Worry, to vex, to torment. In
some parts of Scotland it signifies to strangle, to choke, or
to be suffocated. *Worry carl*, a
troublesome fellow, or ill-
natured churl, who vexes both
himself and others. Possibly
from the Gaelic *uaire*, stormy.
(See WIRRY-COW, *ante.*)

Wow ! an exclamation of surprise
or wonder, without etymology,
as exclamations usually are.

> A fine fat fodgel wight,
> Of stature short, but genius bright,
> That's he ! mark weel !
> And *wow !* he has an unco slight
> O' cauk and keel !
> —BURNS : *On Captain Grose.*

> And *wow !* but my heart dances boundin
> and licht,
> And my bosom beats blythesome and
> cheery.
> —JAMES BALLANTINE : *The Gloamin'
> Hour.*

Wowf, partially deranged. The
Scottish language is particularly
rich in words expressive of the
various shades of madness and
insanity ; such as *wud*, raging,
or stark staring mad ; *daft*,
slightly deranged ; *gyte, cranky*,
subject to abberrations of intellect on particular points ; *doited*,
stupidly deranged—all which
words are in addition to, and

not in supercession of the English words, *mad, idiotic, lunatic, crazy,* &c.

It is very odd how Allan, who, between ourselves, is a little *wowf,* seems at times to have more sense than all of us put together.—SCOTT : *Tales of My Landlord.*

Wrack, to break in pieces, to *wreck.* In English the phrase "*wrack* and ruin" is more often used than "*wreck* and ruin;" from the same source as *wreak,* to act, do, or perform a deed of anger ; to *wreck* spite or vengeance. It is possibly of the same origin as the Teutonic *werken,* the English *work,* employed in the sense of destroying rather than of creating or constructing.

Oh, roaring Clyde, ye roar o'er loud,
Your stream is wondrous strong ;
Make me your *wrack* as I come back,
But spare me as I gang.
—JOHNSON'S *Musical Museum: Willie and May Margaret.*

Wraith, an apparition in his own likeness that becomes visible to a person about to die ; a water-spirit.

He held him for some fleeting *wraith,*
And not a man of blood or breath.
—SIR WALTER SCOTT.

By this the storm grew loud apace,
The *water-wraith* was shrieking,
And in the scowl of heaven each face
Grew dark as they were speaking.
—THOMAS CAMPBELL.

The etymology of this word is uncertain. Some suppose it to be derived from *wrath,* or a wrathful spirit, summoning to doom. Jamieson is of opinion that it is from the same root as *weird,* fate or destiny, or the Anglo-Saxon *weard* or *ward,* a guardian, a keeper, and thence a fairy, a guardian angel. This derivation is scarcely tenable ; that from *breith,* doom or judgment, aspirated as *bhreith,* is more probable, as the apparition of the *wraith* is always supposed to forebode the doom of the person who sees it.

Wrang, English *wrong.* The etymology of this word has been much disputed ; but it seems to be from *wring,* to twist, and *wrung,* twisted or distorted from the right line. *Wrang* in Scottish parlance sometimes signifies deranged—out of the right line of reason. "He's a' *wrang,*" *i.e.,* he is demented. *Wrang-wise* is a wrong manner ; the opposite of the English *right-wise* or righteous.

Writer, an attorney. *Writer* to the Signet, a solicitor licensed to conduct cases in the superior courts.

Wroul, an ill-formed or diminutive child ; a name originally applied to one who was supposed to have been changed in its cradle by malicious fairies ; a *changeling.* Jamieson refers to *wer-wolf,* a man supposed to be transformed into a wolf, called by the French a *loup-garou,* but this is evidently not the true derivation, which is more probably from the Dutch and Flemish *ruil*, to exchange.

Wud-scud, a wild scamper, a panic, called by the Americans a *stampede;* from *wud*, mad, and *scud*, to run precipitately and in confusion. The word is sometimes applied to an over-restive or over-frolicsome boy or girl, whom it is difficult to keep quiet.

Wudspur, a Scottish synonym for the English *Hotspur*, wild, reckless, one who rides in hot haste; from the Flemish *woete*, German *wuth*, old English *wode* and *spur*. It is difficult to decide which of the two words was the original epithet, and whether *wood-spur* in Scottish parlance was, or was not, anterior in usage to the *Hotspur* of the great poet.

There was a wild gallant among us a',
His name was Watty wi' the *wudspur.*
　　—*Border Minstrelsy: Ballad of Jamie Telfer.*

Wyg to wa'. "A thing," says Jamieson, "is said to gang frae *wyg to wa'*, when it is moved backwards and forwards from the one wall of a house to the other." He suggests that *wyg* is but another name for wall, and that the phrase signifies really "from wall to wall." It is more probable that *wyg* is but a misspelling of the Gaelic *uig*, a corner.

Wyte, to blame, to reproach The etymology is derived by Jamieson from the Anglo-Saxon *witan*, to know, and the Gothic *wita*, to impute. But the root of the word is the Flemish *wyten*, to blame, to reproach.

Ane does the skaith, and
Another gets the *wyte.*
　—ALLAN RAMSAY's *Scots Proverbs.*

Many *wyte* their wives
For their ain thriftless lives.
　　　　　　Idem.

Alas! that every man has reason
To *wyte* his countrymen wi' treason.
　　　—BURNS : *Scotch Drink.*

"Dame! deem warily! Ye watna wha *wytes* yoursel."—*Old Proverb.* (A warning to a censorious or tattling woman to beware of scandal, lest she herself should be scandalised.)

This was an English word in the time of Chaucer, but has long been obsolete except in Scotland.

Wyter, one who blames; an accuser.

Wyteworthy, blameable, blameworthy.

Y

Yald, sprightly, active, nimble, alert ; *yald-cuted* (erroneously spelled *yaul-cuted* in Jamieson), nimble-footed ; from *yald,* nimble, and *cute,* an ankle.

Being *yald* and stout, he wheel'd about,
And clove his head in twain.
—Hogg's *Mountain Bard.*

Yammer, yaumer, to lament, to complain ; from the Flemish *jammer,* lamentation ; *jammern,* to complain or lament ; *jammervoll,* lamentable.

Fareweel to the bodies that *yammer* and mourn.
—Herd's *Collection of Scottish Songs,*
Bide ye Yet.

We winna, shauna, *yaumerin'* yirn
Though Fortune's freaks we dree.
—*Whistle Binkie.*

In Lancashire and the North of England *yammer* is used in another sense, that of yearning or desiring ardently.

I *yammer'd* to hear now how things turned out.
—Tim Bobbin : *Lancashire Dialect.*
And the worm *yammers* for us in the ground.
—Waugh's *Lancashire Songs.*

Yankee, an inhabitant of Massachusetts, Rhode Island, Vermont, Connecticut, New Hampshire, and Maine, the six New England States of the American Union. The etymology of the Scottish word has not been ascertained. *Jank* (pronounced *yank*) in Dutch and Flemish, signifies to cry out lustily, and *junger,* in German, is a young man, the English *younker;* but neither of these words can account for *yankie,* either in the Scottish or American sense. Danish and Swedish afford no clue. In provincial English, *yanks* are a species of leather gaiters worn by agricultural labourers, which, according to Halliwell, were once called "Bow Yankies." But this cannot be accepted as the origin, unless on the supposition that at the time of the emigration of the first colonists to America, the term signified not only leather gaiters, but those who wore them. This epithet is often erroneously applied in England to all Americans, though it is repudiated by the people of the Middle, Southern, and Western States. It is supposed to be a mispronunciation of *English* by the aboriginal Indian tribes, on the first colonisation of the Continent. Much controversy has arisen on the subject, which still remains undecided. No one, however, has hitherto remarked that the Scottish vernacular supplies the words *yank, yanking,* which signify a smart

T

stroke ; *yanker,* an incessant speaker, and also a great falsehood ; *yanking,* active, pushing, speculative, enterprising. It is not insisted that this is the correct etymology, but if it be only a coincidence it merits consideration. No true New Englander would dissent from it for any other than philological reasons, in which it is certainly vulnerable, though on moral grounds it is all but unassailable.

Yap, yappish, sometimes written *yaup,* hungry, eager, brisk covetous.

Right *yap* she yoked to the ready feast,
And lay and ate a full half-hour at least.
—Ross's *Helenore.*

This word is probably derived from the Gaelic *gab* or *gob,* the mouth—whence by extension of meaning, an open mouth, craving to be filled. The English word *gape,* to yawn, or open the mouth wide, is from the same root. The eminent tragedian, Philip Kemble, always pronounced *gape* as *gahp,* not *gaipe,* and the late W. C. Macready followed his example. Jamieson travels very far north to find the derivation in the Icelandic *gypa,* vorax.

Although her wame was toom and she grown *yap.*
—Ross's *Helenore.*

Though bairns may pu' when *yap* or drouthy
A neep or bean to taste their mouthy.
. . . .
But a' the neeps and a' the beans,
The hips, the haws, the slaes, the geens,

That e'er were pu'd by hungry weans
Could ne'er be missed,
By lairds like you, wi' ample means
In bank and kist.
—JAMES BALLANTINE : *To the Laird of Blackford Hill.*

Now hell's black table-cloth was spread,
The infernal grace was duly said ;
Yap stood the hungry fiends a' owre it,
Their grim jaws aching to devour it.
—*Jacobite Songs and Ballads : Cumberland's Descent into Hell.*

At that moment *yap* as ever.—*Noctes Ambrosianæ.*

Yare, a word still used by sailors, but obsolete in literature, signifying ready, alert, heedful, or in a state of readiness ; used by Shakspeare and the writers of his time.

Our ship is tight and *yare.*
—*Tempest,* act v. scene 1.

If you have occasion to use me for your own turn, you shall find me *yare.*—*Measure for Measure,* act iv. scene 2.

Be *yare* in thy preparations, for thy assailant is quick, skilful, and deadly.—SHAKSPEARE : *Twelfth Night.*

Nares derives it from the Saxon *gearwe,* paratus ; but the real root seems to be the Celtic *aire,* heed, attention, alertness, readiness for action or duty ; as in the modern Gaelic phrase, "Thoir an *aire,*" pay attention, be on the alert ; be *yare !* allied to the French *gare !* and the English *beware !*

Yark, to smite suddenly, forcibly, and aimlessly ; possibly a corruption of *jerk.*

He swat an' *yarkit* wi' his hammer,
The sparks flew frae the steel like glamour.
—BEATTIE : *John o' Arnha'.*

Yatter (a corruption of the English *chatter*), to talk idly and incessantly; also, to complain querulously, and without reason. "She's a weary *yatter*," *i.e.*, she's a tedious and wearisome gossip. *Yatter* also signifies a confused mass or heap, and is synonymous with *hatter*. (See *ante*, p. 841.)

Yaud or "**far yaud!**" an interjection or call by a shepherd to his dog, to direct his attention to sheep that have strayed, and that are far in the distance. *Yaud*, in this sense, as cited by Jamieson, seems to be a mispronunciation or misprint of *yont!* or *yonder*.

Yeld, or yell, barren, unfruitful. In Galloway, according to Jamieson, *yald* signifies *niggardly*. The etymology is uncertain, though supposed to be a corruption of *geld*, to castrate, to render unproductive.

A *yeld* soil, flinty or barren soil. A cow, although with calf, is said to gang *yeld* when the milk dries up. A *yeld* nurse is a dry nurse. Applied metaphorically to broth without flesh meat in it (soupe-maigre).—JAMIESON.

A *yeld* sow was never good to grices [*i.e.*, a barren sow was never good to little pigs, or, a barren stepmother to the children of her husband by a previous wife.]—ALLAN RAMSAY's *Scots Proverbs*.

Thence country wives, in toil and pain,
May plunge and plunge the kirn in vain,
For oh, your yellow treasure's ta'en .
 By witching skill,
And dawtit, twal-pint Hawkie's gaen
 As *yell's* the bull.
 —BURNS: *Address to the Deil*.

Yerk, a smart blow; *yerker*, a very smart and knock down blow; supposed to be a corruption of *jerk*, with which, however, it is not synonymous.

There's news, news, gallant news,
There's gallant news o' tartan trews,
 An' red Clanranald's men, Joe;
There has been blinking on the bent,
 An' flashing on the fell, Joe,
The redcoat sparks hae got the *jerks*,
 But carle daurna tell, Joe.
 —*Jacobite Relics: Clanranald's Men.*

Yestreen, last night, or *yesterday* evening. *Yester*, both in English and Scotch, was used as a prefix to signify time past; as *yester*-year, *yester*-month, *yester*-week; but in English its use has in modern times been restricted to day and night; and, by a strange surplusage of words, to yesterday night instead of *yester* night, and yesterday morning instead of *yester* morn. In Scotland, its use is more extended, and *yestereen* or *yestreen*, *yesternoon*, *yesternight*, are employed alike in poetic style and in everyday conversation. The word is from the German *gestern* (*g* pronounced as *y*) and the Flemish *gistern*.

I saw the new moon late *yestreen*,
 Wi' the auld moon in her arm,
And if we gang to sea, master,
 I fear we'll come to harm.
 —SIR PATRICK SPENS: *Border
  Minstrelsy.*

I gaed a waefu' gate *yestreen*,
 A gate I fear I'll sairly rue,
I gat my death frae twa sweet e'en,
 Twa sparklin' e'en o' bonnie blue.
 —BURNS.

The derivation of the Teutonic *gestern* and *gistern* is probably from the Gaelic *aosda*, aged or old ; so that *yesterday*, in contradiction to *this* day, or the new day, would signify the old day, the day that is past. Latin *hesternus*.

Yethar, a willow-wythe ; also, a blow with a switch ; probably a corruption of *wyther*, a stroke with a wythe.

Yevey, greedy, voracious, clamorous for food. Of doubtful etymology, though possibly from the Gaelic *eibh* (*ēv*), to clamour.

Yill, ale or beer.

> A cogie o' *yill*
> And a pickle oatmeal,
> An' a dainty wee drappie o' whisky—
> An' hey for the cogie,
> An' hey for the *yill*,
> Gin ye steer a' thegither, they'll do unco weel.
> —*A Cogie o' Yill*, 1787.

Yird-fast or **earth-fast**, a stone well sunken in the earth, or a tree fast rooted in the ground.

> The axe he bears it hacks and tears,
> 'Tis formed of an *earth-fast* flint ;
> No armour of knight, though ever so wight,
> Can bear its deadly dint.
> —*Minstrelsy of the Scottish Border :*
> LEYDEN —*The Count of Keeldar.*

A *yird-fast* or insulated stone, enclosed in a bed of earth, is supposed to possess peculiar properties. Its blow is reckoned uncommonly severe.—SIR WALTER SCOTT.

Yirr, the growl of a dog, English *gurr*. *Gurl*, growl ; *gern*, to grin or snarl with ill-nature or anger.

Yoak, to look, to look at ; possibly from the German *aug*, the Flemish *oog*, the Latin *oculus*, the eye ; the English *ogle*, to look at.

> *Yoak* your *orlitch* [horloge]. Look at your watch [or clock].—JAMIESON.

Yon. The use of *yon* and *thon*, in the sense of *that*, is much more common in Scotland than in England ; as in the phrase, "Do ye ken *yon* man ?" do you know that man. It is also used for yonder ; as, *yon* hill, for yonder hill. It is sometimes pronounced and written *thon ;* as in the following anecdote of a wilful child, narrated by Dean Ramsay :—

When he found every one getting soup and himself omitted, he demanded soup, and said, " If I dinna get it, I'll tell *thon*." Soup was given him. At last, when it came to wine, his mother stood firm and positively refused. He then became more vociferous than ever about telling *thon ;* and as he was again refused, he again declared, " Now, I'll tell *thon*," and roared out, "Ma new breeks were made out o' the auld curtains ! "

Yorlin, a small bird, more commonly known in England as the "yellow hammer." Scottish and English boys have a traditional prejudice against this bird, for some imaginary reason, or no reason at all. It sometimes reads in the old rhyme :—

> Yellow, yellow *yorling*,
> You are the devil's darling.

Yorne, prepared, made ready ; part participle of *yare* ready, or to make ready.

To Norroway, to Norroway,
　To Norroway o'er the faern,
The king's daughter o' Norroway,
　'Tis we maun bring her hame ;
Ye'll eat and drink, my merry men a',
　An' see ye be weel *yorne,*
For blaw it weet, or blaw it sleet,
　Our gude ship sails the morn.

Mr. Robert Chambers, in his Collection of Scots Ballads, 1829, prints *thorne* instead of *yorne,* without note or comment, or apparent knowledge of the unmeaning word.

Youk or **yeuk,** to itch ; *yowky,* itchy. From the Teutonic *jucken,* pronounced *yucken.*

Your neck's *youkin'* for a St. Johnstone ribbon. — ALLAN RAMSAY'S *Scots Proverbs.*

(A taunt, implying that a man's career and character is such as to merit hanging, and that he is nearly ready for it. St. Johnstone, now Perth, was the assize city. A ribbon signified the rope.)

How daddie Burke the plea was cookin',
If Warren Hastings' neck was *yeukin.*
　—BURNS : *To a Gentleman who Promised him a Newspaper.*

Thy auld darned elbow *yeuks* with joy.
　—BURNS : *To Colonel de Peyster.*

A parishioner in an Ayrshire village, meeting the minister, who had just returned after long absence on account of ill health, congratulated him on his convalescence, and added, anticipatory of the pleasure he would have in hearing him preach again— " Eh, sir I I'm unco *yuckie* to hear a blaud o' your gab."—DEAN RAMSAY.

Youllie, a name formerly given to the police in Edinburgh by idle boys or bad characters. " A

low term," says Jamieson, "probably formed from the *yowling* or calling out." Was it not rather formed from the Gaelic *uallach,* proud, haughty, arrogant, and given to the police derisively by the blackguards of the streets when, as they thought, they were interfered with unnecessarily, or ordered to move on ? Or it may be from *yoly,* the French *joli,* pretty or handsome, used contemptuously, as in the phrase, "my fine fellow."

Yowe, a ewe, a female sheep, a lamb ; *yowie,* a eye lamb.

Ca' the *yowes* to the knowes [hills],
Ca' them where the heather grows,
Ca' them where the burnie rowes,
　My bonnie dearie.
　　　　—BURNS.

An' neist my *yowie,* silly thing,
Gude keep her frae a tether string.
　　—BURNS : *Poor Mailie.*

Yowf, to strike hard and suddenly, as the ball is struck at the favourite Scottish game of golf. The common pronunciation of *golf* is *gowf,* and *yowf* is probably, as Jamieson alleges, a corruption of that word.

But had we met wi' Cumberland
On Athol's braes or yonder strand,
The blood o' a' his savage band
　Had dyed the German Sea, man.
An' cousin Geordie up the gate
We wad hae *yowf'd* frae Charlie's seat,
And sent him hame to bide in state,
　In's native Germanie, man.
　—*Jacobite Minstrelsy : Bauldie Travers'*
　　Lament for Culloden.

Yowff, to bark in a suppressed or feeble manner ; said of a dog who is not very earnest in his displeasure.

Ye puir creature you ! what needs ye *yowff* when the big dog barks ?—*Laird of Logan.*

Yowl, to howl, or whine as a dog ; sometimes written *gowl ;* from the Gaelic *guil*, or *gul*, to lament.

And darkness covered a' the ha',
Where they sat at their meat,
The gray dogs *yowling* left their food,
And crept to Henrie's feet.
  —*Border Minstrelsy : King Henry.*

Yule. *Yule* was a Druidical festival in honour of the sun, celebrated at the winter solstice, in ages long anterior to the Christian era.

Yule, about the etymology of which there has been much controversy, was probably named in honour of the sun—the source of all heat and life upon this globe ; from *uile*, all, the whole, whence, by extension of meaning, the whole year, ending at what we now call Christmas, and which in early times signified completion, the full turn of the wheel of the year. The Gaelic *cuidhil*, a wheel, has also been suggested as the true root of the word ; while *iul*, guidance, knowledge, has found favour with other etymologists, because on that day the assembled Druids, in their groves or in their stone circles, laid down rules for the guidance of the people during the coming year. *Iul oidche*, or the guide of night, was a name applied by Ossian to the Polar star. The French *noel*, and old English *nowell*, names for Christmas or *Yule*, are from the Gaelic *naomh*, holy, and *là*, a day. Jamieson, in citing the northern appellation for Odin as *iul-fader*, is in error in translating it as the father of *Yule*, or Christmas, instead of "All-Father," or father of all, which was an epithet applied to the sun as the Father of Light and Life.

Langer lasts year than *yule*.—ALLAN RAMSAY'S *Scots Proverbs.*

Duncan Gray cam' here to woo
On blythe *yule* night when we were fu'.
  —BURNS : *Duncan Gray.*

Yurn, coagulate, churn, curdle.

And syne he set the milk ower het,
  And sorrow a spark of it wad *yurne.*
  —*The Wife of Auchtermuchty.*

LOST SCOTTISH AND ENGLISH PRETERITES.

A LIVING language is like a living man. It has its tender infancy; its passionate youth; its careful maturity; its gradual, though it may be imperceptible, decay; and, finally, its death. After death comes apotheosis, if it has been worthy of such honour—or burial in the books, which, like the remains or memorials of ancient heroes, become the sacred treasures of newer ages. All languages pass through these epochs in their career. Sanscrit, Greek, and Latin are familiar examples of the death and sanctity of great and mighty tongues, that were once living powers to sway the passions and guide the reason of men. In their ashes even yet live the wonted fires that scholars love to rekindle. The languages of modern Europe that have sprung directly from the Latin may all be said to have passed their infancy and youth, and to have reached maturity, if not old age. The Celtic or Keltic languages—all sprung from an ancient Oriental root, and which include Gaelic, often called Erse or Irish, Manx, Welsh, and Breton—appear to be in the last stage of vitality, destined to disappear, at no very remote period, into the books, which will preserve their memory. Were it not for Victor Hugo, and some recent borrowings from the English, and the coinage of Ergot or Slang, it might be said that French had ceased to expand, and had become stereotyped into a form no longer to be modified. Spanish, Portuguese, and Italian hold their own ; and that is all that can be said of them. German, and the languages sprung from the same root and stem, contain within themselves such immense resources, and are so continually evolving out of their rich internal resources such new compounds, if not such new words, as to free them from that reproach of stagnation which may not unjustly be applied to the other great tongues which we have enumerated. But English—which, taken all in all, may be considered by far the richest, though not the most beautiful or the most sonorous, of all the languages spoken in our day—is yet in its vigorous prime, and, though it may be accused of vulgar corruptions and perversions, cannot be accused of exhibiting any symptoms of decay. It is doubtful whether it has yet reached the full maturity of its growth, or whether the mighty nations now existent in America, or the as mighty nations which are destined yet to arise in Australia and New Zealand, will not, as time rolls on, and new wants are created, new circumstances encountered, and new ideas evolved out of the progress of science and civilisation, add many thousands of new words to our already copious vocabulary. Other languages are dainty in the materials of their increment ; but the English is, like man himself, omnivorous. Nothing comes much amiss to its hungry palate. All the languages of the earth administer to its wants. It borrows, it steals, it assimilates what words it pleases from all the points of the compass, and asks no questions of them, but that they shall express thoughts and describe circumstances more tersely and more accurately than any of the old words besides which they are invited to take their places. The beautiful dialect of its Scottish brother has given it strong and wholesome food, in the shape of many poetical words, which it is not likely to part with. But if the English is thus perpetually growing and gaining, it is at the same time perpetually losing. Were it not for the noble translation of

the Bible, and for Chaucer, Gower, and the poets of the Elizabethan age, it would have lost still more than it has of its
early treasures, and would have been Latinised to an extent
that would have impaired and emasculated it, by depriving it
of that sturdy vernacular which is the richest element in its
blood, and best serves to build up its bone and muscle. If
few languages now spoken in the world have gained so much
as the English from the progress of civilisation, it must be
admitted, at the same time, that few have lost so much, and
lost it without necessity. It has been said that a good carpenter is known as much by the shape as by the quantity of
his chips; and the chips that the English tongue has thrown
off since the days of "Piers Ploughman" to our own, betoken,
both by quality and by quantity, what a plethora of wealth it
possesses, and what a very cunning carpenter Time has proved
in working with such abundant materials.

It is one of the current assertions which, once started on
high authority, are very rarely questioned, that the writings
of Chaucer are a "well of pure English undefiled." Chaucer,
though so ancient in our eyes, was a neologist in his own day,
and strove rather to increase the wealth of the written English,
of which he was so great a master, by the introduction of
words from the Norman-French, little understood by the bulk
of the people, though familiar enough to the aristocracy, for
whom he mainly wrote, than to fix in his pages for ever the
strong simple words of his native Saxon. The stream of English in his writings runs pure and cool; the stream of Norman-
French runs pure and bright also; but the two currents that
he introduced into his song never thoroughly intermingled in
the language, and at least nine-tenths of the elegant Gallicisms
which he employed found no favour with successive writers;
and few of them have remained, except in the earlier poems
of Milton. If we really wish to discover the true well of
English undefiled, where the stream runs clear and unmixed, we

must look to the Scottish author of "The King's Quair" and to the author of "Piers Ploughman," claimed by Buchanan, the tutor of King James the Sixth of Scotland and the first of England, to have been a Scotsman, rather than to Chaucer. We shall there find a large vocabulary of strong words, such as are plain to all men's comprehension at the present day, in the Bible as well as in the common speech of the peasantry ; and, above all, in that ancient form of the English language which is known as the Scottish dialect, and which, in reality, is the oldest English now spoken.

Since the days of "Piers Ploughman," a work invaluable to every English and Scottish philologist, the spoken language of the peasantry has undergone but few changes as regards words, but very many changes as regards terminations and inflections. On the other hand, the language of literature and polite society has undergone changes so vast that uneducated people are scarcely able to understand the phraseology that occurs in the masterpieces of our great authors, or the Sunday sermons of their pastors, delivered, as the saying is, "above their heads," in words that are rarely or never employed in their everyday hearing. Among this class survive large numbers of verbs as well as of inflections that ought never to have been allowed to drop out of literature, and which it only needs the efforts of a few great writers and orators to restore to their original favour.

Among the losses which the modern English and Scottish languages have undergone are, first, the loss of the plurals in *n* and in *en*, and the substitution of the plural in *s;* secondly, the present particle in *and,* for which we have substituted the nasal and disagreeable *ing ;* thirdly, the loss of the French negative *ne,* as in *nill,* for 'I will not;' *nould,* for 'I would not ;' *n'am,* for 'I am not ;' and of which the sole trace now remaining is 'willy-nilly;' and, fourthly, the substituting of the preterite in *d,* as in lov*ed* and admir*ed,* for the older and much stronger preterite formed by a change in the vowel sound of the infinitive and the present, as in run, ran ; bite, bit ; speak, spoke ; take, took ; and many others that still survive. And not only has the language lost the strong preterite in a great variety of instances where it would have been infinitely better to have retained it, but it has lost many hundred preterites altogether, as well as many whole verbs, which the illiterate sometimes use, but which literature for a hundred and fifty years has either ignored or despised. Of all the nouns that formerly formed their plural in *n*, as the German or Saxon nouns still for the most part do, very few survive—some in the Bible, some in poetical composition, some in the common conversation of the peasantry, and some, but very few, in polite literature. Among them may be mentioned 'oxen,' for oxes ; 'kine,' for cows ; 'shoon,' for shoes ; 'hosen,' for stockings ; 'een,' for eyes ; 'housen,' for houses ; and the words, as common to the vernacular as to literature, 'men,' 'women,' 'brethren,' and 'children.' In America, the word 'sistern' as a companion to brethren, survives in the conventicle and the meeting-house. 'Lamben' and 'thumben,' for 'lambs' and 'thumbs,' were comparatively euphemistic words ; but thumbs and lambs, and every noun which ends with a consonant in the singular, are syllables which set music, and sometimes pronunciation, at defiance. What renders the matter worse is, that the *s* in the French plural, from which this perversion of the English language was adopted, is not sounded, and that the plural is really marked by the change of the definite article, as *le champ, les champs.* Thus in borrowing an unpronounced consonant from the French, in order to pronounce it the English have adulterated their language with a multitude of sibilations alien to its spirit and original structure. The substitution of *s* for *eth* as the terminal of the present person singular of every verb in the language is an aggravation of the evil. If this change had been repudiated by our forefathers, a grace much needed would have been retained in the language.

Gradually, too, the English language has lost the large number of diminutives which it formerly possessed, and which are still common in the Scottish language and its dialects. The English diminutives in ordinary use in the nursery are many, but are chiefly employed in the pet names of children, as ' Willie,' for little William ; ' Annie,' for little Ann ; and so forth. The diminutives belonging to literature are few, and if we write ' darling,' for little dear ; ' lordling,' for a small lord ; ' mannikin,' for a very small man ; and such words as ' gosling,' ' duckling,' ' kitten,' we have pretty nearly exhausted the list. But formerly almost every monosyllabic noun had its lawful diminutive, as it has to this day in the Scottish dialect, where such words as ' housie,' ' wifie,' ' birdie,' ' doggie,' ' bairnie,' ' mannie,' ' bookie,' ' lassie,' ' lammie,' and hundreds of others, are constantly employed. Every Scotsman understands the phrase "a bonnie *wee lassiekie*," in which there are no less than three diminutives piled one upon the other, to increase the tenderness of an expression which ceased to be English four hundred years ago.

Among other losses of the English from which the Scottish language has not suffered to the same extent are the plural in *en* of the present tenses of all the verbs. We love*n* and we smile*n* would serve many rhymical needs, and administer to many poetic elegancies that the modern forms in English do not supply.

"The persons plural," observes Ben Jonson, a Scotsman, in his "English Grammar"—a work by no means so well known as his poetry—"keep the termination of the first person singular. In former times, till about the reign of King Henry VIII., they were wont to be formed by adding *en ;* thus, ' loven,' ' sayen,' ' complainen.' But now (whatsoever is the cause) it hath grown quite out of use. Albeit (to tell you my opinion) I am persuaded that the lack thereof, well considered, will be found a great blemish to our tongue."

But of all the losses which the language has sustained, not alone for poetry, but for oratory, that of many useful verbs, some of which are still existing in Scottish parlance, and of the ancient preterites and past participles of many old verbs of which the infinitives and present tenses still hold their places, is the most to be deplored. This loss began early ; and that the process is still in operation in the present day, is manifest from the fact that many preterites written in the best books and spoken in the best society forty years ago, are dropping out of use before our eyes. We constantly find *bid* for *bade*—'he *bids* me now ;' 'he *bid* me yesterday ;' *dare* for *durst*—'I told him I *dare* not do it ;' *need* for *needed*—' it was clear to me a year ago that he *need* not perform his promise ; *eat* for *ate* or *ett*—" he *eat* his dinner ;" *bet* for *betted*— 'he *bet* me a thousand to one.' The verbs *to let, to cast,* and *to put*, seem to have enjoyed no preterite during the last two hundred years in England, though in Scottish literature, both of the past and the present, their preterites are as common as their infinitives and present tenses. *Must,* in English, is equally devoid of the infinitive, the preterite, and the future ; while *can* has a preterite, but neither infinitive nor future. For what reasons these and similar losses have occurred in English, it might be interesting to inquire, though it might possibly lead us into metaphysical mazes were we to ask why an Englishman who may say 'I can' and 'I could,' must not say 'I will *can,*' but must resort to the periphrase of 'I will be able,' to express power in futurity ; or why the sense of present duty and obligation implied in the words 'I must,' cannot be expressed by the same verb if the duty be bygone or future, as 'I *musted,*' or 'I will *must,*' but have to be translated, as it were, into 'I was obliged,' or 'I will be obliged,' to do such and such a thing hereafter. These, however, are losses, whatever may be their occult causes, which can never again be supplied, and which at our time of day it is useless to lament.

The loss which most immediately affects the poetical power of modern English is that of the many preterites and past participles of ancient verbs that are still in use, and of many good verbs in all their tenses which without reason have been left for vernacular use to Scotland, and have not been admitted to the honours of literature, except in the poems of Robert Burns and the novels of Sir Walter Scott. These preterites ought not to be lost—they are not dead but sleeping—and only need the fostering care of two or three writers and speakers of genius and influence to be revived. They formed the bone and pith of the language of our forefathers, and the beauty and strength of the Bible in many of its noblest passages, and particularly commend themselves to us in Shakspeare, and other Scottish writers.

Axe, to inquire. This was the original and is the legitimate form of the verb now written and pronounced *ask,* and it is not only to be heard in colloquial use all over the British Isles, but to be found in our earliest writers, with the inflexions *axed* and *axen.*

> Envy with heavy harte
> *Axed* after Thrifte.
> > —*Vision of Piers Ploughman.*
>
> If he *axe* a fish.
> > —WICKLIFFE'S *Translation of the Bible.*
>
> *Axe* not why.
> > —CHAUCER: *The Miller's Tale.*

For the purposes of lyrical poetry and musical composition, the past participle of this verb, if reintroduced into literature, would be a vast improvement upon the harsh sound *asked,* which no vocalist can pronounce without a painful gasp.

Bake, boke, buik, beuk, boken, to bake. Both the preterite and the past participle of this verb are lost to literature, though they survive in the rural dialects of Scotland and the north of England. The language possesses but few trochaic rhymes, and in this respect ·*boken* might do good service to many a poet at his wits' end for a rhyme to ' broken ' and ' token.'

> They never *beuk* a good cake, but
> May bake a bad one.
> —ALLAN RAMSAY'S *Scots Proverbs.*

Beat, beaten. " The preterite of this verb," says Walker, in his " Pronouncing Dictionary," " is uniformly pronounced by the English like the present tense." " I think," says Dr. Johnson to Horne Tooke, in one of the imaginary conversations of Savage Landor, " that I have somewhere seen the preterite *bate.*" " I am afraid," replied Tooke, " of reminding you where you probably met with the word. The Irishman in Fielding's ' Tom Jones ' says ' he *bate* me.' " Johnson replied, " that he would not hesitate to employ the word in grave composition ; " and Tooke acquiesced in the decision, justify-ing it by a statement of the fact, which, however, he did not prove, " that authors much richer both in thought and ex-pression than any now living or recently deceased have done so." Children, who often make preterites of their own, in this respect acting unconsciously upon the analogies of the language, often say *bett* for *did beat.* And the children, it would appear, are correct, if the following from " Piers Ploughman " be considered good English :—

> He laid on me with rage
> And hitte me under the ear ;
> He buffeted me so about the mouthe
> That out my teeth he *bette.*

In Ross's " Helenore "—a perfect storehouse of Scottish words current in Aberdeenshire, Kincardineshire, the Mearns, and the north-east of Scotland—we find,—

> Baith their hearts *bett* wi' the common stound,
> And had nae pain, but pleasure in the wound.

This preterite might well be revived; it is sadly wanted, as witness the following passage from Mr. Disraeli's "Vivian Grey": "Never was she so animated; never had she boasted that her pulse *beat* more melodious music, or her lively blood danced a more healthful measure." If 'danced' (a preterite), why not *bett*, as "Piers Ploughman" has it? The following recent example of the present for the past participle *beaten*, is wholly unjustifiable :—

They were stoned, and the horse in their vehicle *beat* severely.— *Temple Bar Magazine*, March 1869.

Betide, betid, from tide, to happen. The preterite is lost. It occurs both in "Piers Ploughman" and in Chaucer :

Thee should never have *tidde* so fair a grace.
—*Canterbury Tales.*

Bid, and its derivative *forbid.* The ancient preterite and past participle of this verb were *bade* and *bidden, forbade* and *forbidden.* Both of these inflections are threatened with extinction ;—for what offence it is impossible to surmise. Shakspeare says—

The very moment that he *bade* me do it.

That our modern writers do not follow the example of Shakspeare, and conform to the rules of good English, may appear from the following examples :—

The competition is so sharp and general that the leader of to-day can never be sure that he will not be *outbid* to-morrow.—*Quarterly Review,* April 1868.

Mr. Charles Dickens has finally *bid* farewell to Philadelphia.—*Times,* March 4, 1868.

Uncertain even at that epoch (1864) of Austria's fidelity, Prussia *bid* high for German leadership.—*Times,* April 9, 1868.

He called his servants and *bid* them procure firearms.—*Times,* letter from Dublin; March 2, 1868.

James the First, besides writing a book against tobacco, *forbid* its use by severe penalties.—*Tobacco,* by D. KING, M.D.

Blend, blent, to mingle. The preterite of this verb properly preserved by the poets, but seems to have entirely given way in prose and in ordinary speech to 'blended.' Any reason for the change it is impossible to discover; for if it be correct to say 'blended,' it would be equally correct to say 'spended,' 'lended,' or 'rended.' This form of the preterite in the verb 'to mend' has properly been superseded by 'mended,' in order to avoid the confusion that would be caused in the use of the verb 'to mean,' which has its proper preterite in 'meant.' Byron uses *blent* with fine effect in his noble lines on "The Battle of Waterloo:"—

> Rider and horse, friend, foe, in one red burial *blent.*

Blin, to cease, to stop; *blan,* ceased, stopped.

> And so he did or that they went atwin,
> Till he had turned him he could not *blin.*
> —CHAUCER : *The Chanones' Yeman's Tale.*

> Her tears did never *blin.*
> —NARES : *Romeus and Julietta.*

> One while then the page he went,
> Another while he ranne,
> Till he'd o'ertaken King Estmere,
> I wis he never *blanne.*
> —PERCY'S *Reliques : King Estmere.*

Bren or **brend, brent** or **brand,** to burn. This verb is lost, though it might well have been retained in the language. "A *brand* plucked from the burning," and *bran* new, or *brant* new, new as a coin newly issued from the fires of the mint, are almost its sole remnants :—

> Bring in better wood,
> And blow it till it *brend.*
> —*Piers Ploughman.*

Brest, brast, to burst.

> Have thou my truth, till that mine herte *brest.*
> —CHAUCER: *The Franklein's Tale.*

U

The mayor smote Cloudeslee with his bill,
His buckler he *brast* in two.
—*Minstrelsy of the Scottish Border: Adam Bell, Clym
of the Clough, and William of Cloudeslee.*

Busk, busked, to adorn, to dress, to make ready; from the
Gaelic *busg*, to dress; *busgadh*, a head-dress, an ornament.

Busk ye, my merry men all,
And John shall go with me.
—PERCY's *Reliques: Robin Hood and Guy
of Gisborne.*

The king's bowmen *busked* them blythe.
—*Adam Bell, Clym of the Clough, and William of
Cloudeslee.*

The noble baron whet his courage hot,
And *busked* him boldly to the dreadful fight.
—FAIRFAX : *Translation of Tasso.*

Busk ye, *busk* ye, my bonnie, bonnie bride.
HAMILTON : *Braes o' Yarrow.*

A bonnie bride is soon *buskit.*—ALLAN RAMSAY's *Scots Proverbs.*

Cast, to throw. This verb in English has lost its preterite
coost, and its past participle, *casten.* Both survive in Scotland
and the North of England.

They *coost* kevils them amang
Wha should to the greenwood gang.
—*Minstrelsy of the Scottish Border.*

Burns employs the preterite in " The Death and Dying Words
of Poor Mailie " :—

As Mailie and her lamb thegither,
Were ae day nibbling on the tether,
Upon·her cloot she *coost* a hitch.

And again in his immortal song of " Duncan Gray " :—

Maggie *coost* her head fu' high,
Looked asklent and unco skeigh,
Gart poor Duncan stand abeigh.

In the Scottish dialect 'to *cast* out' means 'to fall out,' 'to disagree;' and the phrase "they have *casten* out" is of constant occurrence.

Chirm, charm, churm, to sound like the murmur or sound of a multiplicity of birds. Mr. Halliwell, in his "Archaic Dictionary," defines the word to mean the melancholy undertone of a bird previous to a storm. Nares, in his Glossary, has *charre*, to make a confused noise, a word current in some parts of England. The word is common in Scotland, though almost obsolete in the South.

> Small birds with *chirming* and with cheeping changed their song.
> —GAWIN DOUGLAS'S *Translation of the Æneid.*

> At last the kindly sky began to clear,
> The birds to *chirm*, and daylight to appear.
> —ROSS'S *Helenore.*

Milton makes Eve speak of the "*charm* of earliest birds," a phrase which has been misinterpreted to mean the charming (in the modern sense) song of the birds, while it really means *chirm* (in the old English and modern Scottish sense), the confused and intermingled song of all the morning birds.

Clead or clede, clad, to clothe. The preterite and past participle remain in poetical use as well as in dignified prose, while the infinitive and the present and future tenses have been superseded by the much harsher word 'clothe.'

Clem, clam, clammed, to perish of hunger, to starve. 'To starve' originally meant 'to die,' as we still say of a person that he is "starving with cold." The word has lately come to signify "to die for want of food," and has produced a very ugly and incorrect hybrid in the word 'starvation,' said to have been first used by Mr. Dundas, the first Lord Melville, who, as Horace Walpole informs us, received afterwards the nickname of "Starvation Dundas." The word at the time was supposed to be an Americanism. It has unfortunately fixed itself into our literature; but the original and much better word *clem* and its derivatives still hold their ground in Lancashire and the North of England. The word *clem* does not occur in Shakspeare, but both Ben Jonson and Massinger use it.

> ⎸ Hard is the choice when the valiant must eat their arms or *clem.*
> —BEN JONSON: *Every Man out of his Humour.*

> I canna eat stones and turfs. What! will he *clem* me and my followers? Ask him, will he *clem* me?—BEN JONSON: *The Poetaster.*

> My entrails were *clammed* with a perpetual fast.—MASSINGER: *The Roman Actor.*

"Let us all *clem*," said a speaker at a public meeting at Manchester, during the American civil war, "rather than help the cause of slavery." "I would rather *clem* than go to the workhouse," is still a common and honourable expression in Lancashire.

Clepe, clept, yclept, to call, to name. The past participle of this verb remains for the use of bad writers, and sometimes of good writers who compose mock heroics.

> The compaignie of comfort,
> Men *cleped* it some tyme.
> > —*Piers Ploughman.*

> Peradventure in thilk large book
> Which that men *clepe* the heaven ywritten was
> With stars.
> > —CHAUCER: *The Man of Lawes' Tale.*

> They *clepe* us drunkards.
> > —SHAKSPEARE: *Hamlet.*

> As hounds and greyhounds, mongrels, spaniels, curs,
> Shoughs, water-rugs, and demi-wolves are *cleped*
> All by the name of dogs.
> > —SHAKSPEARE: *Macbeth.*

Mr. Halliwell, in his "Archaic Dictionary," says that the word is still used by boys at play in the eastern counties, who *clepe* or call the sides at a game. Many newspaper writers at the present day, at a loss for a word for 'calling' or 'naming' an inanimate object, talk of the 'christening' of a church, a street, a battle, or any inanimate object. An example occurs in an editorial article of the *Times*, on the removing of the grating from the ladies' gallery in the House of Commons—" 'the grate question,' as Mr. Lowe *christened* it." In this and other instances the old word *clepe*, in default of 'call' or 'name,' would be an improvement, if it were possible to revive it.

Clip, clap, clippe, to embrace, to fondle. Before the English language borrowed from the French the word 'embrace,' from *embrasser*, to clasp in the arms, this verb was in constant use. It occurs in "Piers Ploughman," and in Chaucer, and had not fallen out of fashion or favour in the days of Shakspeare :—

> *Clippe* we in covenant, and each of us *clippe* other.
> > *—Piers Ploughman.*

> He kisseth her and *clippeth* her full oft.
> > —CHAUCER : *The Merchant's Tale.*

> Worse than Tantalus is her annoy,
> To *clip* Elysium and yet lack her joy.
> > —SHAKSPEARE : *Venus and Adonis.*

Then embraces his son, and then again he worries his daughter with *clipping* her.—SHAKSPEARE : *Winter's Tale.*

> Oh let me *clip* ye in arms as round as when I woo'd !
> > —SHAKSPEARE : *Coriolanus.*

> The lusty vine, not jealous of the ivy,
> Because she *clips* the elm.
> > —BEAUMONT AND FLETCHER.

The preterite, once common, survives to this day in the form of an infinitive and of a noun, but in both too offensive to modesty to be further mentioned.

Clout, clouted, to mend, to put a patch upon, from the Gaelic *clud*. The verb survives in Scotland, but has perished

out of modern English literature, although Shakspeare used
it :—

> I thought he slept, and put
> My *clouted* brogues from off my feet, whose rudeness
> Answered my steps too loud.
> —*Cymbeline.*

Many sentences of one meaning *clouted* up together.—ROGER ASCHAM.

> *Clout* the auld, the new are dear, My joe Janet.
> —BURNS.

Conne or can, to be able. Neither the infinitive nor the
past participle of this verb seems to have been used since the
days of Chaucer, who says, " I shall not *conne* answer," *i.e.*, I
shall not be able to answer ; and in the " Romance of the
Rose " has " Thou shalt never *conne* knowen."

Crine, crone, crunken, to shrivel from heat, frost, or sickness.
This verb, with all its declensions, has perished, and only
survives in its diminutive, to *crinkle.* In this last form it is
rather of the middle ages than of our own. See the ballad
of the " Boy and the Mantle " in Percy's " Reliques."

Cut. This verb never appears to have had a preterite,
though a past participle *ykitt* or *ykutt* is cited in Herbert
Coleridge's vocabulary of the " Oldest Words in the English
Language." Whence or when the word was introduced into
English no lexicographer has ever yet been able to determine.
It is neither derived from the Teutonic, the French, the
Greek, nor the Latin, and is therefore, by the exhaustive process, supposed by the most recent compilers of dictionaries to
have been borrowed from the Gaelic *cut,* to make short, and
such phrases as *cuttie*-pipe, *cuttie*-sark, and *cuttie*-stool, all
implying shortness and curtailment. A near approach to
it occurs in the French *couteau,* a knife or instrument to cut
with ; in the Italian *coltello ;* and in the English and Scottish
coulter, the ploughshare, or knife of the plough. It may be

that the original word was *kit*, whence *ykitt*, cited by Mr.
Coleridge, and that it formed its preterite by *cat* and *cut*.
Some little support for this idea may be found in the word *cat*
as applied in ‘*cat*-o'-nine-tails,’ a weapon that cuts pretty
severely; and in *kit-cat*, as applied to portraits that are not
exactly full-length, but cut to three-quarters length, as those
painted for the celebrated “Kit-Kat Club.”

Daff, daft, to make a fool of, to play the fool. *Daffe* in
Chaucer signifies a fool; and in the Scottish and North
English dialect a *daft* man signifies either a lunatic, or one
who has been befooled. *Daffing* signifies foolish fun or merriment. In the scene between Leonato and Claudio in “Much
Ado about Nothing,” when Claudio declines to fight the old
man, and says,—

> Away! away! I will not have to do with you.

Leonato replies,—

> Canst thou so *daff* me? Thou hast killed my child.

Both Mr. Charles Knight and Mr. Howard Staunton, following in the track of other Shakspearean editors, explain *daff*
in this passage to mean ‘doff,’ or ‘put off.’ The true meaning
is to ‘befool,’ as the word is used in Chaucer. When, elsewhere, Shakspeare says of Prince Henry,—

> Thou madcap Prince of Wales, that *daffed* the world aside,

the meaning of the word is the same. The ‘madcap’ did
not ‘doff’ the world aside, for in this sense the expression
would be pleonastic, but *daffed* or ‘fooled’ or jested it aside,
as a madcap would.

Dare or durst, dared. The tendency of our modern and
colloquial English, as well as of our current literature, is to
ignore the two preterites and the past participle of this word,
and to write and say *dare* where *durst* or *dared* would be more

correct. There is also a tendency to omit the *s* in the third person singular of the present tense. The following are examples of each inaccuracy :—

· Neither her maidens nor the priest *dare* speak to her for half an hour [*durst* speak to her, &c.].—*Hereward the Wake*, by the REV. CHARLES KINGSLEY.

The Government *dare* [durst] not consent to the meeting being held. . . . No one can feel anything but contempt for a Government which meanly attempts to gain a cheap reputation for firmness by fulminations which it *dare* [dares] not carry out ; and by prohibiting meetings which it *dare* [dares] not prevent.—London morning paper on the Hyde Park riots.

There is no reason why this verb should be deprived of its declensions, and no careful writer ought to fall into the errors just cited.

Deem, to judge. This word, which now signifies ' to think ' rather than ' to judge,' and which has lost its old preterite *doom*, formerly implied the delivery of a doom, sentence, or judgment. Chaucer calls a judge a *doomsman ;* and in the Isle of Man the judge is still called the *dempster* or *deemster*. The day of Doom is the day of Judgment. Chaucer does not use the old preterite *doom*, which seems to have perished before his time; but in the " Franklein's Prologue " uses the substantive *doom* in the sense of an opinion or a private judgment :—

> As to my *doom*, there is more that is here
> Of eloquence that shall be thy peer,
> If that thou live.

Out of the lost preterite the English writers of three centuries ago formed a new verb, to *doom*, with a regular preterite, *doomed*—a word which does not merely signify to pass judgment upon, but to pass a severe sentence.

Delve, dolve, dolven, to dig, to make a trench or ditch, to bury in the earth. This verb is still retained in poetical composition, and in the everyday speech of the people in

Scotland and some of the northern counties; but the old preterite and past participle are lost. They have found a substitute in the regular declension *delved*. The old preterite seems to have become obsolete at an early period, as appears from the distich of John Ball the priest, the friend and coadjutor of Wat Tyler in the rebellion of 1381 :—

> When Adam *delved* and Eve span,
> Who was then the gentleman?

Chaucer used the participle, "I would be *dolven* [buried] deep;" and in the "Romance of Merlin," a man who was to be buried alive is described as to "be *dolven* quick." "Piers Ploughman" has, "They *dolven* with spades and shovels to drive away hunger." Keats, in more modern times, employs *delved* :—

> Oh for a draught of vintage that hath been
> Cooled a long age in the deep *delved* earth!

If he had said deep *dolven* instead of deep *delved*, he would have had high authority, and would have greatly improved the stately march and music of his verse.

Dight, dighted, to prepare, to put in order, to deck, to attire, to wipe away. This useful word of many meanings is all but obsolete in English literature, but survives in Scottish. The preterite has long been lost. An offshoot of this word in the form of *misdight* (misprepared) occurs in Jack Miller's song, quoted by Stowe in his account of Wat Tyler's rebellion :—

> If might
> Go before right,
> And will
> Before skill,
> Then is our mill *misdight*.

Spencer and Milton both attempted to revive *dight*, but with only partial success :—

> Soon after them, all dancing in a row,
> The comely virgins came with garlands *dight*.
> > —*The Faerie Queene.*

> The clouds in thousand liveries *dight.*
> > —*L'Allegro.*

> Storied windows richly *dight.*
> > —*Il Penseroso.*

In Scottish parlance *dight* does constant service. The lassie *dights* her mou' before accepting a kiss, and *dights* her een after she has been weeping. She *dights* herself in her best attire before going to kirk; and the wife *dights* the dinner for her husband.

> *Dight* your cheeks and banish care.
> > —ALLAN RAMSAY.

> Let me rax up to *dight* that tear,
> And go with me and be my dear.
> > —BURNS: *The Jolly Beggars.*

Ding, dang, dong or **dung,** to strike hard, to beat down. The infinitive and present tense of this verb are still colloquially current, but the preterite and past participle are obsolete, or only survive in the nursery phrase, " *Ding, dong,* bell." In Scotland the verb and all its inflections survive. Burns, in his often-quoted line, says, " Facts are chiels that winna *ding.*" Sir Alexander Boswell has a song entitled " Jenny *dang* the Weaver," which expression was translated by an English critic into the very prosaic form of " Jenny vanquished the cotton manufacturer." The past-participle occurs in the familiar proverbs quoted by Allan Ramsay, " It's a sair *dung* bairn that munna greet," and " He's sairest paid that's *dung* wi' his ain wand." The modern English preterite *dinged* is still occasionally heard in conversation, though lost to literature, as in such phrases: "Horace? Yes; he was *dinged* into me at school;" and colloquially, " Why do you keep *dinging* that old story into my ears?"

The word constantly occurs in serious poetry up to the time of Shakspeare and Ben Jonson, and survives, and is likely long to survive, in the nursery rhyme—

> Ding, dong, bell,
> Pussy's in the well.

The hellish prince, grim Pluto, with his mace, *ding* down my soul to hell!—*The Battle of Alcazar.*

> Do-well shall *dyngen* him down,
> And destroyen his mighte.
>   —*Piers Ploughman.*

> She *dings* you in her hamely goun o' gray,
> As far's a summer *dings* a winter day.
>   —Ross's *Helenore.*

> My chains then, and pains then,
>   Infernal be their hire,
> Who *dang* us and *flang* us,
>   Into this ugsome mire.
>   —ALLAN RAMSAY : *The Vision—The Evergreen.*

The beautiful poem of "The Vision," written in older Scotch than that of the time of Allan Ramsay, is signed A. R. Scotus, meaning, "Allan Ramsay, a Scot." It expresses in covert allusion, the indignation of the Scots of Allan Ramsay's day, at the Union of Scotland with England, and the means by which it was accomplished. Allan Ramsay's Jacobite friends were all well aware that the poem was from his pen, but the government of the day, though suspecting the fact, and willing to prosecute him, wisely refrained from doing so.

Dow, to be able, to thrive ; *dought,* was able. This verb is utterly lost from English literature, but, like many others of its sturdy class, exists in the speech of the English peasantry, and in the speech as well as the literature of Scotland. By a strange neglect, or a stranger ignorance, the makers of dictionaries—from Blount and Philips up to Johnson, Richardson, Worcester, Webster, and Stormonth—have either omitted all mention of it, or erroneously considered it to be synonymous with, or an orthographical error for, the similar word 'do,' with which it has no connection. "I do as well as I *dow?*"—*i.e.*, "I do as well as I can"—is a common phrase in the North : and the super-eminently English but pleonastic inquiry, "How do you do?"—which means "How do you *dow?*"—*i.e.*, thrive, prosper, or get on—has come to be accepted as accurate English, though wholly a mistake of the learned. Even Nares, in his Glossary, has no suspicion of this word, though Halliwell, more acute, gives one of its meanings, 'to thrive,' 'to mend in health;' and Mr. Thomas Wright, in his "Provincial Dictionary," follows in the same track as regards its use in English literature, though he does not seem to be aware of its commonness in the literature of Scotland. William Hamilton, the Scottish poet, writes to his friend Allan Ramsay,—

> Lang may'st thou live and thrive and *dow!*

And Burns says to Gavin Hamilton,—

> When I *downa* yoke a naig,
> The Lord be thankit, I can beg!

In his " Epistle to King George III.," in his eulogy of facts, Burns speaks of them as " chiels that winna ding," and adds, " they *downa* be disputed." Ross, in his " Helenore," has " When he *dow* do nae mair,"—a phrase that shows the essential difference between the two words.

From this obsolete verb springs the adjective *doughty*, strong, able—a derivation which up to the present time seems to have escaped the notice of all the English lexicographers.

Dread, drad, dradden, to fear greatly. The modern preterite and past participle *dreaded* have entirely superseded the ancient forms.

> But what I *drad*, did me, poor wretch, betide.
> —ROBERT GREENE, 1593.

Dwine, dwined, to pine away, to fall of. This verb has been superseded by its diminutive, to *dwindle*, which has the same meaning.

Thus *dwineth* he till he be dead.
—GOWER.
It *dwined* for eld.
—CHAUCER.
Bacchus hates repining;
Venus loves no *dwining.*
—ALLAN RAMSAY.

Fang, fong, fung, to seize, to lay hold of. Most people remember the old law phrase, "in*fang* thief and out*fang* thief," the one signifying a thief taken within the jurisdiction of a feudal lord, and the other a thief taken without his jurisdiction. This is the only remnant of this verb that has come down to our time except the substantive *fang*, the large tooth of a beast of prey or of a serpent; the diminutive *fangle*, to take hold of a new fancy or fashion; and the common phrase *new-fangled.* In Scotland it is sometimes said when the well does not readily yield the water after repeated strokes of the pump, that the pump has lost its *fang* o' the water.

I nold *fang* a farthing (I would not take a farthing).
—*Vision of Piers Ploughman.*

He *fong* his foeman by the flank,
And flang him on the floor.
—BUCHAN'S *Northern Ballads.*

Fare, foor, fore, fure, fared, to travel. This verb is not wholly obsolete, though its preterite is lost. It has come to signify to eat and drink as well as to travel, and also that which is eaten or drunk. It is doubtful whether our beautiful word 'farewell' means "may you travel well through life," or "may you be well treated by the world." A way-*faring* man is still a common expression. 'Auld-*farrand*,' travelling on the old ways, old-fashioned, is intelligible to the people on the north of the Tweed. The preterite occurs several times in the "Vision of Piers Ploughman."

Alexander fell into a fever therewith, so that he *fure* wondrous ille.
—MS. LINCOLN, quoted in HALLIWELL'S *Archaic Dictionary.*

Her errand led her through the glen to *fare.*
—Ross's *Helenore.*

As o'er the moor they lightly *foor,*
A burn was clear, a glen was green—
Up the banks they eased their shanks.
—Burns.

Forewent, preterite of to forego, to renounce.

Writers and speakers still say, " I *forego* the pleasure," but use a roundabout form of expression rather than say, " I *forewent* the pleasure." And why ? *Forewent* is as legitimate a word as *forego,* and should not be allowed to become obsolete.—*Lost Beauties of the English Language.*

Forswink, forswunk, to be worn out with overmuch toil.

She is my goddess plain,
And I her shepherd swain,
Albeit *forswunk* and forswat I am.
—Specker : *Shepherd's Calendar.*

Fret, freet, freten, to devour or eat up; from the French and Dutch *freten,* the German *fressen,* to eat.

Like as it were a moth *fretting* a garment.—Psalm xxxix., *Common Prayer.*

Adam *freet* of that fruit,
And forsook the love of our Lord.
—*Piers Ploughman.*

He (the dragon) has *fretten* of folk more than five hundred.—*Morte d'Arthur.*

Frush, frusht, frushed, to bruise, disturb, rumple, disarrange. From the Gaelic *frois,* a driving gust of rain, and *froiseach,* to scatter, to shake off, and French *froisser,* to rub against. This good Shakspearean word is fairly admissible into modern dictionaries, in few of which, however, does it find a place.

Stand ! stand, thou Greek ! thou art a goodly mark !
No ! wilt thou not ? I like thy armour well,
I'll *frush* it and unlock the rivets all !
—Shakspeare : *Troilus and Cressida.*

Hector assailed Achilles and gave him so many strokes that he all to *frusht* and brake his helm.—CAXTON'S *Destruction of Troy.*

High cedars are *frushed* with tempests.—HINDE, 1606.

Southey uses the substantive :—

Horrible uproar and *frush* of rocks that meet in battle.

The word well deserves favour and restoration.

Gar, gart, gard, to compel, to force, to make, to cause a thing to be done. This verb in all its declensions has become obsolete in English literature, where its place has been but feebly supplied by 'make' and 'made.' "I'll make him do it" is neither so strong nor so elegant as the ancient English and modern Scotch, "I'll *gar* him do it."

> *Gar* us have meat and drink, and make us chere.
> —CHAUCER : *The Reeve's Tale.*

> *Gar* saddle me my bonnie black,
> *Gar* saddle soon, and make her ready.
> —*Minstrelsy of the Scottish Border.*

> And like the mavis on the bush,
> He *gart* the vallies ring.
> —PERCY'S *Reliques.*

Auld Girzie Graham, having twice refused a glass of toddy, when pressed a third time, replied, "Weel! weel! since ye winna hear o' a refusal, just mak it hot, an' strong, an' sweet, an' *gar* me tak it!"— *Laird of Logan.*

Get, got, gotten, to attain, to procure, to come into possession of. The past participle of this verb has lately become obsolete, except in the talk of the uneducated and in Scottish literature. It was common in the last century.

We knew we were *gotten* far enough out of their reach.—DEFOE : *Robinson Crusoe.*

> Ken ye what Meg o' the mill has *gotten?*
> She's *gotten* a lout wi' a lump o' siller,
> And broken the heart o' the barley miller.
> > —ROBERT BURNS.

There is also a marked tendency to the disuse of this inflection in the verb 'to forget,' and people too commonly say and write " I have *forgot*," instead of *forgotten.*

Glide, glode, glidden, to move away easily and smoothly. The ancient preterite and past participle have become obsolete, and have been superseded by *glided*, much to the loss of versifiers in search of good rhymes.

> His good stede he all bestrode,
> And forth upon his way he *glode.*
> > —CHAUCER.

> He *glode* forth as an adder doth.
> > —*Idem.*

> Through Guy's shield it *glode.*
> > —*Guy of Warwick.*

The reason of the substitution of the regular for the irregular preterite may be found in the desire to prevent confusion with the regular preterite of the verb 'to glow.'

Glint, glent, glinted, to shine, to flash, to appear suddenly. In Sternberg's " Northamptonshire Glossary " the infinitive of this verb as used amongst the peasantry of that part of England is cited as *gline*. *Glint* would be the legitimate preterite if this were correct. In Scottish poetry *glint* is the infinitive, and *glinted* the preterite and past participle. In Old English poetry *glent* is the preterite.

> The sunbeams are *glinting* far over the sea.
> > —*Newcastle Garland.*

Cauld blew the bitter biting north
Upon thy early humble birth,
Yet cheerfully thou *glinted* forth
    Amid the storm.
        —BURNS : *To a Mountain Daisy.*

There came a hand withouten rest
    Out of the water,
    And brandished it.
Anon as a gleam away it *glent.*
        —*Morte d'Arthur.*

Gnaw, gnew, gnawed, to bite at a hard substance. The old preterite is lost, doubtless on account of its identity in pronunciation with the more familiar word 'knew,' the preterite of 'know,' a word of different meaning.

Till with the grips he was baith·black and blue,
At last in twa the dowie ropes he *gnew.*
        —Ross's *Helenore.*

    No sustenance got,
But only at the cauld hill's berries *gnew.*
        —*Idem.*

Go, gaed, gone, to depart. The ancient and legitimate preterite of this verb has been superseded by the preterite ('went') of the verb to 'wend,' to turn away. It maintains its ground, however, in Scotland and the northern English counties. Chaucer has 'gadling,' for a vagabond, a wanderer who goes much about; and the language still retains the word to 'gad,' to wander or stray about, making short visits.

    I *gaed* a waefu' gate yestreen.
        —BURNS.

Grab, grub, grabbed, to dig up, to seize. This verb, in all its inflections, has been wholly relegated to the speech of the vulgar, but, like many other vulgar words, has a highly respectable origin. *Grab,* in its first sense, means to dig a grave or hole; and *grub* means that which is dug up, such

                             x

as roots for human subsistence, whence its modern and slang signification, 'food.'

Graith, graithed, to prepare, make ready. A critic in the *Literary Gazette* of March 30, 1860, called a poet to account for using such an unpermissible word as *graith,* of which he declared his utter ignorance. He might, however, have found it in Chaucer, in Worcester's Dictionary, and in Robert Burns :—

> Her son Galathin
> She *graithed* in attire fine.
> > —*Arthour and Merlin.*

> Unto the Jewes such a hate had he,
> That he bade *graith* his chair full hastilie.
> > —CHAUCER: *The Reeve's Tale.*

> Go warn me Perthshire and Angus baith,
> And *graith* my horse.
> > —*Song of the Outlaw Murray.*

Greet, grat, grutten, to weep. This verb, with all its declensions, has lost its place in English literature, though the word *greet* remains with a different meaning, 'to salute.' Like other strong indigenous words which modern English has unnecessarily discarded, it is retained in Scotland. It seems to have been lost even in Chaucer's time, who uses *greet* entirely in the modern sense of 'to salute.' "Piers Ploughman" has it in the sense of 'to lament' or 'weep.'

> And then 'gan Gloton to *greet,*
> And great dool to make.

"It's a sad time," says an old Scottish proverb, "when hens crow and bearded men *greet.*" Another proverb says, "Better bairns should *greet* than bearded men."

> Then ilk ain to the other made his wain,
> And sighed and *grat,* and *grat* and sighed again.
> > —Ross's *Helenore.*

Duncan sighed baith out and in,
Grat his een baith bleer't and blin'.
—BURNS: *Duncan Gray.*

The Edinbro' wells are *grutten* dry.
—BURNS: *Elegy on the Year* 1788.

Heat, to make or grow hot; **het,** made hot.

Let him cool in the skin he *het* in.—ALLAN RAMSAY: *Scots Proverbs.*

Help, holp, holpen, to aid. The preterite and past participle are fast becoming obsolete. They are still retained in the Flemish language.

For thou hast *holpen* me now.
—HALLIWELL: *MS. Cantab.*

And blind men *holpen.*
—*Piers Ploughman.*

Building upon the foundation that went before us, and being *holpen* by their labours.—*The translators of the Bible to the reader: temp.* JAMES I.

Hend, hent, to take, to hold, to seize, to apprehend.

Jog on, jog on, the footpath way,
And merrily *hent* the style-a:
A merry heart goes all the day,
Your sad tires in a mile-a.

It is probable that in this well-known passage from the song of Autolycus in the "Winter's Tale," the preterite *hent* is a misprint for the infinitive *hend,* though it must be admitted that Chaucer uses *hent* both in the present and the past tenses. This is a very unusual defect in an English verb of that early period.

All be it that it was not our intente,
He should be sauf, but that we sholde him *hent.*
—CHAUCER: *The Friar's Tale.*

Shakspeare uses *hent* as a substantive, to signify a purpose, an intention to hold by, in Hamlet's exclamation, when he determines not to kill the king at his prayers :—

> No !
> Up, sword ! and know thou a more horrid *hent* /
> When he is drunk, asleep, or in his rage.

Hit, het, hitten, to strike, to touch violently with a blow. Both preterite and past participle are obsolete. *Hitten* survives in the colloquial language of the peasantry. '

> Your honour's *hitten* the nail upon the head.
>   —Ross's *Helenore.*

The Americans, in default of the old preterite *het*, occasionally say *hot*—as, " He *hot* me a heavy blow ; he *hot* out right and left."

Hold, held, holden, to have, grasp, or retain in possession. The past participle is obsolete, but might be advantageously revived for the sake of the rhyme which it affords to ' golden,' ' embolden,' &c.

Keek, keeked, to peep, to look in slily.

> The robin came to the wren's nest,
> And *keeked* in and *keeked* in.
>   —*Nursery Rhymes of England.*

> This Nicholas sat even gape upright,
> As he had *keeked* on the new moone.
>   —CHAUCER: *The Miller's Tale.*

> Stars, dinna *keek* in
> And see me wi' Mary.
>   —BURNS.

Kythe, kouth or couth, to show, appear, know, make known. This word has become wholly obsolete in England, but survives in Scotland. The sole remnant of it in English is *uncouth*, originally meaning something unknown, unheard of, strange, and now meaning rough or ungainly. Milton has—

> Bound on a voyage *uncouth*,

meaning unknown. The Scotch have the word *couthie*, familiar, or well known.

> And to the people's eres all and some
> Was *couth* that a new markissesse
> He with him brought in such pompe and richenes
> That never was there seen with manne's eye.
> > —CHAUCER: *The Clerk's Tale.*

> Take your sport, and *kythe* your knights.
> > —*Sir Ferumbras.*

> · *Kythe* in your ain colours, that folk may ken you.—ALLAN RAMSAY'S *Scots Proverbs.*

> Their faces blythe, they sweetly *kythe.*
> > —BURNS.

Laugh, lough, leuch. The ancient preterite and past participle of this verb have been superseded by the modern preterite in *ed.*

> Then *lough* there a lord,
> And " By this lighte " saide,
> " I hold it right and reson."
> > —*Piers Ploughman.*

> He cleped it Valerie and Theophrast,
> And *lough* always full fast.
> > —CHAUCER: *The Wife of Bath's Prologue.*

> When she had read Wise William's letter,
> She smiled and she *leuch.*
> > —MOTHERWELL'S *Collection.*

> " I think not so," she halflins said, and *leuch.*
> > —Ross's *Helenore.*

How graceless Ham *leuch* at his dad,
Which made Canaan a nigger.
—BURNS : *The Ordination.*

An' ilka ane *leuch* him to scorn.
—PERCY'S *Reliques : The Auld Guidman.*

Leap, lope, lopen, to leap.   At what time this verb followed the analogy of weep, creep, and sleep, and formed its preterite in *leap* or *lept*, does not very clearly appear.

And they laughing *lope* to her.
—*Piers Ploughman.*

Have *lopen* the better.
—*Idem.*

Up he *lope* and the window broke,
And he had thirty foot to fall.
—PERCY'S *Reliques: The Murder of the King of Scots.*

Tom Rindle *lope* fra the chimley nook.
—WAUGH'S *Lancashire Songs.*

Let, loot, letten, looten, to let, to permit.   This verb has lost all its inflections in literary and colloquial English, but preserves them in the Scottish dialect.

But *letten* him lede forth whom hym liked.
—*Piers Ploughman.*

And aye she *loot* the tears down fa'
For Jock o' Hazeldean.
—SIR WALTER SCOTT.

Ye've *loot* the ponie o'er the dyke.
—BURNS.

But dool had not yet *letten* her feel her want.
—ROSS's *Helenore.*

He boore upon him and ne'er *loot* her ken.
—ROSS's *Helenore.*

Ligge, ligged, to lie down. This ancient word is still in common use in Cumberland and Northumberland, and also in the Border counties of Scotland.

> So that the Holy Ghost
> Gloweth but as a glade,
> Till that lele love
> *Ligge* on him.
> —*Piers Ploughman.*

> What hawkes sitten on the perche above!
> What houndes *liggen* on the floor adown!
> —CHAUCER : *The Knight's Tale.*

I have *ligged* for a fortnight in London, weak almost to death, and neglected by every one.—G. P. R. JAMES : *Gowrie, or the King's Plot.*

List or **lest, lust,** to please. This word has gradually been dropping out of use, but having been preserved in the Bible, is still occasionally heard. The preterite is lost, though the word itself survives as a substantive, and as the infinitive of another verb, to *lust*, signifying to desire pleasure vehemently.

> The wind bloweth where it *listeth.*

The colloquial expression, " to *list* for a soldier," seems to come from this root, and means, to please to become, or voluntarily to become, a soldier. Chaucer uses *lust* in the sense of joy :—

> Farewell, my life, my *lust*, and my gladnesse.
> —*The Knight's Tale.*

Lout, louted, to make an obeisance or a curtsey.

> And then *louted* adown.
> —*Piers Ploughman.*

> " Sir," quoth the dwarf, and *louted* low.
> —PERCY'S *Reliques: Sir Cauline.*

> They *louted* to that ladye.
> —PERCY'S *Reliques: On Alliterative Metre.*

> To which image both young and old
> Commanded he to *lout.*
>> —CHAUCER : *The Monke's Tale.*

> And I am *louted* by a traitor villain.
>> —SHAKSPEARE : *Henry VI.*, Part i.

Melt, molt, molten, to liquefy by means of heat. The preterite is lost, but the past participle is still preserved in poetry and the Bible.

Mint, minted, to essay, to try, to 'aim, to attempt, to prove the genuineness of metals before coinage.

> *Minting's* not making (attempting's not doing).
>> —ALLAN RAMSAY'S *Scots Proverbs.*

> A *minted* [attempted] excuse.
>> —*The Two Lancashire Lovers*: 1660.

Nake, naked, to denude of covering. The preterite survives as an adjective ; the infinitive is lost.

> Come, be ready ! *nake* your swords.
> Think of your wrongs !
>> —NARES : *Revenge's Tragedy.*

Pight, a word that occurs in Chaucer, is defined by Tyrwhitt as meaning, ' pitched,' rather than the preterite of ' put ':—

> He *pight* him on the pomel of his head,
> That in the place he lay as he were dead.
>> —CHAUCER : *The Knight's Tale.*

Stowe, however, at a later period, uses *pight* for ' did put ' :—

He was brought to the Standard in Cheape, where they strake off his head and *pight* it on a pole, and bare it before them.—STOWE'S *Annals : Henry VI.*

Prank, prankt or **pranked,** to adorn, to embellish, to dress fashionably.

> Some *prank* their ruffs, and others trimly dight
> Their gay attire.
> > —SPENSER : *The Faerie Queene.*

> False tales *prankt* in reason's garb.
> > —MILTON : *Comus.*

> Most goddess-like *pranked* up.
> > —SHAKSPEARE : *Winter's Tale.*

Put, pat or **pight, putten** or **pitten,** to place. The modern verb has lost the preterite and past participle.

> I there wi' something did forgether,
> That *pat* me in an eerie swither.
> > —BURNS : *Death and Doctor Hornbook.*

> Ye see how Rob and Jenny's gone sin' they
> Ha'e *pitten* o'er their heads the merry day.
> > —Ross's *Helenore.*

He's *putten* it to a good purpose, has Brighouse.—*The Master of Marston :* London, 1664.

Quake, quoke, to tremble with fear.

> An ugly pit, as deep as any hell,
> That to behold therein I *quoke* for fear.
> > —*The King's Quair.*

> The whole land of Italy trembled and *quoke.*
> > —DOUGLAS : *Translation of the Æneid.*

Quethe or **queath, quoth,** to say. The infinitive of this verb is lost, but the preterite *quoth* remains in colloquial use, and in writings that do not aspire to eloquence or dignity, as ' *quoth* he,' ' *quoth* I.' *Bequeath*, to say in your will what part of your property your heirs or legatees shall possess, is a remnant of this ancient verb.

Rax, raught, to reach, to stretch.

> He *raught* to the steere (he reached to the helm).
> > —*Piers Ploughman.*

> He start up and would have him *raught.*
> > —MERLIN : *Early English Metrical Romances.*

> The villain is *o'er-raught* of all my money.
> > —SHAKSPEARE : *Comedy of Errors.*

> Their three-mile prayers and half-mile graces,
> Their *raxing* conscience.
> > —BURNS : *Epistle to M'Math.*

> > Is this a time to talk o' wark,
> > When Colin's at the door ?
> > *Rax* down my cloak, I'll to the quay,
> > And see him come ashore.
> > > —MICKLE : *There's nae Luck about the House.*

Reap, rept, rope, ropen, to cut, or help to cut the harvest.

> *Ropen* and laide away the corne.
> > —CHAUCER : *Legende of Good Women.*

> After the corn is *rept.*
> > —NARES.

Reave, reft, take off, take away, whence the old English and Scottish word *reaver* or *reiver*, a thief.   This word survives in *bereave* and *bereft*, but is fast becoming obsolete.

> > If he *reaveth* me by night,
> > He robbeth me by maistrye.
> > > —*Piers Ploughman.*

> Therefore, though no part of his work to *reave* him,
> We now for matters more allied must leave him.
> > —HEYWOOD'S *Troia Britannia*, 1609.

> > To go robbe that ragman,
> > And *reave* the fruit from him.
> > > —*Piers Ploughman.*

Means to live by *reaf* of other men's goods.—HOLINSHED'S *Chronicles.*

Reek, roke, to emit smoke or vapour. The present tense of this verb survives in solemn and poetical composition in England, but both the present and preterite are in common and colloquial use in Scotland. " Auld *Reekie* " is a popular name for Edinburgh.

Rown, rowned, to whisper, to talk privately, to whisper in the ear. This word is wholly lost, but might have been preserved, if Shakspeare, like modern authors, had been in the habit of correcting his proof-sheets. The word, misprinted *round,* occurs several times in Shakspeare, and has puzzled all the commentators. Mr. Staunton, in a note on the passage where Polonius says to the king in " Hamlet "—

> Let his queen-mother all alone entreat him
> To show his grief—let her be *round* with him,

says, " Let her be blunt and plain-spoken with him."
In another note to the word in "King John," act ii. scene 2—

> Whom zeal and charity brought to the field
> As God's own soldier, *rounded* in the ear
> With that same purpose—charge—

he explains the true meaning of *rounded* (which should be *rowned,* just as vulgar people sometimes say 'drownded' for drowned) as ' insinuated,' ' whispered in the ear.' He quotes from the Spanish tragedy the line where the same orthographical error occurs—

> Forthwith, revenge, she *rounded* them in the ear.

The word appears correctly in all authors previous to Shakspeare :—

> They rose up in rape,
> And *rowned* together.
> —*Piers Ploughman.*

> The steward on his knees sat down
> With the emperor for to *rown*.
> > —*Romance of Cœur de Lion.*

> But if it like you that I might *rowne* in your ear.
> > —Skelton.

Sag, sog, to bend or give way under pressure, to fail.

> The mind I sway by, and the heart, I fear,
> Shall never *sag* with doubt or shake with fear.
> > —Shakspeare : *Macbeth.*

> That it may not *sag* from the intention of the founders.
> > —Fuller's *Worthies.*

From the lost preterite *sog* comes the adjective *soggy*, often used by the Americans to signify wet boggy soil that yields to the foot.

Scathe or skaith, to do an injury or damage. Shakspeare and Milton use the verb :—

> This trick may chance to *scathe* you.
> > —*Romeo and Juliet.*

> *Scathed* the forest oaks.
> > —Milton.

The substantive *scathe* or *skaith*, signifiying hurt, damage, and injury, survives in Scottish speech and literature, and is not wholly obsolete in English poetry, though rarely used by modern writers.

> Oh ! if on my bosom lying,
> I could work him deadly *scathe*,
> In one burst of burning passion,
> I would kiss him unto death !
> > —*Love in Hate.*

Seethe, sod, sodden, to boil. The translators of the Bible have preserved this old English word, which was in common

use before its modern synonym was borrowed with other culi-
nary phrases from the Norman French :—

And he said unto his servant, Set on the great pot, and *seethe* pottage
for the sons of the prophets.—2 KINGS iv. 38.

> Go suck the subtle blood o' th' grape
> Till the high fever *seethe* your blood to froth.
> —SHAKSPEARE: *Timon of Athens.*

Seethe stanes in butter, the brew will be good.—ALLAN RAMSAY'S *Scots
Proverbs.*

> It is unsavorye
> Y-*sodden* or y-baken
> —*Piers Ploughman.*

Shape, shope, shopen, to make, to create, to put into form.
This verb has wholly lost its original meaning in the infinitive and present, in which form it subsists as a regular verb,
with its preterite in *d.* Its preterite and past participle have
long been obsolete, and do not seem to have been used in English literature after the time of Chaucer.

God *shope* the world.—WICKLIFFE'S *Bible.*.

> The king and the commune
> *Shopen* laws.
> —*Piers Ploughman.*

To which this sempnour *shope* him for to wende.
> —CHAUCER: *The Frere's Tale.*

Shear, sheer, shore or shure, shorn, to cut closely off. The
ancient preterite is obsolete, and has been superseded in the
regular form in *ed.* The sea-shore—*i.e.*, the strip of land
sheared, shore, or *shorn* by the action of the waves—is the sole
relic of this word in modern parlance.

> Robin *shure* in hairst [harvest],
> I *shure* wi' him.
> —BURNS.

Boston was the Delilah that allured him [Daniel Webster]. Oft he broke withes of gold, till at last she *shore* off his locks, and his strength went from him.—THEODORE PARKER : *Discourse on the Death of Daniel Webster.*

Shend, shent, shent, to rebuke, to blame, to shame, or bring to shame.

> What say you, sir ?
> I am *shent* for speaking to you.
> > —SHAKSPEARE : *Twelfth Night.*

> He that shames let him be *shent.*
> > —ALLAN RAMSAY.

> All woe-begone was John o' the Scales,
> Soe *shent* he could say never a word.
> > —PERCY'S *Reliques : The Heir of Lynne.*

Spenser in the " Faerie Queene," and Thomson in the " Castle of Indolence," use this word. According to Dr. Johnson, the last author of note who employed it was Dryden. It survives in Scotland.

Shread, shred, to cut off the ends, to lop. The old preterite has long been obsolete, but survives as a noun ; *shred,* a thing lopped off or cut off, a remnant.

The superfluous and waste sprigs of vines being *shreaded* off.— WITHALL'S *Dictionarie :* 1608.

A *shredded* of trees.—NARES.

Shrew, shrow, shrown. This obsolete word, of which the only current representative is *shrewd,* a perversion of the original meaning, signifies 'to curse,' and ·finds a singular synonym in America. In England a scolding wife is a *shrew ;* in America the same disagreeable person is a 'cuss.' Shakspeare applies the word *shrew* to both sexes, just as the

Americans do the word ' cuss.' " Beshrew me ! " the old ejacu-
lation, meant " curse me ! " At the present day inferior
writers and careless speakers will say, " I have a *shrewd*
suspicion," meaning " a *sharp,* cunning suspicion." The time
at which the word assumed this new meaning in speech or
literature is uncertain.

Shrive, shrove, shriven, to confess to the priest ; *shrift,* a
confession. This verb, in all its inflections, went out when
the Reformation came in, and only survives in poetry and
romance, and in the word " Shrove Tuesday."

Slake, sloke, sloken, to assuage thirst, to quench a fire.
The preterite and past participle are obsolete.

Sneap, sneb, snub, to check, chide, rebuke angrily, to be
sharp to a person, like a cutting wind.

> An envious *sneaping* frost
> That bites the first-born infants of the spring.
> —SHAKSPEARE: *Love's Labour Lost.*

> Do you *sneap* me too, my lord ?
> —BROWNE'S *Antipodes.*

This word only survives in its past participle *snub,* which has
become the infinitive of a verb with the original meaning.

Snow, snew, snown, to drop partially congealed rain. The
preterite and past participle survive in America, but are considered vulgarisms.

> Withouten bake meat never was his house,
> Of fish and flesh, and that so plenteous,
> It *snewe* in his house of meat and drink.
> —CHAUCER: *Prologue to the Canterbury Tales.*

> First it blew, and then it *snew,* and then it friz horrid.
> —MAJOR DOWNING'S *Letters.*

Ben Jonson, in his " English Grammar," cites the following verbs that make their preterite in *ew*—viz., blow, grow, throw, crow, know, draw, slay, and *snow*. The last is the only one of the number that now forms its preterite in *ed*, though un-educated people both in Great Britain and America some-times form the preterites of grow, blow, and know in *ed* —as when Topsy, in " Uncle Tom's Cabin," says " she growed." " I knowed it," instead of " I knew it," is also a common vulgarism.

Stand, stood, studden.

Weel, I thought there was naething but what your honour could hae *studden* in the way o' agreeable conversation.—SCOTT: *The Antiquary.*

Stent, stint, stunt, to desist, to cease, to limit, to confine within a certain bound. This verb is a curious instance of the liberties which Time takes with the old words of a language. The three inflections have each been made to do duty for an infinitive, so that one verb has been virtually converted into three. Chaucer has *stent*, the correct and original form :—

> And of this cry we would they never *stent*.
> —*The Knight's Tale.*

The noun *stent*, an allotted portion of work, though obsolete in England, is common in America.

Little boys in the country, working against time, with *stents* to do.— THEODORE PARKER: *Discourse on the Death of Daniel Webster.*

Stint, the ancient preterite, is the modern infinitive, and forms its preterite and past participle regularly in *ed*. *Stint*, to stint, or stop, or cease in growth, goes through the same inflections. The late Daniel O'Connell called the Duke of Wellington a " *stunted* corporal."

Sweat, swat, to perspire. This ancient word survives in colloquial, but has been of late years banished from literary

English, and from polite society. The curse pronounced upon Adam, " In the *sweat* of thy face shalt thou eat [or earn] thy bread," would have lost much of its native energy if the ancient translators had been as mealy-mouthed as the men of the present day, and rendered *sweat* by *perspiration.*

> His fair steed
> So *swat* that men might him ring.
> > —CHAUCER: *The Rhyme of Sir Topaz.*

> His hackenye which that was al pomelee gris,
> So *swatte* that it wonder was to see.
> > —*The Chanones Yemanne's Tale.*

> Some, lucky, find a flowery spot,
> For which they never toiled nor *swat.*
> > —BURNS: *Epistle to James Smith.*

An anecdote is related by Dean Ramsay, of a sturdy old lady who so greatly loved hearty vehemence in preaching, that she delighted in one particular minister, because when he preached he was in such grim earnest with his discourse that " he *grat* and *spat* and *swat* " over it !

Swell, swale, swoll, swollen. The preterite in *swale* is almost obsolete; that in *swoll* has been newly revived, but scarcely holds its own against *swelled.*

> An' thought it *swale* so sore about hir harte.
> > —CHAUCER: *The Wife of Bathe's Tale.*

Swink, swank, swonken, to labour over hard. This word appears to have been almost obsolete in Shakspeare's time. Some of his contemporaries use it, and Milton tried to revive it.

> In setting and sowing
> *Swinken* full hard.
> > —*Piers Ploughman.*

Y

> Great boobies and long
> That loth were to *swink*.
> —*Piers Ploughman.*

> For which men *swink* and sweat incessantly.
> —SPENSER: *Faeric Queene.*

> We'll labour and *swinke*,
> We'll kiss and we'll drinke.
> —BEAUMONT and FLETCHER: *The Spanish Cureto.*

> For he had *swonken* all the nighte long.
> —CHAUCER: *The Reeve's Tale.*

Thole, tholed, to suffer, to endure, to tolerate. This word is in common use throughout Scotland and on the English border, but has long been lost to literature.

> Which died and death *tholed*
> About mid-day.
> —*Piers Ploughman.*

> What mischief and malease Christ for man *tholed.*
> —CHAUCER: *Visions.*

> What mickle wo as I with you have *tholed.*
> —CHAUCER.

> She shall the death *thole.*
> —GOWER: *Confessio Amantis.*

> He who *tholes* conquers.
> —ALLAN RAMSAY'S *Scots Proverbs.*

> Tenant bodies, scant o' cash,
> How they maun *thole* the factor's snash!
> —BURNS.

Threap, to argue, to complain, to lament.

> 'Tis not for man with a woman to *threap.*
> —PERCY'S *Reliques: Tak' thy auld cloak about thee.*

> Some cry upon God, others *threap* that He hath forgotten them.
> —BISHOP FISHER.

> Some heads well learned upon the book,
> Would *threap* auld folks the thing mistook.
> —BURNS.

In Grose's "Provincial Glossary" a shopkeeper's phrase is quoted, "This is not *threaping* ware "—*i.e.*, these goods are so superior that they are not to be argued about or cheapened.

Thring, throng, thrung, to press, to jostle, to crowd, whence the modern word to *throng*.

> A thousand of men,
> *Thrungen* together,
> Cried upwards to Christ.
> —*Piers Ploughman.*

The Scottish word *thrang*—*i.e.*, busy with a crowd of customers—is a remnant of this word, in which, as in many others, the original preterite has been made to do duty for the infinitive and the present tense.

Trat, the preterite of treat.—TIM BOBBIN.

Wax, wox, waxed, woxen, woxed, to grow, to increase. This word, chiefly preserved by its frequent use in the Old and New Testament, lost its original preterite and participle, *wox* and *woxen*, before the translation of the Bible in the reign of James I., at which time the word *wax*, with the regular inflections, was in common use.

> And when he *woxen* was more
> In his mother's absence.
> —*Piers Ploughman.*

> This man *wox* wellnigh wood [mad] for ire.
> —CHAUCER : *The Sompnoure's Tale.*

> Before my breath, like blazen flax,
> Man and his marvels pass away ;

> And changing empires wane and *wax*,
> Are founded, flourish, and decay.
> —SIR WALTER SCOTT : *Translation of the*
> *Dies Iræ.*

Wink, wank, to close and open the eyes, to make signals with the eye.

> Our king on the shepherd *wank*
> Privily with his eye.
> —HALLIWELL : *MS. Cantab.*

Wreak, wreaked, wroke, wroken, to avenge. The infinitive of this verb is still current in connection with the nouns wrath, vengeance, displeasure, spite, and others.

> So *wreake* us, God, of all our foes.
> —*Sir Bevis of Hampton.*

> 'Tis not my fault, the boar provoked my tongue.
> Be *wreaked* on him.
> —SHAKSPEARE : *Venus and Adonis.*

> And soon in the Gordon's foul heart's blood,
> He's *wroken* his faire ladye.
> —*Minstrelsy of the Scottish Border.*

To have *wroken* himself of such wrongs as were due him by the French king.—HOLINSHED'S *Chronicles.*

The verbs here quoted are merely samples of the literary treasures that lie concealed in the speech of the common people of the northern counties, in the old English authors anterior to Shakspeare, and in the Scottish literature of the present day. What should we say if an English nobleman of ancient and illustrious lineage and great wealth had in the cellars and vaults of his castle hundreds of coffers and oaken chests filled to the lid with coins of the purest gold stamped with the image and superscription of bygone kings, if he would never use nor look at any portion of his wealth ? What, also, should we say of him if, in want of gold for his daily needs, he persisted in borrowing it from strangers at usurious interest, rather than touch his antique treasures? We should say he was unwise, or at the least eccentric, and that it was questionable whether he deserved to possess the great wealth which he had inherited. Every master of the English tongue, whether he be poet, orator, or great prose writer, is in the position of this supposed nobleman, if he will not study the ancient words of the language, and revive to the extent of his ability such among them as he finds to be better adapted to express strong as well as delicate shades of meaning, than the modern words which have usurped their places. To the poets more especially, and, if there be none such left in our day (which we should be very sorry to assert, when certain great names flash upon our memory), to the versifiers who are not likely ever to fail us as long as there are hopes and fancies in the hearts of young men and women, this is a matter of especial concern. The permissible rhymes of the modern English tongue are not copious in number; and such as exist, if not as well worn as love and dove, breeze and trees, heart and dart, are far too familiar to come upon the ear with any great charm of novelty. The dactylic rhymes are still fewer, as every one who has tried his hand at versification is painfully aware. It is the poet, more than the prose writer, who strengthens as well as beautifies the language which he employs. It is true that language first makes literature; and that literature, when once established among a people, reacts upon language, and fixes its form—decides what words shall and what words shall not be used in the higher forms of prose and poetical composition. Old English—such as it is found in "Piers Ploughman," Chaucer, Spenser, and the poets and dramatists of the Elizabethan era, and as late as Milton and Dryden—is a passionate rather than an argumentative language; and poets, who ought to be passionate above all else, otherwise they are but mere versifiers, should go back to those ancient sources, if they would be strong without ceasing to be correct and elegant. The words that were good enough for Shakspeare and his contemporaries ought to be good enough for the greatest writers of our day. But Shakspeare himself is becoming obsolete, and needs the aid of a glossary to explain to educated people many excellent words that are quite intelligible to a Scottish or English ploughman. Is it the fault of Shakspeare or of modern writers that this should be the case? Doubtless the fault is not in Shakspeare, but in ourselves.

—Reprinted and Extended from
" Blackwood's Magazine."

ALLAN RAMSAY'S

COLLECTION OF SCOTTISH PROVERBS.

A BEGUN turn is half ended.
A blate cat makes a proud mouse.
A black hen lays a white egg.
A blythe heart makes a blooming look.
A bit is oftener better gi'en than eaten.
A bonny bride is soon busked,
  And a short horse is soon whisked.
A borrowed len shou'd gae laughing hame.
A bread house never skail'd.
A black shoe makes a blythe heart.
A cock's aye crouse on his ain middin'.
A cramb'd kite makes a crazy carcass.
A daft nurse makes a wise wean.
A denk maiden, a dirty wife.
A dog winna yowl if ye strike him wi' a bane.
A dog's life ;—muckle ease muckle hunger.
A dry summer ne'er made a dear peck.
A deuk winna dabble aye in ae hole.
A dumb man wins nae law.
Ae beggar's wae that anither by the gate gae.
Ae bird in hand is worth ten fleeand.
Ae good turn deserves anither.
Ae good turn may meet anither, if it were at the brigg o' London.
Ae half of the warld kenna how the ither half live.
Ae hour's cauld will suck out seven years' heat.
Ae hour in the morning is worth twa after noon.
Ae man may lead a horse to the water, but four and twenty winna
  gar him drink.
Ae man's meat is anither man's poison.
Ae scabbed sheep will smit the hale hirdsel.
Ae year a nurse, and seven year a daw.

A fair maiden tocherless will get mae wooers than husbands.

A fool and his money are soon parted.

A fool's bolt is soon shot.

A fool may speer mair questions than a doctor can answer.

A fool may give a wise man counsel.

A friend in need is a friend indeed.

Affront your friend in mows, and tine him in earnest.

A friend's dinner's soon dight.

Aft ettle, whiles hit.

Aft counting keeps friends lang thegither.

Aft times the cautioner pays the debt.

After meat mustard.

After a storm comes the calm.

A fu' man and a hungry horse make haste hame.

A fu' purse never lacks friends.

A gawn foot's aye getting.

A gentle horse shou'd be sindle spurr'd.

A gi'en horse shou'd na be look'd i' the mouth.

A gi'en game was never won.

A good beginning makes a good ending.

A good goose may ha'e an ill gansel.

A good face needs nae band, and an ill ane deserves nane.

A good tongue's a safe weapon.

A good word is as soon said as an ill.

A good tale is no the waur to be twice tauld.

A good name is sooner tint than won.

A " good fellow " is a costly name.

A graining wife and a grunting horse ne'er fail'd their master.

A green wound is half hale.

A green yule makes a fat kirk-yard.

A great rooser was never a good rider.

A greedy eye never got a good pennyworth.

" A great cry and little woo," quoth the deil when he clippet the sow.

A handfu' of trade is worth a gowpen o' gowd.

A hasty man's never lasty.

A horse hired never tired.

A horse with four feet may snapper.

A horn spoon hauds nae poison.

A houndless hunter and a gunless gunner aye see rowth of game.

A hungry man smells meat afar.

A hungry louse bites sair.

A hungry man's aye angry.

A kiss and a drink of water is but a wersh disjune.

A lass that has mony wooers oft wales the warst.

A lang gather'd dam soon rins out.

A leaky ship lacks muckle pumping.

Ale-sellers shou'd na be tale-tellers.

A' liars shou'd ha'e good memories.
Alike ilka day makes a clout on Sunday.
A light purse makes a heavy heart.
·A' o'ers are ill, except o'er the water and o'er the hill.
A' fails that fools think.
A' the truth shou'd na be tauld.
A' the corn's no shorn by kempers.
A' the men of the Mearns can do nae mair than they may.
A' the winning's in the first buying.
A' cracks are not to be trow'd.
A' that's said in the kitchen shou'd na be tauld in the ha'.
A' cats are gray in the dark.
A' the keys hang not at your belt.
A's no tint that's in hazard.
A's fish that comes in the net.
A's not at hand that helps.
A' things wytes that no well fares.
A's well that ends well.
A' things are good untried.
A man's mind is a mirk mirror.
A man's aye crouse in his ain cause.
A man canna bear a' his kin on his back.
A man of mony trades may beg his bread on Sunday.
A man at five may be a fool at fifteen.
A man may see his friend in need, that winna see his pow bleed.
A man may woo where he will, but wed where his wierd is.
A man may be kind and gi'e little o' his gear.
A man of words and not of deeds, is like a garden fu' of weeds.
A man is well or wae, as he thinks himself sae.
A man has nae mair goods than he gets good of.
A misty morning may be a clear day.
A mouthfu' of meat may be a townfu' of shame.
A muzzled cat was ne'er a good hunter.
An auld mason makes a good barrow-man.
An auld tout in a new horn.
An auld sack craves muckle clouting.
An ill shearer never gat a good hook.
An illwilly cow shou'd ha'e short horns.
An ill cow may ha'e a good calf.
An ill plea shou'd be well pleaded.
An ill cook shou'd ha'e a good cleaver.
An ill lesson is soon lear'd.
An ill wife and a new kindled candle shou'd ha'e their heads hadden down.
An ill turn is soon done,
An ill servant ne'er proved a good master.
An ill life makes an ill end.

An ill won penny will pu' down a pound.
An inch of a nag is worth a span of an aver.
An inch off a miss is as good as a span.
An inch of good fortune is worth a fathom of forecast.
An olite mother makes a sweer daughter.
An ounce of mother-wit is worth a pound of clergy.
An unlucky man's cart is eith tumbled.
Ane of the court but nane of the council.
Ane does the skaith, and anither gets the wyte.
Ane never tines by doing good.
Ane beats the bush and anither grips the game.
Anes paid never craved.
Ane may bind a sack before it be fu'.
Ane may lo'e the kirk well enough, yet no be aye riding on the
    rigging o't.
Ane may lo'e a haggis that wadna ha'e the bag bladed in his teeth.
Ane is not so soon heal'd as hurt.
Ane gets sma' thanks for tining his ain.
Ane canna wive and thrive baith in ae year.
Ane will gar a hundred lie.
A new besom sweeps clean.
A nod of an honest man is eneuch.
April showers bring May flowers.
A party pot never play'd even.
A poor man gets a poor marriage.
A poor man is fain o' little.
A pound o' care winna pay an ounce o' debt.
A proud heart in a poor breast has meikle dolor to dree.
A ragged colt may prove a good gelding.
A reeky house and a girning wife,
    Will make a man a fashous life.
A reproof is nae poison.
A rowing stane gathers nae fog.
As a carle riches he wretches.
As broken a ship has come to land.
As day brak butter brak.
As fain as a fool of a fair day.
As fu' o' mischief as an egg's fu' o' meat.
As good may haud the stirrup as he that lowps on.
As good a fellow as ever toom'd a bicker.
As good merchants tine as win.
As lang runs the fox as he feet has.
As lang lives the merry man as the sad.
As lang as the bird sings before Candlemas it greets after it.
As lang as ye serve the tod ye maun bear up his tail.
As mony heads as mony wits.
As mickle upwith as mickle downwith.

As ready as the king has an egg in his pouch.

As sair fight wrens as cranes.

As soon gangs the lamb's skin to the market as the auld sheep's.

As sair greets the bairn that's paid at e'en as he that gets his whawks in the morning.

As tired as a tyke is of langkale.

As the sow fills the draff sours.

As the auld cock craws the young cock lears.

As the wind blaws seek your bield.

As the fool thinks the bell clinks.

As the market gangs wares maun sell.

As well be hang'd for a wedder as for a lamb.

As ye lo'e me look in my dish.

As ye lead your ain life ye judge your neighbours.

As ye make your bed sae ye maun lie down.

A saft aver was never a good horse.

A safe conscience makes a sound sleep.

A scawd head is eith to bleed.

A sheaf off a stouk is enough.

A short tree stands lang.

A sillerless man gangs fast through the market.

A silly man will be sleely dealt with.

A sinking master makes aft a rising man.

A slothfu' hand makes a slim fortune.

A sorrowfu' heart's aye drouthy.

A sooth bourd is nae bourd.

A spur in the head is worth twa on the heel.

At open doors dogs gae ben.

A tale-teller is waur than a thief.

A tarrowing bairn was never fat.

A taking hand will never want.

A tale never tines in the telling.

A thrawin question should have a thrawart answer.

A thread will tye an honest man better than a rape will a knave.

A tocherless dame sits lang at hame.

A toolying tike comes limping hame.

A toom purse makes a tartling merchant.

A toom pantry makes a thriftless goodwife.

A toom hand is nae lure for a hawk.

A turn well done is soon done.

A twapenny cat may look at a king.

A vanter and a liar are right sib.

A wad is a fool's argument.

A wee bush is better than nae bield.

A wee mouse can creep under a great corn stack.

A wee house well fill'd, a wee piece land well till'd, a wee wife well will'd, will make a happy man.

A wee house has a wide mouth.
A wee spark maks meikle wark.
A wee thing puts your beard in a bleeze.
A wee thing fleys cowards.
A wight man never wanted a weapon.
A wife is wise enough that kens her guidman's breeks frae her ain kirtle.
A wilfu' man never wanted wae.
A wilfu' man shou'd be unco wise.
A woman's mind is like wind in a winter night.
Auld men are twice bairns. ·
Auld sparrows are ill to tame.
Auld springs gi'e nae prize.
Auld sins breed new shame.
Auld wives and bairns make fools of physicians.
A yeld sow was never good to grices.
A yule feast may be quit at pasch.

Bairns are certain care, but nae sure joy.
Bare backs mak burnt shins.
Bare gentry, braggand beggars.
Bastard brood are aye proud.
Be a friend to yoursell and others will.
Be lang sick that ye may be soon hale.
Be it better, be it worse, be ruled by him that has the purse.
Be thou well, be thou wae, thou wilt not be aye sae.
Be the thing ye wad be ca'd.
Bear wealth well, poortith will bear itsell.
Before ye chuse a friend eat a peck o' saut wi' him.
Begin wi' needles and prins and end wi' horn'd nowt.
Beg frae beggars, you'll never be rich.
Beggars breed, and gentry feed.
Beggars dow bear nae wealth.
Beggars shou'd na be choosers,
Better a bit in the morning than fast a' day.
Better a clout in, than a hole out.
Better a dog fawn on you than bark at you.
Better a finger aff than aye wagging.
Better a fair foe than a fause friend.
Better a good fame than a fine face.
Better a laying hen than a lying crown.
Better a mouse in the pot than nae flesh.
Better a shameless eating than a shamefu' living.
Better a tocher in her than wi' her.
Better a toom house than an ill tenant.
Better a thigging mother than a riding father.
Better a wee ingle to warm ye than a mickle fire to burn ye.

Better auld debts than auld sairs.
Better bairns greet than bearded men.
Better be blythe wi' little than sad wi' mickle.
Better be envied than pitied.
Better be alane than in ill company.
Better be idle than ill employed.
Better be out of the world than out of the fashion.
Better be sonsy than soon up.
Better be the lucky man than the lucky man's son.
Better be unkind than cumbersome.
Better beg than borrow.
Better day the better deed.
Better eat gray bread in youth than in eild.
Better flatter a fool than fight wi' him.
Better find iron than tine siller.
Better gi'e the slight than tak' it.
Better guide well than work sair.
Better haud by a hair than draw with a tether.
Better haud with the hound than rin with the hare.
Better hain at the braird than at the bottom.
Better haud loose than in an ill tethering.
Better hap at court than good service.
Better kiss a knave than cast out wi' him.
Better keep the de'il without the door than ha'e to drive him out of
    the house.
Better keep well than make well.
Better lang something than soon naething.
Better late thrive than never do weel.
Better lear frae your neighbour's skaith than your ain.
Better leave to my faes than beg frae my friends.
Better live in hope than die in despair.
Better marry o'er the middin' than o'er the moor.
Better my bairns seek frae me than I beg frae them.
Better my friend think me fremit than fashous.
Better ne'er begun than ne'er ended.
Better rough and sonsy than bare and donsy.
Better saught with little aught, than care with mony a cow.
Better say here it is than there it was.
Better short and sweet than lang and lax.
Better sit still than rise up and fa'.
Better sit idle than work for nought.
Better skaith saved than mends made.
Better sma' fish than nae fish.
Better spared than ill spent.
Better the ill ken'd than the good unken'd.
Better the end of a feast than the beginning of a fray.
Better thole a grumph than a sumph.

Better to haud than draw.
Better twa skaiths than ae sorrow.
Better unborn than untaught.
Better wade back mid-water than gae forward and drown.
Better wait on the cook than the doctor.
Better wear shoon than sheets.
Between three and thirteen
   Thraw the wand when it is green.
Bid a man to the roast and stick him with the spit.
Birds of a feather flock together.
Birth's good, but breeding's better.
Black will take no other hue.
Blaw the wind ne'er sae fast,
   It will lown at the last.
Blind men should na judge of colours.
Blood's thicker than water.
Boden gear stinks.
Break my head and syne draw on my bow.
Broken bread makes hale bairns.
Burnt bairns dread the fire.
Buy a thief frae the gallows, and he'll help to hang you.
By chance a cripple may grip a hare.
By guess, as the blind man fell'd the dog.

Can do is eithly born about.
Canny chiels carry cloaks when 'tis clear,
   The fool when 'tis foul has nane to wear.
Careless fowk are aye cumbersome.
Cast na out the dow'd water till ye get the fresh.
Cats and carlins sit in the sun.
Cauld cools the love that kindles ower het.
Changes are lightsome.
Come a' to Jock Fool's house, and ye'se get bread and cheese.
Come unca'd sits unserv'd.
Come not to council unbidden.
Comes to my hand like the bowl o' a pint stowp.
Come it air, come it late, in May comes the cow-quake.
Come with the wind, and gae with the water.
Confess'd faut is half amends.
Confess debt and crave days.
Count again is no forbidden.
Count siller after a' your kin.
Count like Jews and gree like brethren.
Courtesy is cumbersome to them that ken it no.
Counsel is nae command.
Crab without a cause and mease without amends.
Credit is better than ill won gear.

Curses make the fox fat.
Cut your cloak according to your claith.

DAFFIN and want of wit maks auld wives donnard.
Dawted bairns dow bear little.
Daylight will peep through a sma' hole.
Deal sma' and serve a'.
Dear bought and far sought is meet for ladies.
Death and marriage make term-day.
Death at ae door, and hardship at the other.
Death defies the doctor.
Deed shaws proof.
Ding down the nest, and the rooks will flee awa'.
Dirt bodes luck.
Do on the hill as ye wad do in the ha'.
Do your turn well, and nane will spier what time ye took.
Do weel and dread nae shame.
Do weel and doubt nae man, do ill and doubt a' men.
Do as the lasses do, say no and tak' it.
Do not meddle with the de'il and the laird's bairns.
Do not talk of a rape to a chiel whase father was hangit.
Dogs will redd swine.
Dolor pays nae debt.
Double drinks are good for drouth.
Double charges rive cannons.
Drive a cow to the ha', she'll run to the byre.
Drink and drouth come not aye together.
Drink little that ye may drink lang.
Drunken at e'en, and dry in the morning.

EAT in measure, and defy the mediciner.
Eat your fill, but pouch nane.
Eats meat and never fed,
    Wears claiths and never clad.
Eating and drinking want but a beginning.
Eith learning the cat to the kirn.
Eith learn'd soon forgotten.
Eith working when will's at hame.
Either prove a man or a mouse.
Either win the horse or tine the saddle.
E'ening red and a morning gray,
    Is a token of a good day.
E'en as ye win't sae ye may wear't.
Enough's as good as a feast.
Ever busy ever bare.
Every ane kens best where his ain shoe nips him.
Every ane lowps the dyke where it is laighest.

Every craw thinks its ain chick whitest.
Every dog has his day.
Every man wears his belt his ain gate.
Every man can guide an ill wife but he that has her.
Every man bows to the bush he gets bield frae.
Every man's blind in his ain cause.
Every man to his mind, as the man said when he kiss'd the sow.
Every man's tale is good till another's be tauld.
Every man's no born with a siller spoon in his mouth.
Every man has his ain draff pock.
Every miller wad wyse the water to his ain mill.
Every shoe fits not every foot.
Every thing has an end, and a pudding has twa.
Experience teaches fools.

Faint heart never won fair lady.
Fair heights make fools fain.
Fair fa' the wife, and weel may she spin,
    That counts aye the lawing with a quart to come in.
Fair fa' good ale, it gars fowk speak as they think.
Fair exchange is nae robbery.
Fair maidens wear nae purses.
Fair hair may have foul roots.
Fair words hurt ne'er a bane,
    But foul words break mony a ane.
Fair and foolish, black and proud,
    Lang and lazy, little and loud.
Fann'd fires and forced love ne'er did weel.
Fancy flees before the wind.
Far away fowls have fair feathers.
Farewell frost, fair weather niest.
Far frae court far frae care.
Farmers faugh gar lairds laugh.
Fast bind fast find.
Fat flesh freezes soon.
Fat paunches bode lean pows.
Fause fowk shou'd hae mony witnesses.
Fiddler's dogs and flesh-flies come to feasts unca'd.
Fight dog, fight bear, wha wins de'il care.
Fine feathers mak' fine birds.
Fire and water are good servants, but ill masters.
First come first served.
Fleas and a girning wife are wakerife bedfellows.
Fleshers lo'e nae collops.
Fleying a bird is no the gate to grip it.
Flee never sae fast, your fortune will be at your tail.
Flitting of farms makes mailins dear.

Fools' haste is nae speed.
Fools are aye fain of flitting.
Fools shou'd na see wark that's haff done.
Fools make feasts, and wise fowk eat them ;
    The wise make jests, and fools repeat them.
Fools are fain of naething.
For want of steek a shoe may be tint.
For fashion's sake, as dogs gang to the market.
Fortune favours fools.
Fortune helps aye the hardy.
Force without forecast aften fails.
Fore-warn'd, haff arm'd.
For faut of wise fowk fools sit on binks.
Foul water slockens fire.
Friendship canna stand aye on ae side.
Friends gree best sindry.
Frost and fawshood have baith a dirty waygang.

GAE to bed with the lamb, and rise with the lav'rock.
Gane is the goose that laid the great egg.
Gaunting bodes wanting.
Gayly wad be better.
Gear is easier gain'd than guided.
Gentle paddocks have lang taes.
Get your rock and spindle, and God will send tow.
Get the word o' soon rising, and you may lie in your bed a' day.
Giff gaff makes good friends.
Girn when ye bind and laugh when you loose.
Gi'e a bairn its will, and a whelp its fill,
    Nane of them will e'er do well.
Gi'e a dog an ill name, and he'll soon be hang'd.
Gi'e a carle your finger, and he'll take your hale hand.
Gi'e a gawn man a drink, and a quarrelsome chiel a cuff.
Gi'e a thing and take a thing.
    That's the ill man's gowd ring.
Gi'e o'er when the play's good.
Gi'e them tow eneuch and they'll hang themsells.
Gi'e the de'il his due.
God be wi' auld lang syne, when our gutchers ate their trenchers.
God help great fowk, the poor can beg.
God's help is nearer than the fair e'en.
God ne'er sent the mouth but He sent the meat wi't.
God send water to that well that people think will never run dry.
God sends us claiths according to our cauld.
God sends meat, but the de'il sends cooks.
God send you mair wit and me mair siller.
God shapes the back for the burthen.

Good ale needs nae wisp.
Good cheer and good cheap ca's mony customers.
Good fowk are scarce, take care of ane.
Good forecast furthers the wark.
Good fishing in drumly waters.
Good will shou'd be tane in part payment.
Good words cost nathing.
Great barkers are nae biters.
Great words fley cowards.
Great winning makes wark easy.
Greedy fowk have lang arms.
Gut nae fish till ye get them.

Ha' binks are sliddery.
Had ye sic a shoe on ilka foot it would gar you shaghle.
Haud a hank in your ain hand.
Haff acres bear good corn.
Hang a thief when he's young, and he'll no steal when he's auld.
Hankering and hinging on is a poor trade.
Handle the pudding while it is het.
Hang hunger and drown drouth.
Hap and a halfpenny is gear enough.
Happy the wife that's married to a motherless son.
Happy for the son when the dad goes to the de'il.
Hardships sindle come single.
Haste makes waste.
Have ye gear, have ye nane,
    Tine heart, and a's gane.
He begs frae them that borrowed frae him.
He brings a staff to break his ain head.
He can haud meal in his mouth and blaw.
He comes aftner with the rake than the shool.
He complains early that complains of his kail.
He can hide his meat and seek mair.
He does na aye ride when he saddles his horse.
He does na like his wark that says *now* when it is done.
He gangs away in an ill time that never comes again.
He gangs lang barefoot that wears dead men's shoon.
He gat his kail in a riven dish.
He has brought his pock to a braw market.
He has mickle prayer but little devotion.
He has come to good by misguiding.
He has an eye in his neck.
He has a bee in his bonnet lug.
He has gotten a bite o' his ain bridle.
He has the best end o' the string.
He has faut of a wife that marries mam's pet.

He has mair wit in his little finger than ye have in a' your bouk.
He has coosten his cloak on the ither shoulder.
He has feather'd his nest, he may flee when he likes.
He has need o' a lang spoon that sups with the de'il.
He has cowped the meikle dish into the little.
He has a hole aneath his nose that will ne'er let him be rough.
He has wit at will that with an angry heart can sit still.
He has licket the butter aff my bread.
He has a slid grip that has an eel by the tail.
He has a good judgment that does not lippen to his ain.
He has a hearty hand for giving a hungry mealtith.
He has a crap for a' corn.
He has need to ha'e a clean pow,
    That ca's his neighbour "nitty know."
He hears with his heels, as geese do in harvest.
He kens na a B by a bull's foot.
He kens his ain groats among other fowk's kail.
He kens whilk side his cake is butter'd on.
He'll mend when he grows better, like sour ale in summer.
He'll no let grass grow at his heels.
He'll tell't to nae mair than he meets.
He loo's me for little that hates me for nought.
He'll wag as the bush wags.
He looks like the far end o' a French fiddle.
He'll soon be a beggar that canna say nay.
He loo'd mutton weel that lick'd where the ewe lay.
He'll have enough some day when his mouth's fou o' mools.
He may well swim that has his head hadden up.
He maun be soon up that cheats the tod.
He maun hae leave to speak that canna haud his tongue.
He may find faut that canna mend.
He may laugh that wins.
He never did a good darg that gade grumbling about it.
He never lies but when the hollin's green.
He needs maun run that the de'il drives.
He never tint a cow that grat for a needle.
He rides sicker that ne'er fell.
He's a fool that forgets himsell.
He's better fed than nurtur'd.
He's a man of a wise mind,
    That of a foe can make a friend.
He's gane as the dog drave.
He's wise that kens whan he's weel, and can haud himself sae.
He's lifeless that's faultless.
He's a gentle horse that never coost his rider.
He's silly that spares for ilka speech.

He's a fool that marries at yule,
 For when the bairn's to bear the corn's to shear.
He's at his wit's end.
He's wise that's timely wary.
He's as welcome as water in a riven ship.
He's like a flee in a blanket.
He's no sae daft as he lets on.
He's sairest dung that's paid wi' his ain wand.
He's a sairy beggar that canna gae by ae door.
He's o'er soon up that's hanged ere noon.
He's poor eneuch that's ill loo'd.
He's a sairy cook that mayna lick his ain fingers.
He's a silly chiel that can neither do nor say.
He's a wise bairn that kens his ain faither.
He's unko fu' in his ain house that canna pike a bane in his neighbour's.
He's a proud horse that winna bear his ain provender.
He's well worthy of sorrow that buys it.
He's like the singed cat, better than he's likely.
He's a worthless goodman that's no missed.
He's a good horse that never stumbled,
 And a better wife that never grumbled.
He's a weak beast that downa bear the saddle.
He sleeps as dogs do when wives sift meal.
He speaks in his drink what he thought in his drouth.
He sits fu' close that has riven breeks.
He stumbles at a strae and lowps o'er a wonlyne.
He that aught the cow gangs nearest her tail.
He that blaws best let him bear the horn.
He that's born to be hang'd will never be drown'd.
He that's born under a tippenny planet will ne'er be worth a groat.
He that buys land buys stanes,
 And he that buys beef buys banes.
He that counts a' cost will ne'er put plough in the eard.
He that cheats me anes shame fa' him, if he cheat me twice, shame fa' me.
He that clatters to himself talks to a fool.
He that canna make sport shou'd mar nane.
He that canna do as he wou'd maun do as he may.
He that comes unca'd sits unserved.
He that counts before the ostler counts twice.
He that does his turn in time sits half idle.
He that does bidding deserves na dinging.
He that deals in dirt has aye foul fingers.
He that forecasts a' perils will win nae worship.
He that fu's in a gutter, the langer he lies the dirtier he is.
He that fishes before the net,
 Fishes lang or he fish get.
He that gets gear before he gets wit, will die ere he thrive.

He that gets, forgets, but he that wants, thinks on.
He that gangs a borrowing, gangs a sorrowing.
He that gi'es a' his gear to his bairns,
    Take up a bittle and ding out his harns.
He that gi'es all wad gi'e nathing.
He that gets ance his nieves in dirt can hardly get them out.
He that has twa hoards will get a third.
He that has a good crop may thole some thistles.
He that has nae siller in his purse shou'd ha'e silk on his tongue.
He that hides can best find.
He that has mickle gets aye mair.
He that has mickle wad aye ha'e mair.
He that has a dog of his ain may gang to the kirk wi' a clean breast.
He that has a mickle nose thinks ilka ane speaks o't.
He that's ill to himsell will be good to naebody.
He that in bawdry wastes his gear,
    Baith shame and skaith he will endure.
He that kens what will be cheap or dear,
    Needs be a merchant but for ae year.
He that keeks through a hole may see what will vex him.
He that lives weel lives lang.
He that lacks my mare wad buy my mare.
He that laughs at his ain joke spills the sport o't.
He that laughs alane will make sport in company.
He that lives upon hope has a slim diet.
He that looks to freets, freets follow him.
He that marries or he be wise will die e'er he be rich.
He that meddles with tulzies comes in for the redding streak.
He that never rade never fell.
He that never eats flesh thinks harigalds a feast.
He that shaws his purse bribes the thief.
He that sleeps with dogs maun rise with fleas.
He that slays shall be slain.
He that steals can hide.
He that strikes my dog wad strike mysell if he durst.
He that spends his gear before he gets't will get little good o't.
He that seeks motes gets motes.
He that speers all opinions comes ill speed.
He that speaks what he should not,
    Will hear what he would rather not.
He that spares to speak spares to speed.
He that sells ware for words maun live by the wind.
He that speaks wi' a drawnt and sells wi' a cant,
    Is right like a snake in the skin o' a saunt.
He that teaches himsell has a fool for his master.
He that will cheat in play winna be honest in earnest.
He that winna when he may, shanna when he wad.

He that wad eat the kirnel maun crack the nut.
He that will to Cupar maun to Cupar.
He that's welcome fares well.
He that well bides well betides.
He that will na thole, maun flit mony a hole.
He was the bee that made the honey.
He was scant o' news that tauld his father was hanged.
He wears twa faces beneath ae cowl.
He was mair fleyed than hurt.
Help is good in a' play.
Hens are aye free of horse corn.
Highest iu court the nearest the widdy.
His wit gat wings and would have flown,
   But pinching poortith pu'd him down.
His auld brass will buy a new pan.
His bark is waur than his bite.
His egg has aye twa youks.
His geese are a' swans.
His room's better than his company.
His pipe's out.
Honesty hauds lang the gate.
Honesty's the best craft.
Hooly and fair gangs far in a day.
Horses are good of a' hues.
Hunger will break through stane wa's.
Hunger's hard upon a heal heart.
Hunger is good kitchen.
Hunger thou me and I'll harry thee.
Hungry dogs are blythe o' bursten puddings.
Hungry stewards wear mony shoon.

I ANCE gae a dog his handsel, and he was hanged ere night.
I bake nae bread by your shins.
I canna sell the cow and sup the milk.
I have gi'en a stick to break my ain head.
I had rather gang by your door than o'er your grave.
I ha'e gotten an ill kame for my ain head.
I ha'e seen mair than I have eaten.
I ken by my cogue wha milks my cow.
I ken how the world wags,
   He's honor'd maist who has moniest bags.
I ken him as well as I had gane through him with a lighted candle.
I'll gi'e ye a bane to pike that will haud your teeth gawn.
I'll gar his ain gartens tie up his ain hose.
I'll never dirty the bonnet I'm gawn to put on.
I'll keep my mind to mysell and tell my tale to the wind.
I'll never stoop sae laigh and lift sae little.

I'll never put the carl aboon the gentleman.
I'll never keep a dog and bark mysell.
I'll never live poor to die .rich.
I'll never buy a blind bargain, or a pig in a pock.
I'll never brew drink to treat drunkards.
I'm o'er auld a cat to draw a strae before.
I'm no sae blind as I'm blear-eyed.
I'm flyting free with him.
I'm no sae scant o' clean pipes as to blaw with a brunt cutty.
I'm no every man's dog that whistles on me.
I'm neither sma' drink thirsty, nor gray bread hungry.
I may come to break an egg in your pouch.
I never liked a dry bargain.
I spake but ae word, gi'e me but ae strake.
I took him aff the moor for God's sake, and he begins to bite the bairns.
I wad be scant o' claith to sole my hose with dockens.
I wadna ca' the king my cousin.
I wad rather see't than hear tell o't.
I wadna be deaved with your keckling for a' your eggs.
I winna make fish o' ane and flesh o' anither.
I wish you readier meat than a running hare.
I wish you as muckle good o't as dogs get of grass.
If ae sheep lowp o'er the dyke a' the lave will follow.
If a lie could worry you, ye wad have been choked langsyne.
If a man's gawn down the brae ilk ane gi'es him a jundie.
If e'er I find his cart tumbling I'se gie't a put.
If he be not a souter he's a good shoe-clouter.
If I canna kep geese I'll kep gaislins.
If I canna do't by might I'll do't by flight.
If it can be nae better, it is well it is nae warse.
If it winna be a good shoe, let it gang down i' the heel.
If it serve me to wear, it may serve you to look to.
If marriages be made in heaven, ye have had few friends there.
If the de'il be laird ye'll be tenant.
If things were to be done twice ilka ane wad be wise.
If the de'il find you idle he'll set you to wark.
If we hae little gear we hae less care.
If ye dinna like what I can gie,
     Tak what ye brought w'ye.
If ye can spend muckle, put the mair to the fire.
If ye brew weel ye'll drink the better.
If ye wad be a merchant fine,
     Beware o' auld horses, herring, and wine.
If ye sell your purse to your wife, gi'e her your breeks to the bargain.
If you tell your servant your secret, you make him your master.
If ye had as little money as ye ha'e manners, ye wad be the poorest
     man of your kin.

If ye do a wrang make amends.
If ye do nae ill dinna ill like.
If ye steal no my kale, break na my dyke.
If ye wad live for ever, wash the milk frae your liver.
If ye wad be haly, healthy, and wealthy, rise soon in the morning.
Ill bairns are best heard at hame.
Ill comes upon waur's back.
Ill counsel will gar a man stick his ain mare.
Ill doers are aye ill dreaders.
Ill deem'd haff hang'd.
Ill getting het water frae 'neath cauld ice.
Ill herds make fat foxes.
Ill news are aft o'er true.
Ill payers are aye good cravers.
Ill weeds wax weel.
Ill-won gear winna enrich the third heir.
Ill-won as ill ware'd.
It canna rain, but it pours.
It gangs in at the ae lug and out at the ither.
It is a bauch brewing that's no good in the newing.
It is a bare moor that ye gang through and no get a heather coo.
It is a good game that fills the wame.
It is a good tongue that says nae ill.
It is a hard task to be poor and leal.
It is an ill wind that blaws naebody good.
It is an ill pack that's no worth the custom.
It is an ill cause that the lawyer thinks shame o'.
It is a lamb at the up-taking, but an auld sheep ere ye get it aff.
It is a mean mouse that has but ae hole.
It is a stinking praise comes out of ane's ain mouth.
It is a sin to lie on the de'il.
It is a shame to eat the cow and worry on the tail.
It is a sair field where a's slain.
It is a sooth dream that's seen waking.
It is a silly flock where the ewe bears the bell.
It is a sairy hen that canna scrape for ae bird.
It is a' tint that's done to auld fowk and bairns.
It is a' tint that fell by.
It is best ganging wi' a horse in ane's hand.
It is better to sup wi' a cutty than want a spoon.
It is by the head that the cow gie's milk.
It is clean about the wren's door where there is nought within.
It is dear coft honey that's licked aff a thorn.
It is eith crying yool on anither man's stool.
It is eith finding a stick to strike a messan.
It is fair in ha' when beards wag a'.
It is good to dread the warst, the best will be the welcomer.

It is good to be good in your time, ye kenna how lang it may last.
It is good to be merry and wise,
   Quoth the miller when he mouter'd twice.
It is good to have our cogue out when it rains kail.
It is good to hae twa strings to your bow.
It is hard to gar an auld mare leave flinging.
It is hard to sit in Rome and strive wi' the Pope.
It is hard for a greedy eye to ha'e a leal heart.
It is hard baith to have and want.
It is ill to be ca'd a thief and aye found piking.
It is ill crooking before cripples.
It is an ill kitchen that keeps the bread away.
It is ill to bring out o' the flesh what's bred i' the bane.
It is ill to lear the cat to the kirn.
It is ill taking corn frae geese.
It is ill bringing butt what's no ben.
It ill sets a haggis to be roasted.
It is ill meddling between the bark and the rhind.
It is ill making a silk purse o' a sow's lug, or a touting-horn o' a
   tod's tail.
It is ill putting a blythe face on a wae heart.
It is kittle shooting at corbies and clergy.
It is kittle for the cheeks when the hurl-barrow gaes o'er the brig
   o' the nose.
It is kittle to waken sleeping dogs.
It is lang or the de'il be found dead at a dyke side.
It is lang or ye cry shoo to an egg.
It is muckle gars the tailor laugh, but souters girn aye.
It is needless to pour water on a drown'd mouse.
It is no the cowl that makes the friar.
It is nae sin to take a good price, but in gi'eing ill measure.
It is nae mair to see a woman greet than to see a goose gae barefoot.
It is nae play when ane laughs and anither greets.
It is no the way to grip a bird to fling your bonnet at it.
It is not what is she, but what has she ?
It is weel ware'd that wasters want.
It is weel that our fauts are not written on our face.
It is time enough to skreigh when ye're strucken.
It is time enough to make my bed when I'm gawn to lie down.
It is the best spoke in your wheel.
It keeps his nose at the grindstane.
It maun be true that a' fowk says.
It sets a sow weel to wear a saddle.
It was never for naething that the gled whistled.
It will be a het day gars you startle.
It will set his beard in a bleeze.
It will be a feather out of your wing.

KAIL hains bread.
Kame sindle, kame sair.
Kamesters are aye creeshy.
Keek in the stowp was ne'er a good fellow.
Keep hame, and hame will keep you.
Keep woo and it will be dirt, keep lint and it will be silk.
Keep out of his company that cracks of his cheatery.
Keep your ain fish guts to feed your ain sea maws.
Keep your kill-dry'd taunts to your mouldy-hair'd maidens.
Keep your tongue within your teeth.
Keep the staff in your ain hand.
Keep your breath to cool your crowdie.
Keep your mouth close and your een open.
Ken yoursell and your neighbours winna misken you.
Ken when to spend and when to spare,
    And ye needna be bissy, and ye'll never be bare.
Kindness comes wi' will ; it canna be coft.
Kindness will creep where it canna gang.
Kindness canna stand aye on ae side.
Kings and bears aft worry their keepers.
Kissing gaes by favour.
Kiss ye me till I be white, and that will be an ill web to bleach.
Kythe in your ain colours that fowk may ken you.

LACKING breeds laziness, praises breed pith.
Laith to bed and laith to rise.
Laug mint, little dint.
Lang look'd for comes at last.
Lang or ye cut Falkland wood with a penknife.
Lang standing and little offering mak a poor priest.
Lang straes are nae motes.
Lang tarrying tines thanks.
Lang sports turn to earnest.
Langest at the fire soonest finds cauld.
Langer lasts year than yule.
Law's costly, tak a pint and 'gree.
Law-makers should na be law-breakers.
Laugh at leisure, ye may greet ere night.
Leal heart never lied.
Leave welcome behind ye.
Leave aff as lang as the play's good.
Learn young, learn fair.
Learn the cat to the kirn and she'll aye be lickin'.
Letna the plough stand to slay a mouse.
Let alane maks mony a lown.
Let a friend gang with a fae.
Let byganes be byganes, and fairplay in time to come.

Let him play a spring on his ain fiddle.
Let him cool in the skin he het in.
Let him that's cauld blaw up the ingle.
Let his ain wand ding him.
Let it fa' upon the feyest.
Let the horns gang wi' the hide.
Let the morn come and the meat wi't.
Let the kirk stand in the kirk yard.
Let them laugh that win.
Let them care that come behind.
Lie for him and he'll swear for you.
Light suppers mak lang life days.
Light winning maks a heavy purse.
Lightly come lightly gane.
Light burdens break nae banes.
Like a Scots man ye take your mark frae an ill hour.
Likely lies aft in the mire, when unlikely wins thro'.
Lik'd gear is haff bought.
Like hens, ye rin aye to the heap.
Like the wife, that never cries for the ladle till the pot rins o'er.
Like the cat, fain fish wad ye eat,
  But ye are laith to wet your feet.
Like the wife wi' the mony daughters, the best comes hind-
  most.
Lippen to me but look to yoursell.
Little can a lang tongue lien.
Little kenn'd the less cared for.
Little gear the less care.
Little wats the ill-willy wife what a dinner may haud in't.
Little odds between a feast and a fu' wame.
Little said is soon mended, little gear's soon spended.
Little wit in the head maks muckle travel to the feet.
Little meddling maks fair parting.
Little may an auld nag do that mauna nicher.
Little dogs hae lang tails.
Little mense to the cheeks to bite aff the nose.
Live and let live.
Live upon love as lav'rocks do on leeks.
Look before ye lowp, ye'll ken the better how to light.
Lordships change manners.
Love and lordships like nae marrows.
Love and raw peas break the heart and burst the wame.
Love's as warm among cotters as courtiers.
Love me, love my dog.
Love me lightly, love me lang.
Love o'er het soonest cools.
Love o'erlooks mony fauts.

MAIDENS should be mild and meek,
   Quick to hear and slow to speak.
Maidens' bairns are aye well bred.
Maidens' tochers and ministers' stipends are aye less than ca'd.
Mair by good luck than good guiding.
Mair haste the waur speed,
   Quoth the tailor to the lang threed.
Make ae wrang step and down ye gae.
Mair hamely than welcome.
Mak the best of an ill bargain.
Mak your hay when the sun shines.
Malice is aye mindfu'.
Man propones but God dispones.
Marry in haste, repent at leisure.
Marry aboon match and get a master.
Mealy mou'd maidens stand lang at the mill,
Measure twice, cut but anes.
Meat feeds, and claith cleads, but manners mak the man.
Messengers shou'd neither be headed nor hanged.
Mickle fails that fools think.
Mickle corn mickle care.
Mickle wad aye hae mair.
Mickle spoken, part spilt.
Mickle power maks many faes.
Mickle may fa' between the cup and the lip.
Mickle water rins by that the miller wats not of.
Mickle pleasure some pain.
Mickle about ane, quoth the de'il to the collier.
Might o'ercomes right.
Mint ere ye strike.
Misterfou' fowk mauna be mensfu'.
Money is welcome in a dirten clout.
Money maks money.
Mony hands mak light wark.
Mony a ane kisses the bairn for love of the nurice.
Mony hounds may soon worry ae hare.
Mony heads are better than ane.
Mony purses haud friends lang together.
Mony fair promises at marriage make few at tocher good paying.
Mony lack what they hae in their pack.
Mony dogs die ere ye fa' heir.
Mony ane's coat saves his doubtlet.
Mony ways to kill a dog tho' ye dinna hang him.
Mony cooks ne'er made good kail.
Mony sma's mak ae mickle.
Mony a ane maks an errand to the ha' to bid the lady good-day.
Mony irons in the fire part maun cool.

Mony aue opens their pack and sells nae wares.
Mony a ane speers the gate they ken fu' well.
Mouths are nae measure.
Mows may come to earnest.
Moyen does mickle, but money does mair.
Murder will out.
Must is a king's word.
My son's my son aye till he get him a wife,
    My daughter's my daughter a' the days o' her life.
My niest neighbour's skaith is my present peril.

Nae butter sticks to his bread.
Nae fool to an auld fool.
Nae friend to a friend in need.
Nae fleeing without wings.
Nae great loss but there's some sma' advantage.
Nae langer pipe nae langer dance.
Nae man has a tack o' his life.
Nae man can thrive unless his wife let him.
Nae man can live langer in peace than his neighbour likes.
Nae mair haste than good speed.
Nae safe wading in unco waters.
Nae weather's ill if the wind be still.
Nathing freer than a gift.
Nathing comes fairer to light than what has been lang hidden.
Nathing's baulder than a blind mare.
Nathing enters into a closs hand.
Nathing sae crouse as a new washen louse.
Nathing's ill to be done when will's at hame.
Nathing to be done in haste but gripping of fleas.
Nathing venture nathing win.
Nane ferlies mair than fools.
Nane sae weel but he hopes to be better.
Nane can mak a bore but ye'll find a pin till't.
Nane can play the fool sae weel as a wise man.
Narrow gather'd widely spent.
Nearest the heart nearest the mouth.
Nearer the night the mair beggars.
Necessity has nae law.
Need makes men of craft.
Need will gar an auld wife trot and a naked man rin.
Neither sae sinfu' as to sink, nor sae haly as to saunt.
New lords have new laws.
Never a barrel better herrings.
Never break out of kind to gar your friends ferly at you.
Never draw your dirk when a dunt will do't.
Never fin' faut with my shoon unless ye pay my souter.

Never gae to the de'il wi' a dish-clout about your head.
Never let on you, but laugh in your ain sleeve.
Never meet never pay.
Never marry a widow unless her first man was hang'd.
Never put a sword in a wud man's hand.
Never put the plough before the owsen.
Never quat certainty for hope.
Never o'er auld to learn.
Never scaud your lips in other fowk's kail.
Never seek a wife till ye ken what to do wi' her.
Never show your teeth unless ye can bite.
Never strive against the stream.
Never venture never win.
Nineteen nay-says of a maiden are haff a grant.
Now's now, and yule's in winter.
Nobility without ability is like a pudding without suet.

O'ER braw a purse to put a plack in.
O'er mickle of ae thing is good for naething.
O'er mickle hameliness spoils good courtesy.
O'er mickle cookery spoils the brochan.
O'er mickle loose leather about your chafts.
O'er narrow counting culzies nae kindness.
O'er rackless may repent.
O'er strong meat for your weak stamach.
Of a' sorrow a fu' sorrow's best.
Of a little take a little, when there's nought take a'.
Of bairns' gifts ne'er be fain,
    Nae sooner they give but they seek them again.
Of ill debtors men get aiths.
Of twa ills choose the least.
Open confession is good for the saul.
Our sins and debts are aften mair than we think of.
Out of debt out of danger.
Out of the peat pot into the gutter.
Out of men's blessing into God's sun.

PAY him in his ain coin.
Penny wise and pound foolish.
Pennyless sauls may pine in purgatory.
Placks and bawbees grow pounds.
Play's good while it is play.
Please your kimmer and ye'll easily guide your gossip.
Plenty makes dainty.
Poor fowk's friends soon misken them.
Poor fowk are fain o' little.
Poortith parts good company.

Poortith wi' patience is less painfu'.
Possession is eleven points of the law.
Pride and grace dwell never in ae place.
Pride ne'er leaves its master till he get a fa'.
Pride and sweerness tak mickle uphadding.
Provision in season makes a bien house.
Put a coward to his mettle and he'll fight the de'il.
Put twa pennies in a purse and they'll creep together.
Put the saddle on the right horse.
Put your hand nae farther than your sleeve will reach.
Put your hand twice to your bonnet for anes to your pouch.
Put your finger in the fire and say it was your fortune.

QUALITY without quantity is little thought of.
Quick at meat quick at wark.
Quick, for you'll never be cleanly.
Quick returns mak rich merchants.

RECKLESS youth maks a ruefu' eild.
Raise nae mair de'ils than ye're able to lay.
Rather spill your joke than tine your friend.
Red wood makes good spindles.
Remove an auld tree and it will wither.
Remember, man, and keep in mind,
    A faithfu' friend is hard to find.
Rich fowk hae rowth of friends.
Right mixture maks good mortar.
Right wrangs nae man.
Rob Peter to pay Paul.
Robin that herds on the height,
    Can be as blythe as Sir Robert the knight.
Rome was not a' bigged in ae day.
Roose the ford as ye find it.
Roose the fair day at e'en.
Royet lads may make sober men.
Rue and thyme grow baith in ae garden.
Rule youth well, for eild will rule itsell.

SAE mony men sae mony minds.
Sain yoursell frae the de'il and the laird's bairns.
Sair cravers are aye ill payers.
Satan reproving sin.
Saw wheat in dirt and rye in dust.
Say weel's good, but do weel is better.
Scant of grace hears lang preachings.
Scant of cheeks makes a lang nose.
Scorn comes commonly wi' skaith.

Seeing's believing a' the world over.

See for love and buy for money.

Seek your saw where ye get your ail,
    And beg your barm where ye buy your ale.

Seek mickle and get something, seek little and get nought.

Second thoughts are best.

Send you to the sea ye'll no get saut water.

Serve yoursell till your bairns come to age.

Set a beggar on horseback he'll ride to the de'il.

Set that down on the back side of your count-book.

Set a knave to grip a knave.

Shame's past the shade o' your hair.

Sharp stomachs mak short graces.

Shoal waters make maist din.

She that gangs to the well wi' ill will,
    Either the pig breaks or the water will spill.

She looks as if butter wadna melt in her mou'.

She'll keep her ain side o' the hoose, and gang up and down in yours.

She hauds up her head like a hen drinking water.

She that taks gifts, hersell she sells,
    And she that gi'es them does nought else.

She's better than she's bonny.

Shod in the cradle and barefoot on the stibble.

Short fowk are soon angry, their heart's soon at their mouth.

Sic man sic master, sic priest sic offering.

Sic as ye gi'e sic will ye get.

Sic reek as is therein comes out o' the lum.

Silence grips the mouse.

Silks and satins put out the kitchen fire.

Sindle seen soon forgotten.

Slaw at meat slaw at wark.

Slander leaves a slur.

Smooth waters run deep.

Sma' fish is better than nae fish.

Soon enough to cry chuck when it is out of the shell.

Soon ripe soon rotten, soon het soon cauld.

Soon enough if well enough.

Some hae hap and some stick in the gap.

Sorrow is soon eneuch when it comes.

Sorrow and an ill life make soon an auld wife.

Sorrow and ill weather come unsent for.

Spare when ye're young and spend when ye're auld.

Speak the truth and shame the de'il.

Spend and God will send, spare and aye be bare.

Speak good o' pipers, your faither was a fiddler.

Speak o' the de'il and he'll appear.

Spilt ale is waur than water.

Standers-by see mair than the gamesters.
Standing dubs gather dirt.
Stay nae langer in your friend's house than ye are welcome.
Strike as ye feed, and that's but soberly.
Strike the iron as lang as it is het.
Stuffing hauds out storms.
Sudden friendship sure repentance.
Supp'd out wort was ne'er good ale.
Surfeits slay mair than swords.
Some ha'e a hantle fauts, ye are only a ne'er-do-weel.
Sour plumbs, quoth the tod when he couldna climb the tree.
Souters and tailors count hours.
Souters shou'dna gae ayont their last.
Souters shou'dna be sailors that can neither steer nor row.
Spare at the spigot and let out at the bung.
Spae well and hae well.
Speer at Jock thief if I be a leal man.
Speak when you're spoken to and drink when you're drunken to.
Stown dints are sweetest.
Sturt follows a' extremes.
Sturt pays nae debt.
Swear by your burnt shins.
Sweet at the on-taking, sour in the aff-putting.
Sweer to bed and sweer up in the morning.
Spit on a stane, and it will be wet at last.
Stay and drink of your ain browst.
Sticking gangs na by strength, but by right guiding o' the gullie.

Tak it a' and pay the merchant.
Tak a spring of your fiddle, and dance when ye have done.
Tak the bit and the buffet wi't.
Tak a pint and gree, the law's costly.
Tak your ain will and then ye'll no die o' the pet.
Tak time ere time be tint.
Tak your venture as mony good ship has done.
Tak your thanks to feed your cat.
Tak wit in your anger.
Tak care o' the man that God has marked.
Tak a hair o' the dog that bit you.
Tak part of the pelf when the pack's a dealing.
Tak a man by his word and a cow by her horn.
Tak me not up before I fa'.
Tak nae mair on your back than you're able to bear.
Tak your will, you're wise enough.
Tak up the next ye find.
Tam Tell-truth is nae courtier.
Tell nae tales out o' school.

Tell not your fae when your foot's sleeping.
That's but ae doctor's opinion.
That's for the father but no for the son.
That's for that and butter's for fish.
That's my tale, where's yours ?
That's the piece a step-bairn never gat.
That which God will give, the de'il canna reeve.
The auld aver may die waiting for new grass.
The auld dog maun die in somebody's aught.
The bairn speaks in the field what he hears at the fireside.
The bird maun flichter that flees wi' ae wing.
The bird that can sing and winna sing shou'd be gart sing.
The best is aye best cheap.
The better day the better the deed.
The book o' maybe's is very braid.
The banes o' a great estate are worth the picking.
The banes bear the beef hame.
The blind man's peck shou'd be well measured.
The cow may want her ain tail yet.
The cure may be warse than the disease.
The cow that's first up gets the first o' the dew.
The de'il bides his day.
The de'il was sick, the de'il a monk wou'd be,
    The de'il grew hale, syne de'il a monk was he.
The de'il's aye good to his ain.
The de'il's bairns hae the de'il's luck.
The day has een and the night hears.
The de'il's aye busy with his ain.
The de'il will take little ere he want a'.
The de'il drives aye his hogs to an ill market..
The de'il does na aye show his cloven cloots.
The de'il's aye good to beginners.
The e'ening red and the morning gray,
    Is a good sign of a fair day.
The farthest way about is aft the nearest gate hame.
The foremost hound grips the hare.
The foot at the cradle and the hand at the reel,
    Are signs of a wife that means to do weel.
The farther in the deeper.
The first dish is best eaten.
The grace o' a gray bannock is in the baking o't.
The good or ill hap o' a good or ill life,
    Is the good or ill choice o' a good or ill wife.
The gray mare may be the best horse.
The greatest burthens are not the maist gainfu'.
The gravest fish is an oyster,
    The gravest bird is an owl ;

The gravest beast is an ass,
  And the gravest man is a fool.
The greatest clerks are no the wisest men.
The happy man canna be herried.
The hen's eggs gang to the ha',
  To bring the goose's egg awa'.
The higher up the greater fa'.
The higher the hill the laigher the grass.
The hurt man writes wi' steel on marble stane.
The king's errand may come in the cadger's gate.
The lazy man's the beggar's brother.
The lucky pennyworth sells soonest.
The langest day will have an end.
The mother of a' mischief is nae bigger than a midge's wing.
The mair cost the mair honour.
The mawt is aboon the meal wi' him.
The mair noble the mair humble.
The mother's breath is aye sweet.
The master's eye makes the horse fat.
The mair mischief the better sport.
The name o' an honest woman's muckle worth.
The poor man's aye put to the warst.
The reek o' my ain house is better than the fire o' my neighbour's.
The strongest horse lowps the dyke.
The still sow eats up a' the draff.
The stowp that gangs aft to the well comes hame broken at last.
The subject's love is the king's life guard.
The smith's mare and the souter's wife are aye warst shod.
The thing that's done is no to do.
The thing that's fristed is not forgi'en.
The thing that lies not in your gate, breaks not your shins.
The thrift of you was the death of your good-dame.
The tod ne'er sped better than when he gaed on his ain errand.
The tod's whelps are ill to tame.
The tree does na fa' at the first strake.
The water will never rob the widdy.
The warse luck now the better another time.
The weakest gangs to the wa'.
The worth o' a thing is best ken'd by the want o't.
There is mony a true tale tauld in a jest.
There is nane sae blind as them that winna see.
There is naething ill said that's no ill tane.
There is nae sport where there is neither auld fowk nor bairns.
There was aye some water where the stirk was drown'd.
There was never enough where naething was left.
There was never a silly Jocky but there was as silly a Jenny.
There was never a thrifty wife with a sheet about her head.

There is skill in gruel making.
There is nae fence against a flail.
There is a time to gley and a time to look straight.
There is a great differ amang market days.
There is little wit in his pow that lights the candle at the low.
There is an end o' an auld sang.
There is a tough sinew in an auld wife's heel.
There is aye life in a living man.
There is an act in the laird o' Grant's court, that no aboon eleven
    speak at anes.
There are mair ways to the wood than ane.
There are mair working days than life days.
There is ae day of reckoning and another of payment.
There came never ill after good advisement.
There is a sliddery stane afore the ha' door.
There's a difference between will ye buy? and will ye sell?
There's as good fish in the sea as ever came out o't.
There is a great difference between fenn and farewell.
There is a hole in the house.
There is life in a throssle as lang as she cheeps.
There is little for the rake after the shool.
They are well guided that God guides.
They are aye good that are far away.
They are lightly herried that have a' their ain.
They are sad rents that come in with tears.
They complain early that complain o' their kail.
They have need of a cannie cook that have but ae egg to their dinner.
They loo me for little that hate me for nought.
They never saw great dainties that think a haggis a feast.
They shou'd please the goodwife that wou'd win the goodman.
They speak of my drinking that never think of my drouth.
They that get the word o' soon rising may lie in their bed a' day.
They that laugh in the morning may greet ere night.
They that give you hinder you to buy.
They that live langest fetch wood farthest.
They that see your head see not your height.
They that hae rowth of butter may lay it thick on their scone.
They were scant o' bairns that brought you up.
They were never fain that fidged, nor fu' that lick'd dishes.
They wist as well that didna speer.
They were never first at the wark that bid God speed the wark.
They never gae with the speet but they gat with the ladle.
Thistles are a salad for an ass.
Three is aye sonsy.
Three can keep a secret if twa be away.
Time o' day to find the nest when the birds are flown.
Time tint is ne'er to be found.

Time and thinking tame the toughest grief.
Time and tide will tarry for nae man.
Time tries a'.
Tine heart and a's gane.
Tine book, tine grace.
Tine thimble, tine thrift.
Touch nae me on the sair heel.
Tramp on a snail and she'll shoot out her horns.
True blue will never stain.
Truth and honesty keep the crown o' the causey.
True love kyths in time of need.
Try your friend ere you need him.
Try before you trust.
Twa hungry meals make the third a glutton.
Twa blacks make na ae white.
Twa things ane shou'd not be angry at, what he can help and what
    he canna help.
Twa fools in a house are a couple ower mony.
Twa words maun gang to that bargain.
Twa wits are better than ane.
That bowt came never out of your bag.
The back and the belly hauds every ane busy.
The black ox ne'er trod on your taes.
The cat wou'd fain fish eat,
    But she is laith to weet her feet.
The de'il's good when he's pleas'd.
The father buys, the son biggs,
    The oye sells, and his son thiggs.
The greedy man and the gielainger are well met.
The greatest tochers make not the greatest testaments.
The kirk's muckle, but ye may say mass in the end o't.
The laird may be laird and need his hind's help.
The man may eithly tine a stot that canna count his kinsh.
The mair the merrier, the fewer the better cheer.
The meal cheap and the shoon dear,
    What souters' wives like weel to hear.
The pains o'ergang the profit.
The poor man's shilling is but a penny.
The scholar may waur the master.
The simple man's the beggar's brother.
The warst warld that ever was, some maun won.
The weeds o'ergrow the corn.
The warld is bound to nae man.
The unsonsy fish gets the unlucky bait.
There is mair knavery amang kirk men than there is honesty amang
    courtiers.
There is a measure in a' things.

There is muckle to do when burghers ride.
There is mair room without than within.
There is nae remedy for fear but cut aff the head.
There was never a fair word in flyting.
There is steel in the needle point tho' little o't.
There are twa enoughs, and he has gotten ane of them.
There are mair married than good house hadders.
There's a bonny reason wi' a rag about the foot o't.
There came never sic a gloff to a daw's heart.
There is fey blood in your head.
There grows nae grass at the cross.
There is little to sew when tailors are true.
They are not a' saints that get haly water.
They 'gree like butter and mells.
They may ken by your beard what has been on your board.
They never beuk a good cake but may bake an ill ane.
They that see you a' day winna break the house for you at night.
They that hain at their dinner will hae the mair to their supper.
They that burn you for a witch lose a' their coals.
They that lie down for love shou'd rise for hunger.
They that eat till they sweat and work till they're cauld,
    Sic servants are fitter to hang than to hald.
They that bourd with cats maun count upo' scarts.
They are eith hindered that are not very furdersome.
Twa dogs were striving about a bane, and the third ran awa' wi't.
Twa conveniences sindle times meet,
    What's good for the plant is ill for the peat.
Tarry breeks pay nae fraught.
Tell your gley'd good-dame that.
That's a tee'd ba'.
That's a tale o' twa drinks.
The bag to the auld stent, and the belt to the yule hole.
The cause is good, and the word fa' on.
The death of ae bairn winna skail a house.
The dorty dame may fa' in the dirt.
The e'ening brings a' hame.
The flesh is aye sairest that's farthest frae the bane.
The gait gi'es a good milking, but dings it down wi' her feet.
The langer we live the mair ferlies we see.
The neist time ye dance tent wha ye take by the hand.
The piper wants muckle that wants his nether chafts.
The poor man pays for a'.
The thacker said to his man,
    Let us raise this ladder, if we can.
The thrift of you and the woo of a dog wou'd make a braw web.
The tod never fares better than when he's bann'd.
There was never a good town but there was a dub at the end o't.

There was never a cake but it had its maik.
There is little mair between the poor and the rich but a piece of an
ill year.
They have been born as poor as you that have come to a pouchfu' o'
green pease ere they died.
They that drink langest live langest.
Thoughts beguiled the lady.
Thoughts are free, tho' I mayna say mickle, I can yerk at the thinking.
Till other tinklers ill met ye 'gree.
Touch a gawd horse on the back and he'll fling.
Tit for tat, as the auld wife said when she f——d at the thunder.
Trot father, trot mother, how can the foal amble?
Twine tow, your minny was a good spinner.

Untimeous spurring spills the steed.
Unseen, unrued.
Under water dearth, under snaw bread.
Up hill spare me, down hill take tent to thee.
Up starts a carle and gather'd good,
And thence came a' our gentle blood.
Use makes perfytness.

Wad ye gar us trow that the moon's made o' green cheese, or that
spade-shafts bear plumbs?
Wage will get a page.
Wae's the wife that wants the tongue, but well's the man that gets her.
Want of wit is waur than want of wealth.
War makes thieves, and peace hangs them.
Wark bears witness of wha well does.
Wealth gars wit waver.
Weans maun creep ere they gang.
Well kens the mouse when the cat's out o' the house.
Well's him and wae's him that has a bishop in his kin.
Welcome is the best dish in the kitchen.
Well worth a' that gars the plough draw.
Well is that well does.
Were it not for hope heart wad break.
We'll never ken the worth of the water till the well gaes dry.
We can drink of the burn when we canna bite of the brae.
We'll meet ere hills meet.
We can live without our kin, but no without our neighbours.
We'll bark oursells ere we buy dogs sae dear.
We canna baith sup and blaw.
We maun live by the living, but no by the dead.
We are bound to be honest and no to be rich.
We may ken your meaning by your mumping.
Wedding and ill wintering tame baith man and beast.

We are aye to lear as lang as we live.

We can poind for debt, but no for unkindness.

We may ken your eilk by the runkles o' your horn.

Wee things fley cowards.

Wha wats wha may keep sheep another day.

Wha uses perils, perish shall.

What ye win at that, ye may lick aff a het girdle.

What better is the house that the daw rises soon.

Wha can haud what will away ?

Wha comes aftener and brings you less ?

Wha daur bell the cat ?

Wha can help misluck ?

Wha canna gi'e will little get.

What the eye sees na the heart rues na.

What's nane o' my profit shall be nane o' my peril.

What if the lift fa', then ye may gather lav'rocks.

What's gotten o'er the de'il's back will gang away under his belly.

What raks the feud where the friendship dow not.

What winna do by might do by flight.

What's my case the day may be yours the morn.

What's waur than ill luck ?

What may be done at ony time will be done at nae time.

What puts that in your head that didna put the sturdy wi't ?

What need a rich man be a thief ?

What said Pluck ? the greater knave the greater luck.

What may be, may not be.

What canna be cured maun be endured.

When ae door steeks anither opens.

When a' men speaks nae man hears.

When drink's in wit's out.

When friends meet hearts warm.

When Adam delved and Eve span,
    Where was a' our gentry than ?

When my head's down my house is theeked.

When the tod preaches tak tent o' the lambs.

When thieves reckon, leal fowk comes to their gear.

When the bags are fou the dron gets up.

When the tod wins to the wood he cares not how many keek for his tail.

When the cup's fu' carry it even.

When poverty comes in at the door friendship flies out of the window.

When lairds break carles get land.

When a fool finds a horse-shoe,
    He thinks aye the like to do.

When a' fruit fa's, then welcome haws.

When I'm dead make me a cawdel.

When ilka ain gets their ain the thief will get the widdy.
When a ewe's drown'd she's dead.
When the goodman drinks to the goodwife, a' *wad be* well.
When the goodwife drinks to the goodman, a' *is* well.
When the heart's fou of lust the mouth's fou of leasing.
When your neighbour's house is in danger take care o' your ain.
When you are served a' the geese are water'd.
When wine sinks words swim.
When the barn's fu' you may thresh before the door.
When ye're gaun and coming the gate's no toom.
When the heart's fu' the tongue will speak.
When he dies for age ye may quake for fear.
When ye are weel, haud yoursell sae.
When the well's fu' it will rin o'er.
When the pot's o'er fu', it will boil o'er and bleeze in the ingle.
When the steed's stown, steek the stable door.
Where the buck's bound, there he maun bleet.
Where the deer's slain some of the blood will lie.
Where the dyke's laighest it is eithest to lowp.
Where there is o'er mickle courtesy there is little kindness.
Where there is naething the king tines his right.
Where drums beat laws are dumb.
Where the pig's broken let the sherds lie.
Where there are gentles there is aye aff-fawing.
Where gat ye that, gif a body may speer ?
    I gat it where it was, and where leal fowk get gear.
Where will you get a park to keep your yeld kye in ?
Where the heart gangs let the tail follow.
While the grass grows the steed starves.
Whitely things are aye tender.
Whom God will help nane can hinder.
Will a fool's feather in my cap gar my pot play ?
Wipe wi' the water and wash wi' the towel.
Wise men may be whilly'd wi' wiles.
Wives and wind are necessary ills.
Widdy haud thy ain !
Wilfu' waste makes waefu' want.
Wiles help weak fowk.
Will and wit strive wi' ye !
Win't and wear't.
Winter thunder bodes summer hunger.
Wink at wee fauts, your ain are muckle.
Wishers and waddlers were never good house handers.
Wit bought makes fowk wise.
Wit bought is worth twa for nought.
Woman's wark's never done.
Women and bairns lein what they ken not.

Wood iu a wilderness, moss on a mountain,
  And wit in a poor man are little thought on.
Words are but win, but dunts are out o' season.
Woo sellers ken aye woo buyers.
Work for nought makes fowk dead sweer.
Wrang has nae warrant.
Wrang count is nae payment.
Wad ye gar me trow that my head's cow'd when ne'er a shear's
  come on't ?
Wae to the wame that has a wilfu' master.
Wae's them that has the cat's dish and she aye mewting.
Water stowps had nae ale.
Wealth in the widow's house, kail but saut.
Well worth a' good takens.
We are as mony Johnstons as ye are Jardines.
We hounds slew the hare, quoth the bleer'd messan.
Wha invited you to the roast ?
Wha can court but cost.
Wha made you a gentleman that didna cut the lugs frae your head
  to ken you by.
What ye do when you're drunk ye may pay for when you're dry.
What ye want up and down ye have hither and yont.

Ye breed of the tod, ye grow gray before ye grow good.
Ye breed of the miller's dog, ye lick your lips ere the pock be opened.
Ye breed of Macfarlane's geese, ye have mair mind o' your play
  than your meat.
Ye breed of the cow's tail, you grow backward.
Ye breed of nettle kail and cock lairds, ye need muckle service.
Ye breed of the gowk, ye have never a rhyme but ane.
Ye breed of ill weather, ye come unsent for.
Ye breed of Saughton swine, your neb's ne'er out of an ill turn.
Ye breed of auld maidens, ye look sae high.
Ye breed of the chapman, ye're aye to handsell.
Ye breed of our laird, ye'll do nae right nor take nae wrang.
Ye breed of good mawt, ye're lang a-coming.
Ye breed of the beggars, ye're never out of your gate.
Ye breed of the butcher, that seeks his knife when it is in his teeth.
Ye breed of the leek, ye have a white head and a green tail.
Ye breed of Lady Mary, when ye're good ye're ower good.
Ye breed of the miller's daughter, that speer'd what tree groats grew on.
Ye breed of the goodman's mither, ye're aye in the gate.
Ye breed of the witches, ye can do nae good to yoursell.
Ye breed o the herd's wife, ye busk again e'en.
Ye breed of the baxters, ye loo your neighbour's browst better than
  your ain batch.
Ye crack crously with your bonnet on.

Ye cut before the point.
Ye come a day after the fair.
Ye cut lang whangs out o' other fowks' leather.
Ye come aftener with the rake than the shool.
Ye canna make a silk purse of a sow's lug.
Ye canna see wood for trees.
Ye can never fare well but ye cry roast meat.
Ye came a clipping time.
Ye cangle about uncost kids.
Ye canna preach out o' your ain poupit.
Ye canna get leave to thrive for thrang.
Ye ca' hardest at the nail that drives fastest.
Ye canna do but ye ower do.
Ye drive the plough afore the owsen.
Ye dinna ken where a blessing may light.
Ye drew not sae well when my mare was in the mire.
Ye feik it awa' like an auld wife baking.
Ye gat your will in your first wife's time, and ye'se no want it now.
Ye glowr'd at the moon and fell on the middin'.
Ye gang about by Lanark, for fear Linton dogs bite you.
Ye glowr like a wild-cat out o' a whin-bush.
Ye get o'er muckle o' your will, and that's no good for you.
Ye gae far about seeking the nearest.
Ye have run lang on little ground.
Ye have aye mind of your meat though ye have ill luck til't.
Ye have a ready mouth for a ripe cherry.
Ye have a saw for ilka sair.
Ye have brought the pack to the pins.
Ye have given the wolf the wedder to keep.
Ye have tied a knot with your tongue that ye canna loose with a'
    your teeth.
Ye have been bred about a mill, ye have mouped a' your manners.
Ye have o'er foul feet to come sae far benn.
Ye have a stawk of carle hemp in you.
Ye have gotten a revel'd hesp o't.
Ye have ae crap for a' corn.
Ye have tane the measure of his foot.
Ye have o'er muckle loose leather about your chafts.
Ye have tint your ain stomach and found a tike's.
Ye have put a toom spoon in my mouth.
Ye have fasted lang, and worried on a midge.
Ye have tint the tongue o' your trump.
Ye have staid lang, and brought little wi' ye.
Ye have gi'en baith the sound thump and the loud skirl.
Ye have aye a foot out of the langle.
Ye have tane't upon you as the wife did the dancing.
Ye have good manners, but ye bear them not aye about wi' you.

Ye have the wrang sow by the lug.
Ye ken naething but milk and bread when it is mool'd in to you.
Ye ken what drinkers dree.
Ye kenna wha may cool your kail yet.
Ye live at the lug o' the law.
Yelping curs will raise mastiffs.
Ye live on love as lav'rocks do on leeks.
Ye'll neither dance nor haud the candle.
Ye'll get nae mair of the cat but the skin.
Ye look like let me be.
Ye look like a Lochaber-axe new come frae the grindstane.
Ye'll no sell your hen on a rainy day.
Ye'll get as mickle for ae wish this year as for twa fern year.
Ye'll gar me seek the needle where I didna stick it.
Ye'll never cast saut on his tail.
Ye look like a Lammermoor lion.
Ye'll let naething be tint for want o' seeking.
Ye'll no harry yoursell wi' your ain hands.
Ye look like the de'il in daylight.
Ye look liker a thief than a bishop.
Ye'll ne'er make a mark in your testament by that bargain.
Ye'll let little gae by you unless it be the swallow.
Ye may tine the father seeking the son.
Ye may drive the de'il into a wife, but ye'll ne'er ding him out of her.
Ye may be greedy, but ye're no greening.
Ye may gang farther and fare warse.
Ye may be heard where ye're no seen.
Ye may gang thro' a' Egypt without a pass.
Ye may hae a good memory, but your judgment winna gi'e mickle.
Ye maun take the will for the deed.
Ye maunna think to win thro' the warld on a feather-bed.
Ye maunna be mealy-mou'd.
Ye mete my pease by your ain peck.
You look like a runner, quoth the de'il to the lobster.
Ye'll be made up at the sign o' the wind.
Ye'll play at sma' game before ye stand out.
Ye'll beguile nane but them that lippens to you.
Ye'll mend when ye grow better.
Ye'll never be sae auld with sae mickle honesty.
Ye never saw green cheese but your e'en reel'd.
Ye never want a good whittle at your belt.
Ye never heard a fisher cry stinking fish.
Ye needna think shame to tak it, your teeth's langer than your beard.
Ye put at the cart that's aye ganging.
Ye're as daft as ye're days auld.
Ye're o'er auld farran to be fley'd for bogles.
Ye're a good seeker but an ill finder.

Ye ride a bootless errand.

Ye're like the wife wi' the mony daughters, the best comes last.

Ye're nae chicken for a' your cheeping.

Ye're come o' blood, and sae is a pudding.

Ye're come to a peel'd egg.

Ye're a widdy-fou against hanging time.

Ye're as lang a tuning your pipes as ane wad play a spring.

Ye're good enough but ye're no braw new.

Ye're no sae poor as ye peep.

Ye're well away if ye bide, and we're well quat.

Ye're of sae mony minds, ye'll never be married.

Ye're come to fetch fire.

Ye're sae weel in your wooing ye watna where to wed.

Ye're never pleased fu' nor fasting.

Ye're black about the mouth for want of making of.

Ye're welcome, but ye winna win ben.

Ye're unco good and ye'll grow fair.

Ye're sair fash'd hadding naething together.

Ye're not fed with deaf nuts.

Ye're sick but no sair handled.

Ye're busy seeking a thing that's no tint.

Ye're good for carrying a propine, ye can make muckle of little.

Ye're like the hens, ye rin aye to the heap.

Ye're fear'd for the day ye never saw.

Ye're bonny enough to them that loo you, and o'er bonny to them
  that loo you and canna get you.

Ye're o'er bird-mouth'd.

Ye're new risen and your young heart's nipping.

Ye're a sweet nut if you were well cracked.

Ye're no light where ye lean a'.

Ye're mair fley'd than hurt.

Ye're Davy do a' thing and good at naething.

Ye seek grace o' a graceless face.

Ye sell the bear's skin on his back.

Ye served me as the wife did the cat,
  Coost me in the kirn and syne harl'd me out.

Ye may dight your neb and fly up.

Ye'll never die on your ain assize.

Ye'll drink afore me.

Ye'll find him whaur ye left him.

Ye'll get the cat wi' the twa tails.

Ye're the greatest liar o' your kin except your chief that wan his
  meat by't.

Ye're mistane o' the stuff, it is haff silk.

Ye'se no want while I hae, but look weel to your ain.

Ye soon weary o' well-doing.

Ye'se get your brose out o' the lee side of the pot.

Ye shanna be niffer'd but for a better.
Ye sleep like a dog in a mill.
Ye shape shoon by your ain shachled feet.
Ye take mair in your gab than your cheeks can haud.
Ye take the first word of flyting.
Ye tine the ladle for the licking.
Your tongue's nae slander.
Your tongue rins aye before your wit.
Ye wad make mickle of me if I were yours.
Ye watna what wife's ladle may cogue your kail.
Ye wad be a good midwife gin ye haud the grip ye get.
Ye wad be good to fetch the de'il a drink.
Ye wad ferly mair if the craws bigged in your cleavding and flew
    away with the nest.
Ye watna where a blessing may light.
Young fowk may die and auld fowk maun die.
Young ducks may be auld geese.
Yule's young on Yule e'en.
Youth and eild never sowder well.
Your meal's a' deagh.
Your bread's baken, ye may hing by your girdle.
Your head's nae sooner up than your stamock's yapin.
Your wind shakes nae corn.
Your head will never fill your father's bonnet.
Your trumpeter's dead.
Your thrift's as good as the profit of a yeld hen.
Your winning is no my tinsel.
Your wit winna worry ye.
Your mind's chasing mice.
Your gear will ne'er o'ergang you.
Your minnie's milk is no out of your nose yet.
Your een's no marrows.
Ye have sitten your time as mony a good hen has done.
Ye have naething to do but suck and wag your tail.
Ye promise better than ye pay, yer hechts ye never brooked.
Ye're ane of snaw-ba's bairn-time.
Ye're here yet and your belt's hale.
Ye spill unspoken to.
Ye was set aff frae the oon for nipping the pies.
Ye was never born at that time of year.
Ye was sae gare ye wadna bide the blessing.
Your wame thinks your wyson's cutted.
Your purse was steeked when that was paid for.
Your neck's youking for a St. Johnston ribbon.

A LIST

OF

THE PRINCIPAL WRITERS IN THE SCOTTISH LANGUAGE.

COMPILED BY G. MAY.

Ainslie, Hew. born in 1792, at Dailly, Ayrshire; his songs, published in "A Pilgrimage to the Land of Burns" (1820), obtained for him considerable popularity. In later life he emigrated to America. In 1855 he published at New York a volume of "Scottish Songs, Ballads, and Poems."

Ainslie, Robert (1766–1838), a Writer to the Signet, and a friend and correspondent of Robert Burns. He was for forty years a contributor to the *Edinburgh Magazine*, and other periodicals.

Aird, Thomas, born in 1802 at Bowden in Roxburghshire; a distinguished poet, journalist, and prose writer. He published in 1845 "The Old Bachelor, in the Old Scottish Village," a collection of tales illustrative of Scottish life, character, and scenes, and in 1856 a complete collection of his numerous poetical works.

Aytoun, Sir Robert (1570–1638), an accomplished poet and courtier, who occupied the post of private secretary to the queens of James I. (of England) and Charles I. His poems are published in the Miscellany of the Bannatyne Club.

Aytoun, William Edmondstoune (1813–1865), Professor of Rhetoric and English Literature at the University of Edinburgh (1845–1865). His earliest literary efforts appeared in magazine literature, notably *Blackwood's,* of which in 1854 he became assistant or advising editor. *Poetical works—*"Ballads of Scotland" (edited 1858); "Bothwell" (a narrative poem in the style of Sir Walter Scott, 1856); "Firmilian, a Spasmodic Tragedy" (1854); "Lays of the Scottish Cavaliers, and other Poems" (1849)—his chief poetical work; "The Execution of Montrose," and "The Burial March of Dundee;" "Nuptial

Ode on the Marriage of the Prince of Wales" (1863); "Poland, and other Poems." The "Glenmutchkin Railway" (a tale); "How I Became a Yeoman;" "Life and Times of Richard I." (1840); "Norman Sinclair" (1861). He was one of the authors, in conjunction with Sir Theodore Martin, of the "Bon Gaultier Ballads."

Baillie, Joanna (1762-1851), a Scottish poetess and dramatist, many of whose songs became popular, and still maintain their place in literature.

Balfour, Alexander (1776-1829), a miscellaneous writer, among whose works may be mentioned "Campbell, or the Scottish Probationer," a novel, published in 1819; an edition of Gall's poems in the same year; a volume of his own poems, entitled "Contemplations," and several other novels.

Balfour, Sir James, a distinguished lawyer who died in 1583-84. His chief work, "The Practicks of Scots Law" (in MSS.), was for a long period a standard work of reference. It was printed in 1754 with a biographical introduction by Walter Goodal.

Ballantine, James (born in 1810, died in 1878), author of "The Gaberlunzie's Wallet," "Lilias Lee," and of many beautiful songs in "Whistle Binkie" and other Scottish collections of lyrical poetry. His songs are of the highest merit, and of great and deserved popularity.

Ballantyne, James (1772-1833). The senior member of the celebrated printing and publishing firm of that name. He was an intimate friend and afterwards partner of Sir Walter Scott, a friendship which commenced at school and lasted through life. To Mr. Ballantyne's judicious criticism are owing many corrections and suggestions in the works of the "Wizard of the North."

Bannatyne, George (1545-1606). The name of this eminent collector of Scottish poetry of the fifteenth and sixteenth centuries has been adopted as the cognomen of a distinguished literary Society. His "Ancient Scottish Poems" was published in 1770.

Barbour, John (1316-1395), a historical poet, author of "The Bruce," a metrical chronicle finished in 1375 and first published from the MS. in 1489. This work possesses great value as an historical record, and has run through about twenty editions, of which the best are Pinkerton's (dated 1790) and Dr. Jamieson's (1820).

Beattie, George (1785 - 1823), was an advocate or solicitor at Montrose. His principal work is, "John o' Arnha'," a humorous and satirical poem somewhat in the style of "Tam o' Shanter."

Beattie, James, LL.D. (1735-1803), a poet, essayist, and miscellaneous writer, born at Laurencekirk, Kircardineshire. His name was first brought prominently before the public by his "Essay on the Nature and Immutability of Truth in Opposition to Sophistry and Scepticism," a reply to Hume. His other works are—"Judgment of Paris" (1765); "The Minstrel," in two parts, Spenserian metre. (Incomplete. Merivale added a third part). "Poems and Translations" (1760). *Prose works*—"Dissertations" (1783); "The Elements of Moral Sciences" (1790-1793); "Essay on Poetry and Music" (1778); "Essay on Truth" (1770); "Essays" (1776); "Evidences of Christianity" (1786). (Life by Sir William Forbes, 1806; Mudford, 1809; Dyce, 1831.) He was part author of the beautiful Scottish song, "There's nae luck about the house."

Bellenden, John (or **Ballenden,** or **Ballentyne**), poet and historian. Archdeacon of Moray, and Canon of Ross (1490-1560). In 1530 and 1531 he was employed by command of James V. in translating Bolce's "History and Chroniklis of Scotland," from the Latin into the Scottish vernacular. He died at Rome in 1550. Among his other poems as unquestionably a man of great parts, and one of the finest poets his country had, may be mentioned "Vertue and Vyse," "The Proheme of the Cosmographe" (the most poetical of his works), and "The Proheme of the History." He also wrote the "Topography of Scotland" (1577); Carmichael's

"Collections of Scottish Poems" contains some specimens of his style.

Bennoch, Francis (born 1812). He has published a volume of "Poems, Lyrics, Songs, and Sonnets," and edited a collection of Miss Mitford's tales.

Bethune, John (1812-1839), son of a farm-servant, and himself a labourer. In conjunction with his brother Alexander he wrote the "Tales and Sketches of the Scottish Peasantry" (1836). Two years afterwards, "Lectures on Practical Economy" appeared; and as "A Fifeshire Forester" he contributed a number of poems to the *Scottish Christian Herald*, and the *Christian Instructor*.

Blacklock, Thomas, D.D. (1721-1791), a poet and divine who was deprived of sight in his earliest infancy. His chief works are "The Graham," a heroic ballad (1774); "Paracelsis" (1767); and two volumes of "Poems" (1745 and 1754). The article "Blind," in the *Encyclopædia Britannica*, was written by him. After his death his writings were collected by H. Mackenzie (1793). He was one of the eminent men of letters in Edinburgh who welcomed and did honour to Robert Burns on his celebrated visit to that city.

Boswell, Sir Alexander (1775-1822), was the eldest son of James Boswell, the biographer of Dr. Johnson. His writings are noteworthy for their lively

2 B

imagination, satire, and humour. Many of his "Songs, chiefly in the Scottish Dialect" (1803), have achieved permanent popularity, the best known being "Auld Gude Man, ye're a Drucken Carle;" "Jenny's Bawbee;" "Jenny Dang the Weaver;" and a poem, published under an assumed name, is entitled "Edinburgh, or the Ancient Royalty, a Sketch of Former Manners, by Simon Gray" (1810). Another work in Scottish verse is "Skeldon Haughs, or the Sow is Flitted" (1816), and "Clan Alpin's Vow." Created a baronet in 1821. He received a death-wound in a duel with Mr. Stewart of Auldearn, afterwards editor of the *Courier*, a London evening paper, resulting from some political satires published in the *Sentinel*.

Brunton, George (1799–1863), a miscellaneous writer of prose and verse illustrative of Scottish life, manners, and localities. These sketches and tales appeared in the *Edinburgh Magazine*, the *Scottish Literary Gazette*, and *Tait's Magazine*. In 1834 he became editor of the *Scottish Patriot*, having previously edited the *Citizen*. After the publication of "An Historical Account of the Senators of the College of Justice," in which he was associated with Mr. David Haig, he, in conjunction with the latter, started the *Scots Weekly Magazine*, which was exclusively devoted to the elucidation of Scottish history and antiquities, and Scottish life and manners.

Burns, Robert (1759–1796), the most popular of all the Scottish poets, and whose fame has become world-wide. The range and variety of his powers are unsurpassed in the literature of his country; including, as they do, such different and such excellent poems as the "Cotter's Saturday Night," "Scots wha hae wi' Wallace bled," "Auld Lang Syne," "A Man's a Man for a' that," "Holy Willie's Prayer," "Tam o' Shanter," "Death and Dr. Hornbook," "The Twa Dogs," all of which have sunk deep into the remembrance and hearts of Scotsmen in every part of the world, and are familiar to all educated Englishmen. His name and songs have become dear to every patriotic Scotsman, and the language of his country will, doubtless, be perpetuated in his works long after it has become an unspoken tongue.

Callander, John (—1789). An antiquary born about the beginning of the eighteenth century. His best known work is "Two Ancient Scottish Poems" (1782); beside this he translated Brosse's "Terra Australia Coqueta" from the French. He also projected, but did not carry out, works on the "History of the Ancient Music of Scotland," and a "Scoto-Gothic Glossary." He was accused of plagiarism in connection with some "Annotations to Milton's Paradise Lost," which it would appear without some reason.

Campbell, Alexander (1764–1824). His first literary effort was "An Introduction to the History of Poetry in Scotland" (1798), together with "Songs of the Lowlands." This was followed in 1802 by "A Tour from Edinburgh through Various Parts of North Britain," generally considered to be his best work; "The Grampians Desolate" (1804), showed a diminution of power. His last work (1816), was "Albyn's Anthology," a collection of native Highland music to which Sir Walter Scott and others contributed verses.

Campbell, Thomas (1777–1844), author of "The Pleasures of Hope," and the spirited songs and ballads "Ye Mariners of England," "The Battle of Hohenlinden," "The Exile of Erin," "Lochiel's Warning," "The Soldier's Dream," and "Lord Ullin's Daughter." He was one of the originators of the London University, and afterwards Lord Rector of the University of Glasgow. He is buried in Westminster Abbey.

Carrick, John Donald (1787–1837), best known as the author of "The Life of Wallace," was a voluminous miscellaneous writer of considerable repute. He was deeply read in old Scottish literature, and became successively editor of the *Scots Times*, the *Perth Advertiser*, and the *Kilmarnock Journal*. His latest work, "The Laird of Logan," is a well-known series of Scottish sketches, to which work he was the largest contributor.

Chalmers, George (1742–1825), a historian and antiquary, whose principal production was his "Caledonia" (1807–1824). He also wrote a "History of Scottish Poetry," a "History of Printing in Scotland," Lives of Defoe (1785), Mary Queen of Scots (1818), Thomas Ruddiman (1794), and several other works, one of which was an illustrated edition of the poems of Allan Ramsay.

Chambers, Robert, LL.D. (1802–1871), a voluminous, historical, miscellaneous writer, and one of the founders of the great publishing firm of William and Robert Chambers. During his forty years of literary labour he produced no less than one hundred volumes, the most notable of his works being "Popular Rhymes of Scotland" (1826), "Pictures of Scotland" (1827), "Histories of the Scottish Rebellions," and a "Life of James I." His "Book of Days," "Biographical Dictionary of Eminent Scotsmen," and his various educational works for "the entertainment and instruction of the people." Since his death, his authorship of the celebrated "Vestiges of the Natural History of Creation" has been publicly avowed.

Cunningham, Thomas (1776–1834), a lyric writer of great merit, and a constant contributor to the *Edinburgh Maga-*

zine, to which he sent not only poems and songs but miscellaneous sketches and stories, all characterised by a somewhat rare vein of pathos, oddity, and humour.

Cunningham, Allan (1784–1842), one of the first of Scottish song writers. His literary productions were extremely numerous, but, perhaps, apart from poetry, his "Life of Burns" is the masterpiece.

Douglas, Gawyn or **Gavin** (1474–1522), styled "the most classical of Scottish poets." He was Bishop of Dunkeld, and translated into the Scottish vernacular the "Æneid" of Virgil, prefixing a poetical introduction of his own to each book.

Drummond, William, of Hawthornden (1585–1649), author of "History of the Five Jameses, Kings of Scotland," which is strongly tinged with royalist principles. His poems and songs are characterised by delicacy and tenderness of treatment.

Dunbar, William (1465– —), one of the chief of early Scotch poets. His "Thistle and the Rose" is a poem of surpassing beauty. Others are entitled "The Golden Targe," "The Twa Married Women," and "The Weds." He interwove Latin with Scottish verses in a very fantastic manner.

Ferguson, Robert (1750–1774), Born and educated at Aberdeen, most of his poems had appeared in Ruddiman's *Weekly Magazine* before he · had at-

tained his twentieth year. A monument to his memory was erected over his grave in Edinburgh at the expense of Robert Burns, out of the profits of the Edinburgh edition of his "Poems and Songs."

Finlay, John (1782–1810). The chief poems of this writer are "Wallace, or the Fate of Ellerslie," and "Scottish Historical and Romantic Ballads," both of these works displaying considerable knowledge and research.

Gall, Richard (1776–1801). His principal poems were "Farewell to Ayrshire" (erroneously attributed to Burns), and "My only Jo and Dearie O;" besides which, "The Braes of Drumlee," and "Captain O'Kain," merit special mention.

Galloway, Robert (1752–1794). The "Poems, Epistles, and Songs" of this poet were chiefly written in the Scottish tongue. A shoemaker by trade, he subsequently became a bookseller in Glasgow. His poems were published in that city in 1788.

Galt, John (1779–1839), a writer, whose productions consisted of poems, prose essays, and a large number of novels, in all upwards of fifty volumes. The following are his principal works:—Lives of Cardinal Wolsey (1812), Benjamin West (1816), Lord Byron (1830); "The Players" (1831); "An Autobiography" (1833); "Literary Life and Miscellanies" (1834); "Ourandlogos" (1833); "Voyages and

Travels " (1812); and " The Wandering Jew." His best novels were entitled "Annals of the Parish " (1821)," and "Ayrshire Legatees " (same year).

Gilfillan, Robert (1798–1850). This writer's lyrical productions were gathered in a volume published in 1831, entitled " Original Songs." In 1835 and 1839 enlarged editions were issued.

Glen, William (1789–1826), a lyrical writer, some of whose productions have found their way into every Scottish home. His Jacobite song, " Wae's me for Prince Charlie," was one of the most touching and popular of the songs of the time.

Grant, Joseph (1805–1835). The tales and poetry of this writer were principally in the Scottish language. His latest work, published posthumously, was "Tales of the Glens " (1836), with a memoir by Robert Nichol.

Hamilton, William (1704–1754). A native of Bangour, he received a liberal education, and early cultivated a taste for poetry. The Jacobite song, "Gladsmuir," his first success, was due to the part he took in the rebellion of 1745. On "The Braes of Yarrow," however, is based his chief claim to remembrance. His works were collected and published in Edinburgh in 1766.

Hamilton, William. Born at Gilbertfield, he, after some years of military service, left the army to devote himself to literature. He was a friend and corres-pondent of Allan Ramsay. Watson's " Choice Collection of Scots Poems " contains his chief writings. In 1722 he issued, rendered into modern Scotch, an edition of Blind Harry's "Life of Wallace," a work which has been frequently reprinted.

Harry the Minstrel, or Blind Harry, as he is more popularly called. His history is obscure, but he wrote in the vernacular the achievements of Wallace, the champion of Scottish Independence. So little is known of him that his surname has never been ascertained. It seems, however, that he was blind from his birth, and that he followed the occupation of a wandering minstrel. His only poem now extant is entitled, " Ye actis and deidis of ye illuster and vailzeand campioun shyr Willam Wallace," the MS. of which is now preserved in the Advocates' Library, bearing the date of 1488.

Hedderwick, James, LL.D., a well-known journalist and poet, in early life sub-editor of the *Scotsman.* He subsequently started the *Glasgow Citizen* and other periodicals. His principal work is " Lays of the Middle Ages."

Henderson, Andrew (1783–1835). author of a " Collection of Scottish Proverbs " published in 1832, to which William Motherwell contributed an introduction.

Henryson, Robert, who flourished in the fifteenth century. The date and place of his birth are unknown. His "Robene and Makyne" is thought to be the earliest specimen of pastoral poetry in the Scottish language. Examples of his verse are included in Irving's "Lives of the Scottish Poets," Hailes' "Ancient Scottish Poems," Ellis' "Specimens," and Sibbald's "Chronicle of Scottish Poetry." His chief works are "The Bludy Serf," "Fabils" (printed 1621); "Orpheus Kyng, and how he yeid to Newyn and to hel to seik his Quene" (printed 1508); "Tailes of the Uplandis Mons and the burges mons" (printed 1815), and the "Testament of faire Cresside" (printed 1593).

Herd, David (1732–1810). Sir Walter Scott, in his "Minstrelsy of the Scottish Border," speaks of Herd as "the editor of the first classical collection of Scottish songs and ballads," and further acknowledges his indebtedness to those manuscripts entitled "A Collection of Ancient and Modern Scottish Songs, Heroic Ballads," &c. This was published in 1769. Herd also wrote concerning Scottish poetry and antiquities in the periodicals of his time.

Hogg, James (1782–1835), who is more popularly known as the Ettrick Shepherd, was born on the banks of the river of that name. Entirely self-taught, he seems, like many others of the national poets, to have been early attracted by the beauties

of Blind Harry's "Life of Wallace," and Allan Ramsay's "Gentle Shepherd." "Donald M'Donald," his first published song, soon became very popular, and was speedily followed by "When the Kye Come Hame," which remains a choice favourite among all who love Scottish lyric poetry. From this time his reputation increased. In all he wrote about twenty volumes, the chief of which are "The Forest Minstrels" (a volume of songs, 1810), "Mador of the Moor " (1816, written in Spenserian stanzas); "The Mistakes of a Night" (1794); "The Mountain Bard" (1807; "Pilgrims of the Sun" (1815); "The Poetic Mirror" (1814); "Queen Hynde" (an epic poem, 1825); "Queen's Wake" (1813); and "Scottish Pastorals, Poems, and Songs" (1801). Besides these, he published several prose works, the chief of which are "The Altrive Tales" (1832); "The Brownie of Bodsbeck" (a tale of the Covenanters, 1818); "Lay Sermons" (1834); "Life of Sir Walter Scott," "Montrose Tales" (1835); "The Shepherd's Guide (1807); "The Three Perils of Man" (1822); "The Three Perils of Woman: Love, Teasing, and Jealousy" (1823); "Winter Evening Tales" (1820), and a comprehensive collection of Jacobite songs and ballads.

Hume, Alexander (1560–1609), a sacred poet whose writings were much appreciated by the Presbyterians. Some of his works have been reprinted by the Bannatyne Club. Amongst the chief may be named, "Hymnes or Sacred Songs" (1599); "Flyting betwixt Montgomery and Polwart;" "Triumphs of Love, Chastitie, and Death," published posthumously in 1644.

Hume, Alexander (1809–1851), one of the "untutored" muses of Scotland, many of whose songs have been set to music. His "Wee, wee Wife;" "Menie Hay;" "Oh! Years hae Come," and "My Mountain Hame," were especial favourites.

Inglis, Henry, for many years a leading member of the legal profession in Edinburgh. He published "Marican, and other Poems" in 1851, and the "Briar of Threave" in 1855.

Inglis, Sir James, a poet and man of letters of the early part of the sixteenth century. It is generally supposed that "The Complaynt of Scotland," the earliest Scotch prose work extant, was written by him. It contains a minute account of the manners, customs, and popular literature of Scotland of that period. He filled the posts of Secretary to Queen Margaret, 1515, and Chancellor of the Royal Chapel of Stirling, 1527, subsequently becoming Abbot of Culross. He met with a violent death in 1530.

James I. of Scotland. After passing nineteen years of his earlier life in Windsor Castle, where he was held in captivity by the English monarch, he ascended the throne of Scotland in 1424. This royal poet ranks high among old Scottish authors. The MS. of his chief production, the "King's Quhair," an allegorical poem, was discovered in the Bodleian Library at Oxford, and was published in 1783. Two other poems, dealing humorously with the rural manners and customs of his day, are also attributed to this monarch. These bear the titles of "Christ's Kirk on the Green," and "Peblis to the Play." "The King's Quhair" is a production of the highest poetical merit, and was inspired by his love for a beautiful English lady of noble birth, whom he saw for the first time in his youthful captivity in Windsor, and whom he afterwards married and took to Scotland as his queen. He was assassinated by a company of aristocratic murderers, who slew him before her eyes, during a struggle in which the tender, affectionate, noble woman displayed in his defence the most touching and romantic heroism.

James V. of Scotland (1512–1542), a monarch who so endeared himself to his people that he bore the name of "King of the Poor." Being fond of romantic adventure he is reported to have often disguised himself and wandered through the country under the name of "The Gudeman of Ballangeich," the name of a pass on the rock on which

Stirling Castle is built. His adventures formed the basis of two well-known ballads and songs attributed to and possibly written by him, the most popular of which is still current and often sung in Scotland, under the title of "We'll gang nae mair a Rovin', a Rovin' in the Night."

Jamieson, John, D.D. (1758-1838). This writer takes one of the first places amongst Scottish authors. Entering the ministry early in life, his first work consisted of two volumes of "Sermons on the Heart" (1789). This was followed in the same year by a poem in blank verse entitled "The Sorrows of Slavery," and in 1798 by another poetical work "Eternity." The publication of various theological volumes was followed by "The Etymological Dictionary of the Scottish Language" (1809-10). A supplement to this was issued in 1825. Amongst other volumes from his pen may be mentioned "Hermes Scythicus, &c." (1814); "Historical Account of the Ancient Culdees of Iona" (1811); "Historical Account of the Royal Palaces of Scotland" (1818).

Kennedy, Walter. Douglas calls this poet, who lived in the sixteenth century, "The great Kennedy." His chief work was "Flyting." Only two other short poems have been preserved, the rest having unfortunately been lost. These are "Invective against Mouth-Thankless," and "Prais of Age."

Laidlaw, William, Born in 1780, died 1845. He was the farm-bailiff, amanuensis, and cherished friend of Sir Walter Scott during his residence at Abbotsford. He was the author of several admired songs, amongst which the best known is "Lucy's Flittin'," which appeared originally in the "Forest Minstrel" of the Ettrick Shepherd.

Lapraik, John, described by Robert Burns, who greatly admired his poetry, and wrote a rhymed epistle to him, as "a worthy facetious old fellow." He was owner of a small farm in Ayrshire. The date of his birth is unknown. He died in 1807. His principal and most popular poem is "Matrimonial Happiness," addressed to his wife—which Burns says "thrilled through his heart-strings a' to the life."

Lauder, William (—1771). This author is chiefly known by his attempt to fasten a charge of plagiarism upon Milton, and although at the instance of Dr. Johnson he withdrew it, he subsequently retracted his denial. He wrote a well-known work on Scottish literature, bearing the title of "Poetarum Scotorum Musæ Sacræ."

Leighton, Robert, born in 1822, is the author of "Rhymes and Poems by Robin" (1855).

Leighton, Alexander, uncle of the above Robert Leighton, and author of an excellent humorous poem, "The Bapteezement of the Bairn."

Lesley, John, Bishop of Ross, a champion of Mary Queen of Scots, and the author of a "History of Scotland."

Leyden, John, M.D. (1775–1811), a distinguished poet, linguist, and traveller. His works are numerous, and in their time were very popular. The bluntness and independence of manner, which met with little favour in society, served him in good stead in his literary labours. He visited the interior of Africa, India, and accompanied an expedition to Java, where he died. His most valuable work was "Discoveries and Travels in Africa" (1799); "Poems and Ballads" (posthumous, 1858); "Poetical Remains" (posthumous, 1819); "Scottish Descriptive Poems" (1803). His life was written by Rev. J. Morton (1819), and Sir Walter Scott (1858).

Lindsay, Lady Anne, daughter of the Earl of Crawford and Balcarres, afterwards Lady Ann Barnard. She is best known as the authoress of the exquisite and universally popular song of "Auld Robin Gray," which she published anonymously in 1772, when yet a young girl. She first avowed the authorship to Sir Walter Scott in her old age.

Lindsay, Sir David (1490–1569 ?), an eminent poet, whose chief works are "The Dreame" (1528), in which he applies the lash with great truth and force to abuses in Church and State, which had arisen from the licentious lives of the clergy and the usurpations of the nobles; "The Complaynt of the King's Passings," another satirical production of extreme pungency; a drama bearing the title of "A Satyre of the Three Estaties;" "The Supplication against Syde Taillis," a satire on woman's dress; "Kittie's Confession," ridiculing auricular confession; "The History and Testament of Squire Meldrum" (1550, the most pleasing of his compositions), and the last and greatest of his works, "The Monarchie" (1553). The whole of these books were written in the Scottish tongue, and are marked by strong satire and broad humour. Many of his moral sayings have passed into proverbs.

Lockhart, John Gibson (1794–1854), best known as the biographer of Sir Walter Scott, whose daughter he married. He was for many years and until his death the editor of the *Quarterly Review.* His humorous and quaint lament on "Captain Paton" is well known, and a great favourite in the legal and convivial circles of Edinburgh and Glasgow. He also wrote lives of Burns and Napoleon the First, in addition to several novels, and a very popular volume of Spanish ballads.

Logan, John, a clergyman of the Church of Scotland, born 1748, died 1788. He is known by several favourite songs, but more especially by his beautiful ballad " The Braes o' Yarrow."

Mackenzie, George, author of "Lives and Characters of the most Eminent Writers of the Scots Nation." This work is one of great research, and was published in three volumes folio.

Macneil, Hector (1746–1818), a popular poet and song writer, his love-songs in the Scottish language having speedily become favourites with all classes. When only fourteen he went to the West Indies, remaining there until 1789. His principal poem, "Scotland's Skaith," appeared in 1795. So popular did it become that it passed through fourteen editions in twelve months. A complete collection of his poems was issued in 1801, and these were followed by two works in verse entitled "Town Fashions" and "Bygane Times." He also published a novel entitled "The Scottish Adventurers," and for a time was editor of *The Scots Magazine.* His best known song, entitled "Saw Ye my Wee Thing," is still highly popular.

Mayne, John, a poet and miscellaneous writer who died in 1836. His chief work, "Glasgow" (1803), has passed through several editions, but his strength lay principally in ballad poetry, his "Logan Braes" and "Helen of Kirkconnell Lea" being inferior to no poems of their kind in the language. His "Siller Gun,"

published in 1808, with notes and a glossary, was at one time very popular, and contains many vigorous scenes and sketches of character.

Miller, William, born at Parkhead, Glasgow, about 1812, chiefly known as a writer of nursery songs and tender lyrics in the well known collection entitled "Whistle Binkie."

Moir, David Macbeth (1798–1851), a poet who wrote under the celebrated pseudonym of "Delta" in *Blackwood*, his chief works being "Bombardment of Algiers" (1818), "Domestic Verses" (1845), and "Sketches of the Poetical Literature of the Past Half Century" (1851).

Montgomery, Alexander. No details have come down to us concerning this celebrated poet. He is best known by his allegorical poem "The Cherrie and the Slae," which subsequently formed the model for Ramsay's "Vision." He also wrote "The Minde's Melodie," and a large variety of sonnets in the Scottish language. A MS. collection of his poems is preserved in the Edinburgh University, and a complete transcript was published in 1822.

Moore, James, LL.D. (1712–1779), a Greek scholar and librarian to the University of Glasgow, subsequently becoming a professor and vice-rector of the same institution. Besides several classical works he contributed largely to the *Edinburgh Magazine* and *Review.* The Scots ballad, "The Chelsea Pensioner," is also attributed to him.

Motherwell, William (1797–1835). The first work of this highly gifted poet was a collection of ballads, "Minstrelsy Ancient and Modern," a very valuable and interesting production. He became editor successively of the *Paisley Advertiser*, *Paisley Magazine*, and *Glasgow Courier*, besides contributing prose and verse to *The Day*, a Glasgow periodical. Conjointly with Hogg he edited an edition of Burns's poems. The most noteworthy of his own songs are "Jeanie Morrison," "My Head is like to Rend, Willie," and "The Sword Chant."

Murray, Alexander, D.D. (1775–1813), an eminent philologist, who was entirely self-taught. His chief works were a volume of poems principally in the Scottish language, "Outlines of Oriental Philology," and a "History of European Languages," published posthumously.

Nairn, Carolina, Baroness (1766–1845), the gifted authoress of the inimitable "Laird o' Cockpen," and the touchingly pathetic "Land o' the Leal," songs which still retain their early popularity. Most of her verses appeared in "The Scottish Minstrel" under the signature B. B. She, however, in later years abandoned her incognito. She left a large number of unpublished songs.

Nicoll, Robert (1814–1837), a favourite Scottish poet; his first volume, "Poems and Lyrics," was published in 1835. In the following year he became editor of the *Leeds Times*, the circulation of which he quadrupled during his one year tenure of office.

Outram, George (1805–1856), who from 1837 to the date of his death edited the *Glasgow Herald*. His best known song or ballad is the inimitable "Annuity," which is often recited or sung in Scottish society, and is a great favourite in all legal circles.

Picken, Andrew (1788–1833), a miscellaneous writer, whose first attempt at authorship was "Tales and Sketches of the West of Scotland." The "Sectarian" (1828, a novel) exhibited great skill in delineating mental psychology; he excelled, however, in his portraits of humble Scottish life, especially in his "Club Book," "Traditionary Stories," and the "Black Watch."

Pinkerton, John, F.S.A., antiquary and miscellaneous writer (1758–1826). "The Runes," "Select Scottish Ballads," "Letters of Literature," "Walpoliana," "Ancient Scottish Poems," "Treasury of Wit," "Iconographia Scotica," and the "Scottish Gallery" are his principal works. His compilations, however, are marked by self-confessed forgeries.

Pringle, Thomas (1789–1834), a poet whose "African Sketches,"

"Ephemerides," and "Scenes of Teviotdale" achieved a permanent popularity.

Ramsay, Allan (1686–1758). This distinguished poet ranks next to Burns and Scott in the favour of the Scottish people. His pastoral, "The Gentle Shepherd," is perhaps the finest poem of its kind in any language. His two great compilations, "The Evergreen" and the better known "Tea Table Miscellany," are essential to the completion of every Scottish library. He was originally a barber and wig maker in the High Street of Edinburgh, and is reported to have been the founder of the first Circulating Library ever established in Great Britain.

Ramsay, Dean (1793–1872), will be long remembered by his "Reminiscences of Scottish Life and Character." He was for some time Secretary of the Anti-Slavery Society.

Rodger, Alexander (1784–1846). The "Poems and Songs" of this writer are well-known. Among the more popular is "Behave Yourself before Folk," which first appeared in "Whistle Binkie." He was for many years connected with the Glasgow newspaper press.

Rolland, John, the romancist in the Scottish vernacular of the "Seaven Songes" (1578), a collection of stories similar to those told in the "Arabian Nights."

Ross, Alexander (1699–1784), a poet whose "Fortunate Shepherdess" is almost as popular as the works of Ramsay or Burns.

Rymer, Thomas, commonly called "Thomas the Rhymer," whose patronymic is unknown, was born somewhere about 1226, and died in 1299. The most popular of the writings attributed to him are to be found in the "Minstrelsy of the Scottish Border."

Scot, Alexander, a poet attached to the court of Mary Queen of Scots. Specimens of his poems will be found in various collections, notably in Allan Ramsay's "Evergreen."

Scott, Sir Walter (1771–1832), a celebrated poet and the most distinguished novelist of the age, whose works in prose and verse at once achieved a popularity which they have ever since retained. Scott, perhaps more than any other author, familiarised the people of the sister kingdoms with Scottish life, scenery, and literature. His admirable works are too well known to need a detailed description, and have been translated into many European languages.

Sibbald, James (1747–1803). He wrote chiefly on the antiquities of Scotland, in the *Edinburgh Magazine*, which he owned and edited. His principal work, a "Chronicle of the Poetry of Scotland," appeared in 1802.

Skinner, Rev. John (1721–1807), a poet whose songs have attained a lasting popularity, the best known being the "Reel of Tullochgorum," and the "Ewie wi' the Crookit Horn."

Skirving, Adam, a farmer in Haddingtonshire, born 1719, died 1803. He was a staunch Jacobite, and is principally known by his spirited ballad, "Hey! Johnnie Cope, are ye waukin yet?" written in a fit of joyous exaltation in 1745, when Sir John Cope, the Hanoverian general, was so signally defeated at Prestonpans by the forces of Prince Charles Edward Stuart, called by his adherents the "lawful king," and by the partisans of the Guelphs "the Pretender." The ballad still continues to be popular in Scotland. Skirving wrote other songs, but they have fallen into oblivion.

Stoddart, Thomas Tod, born in 1810; he published, in 1831, "The Deathwake, or Lunacy;" "The Art of Angling," in 1836, and others of the same type, which have since been remodelled in the "Angler's Companion," a work still much in request. He died in Kelso, where he had long resided, in 1880.

Stone, Jerome (1727–1757), a self-taught scholar and poet, who, from an itinerant pedlar, became assistant-master at the Dunkeld Grammar School. He translated several poems from the Gaelic, but his great work (unfinished) is "An Enquiry into the Origin of the Nation and Language of the Ancient Scots."

Tannahill, Robert (1774–1810), a writer of songs and ballads, some of the best of which were composed whilst working at the loom. Some of them attained a wide popularity, as, *e.g.*, "Jessie, the Flower of Dumblane," "The Braes o' Balquither," and "Gloomy Winter's now Awa'."

Walker, Charles, a travelling mendicant and ballad singer of the last century, well known and highly esteemed by all classes in Aberdeenshire and the East Coast of Scotland, and as welcome to the rich as to the poor in all the districts that he favoured with his visits. He attained the great age of 105 years, and is said to have been present at the battle of Culloden. He was a fervent Jacobite, and author of the admirable but rough ballad of "Bonnie Laddie, Highland Laddie."

Wedderburn, James (1500–1564–65), a religious poet and playwright. His chief work was "Buike of Godlie and Spirituall Songs." He also wrote two plays exposing the corruptions of the Roman Church.

Wilson, Alexander (1766–1813), an eminent ornithologist and writer of Scottish poetry. He in early life emigrated to America, where he devoted a large portion of his time to ornithology, publishing a large and important work as the result of his researches. Several volumes of poems also appeared under his name.

Wilson, John, "Christopher North" (1785–1854), a popular poet, novelist, and dramatic writer, born at Paisley. For many years he was largely concerned in *Blackwood's Magazine*, to which he contributed the inimitable series of papers entitled "Noctes Ambrosianæ." He was Professor of Moral Philosophy in the University of Edinburgh.

Wilson, John Mackay (1803–1835), the author of the well-known "Tales of the Borders," and several dramas and poems, the most popular of the former being "The Gowrie Conspiracy" and "The Highland Widow," whilst his poems, entitled "The Enthusiast" and "The Sojourner" (in Spenserian stanzas), rank amongst his best productions.

THE END.

PRINTED BY BALLANTYNE, HANSON AND CO.
EDINBURGH AND LONDON.

JUST PUBLISHED.

Large post 8vo, cloth, 7s. 6d. ; or half-bound, gilt top, 9s.

A DICTIONARY

OF

SOBRIQUETS AND NICKNAMES.

BY

ALBERT R. FREY,

Author of "William Shakspeare and Alleged Spanish Prototypes,"
"A Bibliography of Junius,"
"A Bibliography of Playing Cards," &c.

WITH AN INDEX ARRANGED BY TRUE NAMES.

"Sobriquet" and "Nickname" are two words often used as if they were identical in meaning, and are as such employed without regard to the difference between them. A "sobriquet," as its etymology proves, is an epithet bestowed upon a person for some quality, good or bad, which he possesses, or which he is reputed to possess; and a "nickname," or more properly an *Eke-name*, is an addition, or *eke*, to the name by which he is legally or generally known. "Sobriquet" is a French word, recently adopted into English, and is of Celtic or Gaelic extraction, from *so*, an affix equivalent to the Greek *eu*, signifying pleasant, fit, appropriate, and *breach*, a mark or spot ; and thus signifies a fit or appropriate mark or designation of any one by which he is familiarly known. An *eke-name* is of Teutonic origin, from *auch* or *eke*, also, or additional, and has been corrupted into "nickname" by the ungrammatical transference of the *n* in the indefinite article *an* to the unaspirated word which follows it. Originally all names, except those bestowed at baptism and called Christian names, were properly "sobriquets" —descriptive of the personal appearance, the colour of the hair or eyes, the profession or trade, or the residence of those to whom they were given, as Cruikshank, Longman, Short, Black, Brown, Grey, White, Green, &c. ; Smith, Tailor, Carpenter, Baker, Driver, &c. ; Wood, Vale, Forest, Rivers, Hill, and many other familiar examples. Sobriquets applied in this manner are by no means obsolete.

The reader of to-day, no matter to what especial branch of literature or history he may devote himself, must have encountered many of such peculiar sobriquets and nicknames. Frequently their origin is difficult to determine, and their real force is lost.

No book has as yet been issued which is devoted to the explanation and derivation of these humorous, and, in some instances, abusive appellations ; and to fill this gap the present work was undertaken.

IN PREPARATION.

𝕬 𝕹ew 𝕱rench and 𝕰nglish 𝕾lang 𝕯ictionary.

ARGOT AND SLANG.

A NEW FRENCH AND ENGLISH DICTIONARY

OF THE

CANT WORDS, QUAINT EXPRESSIONS, SLANG TERMS, AND FLASH PHRASES

USED IN THE HIGH AND LOW LIFE OF

OLD AND NEW PARIS.

By A. BARRÈRE,

Officier de l'Instruction Publique, Professor R. M. Academy, Woolwich.

The work treats of the cant of thieves; the jargon of Parisian roughs; the military, naval, parliamentary, academical, legal, and Freemasons' slang; of that of the workshop, the studio, the stage, the boulevards, the *demi-monde*. It is accompanied by an exhaustive introduction; also by numerous specimens in prose and verse of the flash tongue of different periods, arranged in chronological order up to the present day, among which is the autobiography in parallel columns of a thief in English and French slang.

LONDON : WHITTAKER & CO., PATERNOSTER SQUARE, E.C.

www.ingramcontent.com/pod-product-compliance
Lightning Source LLC
Chambersburg PA
CBHW021322110726
47900CB00005B/1321